KISSES OF THE ENEMY

Rodney Hall was born in England in 1935. He left school at sixteen to earn his way as a performer, and by eighteen was acting on stage, on radio, and playing baroque recorder professionally. He resumed his formal education at thirty-three at Queensland University, Australia. He has three daughters and lives with his wife on the coast of New South Wales.

Rodney Hall's work has been published in Australia since 1962. He has written two biographies, eleven collections of poetry, and five novels including *Kisses of the Enemy*, *Captivity Captive* and *Just Relations*, which have all been published by Faber and Faber.

KISSES OF
THE ENEMY

Rodney Hall

faber and faber

LONDON · BOSTON

First published in Australia in 1987
by Penguin Books Australia Ltd
Published in the USA in 1988
by Farrar, Straus and Giroux, Inc.
First published in Great Britain in 1989
by Faber and Faber Limited
3 Queen Square London WC1N 3AU
This paperback edition first published in 1990

Printed in Great Britain by
Richard Clay Ltd Bungay Suffolk*
All rights reserved

A CIP record for this book is available from the British Library

ISBN 0-571-15092-6

For Bet
with my love

ACKNOWLEDGMENTS

My special gratitude goes to Peter ("Beetle") Collins who so generously assisted, in particular with shaping the character of Peter Taverner; also to Humphrey McQueen for his tirelessly perceptive editorial advice.

Thanks are due to many other friends for various kinds of support, ranging from criticism of the manuscript in progress to the loan of a generator so I could have electric light while working late at night in this remote and beautiful house. For stimulating the novel's progress, supplying information, or simply helping keep the household financially afloat, I am grateful, severally, to Iain McCalman, Giuseppe Stramandinoli, Joan and Don Whetton, Wesley Stacey, Helga McPhie, Linda Collins, Tom Shapcott, Eileen Scollay, and Max Williams. For a dream image I am in debt to C G Jung, and for the notion of form as energy to the example of Leoš Janáček's string quartets.

During two of the four years' work represented by this book, the Literature Board of the Australia Council granted me a Senior Fellowship. Without that income I would not have been able to write what I have written.

CONTENTS

PRELUDE

Straws in the Wind

1

Wind worried a confusion of bunting and *REFERENDUM* signs. Wind ripped the advertised arguments for Yes and No off their hoardings and sent them gusting into the air, tossed conflicting ways with a swirl of grit and ice-stick wrappers. Flurries of tattered reasons tumbled in the wind along Bathurst Street. Slogans suffered ravages to their superlatives. The blankly simple colours of party allegiances frayed and tore loose.

Bemused people hung about the streets appearing, of all things, content. Even the buildings had become less than substantial, mere furnishings for the wind's arena.

The bubble of independence had risen, supreme, gorgeous with our optimism, and almost burst. We felt air under our feet, being far gone in innocence then, during 1992. We had waited a very long time.

High above the city but swooping headlong down, a gentleman laid bare his gold watch, consulted the promptitude of destiny, let an immaculate cuff slip back over it, and attended to his sensations. He would take nobody's word that the future so much as existed until he might tramp in its wreckage for himself and choose which of its delights to dine on. Out through the helicopter window the toy city banked and righted, threshed by the tips of flickering blades, like classic scenery from some old-time movie. Was this supposed to be the dynamic world capital of sexual deviation, as local newspapers loudly asserted, this wilderness of dollhouses and sugar-coated foibles? The helicopter lurched a few degrees south. A cove sparkled, a dish canting, and afternoon's gold beads skittered beyond the Opera House's broken teacups, beyond dinky apartment blocks crowding to obstruct each other's waterviews. Remote-control traffic shuttled across the loom of intersections and model trains came snaking out of tunnels. He glimpsed Long Nose Point as a nursery tale monster seen through the dwindling-glass, a furry silhouette of almost forgotten horror, driven by dark thighs, swimming but never able to escape the game. Pleasure craft stood round down there, transfixed in a pantomime of nodding and bending over backwards, a thousand sails stiff with slanting wind, wind rubbing the water scaly, shoreline foliage a shiver of miniature excitability. Was this the place he had chosen for the glory of his ambitions? The pilot glanced his way, shrugged at what he saw, and brought them in close.

Sydney, flaunting its silliest floosiest mood leaned nearer, festive dress aflutter, bright and tipsy.

Anything could happen. And was just about to try.

Completing a circuit of suburbs and soon to land, swaying low over the business district closed for the public holiday, dipping its spider shadow across tall buildings with fiery windows behind which sat covert meetings of boards of directors whose habit was to think in terms no subtler than multiplication tables, while chasms magnified its arrival with a thunderous malevolent fanfare, the helicopter touched down, bringing the fixed smile and symmetrical teeth of Luigi Squarcia, champion of Yes.

Thommo Thomas, a boatbuilder in vigorous middle age, set aside his electric saw, the heat of which could be felt without touching it, scratched one hairy forearm coated with hardwood powder, bunched and flexed broad knuckles which had only rarely been used to hammer other men's faces, and then generally to persuade them they should allow him the courtesy of speaking for himself, faced the slipway rather than his interlocutor, and drawled.

— I'm happy this way, doing restoring jobs. It keeps me in touch, if you know what I mean.

He completed the scratching necessary for this arm and began on the other. He looked away from the harbour he loved, still with that unsettling expression, straight into the eyes of someone who had asked a question but was probably too clever to expect an answer.

— The history of it, you see, he added. Sailing and all that. The sacredness, I call it.

Both Thommo Thomas's arms were now finished and hung placidly. If a whole scrum of front-row forwards had charged him at that moment, sweating in their rugby jerseys and mud-caked socks, smack, they'd have broken and fallen round his knees.

— I don't mind, he resumed with a gentle smile. People thinking I'm a bit slow.

A housewife at her piano played from a yellowed edition of Erik Satie's *Sports et divertissements*. The window stood open. Sometimes she glanced at the music to remind herself. Sometimes she looked at the framed panels of the tall upright instrument and at screw holes where candle brackets had been before it was hers. Sometimes she looked to one side, out where notes flew free across her lovely garden, across the pond, the honeysuckle hedge down there, the fruit trees, the two red-gums. Hers was an upstairs window. She listened, but not only to the voice of Satie or the hushing of Jaguar tyres along the drive next door, she also listened for her son's voice, who might be calling. This, then, was what she expected in life. If we lived somewhere more neighbourly, she had objected to her husband's choice of address, there would be boys Rory's own age for him to call on.

She turned a page. She knew this piece too. She revelled in the tragic jokiness of another little sport, without the least suspicion her fate was being sealed by an agent with helicopter-combed hair; or that, in a few moments' time, she would be robbed of what limited freedom remained to her in choosing the direction her own life might take. Her wedding ring and her engagement ring, which she slipped off to practise, trembled on the ledge beyond the piano's topmost A.

— Am I getting through? No, our sympathy for Australia is established beyond doubt. We've been allies in war. We've come through all that. Right? You can't quantify it. The sanctity of our mutual trust is not in question. We understand your reticence and we respect it. But in return we cannot settle for less than complete confidentiality. On no account must our sources be compromised. You deal with us on precisely the level you used to deal with the Pentagon. Defence is ours; we put up for it and we got it, so we keep the program going. Quiet and efficient. Let's be clear, we want no publicity. No cowboy antics. We're in business to win. Now we have made our move, the only way out is up, the high road, expansion.

— So, put another way, we are part of your takeover?

— The point is that the right man will have a great deal to contribute. Diplomacy between us has never been a question of kind, only degree. We are proposing to elevate Australia's status yet again in terms of world strategic significance. No change of government, as such, would affect the deal. We're too big for governments. Unless it's a coup.

— It is not a coup.

— The dynamics of peace is what we're talking about. The art is to keep the economy stable while destabilizing the currency. We know our business. Enough to say we have depressed the value of your dollar and we're holding it down. We get our installations completed. . . you with me? . . . then we look at the wider issues. It's a buyer's market.

Crowds surged through roadways cordoned off to traffic. They massed in squares, in Martin Place, Taylor Square, Macquarie Place, outside Central Station and outside the Customs House, waving flags. A pink tide of excitement passed over them: faces turned up (innocent as playing-cards although a swindler had been let loose on the game) toward the magnet of an event.

Roving cameramen captured mileages of tanned girls in shorts, their lovely long legs bare, men lip to lip with foaming cans, the soundtrack a montage of larrikin goodhumour while an unexplained roar swelled, thundered, seeming to come from the unbounded deep of horrible confusion rather than the clear day above, swamping the chaos of *Alleluias* in all the accents of gullibility, till sticky mouths gaped against the glass, the uncomprehended limit they were set, and pouted fishy but soundless opinions on independence.

Beneath the helicopter, hidden from both Mr Squarcia and his pilot, the letters Y-E-S, suspended under the fuselage, wobbled now through a slowing, drifting sky. The ground domed up for the machine to land. The letters collapsed in a stack on the space being swept clean by the whirlwind. Here Luigi Squarcia, unseen gold watch timed for his moment, stepped out right in front of Sydney Town Hall at the polling booth. Arms flung wide in a gesture not quite convincing, fingers grasping the sunlight, he chanted in acquired English.

— Yes. Yes. Yes. That's the message.

So perfect was his elegance, he might have come straight from a beauty parlour run by an asthmatic Hollywood queen with varnished fingernails. And he had. The wind did what it could, the slashing blades gusted his hair this way and the other as he moved. (The wedding ring on the piano trembled again while the lady still played.) Carelessly and with the irritability of a man for whom appearances matter, but only as a means for furthering undisclosed ends, Squarcia pushed the hair out of his eyes. Supporters of the cause shouted back a mighty *Yes!* Who's that fellow? they asked as they got their breath back. Then, with a tremendous thrust of the throttle and clatter of slatted pollution, the helicopter rose on their applause, up, drifting sidewise to miss the Town Hall tower by a millimetre, buoyed on solid enthusiasm, engine firing rapid detonations and rotors whisking, rose jiggling its Y-E-S across the metropolis of a million packed bodies plus another two million on the way home from voting, or travelling in to seal their fate, or watching the action on television as usual.

The voluntary workers busy handing out pamphlets at the booth, anxious to claim their share of such glamorous drama, called greetings.

— A pushover, Lou, a bloody pushover, mate.

But their words did not appease him; he felt irresistible rather than contented. And bland Australianisms merely aggravated his mood by their presumption of an underlying goodwill, their optimism being as vulgar as it was shallow because, Luigi Squarcia knew, failure on his part to respond with some equally fatuous pleasantry of his own was likely to provoke instant aggression.

— You organized a great campaign, said a corpulent lady who sported festoons of rosettes, complimenting him on behalf of the whole team. So I reckon you earned your reward.

Which turned out to be a wet kiss from her own lips, hot when delivered but rapidly cooling.

The champion of Yes smiled, vilely debonair.

When he left, he walked away, leaving them to watch his back while an anonymous public milled round, closing him off. His cream suit could be sighted now and again, each time a stage farther away, but always distinct, never blending with the mass.

— A nice cold beer is what he's after if you ask me, the lady with kissing lips remarked in the manner of one frequently called upon for her judgment. What a stinker of a day. And April already, she added, being a performer and eager for the limelight. I'm fair melting under this finery. She raised her voice to a triumphant fortissimo. Choose an independent Australia! she called. No extra charge for voting Yes!

A drunken poet offered Squarcia odds on the poll. He declined because he knew he would never be paid; and strolled past shops gay with makeshift windowboxes packed full of instant flowers and potplants harvesting dust in doorways. A vast blue flag with white cross and five stars, being stretched from hand to hand the full width of the road, tented a segment of massed bodies. This made him feel sad. The scene of such hope became a flaking fresco, the sky cracked plaster, naive faces mouldering, the hectic colours fragmentary. Sad because he was big enough to bring the whole show collapsing about their ears. They had no idea who was among them, nor why he turned along a sidestreet beyond the cordoned area, scanning dingy buildings the colour of moss and fungus.

A sudden cacophony of children rushed out at him, frenetic with certainty that even adults had gone crazy for twenty-four hours. Luigi Squarcia, educated on the Naples docks, knew how to speak to them.

— There's big bucks to be made out of this, he promised.

— I reckon, one lad agreed.

They scattered, coltish, punching heads affectionately, scuffing a few tattered streamers bowled by wind among the garbage bins, pausing only to whistle at a flash sports car parked beside the kerb. Squarcia glimpsed the chrome of greed in their eyes as they scouted off, pursuing some goodnatured vandalism. It would not take much to push them into purposeful violence. The car was his.

A tuna boat drifted far out to sea on one of those sleeky calm afternoons when the heat is fixed at melting-point. The young men had been in the racks for seven and a quarter hours. Still they heaved at poles and sent huge tuna flying over their shoulders to bounce across deck, mouths torn and bloody, tough fish, fastest in the sea, thrashing in their struggle against death, rolling down into a hold and moiling there among the bristling spines of their fellows.

The young fishermen, and they had to be young, fought off exhaustion, bodies strained and bulging as they hauled at the catch. The skipper stayed in his wheelhouse keeping an eye on them, knowing that, with some guys at least, if he treated them like shit for long enough there was the chance they'd jump ship and not come back even to collect their pay. Labour had become cheap.

In a swell, the boat would roll and at each dip douse the men where they stood in the welcome of pure relief. But no, that glassy sea did not rise to sluice the blood caking skin and drying to a crust in hair. Fresh spatters rained on the crew and fresher blood swiped at them as more tuna were flung past, hooks flicking free from torn lips. The blood stuck. It must be picked off in hard scales thick as the sole of a shoe before there would be any point in washing, scrubbing with a brush to reach the skin. And once the men had scrubbed themselves they needed to scrub the boat, or the blood would eat into the paint.

Tuna thrashed around on deck, making it dangerous for anyone to move from the racks. But the one man strong enough to oppose the boss turned his back on the horizon and, taking ponderous steps like some knight in the armour of a day's butchery, was knocked off balance on his way to the wheel-house and fell. His body skidded along blood-wet decking and rolled down into the fish room among tuna vibrating them-selves to death, to struggle up, treading on glazed lustrous fish as big as himself, and he was powerfully built, slipping off-balance, slashed by spines, sinking, with nothing to hold on to, heaving, staggering, trampling again and slithering over hard silver bodies, the upper ones of which coggled and resonated on the dead beneath, and going down, gravity pulling him surely deeper among grinding roller flanks. Young as he was and unready, he faced death, knowing while he sank that a quick-sand of cold corpses would close over him long before his feet touched the fish room floor. Already lanced with tormenting wounds, he discovered the meaning of fear. Still going down, little by little, up to his neck, and his face lacerated too while he fought to free one arm, to work it above his head, and next the other, he did not hear his own hoarse panting. His entire being centred on the gaff hook a couple of mates poked towards him. He gripped it with a pain he would later describe as joy flowing from his hands, then kniving along the inner arm, ribs, and thighs as his resurrected body was hauled clear into the sleeky nightmare of that hot still afternoon he had intended to cut short.

They laid him on deck. The skipper, watching, said a man wounded by tuna spines could die if the wounds festered. The only cure, he explained, was piss. So he would be first to volunteer, and ordered the crew to unzip and help out. They didn't know whether to believe this or not. But something had to be done for a sufferer in his agony. And they could dredge up no knowledge of their own. By twos and ones, ignorance left them no choice. In the stinging swill their leader shuddered with the frenzy of a saved life while, unnoticed now, the catch below also shuddered.

Only his mate Greg could not bring himself to the act and slouched away, gazing ahead, longing for a first glimpse of the coast which he knew was still too far off. The inconsequential fact that this was Saturday presented itself; as if labelling the afternoon might clamp a tidy frame around the horror going on behind him. . . Saturday, the bloody day of reckoning, no less. Well, he for one wouldn't be there, and he didn't suppose his vote would be missed. The same with the rest. Polling closed at six.

While he watched, the sea swung a few points to port. They had altered course.

— Now you look here, the skipper replied when challenged (and Greg was not a born challenger). I've got forty tons aboard, see? The market's right in Sydney. We're going to make a killing. Just for the extra time it takes to get there. We've got enough fuel. Dead set.

Seeing Greg's gaze flinch and glance out from the wheelhouse, he knew what the trouble was: the injured man being carried away to his bunk.

— Too bad he had an accident. Careless. But if he's going to be okay he'll survive anyhow. Isn't that the truth? the skipper smiled reasonably. We'd take twenty-four hours to reach Narooma. Sydney direct'll take only another eight or nine. What's the difference?

Greg went and stood at a hatch, watched the last tuna dying, and thought about how far one could push the good times.

— What would you have voted if you hadn't been working? The question came at him from the wheelhouse.

He did not answer.

— *Yes?* the skipper laughed.

The building Luigi Squarcia sauntered into stood full to the brim with a chlorinated silence which shivered each echo he left imprinted on the tile floor, to stop only at the cash desk where

ratchet-gates clacked round on busy days. A memory of customers stained the walls with blunders.

The Imperial Indoor Swimming Baths & Hygiene Facilities
Pty Ltd, though listed for demolition to make room for a video
hire centre, still operated in the twilight of its popularity. But the
satellite message had not warned him of decay. He came expecting young spunks, he came expecting girls in bikinis and
flatulent businessmen easing their failures by getting a good
look while not needed at the office. Squarcia paid his coin.

He found the men's changing room empty, nobody there to
legitimize the place by getting changed, nobody there to read
the *It is an offence to* notice. Not even a ghost of damp-limbed
fumblings survived to warm the air. He looked for another go-
between like himself, but caught only scabby images of his own
body revealed in long mirrors, bare arm by arm, leg by leg,
jaundiced comments corroding unlikely places. Alertness pis-
toned through him. Walls whispered at his clothes. Ready, he
said, his delicate manly feet padding fastidiously through a
trough of milky disinfectant out into the grand chamber of the
pool itself.

Here was a world apart, tiled from top to bottom with arsenic
green forests of freak treeferns. An apsidal gallery looked over
the deep end, doubtless still smelling of talcum where Private
Members had frittered almost a century watching muscular
vulgarians vie for attention. At the shallow end, steps extended
the full width of the baths to compensate for the absence of any
other way out, and the word *Children* had been let into the wall
in black ceramic lettering one could read with the fingers. The
chamber also boasted a cast-iron diving tower (the top level of
which had been boarded up as unsafe) and an immense leaky
skylight in the centre of the ceiling where a stained-glass rose
grew from the rot of anno 1901.

The pool, like the changing room, lay empty. This stillness of
water, more still and more mysterious than glass, deprived even
Squarcia of his breath.

He flexed his shoulders to shrug off a sinister visitation and
decided to be amused instead. He regaled his lungs with chlo-
rine, a touch of poison always acceptable and even medicinally
recommended, and plunged in. No one appeared. His slicked
head waited attentively. His body, suddenly become a jellyfish,
waited also. The dive crashed round vitreous walls. So the
champion of Yes set out to accomplish a few laps of the future.
He turned his head critically to watch one wet arm then the

other. He adjusted his stroke, slitting the surface without the least splash.

And at that instant sensed an intruder. He risked drowning to churn round. Choked. Looked up and about. And saw in a glassbead frame. . . nothing. He headed back for the children's end through a web of glaucous light. Ripples of his passing glinted from the water. Halfway home his feet touched bottom. As he waded the rest his chest heaved proudly, hairs lay otter-sleek along his body, pasted to pampered skin. He slushed up the steps to flop at the edge in a puddle of his own warmth, gasping with satisfaction.

— Shit, Luigi Squarcia swore suddenly. That's why!

How could he have fallen for such a basic ploy? Naturally they were scared of him. They wanted him here at the baths while the action took place elsewhere.

Far away in the suburbs, a housewife touched the final chord of her Satie *sport* or *divertissement*, whichever, and listened while a new blank world lapped in to swamp the old.

The cashier put aside her novel and denied everything. No, no other customer had come into the place while he himself was taking his swim, mate, it's pretty quiet these days, you may not have noticed. Absolutely nobody. She should know, she had been sitting here long enough, she grumbled echoes.

— I suppose you've voted already? Squarcia persisted plea-santly, taking a different line, one hand waving towards the outside world, creating it for her at that instant: the heat and wind, shouting yokels and young mothers wheeling partisan babies in and out among knife-strokes of sunlight.

— Later, she replied absently, her mind tugging back to her novel.

— It is a great occasion, Squarcia assured her though he felt convinced no Australian occasion could be great in the Euro-pean sense: majestic with history, purified by ritual and, in procession from one holy shrine to another, following the very footsteps of saints and monsters.

— An occasion, she conceded forlornly in her museum of extinct sporting types, the shadowed lobby walls glazing a sicklier green while she spoke.

He strolled away as if nothing might happen. But in fact, when he slipped one hand into his coat pocket, his fingers closed on an envelope. Well, wasn't he the one to demand an arrangement protecting his neutrality, an old-fashioned connection in a meeting place sufficiently out of the way to have been erased from the many systems of electronic scanning used by government and commerce?

Squarcia emerged into sunshine, appearing to smile at the sound of nearby crowds yelping joyously. But maybe this was a sneer, or the first sign of an impending sneeze. He tore the envelope. The message inside confined itself to a single printed name, *BERNARD BUCHANAN*, which took him by surprise because he had never heard of the candidate.

(But the housewife at her closed piano, still humming its clarities of a past life, knew him well enough.)

Luigi Squarcia bore the chosen name down among blown ice-stick wrappers and the lilting cries of predatory children. He opened his car door, never giving a thought to boobytraps. Quite right he was. The leather seat had been razor-slashed.

Having plumped on the bed when she returned home from voting No as fervently as one could express an opinion with that stub of pencil in the polling booth (and having had words with a loud creature handing out Yes cards), Greta Grierson's gaze sought the inevitable photograph among the hairbrushes and inexpensive lotions on her dressingtable. It was in a black do-it-yourself frame, adequate for the archival misery of three girls facing the camera: one bravely, one defiantly, and one resentfully. Greta herself being the defiant one, all those years ago, because she it was who had insisted a record should be kept, that the children should remember their childhood.

Miss Grierson did not regret her insistence.

The brave little girl on her right, who hardly came up to her waist, expected to be thought of as an adult twenty years later. But a fact is a fact, which no amount of tears will undo. *Stephanie*, said the handwritten legend across the grey sky of those troubled times, yet the letters curved like a rainbow, an escaped halo floating above the child's head. All Greta could think about the name, if she ever thought about it, was: I wrote that.

Greta, the same hand announced in definitely larger and more positive script above herself. This was true. And she did appear defiant, or at least determined, as is the privilege of those who make a tidiness of being right. Across her knees the date had been recorded: *1972*, the year of Whitlam, the year our whole country went mad on the fantasy of going it alone. Even then, when she was only nineteen, she could have warned them life wasn't like he said at all.

So Stephanie put a brave face on loss. And Greta defied the reluctance of her charges. Not everybody surrendered to empty optimism in that memorable year. But as for the third girl in the picture, what do you do with someone who will never be told?

While I know I could not always control my temper though I was famous for being fair; while I accepted that it wasn't enough just to love her; while I had to use the limited means at hand to teach her what to beware of in the world outside; while I did admittedly smack her face that very morning (I am too conscientious to have forgotten even to this day); while I knew her ogling that art teacher was not the first time she set out to mortify me in public; I will never believe Lavinia's resentful expression was the look of a fifteen-year-old who has, as she skited to me, slept all night naked with a man.

The wound remained so intense, Greta needed to live with its reminder. What she seemed unable to escape was Lavinia's description of his furry legs wrapped round her smooth ones and his furry groin pressing like a pad on her furry groin. That was when the slap came.

Had Greta guessed how Lavinia might one day play a part in bringing down the state itself, she would have told the media: Didn't I say so all along?

Contact with Mr Bernard Buchanan, Squarcia decided, should be made in person. Not by him though. . . he must not commit himself yet. . . but by a public figure of spotless (*immacolato*) respectability, a man of distinction (*potenza*).

PART ONE
The Republic

2

Lunch being safely inside two hundred dully rapacious stomachs and swilled there with plentiful wine, the delegates made a terrific rumpus of fleshy male laughter, voices blatant as trombones and glutted by self-satisfaction. The seventy-four different conversations, however, compassed remarkably few topics: money, the suspected treachery of friends, the inexhaustible fascination of women with large breasts, horseracing, computer fraud and Roscoe Plenty's keynote address.

Roscoe Plenty MP argued that any period of upheaval is a gift, an invitation to make profits. And the more fundamental the change, the bigger the opportunities. Though not quite in the class of the Second World War, the coming republic was probably comparable to Federation, well known for having made and broken many fortunes. Plenty himself, a darkbrowed darksouled man still young enough to be mistaken for young, eaten by fires and hungry for adulation, snarled delightedly at every attempt the delegates made to approach him with the appreciative fatuities of their class, that sporty mocking which they traded as the sole vocabulary of good fellowship. Plenty, newly come to public notice as spokesman for the Hot faction of the Right, despite his background in trade union bureaucracy, grinned and gnashed at yet more compliments on the shake-up he was giving his own leader in parliament. Then a colossal voice from a neighbouring group simply bulldozed through this desirable line of conversation.

— If we're not here to cut loose and have fun, why did we

come at all? We could fiddle our stocks without setting a foot outside the office.

The speaker was immoderately fat and animated. The men he bellowed at seemed, to judge by the stampede of their own bellowings, to appreciate him.

— Who's that creep? Roscoe Plenty asked combatively enough to be heard. He was, after all, a man who wore his success without the least adulteration of modesty.

— Couldn't say.

The fat man had begun on a fresh story.

— Don't mention *that*, he said, suddenly tragic. No, I assure you the whole thing was entirely true, every word. He laughed delightedly. I bought it for four thousand dollars, can you imagine? And only two months later, he glared at them to check whether they believed him. I sold it for fifty-seven thousand. Wait! he held up an open hand to silence any scepticism. To a bunch of Aborigines.

They hooted.

— Yes, one of his audience recollected. I believe I read about it in the press, some sort of scandal?

— No scandal, the fat man roared cheerfully. Only penis-envy.

They thought this immensely clever, though a few called in question the actual payment of the fifty-seven thousand.

— Money? the entertainer replied. They've got money all right. Our money. Those good notes we let slip into the clutches of the Deputy Commissioner of Taxation. No, he belched. I assure you. Why should I (he became naive in confession) lie to you? It's the truth, I'm a man of principle. I only mention it because... Now he whispered something from that mottled football of a face, pursing his lips as if to kiss their ears. And then leaned back on his heels, thrusting out his noble belly, and exploded with merriment.

Roscoe Plenty, watching this, suddenly suspected he was its target, that the performance might be specifically to attract his attention. Known to have harsh views on Aboriginal land rights, health and housing schemes, he was still not going to be drawn into the orbit of any nonentity's self-aggrandisement. He turned aside, though a moment too late to miss the quick glare the fat man shot at him, plus a glimpse of the chairman approaching, hand placed on one shoulder after another using delegates to haul himself along, the well-dressed shoulders yielding, men turning side-on to allow him past, showing carefully tied ties round thick coarse necks. As star speaker, Roscoe Plenty presumed the chairman was coming to congratulate him. He affected nonchalance, until the delay lasted too long.

Cursed with an inability to control his impulses, he looked again to see what had happened. And where should the chairman have been heading? For the fat man of course, who listened a moment in confidence and then drew aside, firing another bull's-eye at Plenty's impertinence. The chairman led the fellow away towards the private suite set up as an office. The door closed on them and, a matter of seconds later, intriguingly, the chairman came out alone.

Inside the room stood a famous man, tall, white-haired and with a military bearing.

— Buchanan? he suggested. Delighted.

The door hushed against plush carpet, leaving them to observe each other adrift on background noises from the conference hall where delegates were being asked to resume their seats so the next session could begin on time. They listened a moment longer to the remote hubbub of persons in agreement.

— Bernie, how would you, ah, feel about being, ah, president? the famous man asked, famous eyebrows working with avuncular wildness. A job, he explained to the carpet. We have reserved for you. He looked up sharply.

Astonished Buchanan certainly was, but only in the sense that this unexpected event did so perfectly happen to fit the shape of what he felt missing from his life. And not just the shape but the texture of that which he might have dubbed his peculiar personality. Although he had done nothing to earn it, in the conventional political sense, the candidature instantly belonged to him. There was no dividing line between *Bernard Buchanan* and *President of Australia*, no fracture along which the one might be said to be separable from the other. His astonishment, then, was a matter of recognizing an exact equation in how well he belonged to the role and how well it belonged to him despite his never before having given it a thought. Looked at from such a compelling new perspective, he admired the genius of whoever chose him. He knew at a stroke that his life had been directed toward this objective. Without the least intention of a career in politics, his mistrust against planning of all kinds had trained him for it.

— Just what I always wanted, he joked.

— Impeccable backing. Unlimited money. Guaranteed. The

eyebrows wagged privately for the two of them alone. We are confident. We could have, ah, anybody, the voice continued in an accent to match his white toothbrush moustache. But we chose you. You are unknown outside financial circles. You have no affiliation with established political parties. No, ah, religion. But if all things were equal you could agree to being born again, eh? You're a clean-skin. We like your style, Bernie. We have been keeping an eye on you and an ear to what you say. Good man. Congratulations. He switched off his smile and presented in its place the expression of a worried parent. We must save the nation getting into the, ah, wrong hands.

They both still stood in the posture of greeting. But now the famous man shrugged endearingly, as if to say I'm afraid this trifle is the best I can offer, and switched on his smile afresh, setting the hackles of his moustache bristling. Buchanan nodded.

— When does the campaign begin?

— Most of the work has already been done. All we need from you for the present is your, ah, image. Can you be ready for the photographer in five minutes? The smile grew even more ferociously winning. Our organizer chap will be in touch, with details and developments before they arise. Meanwhile, he added while his eyebrows worked overtime. I suggest you brief yourself on the, ah, Paringa communications base. Fair enough? Good!

3

Dorina Buchanan attracted music. As other people are said to be accident-prone, so she was music-prone. In her company public servants started humming. Minutes after she'd begun watching workmen on a building site they were whistling at the top of their range. Children sang *Sorr-ree* when they bumped into her trolley at the supermarket. Of an evening a cicada orchestra chirred for her. And while she tended her beloved garden, choruses of magpies fitfully improvised a new Webern serenade. She need only push her rusty wheelbarrow for its squeals to develop a pure note. Hailstones fell in rhythms around her. Even her moody son, at eleven, banged the table with a regular ratta-tat-tat. Piped muzak in a lift malfunctioned for her benefit.

Bernard was the only one who could never contribute.

She wooed him with rhapsodies. She crooned while brushing

her hair at night, oh the dark tower and the deep river. Her radio trumpeted fanfares when he arrived home from the office. A susurrus of aeolian harmony hung garnishing the lintel over the diningroom door. Even during the privacy of his bath, her song about a bushranger's death seeped up through empty pipes of a disused installation with *that was his downfall*, and might have driven him mad had he heard it. But he was saved by the importance of his belly rumbling, by the satisfactions of beer gurgling down his gullet and bathwater sloshing on the floor where Dorina would mop it up as soon as he had finished.

So here she was, reading his message as she wandered through the garden and a frog called from the pond, E-flat E-flat.

— Wait, she cried out laughing. Slower! I can use you in Mozart's thirty-ninth.

The message, sent from his conference, gave her strict instructions she and the boy were to enjoy themselves.

— That's all very well, she protested as if someone were there to discuss the matter, and sat a moment in the regrets of her finishing-school posture. But I mayn't like this Penhallurick person. Dear Buchanan, she added. I wish he wouldn't try so hard to be considerate. It doesn't suit him in the least. We might have had a nice time.

— E-flat, the frog suggested.

— Rory darling, she called brightly. Your father has arranged a surprise. We're to go sailing in a yacht, right out to the reef.

Rory came slouching round the corner of the big house and hefted a stone at the frog.

— Very well, she cried promptly. We won't.

But it made no difference. They were trapped in Bernard's good intentions, which this time entailed meeting his old benefactor in business, William Penhallurick. Naturally Dorina had heard a great deal about Penhallurick, but none of this struck her as relevant in the event. Some important things had never been mentioned. For a start, nobody warned her he would put on a yachtsman's cap to shake hands. She actually saw him duck behind the boom and cram it on his scrofulous head, then he sprang out and a hand pounced on hers, amazing her with his eighty-six years. She would, she acknowledged, be amazed by a man-sized preying mantis too. And having possessed her hand, he refused to let go, persuading her how much he admired a fine young woman, women in their thirties being cattle so tender you couldn't help lusting after a prime cut of them. When he finally released her, Dorina dusted off the flakes of skin he had left stuck to her fingers. She saw no need to do so tactfully.

— This, she announced in her starchiest voice. Is Rory.

— He'll have plenty of playmates today, the old man laughed, darting about to gather his grandchildren for inspection. But he did not say anything directly to Rory to make him feel at ease. Instead he began singing a parched folksong from central Europe, each syllable crazed like ancient pottery. His son-in-law, Dr McKinley, who had driven to the airport to collect Dorina, now emerged from the car park with her bag and the wine she had brought as a contribution to lunch. Portly and optimistic, he organized his crew, sent the host up front as lookout with orders not to take his eyes off the water because there were rocks to be navigated, blew a whistle acquired from the sportsmistress he had long ago married and divorced, and set a pace for the piercing bedlam of the sea voyage to follow.

— I voted Yes, the patriarch Penhallurick informed Dorina as they anchored off the reef in water so deep and clear she dared look down only once, as if leaning out of the cockpit of a glider. On condition I get my knighthood before a republican administration can take all that away. What do you say, Philip? he referred the matter to his son-in-law.

— Your only chance, that rosy gentleman commented between blasts of the whistle as he supervised the sheet-anchoring operations, is the Queen's birthday honours list. He waited a moment while the mainsail racketted and thumped. In June, he concluded when sudden quiet wiped the air clean.

The old man poked at his ears, shedding a couple of scabs.

— I'll just squeak in, he agreed gleefully. With a week or two to spare. The luck of the wicked. What do *you* say? this time the question was put to Dorina.

— Shall we have lunch straight away or after a swim?

— Food! the ogre stuck his yachtsman's cap back at a rakish angle and capered about the deck. What do you say? he asked his assembled grandchildren.

— Food, they yelled.

Dr McKinley, who began singing a sentimental aria as he went below, passed Dorina the picnic basket, then hoisted a cooler on to the galley table and began distributing cold drinks.

— Glorious food, crowed the owner of it. What do you say?

— Thank you, Dorina said.

During the flight from Sydney she had explained to Rory that sailing is the noblest means of travel. Now, able to form an

educated opinion, she classified it quietly as a particularly maddening means of reaching B from A.

While they ate, the host insisted she join him on a seat against
the aft rail.

— I have a lot of faith in your husband, he confided, his voice
foreign. He shot her a glance so shrewd she realized with shock
the real man had not yet been encountered, she'd been tricked
into seeing only a decrepit clown.

— Your support, she replied. Means a very great deal to him.

— And your support, Dorina?

— Mine goes without question.

— But what if unexpected demands are made on him?
(Again the piercing glance.) Let us say the demands of great
success?

— Surely, she retaliated. You cannot be asking about our
private affairs?

— I have Bernard's interests very deeply at heart. He
thumped his heart to show it was there.

Dorina took her time. She knew that the conversation, like the
yacht, hung suspended over deep canyons, the casual tone an
illusion of calm beneath which malice drifted, monstrous,
somnolent-bodied, but alert. She crunched a lettuce leaf and
savoured a mouthful of sauvignon blanc.

— Have you a reason for believing such success might come
to him?

— Ah, he confessed, eyelids drooping demurely. When you
are as rich as I am, you make sure you are ready for anything.

— We cannot know, she then explained. How we will behave
in unfamiliar circumstances. That is what makes life interesting.
But I may say I am not the kind of person who expects to get
away with anything.

His eyes, now fierce and cold, searched hers. This, undoubtedly, had been taken as a challenge.

— Morality, he granted after an uncomfortably long pause. Is
a strong position. Good.

The children, having stuffed themselves with luxuries, set
about sorting masks and flippers ready for snorkelling. They
cheered when their father brought spear-guns too and placed
them, glittering, on deck.

— I don't see morality as needing strength to justify it,
Dorina countered. It may equally well be weakness, or an excuse
not to think for oneself. I just know that, for me, life without it
would be inconceivable.

Warm sea patted the yacht gently. The whistle shrieked.

— Bernard, I am happy to discover, Mr Penhallurick closed the interview. Is a lucky dog.

— Stand back, Dr McKinley brayed at the children though Rory was already standing back. Ladies and grandfathers first! Now, he bowed to them. Choose your weapons.

— What a great fellow this is, the old man chortled delightedly. To acquire for the family.

— I don't think I shall swim today, Dorina apologized, not wishing to have it known that she couldn't swim, particularly now. The wine has given me a headache. And just look how burnt I am.

So, granted guest's dispensation to take refuge from the sun, she climbed down into the cabin.

— Come on Grandpa, shrilled a child. Here's a mask for you to wear.

— I'll be in it all right, the old man answered. You won't beat me.

Dorina lay on a bunk against the thin shell of hull, bankrupt of adventurousness, indignant at having been investigated, but relieved that her skin failed to live up to normal standards while the McKinleys toasted themselves browner, providing her with a legitimate escape. She did rest, lulled by small-fry scuffling overhead. No, count me out, she murmured, smiling with anticipation of their happiness.

A distant cry came to her, nothing to do with the snorkelling preparations above; came to her, incredibly, from below, from underwater. A long-drawn plaintive ululation buoyed her up, so music-prone she was. It set the hull vibrating as a membrane. She wished she could make the call come clearer. The muffled hooting sounded again. She had never heard its like before.

Fascinating, she told herself. Nonsense, she added.

Yet the dreamsound drifted, impossibly, sustained by remembered heartbreak. When gone, Dorina doubted it had ever been. Her real concern, as she admonished herself, was Rory with his dogged refusal to make friends. Had he at last struggled free of the barriers he trapped himself in, barriers he was more likely to have inherited from her than from Bernard? She did so hope he would be happy. She meant, also, for the rest of his life.

Dorina had her own problems too. Lately she'd become aware of a familiar strangeness in her body; of feeling, as she might describe it, ill with good health. Nothing was confirmed, but some biological festival jostled the blood, life crowding faster through her. She had not consented to this. No. She lay on the bunk, suspended above a treachery of clear-sighted depths, blaming herself for not relaxing.

The first siren-sad calls had long faded when an answer came, a second voice booming directly beneath the boat, a moan which welled, loomed, shockingly close. She sat up. The celebrating blood drained back to her heart; fear ghosted over her cold burnt skin. As she listened, several more cries floated in from remote valleys. Dorina summoned her courage and her robust critical sharpness as well. Yet, however she might try, the water voices could not be denied. Bass notes growled, so deep her fingers on the hull heard better than her ears. Then she acted. She clattered to her feet, unsteady in the gently rocking yacht.

— Philip, she called. Philip, please come. Come quickly.

Dressed for diving, he descended the ladder, flippers appearing first and ludicrously aflutter, bare legs followed, then plump belly, florid chest, neck with a grey frizz of hairs normally concealed by a collar, intelligent mouth ripe with use, nose dilated to exhale the whole sky on this glorious day, and finally the questioning eyes.

— Ssh! she ordered and held one hand behind her ear with a conventionality that irritated him.

Then he heard what she heard. His face shone with success. This was a marvel he knew and had expressly organized. He would present them all with the ultimate entertainment.

— Fantastic luck! he whispered. The whales are singing.

He sloppered up on deck to fetch the others. Dorina lay back in her bunk with the pleasure of someone whose high standards are at last, and especially because only this once perhaps, met.

She forestalled any danger by addressing her mind to the question of water in general. We came from water, she conceded. Out of some ocean liner, or off a clipper having rounded the Horn, from some raft held together by lashing, from ugly little coracles refusing to be steered, right back to a basket in the bullrushes, I suppose. Or a dug-out canoe, she corrected herself. Also in the wider sense, having been big newts waddling up from swamps, fresh out of the slime with grand ideas of standing on our back legs and drinking from cups and saucers. Well, she acknowledged the whales, they were ideas grand enough for us to be able to draw the shape of your ocean as it defines our land. Could there be such a thing as Australian whales? How to explain the case for yes or no? Will this change the seabed? Will the plankton emigrate? The point is, we shall feel prouder of you, if you see what I mean and the value of that.

The McKinleys tiptoed down to join her, Rory among them. Dorina immediately saw he was no longer shut off and sulking. How very young the boys looked. Mr Penhallurick followed, a little less spry than he'd been on deck; his flippers, no sooner strapped on than tugged off again, left red welts across chicken feet. At Dr McKinley's cue, the entire crew listened. Dorina smiled, welcoming them, as if the whale-song were some peculiarity of her own, herself the hairy woman in a circus cage reassuring country bumpkins she was not at all shy of displaying her deformity. She lay back as she had when the marvel first visited her, maybe in the hope of catching something she missed the other time round. Yet, if it came to the point, did she want this? Did she wish actually to receive a message? Even the possibility that there was a message put her in the dilemma of either refusing to listen or catching herself eavesdropping: both contemptible. More troubling still was the implication that if the calls were warnings, as she believed they were, then they spoke of what was to come, the nightmare vocabulary of a future burdened with treachery too deeply known in our secret selves to be opposed. What if rational speech might be howled down in this future, leaving us deaf to human music? No, Dorina refused to allow it. She insisted whales behave like whales. All this, she persuaded herself sensibly, is simply biology. They call to keep contact with the family. That was it. They survive, these vast animals, hot at heart, by banding together down there in an art form. A consort of whales.

Dorina risked glancing at her companions' tourist faces and knew they would hear the roar of Fitzroy Falls with the selfsame delight. She wished it might be otherwise, but they caught none of the sadness, none of the appeal. Being alone, she thought, grows tiresome. Small waves slapped warnings against the hull. Once, a scarlet note flaming above the inky basses spoke too desperately to be art. Her dispassionate theory collapsed, she shivered with dismay that a whale might cry help to someone as impotent as herself. She imagined the massive mammal already beginning to rise beneath their yacht, the surge of its approach, the waxing and dim vastness of its climax, barred with shafts of shadow and crusted with barnacles. She recoiled from the hull lest she be swallowed. And Dorina was not alone in her distress; she noticed Mr Penhallurick scramble back up on deck, his livid feet betraying him.

Whales hooted high soprano notes and the McKinley clan joined in, mooing and shrieking; just as, on the voyage out, they had gone crazy each time the boat heeled through a swell.

Dorina's childhood having been so filled with sickening luxuries and violence, she could never wish more youngsters to be brought face to face with reality as she knew it. Better the illusions any time. Most of those years were spent in dormitories or foreign outposts where her father speculated on how the world might be changed: as if things weren't terrifying enough as it was.

— Let's go, the smallest McKinley proposed like a comically diminutive adult. And see if they come up spouting. Shyly, imperiously, he led her to the ladder.

Once out in the open again, she looked round for the old man, perhaps to speak to him, but he sat in the bows, evidently wishing to be alone. The grandchild's fingers clung to her, certain she would share the next adventure, this lady who had been first to hear the whales. She must bring him luck.

Dorina rejoiced in the complicity. She accepted his hand like any motherly person and allowed herself to be sat in the blistering sun and directed which way to face and what to look for.

— Have you ever seen a whale before? he wanted to know in his husky voice.

— Have you?

— No, he confessed out to sea.

— Nor me.

But what if Dr McKinley had been wrong? What if his psychiatric patients struggled up from the couch and took fits of frustration against his incompetency? What if the backing of the Australian Medical Association were not enough to make his practice respectable? What if the noises were not made by whales at all, but by currents among the coral, the yawning of caves scoured interminably, the legato gasp of subterranean tunnels? Suddenly sceptical, Dorina stared out over the boring sea as instructed, still holding her companion's salty hand but losing contact. Regretfully she watched that meaningless expanse of brilliance. The boy was already mesmerized by disillusion on a cosmic scale. There would be no whales. Childhood, she once remarked to her husband who surprised her by nodding agreement, is the only time in our lives when anything has three solid dimensions. Solid grief. Solid joy. Because, she attempted to explain to him, we are still wholehearted then and irrational. As she elaborated this idea, she watched Bernard's interest wane till he helped himself to a bottle of beer from the refrigerator. Dorina was recalled from her reverie by hearing Rory belowdecks utter a belch of laughter: at last. She felt responsible toward this other child too, whose hand still waited in hers. How was his letdown to be healed?

— No, she spoke up, turning away suddenly. I cannot stand any more. But recollected her duty and smiled. They are too sad, she explained.

Dorina noted the child's expression now she and he faced opposite ways like occupants of a nineteenth-century lovers seat. His eyes, the sea's identical blue-touched-green, were truly part of the sea and unafraid. It was in these eyes she saw the whale rise marvellously black and glossy, throwing off blinding jewels of sunshine, dilated with pride at its own mythology, saw it break the surface, cascading silent arpeggios.

She spun round but the whale had gone. Gently seething water covered all trace of its plunging body.

— What was it like? she begged.

He took a moment to locate his tongue.

— Big, he croaked.

This is, she instructed herself goodhumouredly as she returned to the vigil of watching, what faith means: somebody else's witness. The endless panorama had seduced her into expecting to find words for the sacred. Then a second whale slid up through the dreaming sunlight, a long low back not as huge as she had imagined, debouched an exhaust of fine spray, and sank out of sight. She reached for the little boy's hand, because they had released one another in the meantime, and squeezed it. He let her do so. She had brought him his good luck. Then freed himself, the better to concentrate.

— Dad! he screeched without once taking his Pacific eyes off the spot, the arteries in his thin neck startled full of blood. Up here Dad!

If it is true that I am pregnant, how shall I ever break the news to Buchanan? Dorina asked herself. And how shall I cope with his reaction? He has a way of running other people's lives. My life. If he is angry, of course I shall be angry with *him*. But if he is pleased, I think I might still be angry about that.

Rory was the first up from the cabin.

— Look darling, she cried excitedly. Over this way, the whales are leaping right out of the water. It's a thrill you must treasure all your life. You'll be able to tell your father when he comes home. Nothing so exciting can possibly happen to him at his conference.

Trapped in a cube of hell called childhood, Rory watched his mother ruin everything from the outset of the adventure, pursing her lips at this as dangerous and that as too simple. He raged because he could not endure sharing anything with her. Also because he could not endure sharing her with others. Most of all he was wounded by his own petulance, humiliated by knowing his mother felt ashamed of the way he misbehaved. Nothing less than singing whales had a chance of healing the fierce loss in his heart. But now here she was again, telling him what he must remember. Then a young whale surfaced quite close, rolling on its side, on its back, sunning a pale belly, snaking one flipper up and up into the air like a black tentacle and letting it fall flat to one side, slapping hard on the hard water. Again. With great lolling joyful whacks this lazy calf amused itself, and Rory found he had, without effort, joined in the hysterical cheers of the McKinleys.

Dorina noticed the old man move to be nearer them and busy himself doing something. Then she saw what it was. He clutched at a lifebelt, tugging to free it from its bracket. She went across, steadying herself against the boom, and spoke gently to him.

— When I was a child, she began. We were caught up in a revolution. We lived abroad, you see. There was nothing one could do but hang on to one's nerve. The whole thing had got so completely out of control.

Mr Penhallurick did not look at her. But he listened. And he let go of the obstinate lifebelt.

— I too, he admitted eventually, hoarsely, in his thick foreign accent. Outlived a revolution. Though I was not a child. The blood returned to his lips.

This time it was she who took his hand. A breeze reached them from the mainland and sang tenderly in the rigging.

4
_____

Buchanan returned to his hotel room to find a dossier on the table: the complex negotiations for Paringa, plus drafts of a satellite agreement bearing a departmental gloss: *We regard the term satellite as conveniently covering a range of possible defence strategies not yet able to be defined more accurately, owing to their being still in the development stage.* He scanned it, getting a feel for the length, the responsibility of such documents. Was he to be allowed to take it to Sydney with him? The oddity of his situation now struck home. He did not know who had delivered the dossier, or who expected it back. He had nothing to prove he had even been asked to stand for election. Not a word in writing. He was on his own.

More disquieting still: he realized that if everything went according to plan, he may never be on his own again. The next few days might be his last as a private individual at liberty to please himself and go where he liked without a platoon of detectives clomping in his wake. He smiled for the photographer. He looked grave for the photographer. He submitted to being lit from all sides, floating like a vain but vulnerable yolk in an egg of hot white light. He folded his arms, sat, stood. These few days might be the last in which he would be at liberty to follow a whim. The camera clicked and clucked while its operator sighed small satisfactions, small doubts. And his whim for the present was characteristically audacious: if not now, when would he ever have the chance to see this Paringa site on his own terms, free to poke around without being shown what to look at by public service con-men, without being condescended to by the military? Good one, sighed the photographer.

Buchanan consulted some excellent maps in the dossier and calculated how long it would take him to drive a thousand kilometres by the crow, the last three hundred with no fuel depots. He would carry extra cans. No worries.

He set out early next morning, the dossier shut in his brief-case and locked in the boot. Nothing now could go wrong. Friends whose existence he never suspected were to make fools of his enemies. Buchanan the Good, not an ounce of music in him, siffled. He thought briefly and affectionately of the impossible Dorina. He chuckled, he flew, our corpulent messiah, reassuring himself: anyhow, if this American base is to be on our soil they'll have to understand we're a pretty independent crew. Thus he set final approval on his escapade; he was demonstrating a political point. Bold with joy, he made this his first mission. The loneliness of the drive would be a tonic, a chance to clear his brain. Beneficial all round, considering the excitable state of a chosen man. He drove. He relished his freedom.

Far out on the barren flatlands the last parrots advocated turning back. Sand-dunes nosed at the verges of a stony plain like cliffs jutting into a harbour. Still he drove, charmed, in a capsule of airconditioned luxury. His heaped-up body relaxed. The farther the Mercedes progressed, unrolling that halfcircle horizon as a bow-wave, the more isolated our leader-elect became in a devastation of heat. He stopped only to relieve himself, amused at the possible benefaction of so much liquid in one spot and expecting seedlings to sprout while he watched. He enjoyed a cold beer. And topped up the tank from the first of the fuel cans while he was at it. The tyres rumbled over a road which was no more than straight depressions worn through identical smooth stones paving the whole desert. Buchanan's cool capsule travelled balloon-buoyant across waste land vast as some entire countries, till it reached the very core of desolation, the heart of nothing. There the engine died.

With no warning, simple as a lone dinosaur surrendering the huge effort of supporting its own extravagance and humbly, fatally lying down, the car jolted, coughed, and rolled out a final ninety metres of wilderness, a last lap to extinction. The fat man sat shocked; his foot still depressed the accelerator, his hands still steered.

The airconditioning hummed confidently. The control panel showed no warning lights. The clock went round. For a long moment he believed the car once more sleeked smoothly toward destiny. But commonsense took control. The cooler would, of course, drain the battery. He reached out. And switched on a blast of immaculate silence. His own breath treacherously eroded the stock of cold air.

He had better look at the motor, not because he knew anything about motors or had the least skill at fixing them, but because this was what a man did when a car broke down. His good news told him nothing could go wrong, that angels watched over him. Echoes of laughter confirmed his great future. Still bold with joy, he opened the door. Heat slammed him tightly back on his seat, a huge suffocating hand of it slapped over his face. He could not squirm free.

Long before: the invading sea had rushed in and tumbled rocks, cracking them to even sizes, grinding them together and washing them smooth. Centuries, impossible to count, rose in a succession of suns to witness the stone-smashing. The sea broke those broken stones again and rounded their roundness until the seething froth retired on its last tide amid squalls and chaos. Ten million years (still palpable) sealed petrified bones of the sperm whale's progenitors buried far inland along the courses of extinct rivers. The desolate bed of the sea's labours dried and set to a stony plain. Only scorpions defied the heat, plus a lizard camouflaged as stone and indifferent to sympathy. In other deserts sand lies a kilometre deep, its upper layers shifting gracefully as a woman beneath a time-coloured blanket. But here were only stones. The stones did not move once the sea had gone. Wind could never budge them. There was nothing else to try.

So the car came to stand on this plain, marooned and singular, the largest intrusion for a million hectares around. Inside a driver sat glued to the seat with sweat he could ill afford to lose. In the flicker of an eye, when his attention was not focused, two days escaped him. The sun forged through his stopped reality. A wary scorpion patrolled the sharp rim of car-shadow, tail curled crusty with arrogance at having been the first airbreathing animal and still alive. The burning horizon severed land from outerspace.

— Can you imagine, Buchanan asked faintly to alleviate the threat. Walking half a kilometre? With only another one hundred and twenty-three and a half to the nearest water?

The moulded sky refused to give room for the sound of words, so this joke stuck to his face. He tried a few grimaces, hearing his skin crack, resistant. He even made the error of adjusting the mirror to take a look. The seat held him firmly in the mirror's range. Dismissing the temptation to be shocked, he inspected blisters and the erupting strata of dried words plastered fine as skin on his cheeks.

— About my usual, he conceded. Bernard Buchanan, he added a little later, recognizing the face.

The sun persisted in drifting. But not smoothly, no. It jerked and slipped in his vision, rushed a little toward the strict horizon, held back slyly, developed a squashed top and a belly on one side, mocking him, and finally trembled stickily into a heat haze of its own delirium.

— President! Bernard Buchanan whispered in the late light, eyes deflecting the title to his mirror where the promise belonged.

Then he turned to face the young man sitting beside him. Because, in that flicker of an eye when his attention was not focused and those two long days ghosted by, a stranger had arrived.

They both turned, in fact; the one clockwise, the other anti-clockwise. Interlocking cogs. Their eyes met. But Buchanan dropped his, shamed by the fellow who had done all that could be done to attract rescue, having stripped the vehicle of objects useful to survival, only to retreat, finally, behind an expression of vacant confidence. An expression, the fat man thought, more appropriately worn by an assistant, some poor sod relegated for life to holding a clipboard or passing a scalpel, who awaits, even so, the unattainable satisfaction of his own command. Out here such a look came distressingly close to heroic.

We, Buchanan had been told by the famous man with the toothbrush-moustache accent, have full support from all but one of the, ah, commercial television networks, we have newspapers and magazines, everything set for victory, radio talk-back shows, you name it. Ah, we don't do things by halves. Just brief yourself on the Paringa thing.

Once he'd reached the fringe-desert, the candidate saw for himself the region's saleable isolation. Bare tracts of country offered ideal exposure to the sky. Such a sky it was! Perfect in clarity. Probably the world had nothing finer to commend. It was the sky they were buying. Buying, because the whole contentiousness of the issue lay in the government's negotiations to sell title and deed in perpetuity to a foreign commercial enterprise.

At dawn the desert lay bare as a temple courtyard, wind blowing infertile dust in eddies and a few spiky flowers of light crackling red at one corner of what was otherwise empty. So intense the attendant silence set, he believed in sudden panic that he had been struck deaf.

A memory from those two lost days came back. The sun, wedging a blade between his eyelids, had prised them apart. He recalled levering one powdered arm into position (had he collapsed, then?) and letting it fall across his face. This would do, this gesture old as Pompeii, till he woke to a heavenly illusion of shade. A voice spoke from the midst of the burning day, telling him he would be saved. A bottle rested against his mouth and dripped water. Someone's hand smeared life into his face. He squinted at the flaring void. Now, said the young man, if you lock your arm around my neck, that's the style, I'll lift you on *nmf* your feet okay and *nmfa* we'll have you back. . . right?. . . inside the car.

The fat man's itching skin itched at the memory. He had indeed been saved. The sun jerked and drifted through that precious real-estate sky; the car seat held his flaking despair in a mirror's prison; the handsome eyes of his rescuer turned away from him, as if the desert promised more interest. The word *president* had slipped out, had given Bernard away. What a fool he must appear now, with his glorious optimism. The clock went round. Sudden night welled hardly less searing than the sun.

— Another day Peter, he observed, manoeuvring his brown-paper tongue in its rusty can to let the syllables free and shuddering a shudder not missed.

— Chasing a wave, the young man remembered softly after a while. You can wait for hours, you know. Just floating, paddling, calling yourself a mug. Then the big one comes. You ride the slope and you pick up power. The board moves fast, he smiled and paused a moment as it caught his breath. You've got to take a wave for all you can get. You need to be pretty strong, pretty fit. But in those moments you fly. And that's when it can be scary too. No worries.

Bernard Buchanan looked far through the fiery rim of his eyelids into the first shadow seen all day, the shadow of earth itself tilting away from the sun. The cosy idea of a rescuing wave did him good.

— That was a bloody long speech, he remarked. For you.

— Yeah, Peter Taverner agreed with a grin so sudden it illuminated the dim cab with piercing advice of vitality, the light's last reserves glowing from blue eyes and strong teeth.

The fat man reclined his seat and rolled to one side, unsticking his back so it sounded like flesh tearing under strain.

— Bernard, his companion said. Sweet dreams mate.

— I forgot, he apologized as he handed over the flask. It's your water after all.

— One sip each, do you reckon?

— To hell with it, Buchanan cried so his voice rattled. Let's have two. We're sure to be rescued tomorrow.

Peter gave him a mock punch on the shoulder.

— That's the old Bernard, he said with certainty, though they had never met before.

5

The principles of stress and counterstress in the Human Pyramid depended on that outward thrust, common even to stone pyramids, pushing against the sides, as well as, by gravity, thrusting downward. From apex to base these several pressures were visible in the stretch and strain of muscles. All twelve men, wearing patterned black and white singlets and tights, had been chosen for their ugliness, that the individual could be shown, through the agency of training, to transcend his misfortune in a collective beauty.

Once the pyramid assembled itself tier by tier, the last man ran up diagonals of knees and elbows, finally straddling the heads at the top, to raise his arms and form the peak of a triangle in a gesture which was at the same time a sign of victory. So, wavering momentarily, they firmed. They posed for applause.

At first, one watched with admiration the general shape and then, scanning it from point to point, appreciated the details of stress seeming certain to pull the figures apart: the holding together of linked arms, the swell of resisting limbs, torsos heaving, black tights glinting long muscle flanges almost metallic in the gloss of encasing fabric, sweat-slicked arms and shoulders, some pale and hairless, some freckled and furry, some dark and etched by anatomical lessons. And then, mysterious as an epiphany, the patterns on the costumes flexed till they were seen to form letters. The letter A emerged at the apex; below it an L, and below that a P. The audience burst into a storm of cheers. The pull of the pyramid flexed again and while the vertical ALP remained visible, a horizontal triad of the same letters formed, intersecting at the L.

The circus band, silent till this moment, burst into cacophonous bleatings of triumph, an ill-tuned fanfare dipping its ocker lid to that grand tradition traceable back through movie vulgarizations to genuinely royal occasions, through gratitude to God right back to the ten-metre African trumpets mounted on two camels and the skin-bound horns of Egypt before, to the rose-belled tubas with which the Hammurabi declared their victory over Sumer in the valley of tombs.

Astonishingly, the man at the top smiled. The only one of those impersonal faces (faces concentrating on inward messages dedicated to holding their balance a moment longer) to break into an actual expression of success. His name, though not a single person in the auditorium knew this, was Nick.

Then the structure yielded, using natural forces as a springboard, simultaneously leaping out, exploding the pyramid to line up before the audience's flickering hands and wide-open faces. The Labor leader, Darryl Robinson, sidled from the wings to congratulate them. Through wafting sweat, on a stage space still imprinted by that tricky acrobatic pattern, speeches began.

So the first campaign got under way for the coveted presidency. Robinson, what's more, did seem assured of success. The
present government, in the usual conservative tradition, had no
policy; they floated along on commercial opportunism, stagnat-
ing in backwaters or being swept rudely out of their depth by a
flood of speculation. Miraculous innocence became their habitual achievement. . . always the blame lay elsewhere. As an
Opposition leader, Robinson seldom needed to aim shots; the
enemy scored his points for him. He came to rely on winning by
default in the long run.

— Thank you. Thank you, he smiled and held up his empty
hands. Friends.

He was so pleased with himself, he missed noticing the sighs
of experienced journalists. They knew him well enough to
anticipate a boastful encomium on his own skill and integrity,
reasonably certain that once he got to the juiciest part his nerve
would fail. He would not falter so much as grow blurry while he
felt an icy spool of scepticism being drip-fed into his blood-
stream. Nobody did this to him. He managed it all by himself as
his one true virtue.

The current jokes about his speaking with a forked tongue
referred mainly but not exclusively to the fact that Darryl
Robinson looked rather reptilian. Although such scaly long-
nosed types might pass for handsome among certain Australians, and at least as homely among a good percentage of others,
his seasons before the mirror had much the same effect of
creeping distress as his occasional virtuosity on the hustings. He
sensed great events growing beyond his control.

It would also be true to say that many journalists sipping
coffee between jottings and checking the tape in their miniature
recorders already knew something about editorial policy in the
election coverage, the villainy of which Robinson could hardly
be blamed for failing to anticipate.

At this stage, Roscoe Plenty had not yet announced his
surprise plan to contest the election too.

6

Stars flocked down as night wheeled through the epochs of
hunger and drying out. Peter Taverner lay curled on the back

seat. Buchanan remained in the front. The men slept neither more nor less than during daylight. And their hearing, in the dark, gave no firmer grip on testable reality than their sight in the blinding sunshine. But the air took on a drinkable mildness, even with a touch of cold.

Comfort crept through the fat man's body, the loose rolls of his waist and paps sagged to their familiar shape. He enjoyed a sensation of lightness, of capability. He got up to use his legs for the sake of health and walked away from the car, out across the stony wilderness. To his joy he found his body remembered other functions of its prodigy. So many years lost since those public notices: *Gents are requested to adjust clothing before leaving*. He was old enough to have grown up in a courteous world. Bernard loved the night, this was another issue on which he and Dorina could never agree. There was in him, perhaps, a yearning to live at night and sleep away the day while she sang in her garden. Without a moon, black space stretched taut, spiked by planets.

Ankles turning, lungs wheezing, he wandered painfully away from the Mercedes and that fellow left asleep. Stones chimed like porcelain underfoot. The man chosen to stand for president stopped again, to find he watched one star progress evenly and steadily among the rest, maintaining a ruled line. That, he deduced with bland interest, but nevertheless in the manner of a person thus claiming to belong to a safe world from which he had been unfairly expelled, is a satellite. I haven't seen one since the day we all rushed outdoors to watch Sputnik and the national news broadcast details of where and when to look. This particular satellite, though, might now concern him personally, might indeed be the first stage of the US space station.

He pondered his foreign backers ready to break their necks (and anybody else's) for a communications base, acknowledging that the term conveniently covered a range of possible defence strategies not yet able to be defined more accurately. . . And why shouldn't they have what they wanted? Another base could do no harm. It was to our advantage, going with the strength. Bernard nodded darkly. The silly New Zealanders provided a lesson in the wages of folly, having defied America long enough for multinationals to foreclose their mortgage and call in their loans, till all that was left for payment in reparation was the country itself. Hadn't a compliant Australia already been offered the South Island as an eighth state for the future republic?

The satellite seemed almost homely. He talked to it, reviewing his life for its interest.

— People who are not fat think of fat people in social situations as funny or a nuisance; whereas when you are fat you think of yourself as lonely. Nothing will change this. I am not free from it myself. Fat people are secretive, and that's not a bad thing. Also ambitious, which is fine. Because we want to be loved.

Buchanan the Good stared at the close and infinite night and shook his busy head, feeling the crusted skin crack some more. Shoes kicked clinking stones, stones undisturbed for the ten million years you could still feel surrounding you. What a mercy the young bloke had chanced by. For company. Yet this mercy made his suspicions ache, this mercy tormented him more sorely than blisters. Grateful beyond expression, he was. But the big questions were not answered. How did Peter come to be here? What was he up to? Buchanan thought of the young man's appearance; hair and the beginnings of a beard so blond in contrast to his tanned face, he might have been a photograph's negative.

Feet growing tired and knees weak, the chosen man sat where he was. His satellite went into decline.

— Once, I was a kid on a bike, he reminisced and the space station paused to listen. I had wings.

The cosmos caught him in its net of constellations. He must have dozed off.

— How? he demanded, woken by the ache. How did the bloody fellow arrive here on foot?

He must get up. He must retrace his steps. But where? He had lost any sense of direction. The air hummed with immeasurable frequencies. He looked up, puzzled. He faced about. His space station had gone. And the lustrous black sky itself was being, as he now saw, cancelled by an opaque blanket. One last stripe of stars narrowed between an upper and a lower horizon. For fugitive minutes these surviving stars sparkled like a distant sea. Then the straight edges of the world below and its swooping counterpart above clamped tight, sealing him in like the sliding door of an observatory dome, sightless. Buchanan scrambled to his feet. Was he to be swamped by a freak thunderstorm? In desperate need of a drink, was he to be drowned? Yet no, surely there would be lightning.

— Why doesn't he tell me? he persisted with a thought left

over from before falling asleep, as if this might also restore the world he knew how to suffer.

Once upon a time Bernard Buchanan was given such wonderful news he floated, he flew, stimulated by the trumpets of self-confidence he entertained himself, becoming his own first disciple.

— Peter, he shouted into the night memories. Peter.

Nothing at all could be made out from the blackness he stumbled through. His lovely green car stood somewhere, invisible. The dark flooded so close he could hear it rushing from an empty tunnel. And now he smelt dust. Dust storms were notorious in the outback. One saw films: dust smudged huge as an advancing cliff that roiled and surged, a stupendous wave hanging and then breaking, millions of tons of the stuff hailing down along a front extending for a hundred kilometres. Dust deposited deep enough, at its worst, to bury a house.

— Peter, he called patiently, not being one to allow panic the upper hand. But the stillborn word went nowhere, all space thick with an impending fall. He doddered over cobbles which, he was convinced, now sloped uphill. Again he collapsed, trembling and hearing his knees, as mechanisms, crack. Peter! he cried under that gag, in a voice his mother would have recognized with despairing impatience. Peter! Silence settled thickly about him. He decided to remain on one spot, wobbling as he was (That's right, he gasped), and call at regular intervals, conserving the tatters of energy.

Once, at an opera Dorina insisted they should see, a tenor with electric black hair stood rigid on stage under blazing lights and the stares of the audience while the action passed him by. He stood till you suffered for him. Then, when it seemed too late, opened his throat and sang heartstopping high notes. Even Buchanan, tone deaf as he was, caught the power of the moment. Yes, and he too would stand, simply, on this unique intersection of longitude and latitude, shouting till his thoughtless guest chose to wake and hear. He would not, at all events, be out here beyond sunrise. The misery had a limit to it. Even in pre-dawn light his car must be visible for twenty kilometres.

But he was not a man to submit to patience, not the type to conserve energy prudently. He felt a desperate urgency, fighting for life. Fear drove him to lurch about, yelling the only name of rescue, yelling it now with naked hatred. Peter! He tilted his head to look up, to learn whether his eyes were open. He could not tell. He fought blindness and the dreadful sensation that he may not be shutting them when he thought he was. Nor were his ears offered hope. Only the deadened syllables he may just as well imagine he shouted. After several attempts, he questioned whether he had made any sound at all, and took to gripping his larynx between thumb and finger to feel it vibrate *help*.

The weight of dust stifled him. Any minute he might be buried alive. Already his existence was revealed as tentative: raising the free hand in front of his face, he smacked his nose and seemed satisfied. He stumbled upon the scent of water one hundred and twenty-four kilometres away. He heard that hard young body turn in its sleep. He prayed for the satellite to rise again and be seen. He dislodged hope from his ragged throat. Peter! feeling the word with his fingers, while dehydration wormed its way to the juicy centre of complacency, and hunger dug new cavities in that ample belly. Terror pressed against him warm as a woman.

He walked the rim from which the sky rose, a void burnt black by the sun's naked flame.

Bernard Buchanan stopped. Stamina gone. Swayed where he stood, freighted with knowledge of helplessness. Perhaps here was the place designated for him to die, and no struggle on his part could alter it. Here on these salty stones must be the cleanest grave the world offered, the driest and most sterile; though the choice of moment showed fate as not above malice. What price his amazing luck now? Having invited him to be their candidate, propositioned him and got him, how could those powerful people be careless enough to leave him to die? He moaned, desolate as a child who knows nothing beyond the passion for sustaining his grief.

Unaccountable, how the blackness pulsed and exhausted the air, how it began speaking to him in thrilled stammerings. He poked at his ears. A wind was rising, yes, but he felt no dust. The strange aroma not so much dust itself as dust-like.

He imagined somebody had come to stand beside him. He felt their bloodheat and heard them panting. Who is it? he croaked in his thirst. Night made no answer. He groped at the void; he lashed out. No longer one hand at his own throat (who cared if sounds were escaping now or not?) he swept both arms in wide arcs of fear.

— Is that you Peter? he whispered for the animal dark. He moved sharply to one side, foiling any attempt to stab him.

What if there might be more than one attacker? Impossible.

He dismissed the idea. Where would others come from? But men are ingenious, and criminals especially. Not to mention the superpowers once it comes to matters of strategic secrecy. Why had he accepted the file? He'd be all right if he had played it cool. Gentle breath disturbed hairs at the nape of his neck. He knew Peter Taverner was capable of surprising him. Everything about the young thug smelt alien: his carelessness of safety, his indifference to property, his self-reliance, his sensuality and, most of all, his being there in the first place.

Someone dangerous as a big cat stalked Bernard Buchanan. There could be no mistake. He touched his larynx again, this time to be assured no sound did escape to give him away. The destroyer shadowed him, knowing his weakness, in the inexplicably roaring night. He felt cat fur ripple near enough to stroke.

The candidate imagined firing the revolver which lay in his desk drawer but which he had never taken the trouble to learn how to aim.

He worked his way round on one spot, trying to sense which direction felt thickest with threat.

— I came by myself, he said angrily while his fingers listened. I didn't ask you along. Leave me alone, he whispered. Don't leave me, he whispered, reconsidering.

Momentarily a block of stars showed through a hole in the covered sky, giving sufficient light to check his own dim blubber ghost poised the usual height above the ground. But no one else. The stalking beast not close as he feared, no glimmer of eyes. Nothing. Then the dark plugged him in, thick as earth to a grave.

The dust-like aroma gusted on a rising wind. He thumped his ears to clear them of the intense thrilling. He tipped his head on one side and banged it with his palm. He tried the other ear, even jumping on the spot to jar his frame and shake the muzziness loose. His mountainous panic shuddered at the impact. Star-hot stones chuckled underfoot as he walked. The pitch of the firmament reached him as a hundred million tiny grinding jaws, a canopy of jaws, enough to chew a nation's history to fibres so fine they could be lost in spray and drift out to sea beyond the reach of patrol boats at the two-hundred kilometre limit. Peter! Buchanan trembled, hoping to be rescued. The pulse spread, softer but wider than thunder, a swelling roar, as dense to the ear as the blanket of darkness to the eye. Then something smacked against his cheek. He let out a yell of dread. The brisk but painless impact of a small object thrown, or rather shot from a catapult. He strove to call Peter Taverner again, but no sound came. He clutched his neck to be certain. He had been shocked dumb. Then he felt his trouser leg being fingered. He kicked out: he stamped, the ground clinking underfoot. Nothing. Nothing but a saurian sky alive with rumbles and murmurs. Blood thudded at the base of his jaw. Haunted, he snatched at breath. Without further warning, a cataract of chirring sky tumbled about him, fluttering, clinging, nibbling, his skin and clothes infested. The carnivorous cloud swirled over him.

— Peter! he shrieked from a throat tight in the grip of his own hand, the blubber of obesity hanging round him thick with parasites. Crystals of salt grated in his eyes.

Instantly, the darkness blazed alive. He staggered under the blow of light, one fat arm shielding his face. He tripped and collapsed into the shimmering ferocity of that agonizing white. Brilliance drenched him and flooded his head. He fell from infinity through angels' wings. All space bristled alive. And then a man's legs waded through the horizontal beams, kicking up protests of insects, setting dark spokes of shadow flickering across him. The terrible night split apart at a human voice.

— Beauty! This is fucking unreal!

Someone's strength accepted the burden, supporting his abandoned body. Someone he had not thought of kindly, nor cared about, helped him to his feet and dragged him through crackling locusts, to one side of the four headlamps on high beam. So he had found his way back to the car. He was there. He had been almost close enough to touch it.

— I was miles away, Peter laughed with delight at the rarity of the scene, shoving him in, stuffing him home behind the wheel, rough with acceptance of their differences, then sprang into the back seat. They shut the windows, crushed those insects already inside, and watched an entranced swarm whirl through the light; membranous wings flickering wafer jewels.

— Christ, Bernard gasped, reaching for the switch.

In the sudden dark, heart pounding desperately, glad he could no longer be seen, the sound of the plague swelling round them till he felt rather than heard it, the candidate slumped where he was. And sank into an exhaustion of horrors.

7

Peter Taverner had arrived on foot. His own vehicle having broken down seventy kilometres further along the track, he accepted the inevitable and set out to walk back. He did so in high spirits. This was nothing. To a man who once faced death among the grinding flanks and spines of a hold full of dying tuna, the prospect amounted to a holiday.

First he had succumbed to the magic of the semi-desert, that land of sticks and prickles, stark yet teeming with animal life, of sand dunes with soaks held mysteriously between them, the water cold and fresh where wallabies drank, oases thick with fly-swarms and thousands of birds, sanctuary even for frogs plus a couple of wild goats wandering the world and glad to have put captivity behind. Then he had come upon the stones and gradually out-walked all signs of life, leaving the prickles behind and the pools of deep space in their sandy hollows. Even the flies gave up and went home. Alone and without support, he felt stimulated.

This was a solitude few dare to cross. Hints of more country beyond lay in the colourless haze pencilling a perfect arc along the horizon. Such sky here is constant. If ever a cloud intrudes, small and white though it may be, that cloud will hang around heavy as a misshapen moon, with no chance of drifting clear. Far as it moves, the ground beneath remains unchanged. While the sun sends a strange visitor gliding coolly over the hot stone floor: a shadow. And sudden clusters of insects, supposed not to exist, play in it as birds dip their wings in water. Stories survive of British explorers heading out across this wilderness ten million years too late to discover the inland sea of their hopes, horse hooves knocking the gibbers together, eyes glinting silver with the deadly glare; and eventually bones scattered as pathetic reminders that such deserts offer no here and no there. Peter Taverner found it to be all one. Never before had a religious feeling come to him. Twice he looked back at his car: once when it seemed quite big and ready to be driven away, and once when it had dwindled to a toy. This second time he stood thinking his thoughts while eternity eroded the distant hills to westward. Between him and his past the plain shone with black stones which clinked and tinkled underfoot. Yet such harshness filled him with joy. Each stone appeared as an original and worthy of note. Peter Taverner walked on. He would not look back again. But soon he did stoop to observe a last flower. The tiny living thing blew about on its flimsy stem, so rare a survivor. He recognized the power in his own body as elasticity.

— I thought they had this under control, I thought there were guys looking into this, with all the money people spend on things, he had said to Julie and Sue and Frank the Fixer (though none of them could be aroused to indignation as it turned out). Someone has got to go up there and claim that desert.

He could not adjust his mind to accept how naive he had been only last week. But glad he had come. Yes, even when the catastrophe hit, too late to salvage his wagon, he found nothing to fear in walking two hundred kilometres. Wearing light clothes, carrying water and food in a bag, he set off across shimmering stones where his boots appeared never to touch the ground. South-west he walked following that joke of a road, still carrying in mind an image of the place he had come to see. Paringa.

Globular hills on either horizon crept their infinitely slow fate, lagging and rotting mauve as he outstripped them, creeping a little closer together behind him just as he was almost lost to sight.

He walked in the simplicity of uprightness. This was Man. Man who has economized motion to using only two legs. Man who dreams and laughs, who recalls the future and invents beauty.

He mopped his face with the T-shirt he had stripped off, only then noticing the tag: 100% COTTON HAND WASH COLD DRIP DRY MADE ON PLANET EARTH. One day ago he would have laughed understandingly. Now, in this desolation, which other people called desolation, he had a nasty feeling. All those who stood against dehumanization, against the rape of the land, against suffocation under technology, were they fools? MADE ON PLANET EARTH. What a wank. He would tear the label off. But no, he left it.

The stones jingled as he walked through the day's killing loveliness. A sudden wing of light swept him along, his angel skeleton clear as glass but pliable. He had already grown beyond all prior experience. He would never be that familiar youth again. Even when the full moon, risen to its last days, floated among expectant stars, Peter Taverner still swung ahead without haste. Not until the stones grew cool enough to lie on did he take a break, eat a little food, drink a little water, and stretch out.

He dropped into sleep suddenly as rolling over a cliff.

When he saw a mechanical bug gliding on the waters of mirage the following day, he stopped and narrowed his eyes, concentrating to make it vanish. That was a vehicle all right, with no alternative but to approach along this very road. Yet the afternoon swirled past in willy-willies of dust and the car seemed no closer. If it had not moved for some hours, its stillness posed questions even more obscure than the fact of being there at all.

The Mercedes stood helpless as he drew near, one door held open by wind, and the driver's body lying in the roadway.

— Hey man, what's cooking? he asked, filled with the qualms of addressing a corpse. What're you doing here?

The transcendent day came down to this. And once again he felt glad.

Despite being in poor shape, the fat bloke was alive and did not appear beaten or wounded. He'd got himself into a mess all right and you had to admire a man so unfit for venturing this far from safety. Peter tried the motor, which would not start though the battery responded strongly and the gauge indicated a tank half full. The familiar pattern. A cold sensation crept round the back of his scalp. Here was a repetition of his own breakdown. The fuel cans in the boot of the Mercedes confirmed the improbable: filled with salt water, every one, so you couldn't even survive by drinking the stuff. He had scarcely questioned the motives of whoever pulled this lethal trick on him, but now it was no mere trick. At one stroke it had become a plan. He racked his brains for some explanation of how his coming could connect with a rich man in a rich man's car.

He began stripping the vehicle of everything useful for survival. He constructed an evaporation plant filled with salt water and set a small container to catch the fresh drops it produced. He even, after some hesitation on the grounds of good manners, opened the briefcase. *PARINGA. CLASSIFIED. SECRET.*

He looked inside under the heading *Summary*.

Stage One of a two-stage experimental defence strategy involving an earth ''leg'' of 1500 kilometres to ensure maximum accuracy in all military applications. Stage One, the mother unit, to house the reactors, the main research facility, military airforce base, and administration. Stage Two, location still to be agreed upon, but ideally in the Port George district on the east coast of New South Wales, will create the base of a triangle, the apex being the satellite space station.

Negotiations include a proposal that Stage Two, entailing rather less secret equipment, ought perhaps to be established as a joint operation with our own Australian Space Agency and built under contract by Australian labour.

He heard Bernard Buchanan moan. He closed the dossier and glanced in at the sufferer, who settled back, fitfully, to sleep. Again, Peter Taverner trespassed on the secret information. He found a confidential note from the Defence Minister:

Whatever public stance the government adopts to safeguard the project against the sort of anti-nuclear hysteria we expect, the facilitating company, Interim Freeholdings Incorporated of Delaware (IFID), has made amply clear during negotiation that unless granted unqualified freedom of action, which is to say in access and actual ownership of the land, the project will not go ahead in Australia at all: another South Pacific venue will be chosen. And their defence treaty with us would be revoked. This is in line with previous indicators from the US Defence Department. It is a point to be stressed at all times. There is also the likelihood of American investment being cut right across the board by as much as 20%.

The desert sky stung him on the chest and mouth. Again Bernard Buchanan moaned and then called out too. The young man replaced the dossier, latched the briefcase quietly, and closed the boot with a thump.

— You've got a problem with your fuel tank, he replied. You've filled her up with water.

At night Peter made himself comfortable on the back seat, stimulated by the turn of events. He or his kind, footloose and unhampered, might set off for the remote outback and never be traced. But a fellow with a Mercedes and a crocodile-skin briefcase could not expect to be gone an unaccounted-for hour without alarms being set off.

He half woke, his eyes sore. He remembered. Lots of people might want a man with secret documents dead, but others would just as certainly want him alive. The strategy was to keep him going as long as possible and simply wait.

He slept.

Ages and ages ago Peter Taverner had shut the louvres in a house at the coast; the squeak and clash of glass at the end of a sweltering day, his sunburnt back chafed all night. The small panes of glass clashed again to shut away sounds of an ocean bombing rocks below. He was twelve that year or fourteen and thought he could shut out the Pacific. With one brown hand on the corroded aluminium he tugged the stiff lever and clashed the glass against a pounding so huge the headland itself trembled underfoot. And his bare feet ran scattered over the sandy bare floor, up on a squeaking bunk where he tugged the slats of sheet over his ears and still heard the world roaring, still felt a tremor of life rise through the house stumps, flutter the floor with its hopping grains of sand, excite the iron frame of the bunk and springs tingling so his own blood echoed the next wave through the frail panes of shame, his training not to wet the bed like a baby shattered at one tide of sex, his young body laid waste by the vigour of desires, the erection that would not subside, would not lie limp and, against his prayers, his louvres, defying respectability, triumphant in claiming its right to dominate his life, sprayed the covers with promise of victories. So a new vanity lurked beneath his shame and incomprehension.

Night intervened with welcome cooling of the air and less call to be sociable.

Yes, he was fourteen that year because he had known himself capable of loving as a man: all-eyes on the beach, devouring every girl and every woman not too wrinkled to be admitted as a woman. The cut of a child's costume stretched too tightly round her thighs, the sheer mass of a matron's breasts, the enigma of dimpled shoulderblades. Each night as he reviewed the day's revelations he wrenched at the corroded lever to slam the louvres shut, believing he must lock the Pacific behind small panes of glass, run, scuffing sand under his soles, leap on the bed where he could feel the ocean's detonations as strength tingling through his muscles, and the remembrance of a tender inner leg, a shaved armpit. That Pacific roar rose in mind solid as a warning he must not ignore.

He woke yet again. Something wrong with the Mercedes. Where the hell was Bernard? Gone. Had he been tricked, marooned, his water supply shared with a man who only waited to be picked up to leave him here to die? He sat under the muffled clubbing of his blood. You simple fellows, he recalled Bernard's cracked lips murmuring, are the ones who scare shit out of me. At the time Peter had taken this for a joke.

The night was invaded by an inexplicable noise, loud as a river in flood, so loud he had to disbelieve it, to call it part of his

dream. And Bernard? Was it possible he had taken off by foot
with a view to never coming back? Captain Oates, slipping out
into the night to die rather than consume any more of the tiny
water supply, endowed with the stamp of a hero? The gesture,
if made, had come too late. He'd thrown in his lot when he
helped the fat man back to the vehicle and sat with him. The
only way of surviving exposure on such a long walk was to
keep going. The blackness set so thickly he sat in an invisible
car, sensing its surrounding shapes as a blindman who walks
towards a wall will suddenly stop. The same nerve endings told
him the confines of comfort: also that the space thrusting in
through his window communicated directly with stars.

Using his bare hand he could smash a brick, one chop and
that was it. So of course people felt nervous of him, perhaps he
intended them to. Something, after all, must lie behind those
hours of gruelling training. The will had to begin somewhere.
Yet he considered himself gentle, and especially gentle with
women. In any case, Bernard had no knowledge of this, no
excuse for being afraid.

— Peter, came a sudden shriek, so the brick-chopper went
into action. He leaned over to reach the controls and groped to
flip the headlamps on, illuminating a fantasy: a hubbub of insect
wings fluttered as far as the beams penetrated, denser than hail
where his companion crouched, face on one side, mouth agape,
stick flickers and dartings of locusts clustered all over him.

You couldn't help laughing at such a pantomime of danger.

Long after they were both inside the car and the last intruders
crushed, Peter Taverner heard in that syllable — Christ — the
disgrace of a man defeated. He lit a cigarette, the explosion of his
match making Bernard jump. A flare of light flowered in cupped
hands raised like a monstrance to his face caught reflected in
black glass: sharp-cut nose and suntanned cheeks with their
pale stubble.

He slept.

Across fiercely hot stones morning swooped already to gulp a
mirage of amber hills. The bare landscape was licked clear of
locusts where the car, a glossy bean, waited to crack open at the
centenary of rain. The absence of locusts so astounded the
watching men they were glad of squashed bodies on the carpet
to prove they knew what had happened to them.

— Bernie, yelled the young man excitedly when he got up for
a piss. Check this out.

They looked together, that unlikely pair. The fact, incredible as it was, became their closest moment of sharing. The grass-hoppers had gone, but so had the car's green duco. Stripped. Buffed back to raw steel, naked and glittering, the whole of the Mercedes a reflector outshining the hubcaps Peter had removed and laid flat on the ground to attract notice from the air.

— Christ, said the presidential candidate again, but now with the voice of a man who discovers something hopeful in the world's unpredictability.

Roscoe Plenty got off to a flying start. His black hair and black eyes, his glamorous anger and stereotyped ideas, made him instantly popular. Of course he was already known as an up-and-coming young minister in the tory coalition, a convert from the left and given to the convert's traditional ferocity against former colleagues. But this was different.

While Darryl Robinson only *toyed* with a leap to the right, Roscoe Plenty had made it and made it properly, not getting hung up on the fence. Very likely the powerbrokers most often cited as his hardcore support considered him unreliable. But for a politician out front with the courage of his folly, Plenty was difficult to beat. And though welcoming an end to the monarchy in this country, he conceded he and the Queen did hold one opinion in common, that the greatest misery was to endure a night at the opera.

During Roscoe Plenty's years as a trades unionist, whilst he dreamed lustfully of parliament, he did not waste time. He perfected his image for when the small screen would become his forum. The Nationals welcomed him in parliament as a turncoat because he brought them an illicit seat. So far so good. But the presidency promised to be something else entirely.

Overnight, he declared himself. In the wild sweep of an impatient hand, in the brassy voice of a bully, the electorate discovered a new contender. These things, like love and lifelong hate, happen in an instant and seldom need speaking of. Confidence in the moderate right had slowly collapsed and was already in ruins when a wellknown academic historian spoke up in Roscoe Plenty's favour, incidentally scoring a side-swipe against Asian immigrants. So within days of the Yes vote being declared, the battle lines were drawn. Meanwhile, Buckingham Palace clerks were still shuttling memoranda which politely conceded that Her Majesty, as Queen of Australia, had indeed (and regrettably legally) been declared no longer wanted.

Roscoe Plenty scrutinized his image, subjecting each respectably labelled detail to ruthless criticism and, once he'd taken off a sporting badge, found that image perfect.

He had completely forgotten his flash of jealousy when a fat man at an Adelaide conference upstaged him, gate-crashing the compliments to say: If we're not here to cut loose and have fun, why did we come at all?

The wreck sparkled blinding daggers. In order not to suffocate, the two survivors had opened all the doors and tented a towel across those on the sun's side, securing it to the roof under five heavy stones. Heat shimmered in a centuries-long explosion, snatching air from under their noses. Each man sheltered the side of his face with a cupped hand to make breathing possible. For the fourth day, the road wavered toward an infatuation of rescue. There were no shadows beyond their car. Although the hurling world might be arrested by a single bird call, none came. The wind itself arrived silently, encountering no obstacle until it reached the clean steel edges, and there the Mercedes whistled the sibilant keening of sinews under a saw.

— I ask myself, Bernard began but got no further, staring at the probability of death, himself an awful sight with wild eyes in red-crusted rims, white flecks curdled on his lips, and skin beginning to work its way through the shirt fabric. The living head dared not move and dared not require movement of any other member of the body it was responsible for. He looked as his mother had when she was giving birth to him.

— Why? he mustered strength to add a lot later, ungluing his mouth. That's what I ask.

Right up till yesterday he had taken hold of the wheel, driving still, true to a belief in progress which had fuelled his career. Lips pursed, the skin crazed.

The passenger, now in the front seat, suppressed a hungry rebellious energy to reply twenty-four minutes later.

— If it helps to talk, keep it coming.

The entire 360 degrees of Australia melted in deadly brilliance. Among stones a lizard caught one trespassing insect. In this land the tongue is a weapon.

The driver chose to counterattack instead.

— Do you bludge around for a crust?

— I do odd jobs, the other replied politely. A bit of fishing, bit of labouring, he shrugged. Bit of dope scamming.

Buchanan was satisfied. The only thing which could have shocked him in their predicament was a lie. Even so, he felt the temptation to establish, by contrast, his own impeccable respectability; to boast, in other words, of having been selected as presidential candidate. If only to claim a higher tragedy for his fate. But something decent in him would not allow this. Death is death. And the young man made no sentimental capital of his youth. One fleshy cheek grew pregnant with a blister. Lapped by translucent air, afloat inside an eyelid-coloured shell, not knowing if he was head down or up, the president-to-be opened his mouth on the confession of pure fire he had wished to make before. He was a streak of purple light illuminating a hill he would never now reach. One of the tyres gave way and began quietly collapsing.

— Are you dead yet Bernie? he thought the fellow asked. And that was when his confession clattered out, as hot stones, long after he intended the phrases and had given them up for impossible.

— As the jury foreman. . . Not guilty, My Lord. . . I took offers afterwards. . . a great future.

Like a latecomer his swollen tongue knocked on the roof of his mouth. But there was no more to be said.

— So someone wants you out of the way?

The idea that his breakdown might not have been an accident had never occurred to Bernard. It woke him up. The white line round his lips crumbled to a reflective smile. As victim of a murder plot, his self-respect was restored. He accepted sleep. And dropped off. But then woke immediately.

— When we get out of here, come and see me.

His hand shovelled around in a pocket and produced a visiting card. The card dazzled Peter who took it by two pure corners, astounded at the invention of print, at letters in their ageless beauty, the symmetry of this small object so exactly manufactured being evidence of civilization. He might have said something unwelcome had his mouth not coagulated with homesickness.

The tyre bagged completely flat, but the men hadn't felt a thing. The sun roared round to slant in at the back window. Through a crack of vision between swollen eyelids, the Mercedes thorn on the bonnet became a gunsight awaiting a target.

— Conscience is, the fat man intoned from the frontier of, perhaps, heaven. A punishment.

— I don't gag, mate. I don't do things I'm going to be ashamed of.

Yet Peter's words disowned him. They belonged to the naivety of a fairground. Gaudily painted mechanisms (it's a question of pride) simulated real horrors under the guise of fun. Wooden horses and flickering mirrors passed. Gyrating cradles of lovers, always lovers, came spinning so high and fast in the Wheel of Death that they were plastered flat and could be stood on their heads without falling out.

The water stock was finished; the fact grew terribly clear. But he had only recently noticed the road begin to move without them, stones oscillating as smooth ballbearings, gliding under the car without sound. Ages of this silence later, catching the shock in some other bloke's eyes, Peter checked the way ahead, an interior of where he might be. Dark jungle gaped. Ghost light wavered, laced with trailing vines. The spaces between stood solid as mountains. While below he clearly saw children, he watched them, from the fairground, going berserk, setting fire to their fathers' laws and stoning a ramshackle palace of windows flashing open again on the heat of day. Inside he could see, past that fat man with crocodile briefcase, diplomats poisoning one another's wine in the cause of morality. He was doing nothing but staring through the void of a rectangle, a blank card, a blank windscreen, shuddering at each concussion of emptiness.

He woke. The desert stones shook flat again, those gonging stones, waiting. A sunpath lay on them as if they really were an inland sea. Peter Taverner kicked the empty waterflask on the floor. Dug his eyes with blunt thumbs, causing sparks to crackle from corners. It must be late afternoon. Why were those investigators so slow enquiring after the missing tailored shirt with a fat man in it? Surely voices could be heard on the wind? He must get out to check his evaporation plant and collect fresh water.

— Heaven help us, Bernard muttered in answer to this piousness. His puffy lips scarcely parted. Don't you ever have fun then? Cut loose?

He pressed the car horn. A solid jet blaring. He created it. This was the presidential voice. This was how he would sound. Someday he must find occasion. The blister ripened on one cheek and deep angry furrows set permanently between his brows.

Peter considered the challenge a long while before replying. He felt better. It was a serious question.

— You can only rely on yourself, he offered.

— But I am relying on you.

— Forget it.

Forget it! the fat man sneered bitterly to himself. To forget, one needs a future.

A dust cloud swayed into the distance, bruising the rim of sky. The heat haze dwindled. Wind weakened. The car shadow seeped out big as a building, dark as blood from their obstinacy.

It crossed Buchanan's dozing mind that his companion, by telling nothing of how he, too, came to be in this predicament, withheld a vital clue to making the whole pattern of crazy fragments fit.

Stones sparkled with knowing their secret music. Sudden gusts of grit needled the skin. The world rolled over.

The towel hanging limply against the car flapped once on metal buffed raw. And right then, heralding another plague, locusts droned loud as a distant plane and the air crackled radio messages. A huge hot shock of shadow knifed above them. Flurries of dirt swirled through the open car, ripping the towel from under its stone anchors and chasing the turbo-prop aircraft as it landed on the road ahead.

Like a terrified confession, the towel tumbled and recovered, stood up and fled, desperately clutching at rescue, and skidded eventually to its death on the abrasive ground, twitched once and lay still.

8

Dorina arrived home with an uncomfortable case of sunburn and without Rory, who had so redeemed himself that the old man said you must call me Uncle Willy and stay on with us at our beach house. Dr McKinley put the change down to his own exemplary handling of a ticklish situation.

She was alone, then, wandering from room to room savouring the pleasure of being home in Sydney, restored to her empire of intimate smells and the arrangements she had had a hand in. At this distance, the haunting of underwater cries took on an almost mythological grandeur. She heard mournful new sonorities while working at a Debussy program nobody would invite her to perform, cavernous basses sighing down the minor third, warnings beyond her powers to interpret yet familiar as the rings she wore, which she slipped off when she played and left on the ledge at the treble end of the keyboard. But I am not unhappy, she protested, this is quite fun, being alone.

The telephone sang out.

Dorina received the news with astonishment. Then she set to, capably, rather stimulated by the prospect of having her husband as a convalescent in the house. He had been up to something absolutely inexplicable, which also sounded rather marvellous: driving, it would seem, into the outback of South Australia right up near the Queensland border for heaven's sake, without a word to anyone. And did you say he was rescued minus the Mercedes? She dumped the phone back on its cradle and stripped off her gardening gloves with the air of a person who has been waiting to get down to business. She left her garden hat on as a statement against vanity, then got busy. What must be done? Dear Buchanan was hopeless, of course, about the small things. And how did he come to be marooned without her, when he knew perfectly well she had complained of a lack of adventure.

If the truth be told (and she did tell herself), Dorina might well have planned some disaster to get him off her back, but not this. Then again, she loved him and had loved him a long time. Provided Rory did not turn out the same. As for life! she declared, busy about her duties, she had enjoyed so much of her martyrdom, dinner parties, the theatre, even that heterogeneous crowd of people who called themselves friends and were ashamed when they turned out not to be and could no longer hide it. But I never mistook them for friends, poor things, she'd say, they have nothing to apologize for.

Oh, she was wicked too, hankering to fly in the face of convention, to create some unpardonable furore, and half longing for a sudden end to Bernard. If only something clean and final would happen, some change which Dorina would recognize the moment it came. Not revenge. His having to suffer would be awful and irrelevant. She believed she would regret none of her life if only he ceased to dominate it. But even then her sense of fair play rose in outrage on his behalf: had he contributed nothing? Most certainly she wasn't a person to plunge them into the crisis of divorce, ruining Bernard perhaps. No. Also such searching of self. A form of indulgence. Who wants to know? she'd cry. She referred to psychology as poking among the intestines of the mind. I'd sooner have a good dinner, she declared. As for self-analysis, she shuddered; she desired above all to accept life exactly as it was, beyond pretence, beyond doubt, whole. Oh no, that caper was not for her. The whole was what she longed to change, unable any longer to doubt that she had become Bernard's prisoner, trapped by his routines and needs. The urge for liberty burned strongly.

She arranged for a doctor to call, reviewed the food stocks, cut her very finest flowers and bundled their weeping stems into a vase, rearranged the bed and chose some light reading for his bedside table, put a pot of broth on to heat gently, checked there was ice in the fridge, and then paced the carpet to the tempo of an inappropriate recording she slapped on but couldn't muster the penitence to change for a lighter-hearted piece. She had something else on her mind, some more final bondage, something so momentous it put even Bernard's brush with danger in the shade.

— Poor darling, she kissed him and stroked his thinning hair off his forehead. How on earth you contrived to get yourself in such a mess baffles me. Of all possible crises I never imagined this. Buchanan, you are the limit. She released him from the assistance of the ambulance men and herded him tenderly into the hall. Thank you, she called, forgetful, with her back turned and hat flopping. Send the bill will you? Now straight to bed is it, and what a fright your face looks: you've got the most disgusting thing there, swollen and cracked. She kissed him again as if he'd done it to himself on purpose. They made you sound an invalid but you are walking quite satisfactorily. Does anywhere hurt?

— I'm so grateful, her husband murmured from the swabbed soreness of exposure. So tired and grateful.

— The bed's ready with extra pillows, just perch on the edge here while I cope with your shoes, she bossed him to protect him from tears. You can begin telling me once you're comfortable. A proper Leichhardt, I gather. Her hat grew sentimental in spite of her.

The subtle aroma of home calmed him into believing he was, at last, safe. He breathed deeply, the air itself a tonic.

— I'm so grateful.

— Nonsense, you're never grateful. That's part of your charm, taking the good things as your due and making a conspiracy out of everything else. She eased his clothes off to save his tender skin. She sponged him, folded his arms and laid out his corpse, then regarded him with satisfaction. No dear, gratitude has to be felt towards others, relief is what you're enjoying. But why you didn't stay in hospital is what I can't fathom.

Gliding on a trolley through the sterile wilderness, along polished corridors, a dream fear had robbed him of his courage, the insecurity so total he could relate it to nothing else. He expected Dorina to insist on an explanation but she didn't. He could not have told her. He turned his face to the wall and gazed into that shimmering flat landscape he must carry in nightmares for the rest of his life.

Her tall body creaked as she bent to care for him. Angular with breeding, she tucked him in. The domestic fatuousness of the situation struck her as dangerous: the nation run by wives tucking their idiots safely away, wars entered upon as neighbourhood louts might draw blood to make off with a lolly. Will we never grow up? she demanded. She hated childishness in adults. She was much cleverer than Bernard. She should have been the financier if brains had anything to do with it. Instead she found herself condemned to burlesque.

— That journey was a quest, he murmured somnolently. It nearly finished me off.

— My stars, she laughed a theatre person's laugh. The words you dredge up!

He examined the ceiling and wall where a wavering net of light played, reflected from the goldfish pond outside.

Of course, Dorina had news of her own to tell, but she could not muster the humility, nor the strength to withstand his reactions. Yet she was tempted. Now above all times he might be sufficiently incapacitated to behave moderately, throat so burnt to the roots of the windpipe his voice emerged as a toneless whisper. She'd be spared the inevitable emotional outburst. She bent closer. Should she? Even inside his ear the skin peeled; she noticed and took pity. She patted his arm. A pair of wattlebirds in the trees outside began an interchange at the same time vulgar and impersonal, squawk and squawk-squawk, squark. That, she confirmed, is how we must sound to them more often than not. She said nothing of what clamoured to be said. He would be thinking about himself. So Dorina took refuge in a touch of sharpness brought on by fears that his health might still be in danger.

— And did anything happen at your conference, Buchanan, apart from drinking and the obligatory little flirtations?

— I resigned.

Burnt as he was, he contrived to turn and watch the effect of his whispered words. She met the seething rabble in his eyes. Would he never find life measured up to the living of it?

— Good for you! she was unaffectedly enthusiastic about any change she had not thought of for herself.

He rolled back to the desert, a place so dreadful you could willingly give it away to any foreigner found fool enough to accept the gift.

— It was a secret, he told the wall.

She experienced a further stab of hope that she might have underestimated him.

— So you *intended* resigning? Well I suppose there will have to be adjustments.

Mr Penhallurick had asked: What of your support, Dorina, if the demands of great success are made on Bernard? No mention, naturally, of the need for her support in case of failure.

Now she did take off her garden hat and hold it gawkishly, head on one side like a person accustomed to trouble, hair tied in a soft roll, and her neck revealed as tender. Unlike her school friends, Dorina had never longed to be beautiful, seldom more than fleetingly anyway. She had wanted desperately to be brilliant though. Not feared, but not necessarily liked either. Just brilliant.

— What a wrench it would be, she added. If I had to leave my garden after all the work I put into it.

— I shall find something else, he began to fall asleep. When the country turns republic, I might try for president.

— Oh yes, she saw the brutal humour of it. You will.

Hadn't she watched a millionaire strike his chest and swear he had her husband's interests deeply at heart?

He woke again as the huge swift knife of darkness sliced through heat haze. He heard the plane's engines only after it had passed, during the moments he was sure it would crash. He faced the punishment his Presbyterian mother used to threaten when he was wicked: archangels with glittering swords swooped down to bar his way, flickering and slashing. There was no escape. He rocked his head in distress: and found it cradled in Dorina's hands.

— I'm grateful, she spoke softly, having taught him the correct usage of the word. Grateful you are safe. Grateful I didn't know what danger you were in.

Finally the awkward shapes of their love settled on them and he closed his eyes without fear.

— Bernard, she whispered feeling the moment was, at last, right. I have something important to tell you.

But he had already set out across the unbroken landscape of a twenty-hour sleep.

9

Some say Luigi Squarcia ran away to sea at thirteen, others put the age at fifteen. Some, with a better ear for modern doubletalk, say he hitched to Sweden and lived as a male prostitute till his Mediterranean charms grew too hairy for a fastidious clientele. He himself claimed to have lived in India and travelled by train to Poona; first treading between the hundreds of slumbering paupers on the Bombay railway platforms and then watching his hill-bound locomotive weave its way out of that vast and sprawling city of flesh between parallel ranks of bottoms, as the shitting citizens squatted either side of the track in their pre-dawn ritual of modesty. He turned up in Trinidad among the most sensuous people on earth and in Curaçao wandering past those grubby Dutch houses, only to find himself mistaken for a Spaniard who had evaded the police during a whole humiliating year after he exhibited a white travesty of the famous Black Christ.

He belonged to the class described as living on their wits, meaning that they have accepted the corruptibility of others. Also that nothing is more reliably paid for than the gratifying of this corruption. He had charm too, which is to say no moral scruples. He regretted the limited variety of carnal desires, whilst scorning those who fell victim to any one of them.

Italy was no place for such an Italian. Surrounded by the effluvia of wealth, the baubles of art and constant domestic impertinences from Mother Church, he decided America offered the air he needed most. Perhaps it did. He spent nights in Hyatt Hotels at the expense of Christians and nights in the gutter at the expense of his health. New York, he discovered, was about as clean as Bombay. But though he met influential people they were not interested in listening to him while they rutted. They, however, talked with breathtaking virtuosity about their problems. O America! Show me someone rich and simple, he cried in the language which, despite his dislike, he learned quickly.

He was nineteen, good God, practically an old man, already the father of an unknown tribe, when he escorted a bony geriatric lady to Miami Beach and helped her swim, held her arm and instructed her how to bend it this way (creak), he himself having style, now bring it under here (creak), now kick your legs (crackle, crackle) and lo and behold you're as good as a motor boat.

So, that night when she'd accepted him in her dry rubber privacy front and back, having had her weep, and stroked his nipples and bellyhairs, she confessed he was the highlight of her life and would he like to ask her anything? Yes, he said, are you an Australian? She was immensely pleased to have her accent recognized, as if she had at last proved a credit to her kin. I am, she admitted, ashamed and boastful, being a girl from Whitey's Fall spending the last of the gold on happiness. And, she proposed, if you promise to love me I shall take you back home to show you to the girls. She packed her built-in deckchair of wooden limbs and they boarded a ship.

He never forgot who was who or what had been done to them. This, plus his Washington bedroom book and his trade on the beach at Monte Carlo leading to friendships with several heads of state, were Squarcia's only assets which couldn't be seen when he stepped into the shower. He found himself in a paradise of carelessness. Nobody else could bother to do up their shoelaces, let alone rub two ideas together. He became a man marked for success or else an extended stay in Parramatta Jail. He acquired a list of clients.

Did he stop short of evil? the historian asks. What a question. It was the vigour in his blood, evil. That is why he was so popular. Wearing Savile Row suits, with a heavy gold chain round his wrist, perfumed and massaged, he sold his own customers to the highest bidder. If it came to the point, he would turn up at the funeral with a laurel wreath. Here in Australia, he explained, you generally don't need to have people killed. They can be swindled without ever suspecting anyone less duplicitous than God. You can take over their companies and their wives, market their young for drugs and have laws passed by your clients to ensure your safety while you do so, offer them pap in return for the products of their good soil, shut them away from the finest climate in the world with television's leavings, convert them to the population control of defective automobile design and promise them impotence in return for their traditional self-sufficiency and these wonderful folk, confounding all probability, will declare it to be their way of life. Nearly twenty years after first arriving in Australia, Luigi Squarcia stood as a testament to such opportunities. No information was wasted. His record remained unblemished.

He had never been in love.

Squarcia adored politics. He adored committees and haggling over policies behind locked doors, games with the press, ladies conducting afternoon teas to raise funds by raffling unwanted necessities, and attending subscription dinners at exorbitant cost to hear guest speakers air their banalities. Most of all, Squarcia adored the Australian Labor Party. He found Labor ideas so comically righteous, and when branch meetings debated motions as honourable as rockinghorses the lowliest member might get up on his back legs and bore the meeting to the brink of violence before anyone infringed his rights so far as to tell him to shut up; and yet even senior senators could be compelled by an obscure doctrine of the infallibility of the collective commonplace to submit to verbal drubbings by a book of rules. Even more than this, he loved the spectacle of ALP ministers fresh in office, beginning to read between the lines, seeing emerge about them the labyrinth of forces totally beyond their control in which they had to seek their own accommodation or be lost, learning to put a brave face on it for the sake of hard-won status, twisting and squirming as the knife went in, stuffing the wound with money and locking away their principles to keep them intact for a more favourable day.

Luigi Squarcia had, then, a gift for politics, which protected him from ever becoming a politician. Though he sometimes mused about the pleasures of fame, he recognized the superiority of his position; the mob could never vote him out of office, nor could jealous rivals demote him to ministries of cottage crafts or pest control. Once he'd begun operating on behalf of Interim Freeholdings Incorporated of Delaware, thanks to those Washington connections, he dealt with nobody below inner cabinet rank. Squarcia was unique: he had no assistant, he delegated nothing. Every task undertaken he attended to personally. Even the Yes campaign for the republican referendum he decided entailed his future too closely to be sub-contracted. He did it all. Of necessity he lived in an aircraft.

Canberra is as beautiful as white buildings cleaner than blocks of soap can be. Glossy traffic collides around the clockwork roadways in suburbs where suicides may nod quietly to one another across saturated lawns. This small city of privilege boasts gourmands and voluptuaries who taste their respective delights free from the pressures of a metropolis. And yet, within the orderliness lurks a sinister memory; the efficient town plan redolent of Van Diemen's Land, of the military barracks and convict cells at Port Arthur, being so scrupulously hygienic and with regulations to cover every contingency.

On the afternoon of the first of May, Squarcia's personal jet circled the giant garden in which the city nestles, a hundred thousand imported trees triumphing over the trauma of autumn with spectacular yellow and crimson foliage. On the other side of the aircraft the surrounding Australia, grey-blond grasses and brown-green leaves, tilted away from him. Next thing, he was driving his superior car, the seat leather having been expertly repaired, speeding between rows of poplars, the highway a mad swirl of fallen leaves puffing to a cloud of yellow and brown butterflies up over the vehicle ahead then settling back on the tarmac ready for him. He was to meet Buchanan. He could be certain the arrangements were perfect: he made them himself. A colonial property not far from the city had been offered for the occasion. Signed and sealed and thank you very much.

— What I've got, Squarcia crowed, leaning across to catch a handsome glimpse of himself in the mirror, soul soaring to the intoxicating drone of the motor. Is spunk.

Bald men (no women among them, because even the most advanced corporations are slow to catch up with the times), listening to him quietly as they sat in their boardroom, sixteen thousand kilometres away, smiled and wagged heads indulgently. That was their Squarcia, after all.

Bernard Buchanan did not wait to thank the driver; he was too keyed up. He banged the hire car door behind him without looking round, his whole attention already on the house, homestead really, for it was a farm till the land grew too valuable to resist subdividing it. Chrysanthemums on long stems either side of the path brushed his trousers. The welcoming smile of his hostess hovered, already on display.

He had survived and would triumph. He felt himself carried through fiery petals and an odour of growing things, never mind Dorina's inexplicable refusal to accompany him. But during the flight from Sydney he had not rehearsed thank you to the driver, nor even hello to the hostess. He had not rehearsed elation either. What was too late was too late. There could be no way back to private life now except via failure. Failure it must not be. This walk was a walk into the merciless, the fascinating spotlight. Buchanan panted with urgency. He must reach his reception (flesh holding him back, the spirit rushing him on) and begin his rise to fame.

— Hello, the lady called in her shaky voice of a newspaper heiress, immaculately groomed figures shuffling through the lobby beyond, as he forged among the petals.

He knew her. He had met her once or twice: Mrs Alice Penhallurick. Soon, so those in the know were tipping, she would be Lady Penhallurick. Thirty years younger than her husband, she was nevertheless far more addicted to the digni- fied slowness of age. She belonged with these people. And part of the complexity of his present feelings lay in the fact that he did not. He trod ankle-twisting stones, his bearings lost. Betrayal billowed through him as arid as a cliff of dust. Buchanan found himself wondering who among his wellwishers might arrange for a man's fuel tanks to be filled with water. In which of these silverhaired heads had such a plan been further refined to suggest saltwater which could not be drunk for survival? He did not hesitate, though, leaving the past. Already he found it difficult to believe anybody wanted him dead.

— Hello, she called a second time as if asking whether her first attempt had been good enough.

— Hello Alice, he boomed now, breathless but not yet so close as to be said to have arrived, looking up at her dumpy figure. She wore her dissatisfied face in a pleading smile which told him she was not at all sure she could make a success of the reception, suddenly revealing the shy girl she had grown to be.

— This is so exciting, Alice offered phlegmatically, clasping one hand with the other and twisting her diamond rings. Everybody's longing to meet you. Did you have a comfortable flight from Sydney? What a pity Dorina couldn't come.

The livingroom talk subsided politely. Guests transferred whisky glasses to their left hands ready to be introduced. He forgot nobody, he would recall each one when he came to power. He would know who his supporters were. And, among them, he would be sure to have whoever planned his death.

— Did you meet Mr Squarcia yet? the hostess asked, precipi- tate with shakiness. I must find him for you. Mr Squarcia is a treasure.

— Never underestimate Squarcia, he was advised by whoever offered him the cigar he declined.

— Squarcia will see to everything, a solicitor explained. We

have put him entirely in charge of your campaign. Lucky man.
Poor Roscoe Plenty was busting to get him.

— You can't do better than Squarcia, the breeder of champion cattle assured him without suspecting that a needle of
resentment had entered the fat man's heart. Nor that he
thought: these creeps don't even know me.

One backdrop of gossiping guests was rolled up and an even
more crowded one pulled down in its place before Squarcia
consented to be found. They turned the volume higher on the
recorded chatter. Few people bothered to speak more than
perfunctory words to the candidate, though many craned to
look, mouthing: Is that so? Or perhaps even: Can you be
serious? Squarcia emerged from what might have been an illicit
embrace judging by his high colour and elastic tread.

— Here is a copy of your standard speech, some answers to
questions, a draft of your proposed itinerary, also the address of
an acceptable tailor.

With the genius of the accidental, a woman laughed raucously
from her pearls in the midst of an unrelated conversation. The
fat man extracted the itinerary, which he folded away in his
wallet for later. The rest he scrumpled into a ball and passed
back to his campaign manager. Squarcia accepted it without a
tremor, weighing it in his hand for what it might tell of the
future. Chandeliers twinkled the colours of meretricious
jewellery.

— Be sure two seats are reserved on any commercial flight
I'm to take, Buchanan replied boorishly as he snatched a beer
from a passing tray. That way I can spread myself. I don't like
feeling cramped. Good luck!

Squarcia checked the faultlessly folded handkerchief in his
breast pocket. Oh but I am bored already, he thought. Dear
Maestro Machiavelli, send me a prince in place of this toad.

— How am I to sell you? he asked. That is the problem.

A publicity secretary approached and departed declaring
what a joy it was to see the two of you getting on so famously
because we cannot do without our Mr Squarcia. The devils-on-
horseback came sizzling from the oven. Ice rattled in empty
glasses.

— Politics will be a challenge, the candidate made a grumpy
effort to rescue the situation because, after all, they would have
to work together for his aggrandisement. He puffed his cheeks,
so recently host to an unsightly blister, to the semblance of a

smile and tilted his head back to offer a view up hair-clogged nostrils.

— Anywhere else in the world you would be dead, Squarcia suggested. In any professional country, he explained.

A mining magnate presented himself for inspection, committed a few industrial clichés and navigated towards the lavatory to lodge a report. The reception, in full swing, was already a success.

— Meet our man, Mrs Penhallurick continually invited this one and that, whom she brought across for the purpose.

Meat, all right, Squarcia thought. Okay, but this makes my job tougher than I like. (What, Lavinia Manciewicz challenged him the previous night, do you take seriously Lou? Not her gasps as we reached a climax, he assured himself, groanax of the thoreau. Puns, he replied having seemed to think it out so her feelings would not be hurt: transcreated litter. The anguish lingo, he'd added.)

— What. . . ? they were asking him.

— By politics I mean having the delectable impertinence to manipulate fortunes not yours, Squarcia improvised for the sake of keeping some smalltalk going. But it's the only way for civilization to stay afloat under its cargo of dead ideas. Whatever we do, don't let's fall for our own advertising. We pay to take the rest of them in, he quipped charmingly. A big dose of someone like us could be fatal.

— Or is politics, Buchanan joined in, interested for the first time that afternoon. Being subtle enough to keep the truth to yourself?

— I shall take you on, I suppose.

— If I don't kick you off first, came the hot retort.

— I'm so gratified you two boys are having a joke, Mrs Penhallurick joked again in passing. Victory is so so important to us all. Especially at this time.

— Who is to be the candidate, Squarcia or me? Buchanan demanded of the minerals magnate.

— Ask Squarcia.

Money talks beautiful good sense.

— Ladies and gentlemen: a toast. Charge your glasses. To President Buchanan. We can't lose!

The silverhairs, the chicken-necks choked with pearls, the hard eyes in soft painted faces, the grasping hands hidden in pockets became details of a tableau while the assembly gave this matter respectful attention. They drank solemnly. Then alcohol resuscitated the art of conversation, mouth to mouth. A contingent of graduates from a ladies' college arrived to charm the company with naive chic. Music escaped the record player, though Bernard Buchanan by habit did not notice. Lampshades blushed as evening came on. A tiny light glimmered from one car waiting outside while the chauffeur read his newspaper and missed the news. Priorities regrouped round a meringue mountain stuck with cream and hothouse strawberries. Gluttons led a sally of clapping, some even putting down their drinks momentarily. Spilt claret ate into a cedar tabletop. It was a comforting success. Mrs Penhallurick shed her nervousness and took to blowing her nose as a contribution to the niceties, a sure sign of her feeling at ease. *The Woman's Home* took photographs of bosoms. And Squarcia laughed in Italian.

The following morning's newspaper surprised Bernard Buchanan. Not only did the reporter quote some sound statements on policy which he couldn't recall having made, but with impressive cunning she got a few of her facts right. Dorina remained strangely detached and unimpressed, though the kettle sang *Amen* and the toaster clashed its tiny discordant cymbals.

10

Rory came back to Sydney, alight with wonder, utterly besotted with sailing. He would join the navy just as soon as he was old enough, if he hadn't already run away to sea before that. Suntanned and bright-eyed, he held his mother spellbound with tales of how Dr McKinley let him steer the yacht, could she imagine, let him help set the sails and take them in again. Out tumbled fluent information about cleats and sheets and the lee of some island or other, of rocks on their starboard bow, of heading a little more up-wind, of jibing and how he nearly ran her aground. The exciting part of life had begun. Thanks, he remembered to mention, to Uncle Willy. Yes, Mr Penhallurick had said to call him that.

Once the catalogue was finished, the truth of his fate dawned on Rory and he began complaining about home where he had nothing to do but the usual old boring things. Then he took to dreaming on his bed with the dog Churchill dreaming beside him, different dreams but nevertheless in tune. He was surprised to hear a growl develop deep inside the animal as if the growl were a separate creature, swelling, taking shape, leaping clear of that friendly throat as a fully-fledged bark.

Doorchimes sounded belowdecks.

— No. We expected you.

His mother's remote voice told him that, though she treated whoever had come politely, she didn't like them at all. Her customary encouraging tone (her dreadful suffocating motherly warmth that he squirmed under) was missing. Then the lord's greeting came from the kitchen doorway.

— Come along in, Lou.

Crouched at the top of the stairs, Rory spied on his mother as she stepped aside for a stranger who bowed to her as he passed. Didn't he know you should telephone first and see if people wanted you? Churchill, imprisoned in the bedroom to keep him from giving the game away, could no longer withhold a couple more muffled warnings.

— This is my wife Dorina. Dorina, I'd like you to meet Lou Squarcia, the organizer.

The Organizer! Agog, Rory pressed his forehead between the slender wooden balustrades.

— We have some business to discuss, the visitor explained in a voice like no other, harsh yet unhurried.

— In that case I shall amuse myself at the piano.

She came climbing the carpeted stairs and passed him at his vantage point, too preoccupied to worry about an eleven-year-old or a dog's agitation. Across the bare floor of the music room, her footsteps were rather less indignant than he expected. In fact they were more like his own when he was sad. He had heard this sometimes, so hollow it could be a different boy walking and not himself after all. They stopped. The piano stool screeched against the boards. The first notes of one of her droopy pieces spoiled his chance of overhearing the conversation below.

Rory was already halfway down, alert; then the whole way. He was creeping on all fours out of sight of the enemy, through the diningroom, to take cover right under the servery hatch. The piano sounded in the background.

— . . . the way it is. My clients, the harsh voice resumed. Never make mistakes. I like to help them keep this reputation.

— Um, his father commented, and then asked. Um?

The organizer chuckled agreeably enough.

Fluff balls under a tea trolley parked in the corner bore witness to his mother's attitude to housework. Rory's own fingerprints stippled the dust around him. Evidence. He settled his back against the wall, careful to make no sound. Contemplating his bare legs, he picked at a crust of blood where he'd grazed his knee on that rock when they last went ashore. Could it still be only yesterday? Was everything the same up there on the reef, even now?

Chairlegs curved outward and inward and out again to the foot, the dark wood glossy. He could not see flowers on the table from where he was, but he smelt them. Always boring flowers in the house, always boring music.

— That's Debussy, said the harsh unhurried voice which might have been alien itself as well as saying an alien word. Your wife is quite professional. Congratulations.

Sounds escaped of teaspoons in cups, a chair creaking. Tension chilled the diningroom. Rory could feel his face tighten to shapes he had never thought were his.

— Your clients have not yet had the manners to contact me. I don't even know who they are. I have only your word they exist. Plus a corporate name mentioned in a government file.

— They make some conditions. But you've been warned already, I think. I am here for a signature on the contract. I can witness it. Simply your promise of good faith before real money is invested in the campaign. Fair enough? We have to give scrupulous attention to our public image. We're at a fragile stage.

— Voters being toey about foreign investment?

— Not to mention foreign ownership. I am to draw your attention to item twelve in particular.

Furniture creaked and moved. Rory's heart stopped. Were they standing up already?

— My instructions are that you may have ten minutes to read it. I shall be outside in the car if you want me. Oh and *we* supplied you with that dossier. The Public Service would appreciate having it back before it is missed. Also, I ought to remind you that not so long ago your excellent car proved less than safe. But that a rescue plane did arrive. Just in time. Ten minutes, then?

Rory made his break. The delay needed for the lord to hoist himself clear of a chair was about enough for escape. Off he shot, swinging round the banister post and hurtling velvet-footed upstairs. The music had stopped before this. His mother watched him from above. She knew he had been eavesdropping but hastened down past him, like the sport she was, without a second glance.

— Can't you find another campaign manager, Buchanan? she called, scarcely waiting for the front door to shut, and meeting her husband as he stood irresolutely with a document in one hand.

— Please don't interfere, Dorina. You don't know who you are dealing with, he protested hoarsely. Squarcia is the best.

11

By the end of May the cold weather had set in. A wall of air floated across the ocean from Antarctica and pushed the Indian summer, with all its sweet late ripeness, north toward other countries with other amenities and speaking quite other languages. High smudged cloud reduced the light and muted primary colours. Even the silks worn by jockeys were shot with sombre tones. Rain began, as always, on a Saturday, drifting in just as they called the fifth race at Randwick. Members clustered near the enclosure fence. Mr William Penhallurick, himself like a mummified jockey, stood listening to a question he was being asked by Roscoe Plenty. Anyone could tell from his stillness he meant *no* without wishing to have to put a name to it. But Plenty was not a man to take hints. While talking, they watched the horses led in: brittle action of slender hindlegs, flutters of haunch-muscle, glossy coats stuck flat and dark patches dripping, the great shining inward-looking eyes of racers.

Light rain stuttered against the drum of their black nylon umbrellas which had developed a pleasant clumsiness, butting together periodically and shedding, in twin tremors, bright unwanted drops. The jockeys appeared thoroughly out of temper, carrying saddles, whips knocking against high boots, pointed faces handsome as ferrets, breathing the steamy breath of those great warm tyrant beasts.

If Roscoe Plenty looked up now and again, cold and quick as an eagle, it was because his secret hollowness haunted him, as always, even here where he was most relaxed and in his own realm you might say, being president of the club. In the same way, it was his habit to interrupt people suddenly as if to test whether they could actually hear his voice at all. This was why he bumped against that waiter at the Hydro Majestic a week before and was so gratified by the impression he made. This was why he perpetually enquired when, how, then why were you where and what did you see? He craved witnesses. He wanted to be told some very particular information. He wanted, simply, to be shown what he was like, yes, physically as well as psychologically, what personality he had, what signals he gave out, and whether all this showed anything of the white heat raging through him. No one guessed he was asking to be told information so basic. When Roscoe Plenty looked in a mirror he did not see just a crisp illusion detailing every quirk of his face back-to-front. This superficial image got in the way. If he smiled he could make out, behind the mask, a jellied shadow of possible joys. The mirror darkened with him in it, promises receding to levels he could never learn to focus on. He knew his colouring all right and the woolly bulk of his silhouette, but he also caught fleeting hints of black centres deeper and more devious than the general obscurity. Once when he was drunk and pressed his nose against the glass he saw, plain as you like, terrible schemes inside china-white shells. Another time he slapped a niece, just for the desire to watch, printed red on the child's bare thigh, an emerging representation of his own hand; and he pressed an apology of money into the howling child's palm as thanks for encouraging him. Not even in his schooldays had he been sure what he might be capable of. Other boys would fly airliners or posture in front of adoring audiences, but he could only say this: that no teacher need explain why Nero fiddled while Rome burned, he knew already and considered this emperor heroic for the magnitude of his doubt. The Kings of England left him cold, smug snobby lot they mostly were, but Warwick the King-maker struck a chord. Roscoe Plenty understood Warwick, and could have anticipated that after victories as a fighting soldier he would take to the sea until he was in command of the entire navy, that having been appointed Admiral of the Fleet he wouldn't stay still a minute till he had cast aside this honour, got himself nearly killed in a brawl (ah, then he must have come close to seeing!) and ended by having to be content with an indefatigable career of choosing who would rule the land, of propping them up and bullying them to the right crisis of ambition. The spark struck from steel in battle and the reflected glitter of crown jewels were the only light by which such a Warwick caught any glimpse of how he really was. Roscoe knew from his own torment. He, too, perceived the uses of power and the comfort of brutality.

One of the horses uttered a shuddering whinny.

— Just how I'd feel if I had to race today, Mr Penhallurick joked, rocking on the balls of his feet to that nightmare obsession with keeping young.

The umbrellas collided, clear drops jumped off them, a last jockey scowled from his silks like some irritable emblem from a Third World flag. At the rail on the opposite side of the enclosure a woman, standing among the crowd of known and semi-known faces, fingered her purse. Finally, unable to restrain her excitement, she extracted a wad of banknotes and counted them on the quiet, just to satisfy herself.

— There's a real filly for you, said the ancient rake. And a winner too by the look of her. What do you say? He nodded with offensive spryness.

— She must be thirty, the politician objected. I prefer them young.

— Don't give me that. Women in their thirties are prime cattle, just ripe enough and juicy. He capered under his jiggling umbrella, smacked his lips and scratched his flaking cheek (the scrofula an inherited complaint, once known as the King's Evil and believed curable only by the touch of a living monarch).

The punter, seeing she had been observed, stuffed her winnings away, embarrassed, and backed off from the fence to mingle with anonymous gamblers taking a critical look at the field.

— The club, the old man introduced the subject. Has a surprise in store for you and I'm here to sound you out. The executive feels we should resurrect an old tradition and have a portrait painted of each president from now on, starting with yourself. Before you become the President with a capital P. What do you say?

Roscoe Plenty's impulse to prevaricate for the sake of disguising the unguardedness of his pleasure was cut short by a voice right beside them.

— Birds of a feather!

He swung round to confront the intruder. But finding this was Luigi Squarcia, whom he also hoped to lure away from Buchanan's team, just as he hoped to bribe Penhallurick himself with the one flattering appointment he knew the old man craved. He leered amiably.

— *There* you are, he said.

— And I, Mr Penhallurick continued as if he had broken his sentence only for the length of a comma. Have taken the liberty of asking Lou to recommend an artist. He knows the world.

— Unless, Squarcia smiled at the notion, also as a man secure in the knowledge that his motives are too devious and farsighted for others to guess. You have your own choice of a painter in mind, Roscoe.

The cluster of people round the enclosure, consulting programs and form-guides indolently, contemplatively, dispersed. One systematic lady lingered to scribble marks in the margin beside the list of starters, her pen glinting in rainlight. Squarcia, too, turned on his heel and paced the wet lawn, eyes down, watching his perfect shoes and the way he placed them.

— Who do you suggest? Roscoe Plenty asked eventually, firing a look at first one then the other of his companions by way of affirming that they were there to attend him and furnish him with the most reliable advice to be had.

Penhallurick, under his ebullient umbrella, shook his head, losing a couple more flakes of dead skin, and left the answer to the man who would know.

— Would you like to be introduced right now? the harsh voice suggested almost teasingly.

— A race-going artist?

Squarcia didn't bother replying. He merely raised his hand. And there, over by the members' stand a woman waved vivaciously in return.

— That's the filly, the old fellow discovered gleefully. And look who she's with. One for you!

A younger, much prettier woman was speaking to her animatedly, pleading perhaps, bullying, then marching off with affectionate despair, hesitating for a backward glance, but finally walking away, resigned. Plenty had already stopped in his tracks though the rain grew more purposeful and they had reached a patch of mud.

— What do you say? Penhallurick called back to him.

Squarcia crossed quickly to where she waited, reached out, clean cuff displayed, and drew his painter forward by the arm.

— This is Lavinia Manciewicz, he introduced her, guiding her past the old man's clutches and his extravagant welcome, to confront her intended sitter.

— I understand! she observed shrewdly. Mr Plenty doesn't wish to be painted by a woman.

Roscoe Plenty stood in the mud without the wit to lie, unexpectedly deflected from his audacious plan of inducing both Buchanan's manager and Buchanan's backer to switch to his own team before the campaign was too far advanced.

— Do you think of the portraitist as possessing your image, mastering you in some way? she pursued, presenting herself as having a flair for clothes without the bother of dressing fashionably.

— Women are amateurs, he growled.

— Ah now that depends, that depends, Penhallurick objected in the interests of females at large.

— Miss Manciewicz, Plenty apologized. I would never have troubled you. . .

— If you had known, she completed the insult for him and then laughed carelessly. I've had such a good day, she added. And the fun of hobnobbing in the enclosure. Luigi! she saved face by presenting her arm for Squarcia to take.

They strolled away together, in step. She turned toward him, laughing afresh, and the single word *silly* drifted back to the others as the loudspeaker system bellowed a commentary on the race just begun. She slipped her arm round his waist when he put his across her shoulders.

— What a filly, Penhallurick enthused, returning forlornly to join his companion. What a dog. What do you say?

The crowd roared as thundering hooves approached and horses wheezed mad combative desperate breaths. Then they were past. A chaotic hubbub of moans and delighted yelps followed as the punters subsided in their seats, binoculars still held in dazed hands, hopes dying reluctantly. While some began elbowing their important passage among the envious to collect from bookies, most ruefully acknowledged their loss.

— The news is positive, Bill, Roscoe Plenty counterattacked suddenly, springing his surprise with that cold eagle glance to catch the reaction, seeking himself in the shock value of what he had to say. The knighthood is yours. I've seen the approved birthday honours list, so this year it's official. Knight of the Order of Australia.

Once upon a time a boy was offered a silver shilling if he would sell all the tears of his lifetime. Naturally he didn't think twice, a shilling being a great deal of money in those days. In any case he was almost a man so he had used up most of the tears he would expect to shed and it is well known that men never need to cry. Gladly, he said, yes. He took the shilling. And took the shilling. And now here he was, soon to be called Sir, staring from dry red-rimmed eyes at a future in which the price of happiness ever after was just one tear.

— Thanks to your wife, Roscoe Plenty added woundingly.

Her respectability and her chain of newspapers. (Oh, was he getting reactions; was his presence being felt this time!) He plodded about in the mud while the crowds simmered and gathered their energy for a fresh orgasm of risk. But chiefly, he said with belated emphasis. Thanks to your own great contribution to the nation, Bill.

Squarcia and Lavinia Manciewicz consulted the odds offered for the last race. She teased him with her success and pointed out how little use his practical calculations proved when what was needed was good old-fashioned luck. And luck, anyway, was the whole point of the fun; knowledge being almost immoral.

— If I'd won the money because I knew I had made an intelligent choice, she concluded. I would have accepted it as no more than my due, like wages. There'd be no pleasure in it. What's so exciting is that I don't deserve what I got.

Squarcia looked pleased as he thought about this and perhaps tucked it away for use at a later date.

— In that case, he offered. You can choose for me as well in this race. You can back your fancy twice over. Two stabs at undeserved riches. And if I win I shall have double the pleasure because I know as little about you as I do about the horses.

She studied the list so she need not so clearly have understood his meaning as she, undoubtedly, did.

— Who, he pursued his advantage. Was the pretty blonde you were talking to? I thought you promised me you didn't mix with racecourse types.

— My sister Stephanie, she replied absently, secure in the certainty that this was not what he expected. She's a journalist.

Lavinia made up her mind about their horse, took her money and his, and placed the bets, both the same. He noted with approval that she wasn't cautious enough to want a little each way.

— Yes, she explained further, handing him his ticket. She hoped to meet you. She thinks you're a celebrity on the quiet. Among those who really know, was the way she put it.

Squarcia looked modestly at his beautiful shoes.

— She's after inside information on your Bernard Buchanan and she's wild to find out what Roscoe Plenty was saying. Two candidates with the one stone. What a beast I was. I told her I'd rather she didn't try making use of me. She's so new to the game, she couldn't handle a refusal, Lavinia added in a parental tone of voice. She's a dear. She wants to take the world by storm, but she doesn't know how.

— Stephanie, he murmured.

12

From the long night journey by car twin beams sheered ahead to a right-angled corner of the sort which gives no idea what you will meet next, and swung in among starved public services: streetlamps glimmering sullenly on a decayed toilet block and a telephone booth with the glass smashed. Tyres whispered comfortably. The very breadth of the street told how many hours it had stood abandoned. Trees down the centre masked the effect of smalltown shops and muffled the courthouse. Port George post office stood forward while four pubs set diagonally on two consecutive crossroads gazed blankly toward rival attractions. The whole place had turned in on itself, perhaps for generations. Even the big posters of Bernard Buchanan, shining fat with fresh glue, hypnotized one another from either side.

VOTE 1 BUCHANAN
AN INDEPENDENT FOR INDEPENDENCE

At one in the morning, such was the blank of their welcome after a two-thousand-kilometre drive. Somewhere in an unidentified house, the address carefully memorized, friends expected them to call, camp on the floor and surf with them in the morning, expected them with that impatience of a household needing only money to switch on the good times, the sort of friends who'll come up and talk to you when they don't know you, who with no character of their own adopt the nearest to hand, so if everybody's going to the pub they go to the pub, if everybody's going to Keith's place they go to Keith's place, if everyone's raging they rage.

A breeze smelling of the sea filled the open car.

— By rights, Greg suggested. We shouldn't've stopped for those beers on the way. We'd've been here a coupla hours ago.

The driver did not reply. He heard with that mixture of contempt and affection travelling companions commonly develop. But kept his mouth shut, suddenly alert, anticipating an event, some enjoyable surprise. Meeting only the gaze of a photograph. Those bulging eyes. So Bernard really did have ambitions. Peter Taverner still could not account for the link between himself and this man whose life might be in danger just because he (Peter) had withheld telling one vital fact: his proof that their ordeal in the desert was planned, and planned by people who knew how to get inside information. Water could not have been put in the spare fuel cans of both cars on impulse, nor by accident, not twice over. Somebody was serious. And most probably, as part of the plan, they presumed their two victims would compare stories and draw the right conclusions. He had not given Bernard the chance. He had not mentioned his own car.

Port George, even now drifting past on either side, was the place named in that dossier as the site of the next US base. No such exalted destiny appeared likely. But curious connections had been made.

— We've done it! Greg spoke again, watching dismal timber shopfronts glide by and even more dismal brick-veneers swaying crooked with drink, blobs of dull light from overhead lamps splashing his companion's bare arms. He heard the comfort of tyres on smooth bitumen. They reached the end of the street.

— I'm busting for a leak, Greg the comedian groaned.

The car stopped. Right there at the end of the double row of defeated shops and the single row of peppertrees between. Without a word the driver looked across at him, expecting action, raising his eyebrows with expectancy, an expression he had never shown Bernard Buchanan.

— Get on with it then, Keg, he said indifferently.

Greg opened his door and let himself fall out, flashing a grin back into the vehicle. How could he welsh on a challenge? He unzipped his pants and aimed at the uncertain gutter, watched the piss become an independent creature, an elegant parabola, watched with that marvelling concentration of discovery characteristic of drunks, not only for its formal perfection but for a hint of luminosity. He watched, emptying himself. The jet of urine sparkling, unaccountably floodlit, dazzling him, crystalline flickers brilliant against the dark background, steady enough to appear breakable, caught like that in the headlights of a police car.

The crisis had happened. The flow died to a painful dribble as the culprit tried holding himself in. The police drew up beside them and sat purring in the middle of the street. Drab shops showed a cold glaze of reflected light. Trees rustled in a breeze from the port. Friends, who were not so close after all, lounged waiting for the good times to arrive, packets of marijuana already sealed and put ready, worth a couple of grand.

Two policemen got out with that weary air of men ready for the opportunity of violence.

— You got a licence? one asked.

The culprit (thinking, What the hell! anyway unable to hold in a moment longer) let go and continued relieving himself.

— Does he need a licence to piss? the young man at the wheel answered incuriously.

— A-ho! the uniform declared. Somebody is asking to be taught about the law.

He peered into the car with fox eyes.

— South Australian numberplates, his colleague reported. Underneath all the muck.

Greg finished pissing. The pleasure had certainly gone out of it, the beer a waste. He sank back in his seat, hollow and cast off by the action, no one interested in him now.

— Blow into this bag, they instructed the driver.

How do I get away with this? Peter blew shallow puffs, releasing as little as possible of the air from his lungs. Even so, the crystals turned green. Enough for him to be taken and put on a Breathalyzer.

We shouldn't've stopped for those drinks, by rights, Greg Sullivan thought in the outrage of his inconsequentiality. But did not think, we shouldn't've stopped for me to let the drink out.

— Your mate can watch the car, Fox-eyes offered Peter, leading the way across the road and into a police station now manifesting itself complete with oblong blue light burning outside.

The busy scene at the desk bore no relationship to the dead town behind them, to the unlicensed piss cold in its gutter, or to Greg (also known as Keg, Mug, Dag, Nagger, the Shagger, Legs, Piggy and Eggo) gazing bleakly at shopfronts. Three detained persons already leaned aching elbows on the counter, morose and blind in the bright office, scrutinizing half-consumed mugs of staff coffee on the desks, typewriters under waterproof hoods, and among papers a telephone receiver lolling off its cradle with somebody listening at the other end out there surrounded by night. A constable and a desk sergeant stood behind the counter filling in forms. They emitted sporadic monosyllables of advice to offenders who awaited their fate docilely; countrymen, having quite likely seen these police grow up from lads, being uncles maybe. The Breathalyzer showed point one three, so a formal arrest was made. Then Fox-eyes extracted the driver's licence from a wallet which the younger policeman had handed him with the explanation that it had been found under a seat. He spread it open for inspection.

— Peter Taverner. New South Wales licence, he observed with interest. South Australian vehicle.

The other officers glanced up and then went back to their business. The waiting offenders who had already begun to behave like customers, also feeling this was none of their affair, concentrated on preserving that humble demeanour least likely to aggravate their petty offences. Fox-eyes lit a cigarette and pulled at it reflectively but with an animal hunger.

— You carrying drugs or something? he spoke at last.

— No, said Peter, goodhumoured again.

— Had your fingerprints taken before, Mr Taverner? he asked in a quiet voice.

The young man shook his head cheerfully.

— Then I'll show you what to do. Come round my side of the counter. This here is the ink pad. There's where you'll put your marks on the paper, okay? Spread your fingers like this and press down firmly on the ink. Got to get them well inked first.

— Pad yeah, ink yeah, no worries, let's get out of here, the client agreed cooperatively.

— Hey, the other constable called holding up the wallet. Look at this, will you! He drew from the back compartment a wad of banknotes.

Peter Taverner stood, his hand outstretched, black with ink, ready to contribute to the records, Fox-eyes already guiding it firmly, finger by finger.

— That's my money, he objected. Mine and Greg's. The ink, the arrested action, caught him in a helpless gesture.

—Two thousand dollars? Where would you get two thousand dollars?

The young man returned to the task in hand, to have the fingerprinting done and over with.

— Working harder than you bastards ever did in your bloody lives, he growled, furious now, the alcohol burning in him. Tuna fishing.

— What's that? snarled Fox-eyes, his broad face flushing and his little eyes growing closer together (so the meek offenders, listening while they feigned deafness, kept their gaze lowered to remain as invisible as they were) while he locked one arm around Peter's head, bearing down with the weight of his massive self-confidence, thumping the head with his free hand.

— I was a canecutter, son, he roared between blows. In north Queensland.

The victim, neck cranked sideways, thought to himself: That's fucked everything, canecutters are said to work harder than anybody. From the pain and awkwardness of his position, he sought the desk sergeant's eyes.

— Is this usual? he asked as if talking to a friend.

— I can't see a thing mate, that public servant replied.

So, head twisted askew, suddenly enraged at the prospect of losing money which he needed to do a deal in the morning, he edged his body round to obtain leverage, placed his right hand flat against the attacker's ribs, printing an ink record of the event there, wrenched himself free and rammed Fox-eyes back on the wall, breaking his hold and dodging away.

— What's all this then? he yelled. Half the bucks belong to my mate and half are mine. That's our pay, we earned it poling tuna.

Another policeman jumped him to pin him down. He evaded the attack, shoved the man aside leaving black smears on his shirt too, and leapt over the desk. All four officers moved in. Terrible emptiness overcame him. Caution about consequences occurred too late as always. He was feeling pretty strong. And strong in the traditional knowledge that justice and authority are seldom on the same side. A touch of the show-off behind his defiance, he hit back. For their part, they did not need to think: the call had become too urgent for reasons. They had been awaiting this through the boredom of their usual vagrants. With the hissing ferocity of men abandoned to a fight they lashed out, pursuing him as he dived between them and up again with an agility that inflamed their excitement. Treading on a typewriter, he vaulted the counter and swung around, back to the wall, sprang out at them, delivering quickfire blows. He felt no pain, only an instinctive rightness, an energy flow of which he seemed to be not the source but somehow an extension. The inventiveness of his fighting took them wholly by surprise. They charged and blundered about the office, obstructed by its familiarity for purposes now irrelevant. He used it. The desks and heaters, the filing cabinets and flying documents were his territory, employed as springboards and baffles, tactical possibilities of perilously slight advantage. He had taken some punishment but given more, when the two youngest assailants cornered him. They clung to his arms and tried dragging him towards the open cell. This, he knew, was what he must fear. No going back. The cell meant defeat. He could see a telephone directory put ready inside in the hope of such an arrest; he knew this was for beating up prisoners so nothing but general bruises would show afterwards. Where the hell was Piggy? A mate could be useful here now. One tugging each arm, the enforcers of law dragged him towards the cell. As they edged their way inside, squeezing through shoulder by shoulder, he braced his feet against the doorframe. In this position he matched their combined strength. He defied them. Whatever happened he was not going to be locked in there. All the while, he discovered he had been talking. Not pleading, no, nothing servile, but reasoning, saying look if this goes on somebody is going to get hurt, really hurt, knowing it would eventually be himself, but knowing too that before he went under, one of them would go first, or several. Though they wrenched and yanked at his arms he was too strong for them. Stuck in the doorway like that, themselves in the cell and him outside, the struggle reached one of those stalemates fighters know so well. A moment of calm, the brain suddenly clear of anger and confusion. They strained against the stillness, noting that the bystanders had all taken the opportunity of going without a word, slipping off into the ignominious night. The senior constable, bleeding quite badly from the mouth, recognized this momentary lull as his to control.

— Okay, he said. So we believe you. So you have been tuna fishing.

The constables let go. Peter backed away from the open door and from the telephone book waiting as innocent as a member of the family. He stumbled on a flimsy wire basket and spilled its correspondence. All five men took stock of themselves, the torn skin on their knuckles, grazed elbows and bruised faces, a welter of evidence in the fingerprints inked and smudged across their clothes. Then of the wreckage in the office: overturned chairs, toppled typewriters and files on the floor, one of which bore as a legal seal a bright splash of blood.

— We'll even let you out, Fox-eyes went on, quiet with the chance of victory. On bail. The power was his, he had the lines. Panting and heaving one arm round to tuck his shirttail back in, he licked his lip not only for the blood but to taste the satisfaction of a man who fights because to be a man he must.

— A thousand dollars.

The energy flow cut. That exterior power on which Peter Taverner had drawn now dropped him.

— A thousand dollars' bail! he repeated, astounded. For nothing more than drunk driving? Plus, I wasn't even driving, I was sitting in my car parked at the kerb, and you know it. You wouldn't ask that much from a murderer.

— A thousand dollars, the policeman confirmed to his admiring colleagues, immensely pleased to have concluded the battle by a stroke of unbeatable intellect. Half this money is yours you said. Half the two thousand. I'm not unreasonable. I'm not asking for anything you haven't got. So if you want to go free you know what to do. Otherwise you can stay in our cell for nothing. He smiled impersonally. We'll let your mate off any indecent exposure charge as a bonus. This is Port George hospitality.

— A thousand dollars' bail! the magistrate exclaimed and looked around the courtroom in bewilderment. Mistakes like this were not supposed to happen. He stared back at the papers before him in case the figure had become a hundred in the interim, but it had not.

— That's just what I said, said the accused.

— Kindly address me as Your Honour.

— I said you'd put a murderer on that sort of bail.

— This is not a matter for you to comment upon young man. And call me Your Honour.

— I didn't do a thing, mate. Only driving under the influence, plus an unregistered vehicle.

— Call me mate once more and I shall charge you with contempt of court.

— Only driving under the influence, Your Honour.

— Three hundred dollars' fine and forty-seven dollars' costs. Drunken driving is a serious offence, I'll have you know. Take this as a lesson. Don't let there be a next time.

— Eggo, Peter Taverner rejoiced outside. I got six hundred and fifty-three dollars change. Let's have a bloody night on the town.

13

Bernard Buchanan saw only a procession of supporters, hecklers, interviewers and organizers who flocked round, melted away, cheered, and sank toward an alcoholic vanishing point.

He had no chance of knowing what was going on, which soon frustrated him. Life was back to front. No longer was he one moving among many, an observer as well as a participant in society. He had become the single constant reference point. Everybody came to him. They came to fetch him, to feed him, to flatter and be known by him; they wanted to talk seriously about himself; they escorted him as if he could not be trusted to find his own way; they never let him carry his bag or even hold his airline ticket. Wherever he arrived he was met, wherever he departed from he was seen off, his meals had been thought out and ordered long before he knew what he wanted to eat, the barber attended him in his hotel suite and they confiscated his watch so he would not be tempted to worry about the time. He felt like a blindman stifled by protective goodwill. The tighter his schedules, the more he felt he was standing still while life whirled past.

He talked. He repeated what he had said before until it grew to be policy. He meant to stick to facts. He meant his analyses to be searching. But there was no time to find out, never time to think. Squarcia or one of Squarcia's minions would that moment knock discreetly and enter without waiting for a reply (he was never allowed doors he could lock from inside) bearing some small luxury on a tray or some digest of information selected and prepared by a computer. The nation itself was brought to him: as rooms full of faces, boxes of pale confections which he might choose from and taste. And when they were suddenly taken away for the night, for lunch, for seventeen minutes and five seconds (he never knew), he was left alone in a room, embalmed in boredom, prone on his hotel bed, empty and disoriented but tense, alert for the next invasion to rush in with outstretched hands.

From time to time they picked him up and sat him down among statisticians to be told how the public reacted to the early days of the campaign.

— Our platform, after all, Squarcia apologized. Is called National Pragmatism.

— So, said the candidate offering them a plastic smile. You've been conducting opinion polls? Irritating drunks in pubs, is that it? Gatecrashing visiting hour at hospitals for the incurably ill and dying? Quizzing the man in the street for answers to some tricky questions on the future of civilization? The old scientific spirit?

— The main points are here, a senior statistician replied,

courteously ignoring this outburst. Firstly, only 20.5% of adult voters care about policy issues and 70.82% of these describe themselves as firmly committed already. We should compare that with the figure on page two, you see, the 71% who admit to judging a candidate on the basis of personal style. Our agency is at work on your image right now. We have to take serious account of the 17.4% of our sample, here, comprising 32% female and 1.7% male who base their choice at least partly on sexual appeal.

— I dare say 99% of citizens not actually in lunatic asylums, Buchanan burst out in a fury. Would agree that pollsters are a pack of swindlers getting their hooks into hard-earned campaign funds. And to tell us what? Either simplistic garbage I could have told you over two dollars' worth of beer in five minutes, or else impertinences I wouldn't offer my lowliest employee.

The experts, not knowing what to make of this, left their clock faces on, all reading the same, all open to public scrutiny.

Squarcia smiled. Buchanan scowled.

— I'll wager I win more support by drinking in the pub of an evening than I would dangling my dick in front of the nymphomaniac fringe. You make fools of yourselves believing the things people write on official forms. He burst out laughing delightedly: Look, I'll give you a sporting chance. You take a Melbourne sample of my popularity now, and then another after my speech there at the Town Hall on Saturday. If there's less than 5% difference, I shall come to heel and listen to your silly nonsense. But if there's more, you have to accept the boot. Okay? And no talk of compensation. Is it a deal?

— It's not so bad being fat, the candidate explained to Squarcia afterwards, as they sat in a car and a plane and a car again, the barriers down and a mellow confidentiality growing between them. . . or at least on Buchanan's side. I felt it most as a boy, he explained. My one escape was my bicycle. Sad. Do you understand that, Lou? A bicycle. I'm telling you. . . pretty old battered old thing. I flew. I flew on that bike, you know, weightless like this. He demonstrated with his arms as wings. The road down there streaking by. See? You know how a headlamp, excuse me, trembles. My bike never had a brand name, he sighed regretfully and then turned this into an asset: unique. He shrugged. Worn off, I suppose. Secondhand you see. Probably thirdhand. The apple of my eye, his voice came warmly. Crazy old thing. I kept it oiled. Always riding. Shouted for the kids to come and join me. Kids who never spoke when I was walking. They wheeled out from their backyards. They knew we'd have a good time, because of me and my mood. He recalled a mystery: That machine never seemed to notice my weight. Hit the pedals and it soared. We thought we were speedway heroes. Skidding wheelies in the gravel. Did you do wheelies in Italy, Lou?

Squarcia refrained from saying he had never ridden a bike.

— Too careful I suppose, Buchanan wagged his head respectfully. The others laughed at me, you know, because my knees stuck out or my arms jiggled or my bottom sagged over the saddle. But they laughed with admiration, I'm, excuse me, telling you. Because I was the best. I was the leader. I knew all the rules. He remembered something joyfully: I made up the damn rules. There was a different me inside me. They sometimes saw it. But I always knew it was there the whole time. See me, freewheeling downhill, legs splayed out for laughs, and I got them, cycling with no hands, lolling back. . . I discovered clowning. Lou, I'll tell you something secret, you must never tell Dorina, Lou, or she'd use it against me, but I used to thank God for my bicycle. Do you know that? Yes, I did, in my prayers at night, or sometimes out loud. Hallelujah. Down a slope and swaying graceful as buggery into the bend at the bottom. Funny thing, life. He looked up like a small boy caught in the act of some naughtiness: Most times I couldn't stand a bar of God. I blamed him for making me fat you see. But I forgave him because of that bike. He became brisk: The bike taught me that there was something in me that wouldn't be repressed. Like our fiasco with the hair-splitters today, eh?

They sat companionably for a moment. But the alcohol was still at work.

— Maybe some people find me repulsive, Bernard now suggested with tragic solemnity. You see? Then he was off on another tack entirely and leaned over to share a confidence. Once some man came up to me in a park. I was still at highschool. Not what you think, Lou, no, get your mind out of the gutter. This man talked in a quiet voice about the cost of heating a house. Fancy me remembering that, he said admiringly then exploded with laughter. Took me for somebody a lot older. Shortsighted perhaps. And that is what we will never know. Lou, he announced, grand and serious, I have excellent sight myself. He patted Squarcia's hand. Maturity, he whispered, can make a fat man attractive to certain women. Did you know that? And maturing bonds too. Being poor. . . but you wouldn't have any idea. . . felt like a physical wound. He wiped a tear aside. Think of it, for years walking round nursing a hole in my pride. That was me. There I go. My qualities stem from the two burdens of my life. He turned up the full orchestral brass: fatness and poverty.

He drained a bottle. Drink made him more dignified. His enunciation, though slower, did not deteriorate. Squarcia approved.

Squarcia had a story of his own, but kept it to himself. When he was about the same age as the bicycling Buchanan, his father gave him an ingenious toy boat. Cheap and simple, it was powered by steam. The speedboat's cabin comprised a tiny water tank under which the operator fitted a stub of lighted candle. As the water boiled, steam was ducted through twin exhausts just below the surface to propel the boat by its own power. The thing had a beauty which never failed to charm him. So much so that the smell of a smoking candle, instead of soberly recalling the duties of church, took him straight back to the ponds and water troughs in his native town. The candle had to be seated just right not to upset the balance. A skilful off-centring drove the boat in a perfect circle.

Twenty-five years later, when his father was dying of nostalgia, Luigi was heartless enough to recount these details. You know, old Squarcia grunted, shocked by the tiny dreadful additional pain, I remember your damn boat. His shaggy white moustache with the nicotine stain fluttered. They were the last words he spoke. So Luigi had the satisfaction of knowing he had been a comfort at the end.

For his Melbourne speech, the fat man sprang a surprise. He walked on stage at the Town Hall, before the country's most politically critical public, with a stuffed goanna tucked under his arm, the tail trailing behind him and the head well above his own. He propped it against the lectern where it rocked for a moment, stiff as a stick. He patted it and held up an admonishing finger, after which he faced the audience and delivered himself of an overfed smile.

— You may think, he began in his fruity voice. This is a stuffed lizard here. But no, actually he is a most serious person and the toughest competition I face in this campaign.

The audience laughed with surprise.

— Yes. His name is Robinson. He has a thick skin. (He knocked at the hard scales with one finger. Further laughter.) A narrow skull, but quite adequate to hold the quantity of brains inside. (He showed them. And now they began to enjoy themselves.) His most dangerous argument is his fingernails, which he hasn't trimmed for far too long. (He shook paws with the goanna.) I have invited him here, friends and neighbours, to put his own case to you before I put mine. Nothing could be fairer than that. This is the original fair go. Agreed? All right then. Now Mr Robinson, would you perhaps open the debate by explaining as clearly as you can what your policies are and giving us a list of solid facts, free from your wild socialist promises.

Buchanan stood back and struck a respectfully attentive pose. He waited for the stuffed goanna to speak while the audience grinned delightedly. He cupped one hand behind his ear. No? He leaned closer. No?

— There you are then, ladies and gentlemen, he declared. That's it. You've heard from his own lips what he has to offer if you vote for him.

This time no one needed to lead the applause. The place shouted with laughter. And the laughter went on and on until drowned in a storm of clapping. The goanna even began to look like Darryl Robinson, stiff-necked as a transported aristocrat and with the beady eye of an old Geelong Grammarian. Beyond doubt the campaign would make its own running. There'd be no following any lead suggested by opinion polls. Interim Freeholdings Incorporated of Delaware had picked a winner.

— Ah, the humiliating intimacies of morning tea, Buchanan declared urbanely on being welcomed by yet another hostess and stooping to kiss her grandchild till the cameras stopped clicking.

— Glad to be here in the Sentiment Belt, he roared as he patted an elderly paraplegic on the head.

— My life, he responded to a toast. Is one round after another of cocktail parties, fêtes and club dinners. Unbearable. Everyone chuckled delightedly.

At these times he missed having Dorina to share the burden as other wives (and even one of Plenty's mistresses) did. She'd told him calmly that she had not been consulted about surrendering their lives to the public, or she would have made perfectly clear her refusal to do so. She wished him success on the treadmill but declined to join him, thank you. She regarded herself as already a widow and Rory a fatherless child.

Buchanan recollected her words and her anger while being shown over shopping complexes and trudging across treacherous sand at surf carnivals among all that narcissistic carnality. Pub crawls to meet grassroots campaign helpers were a little easier to bear, though cumulatively they depressed him too. His feverish bonhomie blossomed. Must he depend on these drongos to persuade supporters to the cause? He slumped badtemperedly in a chair and grimaced at the microphone while put through his paces on talkback radio. He cut short a question which touched on family matters, winking and smacking his lips and declaring all sexual subjects taboo in the interests of modesty. Then scowled.

Typical was the morning he set aside to be with Dorina and the boy; nothing would drag him out on the campaign trail. Things were going so well, he could afford the break, his sole engagement being cocktails that evening with a High Court judge, a function to be held at home. It was a Sunday, with weather beautiful enough for spring. Rory suggested they hire a motor launch and his father promised some fishing also. Pittwater had been chosen for the trip when the phone rang.

— We're after the swinging vote, Squarcia explained as they drove off with promises of being gone not longer than an hour. Buchanan waved to the boy who stood, bereft, in his jaunty shirt and yachting cap.

Dorina remained indoors.

Squarcia had big news. The Prime Minister rang to let him know, confidentially, that he would be quite prepared to work with a National Pragmatist president. This would be a total slap in the face for his coalition partners. Even to take such a risk in private, he must believe the result a foregone conclusion. A tremendous feather, Bernie, for your cap.

— It's my day off, Buchanan fumed. I have spoken to all the minorities, every group of cranks there is: women, ethnics, you name it, Actors Equity. What else is there?

— I am counting each vote as precious, his manager replied.

They swung off the road, hushed over some turf between a pair of gateposts supporting a *MENS SANA IN CORPORE SANO* arch executed in wrought iron, and stopped.

On the field a game of cricket was in progress. Teams dressed, respectively, in hot pink rompers and crimson tracksuits were watched by a crowd of perhaps two hundred. The hot pinks, a side of giggling men, collapsed with merriment each time they misfielded while the crimson batspersons, earnest females calling for runs in baritone voices, charged liked rhinoceroses. The entire occasion exuded goodwill. Squarcia led his candidate to seats put ready, and a lad fielding nearby gave them a cheery wave. Meanwhile the bowler froze mid-stride and batspersons lifted their bats in salutation. To make matters wholly intolerable, teams and spectators clapped. Plainly the visit was expected.

— Acknowledge, acknowledge, hissed Squarcia.

Inwardly raging, Buchanan raised one paw for the sake of the swinging vote.

— Let me remind you before you have anything to say, said Squarcia in an undertone. That, after wives, gays are the biggest minority in the country, bigger than the Greeks. You get their votes and afterwards you can jail the lot if you feel like it.

Play on, someone called. The bowler ran up, swung his arm, and at the last moment changed action, lobbing the ball underarm. The field ached with laughter. The ball sailed gracefully across the swiping bat and collected the middle stump.

— Shocking! the batsperson declared. Shocking bad sportsmanship.

— Boo! called the crowd enthusiastically.

— Give him a thump, one of the waiting bats advised.

— Oh no, she retaliated sharply. I'm out and if I'm out I go with good grace. It's purely in the interest of standards that I lodge my comment.

Even the umpires were helpless with mirth. She snapped off the gloves and trudged back to her seat stewing revenge for when she'd have a go with the ball. A pretty young girl took her place at the crease.

— Wait! she called as the bowler got into his stride. Not ready. She arranged her long hair behind her ears. It's this marvellous shampoo, she apologized.

Having put everyone off their stroke, she faced up to the bowler who cocked his wrist at a menacing angle (found to have been much admired at school all those years ago) and sent it down with such exaggerated backspin it almost stopped dead where it hit the pitch. She tapped it away.

— Run! yelled the other bat.

— Will you fetch this one? the languid square leg pleaded and a bald colleague galloped all the way from mid-on to oblige.

— Thank you Roger dear.

A Ganymede emerged from among the cars, bearing glasses and champagne on a silver tray. He wove elegantly round the field serving drinks, occasionally ducking the ball, skipping niftily out of the way of flying batspersons and collecting rather more than his share of applause.

Now the defending pinks stood round sipping while the game warmed up. A couple of wickets fell. Out came the handkerchiefs for mopping brows. The wicket-keeper lay flat on his back, complaining in a voice audible to the spectators that this was the longest he'd been on his feet since the gay mardi gras and then he had had a couple of nude chaps to hold him up, having gone as the *Kama Sutra* between bookends.

— But do you realize, the savage Buchanan growled. That I never know what is happening? No one has even told me about IFID and why all this promotion was laid on in the first place.

— So you are learning to trust me? Squarcia smiled infuriatingly. By the way, I thought you would be amused to hear that one of your rivals has been making advances to me.

At the first ball of the new over, a splendid drive came bounding straight for Bernard Buchanan. This, then, was the burlesque his fantasy of power had dwindled to.

— Half a minute, suggested deep mid-off, placed his glass on the turf and trotted to intercept it, missing by a comfortable margin. Over the boundary rolled the ball, smack into the (perhaps) presidential boot. No escape. Seething impotence, B Buchanan clutched at it, stood, and hurled it viciously at the fielder, who ducked with more agility than one might have supposed him capable of. A wandering short slip hopped out of its trajectory and spun round on his toe to watch it skittle the wickets. The crowd roared.

— Yes, Roscoe Plenty would like me to be leading his team instead of yours.

The Ganymede executed a quick round of the players, topping up their glasses which they raised. A toast.

— Acknowledge, acknowledge, hissed Squarcia beaming with all his glittering teeth. This is real votes.

— Come and join us, boomed the lady with the bat. What a sport!

Too late to quell their enthusiasm: the whole team of crimson females that moment sprinted across the field in his direction, kicking up their heels, ponytails bobbing. He remained standing to ward them off. They gathered round with laughing friendly faces and coaxed him on to the pitch while Squarcia gave his blessing. Tugged by the lapels, pushed by hands on his bottom and back, a child inside him crying at the humiliation, he found himself at the crease and taking strike. He had always been useless at cricket. In that moment he faced the fact that he had probably never succeeded in hitting a ball during all his school years. The bowler, no longer the flaccid dilettante of a few minutes ago, out to prove his manhood against a real adversary, galloped across the grass, flinging his whole weight into the delivery of the ball. Buchanan, mad with anger and fear, shut his eyes and swung the hateful bat to kill. Crack! He opened his eyes, as his shoulders jarred, to see the shot he'd made soaring high above the heads of the champagne tipplers. Up it went, safe from even the most spectacular catch, to lob on the full among the waiting batters. Six. They went crazy with enthusiasm. He was a hero. He passed the bat to the umpire. Grinning with delight at his performance, he set off at a pounding stride to give Squarcia hell. The spectators cheered and Ganymede darted in his path, deposited a glass of champagne in his hand, and said something that sounded curiously rehearsed.

— The kisses of the enemy are treacherous.

Perhaps these words seemed all the more extraordinary for being spoken in an American accent, one of those true and gentle accents completely unlike an Australian putting it on. The fat man thought again of IFID and IFID's limitless generosity. Obedient to convention, he held the glass aloft like the champion he always longed to be, shook hands liberally with well-wishers of both sexes, assured them he stood for universal goodwill, quaffed the lees of the champagne, noticing Ganymede's cruel eyes as he gave the glass back, headed straight for the waiting vehicle, sank into his seat, pressed a button for the window to slide shut on his winning smile, spoke curtly to the chauffeur, and was swept away in a puff of gasoline fumes under the sign *ONAS EROPROC NI ANAS SNEM* which exasperated him unreasonably.

—You imbecile, Buchanan shouted. What if the press had been at that circus. I'd be smeared. I'd be branded.

— Of course the press was there, Squarcia soothed him. I invited her personally. You did magnificently.

— The Presidential Election, the fat man roared giving it capital letters. Is a deadly bloody business and too serious for that kind of cheap junket.

— If I remind you your present run of success began with a stuffed goanna, you won't hold it against me, will you?

— And supposing I've caught AIDS?

A brooding silence suffocated the three men trapped in their padded vinyl roles. When deposited home at his own gate almost two hours after he had left, seeing the garage empty and Dorina gone, Buchanan felt he had a right to the last word.

— You mention the Prime Minister's overtures once more in that lollipop voice and I'll flatten you.

He slammed the door as if Squarcia's smiling head were caught in it, only to hear that harsh calm voice reminding him of his schedule.

— There's nothing now until six this evening. Why don't you have a rest? I shall get here a quarter of an hour before the judge is due.

Bernard Buchanan realized time was against him. Even as the fridge door opened, apparently of its own accord, and he gazed in, during a few minutes remote as Christmas, at the illuminated delicacies his wife had prepared for the visitor. Even while he promised himself he could cross the kitchen and rectify the matter of openness letting all the cold air out or the warm air in, depending on which university you went to and it was quite a cool evening just to confuse the issue, space confounded him with a conundrum he could not get right.

— Time, he explained to the self he could see doing clever manual things he'd lost the knack of. Is against you.

Bottles rattled as his hand migrated among them, testing them by sound and weight. The rather dignified alcove of white tiles where Dorina's stove usually stood, yes and still did, struck him as appropriate. He leaned there to steady the swaying. Peeved, he was looking round an altogether altered kitchen, when one fly walking across the table gave him an idea instead of posing another question, an idea he musn't lose, a perfectly insightful idea revealing the nature of life, which he almost found words for, almost. Words he might just about bite on, but which his tongue couldn't manage. There was rather too much rotation in the room to encourage real research, but he sank back partially satisfied by his willingness to learn. He cared. The awful outward rushing sensation, that cosmic aspect of touch no other sense can equal, the rush into nothingness without the least possibility of being stopped or rescued, roused him to enough energy to open the wound of conscience, coagulating, gory, and weeping clear fluid.

— Is it my right? he muttered with his clustered chins forced well down against his chest.

He was his own master, surely. But would he continue to be in the future?

— If the client, he began again. Could have seen me hitting that six. His arm swung him round to face the tiles, to actually lean his cheek against the tiles till they grew warm and he settled there.

— How can they make me do it. . .

The conundrum worked itself out in the wonderful way of such phenomena.

— . . . afterwards?

He discovered the end of the swoop through space, though the damned light in that damned fridge kept catching his damned attention and nagging at him for some damned thing.

— I know, he informed a most attentive Churchill suddenly found to be licking his face. Exactly what you're doing.

Dorina would go to any lengths to save Buchanan disgracing himself in front of a judge. Even if the judge was, as he was, an old acquaintance. She and a tearful Rory had arrived home to find the immovable bulk of a drunken collapse stacked in the half-light, a monument against the kitchen wall. She sent the boy to have a shower and get changed into warmer clothes. Then she snapped the light on. The monument heaved with pain, raised one dusty arm to shield its eyes but let that fall like everything else in Pompeii. This would do, this time-form of a kitchen, no opportunity to tidy up before the catastrophe of uncoverers and sacrilege. Dorina shut the fridge door. He groaned.

— What time is it darling? she called upstairs to Rory, needing him to tell her, but also knowing how he loved to consult his watch.

— Five thirty-seven Mum. Five thirty-eight.

Good lord, she had come home at the last minute knowing how quickly she could make herself presentable, knowing she had put everything ready to receive the visitor, envisaging Buchanan pacing the house and sweating with worry. She only wanted him to see how she and the child felt, no more than that. Hadn't she agreed, with her diplomatic family background, on the need for the utmost discretion in a case like this? Wasn't it she, in fact, who conceded that Judge Mack might come casually as a friend, with her to talk to as well, and the usual concomitants of cocktail hour? In his delicate position, especially as a possible candidate for Chief Justice, he could not risk compromising his perfect impartiality, let alone be suspected of feathering his nest in the event of a change of government. Not even, which was how she had yielded to analysis, could he be seen to have preferences, to confer extra dignity on particular people as a consequence of his interest. This she clearly saw.

Dorina hunted in the phone book for the judge's number. She must put him off somehow. They had, after all, known one another slightly at university. His name was not listed: doubtless he needed a silent number as a matter of policy. He had taken her out once, but on what occasion she could not now bring to mind. She rang Enquiries and explained that the circumstances were desperate. But no, madam, there was nothing they could do, unlisted numbers being a safeguard against people shooting at judges as she'd probably heard, and respectable sounding ladies like herself not necessarily beyond feeling the same angers as anybody else; their best advice, really, was for her to contact some mutual friend who might have the number written down. Dorina could not explain that she and the judge had no mutual friends. Then she thought of enemies, of old Penhallurick. Thank you, thank you, she murmured hastily. Her pianist's fingers knew what to do. Having dialled again, she listened with fallen hopes while the answering service invited her to leave a message after the tone. Rory appeared, pink and alert.

— Is he unconscious? he asked with interest.

What should she shield the boy from?

— I don't think so, now, his mother answered replacing the handset at the exact moment the door chimes sounded. Churchill's tail stiffened and he went out barking. Dorina patted her hair. And dusted her knees, because she had knelt beside Buchanan when she first came in. A fly sang round the lightbulb. How could she fail to respect this drunkenness, so plainly a clumsy apology to her, even to putting at risk his powerplay? She began to see what it meant to him that she refused to help in his campaign. Yes, now it came to the point, Dorina was glad to have to cope. She composed herself for an ordeal.

— Stay with him, she suggested to their son, and closed the kitchen door behind her as she went to answer the call.

Rory heard her surprise, the relief in her greeting. His father, one eye open and the other still stuck shut, began heaving his huge bulk up on his feet, swaying away from his shadow on the white tiles and crashing back against it.

— Do I have the right? the drunken mouth croaked, some cumulative anguish erupting.

Next thing the door opened.

— We'll have to say he's ill in bed. I've never seen him like this during all our years together, Dorina apologized in distress, opening her palm as if rolling the ball of Squarcia's attention right to the culprit's feet.

— What if he won't stay up there?

— I won't, Buchanan roared. I won't.

— What if he tries to butt in?

She and the visitor stood together, for the first time, while they imagined crashings and bellowings. Bernard took a step towards them, maybe to supply a demonstration, clutched at the table for support, and swung across to the refrigerator. He balanced his weight and scratched his head.

— So I did shut the door, he muttered, rather pleased.

— Is he drunk Mum? Rory whispered in wonder.

This seemed to be all the confirmation Squarcia needed. The situation was not beyond at least partial salvage. Judge Mack getting to know Dorina again, yes, might work both ways to Bernard's advantage. A second cocktail call should improve their chances of passing the arrangement off as casual. For the present, then, he needed help with housing the evidence. Lavinia, of course, would cooperate. One could be certain of that. And she was home, as he knew, having just come from there.

— Hold the fort Dorina. I shall leave him with a friend. It's not far to drive. He can sleep it off. With luck I'll be back by the time the judge arrives. I know we can rely on you to cope, he added as a gesture of peace, also because he meant it. She was, in his estimation, professional. He sent Rory to shout for the chauffeur. They all crowded round Buchanan, hoisting him out along the passage (who had once not so long ago been hoisted by a single man) and bundled him into the back seat.

— We'll say he's had a minor accident while, Squarcia panted. Campaigning.

They drove away with the hero of the moment.

14

Crime Commission Draws Blank

The fourth New South Wales Commission of Enquiry into Crime today admitted lack of sufficient evidence for police to prosecute criminals at the centre of drug trafficking. Justice Mack said he deplored the tendency to try manipulating Commission hearings for political purposes. . .

— The sub has cut my reference to the naming of certain well-known businessmen. So you see, that can mean only one thing, Tim Davies pointed out. He already knows about Penhallurick.

— If he knows, you mean, everybody knows? young Stephanie asked, staring into her own copy on the display screen, occasionally tapping the keys with second thoughts. Or everybody with power to do anything about it?

— Precisely.

— Just as well the sub did cut it then, she observed absently, head down and hard at it. He's done you a favour.

Tim conceded the point with that sweet ruefulness he bore as a hangover from school days.

She did not notice.

She tried reading her piece as if she were somebody else. *Buchanan Knocks Them for Six.*

— I seriously question this Buchanan character, Stephanie confessed. But he puts on a terrific show. Best-humoured stunt you could imagine. Superbly managed. One hit and he left it at that. Couldn't improve on a perfect shot. The gays are eating out of his hand. Not a shadow of ostracism over AIDS. I just suspect him. There's something insubstantial in what he does.

— Think he's a lightweight?

— God, I feed you good openings, she laughed.

— We'd better get used to him. Lady P is all for him. Plus the opposition papers too. At this stage he can't lose. Though he was blind drunk yesterday when they brought him to your sister's place to dry out. I think he might have a problem.

— You met him? Stephanie cried in chagrin. Drunk? Oh God I wish I'd been there with a photographer. Why didn't you ring me? You've done it yourself, she accused him enviously.

— What, and put Lavinia on the line?

— You're too soft, she returned. To ever be successful.

Stephanie looked at Tim affectionately. But of course she was furious with him.

— Would you be surprised, she said to rescue him from the painful subject of his failures. If I told you it's not the unsavoury nearness of your body I find obnoxious, but the stink of the dead cigarettes you leave behind in my ashtray? Haven't you heard of the health revolution? Others kicked these bad habits years ago. They're all outside jogging and shopping for protein supplements with papaya enzymes.

— Then they need me for a benchmark, he proposed. Prime wreck, I am.

Lady Penhallurick herself walked in through the outer office with the busy timid bossiness of a galah, like, in fact, the Miss Alice Neilson she had been for most of her life, notorious as one of those owners who haunt their papers. The staff took no notice. On this occasion she stopped near the features editor's door to exchange a few words with his empty teacup, meanwhile watching two journalists she knew by sight but not by name, a tall thin fellow parked on the corner of one desk lighting a cigarette while smiling at a pretty fairhaired girl intent on the screen in front of her at another.

There was in Lady Penhallurick's expression, as she watched this young woman for a moment beyond the time convention allows for routine greetings, a certain emptiness akin to longing.

15

— I stand, even if I eventually sit because as you see I'm a shadow overweight, Bernard Buchanan trumpeted. I stand, I say, for an independent presidency. And I believe this is the best possible beginning for our new Australia, to be independent of political parties exploiting that outdated wrangle between employers and employees. For goodness' sake let's have something fresh. We're sick to death of the same old tunes. Well, aren't we? All we need from a government is sound financial management. Who better to offer this than a sound financial manager? I carry the evidence of my success wherever I go. (He patted his belly.) My pledge is fair practice, hard-headed opportunism, a free-flowing style, and a realistic program of nationalism. It's not just that I've got the best promotion agency working for me, thank you fellows, but the best ideas.

— We don't want a fair go, Buchanan boomed to the Lions' Club. No, he assured the Ancient and Honourable Order of Buffaloes. We shall make do with nothing but the best. Isn't that it? The others be damned, he promised. A fair go is a load of old bullshit inherited with the farm. How, he cried to Rotarians dizzy after a well-lubricated lunch. How we have been sold a pup! Heavens above, take our resources, our open-minded attitudes and adventurous spirit. We ought to be happy as Larry, raking it in. Instead, what have we got but strikes and lockouts and the endless muddles of egg-head economics professors. Will we honour international contracts? he quizzed the Returned Servicemen's League. Hell! Contracts made on such suicidally generous terms that we look like giving the stuff away to all those little people? Is this what we fought for in two world wars and the other wars following them? he asked the questioning faces. No. No, he gave them the very answer they would have made had they thought of it. And no again. We shall say, if you still want the goods then you have to move with the times, you've got to accept that a trade agreement is not Holy Writ. The sugar price was not prophesied by Isaiah, was it? The world parity price for coal wasn't laid down in the Acts of the Apostles. OPEC doesn't stand for the Orthodox Pronouncements of Enlightened Christianity, does it? Look, speaking personally, I wouldn't want to change a comma of the ten commandments even if I could, he informed the ecumenical conference of Churches of Christ, but I'll tell you what, there's not a single treaty we should leave as it is if we have found it doesn't serve our interests. What are we, craven or something? Can't we sign our names again? Once we have thought out terms to a deal, aren't we ever allowed to think them out again? Haven't we, he demanded of the Melbourne Chamber of Commerce, the guts to say by God what mugs we were when we let you put that one over us? Come on Australia, let's get up on our back legs, face our mistakes, put them to rights, give ourselves a break and tell our trading partners, if you don't like this, stick it in your pipe! We behave, he told the Western Districts Football Club, as if we were a great power needing to keep a cool profile. What for? They get all the benefits of world influence and we don't even have the pleasures of the carefree. I'm saying: Wake up Australia, wake up to the reality. We are a third world country and that means we can do as we damn well choose. Tourists? Of course we want tourists, we love them, the National Press Club was assured. Tourism is at the heart of the matter. That's money for old rope. You've only got to get your rope out and put it on display. (Male laughter.) We should turn on the best show we can for them and I reckon you fellows would probably make as good a fist of that as any in the land. (Further male laughter.) When I come to power you'll see how much can be done, just by applying a bit of get up and go. We'll have to fight them off, I'll make the place so bloody attractive. This is National Pragmatism as it will be in practice, hanging on nobody else's apronstrings and no bastard hanging on ours. Instead of giving out overseas aid, we might cop a few bucks ourselves for a change. How about that? The Country Women's Association clapped. The whole country had begun clapping. Wherever he went, word went before. He had a winner's confidence. The gentlemen who had taken so much trouble to watch over his welfare when he was stranded in the desert, who had listened to his bicycling autobiography plus a hundred hours of private conversations and still not found him wanting, smiled yet again.

16

Glittering Future Forecast by Candidate

— Exactly, moaned Stephanie shaking her curls and fixing Tim with a glare as he stubbed out a half-smoked cigarette. But what happened to my analysis of his grounds for this jolly stuff? That's my clean ashtray you're violating, you know.

— I know, Tim grinned whisking the pulls off her desk, the large sheets flapping elegant as a bride's train.

She contemplated her description of Buchanan as a feisty fast-talking ring-in from the sticks. Should it, she wondered, be the Styx? Some delinquent had borrowed her pocket dictionary and not returned it.

The sports editor came to the door of his glassed cubicle. He beckoned to a man at the far table who, without seeming to have noticed, stood up, improbable as a levitationist, head still bowed by the gravity of his opinion on the football semi-final, and sleepwalked obediently.

— Listen, Tim suggested. I've been thinking about twentieth-century literature. We live it here. That's my idea. Read Camus or Hemingway and it's all people smoking cigarettes; read Muriel Spark and they're drinking tea. The clink of a spoon, the contemplative puff. Scribble of smoke screening a significant look between a man and a woman. Bloodwarm tea wet on the lip. Pure literature.

— I was trying to hold on to my bad mood, Stephanie protested, laughing crossly.

— They're threatening to throw me out of my flat.

— For misbehaviour?

— That sort of thing, he confessed after a moment's pause.

— Well you can't move in with me.

— Shame on the woman for her heart of flint. What are you, a Hebridean Islander or something?

— No, I'm in love, she said suddenly, radiantly. But not with you, she apologized, just as suddenly shamefaced. And laughed.

— God preserve us the poor creature, Tim wailed in an Irish accent. And she doesn't even recognize her own copy on the latest extravagances of the fat man.

17

Roscoe Plenty did not like being observed impartially. When Lavinia Manciewicz showed him in, then installed herself in the most comfortable chair and lit a cigar, she subjected him to the kind of scrutiny he'd have punched a man's face for.

Morning light streamed across the studio, highlighting a rubble of found images, odd objects hoarded for their texture and shape. Large tables along two walls bore the detritus of productivity, twisted paint tubes, jars, splodges of hardened pigment. Every breath reeked of linseed oil.

The artist rocked back in her chair as she sensed his reaction, staring without concern for his feelings. She began sketching straight away, quite fired by what she saw.

— So you're going to prove me wrong about women being amateurs, he said, shooting her that cold quick eagle glance, hoping to surprise her into showing him the true shape of who he was. He watched her supple body as she bent over the drawing.

— I like your head, she explained absently.

Her first sketch depicted a darkhaired man about forty: he has thick eyebrows and cunning eyes, his mouth is a slash that dips to one side, his powerful shoulders bunch tensely and striated sinews lace his neck. Her second sketch was of two hands: the one is gross and curled round an unseen object that it will not let go, the other reaches out from a knobbly wrist, rapacious. Her third sketch was of a cheek: the jaw clenched and a corner of eye darkly glittering.

— The quality that will make you hard to paint, she explained at the end of the sitting. Is how fast you move.

He liked this and rose abruptly to prove it. As he swung round to replace his chair, he came face to face with a new painting propped against the wall, colours still slick with freshness: an unfinished portrait of Bernard Buchanan, there could be no doubt, staring at success across an acreage of broken glass punctuated by a couple of standing beer bottles.

—That's dear Bernard, she introduced them with a lightning check on his response. But you politicians all know one another, don't you? Playing the game? Hammer and tongs in public, and afterwards a drink together in the bar? That's what we hear.

— Dear Bernard? he fired at her.

— In the future, she confirmed ambiguously.

He could spare time for only one more sitting. If this were not part of his play for Bill Penhallurick's support, he would never have considered it.

She made exploratory sketches, pored over the photographs he brought and conducted a close examination of his skin texture. Like a dentist, she had perfected a technique for such closeness that precluded intimacy. But this, of course, was reckoning without his reaction. He watched and calculated. He understood why she appeared to have power: she chose not to acknowledge his status. She treated him exactly as she might treat someone harmless. She greatly admired Stanley Spencer, she told him, for creating a mystical suburbia. And for his cardigans. For dressing women in cardigans, she explained, and then painting every stitch. Roscoe Plenty would like to have thought up a joke about cardigans.

— What happens, he said. If I offer to fuck you?

She drew him with a snout and fangs.

— Um, she replied like his grandmother taking a message from God. She drew his nose, two eyes and a frown. That was how the painting began.

His face filled the big square canvas, just a glimpse of jawline across the lower righthand corner and part of the chin to the left. No hair or ears shown. This was a portrait of a nose. This was a landscape of moulded forms in which the terrible eyes and the mouth opened a way to unguessable depths. It was a country she painted, a passion, a ravenous predator. In through your window thrust the face of the giant and his breath lent a glow to the skin. But he was not looking directly at you, no, he was looking at his hands because you could see them reflected, one in each eye, the grasping hand and the reaching hand. She stuck the paint on the canvas in thick daubs, she smeared it and worked it, she caressed the surface, she seduced it, she laid her colours on thick as putty, dug at it with brushes, slicked it with her thumb. Her eyes laughed and her lips were grim. She grew gaunt and sweaty. She paced the room, swinging round to attack the painting with a fresh idea. She forgot him altogether, she shouted if he moved, as she might shout at the table for upsetting her still-life. He fixed her with his hypnotic rage and asked if this was relaxed enough. She smothered the red slash of his lips with ochre. At the temple, the skull became so prominent the pallor of bone showed through the skin. The hot secrecy of his nostrils she camouflaged with jutting bristles. His cheek she laid as a slab of stone. But his eyelids she kept for her climax, each a membrane ready to tear with strain. He told her about his travels and the Arab with a knife who chased him through Tripoli backstreets, how he used his commando training and broke the man's arm in his own good time. So you knew this was the least of it. She worked it all into the impasto frown. Then he concluded that the incident had happened only months after an American raid, so the Libyan probably mistook me for an enemy. She disguised her horror by opening the curtains further to blind him with light. Roscoe was a family tradition, he answered her enquiry, my father's a Roscoe and my grandfather was too. The generations of Roscoes stained the side of his nose. She smoked aromatically while she tackled the problem of correcting his brows. He told her cigars could give her lung cancer. She pounced at the portrait, her brush touching it with an unexpected glint of tooth.

— I'd say no to a fuck, she said.

He might have accepted silence. He might have accepted abuse. He was inclined to be tolerant of women. He could call on huge reserves of charm if provoked in subtle enough ways, as many had witnessed. But this one didn't understand basic civility. Right from the beginning, she hadn't known how to behave. At the racecourse she bluntly confronted him. She needed to be taught a lesson and he was just the teacher for her.

— I hope you will at least, he said. Come to dinner. A small party to view the portrait when it's ready.

She protested that he might not like her work. But he did. This was what he had waited so many years to see. He recognized the truth of it, shock sending adrenaline through him. His vanity responded. Yes, this was the shadow haunting his face in the mirror, this was precisely what no photograph showed. But his excitement was much more than vanity; on the spot, he grew to fulfill the ferocity of that face with its wolverine mouth. His satisfaction intruded on her own worries with the portrait and drove her to the window. Rain poured down outside. Only now did she become aware of the tuneful drains gurgling, a delicious speckled sonata pattering on the brick terrace. The healing began. Some washing along the line below hung in lank grey loops. She would use that, one day. Lavinia's studio, set high, commanded a view of Paddington backyards, chimneys, walled cubes of garden, fences with secondhand building materials stacked against them, the turn in a narrow lane where one garbage bin without a lid drank the downpour, and an umbrella bobbed along the lane, a woman's green umbrella answering her own mood, the very colour she had wanted for her harbour painting, it sparked a reflection in a wet wall. If she watched half a minute more, she'd glimpse the woman's back as the narrow lane opened into the street, childhood settled on her: a flesh-eating butterfly.

— It depends on the date, she replied in a green voice.

She used to get bitten by ants. They always found her. Everybody said she was imagining things. My life is wrong, she once confessed to her baby sister. Or at least what I mean is, happening. My life is happening without me. And rocked the baby too hard. The woman with the green umbrella reached the street. You could hear heels on the pavement because she was hurrying. Lavinia recognized her, her mother, wasn't it? Surely? Arrested by a voice in the mind, the woman down there stopped, tilted her umbrella, and looked back through the meshes of rain: a stranger with half her face blotted out by a plum-coloured birthmark.

— Set a date to suit yourself. The dinner will be in your honour, said the wolf.

Lavinia Manciewicz began as a rejected student. Unable to guess what others wanted of her, she answered truthfully and was judged self-opinionated, behaved modestly and was accused of having no ambition, painted as she thought and was advised to take up secretarial studies instead. Even now, when she considered her career, she couldn't imagine how everybody missed seeing her as she was. The rain intensified, the sheer weight of it on the roof set the house thrilling with life. A lovely jade light, having nothing in common with the rich umbrella colour, touched the edges of objects with glass. She noticed Roscoe Plenty's agitation. She knew he was dangerous, but a butter-green light swathed him in illusions of gentleness.

— Who's cooking? she asked in a tone that might have been thought mischievous.

— I'm a bachelor.

She knew this and he knew she knew.

If no institution would teach her, she had decided, to hell with them. She bought books and paints. She half-lived at the gallery. She began a program of throwaways. People keep too much, she declared with the certainty of an eighteen year old. She slapped the colours about. She chose the most unexpected angles of the most impossible subjects. She looked intently. Her eye trained her hand. Who said she couldn't see? Who said she hadn't the drive, the talent? She had talent enough to make them squirm. Talent enough to show what she saw, and that, after all, was a function worthy of respect. The first time Lavinia was admitted to an art school class was as a tutor, showing the hopefuls how to lay rust red beside cobalt blue to make the tonal balance sing, to make horizons of paint quiver with outback heat. They asked her what was the rule and why. But each time she planned to say her piece on how insultingly she has been treated and pay back those who had injured her, it seemed pointless. Worse, a waste of energy she needed for the next painting. They thought her sweet, they said among themselves, but rather unworldly. My life, she objected silently when she overheard this, has been harrowingly domestic. She forgave even the man who seduced her for her lovely nature, so she could get on with what mattered. She knew he intended seducing her and explained her lack of resistance by saying the time had come to knock her virtue on the head. Plus being twenty-two. Whoever can stand the strain of not knowing at twenty-two? And maybe I did have a lovely nature, she admitted.

— It's your success we're celebrating. I'd like you to invite one guest of your own. Someone special. The food will be perfect. I don't do things by halves.

She could imagine. She saw straight away the drab tartan skirt Greta would wear, the fine wool of her jersey, a too-large brooch at the throat, her simple pearl stud earrings, the church-goer's handshake she'd offer all round, touch of the good sport once, the implacable judgment she would form of each person from what was, after all, a position of genuine moral strength. But Greta it must be. This was a chance. Dear Greta, her plain goodness, her years of disapproval, her respect for authority.

— Thank you Roscoe, Lavinia replied turning her back on the window, the rainy roofs of Paddington, and the sound of a child shouting excitedly.

The table for eight at La Métropole looked out to a courtyard of floodlit ferns and planetrees, Australia half a world away. A specially built alcove masked off the main restaurant, while on the wall of this alcove the portrait had been hung. As a sensible French establishment whose pride was its cuisine rather than theatrical ingenuity, La Métropole spared its clients the usual task of penetrating subaqueous electric candlelight to pursue their intimacies. Here was a scene made cheerful by lights and heels hurrying across a slate floor, by the flash and clatter of hot dishes and the popping of corks.

Of course old Penhallurick, now Sir William Penhallurick, that scrawny rooster shedding profligate excesses of dry skin, was there representing the club and bringing his wife Alice, who had last been seen in public as hostess for Bernard Buchanan's nomination party. Lady Penhallurick blew her nose periodically to express her opinion, then returned her plump little hands to her plump little lap where they settled to the task of checking all her rings. Latest of a procession of tragic wives, she was, to the surprise of many, a mere thirty years his junior. Opposite her, and substantially fatter, Bernard Buchanan overlapped the edges of his chair, snug in a mantle of approval by unknown backers and promotion by just about anybody with a name. She smiled at him, she and her media empire being among those who would make him. Lady Penhallurick watched the wife, Dorina being parked sticklike two seats away from her, while Luigi Squarcia, the treasure, accepted a place between them, favouring both with equally affable smiles. Why had Dorina been chosen for that seat beside the host? Why not herself?

Lavinia stood at the alcove door, dazzled by the white cloth, the glassware and jewels. Beyond, rainsoaked trees shone an unlikely green against the silvered night. Remembering her responsibilities, she stood aside to usher in her guest.

— This is my sister Greta Grierson.

Clearly Roscoe Plenty was surprised at her choice and perhaps displeased as well. But if so, he covered his feelings adequately by making a ceremony of the introductions, beginning with Sir William and working clockwise round to Bernard Buchanan.

— Miss Manciewicz, he ended. Mr Buchanan.

— Mrs Manciewicz, Bernard corrected him and Dorina, suddenly alert, watched the look they exchanged.

Lavinia herself, so keen her elder sister should not feel out of place, noticed nothing of this tension. Poor Greta, loaded with responsibilities when barely seventeen, had been a wonderful success as a surrogate mother. Especially for little Stephanie. But also for herself. No wonder, then, she now felt some guilt for her sister's sedate spinsterhood. Stephanie might also have been invited, had she not been a journalist and likely to misuse the celebration. Plus, as it turned out, the possible embarrassment of her discovering she would be dining with the boss.

Soon enough they were seated and chewing crusts of French bread whilst awaiting the soup. Sir William was casting moonish eyes on the two fillies, Lavinia and Dorina, and mopping up crumbs as he dropped them, licking his finger and dabbing it on the cloth, not to miss a particle of free food. A middle-aged woman, unmistakably the proprietor, came for their orders. Squarcia took it upon himself to have invented Europe, and conducted the whole show in fluent gutter French.

The occasion began accumulating embarrassments. Dorina, on her guard against Roscoe Plenty's possible intentions, spoke infrequently and tactically. In any case, she felt ill and perpetually listened for some familiar music which had faded out of earshot. Sir William, bent on being the star of the occasion, took an instant loathing to the portrait in which he could see a successor to some of his own dear privileges. His wife kept up her cheerful nose-blowings. Bernard Buchanan had already enjoyed his single moment as voluntary centre of attention in correcting Lavinia's name. Miss Greta Grierson sat paralyzed by the threatening smells of cooking that expected to be lusted after. Roscoe smiled so genially the temperature fell. And Squarcia rehearsed the future, giving the present only enough attention to keep the pot boiling by provoking Lady Penhallurick to talk too much.

— I do think, she confided to Lavinia. Your painting makes our handsome Mr Plenty look a proper villain.

Lavinia laughed with surprise and pleasure.

— Not that I'm daring to make an artistic judgement, the lady insisted. I don't even know what I like! Not like my father who knew everything. But I can see what I see, she warned her husband, by directing this remark at him, not to try putting her down. I do have eyes and we're all entitled to an opinion, I should hope. We aren't ruled by the communists yet. What's more, opinions never upset real artists do they? she begged. It's having no opinion that's wounding.

But Sir William did not intend rebuking his wife. This was one of those occasions when he considered her naive directness hit the mark dead centre. He eased his collar, dislodging a few crusted flakes of skin, and made eloquent use of gestures to encourage her to continue.

— Tell me Lavinia, she went on to cover the awkwardness. How much do you charge for a painting like this?

Dorina was simply dismayed at the prospect of a whole evening of such conversation led by that woman flaunting her husband's title when everyone knew it had been bought. Already the chilled vichyssoise smelt indigestible. Or no, she chided herself impartially, last time I was pregnant I had just the same problem with bouts of nausea. Yet, instead of raising the full spoon to her waiting mouth, she returned it to the bowl. Then she gathered her reserves of determination and tried again; Bernard must not guess what might be wrong. She hadn't come upon an opportunity for breaking the news to him and would be mortified at being, as she put it to herself, found out. Rain on the roof sang to her, remote and peremptory as her whales.

— I should imagine, Dorina said to save the artist. A work of art and its price have nothing to do with one another. Surely the only thing money buys is the right to hang it on a particular wall? She tasted her soup at last.

Bernard harrumphed indiscreetly and grumbled about how excellent the flavour was. Lavinia shot an interested glance at Dorina, noting that she looked as if she might peg out any moment. Greta Grierson mopped an imagined spot on her woollen bosom. Sir William rallied to his wife's side.

— I'm damned if the club's money was spent on rights. We bought the picture. Am I correct?

— You did, Lavinia conceded but her tone gave her away.

— William was talking in terms of thousands, you know, Lady Penhallurick explained to Squarcia.

— Naturally, he replied. I was always led to believe that once you are given a knighthood even your grocery bill has to be settled in thousands.

This was a kindness Lavinia did acknowledge with a smile. But the price of food was her sister's special subject and so Greta corrected him immediately, ignoring the hearty nods of the sufferers.

— I'm always shocked by how much people waste, she said. And the worst is wasted food. When we were children, though Lavinia was so young she'd hardly remember, we often went without. Since then I can't bear to throw away a stale crust. Suddenly her soup smelt delicious and she overcame her suspicion at its being cold. She drank a spoonful. My goodness, she whispered with a new understanding of the frailty of those who succumb. She looked up, afraid her revelation of greed had been recognized for what it was, looked especially towards her sister, poor little Lavinia needing care and instruction all those years, and then abruptly beginning the downward course of answering back, collecting her sheaf of failures like prizes, setting her face against everything wholesome. Just to say: Accept me for who I am. The little idiot didn't know who she was herself. No wonder their unfortunate mother gave up and left them all. Betrayed them without a word of excuse. Heaven knows, it was Greta herself who reared the younger girls. Thus (as she might have summed it up) having put Lavinia in a basket, this suet pudding of a woman with her skin boiled pure, her plump succulence bursting at the strings, her untasted promise, armpits dusted with talcum, observed the rest of the party. If she accepted that Lavinia had, to this extent at least, made a success of her career, it was only to add the qualification that good things never last if they haven't been worked for.

The host was speaking through lips too moist for a man, yet altogether coarse and masculine, his dark eyes calculating. One hand toyed with the pot of flowers, turning it and turning as if winding something up, while the biddy next to him made sour faces in her soup, her adam's apple gristling its way up and down to let the food through, and once peered over the rim of her spoon with what Greta described as a look to put us all behind bars. The titled lady of course wasn't titled. High society, like food prices, being very much in Miss Grierson's line, she understood that Lady Penhallurick was as much a lady as her husband was a knight. Watched her giving little gasps with open hands, tiny fat catastrophes, and delving in her sleeve for a handkerchief to blow her nose. The nose received this punishment with bad grace, small though it was, the skin reddened and an angry flush remained there during the whole occasion.

How hard to believe the dinner was in honour of Lavinia and that horrible painting of hers. Surely there must be some hidden, unlucky motive, and the silly girl being used. Impossible to believe anyone saw the portrait as other than an ugly daub. She herself once painted, devoting her energy to truly lovely parrots done on the pastel-coloured pages of friends' autograph books, hers always the choicest contribution among platitudes and doggerel, the bird feathers touched in one by one with the driest of watercolours. She taught Lavinia, you could say. And now Lavinia had lost even her youthful bloom, her one asset. She is a woman, Greta realized with resentment. There is nothing left in common between us. All trace gone of the girl I used to know. These revelations were interrupted by that bloated type opposite, his threatening toad shapes leaning forward to speak to her, neck bulging out over his collar and thin hair stuck damply to his head. But he changed his mind and sank back. She dusted her sleeve, as she rid herself of scrofula flakes from the specimen next to her; as for him, Greta detected something foreign in his voice so she wasn't fooled by that grand name, oh no. Had it not been for Mr Squashia or Squarechair, she wasn't sure she could go on sitting. He alone made no pretence of being what he wasn't, no attempt to hide his Continental origins. Greta Grierson, like so many of her peers, admitted two classes of European migrants, the foreign and the Continental. So Continental was he that she could imagine him as her guide, perhaps her escort, his firm hand under her elbow, helping her up the Eiffel Tower or warding off beggars at the Taj Mahal. But enough of fantasies. The spoons clattered emptily and one guest after another laughed a false laugh. Icy wineglasses were lifted to their lips. The hungry mouths sucked in alcohol or spat words. Why must she be put through this torture, so out of place she was, and feeling judged.

Lady Penhallurick blew her nose and checked her rings.

Whereas nobody had difficulty calling Lavinia Lavinia, though she was a stranger to half of them, they found the name Greta eluded the memory. Every so often a Miss Grierson would be let slip to freeze the conversation.

— Thousands Miss Grierson, Lady Penhallurick confirmed. At the supermarket! and her plump neck swelled with enthusiasm. Mind you, I'm a tiger for a bargain. This ring now, this one here, the diamond and sapphire, you wouldn't credit how cheap we managed to get this.

Dorina gulped her soup, nauseated at what she had been

through so recently, that frightful drama of finding Bernard drunk and then having to soothe the judge. But I married him, she protested, to escape public life, to have an ordinary private family.

— I mean, it's worth a fortune of course, but Sir William and I went into it knowing exactly what we'd pay, exactly how to beat the fellow down. And he was the expert, she crowed triumphantly.

— Alice! her husband remonstrated, topping up his blood-alcohol level. He assembled fingers round the glass to try them out.

Bernard had no patience left for such occasions. He was tired. As his chance of success increased he felt, ironically, more easily dispirited. Now he seemed likely to have to live with the consequences of that contract he'd signed, it troubled his conscience with the ache of an indefinite anxiety.

Lavinia's sister suited Roscoe Plenty's intentions beautifully the more he observed her. He considered her with the dark, brilliant scrutiny the painting had taught his eyes.

Plates and bottles being removed and replaced, Squarcia sent his commendations to the chef on the *poulet à la Marengo*, he even produced a spicy joke he'd rehearsed, concerning Napoleon's viceroy in Italy (a connection none but Dorina understood); however, he was mildly critical of the chablis and consulted the label several times before relinquishing it. Lavinia now looked out to the freedom of the garden where, for a flash, the green tree mimicked a woman's umbrella; she was ashamed at having willed the poor thing to turn and show her birth-marked face. Some of us, she thought, carry a stain through life no less disfiguring for being invisible; but immediately regretted the idea as trite. Bernard caught her eye, guessing they might have seen the same unexpected interloper out there. And yes, she did seem to acknowledge a ghost. They each remarked silently on how withdrawn the other was. Or some premonition, perhaps, bought them closer together.

— I think, Sir William declared in a too-loud voice, I should say a few words. He shuffled to his feet and wobbled there. He may have fallen over without the table to hang on to. I had my own portrait painted once. So I'm no novice to the world of artists. Sat for three days with only food, sleep and the natural functions to break the monotony. Of course in that case it was a much more traditional job. You young people would call it old-fashioned. This dinner. This dinner is private. Is a private celebration. The club will put on something more public, never fear. The idea of portraits of club presidents is a cultural one. And Roscoe is the first. May there be many more. He peered at them, their lack of response putting him off his stroke. He showed signs of sitting down but recollected his reason for making the speech in the first place.

— Of course, a patron is nothing more than a name to list on the letterhead. The suggestion of who to commission is the point. That's what I'm getting to. And the suggestion was an excellent one which came from, I'm pleased to say. (He was a child in an adult's suit of clothing being listened to with particular concentration by Bernard Buchanan.) Pleased to say, he concluded, having lost his thread.

— You're making a fool of yourself Bill, Squarcia observed.

— This lovely lady on my right, the knight went on, clawing at Greta Grierson's shoulder. Is the proud possessor of a sister. That's the point I'm getting to. We've never met before, this lady and I, but I'm sure we will meet again.

Greta raised stricken eyes, expecting to suffer some withering rebuke from Lady Penhallurick. But Alice was dreaming, she was floating along on the rhetoric, she was recollecting that voice of his in scores of dignified situations. She had heard him launch ships and lay foundation stones, she had applauded while he warned the young against communist teachers, she had been mesmerized by his tales of remote Hungary, its fleeting republics and fleeing kings, dank castles and incomparable wine. He had the grace to lecture guests on the refinements of the food she served them. His was a voice the Pope himself had heard. No point in her resisting; and she never had, as she never gave the least quarter to gossips who tried to warn her; oh yes, they had things to warn her about and other women's names to hiss in her ear, plus the begging remnant of families ruined in the companies he had sunk in his time, so they said, the evil ones who had no idea of his little kindnesses and how he had never looked down on a single one of their tradespeople or the cleaner who came twice a week and to whose children he gave Easter eggs without fail. What about them, she'd reassure herself while she blocked her ears to the libels of drowning and crashes, poison and knives, the ghastly libel that this voice had been heard in court guiltily defending itself. Hadn't the slanderers been told about justice or the acquittal by an impartial jury? And why was he not marked if this were the truth? How could he escape without scars on his personality which she, alone of all people, was close enough to assert were nowhere to be detected. Self-appointed moralists committed cruelties with no cause whatsoever, hurtful offences like splashing black swastikas on their lovely white BMW, writing begging letters to her on behalf of orphans from some pogrom she ought by rights never to need hear about. But always his voice at breakfast chanted its comfortable litany between the tiny whacks he delivered against the boiled egg with his teaspoon: Another day, Alice, no regrets old lady I hope, this egg's perfect as always, let them say what they like, that's why I leave it to you to read the newspaper, so you can tell me what to expect. And if the worst were true, after all, if he had committed murders, she'd tamed him hadn't she, alone in showing enough courage to see his qualities and save his soul? Even as she denied everything, Alice thrilled, secretly, to the one risk she had ever taken in her life, and such a risk.

I ought to have told Buchanan on the day they brought him home in the ambulance, Dorina reminded herself. She swallowed bile. It would have been so much less complicated then.

— You can't tell me anything about the arts. Sir William fired at them aggressively. He adopted his pulpit manner as the seductive idea of recounting an anecdote possessed him. Years ago, I made my first visit to the Adelaide Festival. This would have been back in '76. I was catching a direct plane from Sydney. I know my dear, he placated his wife who was signalling that she had heard this one before. But no one else here has heard it. Well, they'd just finished clearing away the meal when what should we hear but bagpipes. Yes, cruising at thirty thousand feet, bagpipes!

Everybody laughed except Greta, for whom anything Scottish bore the suggestion of solid normality, and Dorina, still withdrawing from the absence of her own music.

— What's more, these bagpipes were getting closer. Can you believe it? We couldn't see back past the curtain to the economy class, but the hostess told us it was a member of a pipe band going to Adelaide to compete in some competition. Well, there he was, yowling up and down the aisle. So I lodged a complaint straight off. If this is what we've got waiting for us at the festival, I said, turn the plane round and head home for Sydney. I can't stand hearing a cat murdered.

Roscoe Plenty slapped the table with delight, setting the cutlery jingling. And a nervous waiter glanced round the doorway to see what had gone wrong.

— If there were any overseas visitors on that flight, Dorina objected. They would have thought us the most cultured nation on earth, having live music in our planes.

—Then what happened Sir William? his wife urged to cancel the dampener of this unsporting comment.

— You weren't there, my dear, he rebuked Dorina kindly, in return for her kindness to him when whales threatened to wreck his yacht, not being a man to forget. I caught sight of him later. They pointed him out when we left the flight. Full-grown fellow he was too. The pipes died with a squeal. The passenger across the way from me clapped his hands silently. There's one thing about art that's better than war or bankruptcy, a single word and you can have it stopped.

Now Miss Grierson did, perhaps, smile faintly, privately.

— I haven't forgotten, he rebuked his wife for her reminding looks and held up one hand as if pleading innocent. Unwittingly this gesture gave him away. In the extrovert pleasure of a storyteller, armies came to attention, the golden youth shouted their joyous *Sieg Heil*, he smiled the smile of a man who has the ultimate backers. Safe to do anything. At his gesture the garden outside glowed brighter. Another good thing about art, he rescued the situation. Is that one word and you can get it going too. This is how we came to commission the portrait from Lavinia, not only a prime filly, but a talented hand with the brush.

Dorina, though she was angry at Lavinia for having allowed the drunken Bernard to stay in her studio all night instead of sending him home by taxi, now felt extraordinarily sorry for her, having to suffer these philistines and, even worse, having to surrender her marvellous painting to them.

— I am here, Sir William intoned, shedding some more dead skin. To propose a toast. To Lavinia Manciewicz, the painter of the portrait.

They stood, Bernard taking a long while to muster his way-ward flesh, as in bags and nets, copious panniers of fat, and assembling it to a shape his suit could still contain. While he did so, Plenty switched attention to him and him alone, testing if this might possibly be the moment, then darting a look at Penhallurick and Squarcia to surprise them, maybe, in some expression of sympathy.

— To Lavinia.

Greta, whose alcohol limit was a glass of sherry a week, joined in rather too suddenly. And now she did have a stain on her jersey. This appeared to be her chance, having steeled herself all evening to say something publicly. She took advantage of the arrival of dessert, once they were all resettled, to blurt out her contribution to the smalltalk.

— A friend of mine, she said. Has married twice, each time to a man called Tom Anderson.

The tipsy Penhalluricks boggled.

— On purpose? Sir William squawked in an envious falsetto.

— She married on purpose, Miss Grierson replied giving the question careful thought. But not in either case because of the man's name. So far as I know.

The dessert was consumed amid *ahhs* and smacking lips.

— I, Roscoe Plenty announced keeping an eagle's eye on the wollen jersey and pearl earrings. Have my own thanks to add. He smiled warmly round the table, the nice man. I don't like having my photograph taken even. No, photos make me look too handsome. They never seem to show what I expect. But this painting does. It's good. Unflattering if you like, but powerful. I like it. I'm delighted with it. I thank the club. And I thank Lavinia. And I take it as a special compliment that you've done me so much better than you did Bernard.

Dorina felt the cold blade sink in. What portrait of Bernard? But if Master Plenty imagined she'd give him the satisfaction of a public enquiry he couldn't be more mistaken. It was Sir William, sounding peeved, who gave him his opening.

— So you've painted Bernie?

— I have a soft spot for Bernard, Lady Penhallurick warned.

Squarcia spooned up his dessert nonchalantly as the evening, ponderously superficial, showed its first flicker of life. Soon he would discover, apparently, why they had been invited. The Presbyterian brooch glowed with new light.

— Was it another official portrait, Lavinia? her sister asked, antennae bristling, picking up alarm signals.

— Hardly! Roscoe laughed coarsely to encourage his guests to join in. She painted him without clothes.

The idea, so distasteful, of a nude Buchanan made Dorina shudder slightly. He was watching her too, from a blank face which made it worse, from a face which had no idea of what she herself was going through at that moment, a face as good as saying great heavens haven't I suffered enough in recent times without hearing this? Dorina had been brought up to remain outwardly unruffled. Why did he not reply? Wasn't he content to have made so many enemies, without allowing friends to turn vicious? Her adam's apple popped down and up with each measured mouthful of coffee.

— Bernard does not have your good looks, she then announced with crushing disinterest. But his warmth is ample compensation.

This is more like it, Squarcia thought, watching Plenty's unpreparedness for so calm a rebuff.

Lady Penhallurick checked her rings.

— You, she challenged her dear drunkard. Haven't had yourself done, I hope?

But Sir William didn't take this as a joke at all, directing at her an angry dismissive gesture which, unfortunately, connected with his glass and splashed its contents over the cloth. Squarcia made use of the break.

— Since we have been, shall I say, cohabiting, Lavinia has worked on a whole series of nightmare images. I beg your pardon Bernard. She never normally (here he smiled at her, possessively) leaves them out for just anyone to see. In this instance, however, I laid a trifling wager, he lied. A whim. So it is my fault.

Greta, he knew, was collecting courage to walk out, but there were always sacrifices to make. He had his candidate to save in this influential company; he couldn't save Lavinia's sister as well. He was more than a match for the tempestuous Plentys of the world. There was only one person he could turn to.

— That will be ten dollars you owe me, he said to the unsuspecting Dorina, who rallied, put aside the tortures of her conscience and the queasiness of her condition, promptly opened her purse and produced a note which she slapped in front of the odious creature. Thank you, said Squarcia sweetly and folded it.

Lavinia regarded her with instant hatred.

Now Miss Grierson did find strength to stand. She shook off Sir William's flaking claw. It would never have occurred to her that none of this might be true, such lethal games with a person's reputation being unthinkable. She gathered up her handbag mutely. She could not bear to look at her sister. She walked out of all their lives, bearing her martyrdom on her arm, a past of unjust responsibility, her grief and humiliation held together only by fine wool stitches.

The bitter rejoinder in Lavinia's mind, for this was the absolute end of their brief affair, must remain unspoken. Her eyes filled with tears. The only person she cared to save had gone. So great was the price to herself, she did not see that Luigi Squarcia was protecting her too.

— I agreed to a portrait, Buchanan spoke abruptly, addressing them all. And how do you know it was not for your benefit? Maybe I did it precisely to invite a shoddy scene like this for showing me who my friends are.

Dorina looked up, immediately alert to the pride she felt in his spirited tone.

— You don't know. Unless I tell you, he insisted. You won't know either. I have a long memory. Tomorrow, don't be surprised if you think back and feel uneasy and ask yourself: Did I show my hand, the few pathetic cards I'm bluffing with? That's what you'll find nagging you. In ten years' time it will still be nagging you when you want to know what went wrong and how I knew what I knew. Your sister, he spoke to Lavinia alone as he stood and Dorina stood with him. Showed admirable good sense.

The Penhalluricks, too, appeared relieved that he had finally defended himself, but it was hard to tell with Sir William how genuine this might be; or with his wife whether the principal issue might not be the preservation of her list of acceptable dinner guests.

Roscoe Plenty, having hoped to drive home his first wedge, found himself left in the cold. But at least the subject of electioneering had been avoided, with not even one joke about their respective campaigns. He was saved having let it all hang out.

With a contraction of the heart, Dorina knew that declarations were being made nonetheless, that both Squarcia and Penhallurick refused Roscoe Plenty's bait. Till now her mind, in its formidable strength, had put up a barrier of scepticism. No longer. Deep within lodged the fact that there would be no salvation by laughter. Buchanan's surliness did not hide his true state, his besotted enthusiasm for the unthought-of powers being put in reach. She feared consequences. These powers might leave him relatively unscathed, he might just ride them with the very childishness she deplored more than all his other vices, but *she* would not escape. The wave lifting him into the limelight must eventually dump him, but while likely to do no worse than tumble him painfully on the sand, it would drown her. And drown Rory as well. No, perhaps not Rory; for who knew what resilience the boy kept hidden under his dogged unsociability? Buchanan's fat hand on her elbow guided her out. She glanced once more at that splendid powerful painting. And nodded thanks to the staff.

Rory might survive, with luck.

18

— Is it to be the old bitch herself coming? I know about the ceremonial whatnot, sure. Then why shouldn't we give her a roasting? She'll have to fly, won't she? She can have a taste of her own medicine. Needs a touch of finesse in the planning, of course.

— And you can rely on us for that.

— You can. We shall have a hell of a good time.

— And if this Buchanan fellow was to win? He wouldn't be one of Black Cromwell's men, would he, what with him having a human name like he has?

— He wouldn't be used to baiting the police either, that's as much as to say in his condition he doesn't get his amusements on the hoof. Mind you, I am only guessing.

— That dome wasn't built in a day! Never.

— It's his wife I'd be feeling for.

— Now we've no cause to intrude on a man's domestic confidentiality, the poor misfortunate creature. We're losing the bloody thread.

— If you ask me, Buchanan is as Buchanan does. And anyhow he might not win at all. We could be dealing with Robinson. There's a man that sticks his English family up your nose, now.

— When were we ever put off by the fear of consequences? The point is clear. This is the last place on God's earth where they'll think she'll be putting herself at risk.

— Is it a written invitation we're waiting for, then?

19

Bernard Buchanan examined his hands. He could not read the future. But the past was there all right.

I was never happy, he remembered. I always wanted my mother to be. . . what? . . . famous? . . . unconventional? Excessive. Yes, and perhaps she was, though not in a way I could skite about when I needed to. Everybody called her Mum. Even her husband the school inspector called her Mum. Except me. In my case, I spoke of her as My Mother. And there you have it.

My mother never liked me kissing her after I was thirteen. She used to shy away and hold up horrified hands, laughing and telling me I would not make a man if I couldn't restrain myself from kissing her. She had a consuming interest in my growing to be a man. I was made to wear my football guernsey and boots on the weekends even though not in the team. She only let me off on Saturday afternoon to listen to the race commentaries. These were our closest moments; she gave me all her attention when we discussed the form guide and wrote out our bets on sheets of lined paper so we could crow over the horses and swap stories of how rich we would be if we'd put money where our intuition was. She was the one who arranged for me to have that bicycle. My father, who despised the racetrack hobby, didn't care one way or the other about the bicycle, he said. But Mother convinced herself this would be an orthodox step towards manhood and might help me lose weight. Far earlier than this, perhaps back to the pram, she had begun her campaign. I had been ogling, she assured her friends. I could tell a girl baby from a boy almost before her parents could. My childhood had been a ceremonial march-past of prospective female flesh in review order. At six I had been caught with a hand up Sheila's skirt. At seven I heard Mother proudly warn a neighbour I took the knickers off their ten-year-old twin daughters, both at the one time; at eight and a half I was the suspect in a child-rape case and she called the police, to their amazement, so that I was shut in the kitchen with a sergeant who pulled my pants down and handled me to see if he could tell the possibility; at nine she took me to bed and let her fingers make awful hot waves under my pyjamas; at ten she threw me out for refusing any guests but boys at my birthday party; at eleven she recollected in public how I sat on the potty as a toddler and bending right over had observed two things hanging down, a small one and a big one that finally dropped; now of course, she smiled, it would be a big one and a big one. At twelve she instructed my sister to take out a tit for me to feel; at thirteen she purchased a prostitute for me and promised to pay more for the time we didn't spend together than we did, as an inducement to quick results and a way out of her torment. At fourteen I was disowned by her as a flabby disgusting pansy with your little thing hardly better than a finger, when at least you should be as good as your father, whose one good side is that.

She made wonderful rice pudding, sweet and creamy. And most of the time she loved me.

When you were only a twinkle in your mother's eye, as my father described the period before I was born, putting me in touch with a great many years I'd otherwise have been excluded from. I had looked into her eyes and witnessed myself there, so I knew what he meant though I couldn't imagine the marvel of how it happened. I searched her eyes for other children in case I'd have to put up with more than the sister I already had, an older sister who couldn't see what I saw in me, as she put it.

At school I used to wrestle with the younger kids and sit on them till they began to howl. They appear to have liked this because they were always hanging round me.

You could get into the cinema for sixpence when I was a kid. This was the wonder of those Saturdays when I escaped the races, lolling in the huge eight-seater canvas deckchairs, patrons smoking all round, and us with them; chucking lollies at friends and rolling lemonade bottles down the sloping wooden floor to hear them rumble and bounce and then clatter up against the stage at the front right under the nose of Johnny Weissmuller that moment swimming after a crocodile, catching it and breaking its back, and the boy next to me toying with his horn while the girls spat between the rows to show what they thought. How would an English lord and lady describe us?

I could never put myself in my mother's shoes. I wish I could say I knew what made her tick, but I'm not subtle enough to be dishonest.

As for my father, he couldn't allow things to happen without a motive. Why? he would ask. Give your reasons. Let them tell you what's behind it. There must be something in it for her. Who's guiding this decision? And so on. I saw him only in the evenings and I tried to keep it as short as possible by demanding help with my homework, help which I knew he would never give. He'd say, what's behind this? Your motive, if I'm not mistaken, is to avoid acquiring knowledge. You simply want to reduce the labour of thinking to the negligible gesture of writing out what I have thought for you.

I was not allowed to attend the school where my father was headmaster before he became the district inspector. This way he preserved his reputation for impartiality. So we occupied a house midway between his school and mine. Bare winter trees, polled windows, each a cluster of punishments, a founder's nostalgia for Yorkshire, stood guard round the playground as I remember it. Imported trees, a wretched relic of imperial sentimentality. Listen to this, I'm telling you. The wind through those trees was pure scent from hundreds of miles of gumleaves. The canes rattled. Inside the classroom I had to write *disappointed* five hundred times to atone for the once I'd written *dissapointed*. I also felt terribly in need of admiration. Friendship was not enough, though I had few opportunities of weighing it. My ears so sang with this need that everybody could be heard walking around in sand.

Usually when I looked outside it was blazing hot: thin persons' weather; or rain on the streets, and at night from my bedroom window rain slanting into lamplight, rain in the morning as feathery as mist, rain cooling hot railway tracks with tiny curls of steam I would have liked to point out to a younger brother if I had had one, rain pocking the surface of the cold river, rain as a taste of yesterday, rain hanging from fence wires and dropping to the ground after the clouds had gone, sparkling.

I was at school the day my father died.

Kids, pouring into the yard for morning break, fell quiet at an unprecedented sight: not the sea escaping in a rush and a new land rising, dead to the sun's nourishment, but the school flag drooping from the flagpole. That flagpole was supposed to be bare, with just the rope slapping its side in a wind. And now this satin flag rustled, fold lapping fold and sending shivers along the spine. Green as snow. We once had snow on the paddocks, do you know that? The emblem had always mystified me, it was a lamb strung up by the strap round its belly, feet dangling straight down. A dead lamb, you see, dangling there above a motto. The motto itself was all too true: *Labore et labore*. While it slinked in the breeze, the lamb's head peeped out between folds and slipped back again. Funny what a child notices. And things happened to the motto too, one sheeny curve reading *Lab* and the next one *bore*. I can remember that. A bit of the tight belt and *abo abo*. But I was missing the point. The flag was not out there on show for the sake of the handworked satin. The flag was there in order to be flown at half-mast.

Our science master appeared on the stairs and blew his whistle. I thought that whistle unbearably shrill. I am here to make a sad announcement, he told us, looking at everyone except me. And this was how I learned my father had died. So much for Archibald Buchanan, BA, BEd. My mother refused to let me see the corpse. She was afraid the shock might arrest my development. Instead of a mild old tyrant reeking of cold pipe smoke, I was left a memory of a whistle, an insincere voice, and that pale green flag. The fabric was so sleek. I can tell you. It was treacherous as water.

20

— More on the Crimes Commission, Tim sighed. Never-ending. Onion. Layers under layers. Once let the sleuths loose and you have mayhem. What they call corruption, I call respectability anyway. Respectability as we have come to know and revere it.

— Don't be cynical. Of course old Alice has to stick up for her husband. No good hoping you'll get through with that one. Unless you go to work for the opposition. Or buy the *Sydney Courier* off her.

— What opposition? They're all running the Buchanan ticket and we don't know why.

— How about actually finishing that cigarette? It'll give you time to reach your own desk to put it out.

— Not a one dares touch Penhallurick. Tim stubbed his newly lit B&H Sterling Extra Mild. Sorry. Not thinking. Alice is married to him, okay? But none of the other bastards are. They can't have that excuse.

— Then you tell me why they won't nail him.

— Something big, Stephanie my chicken. Bigger than we know.

21

An immense swell of nationalist excitement had brought city services to a halt. The characteristic shyness of display, remarked upon by so many visiting experts, was cast aside. The dun husk cracked: exotica blossomed. Citizens, sagging with sentiment, chanted and listened to speeches, were seen standing in the mid-traffic contemplating the promise of the future. Rock bands reduced the process of reason to a deafening repetition of the fatuous. Brawls broke out for the sheer exuberance of the thing, strangers embraced, T-shirt slogans became mandatory badges of patriotism and those not wearing them could expect, when hauled up by happy vigilantes, to have to explain why not. To add to the colour, supporters of political parties flaunted their banners with the fervour of football fans. Bookmakers offered odds and elevated the show to pure mathematics. Indescribable violence crept into the bedrooms of couples with opposing political loyalties, a violence many eventually found solvable by one or both going over to the Independent, Buchanan, and his program of National Pragmatism.

With a fine carelessness, families squandered their savings, expecting a new era. While those in power used the interim to secure their privilege under revised titles, the powerless gave away what little they had and filled the sidewalks with their hopes, we did. We turned our backs on every lesson of history. We forgave our enemies and fell out with friends. The noble vision, the final satisfaction of claiming nationhood, cut loose from reality as a hot-air balloon. Independence was no longer to do with our work, our families, our religion, or the food we produced: it was this high free floating globe, rotund with satisfaction but lighter than air. We believed everyone would love us. The cities became a ferment of alliances. Coffee shops stayed open all night and pubs echoed with more than the usual brouhaha of platitudes. Megaphone sales reached an all-time peak.

— Why did IFID choose me? Buchanan asked suddenly when the last door shut. Why didn't they simply back one of the political parties? How is it I don't know the answer so I can't even lie about it?

— You express things so clearly, Squarcia acknowledged.

— Are we being bugged? he joked with the ludicrous over-acting of the extremely fat.

— Only by ourselves.

The candidate considered this remark in bad taste. Squarcia laughed the bitter laugh of a man who has no alternative but put his life in the hands of an idiot.

About this time, a couple of bodyguards appeared everywhere with Buchanan. One day they arrived and took up their stations. Where they came from, he did not know. Soon people began asking their permission to speak to him. They dealt with the press on his behalf, guiding him under the blaze of lights, keeping journalists at bay as he positioned himself behind a battery of microphones, gently disciplining the plague of photographers trying to get in under his guard for that revealing expression their competitors might miss.

— Everything is a commodity Bernard, Sir William Penhallurick told him privately, ogling like a lover in a 1920s silent film. If you view it correctly. Health, he explained. Happiness, you name it, can be packaged and put on the market for people to choose. What do you say? They buy what attracts them. That's fair, isn't it?

— Just like the tobacco merchants sell lung cancer, Buchanan chortled. Then he turned disagreeable: Just like the lolly peddlers sell us heart disease.

— What do you say? Sir William enquired, lame with sentiment.

22

Four Judges Named as Perverting the Course of Justice

At the Crimes Commission hearing yesterday four separate accusations were cited that judges have acted to pervert the course of justice. Two involved the acceptance of bribes, the others were said to be cases of attempting to save old colleagues from the impartial severity of the law. A Justice of the High Court, Judge Mack, said our judicial system was envied throughout the world, that the public could rest assured each charge would be scrupulously investigated and if any evidence emerged supporting the allegations, the full weight of the law would be brought to bear on the offenders.

— Rest assured, sang Tim irreverently to the chuckle of keyboards around him. Then he read another paragraph from his notepad, a jotting made simply to help clarify his own ideas.

What about the twentieth century? We approach this election as if nothing more than horse-and-buggy harmlessness might lie in store for us. Perhaps the century hasn't touched us, we are so busy catching up on what we missed from the eighteenth: the rise of industrialism, the heroic flavour of revolutions.

23

Lavinia, facing a companion who looked more like her grand-mother than her grandmother had, told her about the spurt of lust she'd felt for Roscoe Plenty.

— Desire, the ancient woman corrected her.

— Lust, she went on. An uncontrollable craving to provoke, contain, and match his energy.

But the longer she went on, obsessed with the need to be honest, the more the grannie received her confessions so calmly she was, perhaps, not comprehending. Her fingers in their loose glove of skin fumbled to re-settle her skirt. She feigned interest though and commented that she seemed to recollect a Plenty or two. And to be christened Roscoe amounted to the misfortune of competing with ambitious parents, particularly if they were of a farming family. She mouthed congratulations when she heard how well the portrait had been received as a work of art, whatever the cost to the emotions. A flicker of anticipation disturbed the wrinkles, decay itself an active agent of knowing knowledge a young mind could not yet grasp.

— The wonder is, the grannie mused. That you ever came to meet people in such powerful circles.

— Pure accident, she accused herself.

— What if, and the faded eyes looked beyond her now. Talent must be punished? Have you thought of that?

— Let me pour your tea.

For talk and tea things were undoubtedly there between them now.

— I've had mine, but you go ahead.

Lavinia dropped a slice of lemon in her cup, listening as the old lady went on.

— I once read a poem about myself. The poet described me at a symphony concert, knitting, knitting the sounds of the orchestra into a scarf, you see, the emotions of the music, the colours, the whole climax. That's why you will never catch me wearing anything machine-made. So I can walk round in a cocoon of harmonies. Do you like that?

Lavinia thought it dangerously flattering to art.

— I like the way you told it, she said.

Half-familiar suburban traffic rumbled past, between them and a local post office where staff were sorting loveletters.

— You are afraid of me, the grannie complained.

Lavinia Manciewicz was a person intoxicated by beginnings, the tentative budding of ideas. To her a hint was more delicious than the full flavour. In the tentative stages you haven't lost yourself. The feel of a man. Now *that* she did love, the strangeness before it became ugly with repetition, kneecaps, knobbly forearms, a tuft of down on each shoulder angelic in its way. The men she had known smoked and smelled half-pickled by smoking; cured, she'd say except that this carried promises of medicine and the church, both inappropriate to the warm rough playful danger she looked for. A man cutting his nails had a non-woman's manner of doing even that. She had watched one pissing once in the pride of his standing and knowing she was there. Lavinia liked that pride. Also big warm hands groping so predictably. Of course she liked it. Hairs sticking to a sweaty chest afterwards and damp armpits. Even the bungled cup of tea brought her in bed, a tribute delicious beyond the comprehension of mere taste buds. She had tried all sorts of men. Mainly lean ones like her ex-husband for example, because she preferred leather and cord and quick reflexes; but others too, for the education. Even a fat man, just the once. Not that his fatness mattered so much to her, but to him intensely. He could not lose himself with her. There was an apology implied even in the way he turned the light out. Anger as lust. The Holy Fathers would want to hear about that: oh yes, doubly culpable to compound the deadly sins. Which? Which was it, then? They are defined and ought not to be confused. The priest a man also, also a smoker, as heard in his polite cough getting out of hand.

— You are afraid of desire, the grannie added by way of consoling herself.

Complete emotion, like complete anything else, struck Lavinia as sealing off possibilities. Chance, she loved.

— Yes, she replied when she saw the postboys' bright red motorcycles lined up along the kerb by the telephones. I am nervous, once I get there, of being stuck with it.

Lavinia Aged nodded. She remembered, after all.

24

Zoltán Kékszakállú was a mere ghost of his former self. He had never been a big man but he was ambitious, with a lascivious wink-on-the-sly grease-your-palm style of energy. An enthusiastic admirer of the Austrian, much the same age as his own father, who very nearly achieved the second most platitudinous of all male fantasies; Kékszakállú, though, would have no idea what to do with the world if once he had it under his heel. His demonic pouncings and posturings had a smallness of concept. The best he managed was to succeed with seven wives, each legitimately bound to him by Christian marriage and six of them dead within a mere thirteen years. So, to give him his due, he was busy. Right in the middle of this matrimonial success story, he proved his ingenuity in business as well: he became a millionaire by availing himself of the beneficence of taxpayers in the country he had migrated to. Yet at the end of his progress along ceremonial avenues, both private and public, what should he see as his ultimate reward but a knighthood. Nothing more imaginative than that. With longterm planning he changed his name to a rather more catchy English one. So Kékszakállú began a new life which reached its respectable apotheosis when he became Sir William Penhallurick. But he didn't forget. Oh no, he was jumpy as hell still. He trusted no one. And this time he had a wife who guarded his peace of mind. Any remark he could not fully understand, or completely hear, he took to be a barb against his reputation. Two clerks discussing a motor accident as he entered his office one morning found themselves sacked on the spot without ever knowing this was how the boss's fifth wife died. Out at an informal dinner party one evening the host had left the radio on in homely Tasmanian style and Penhallurick reacted as if burnt on the shoulder with hot steel; he clasped one hand on it, standing up with violent suddenness, when the announcer began the headline news with the account of a woman drowned at sea together with the boat owner's best friend, a terrible fishing accident, and later in this bulletin we will bring you part of an interview with the heartbroken husband, hero of an epic struggle against death. Penhallurick rushed from the house and made a long-distance telephone call to ask his surviving wife was she all right up there? No mysterious poisoning without trace, no berserk gunman claiming four random lives in a shopping centre, no tragic electrocution in the kitchen, and no busload of tourists raped and burnt by insurgents in the remote highlands of a far continent could be mentioned without sparking a crisis. Nor was this all. His tetchiness made him singularly hard to do business with. Such broad subjects as government subsidies for industry, the Second World War, improvements in car performance, duty, and marriage for money caused this little Hungarian émigré such pain he would lash out regardless of his own safety. At one stage he recounted proudly that he had begun with two clapped-out trucks in 1940 and emerged from the war years with seventeen bulldozers, six graders, four mobile cranes, thirty-one trucks, and a Cadillac. He gave away the pleasure of such boasting, though possibly truthful, because he couldn't fight his way clear of the maze of explanations his admiring hearers asked for; all very hush-hush, he would say with one crooked finger on his lips, winking grotesquely to imply that later in the privacy of trusted company he could and might tell all. He couldn't, and never did, maybe not even to himself. At eighty-six Sir William Penhallurick still thought of his life as a sequence of unrelated fairytales. There was this one about a tragic and beautiful girl who married the enigmatic foreigner, fascinated by his obsession with success, who fell ill and died in his arms mingling her tears with his. There was another about the employer so dear to his enormous staff they nicknamed him Poppa, who once upon a time, when holidaying abroad, heard of a crisis which could bring the business to ruin, so he begged his wife's indulgence for a few days and left her to continue enjoying herself while he flew home to save the future, only to find he had escaped by the last flight out and that revolutionaries were exterminating every foreigner they could catch. Other such fairytales included the one about a young man who travelled a long long way across the sea, and it must be remembered that no Hungarian who has stayed within the boundaries of his homeland has even seen the sea or formed a very clear impression of its immensity and treacherousness. So this poor lad, with high heart, this veritable prince in rags (or near enough) landed on the shores of the world's strangest and most remote continent among people who spoke no language of his consolation. There he worked by the sweat of his back. He married a wife as beautiful as the dawn, who died as bloody as sunset. But true to his high heart he recovered from this accident and married again, and when that wife died he married yet again, this time to a woman just rich enough to buy him a secondhand truck for his wedding gift. He worked with the truck and they lived a happy if humble life while he carted waste bones from the butcher, his truck a trembling mass of skeletons with hanks of meat still hanging from them, rib cages bouncing at every jolt in the road and, though he wore a smock and a hat for the loading, his hair stank of flesh. He scrimped enough to afford a second truck more dilapidated than the first. Then history waved a wand and all was changed, in a moment, in the twinkling of an eye, at the first trumpet of the Second World War. The very time of mourning his thirty-third birthday and third wife, friend Adolf declared an end to stagnation. Time for the prince to throw off his rags. Kékszakállú put his trucks, worn out though they were, at the service of his adoptive country. He was engaged on strategic projects and too necessary to be spared for the army. So when the call came to help on the north-south highway the Americans were to build, that great defensive asset spanning two deserts, he was there you can count on it. Alas, dear friends, what should happen next but one of his nationally necessary trucks ran over the edge of a quarry and crashed hopelessly to the bottom. Thanks to divine mercy, he was not in it. Was this the disaster it seemed, the truck being uninsured as well as uninsurable? Not at all. Australia appreciated his devotion enough to supply a completely new truck under wartime exigency provisions, new down to the chrome door handles, a truckdriver's dream, which he accepted with both hands. Who took the least notice of whispers that his old one wouldn't even start? That he, his twelve-year-old daughter and his wife had pushed it there, straining to heave the reluctant rattletrap along tracks and finally delivered it to its fate minutes before sunrise, had retraced their route, stepping backwards to expunge their footprints all the way, half dead from loss of sweat, slamming themselves in their hut to shock their nerves upright? The point is the work, the service, the inestimable value the nation was to derive from its generosity. The prince never wore rags again and the smiles of the family gathered round him were his reward. His one regret was the sadness of losing this wife too. Life, in teaching him to bear his bereavement with equanimity, offered generous opportunities for practice.

The end of the tale has already been told, the enumeration of his earth-moving fleet. But his heaven-moving prayers ought not to be forgotten. His were the rewards of a righteous man. And though many years later God saw fit to test him in a court of law where he was accused of arranging for his sixth wife to be murdered by a gunman, the jury found him not guilty. Guilty, only, of age. He was, by then, shrivelling. The one-time prince, now a prince indeed, prince among reactor builders and importer of dreams at a market value of fifty thousand dollars per kilogram, so that others could distribute small packages of relief for persons addicted to suffering, settled for enjoying his last wife, Alice, who confirmed the wonderland of his cleverness, who never contradicted him and showed no distaste over his scrofula. He gave up the barbarous vitality of younger days and devoted himself to luxury and to advising the next generation on how to succeed. The Queen of England and Australia knighted him for having amassed so much money.

Meanwhile he had become a member of that select group who saw to IFID's antipodean strategy for world peace, grateful that the latter stages of the presidential campaign were free from the worries of the outset, the cause doing well. His own part in selecting Bernard Buchanan had been so active, a crippling share of the blame would have fallen on him in the case of failure to secure a majority. But now, as there seemed little chance of that and no end to the eagerness of other exploiters to seek his guidance, it looked as if he would, at last, rest content.

25

Sydney. The Peace Party has declared war on Buchanan's National Pragmatism. A spokesperson claimed at their Circular Quay meeting last night that they had evidence of an American plot to annex Australia and New Zealand. She reported what she termed reliable sources as saying that these South Pacific countries were no less valuable to the United States than Nicaragua or Grenada. This is hardline imperialism, she declared to a mixture of boos and cheers from the small gathering. And the truth is, she went on, that Buchanan will be the tool for the takeover. When one heckler shouted out: It can never happen here! shouts of agreement came from all sides. Perhaps it is true, after two hundred years of plenty, that this is the creed in Australia: Don't tell us about it, it can never happen here. But can it?

Tim was out on a job. Stephanie watched her story come up on the screen. She was just about to make an adjustment when the cursor moved of its own accord. A hole appeared in one line. Letters changed. The cursor travelled this way and that, wiping away blocks of her text. Apparently the sub-editor was already at work on it. He seemed to need no pause for thought. She watched words float out into the margin and up or down, looking for a home. *One heckler* went to the top, *evidence of* vanished, *plot* became *plans* and *the creed* changed to *our belief*. *Perhaps it is true* rose to the dignity of fact as *The truth is*.

Sydney. A heckler at yesterday's Peace Party rally shouted out: It can never happen here! The interruption came after a party spokesperson claimed that there were American takeover plans for Australia and New Zealand. The heckler carried the day. Shouts of agreement came from all sides. The public made quite plain that after two hundred years of plenty, we don't need to be told what to think by stirrers. The truth is that this is our belief: It cannot happen here.

In a further reshuffle, the last line was streamlined to *The truth is that we do believe it cannot happen here.*

26

Bernard Buchanan straightened his suit over that immense belly, now immenser with emotion. Out in the streets, as he knew, all noise had stopped, the long prospects were empty, suburbs though alive with lights lay desolate as planners' models. And to take a higher wider view, there were many such places strung round the coast, as on a necklace, the modest glitter of villages leading to substantial towns, to the vast multifaceted rhinestones of our few big cities. And all of them confronted the lonely sea where nightflying birds swooped beachward in search of pickings, where tides lapped inshore leaving quickly fading hopes of phosphorus, and long-shelled breakers rolled across sand still warm with the contentment of people who want nothing more complicated tomorrow morning than a suntan. Everybody stayed home to watch the first hours of the republic on television.

Buchanan, as he listened to what he was told, still preserved the forms of common courtesy, smiling at the thought of his chief rivals attending premature victory parties: a rally outside the cathedral, some wild exhibitionism in a theatre, the wall-to-wall seediness of a city hotel suite for Roscoe Plenty, and Darryl Robinson's burnt sausages at a surburban barbecue. He smiled, almost wistfully, for what he had lost. He listened to the last-minute advice of remember to look the camera in the eye and say such trust makes me humble, have you got that, humble, the responsibility is grave, good luck. He knew those victory parties out there must by now have taken on one and the same tone of weariness, with a bitter edge of futile excuses.

— I am thrilled, he bellowed jubilantly, having floated into view even on those screens set up among his rivals' shattered celebrations. At the trust you have put in me. I'm glad you did it. Because no one else could save this land of ours. If I had not believed I was the best candidate, I would not have stood for election. I love you all. I love you because you are Australians and this is the most emotional moment of our history, this is the moment when we truly become our own masters and take an equal place in the councils of the world. There is no issue, no person, too small for my interest to be aroused. Please believe me in this. I am at your service to lead you and listen to you. We all know how desperately the country needs shaking up. I pledge the first act of my government will be to put an end to unchallenged privilege. In the Public Service, for example, the entire rotting structure is still being ruled by seniority and permanency. This will go as soon as we can move an act through parliament. From now on all that counts is talent. Talent. The best shall have the best jobs; the best minds shall have those jobs based on intelligence, the best bodies those requiring physical agility; the best students shall go to the best schools; and the best pay shall reward the best productivity. We are tired, he shouted, of being dictated to by small-thinking individuals, the cautious, the timid, those polite souls who never tell the truth out loud for fear they might have farted. Good manners have gagged and strangled us.

The interviewer stayed off-camera, not daring to interrupt. He recognized the magnitude of the occasion.

— There are as many Australians in Australia today as there were Englishmen in England at the time of Shakespeare and the defeat of the Spanish Armada. Think of that. Where are our Shakespeares, our Drakes, leaders of the stature of Elizabeth I? I shall answer that. They are here among you, watching me now on the screen. The only reason we don't know them is because we don't deserve them. The snivelling cowardice of our policies in the past has stifled any heroic temperament and kept them in obscurity. No longer. I'm here to promise you the end of littleness. Gone forever. A new age is burgeoning, an age of great spirits, brave initiatives, independent thinking. The age of bigness. I'm big. I'm not what you could call plump or nuggetty or portly or stout. I'm fat, aren't I? Who better to lead you into this age of bigness! Since 1788 we have been followers, trailing along in the wake of Britain and the United States, cravenly aping those we call our betters. I say they are our equals, maybe, but not our betters. And very soon they'll find they need to imitate us if they are to keep up.

In the celebrity viewing room, that rudimentary cubicle, Sir
William Penhallurick telephoned the Chief of the Federal Police;
he spoke little and listened a lot. Then he hung up and turned
to Judge Mack who sat forward on his chair, half an ear to
Buchanan's unstoppable rave and half an ear to the phone
conversation, the tension strung through every extremity of his
body eloquent of his fear that things had gone too far and that
his own future might be in jeopardy. Mr Luigi Squarcia, by
contrast, lounged somewhat apart from them, scarcely able to
contain his amusement: good old Bernard making a real show of
ruling while he still had the chance, filling the screen with bold
gestures and gathering energy as he went along. Sweeping
changes, nothing to do with IFID's guidelines, were being
announced. The armed forces would be revamped and given a
greatly increased budget as the Australian Strike Force. Finances
were reviewed and he foreshadowed radical reforms, not merely
to rates of tax but to the principles of taxation. This is a shake-
up, he declared, immensely pleased with his own evangelical
enthusiasm.

Justice Mack fretted. Another ten minutes and the country, he
could tell, will panic. All the groundwork I've put in on Buchanan to be sure of my rights gone to waste. We'll have to look for
someone else. How do you feel about this, Luigi? his hand
asked, stubbing and restubbing the most expensive of cigars.
But Squarcia volunteered nothing while his creation, his professional politician, spouted molten gold ideas. Well beyond the
critical ten minutes he spoke, till, right round the country, his
enemies began packing the smallest bags they could manage
with, woke the children, and drove their families to an international airport, or in the quiet of night slipped the moorings of
yachts and puttered away through the heads to set sail for New
Caledonia. The judge exchanged frowns with Sir William Penhallurick, who had taken to clutching his pockets as if they were
filled with cash and he had found himself in the confidential
company of a bandit. Both men rose. They went out, sombre
with matters to discuss which Squarcia must not overhear.
Squarcia, indeed, having turned into a foreigner and dangerous
with the unpredictability of foreigners.

— All vestiges, Buchanan roared. Of royal apron strings will
be slashed. What benefit can they be, he reasoned, never letting
the camera escape his direct glare because he spoke without
notes. These outdated links? One clean cut and the task is done.
I'm pleased, he said. To see the back of the Governor-General,

nice fellow as he is. Good riddance to a discredited office. (His nose grew visibly redder despite a coating of powder.) I am here to strike the Union Jack from our flag. May all its history of blunders and condescension go with it. I claim the honour tonight of being the first to unfold our official flag, the only uniquely Australian flag we've ever had. He spread out the splendid standard of Eureka, dark blue quartered by a white cross with central star and a star at the end of each arm. He held it in front of him as if about to begin some coy vaudeville routine.

— As for the Queen herself, he ogled. Well, she and I will meet on occasion, I dare say. I wish her well and a long life. When she comes next week to close the old parliament I shall offer her a kiss on the cheek. (To the disgust of those who didn't matter, he winked suggestively.) But I never have and never will bend the knee to her nor her kind. If she wishes to meet the Australian head of state as an equal, we shall welcome the occasion. But not as an inferior, ever.

Squarcia, now alone in the cubicle, saw clearly that Bernard, far from finishing, had barely begun. Ideas streamed out. He was inventing, chanting, singing a whole history to come, his voice inducing a trance capable of shaking the nation. Down to the least domestic detail he gave it to them, the remaking of society, bringing one stage closer Squarcia's own ambition to return to Italy in glory.

— Let me assure you of this. There's going to be no more Coca-Cola in our country. If they want to go on trading here, they're going to have to call it Coca-Koala, he joked. Now I know you believe politicians don't really rule, that they say what their Public Service experts tell them to say. Well, this may have been true in the past, but you can be damned sure it won't happen any longer.

For two hours he postured and ranted while astounded cameramen kept him in every home. The interviewer, prepared to listen to a brief victory statement, finally sinking back in his chair, weak with nervousness at what he guessed, became the first person to have the honour of being seen agreeing inanely with Buchanan's dictatorial pronouncements. The crowd in the public promenade of the tally room, who began by cheering spontaneously, developed a wary reticence; then, as they sensed the birth of an unforgettable epoch, grew animated with excitement. Instead of change slyly developing in business cartels over lobster lunches among powerbrokers unknown to the public and scarcely ever speaking on their own account, here was the cyclone in person.

All across the nation the hum of paper-shredders droned loud and lamenting as bagpipes. Dossiers fanatically detailed over decades were thrown to oblivion so the frail craft of individual reputations could ride out the crisis. Longstanding hatreds were sacrificed and the smoke of ritual fires rising from old correspondence and old certainties made the eyes smart. For the time being, enemies were forgiven because everybody who was anybody felt the threat. So powerful were the president's words they went shouting down the corridors of jails and stirred the masturbating prisoners as one to cry aloud an inchoate syllable of hope; they echoed in whispers through bank vaults where the authentic keys were busy. Horses in the home paddock woke to a crash of dishes from the station kitchen. Roads out of cities began to fill with dark shapes. Telephone exchanges were jammed by frantic subscribers, savings societies predicted an onslaught of withdrawals and the Hot Air Balloon Club of Queensland devised a brochure advertising wind-driven exploration trips to the Australian Capital Territory.

The first president spoke without taking breath, huge belly and rank lungs holding reserves for just such an emergency. The words poured out of him, developing virtuoso variations on themes he heard in chapel at school. He adopted the tone of a prophet and the certainty of a French lunatic. His immense bulk swayed slightly to the rhythm of the spheres. He hypnotized the camera, those ox-eyes in their puffy lids instantly recognizable as the image of authority. His hands gestured sparingly, running through a repertoire of smoothing chopping punching and being laid open to inspection. He never consulted the clock. Then he announced his final promise for the night. We need, he rumbled confidently, more people. And more respect for who we are. Let me explain it this way. Today you have confirmed your will to be independent of Great Britain and this you shall be. But once we stand unsupported we need the strength of internal unity to survive. If we are divided, amorphous, a nation of no definable character, we'll go under to the first invader with the guts to move in. And why not? many will say. After all, we have thousands of alien-born citizens living here permanently as it is; they may as well invite their armies to keep them company.

— Perhaps you might say that the answer is the one we've heard many times before: get rid of the foreigners, repatriate migrants and call ourselves racially pure. What sort of economic suicide would this be? Sheer idiocy, let me assure you. No, we are a sophisticated people living in sophisticated times. We need clever solutions, not a rehash of past failures. We need swift growth. Ours is a capitalist economy. Nothing is more welcome than growth. With this upturn in the economy we can compete against our trading rivals and beat them at their own game. To be successful, our products must be priced within the going international rates. Now I am not the man to say to Australian workers, You have to work for less, lower your living standards and your families' expectations. No way. The workers and their union movement have fought long and tenacious battles to gain the footing they have and claim a just share of our national wealth. In your heart of hearts you have to admit this is true. So what do we do? The answer is not far different from what it was under Robert Menzies in the 1950s. More migrants, not less. But with this difference, we do not invite them here to stay. They remain guest workers. No question of bringing their families and settling, just a chance to share in our bonanza and take home their legitimate pay packet, the rest belongs to us and the land is ours for the future. So that's what we shall do. I'll bring you masses of willing workers, workers by the thousand, who won't hesitate to soil their hands and relieve you of the dirty jobs, the hard thankless slavery of the labourer on the lowest social rung. You'll all move up one place. Everybody stands to benefit. And if it's security you want me to talk about, ask yourself this: If there are enough Indonesians here, would Indonesia ever attack us on any pretext? If there are enough Russians or Chinese, would Russia or China attack? I think you see my point. All the more because they will not have renounced citizenship of their own countries. Next you will ask, What about the migrants already here? Let's be realistic, migrants have helped make Australia great, we have a responsibility to them. Those who have been naturalized and have certificates we shall allow to keep them. Fair enough? But that's it. No more. Any migrant who has come here to enjoy the Australian way of life and has not felt he or she owed us sufficient allegiance to apply for citizenship has blown it. Too late. I am here to announce that we closed the books two minutes ago. They can return to the countries stamped on their passports. We estimate this will create over ten thousand skilled job vacancies immediately. Some might wish to remain among us and transfer across to our guest worker scheme. Well that's all right too. And a few places may be offered to those specially qualified as teachers to introduce the new arrivals to what is expected of them.

— Finally, I am foreshadowing another significant policy. We shall offer natural-born Australians incentives to enlarge their families. Fertility is to be the symbol of our new age. Speaking as the happiest man in the world, and the proudest, let me bid you goodnight. May God bless you and may your dreams of a true nation be fulfilled in the exciting years ahead. The age of bigness has begun!

He was off the screen. He was there in person. He was advancing on Squarcia, a mound of glistening blubber, pushing the walls away from him, eyes still ablaze with vast prospects, hands blinded by the limelight.

— Okay, he panted noticing the others had gone. So they couldn't stand the pace.

— I have to admit, Squarcia conceded. You gave the first political speech this country has heard in a long time.

— Lou, the new man replied mopping himself with a hand towel. You are being obvious, which is not like you at all. I am the emperor of their selfishness. Now, we begin work right away. By tomorrow morning I want to announce appointments. If you have any general words of wisdom get them off your chest so we can buckle down to practicalities.

— In my view, Squarcia replied, quick on the uptake. You need to divide the population in two parts: those whose power you annihilate and those you buy with favours. The old tradition, in other words.

— We're in business.

Buchanan stood aside so Squarcia could open the door for him. Ankles protesting at the sudden extra weight of regality, he walked out among the favoured and the damned.

While truly professional countries (thank you, once again, Luigi Squarcia) were already well into the age of terrorism, Australia had remained out of it, managing at best the ridiculous fuss of an improbable bomb scare that went wrong and blew a garbage truck to smithereens, plus, years later, a police station having its front blasted off. Our successive ambassadors to the United Nations got on their hind legs to say that whereas we roundly condemned Country A for its recourse to violence, neither could we condone Country B's military reprisals, or that unilateral action against legally established oppression deserved Security Council support only insofar as it did not infringe the rights of the oppressors also. This was about the size of it. The unthinkable had not yet happened here.

Buchanan was elected but not yet installed when parliament confirmed that Her Majesty the Queen, in response to their invitation, had landed to grace the ceremonial hand-over of power and declare the old session closed.

The aged monarch arrived, duly, to make her way from Sydney to Canberra. True, she entered the capital in an unorthodox manner, but this was a unique occasion. And she was punctual as ever. Perhaps close associates guessed by the hint of strain in her neck or the hectic brilliance of her eyes what she had been through. But not the rest of us, let us admit it. Who could honestly say they knew the Queen had, that very day, inducted us into the modern age of professionalism? Who suspected she had survived several compound, successful plots? Not a single crease showed on her dress, nor a smudge on her shoes. She was perfect.

After the cheering died down and a saddened British public received her home bearing the loss of yet another treasured foxhole, rumours began to leak concerning near-disaster, and soon spawned apocryphal additions to lend a peeling gilded frame to the picture. People will have their say, after all. The first hint that anything might be wrong came, surprisingly, to a tiny station along the railway line. Despite all published schedules, this was the way the Queen would travel. Right through Boondarulla Halt on the bumpy route connecting Sydney and Canberra, along tracks too ricketty even for the secondrate almostfast locomotives on which the state was squandering foreign exchange while ministers with appropriate portfolios loafed in Baltic kursaals and took quick recuperative trips to the Caribbean.

Beyond question Her Majesty's landfall aboard the royal yacht *Britannia* had triggered sentimental reactions of contradictory and even farcial kinds. First came the backlash against the decision to declare a republic at all. Waves of permed bourgeoises, who roundly denounced the vulgarity of street demonstrations when other people mounted them, feverishly tore down the backdrops from a production of *The Winslow Boy*, painted them over, whited them out altogether, with never a second thought for the obliteration of the stern classroom, narrow desks redolent of masochism: whited them out and daubed royalist slogans in brutal lettering, nailed them to poles with the passion of perpetrators of a crucifixion, and flaunted them (with the least possible regard for good taste) through the streets of all the main cities and even, in the face of bucolic suspicion, through countrytowns to the disgust here and there of a resident tethered goat plus the usual three leaning drunks required by outback architecture to support a pub's front verandah. Persons of refinement though they were, they rampaged round orderly cities, smashing shop windows to show their feelings and overturning cars sufficiently shabby not to be theirs. They foresaw an end to privilege, such was the extent of their political insight, and they let loose the human beings hitherto kept politely suppressed. They took to looting shops in the manner of New Yorkers during a power strike and tearing clumps of greasy hair from the heads of radicals who dared question their manners.

At the other extreme, a bellicose society of Irish descendants announced that they would hijack Her Majesty's flight from Sydney to Canberra; not because they wished to prevent her formally severing dominion ties with Great Britain, but because they might never get another chance without going to Ireland, or at very least England.

So the Queen, when she disembarked from her yacht, one iceblue shoe after another, took a hastily prepared train with a couple of departing waves of an ice-blue glove plus a marvellous imitation of a smile. Never mind the bumpy line, it would be considerably less bumpy than an exploding 787, or even a 787 bound for an unscheduled haven in Pakistan where she would be met by a mob seething resentments spawned at Notting Hill Gate and West Hounslow.

The train left without a hitch. Actually, with one hitch, but nothing more than a hitch. A red light stopped the locomotive just near the outer limits of the metropolis: long enough for a lethal joke, a political coup, a disastrous laugh.

What can we believe? Fact was so soon to become real estate and open to the highest bidder. In those nostalgic days of compound lying when hoodwinkers enjoyed full employment, this was the story as told.

The illfated van uncoupled while the light remained red was the one fitted out as a royal bathroom and toilet. The train drew away, leaving it behind. Harmless larrikinism. . . our hoary joke about the things a sovereign did not need to do. The journey, making the best time on that shoddy line, would take four hours.

So when the call came down the track, relaying an urgent

message from the driver who was a keen republican but a man of honour, it said *Prepare ablution facilities at Boondarulla Halt for royal patronage*.

Royal patronage. What a phrase, what visions of heraldry, shields, crests, superscriptions and mottoes, what glimpses of black-gloved hands on the car door, a pale stockinged leg stuck out for a try at coming down to earth, what bowing functionaries and whispered assurances, flutters of excitement and covert throat-clearings, what profligate empires of red white and blue flowers wilting beneath the weight of their own perfume, what flickers of diamonds from under fur wraps and hasty rhythm of lone high heels, ranks of girl guides and singing throngs of children cross at not getting a good view, what smug commercial advantages and insufferable polishing of silverplate and plateglass. In the light of which, the preparation of Boondarulla Halt may be seen as being little different from the continuing routine of those thrust by fate in the majesterial path.

Forty minutes before the train was due at Boondarulla Halt, a convoy of vehicles, driven with murderous disregard for safety, bucketed over the level crossing and slewed to a stop outside the tiny station. Doors appeared all round, car doors, van doors, truck doors, ejecting painters and cleaners and disinfectors, the local carpet merchant with a lapsed roll of hall-runner he'd been trying to flog for seven years, gardeners bearing a potted forest and enthusiasts with rakes to assemble the platform clinkers into parallel lines. Scrapers, rollers, brushes went to work. The quiet countryside squealed and choked. *WET-PAINT* signs were propped respectfully round the walls. Mirrors with gold frames were installed, perfumed toilet paper, a lambswool seat cover with the *GENUINE MERINO 100%* label dangling in full view, plus scenic photographs of the dear old Thames Valley to forestall any feelings of not being at home and, hopefully, to divert attention into the bargain, especially when the time came for her to realize that the modern porcelain bowl, though filled to the orthodox level with water, was not connected to any disposal system, there being none available, and the matching porcelain tank screwed hastily to the studs of the corrugated iron walls waited, perforce, dry. She, it was not doubted, would carry this off with royal aplomb and be sufficiently grateful to retire in so desolate a spot secure from public notice to leave behind what was best left, most dispensable and forgettable, after all.

When the train sighed to a relieved stop at the platform, two security men and a maid alighted to help the Queen negotiate the rather steep step down. She who had refused to show nerves in the face of charging elephants or war-dancing natives or the blitz, nodded, grimly nervous, and strode in the direction indicated by the Boondarulla railway clerk, part-time, and his wife. There was only one building, a closed ticket window at this end and toilets at the other. The last train to stop here had departed seven months previously. The security men took up positions outside the embowered entrance beneath a cluster of orchids concealing the *LADIES* sign. The Queen and her maid cut a frigid passage straight inside. Perhaps the heat of a tin building of this kind would be new to her; hopefully she might remark upon it later as a point of interest and proof of her composure. Meanwhile, those still aboard the train were warned that they would have one minute to find any relief necessary for themselves once the engine had pulled them a decent distance out of the station and round the bend (which had been the reason for choosing Boondarulla in the first instance), prior to returning for its royal passenger, who could then appear to be boarding it fresh, as if for the first time and after some ordinary public function among the kookaburras.

All went smoothly as a plot. The locomotive rolled away its remaining carriages, carriages glittering clean and handsomely padded. And quietly kept going.

Summer sunshine scored the skin like powdered glass. The maid wilted. The bodyguards tugged at their collars, glaring across scraggy grass, past battered and rusted road signs, at the far-distant windmill and outbuildings of the nearest house. Her Majesty the Queen, having perfect self-control, stood on the raked clinkers, betraying no sign of surprise, let alone discomfort. The clerk, part-time, and his full-time wife had fled and now crouched underneath the tank, dreaming of their bicycles shut away in the office.

— There was simply no excuse, Darryl Robinson the reptile leader of the Opposition explained afterwards in the House of Reps. For this shameful event to have taken place. What comfort is it to our national self-respect that the hijack of the train misfired; that, in fact, a second conspiracy took over; that Her Majesty, here to honour our independence with true magnanimity, should have been rescued from the first gang of kidnappers by the intervention of a second! What comfort is it, I ask the honourable members of this House, that these were more genteel villains and their purpose the preservation of her person rather than a threat to it? The point. . . the point is that both acts were acts of terrorism. On our soil. Terrorism of the mob and terrorism of the elite.

27

The Queen herself took control: faced with a dignified, perhaps even exemplary, crisis she had the wit to recognize she had been saved from the ignominy of her predicament. She called out to the gunmen, not in the Christmas voice of *my husband and ai* so well known around the world, but in a tone seldom heard from her since she serviced army motor vehicles during the Second World War, when perhaps she had no more onerous expectations than to continue awaiting the birth of a baby brother, or even a son, to save being obliged to surrender the rest of her life to the public. And while she was later escorted by her second party of kidnappers to a gleaming black car, she could already review her conduct with satisfaction.

Two gentlemen stepped forward and bowed. To her inexpressible surprise, they addressed her in the stately polysyllables of Old High German. The senior of these dignitaries was a man in his sixties with an ivory complexion, a respectable Roman nose, and thinning grey hair combed back severely flat from his forehead. On his lapel he wore the ribbon of an order so obscure even she could not place it. His aristocratic deportment was flawless.

They treated her with respect verging on reverence as she and her maid took their places in the back seat. So huge was this compartment that the two gentlemen were able to fit, perched on folding seats, facing them. A brace of military types, having saluted with punctilious regard for the straightness of fingers and the uniform angle of forearms, took the front seats as soon as they had performed a ceremony of unfurling little square flags, one mast on each wing. In this flamboyant manner the vehicle set off at a glide along that rough road, to the mild amusement of a couple of heifers with plastic numbers stapled to their ears.

Prefacing his remarks with a catalogue of profound respects, the gentleman with the nose and the obscure decoration offered to explain this apparently unorthodox behaviour. Her Majesty listened with courteous coolness, able to understand every word he spoke (a fact he noted with deep satisfaction); then she interrupted, asking him in English to identify himself. Friedrich Gustav Graf zu Adlershof, Chancellor-apparent of the Free Hannover, here incognito to welcome Your Majesty in person. You may ask, he asked on her behalf, what business have we with Your Gracious Majesty in this remote place. Alright? I answer, we want you back. We of the new Kingdom of Free Hannover are ready to secede from the Federal Republic of Germany and forge our own future, free from the trammels of a materialist bourgeois nation which has plunged Hannover against its will into the odious anonymity of the European Economic Community. You, he concluded, are our true leader, our moral and spiritual head, the living greatness of our royal house, legitimate heir and descendant of the Electors of Hannover who succeeded to the English throne in 1701, thereby evincing foresight so profound its import could not, till the present moment, be appreciated. England has preserved you for us in our day of independence.

While this explanation, which threatened to be no more than a preamble to yet greater mellifluence, was being delivered and the limousine swept along at impressive speed, Her Majesty was thinking.

— Very well, she declared at last, cutting him short with an imperiousness under which he melted. Drive us, she commanded in German, to Canberra. As we are to be welcomed again into our ancient estates, we must be seen to fulfil all the obligations expected of us. First, we owe it to our former subjects to honour them with a ceremonial closure of parliament. As she said this, a curious emotion awoke in the monarch. Was it so strange that she should behave like a queen? Why didn't all her days give her this direct and measurable satisfaction? How long, how long it had been since she lived on her very considerable wits. I cannot have become, she protested silently... irrelevant?

Roman Nose bowed his head, snapped open the glass panel, and spoke to the military personnel.

— Also, the Queen raised her voice slightly, still speaking German and with a touch of conscious pleasure. We are never late.

— Your Majesty's reputation for courtesy is in our hands, Roman Nose's companion agreed, to give himself some function in this great event, and nodded gravely.

The limousine executed a graceful loop, took a new course and picked up speed at the highway. The splendid standard of the royal house of Hannover streamed out stiff and trembling, gold tassels excited in the glittering sun.

The Queen did, indeed, feel quite at home.

— May I now present Your Majesty with our formal invitation? Count Adlershof requested. Permission granted, he then read from a document: We, the Lords Spiritual and Temporal of the Realm, being in this issue assisted with the Officers of the Provisional Privy Council, with numbers of other principal ladies and gentlemen, with the Mayor of Hannover, Aldermen and Citizens of the city, do now hereby with one voice and consent of tongue and heart, proclaim our invitation to your High and Mighty Majesty in person, Queen of England and Australia, Head of the British Commonwealth of Nations, to become our only lawful and rightful liege, by the Grace of God. God save the Queen.

It was, in its way, perfectly satisfactory.

By the time they arrived at Canberra and the Queen could be certain she was to be safely delivered, the adventure gave her a high colour. She condescended to ask after her new dominion, recollecting a few pertinent details of the life and of the uninhabited Herrenhausen palace at Hannover, each of which was gratefully acknowledged. She even allowed herself a brief flutter with the domestic excitement, which so fills the life of a young working-class bride, imagining what it would be like to furnish the place as she might choose to have it. That horrible museum-deadness would take a lot to shift.

As her limousine approached the city, huge crowds swirled and clotted ahead. At long last Walter Burley Griffin's ceremonial town plan came to life. The stark open areas and barren vistas of grass were transformed by enough people to appear genuinely impressive.

Police barred the way, ready to deal with obdurate foreign diplomats. Being Canberra police, they knew this class of person. But the driver drove straight up to one constable, pennants flapping lazily when the vehicle slowed, and enjoyed (as doubtless he told delighted children at home in Hannover) watching the mask of officialdom drop. The policeman's face changed from annoyance to fury to uncertainty to amazement to deference to self-importance.

Motorcycles, sirens howling, cut a swath through flagwaving spectators who were presented with an extempore preview. Astounded citizens hurrahed and thumped cheerfully on that immaculate car roof, setting up a drumming so intense successive hands maintained the one continuous rhythm. Thus, to the drum and the siren, Her Majesty arrived at the front entrance of Kingston railway station, confounding the confounders of the hijack plot, exactly at the minute the train (still scratching its head at Boondarulla Halt) was due.

The official party pivotted to welcome her, the president-elect stepping forward, bouncing with gallantry, wearing a face cherubic in its murderous innocence.

28

Anybody who has lived through disturbed times will understand that public records remain erratic long after the restoration of order. However efficient a new system, they do. The events of the near past blur elusively or leap out at us with disproportionate clarity: some incident is documented in detail worthy of a medical record from the intensive care ward, but what it means, what led up to it, who the antagonists were or why it was ever considered of the least significance, is obscured. Then, by contrast, a vital turningpoint (vital enough perhaps to be called historic) is merely alluded to in footnotes which researchers trace back to missing files and empty shelves.

Film and videotape reports are so easy to wipe. Who can be blamed? And these *were* difficult times. They still are. We faced a whole new situation: the beginning of a period known now as the Shortages. During the Shortages problems were not simply the obvious ones of inadequate food and petrol supplies, shortfalls in housing and public services, they also affected information. There were shortages of truth and of anything near truth. Public records, converted to electronic storage banks, were then subjected to a KILL instruction, either during the fall of the old regime or the rise of the new, or even afterwards when we thought the worst of it was over. As for private letters. . . who still wrote them? Who still pretended, under the eye of the Public Relations Ministry, and later the Department of Internal Security, that there was such a thing as privacy? Post office surveillance teams invested in an immense scrutiny program, a model of its kind, X-raying, electronically scanning, opening and resealing, photocopying an unprecedented wealth of clutter and feeding it into computers under the categories of subversion. Nobody wrote confidential letters. Every letter was public and at least partly addressed to the nation's Watchdogs. Many were entirely used simply to lay out alibis in case allegations of disloyalty might be made against them, others were cheap means of getting in first with damning information against neighbours.

So it is that when we come to review this period, we find a montage of cut-and-paste images, a flash of action slipped in between monumental chunks of ceremonial architecture, an isolated gesture frozen to enigmatic incompleteness, a word shot in the chest or some fugitive trying to leap craters of cowardice.

If we are to glimpse the royal exit, then, we must make do with a ripple of diamonds in the Queen's hair, the donning of spectacles, the measured delivery of clichés till they amassed a stately poem in the chaotic winds of anticipation, the very slowness creating a pressure of excitement, and finally, the surrender of the Union Jack.

The closure of parliament fulfilled every promise of grandeur by sheer force of staging. President-elect Bernard Buchanan, on best behaviour, refrained from insulting the Queen. Nor did he try leaning out over the vast acreage of his belly, as promised on TV, in an attempt to plant a kiss. Perhaps rumour of her close escape pulled him up in his tracks. Perhaps he was a trifle envious of the gentlemanly brigandage of those Hannoverians, right then waiting to claim her after the show. And envious of the aplomb with which he knew she would confront the next stage of her crisis.

Our new presidential government, based on the American model to give the man at the top free rein in waiving decisions made by the elected representatives of constituencies around the country, was now set to take power. Her Majesty sat. The Chief Justice of the High Court took over. His was to be the privilege of installing her successor as head of state.

— This day ever after, Bernard Buchanan intoned as he placed one porky hand on the Bible. He looked up with an impish grin. Our lives, he said, will never be the same again.

— Amen, some fool was heard to say.

29

Jack Cohen, wearing the uniform he hated but loved to be seen in, plonked his school bag on a bench, stuffed his hands in his pockets, puffed at a cigarette jutting straight out from his face, squinted against smoke which was on the verge of overwhelm-

ing him, and ignored the greengrocer standing in a shop doorway making ready to commit some unwanted gregariousness.

The bus was due.

Across the road an alarm siren suddenly began howling
tireless oscillations that throbbed and wailed somewhere in one
of the buildings. The greengrocer looked interested, watching for
a sign of fire or burglars. Jack Cohen, after a decent interval to
preserve his formidable cool, looked also, but quite separately.

The old Orpheum Cinema, now converted to housing a video
hire business and a mini-market (Coca-Cola), abutted Nikito's
Liquor Store, a chemist (Palcolor: leave films here), the Sham-
rock Butchery (vacant), a fishmonger, and a brick bank. . . in one
or another of them the siren wailed. Still no one took the least
notice. Cars changed gear as they accelerated, buses passed, but
never the right one for Jack, delivery vans delivered goods,
traffic lights flipped from orange to red to green to orange to red.
A two-way shuttle of vehicles drove in and out of the siren's
range, flashed their indicators when turning, drivers watched
the road, wheels splashed through a puddle outside Buchanan's
Real Estate agency (Under New Management), tyres squelched
past the Tandoori Take-Away and a milkbar. But still no fire, still
no burglars. The throaty roar of semi-trailers fading towards the
city left plateglass windows trembling in Mimi's Boutique. Jack
Cohen withdrew one hand, tweaked his cigarette, and held it
ahead of him while he inhaled the fresher air of gasoline fumes,
replugging his face with its adult disguise just as an ambulance
approached. One siren, by coincidence, meshed with the other,
sirens at different pitch, but two of a kind, melding and then
separating, the latecomer unravelled by distance and the
diminuendo of a merely passing emergency. Long after the last
flickers of that ambulance's twirling red light glanced off wind-
screens and reflective shopfronts and the bus still failed to
arrive, the greengrocer framed a suitably intellectual observation
for interesting the grammar-school boy.

— They let those judges off then, he remarked polishing an
apple.

The smoker reserved all his attention for the smoke.

Still no sign of a burglar or a fire showed from the stricken
building, whichever it might be. Traffic lights changed. Cars
splashed through the puddle. The siren howled in fixed cycles.

— I'd have said they were guilty, the man offered companionably now he had broken the ice.

Scorn tightened the boy's profile. One hand retrieved his

cigarette and, having flicked some ash with several taps of a practised forefinger, lodged it back again in place.

— But then I'm always against the underdog, the greengrocer confessed expansively. Like most people, I want to be on the winning side. He took a huge white wet bite from the apple he had been buffing. And crunched it. A trickle of juice escaped down his chin.

Delivery trucks passed, cars shuttled by, a dog sniffed at the door of the empty butcher's shop and walked away, confirmed in its dissatisfactions. Still the expected bus did not come. The cigarette was almost finished. The greengrocer crunched up the judges.

The siren wailed: no one was going to do anything about it now. So much for security.

30

Dorina Buchanan stood a while in the music room, the room she would miss most. (Bernard waved her needs aside when they had moved in all those years ago: I don't care where you put your piano, he'd said, as long as I can't hear it.) The house was already denuded. She had refused to let public servants direct the shifting of her belongings to the high-security residence which would be her future private home. No, she'd decreed, categorically no. Rather than mince words to the customary middle-class pap of insincerities, she told them: You have forced this removal upon me, but I do assure you I am not part of the furniture yet. I shall oversee the whole disaster myself.

So now she was left no choice but to cope with the consequences of her obstinacy. All right. But she might weep at any moment.

Removalists clumped across floors stripped of carpets. Her pictures (many of them had been her father's), cushioned in shredded paper which might once have told secrets, lay bedded in crates. If she were to close her eyes in this hollow house, and she did, she could hear a forest tossed by forlorn wind. The perfumes from her garden mingled to a unique blend which was Dorina's special creation, as unintentional as it was personal. Perhaps, now, for the first time, she recognized this as not quite like any other smell. She stood in the music room, breathing its familiarity. A refreshment and a farewell.

Churchill looked in, rheumy-eyed, to see that she was all

right. He found her dreaming as usual, while wagtails and silvereyes piped from the windowsill to acknowledge her talent. So he shook his head, jingling his licence tag, and padded off to check on the workmen emptying the place of his securities. This was, she confessed, a room with secrets. The glorious festivities she'd planned were never played out downstairs as they should have been. Instead, the world's brutality invaded her retreat: here on her own telephone extension she had heard, having lifted the receiver to call a friend, Luigi Squarcia's voice mid-sentence. . . incalculable asset, he was insisting as she replaced it, suddenly snatching it back when that voice, in miniature, clearly mentioned her name. . . the grannie vote, he said. But it's all sentimental tripe Lou! an unsuspecting Buchanan objected from the kitchen. Rory, she heard Squarcia concede, would probably play up and stick his tongue out at the photographer. What you need Bernie is a new baby in the family or a pregnancy because there's nothing like a pregnancy for netting votes. Then I'm sorry to disappoint you, her husband had replied, Dorina is not pregnant and I'm damned sure she wouldn't be fool enough to oblige just for your sake. . . Are you, that harsh calm voice came down her illicit line after a pause, perfectly certain she isn't? Dorina, in the music room, gripped the phone till her hand hurt. How did this creature know what even her husband had not guessed? Automatically she'd glanced at her stomach. But after only four months nothing showed. So much for confidentiality in the doctor's surgery. She'd held the instrument at arm's length to prevent it picking up her breathing: even her blood raced violently enough, perhaps, to be detected.

After this shock, Dorina had sat a long time at the piano without playing, simply reading an open score and hearing the music in her head, more perfect, more sensuous than ever in performance. A lush gentle Brahms andante for the baby, yes, perhaps with foreboding, before it was too late. And, in answer to the same impulse, she had put *Pictures at an Exhibition* up for the unborn to feel the thrill of that striding promenade, the witty cackle of hens, Mussorgsky's sprawling Russian virtuosity of art which swallows life whole in all its vigour and the dignity of ordinariness. Some instinct had told her to run, to escape while she could. But she'd been too civilized, too constrained, and had sat before the printed music, weeping instead.

Now looking back over the weeks between, even as her mind traced the inventive surprises of harmony, old oaks in the garden turned yellow then brown and cast their skeletal shadows on the crust of losses in the dirt. Her abortion had been simpler than she feared. She could afford the best. And her body, as if to spite the horror her conscience nursed, recovered quickly.

She crouched on the piano stool in that room at the back of their empty house, crushed under terrible thoughts. She heard a table being dragged across the floor below, emitting frightful shrieks of protest. She would have to go and keep an eye on what they were doing or there might be nothing worth saving at the other end.

Dorina sighed as she surveyed her domain, which had turned out, quite to her surprise, the airiest and most charming part of the house. Even while the place was being stripped, this one refuge still looked familiar, having always been bare, with music piled on the floor and a few treasures on occasional tables. Her basketwork chair, drawn up at the window, remained facing the garden, the tall upright piano with its German tone, solid as a mausoleum. She felt collected enough at last to stroll downstairs. Good Lord, she thought, inspecting the emptied rooms, however did they hold all our stuff?

— Clear the decks, lady! a workman called irrepressibly.

Dorina watched her precious escritoire sail out the front door carried at a trot by a pair of philistines. She caught her breath, but interference could only make accidents more likely. She saw the inlaid rosewood piece come to rest on the truck's tailboard, lustrous after its heady descent from the sewing room, as she'd bitterly dubbed her boudoir, which was promised her as a place where she could enjoy privacy. They were whistling tunes completely unknown to her: popular vulgarities, she supposed. During thirteen years of marriage she had hoarded enough to burden a dynasty.

She looked out across the road at the church with its cramped garden of shrubs and clipped hedges. But this is Sydney, she objected, not London. Her fashionable North Shore neighbours flocked here on Sundays. She watched them sometimes during the main part of the social function, standing elegantly in the sunshine, pricing each other's outfits. But she was not tempted to join them, not even for the chance of recapturing forgotten nostalgia from her childhood. It's amazing, Dorina thought, how all denominations trip over their own feet to be up-to-date. Such an idiotic idea, to wish to speak to the ordinary person in the ordinary language of her kitchen, would you believe! The last thing people want is more of their meaningless lives. That's religion brought low, reduced to the level of advertising. We've lost sight of the importance of lofty language and lofty music, that the remoter from modernity these things become, the more charged with mystery and timelessness, the more powerful and immediate, the more *they* become the reality.

She reached for her glass of Lillet put ready on the mantelpiece and sipped the delicate wine. The bother of moving; and all because of Buchanan's inexplicable political ambitions. Never again, she declared. The living space where she stood had been denuded. To one side Turkish rugs stood rolled and propped on end, and several lay where they had fallen. Through an archway she herself had designed, she had a clear view of the last three crates of books waiting where the telephone belonged in the vestibule, and a laundry basket of miscellaneous objects near the door to the diningroom. The white case of her hairdryer could be seen through the wickerwork and a few layers beneath it the holly berries on a Christmas gift she would neither open nor throw away. The odour of hollowness was so unfamiliar-familiar she felt momentarily she could face anything. She held in her hand a clipboard of ridiculous lists she had no intention of checking. Dorina decided on another sip of Lillet. There was no ice. Churchill barked once, but fell silent, intimidated when the hooting sound lifted dust from echoing floorboards. He ought to have gone to a kennel for the duration and would have been dispatched but for her sudden premonition of loneliness. This was my grandmother's escritoire, she had told the men. We won't hold that against her, love, one responded gallantly. What was to be said to such benign ogres? She laughed obligingly though she felt bereft. There are a dozen bottles of beer in the fridge, Bernard explained before flying to Canberra and leaving her to cope, be sure you give them to the removalists in time for their break. She had not forgotten, but it eased her loss to deny them the diversion of carrying her afternoon furniture while drunk. The fridge had gone and the beer too. He would be able to gratify himself with instructing her in the ways of men and her own follies when this item came to light at the other end. For the balance of his settling into the presidential mansion in the capital, was she, she asked, required to cope entirely with arranging the new Sydney house, or might she retire to a hotel to recover? He said she could please herself. Dorina took the glass, tucked the clipboard under one arm, snapped her fingers for Churchill to follow, and directed her desolate footfalls along the passage to the kitchen. There she peered through the servery hatch into the diningroom where Rory had squatted several months earlier to eavesdrop on his father being presented with the ultimatum of a contract. I liked this house, she objected. I loved it. But she had already, fatefully, begun to think of it in the past tense. Churchill sneezed.

— You're getting fat, she explained while he lip-read. Nevertheless she was aware of dust irritating her own nose. The darker rectangles on the wallpaper where furniture had blocked the daylight pleased her. I shan't be leaving it wholly empty of ghosts, she said. That's my sideboard to the life. The worn and faded appearance of her immaculate home filled her with jubilation. To expunge these years of contentment would be more trouble than the usurpers might ever have anticipated.

— Take care, she cried out. With those hideous paintings.

A seashell came bouncing down the stairs, dislodged from the windowsill where it had lain forgotten during six years, since that attempt at a family holiday when Rory was five. Dorina rescued it. She wiped the dust off and was surprised at how fresh it appeared after such minimal attention.

The front door chime rang, an absurdity with the whole house wedged wide open and men trooping in and out in pairs. Besides, its bland tone had become an offence she ought to be spared. She put the shell in her pinafore pocket, equipped herself with the remains of the vermouth, signalled to Churchill to accompany her on the flank and set off to suffer the refreshment of a surprise. I'm still young, she protested. At the end of the passage she caught sight of blond hair shining in the direct sun and a completely unknown profile, and then the double wardrobe floated between on its side. She saw herself momentarily in the mirror doors, split horizontally, the wordless assistant at a conjuring trick, her feet in first position, the remains of her drink unspilt, the merciless light of an empty house showing her a woman with hips and elbows, and a face almost as undistinguished as a man's. Once the wardrobe had turned end-on and wobbled out the door on four hairy legs, she found the visitor looking straight at her. Dorina recognized him from newspaper photographs of the rescue story. She strolled up impersonally.

— I do detest built-in furniture, she said.

— Have I come just in time? he asked holding out the familiar visiting card. This touch of panache put her, she felt, at a disadvantage.

— What is the point of my asking you in, Mr Taverner? We've nothing. Bernard flew to Canberra yesterday, I'm afraid.

— Hey Fred, one of the carriers shouted from the truck to the window above the porch. Stay up there mate. I'm coming up. I need you for the bloody piano.

— Who has a piano *upstairs*? came the reply.

She and he decided simultaneously on the garden. Churchill sanctioned the idea. The young man's face, Dorina noted, was both self-contained in expression and generous, which intrigued her. Beneath the obvious masculinity with its promise of violence she thought she noticed some glimmer of loftiness.

— My husband says you saved his life, she began as their shoes crunched the gravel.

They circumambulated the goldfish pond and glanced briefly at the beastly fish Dorina had enjoyed keeping but would pass to the new owners with relief.

— There's something I ought to tell him. I should have told him there in the outback.

— Pure Chinese aren't they, she remarked to keep the subject off Bernard and threw a handful of gravel to stir them into motion. Pretty little gluttons.

— You have a real touch with the garden. He walked with a lilt while he recognized the garden as her work, appreciating this and this, till only by the exercise of self-control could she take her eyes off him.

— What makes you think it is I who keeps it?

He presumed not to reply. And, because she couldn't even guess his motive, this provoked her mildly.

— You talk as if we know one another. I should introduce myself. This is Churchill and I am Mrs Buchanan.

He stopped and held out his hand, neither apologetically nor cavalierly. She observed his clear direct eyes. The hand was so hard yet so considerate she trembled with a spasm of fear. They met formally then. But already the signals of familiarity had been exchanged. They came from two worlds of privilege: hers of sophistication, his of strength. She was certainly much too well bred to be fooled by his knockabout clothes. And he had the tact to see immediately that she liked being treated as a person immune to sexual flattery. Poor Bernard was as far as ever from any such understanding of her. Her hand trailed along the honeysuckle hedge, raking at the perfume of a lost time. Her eyes filled with tears.

— Well Churchill, he enquired squatting down to address the

labrador and give her time to recover. I was bringing news about how your master's car came to break down in the desert.

Removalists' voices echoed in the upper rooms, one of them letting out a yell of laughter. Mrs Buchanan pulled herself together. She thought of Rory who, having little talent for relaxation, was better off battling it out with his teacher at school than seeing his room violated. Or would he have treated this as an adventure? Mightn't she be the only one to dread the move?

— Not even a cup of tea can I offer you, she apologized.

A sonorous thump from indoors resounded through their bones. She reacted like a nervous hound.

— Maybe you'd be better off staying in there. They'll be more careful with you around, that's for sure, Peter Taverner suggested.

With the thought of those men shouldering heavy loads, she glanced at her guest, who stood up. (Buchanan had said: He took my whole weight, lifted me on my feet, and supported me back to the car.) The path led into the kitchen garden. They followed it to where beds of vegetables fattened with moisture. He helped himself to a pea pod which he chewed whole, his gesture making clear that he saw her as having already relinquished ownership, crunching it greenly and exclaiming at its freshness. The dapple of shade patterned his fair hair and a spot of sunlight caught his eye. He discovered a melody haunting him. Curious, because he couldn't recall having heard it anywhere before.

Dorina longed to be settled. Her ideal was a family property passed on with all its contents complete. She hated buying furniture and hated arranging it. One wasn't born with a mind, merely to surrender it to domestic trivia, just as life ought not to be cluttered with objects one was personally committed to. Oh no, to be owned by purchases, never. She had no notion how deeply she shocked the company wives with such opinions. Dorina consulted the clipboard she still held.

— How we cling to our prisons Mr Taverner, she sang gaily and birds flocked round with their haphazard chorus.

— But given half a chance we're out like a shot, he contradicted her. Freedom. It's a question of boundaries. . . whose boundaries you want to operate in.

She looked at him with absolute delight at so articulate an idea. He went on after crunching another pea pod.

— It's all a game. You don't have to play by anyone else's

book. (He took time for thought.) There's two moves you can make: you can stay or go. Prison's only a prison if you can't recognize the door.

— How did you and Buchanan, she exclaimed, ever find a single thing to say to one another?

But the implications of this were too sudden even for her, so she re-read her checklist as a refuge. *Filing cabinet grey 1, Filing cabinet grey 2, Filing cabinet green 1, Filing cabinet small, Smoking chair.* What a peculiar thing to put, she thought. A smoking chair. She set her empty glass under a tree for someone to find.

— Are you ready to take the weight? came a hollow question from the open window upstairs.

Come to look at him, this young man might be more at home with them than with her. She was amused at the thought, but a little jealous too. The chorus scattered in mad high spirits, regrouping to a line of small birds perched along a wire, just as they had when Dorina was a girl at boardingschool dreaming of being wanted. Yet the only time she prevailed with her father and he decided not to leave her but to take her abroad with him to his diplomatic posting was worst of all. The day came when his love of the Pacific Islands was put to the test.

The lessons had gone wrong from the first bell onwards. The arithmetic teacher didn't attend, so Dorina's class was set to work on religious studies to keep them quiet. Then the English mistress, Miss Gardiner, couldn't stop her lips trembling. She talked in an unconvinced manner about *A Christmas Carol*, making no headway with the challenge of explaining what snow was like and why cripples sat in corners and the nature of a Christmas pudding. Her descriptions had no energy, her sentences lacked essentials (in some she forgot what the subject was, in others the verb was so long delayed it lost any active life in her meaning), her words quivered. Miss Gardiner's face, so white above her secretarial collar, had been simplified to an oval of fear. She stuck to the task till playtime. Dorina Lambert sat with Penny McConachie eating the mangosteens her house-keeper had packed for her. She looked across the coarse-bladed grass to the surrounding jungle and along the track that led, as she knew, to a kampong not five minutes' walk away, a place she loved to visit, with baked earth between the houses, neigh-bours on their diminutive verandahs (diminutive was the very word she herself had thought up and written in a letter to Aunt Sybil in Adelaide), batik hung to dry, and white chickens jabbing beaks at the dust. The village people were so kind and gentle, preparing tapioca and sucking on limes. And sometimes the white-coiffed Muslim girls would troop demurely past the gate on their way to the native school. Coconut palms swayed in the wind. Over to their right, the corner of a rubber plantation was the beginning of Mr Van Dooren's property. She identified all the trees in the area and whether they bore fruit. Penny, who had seen something, let out a scream, gathered her bony legs, and ran for the schoolhouse. In the panic of not-knowing, Dorina followed, beginning to realize she was part of a stampede, teachers, matron, the children milling desperately along corridors. Instinct told her to escape from them also. She stood up against the folding screen which was sometimes used to divide the hall into two classrooms; its leaves of wooden venetians did not fit flat against each other as they were supposed to. Dorina edged sidelong into the gap and pulled the concertina door as close to the wall as she could manage. She was hidden. Half an hour ago, she promised herself, Daddy would have left the consulate on his way to fetch her and any minute he would come to the rescue in the car. A terrible silence suffocated the school; the running feet no longer drummed on the boards, the hysterical voices gagged. She willed her father to come now, now when he was truly wanted.

Her watery green eyes peered down, the fixed angle of the slats allowing her only a view of the floor. The hush thrilled with electricity, a crowd not daring to breathe. She strained to hear anything, so she would have some idea. But the messages seemed to come through the pores of her skin. In the silence a foot appeared on the strip of floor she could see; a small, man's foot, all sinews and joints, blotches of dirt stuck to the skin with (her hair froze) blood. Soundlessly it was gone again, leaving a tiny trace of dust and one flake of grass. She bared her teeth to stop them chattering. She felt the weight of somebody leaning against the folded doors, the leaves of it sandwiching her tight. A curious smell reached her, oily and obnoxious, an animal smell that meant something. With a sudden rustle of cloth against the wood, a body blocked her slit of light. Her nose no more than an inch from his spine. She tingled with thumping blood, guessing this was a mob with knives. She was eight. Lightly as she breathed, Dorina could not believe the sound would escape detection. She had been taught that dogs will smell your fear however bravely you act. This was why the murderer waited, to look for where the scent of a victim came from. Fee Fie Fo Fum. She had had lots of practice in hiding games; the terrors of being chased for home and running just out of reach of clutching hands were on her side. She felt cold. Had they all been naughty in the school, to be punished? The taste of fruit stuck in her mouth sweetly, producing saliva which she tried not to swallow. Little Dorina fought the scream ringing inside her head. The man moved one step and then another. Suddenly he was breathing noisily, panting, and he bounded away on a hundred feet. Bare heels thudded throughout the building. Almost immediately came the shrieks of terror, the whooping cries of baboons, and even more terrible soft noises, helpless yielding body sounds, the snicker of steel blades, tiny wet flops, giant insect wings. A body of bones hurtled against the folded screen with a thunderous rattling that would surely crush her to death where she stood. A beast growled at the back of its throat. A kissing sound followed. Then she saw another foot, this time wearing a sandal and a brilliant new shock of blood with a twinkle of reflected sunlight in it. The foot moved away, but whoever had fallen against the screen stayed there. Men's voices chanted native words in high wild tones somewhere out by the playground. Afterwards the whole school was a feverish chaos of groans and weeping, so that she herself eventually let go and cried. But she did not come out of hiding; she forced her fingers in her ears till they felt sharp as daggers. When night came and the hubbub of pain died down, she found one last mangosteen in her shoulderbag and ate that. Then she crouched where she was, relieving her bladder straight on to the floor; though this had happened before, she was not aware of it. Shivering violently in the heat, she was kept awake by cramps. But even when she did doze, her nodding head struck the door panel and shocked her alert. Until finally she knelt on the floor damp with her urine, wedged her shoulder in against the hinge, and fell asleep upright.

At dawn Dorina woke so numb it was easy to stay hidden, her fear intense enough for its delirious edge to have dulled, intense enough for crouching to become the normal position of the body, for hiding to be a comfort, the will to escape manifesting itself as a force to be feared, a seductive invitation by a half-naked man with sinewy ankles, his butcher's hands busy, up to his elbows in familiar blood. At that young age, though she had proved admirably able to control her body, Dorina experienced far worse problems with her mind. She clamped down hard and refused it all permission to think. But when it slipped free, as happened again and oh yes again, it bolted off along corridors skidding on maps of viscid darkness and plummeted down bottomless wells, or tripped and fell into the arms of the beast that was man, the mutilator of schoolchildren.

Late in the morning her father did arrive, he and his consulate servant crying out in horror at what they saw. Even then she almost missed him. Just as they were leaving via the locker room, she heard his furious voice say: They have forgotten themselves this time! She recognized him. She had been waiting twenty-two hours for this moment. She struggled to part doors too heavy for her with Miss Gardiner's corpse jammed against them. Then she called out. Save me, Daddy, she screamed, save me! So that he told her afterwards this had given him the greatest fright of all, this piercing shriek from inside the folded doors.

Standing under the peach tree she had always called hers, Dorina could find nothing to say.

Her guest helped himself to another pea pod, seeking the right tone and a possible opening for asking her why not one item had appeared in the newspapers about her husband's misadventure in the desert and who had stopped any investigation being made, because if they had found out what Peter already knew, they must have known it was a crime and not an accident.

As if he were also wondering why Buchanan, of all people, had been selected as the candidate, Dorina remarked:

— Really it could have been anyone.

The ivy-smell of honeysuckle leaves reached her eventually. The house itself gasped with shock. Then uttered a perplexing rumble. Just as she had heard the rising whale all those months ago emit its yawning boom, to be answered by twitters of an ungraspable sadness, now a pure screech followed. Mingled with this piercing sound came the snap of timbers plus a man's voice shouting one syllable and, a moment later, the most sumptuous crash, a bang so reverberant the garden quivered. Singing cavities moaned with siren echoes to satisfy every frequency audible to the human ear.

Peter Taverner and the president's wife, having run together, in yet another intimacy, stood at the doorway while the disaster described itself.

Huge wounds gashed the plaster wall with an advertisement in Arabic script, starting from the top of the stairs and sweeping down to where a banister hung, smashed and gating out over its splintered butts. The piano hummed in the vestibule, centre-stage like a virtuoso, upside down. The keyboard flap dangled open and the little useless brass casters pointed in different directions. A triangular dint had been stamped in the floor-boards where the instrument first struck before taking the tiny tremendous bounce to its present position. A corresponding corner of the lid was crushed. Powdered plaster hung in the air, seething down a shaft of golden daylight from the landing window where a seashell had once suffered years of neglect. The older of two workmen leaned against the wall at the top, a broad webbing halter across the back of his neck, his face contorted with fury.

She dropped her eyes to the clipboard and scanned the heading *MUSIC ROOM. Piano 1. . .*

A couple of steps down from the landing, right by that gap in the banister, the young carrier sat, knees apart, head in hands and lucky to be uninjured. He looked up to apologize but could not tear his paper mouth open. His eyes had turned black with shock. The instrument still gave out its bombilation, chest humming loudly as a creature now discovered to be in pain.

— I think, she said hoarsely. I deserved a grand piano anyhow.

Quarter of an hour passed. Dorina felt recovered and in no need of her visitor's support (for, curiously, he did give the impression of supporting her). She let the conversation lapse and accompanied him to the front door. There, by the gate, stood two strangers. What was so arresting about them was their manner of standing: branded by a blend of intimacy and vigilance. Bodyguards. Dorina stared at them. They would stand that way and watch her die if it suited their employers, she thought. At the very least, they would attract someone to wish her harm. Feverish with shock, she spoke up.

— The house is not for sale. It has already been sold.

They watched her politely, being quite used to the eccentrici-ties of those locked away by fame.

— Did you hear me? she insisted bravely, recognizing the end of her life as a private citizen, the end of her privilege in being a person of no account.

— MacGregor, madam, the one replied. And Conran.

— This is not my scene, Peter Taverner said, flashing her his last smile and treacherously leaving, treacherously because he knew she was now afraid of being alone with them.

On this very day in California the final handover of Central Command took place quietly, circumspectly and, one might almost say, casually. Two parties of officials toured the great windowless building murmurously. This was the nerve-centre of a worldwide network. Information poured in without break from secret locations in Greenland, Alaska and Iceland, from stations in Chile and Grenada, the Seychelles off the East African coast, from Guam and Hawaii, of course, and even from Australia. Twenty-four hours a day, satellite transmitters maintained global contact with far-flung arsenals, weapons systems and military bases. In the Pacific alone there would soon be thirty, including actual nuclear stockpiles on Wake Island, Hawaii, the Filipines, and in South Korea and Alaska.

Here men and women sat mute at the controls: as if earth were a great airship whose destiny was plotted in this dark cockpit, with its glowing dials and discreetly floodlit consoles, by operators so dedicated they declined even to glance round at their change of masters. For the present, it was enough that their work should remain perfect.

PART TWO
The Book of Nightmares

31

Seven years after coming to power, a power which had grown beyond challenge in his own country, President Buchanan planned his only overseas trip. The fact was that he had been summoned for a conference he could not decline to attend. Referring to the journey as if it would be a pleasure, he perfected these plans at night, while his staff milled around and the presidential mansion blazed with lights which confused the insomnia he endured as a state obligation and to accommodate which even parliament had to conduct its sittings in the small hours of the morning. Those beneath him, constantly jockeying for favour, grew feverish with excitement at the prospect of having three weeks to reshuffle their power base and see to smoothing matters over before his return.

— Hold everything! he joked from where he officiated in his study at the presidential mansion. He had momentarily put aside the tourist brochures and switched himself through to the large screen in parliament.

This was his prerogative, to intervene when he felt like it and overrule the Speaker by using a neat master control to cut the fellow's microphone off. His style remained characteristically genial.

— Incidentally, I am thinking of announcing an early election for you people, he purred and watched them scramble.

Numbers-men from all thirteen parties went mum, eyes darting frantic signals to their minorities to cool it for fear of losing their seats. Roscoe Plenty was a case in point, that poor boy who cried wolf so often he became one (hottest of the Hot faction in the Right Coalition, which had been huddled together out of the ruins of the former Nationals, the old Conservatives and the even older and more seriously misnamed Liberals, plus six other splinter groups united only by internecine war), had to stifle his nausea and recant. He'd been left no choice but to pay court to the man he once set out to ridicule at a dinnerparty specially arranged for this purpose.

— In support of the motion before the House, Mr Speaker, Roscoe Plenty said darkly, knowing what was expected of him. Let me point out to honourable members that the philosophy of rationing is not, as Mr Robinson has suggested, to deny people the necessaries of life. Quite the contrary, it is to supply them. Not to provide exclusive access to those who can afford black-market prices, but to legally ensure every individual a fair share. Surely. Surely, Mr Speaker, a so-called socialist like the honourable leader of the Opposition doesn't need me to persuade him this will not contravene his own code as I understand it, nor his platform? Furthermore, I'd remind you, sir, we have survived rationing perfectly well in the past. There are even some members present today who grew up on rationed food during the 1939-45 war. They don't seem any the worse for the experience. Nor, he glared in a fury of wit. Do they lack stamina to argue a point when hopelessly in the wrong.

— That will do, the president decided amiably. We shall take a vote on the motion before you clog your brains with facts.

— Plenty, Squarcia suggested quietly from his usual armchair in the presidential study. Is exactly the creep for your new Executive Council. He has nothing to fall back on. Everyone hates him, including us.

Prior to departure, the preparations were lavish. They occupied the mansion staff for months. For months the great man titillated himself with promises of a second honeymoon.

Seldom before were such cushions assembled, such perfumes, such warehouses of gifts and gorgeous ornaments, such hoards of Turkish delight and preserved rose petals or such sachets of rare herbs. Good Sabine and Bergamo pears, Ribstone Pippins, plums from Tours and cherries from Pantagruel's orchard were placed on order, these being the regimen Dorina recommended to keep his sleeplessness free from misleading dreams which might confuse his judgment on state issues.

— How come the country is so far in debt, Roscoe Plenty protested in bewilderment when he accepted the portfolio of

Treasurer. Look at these figures from my department, Bernard. Fifty-three per cent of our gross national product is paid each year as interest on overseas loans. Effectively that means we have been taken over. Who's to prevent those foreign share-holders selling to one another? You may think this is a wild idea, but I can't see what is to stop a monopoly simply buying us out.

The great man beamed, blossoming red roses.

— Next they'll want to put their own man in your chair!

The roses turned pink and gentle. Could a colleague so high up the ladder have remained innocent? Buchanan grew serious and affectionate, making ready to say what was in his mind. But Squarcia intervened.

— It comes of your unionist past Roscoe. You don't think in financial terms. A businessman, as Bernard once said to me, borrows before he needs to.

— Do you know, Plenty turned on him. That out there we have created a new class of citizen? I call them the Babes-in-the-Wood. They are lost and their nerve is failing. All they want is fairytales. Bernard is a fairytale, for a start. The land of opportunity is a fairytale.

The lean wolf had become a thin wolf and no longer threatening. His black looks were grey looks.

— Quite right they are, Roscoe. Do you know how I made myself rich? Buchanan confided. I remember you at that Adelaide conference and how you resented me for being rich. Well this is proof that I *am* a fairytale. One day I asked myself: Can anyone stop me behaving like a successful man? And what other pleasure does success bring but living in style and getting things done? So I appointed myself rich. I got things done. I went out and bluffed my way through. I came back with an office, a secretary, a car, a cupboard full of new clothes, member-ship of the Chamber of Commerce. . . and all on credit. Marvel-lous thing, no need to be afraid of it. People judge you by what they can see, so after this they couldn't load me with their money fast enough. They begged me to take it. He clapped his hands in a single explosion of triumph: Easy! Same with Austra-lia. But don't, he wagged a warning finger. Let it worry you. Just coast along with Treasury as you find it. A nice easy old baggage. You needn't know anything. The last person we want for the job is some meddlesome accountant, let alone an econo-mist. You'll soon get the hang of our methods. He brightened further: And I am always here to guide you. My door is open at any hour.

— Highly satisfactory, Squarcia commented after the new minister had gone.

— Just what I thought, Buchanan snapped. He's fantasizing about taking over from me.

— Going through your gestures with you, Squarcia added with the flash of a flick-knife. And improving them.

— Considering I am the one who declared day night and night day! the president pointed out with a mystified wag of his head, remembering the very occasion he had made the declartion four years previously.

32

President Buchanan's insomnia had begun with the absolute orderliness, the ceremonial protocol, proper to an event worthy of history. The exact day of the exact month was documented: 24 February 1996, which is to say just as his fourth year of glory began, the last year of his first term or, as he himself preferred to style it, the year before the beginning of his remarkable second term.

He did not give in. He was not the giving-in type. He fought it by recounting a catalogue of his triumphs. But this stimulated him and made matters worse instead of sending him off; he brooded on failures, which simply roused his fury; he made an alphabet game from the list of enemies he had put out of the way in jails, in penury, in luxury sinecures; he told the fiction of his own fame; he transformed Dorina to a compliant homely wife, to a silk-underwear stripper, to a moneyed ailing admirer, but he was left with her as she was, obligingly warm and a good deal too communicative, forever advising him that he didn't know what he was doing; he imagined facing death in the desert beside a young hitchhiker whom he had rescued, and ended by asking when will you rescue me with the life you owe me, Peter?

He fought the insomnia with soporifics of budget cuts.

He re-worded tax increases to sound like reductions.

He remembered signing a contract that tormented him.

In his amateurism he lay on his side.

He lay on his belly.

On his back.

He commanded each limb to go limp, starting with the toes.

He achieved limpness. But he also achieved a wakeful appraisal of it, till he fell ill with rancours against his allies. He proliferated hatreds, beginning with Squarcia for having witnessed his uncertainty before the epoch of success. He gagged at the memory of deviates making blameworthy the blameless sport of cricket (never mind the South Africans). He reviewed his circle of ministers and supporters, picked them over, not one escaping suspicion, and planned how he would be rid of them, occupying the wakeful hours to be ready for a morning of sifting through their domestic ruins, where with luck he might find hints of guiltless loyalty. Treasures. He re-lived the humiliations of fatness and schoolchildren's taunts when they discovered that the visiting inspector, a hated figure of authority, was his father. Towards dawn he drifted downhill on a brandless bicycle and swooped round corners, his bottom sagging over the saddle, he yahooed with feigned glee. He wondered what the hell highspirits were anyhow. And merciless day welled in the sky.

Night after night Bernard Buchanan struggled through his ineffectual mutiny against insomnia's seduction. Night after night he felt a cool lewd hand return to smother his parts, fingers exciting his nipples and teasing his bellyhairs. He got up, persuaded that superfluous energy must be what kept him awake, so a burst of activity might burn it out. He pressed the bell and woke his bearers, whom he would order to carry him to the office. But when they presented sleep-reddened faces, sheet creases embedded across their innocent cheeks, and eyes resentful with bloodvessels, he was so infuriated he accused them of mocking his affliction. He shouted till his voice cracked, till perhaps he might burst into tears or shoot them on the spot. If he'd been able to put any weight on his ankles he would without question have had the satisfaction of stamping his foot. As it was, he sent them away with the explanation that he was trying out the system as an emergency drill; and exhorted them to be smarter off the mark next time. You have to be as quick on your legs as I am in my mind, he growled, or the state might go under at a single misfortune. Your Excellency mumble mumble Excellency, they protested mildly and left him seething dissatisfactions so he spent the remaining hours before breakfast designing an orchestra of alarm bells plus electric shocks to be circuited through their bed frames. And this was the way things stood in the seventh year of his martyrdom to the *bono publico*, a long remove from when he'd needed only two musclemen to lift him from his chair or lower him on to a bed and knew their names Harvey and Noel better than his own son Whatsit. The sleepless nights were twice as long once he had graduated to four musclemen and began to rehearse them from right front clockwise to left front, Harvey Craig Scott Noel, keeping his eye on the two he knew, HCSN should remind him: Here Comes Someone Notable. He dreamed while still awake of calling Scott Craig, of being carried through a crowd and suddenly left, dumped for no better reason than a bearers' strike against name-forgetting and confusion of identity, or more pertinently against the increased load. Now he had grown so much fatter with autocracy he needed eight of the bastards plus a full range of carrying vehicles with poles and crossbeams designed for lifting comfort by the hand or on the shoulder. Still awake, he dreamed of humiliating them, having them stripped and himself their master, overlord with whip upraised; but somehow Dorina intruded on the scene and made deflating comments of the Dorina kind so there seemed little point in pursuing the satisfaction. As he lay flat on his back, his belly a dome obscuring not only his feet but even his steepled knees, he panicked that soon he would not see who was coming in the door, that he'd hear the catch and have to wait, sweating for a glimpse of the intruders and what they might be holding. He planned a palace of security mirrors affording him a view of all parts of the bedroom in light-refracting fragments, which he ordered installed that very morning while he munched at unwilling muesli, testing his eyelids for weight, his sticky mouth for the residue of slanders. And so the insomnia went on, growing oppressively more frequent, his gross limbs lolling voluptuously in the caresses of the tormentor. He strove to induce orgasms, painful with sluggishness, to satisfy her, baffle, waylay, interest her. But lying down, his arms proved too short to reach round his successful stomach to perform these rites. He was even denied the simplest male comfort of cradling his idle parts. He had to bend forward, as when he reached for his fly to urinate, before the tips of his fingers made contact. Nothing served, she remained unbaffled.

The insomnia had him.

He offered a reward for a cure and tried each recipe on the spot, calling on salt and ice and warm virgins, on wind quintets and three other pontoon players, on art critic after art critic, on Dames of Academe to cauterize his wits with their prejudices; he submitted to watching commercial television, and learning

Esperanto; but formidable as these boredoms were, they failed. He was not without humour. He laughed the agony of a man who laughs in pain. His mind screamed for release, for one minute's oblivion, rescue from the grinding whirligig of stimulus. Give me, he cried, what every least pauper takes for granted. And instead, he was given a pep talk by a young man with eagle blood, a spinner of curses, a philosopher of all the great issues dead since philosophy became a paid profession. This tormented but ecstatic youth said you are one of the blessed and don't forget it. He raved on to the extent of claiming insomnia as a precious energy, a gift of the few, an opportunity, an opening, a clear way from the thickets of daytime confusion, a power to govern. When do you think Bach composed his greatest music? He had to teach all day. Nineteen children and 205 cantatas, that's what he made of his sleepless nights. Insomnia is the unclouded eye, he shouted enthusiastically. Mr President, you have grown so great you dare not risk what might go on behind your back. You are being taught a lesson you are too conventional to learn.

That did it.

Buchanan rolled his eyes ferociously, but the young man laughed a bird-of-prey laugh and asked: How else do you explain wasting your precious hours filling the mansion with mountebanks? How do you excuse the warm virgins, the dead mice, the *Times Literary Supplement*? We hear you have even promoted the Treasurer to Chief Minister.

— Okay, the president waved a bored hand, the reward is yours.

But this insensitive youth chose not to hear. He employed the late hour enlarging his lecture on a new age of the intellect about to transform unworthy mankind, raise life to higher powers, and so forth, till Harvey Craig Scott Noel & Co carried him out, a picnic of lightness, and locked the door behind him, acting upon the great man's challenge to be quick on their legs as he was in his mind: exactly as he reached for the bellpush, they presented themselves, clear-eyed and unmarked by sheet creases, having already disposed of the philosopher and shut his inextinguishable profundities out of hearing, just as His Excellency was about to request. Buchanan fretted with annoyance. They were supposed to be musclemen, nor smartarses. Besides which, equilibrium would take a long time restoring itself after being rocked by those ideas.

That was the extent of the president's contact with the ordinary person in the street.

— What did he want? Should I kiss his foot to shut him up? Buchanan asked his hundred images in the refracting mirrors of security. Send me the illiterate; they're modest when they're right, and only start murdering people if they haven't got a clue what they are talking about. From now on, he proclaimed into the telephone, this nation of ours is governed from 11 pm to 7 am. Those are my hours. If you don't like them you can resign on the dole.

From then on he contacted his IFID advisors (even if only to argue the toss with them) while his own population slept, more dead to their interests, even, than when awake.

— Aren't these the good times? he demanded of sleepy colleagues. Who's complaining? Don't give me radiation as an objection against what might happen three thousand years from now, good Lord the fucking arguments are getting wilder by the minute. Yesterday they were complaining about the misery of the aged without pensions to scrimp on, and today they're begrudging us our national good fortune because it risks short-ening their lives by a month or two. Less time to grizzle, in that case, we'll tell them. I mean, what do you deserve if you put nothing in the bank?

— Margaret, he instructed his snoring press secretary, her hair flopped over her face, and hands laced behind her back to help the semblance of remaining upright. Margaret, issue a press release to this effect. She dreamed it, the statement beginning His Excellency the President of the Republic has himself faced starvation in the desert. . . and going on to urge the opportunity of chance aircraft landing nearby on the say-so of a satellite. Wonderful epoch, nothing impossible, least of all if it appears unlikely. She pressed the Go button in her sleeping mind and the newspapers blazoned his scornful encouragement as he packed himself into pyjamas and his bearers breathed breakfast over his going to bed.

The Ribstone Pippins had arrived and the Tours plums in cold storage. A dispatch note assured the presidential housekeeper that a second consignment of cherries procured, at last and with difficulty, from Pantagruel's orchard, would be loaded aboard the next available Air France flight, the first batch having been confiscated by terrorists (together with 374 French citizens) in Beirut.

— When will you have had enough of Squarcia, I wonder?

Dorina's voice came down the long-distance line from Sydney to Canberra, sounding startlingly close.

— It isn't a question of having had enough of him, the all-powerful Buchanan replied irritably. Squarcia cannot be touched. And that's all there is to it.

Squarcia himself, in the monitoring room, examined his manicured fingernails knowledgeably: Poor old BB could not admit that this would entail taking on IFID as an enemy too. Not even when speaking to his wife from the perfect privacy of his study could he admit it.

At times, only history itself appeared to offer comfort. But even the past had a habit of overdoing things. George Gipps, who arrived in 1838 to administer the colony of New South Wales, was sent for one reason: to supply President Buchanan with proof that scrupulous fairness, disinterested concern and incorruptibility are the very last qualities compatible with being popular. What schoolchild who can rattle off a rigmarole about Lachlan Macquarie's wretched town plan plus caricatures of John Hunter versus the Rum Corps or William Bligh under the apocryphal bed, has a single platitude to trot out about George Gipps's eight years of tireless dedication to the common good, to the established traditions in law, education and morality?

Major Gipps landed, dusting salt from his cuffs, a career soldier knighted for administrative genius, blessed by a brief so leaking virtue an Ebenezer Methodist might have stitched it into a sampler, framed and hung it above the fireplace. What, then, emaciated his cheeks and shrivelled his firm hands? Bernard could answer this, Bernard who grew fat on power, though he was unsure now whether it was night or day, though he closed his shutters, his windows and his curtains, refused all petitions and declared himself a protected species.

— You can't put on a skerrick of condition, Gippso, until you toss away your book of rules. You had the perfect chance to play the despot, here in the farthest corner of God's earth, to have a laugh and try your hand at experimental private enterprise on the side. And what did you do but purse your lips and bore the socks off the local larrikins, questioning the ethics of expansion? Well you deserved what you got. Thick as two planks. A proper little King William IV's man. A prick you were, the way you bullied the rich to pay their taxes with your insufferable Tory courtesy.

Gipps, as Buchanan pointed out in *The Authorized History of*

Australia, misunderstood the quest for authority: he didn't know how to choose his friends.

— Your problem my lad, Bernard explained further. Boils down to the fact that you never seemed to enjoy yourself. You couldn't even sit back and watch a catastrophe for its own sake, you had to preach a sermon on it: Good is ever springing out of evil, you wrote. My big toe is ever growing out of my foot! And *what* good?

— I explained to my Lord Stanley, Gipps responded vigorously. That disasters which recently overtook great numbers of our settlers had had the effect of driving many estimable persons into the bush with their wives and families where their influence could hardly fail to be advantageously felt.

— Exactly! Would any fat man ever mouth such mealy-squealy slop? I can speak with authority for my own administration and assure you that recent disasters have had the effect of driving many estimable persons to the wall, and tough luck on them: their absence has been advantageously felt by their competitors.

— What I said, said Gipps tartly, standing near the bookcase in Buchanan's office and tucking a handkerchief in his sleeve. Is that the right of the Crown must remain absolute.

— Absolutely, Bernard shouted from where he sat behind the desk. Absolutely. You were called a despot for it. And I rest my case as head of a proud republic.

— You simply have not done your sums Mr Buchanan. Based on the equitable proposition that a man must pay for the use of land in proportion to the advantage he derives from it, you may well find your power more apparent than substantial. You are failing to levy proper charges with impartial firmness. He turned to face his antagonist as he summed up his case. What you call legitimate power, Mr Buchanan, I should rather call a conspiracy.

— You yourself, Bernard replied with the unction of hindsight and dumping clumsy fingers on the heap of his waistcoat. Once wrote that one might as well attempt to confine the Arabs of the desert within a circle traced upon their sands as to confine the exploiters of this country within any bounds that can possibly be assigned to them. If you'd only had the spunk to join them, you'd have been the most famous of our colonial governors. Even if you had declared a couple of public holidays you'd have done better than you did.

Just as the argument promised a bit of fun, that spoilsport

Roscoe Plenty, the new Chief Minister, presented evidence of learning to be clever. In the dead of the working night, he walked right through Gipps without noticing.

— What I cannot comprehend is how we got into such deep water. Our dollar was strong, he complained. I made sure it was strong.

— That's the reason I shifted you from Treasury, the president answered scathingly. If the currency firms, foreign money floods in, and the deficit shoots up. Logical. What else do you expect once you have an open banking system? There's no help for it but to sack your Treasurer, he laughed suddenly. The great thing about a floating currency is that it can go into reverse any time and either way. No warning.

— I wonder if I'm asleep or awake. I don't have your gift for optimism, Bernard. I came from the wrong side of the tracks. He sneezed. There, he added as further proof of the disadvantages he had to rise above. Now I've got a cold.

— Do you think I didn't come from the wrong side too!

Sir George Gipps smiled as part of the bad dream and tipped his head back, nose in the air, musing.

— Well, you know my style by now I should hope, Buchanan recovered the situation. Our job is to keep people from agitating for unreasonable conditions. One thing we cannot afford is a full flow-on of the East Coast Luxury Standard. We sit tight. The money market ought to come good now you are out of the job. How does it feel to be kicked upstairs? I do not rule with armed troops in the streets. Nobody is forced to conform, he crowed. I rule because the people love me.

Two days later, in the hour before dawn, armed Watchdogs marched through the dark streets of Brisbane and Melbourne, took up their positions and stayed there. Next came Port Hedland and Newcastle. A flying squad confiscated the beer supply at Katherine, paralysing the town. Then Sydney fell and Canberra.

Denied yet another pay rise while prices soared, the population from Broome to Hobart, employed as well as unemployed, began to have doubts. Began, even, to become restless.

Preparations were complete for the president's overseas trip. The obligatory engagement was not the Convocation of World Heads of State (which he certainly intended to amuse himself by taking in on the same journey), but a private conference immediately following it.

33

Greg Sullivan, who had spent his youth bumming up and down the coast as a surfer of indifferent ability, a pleasant, if unexciting companion, known variously and not always kindly as Mug or Shagger or Eggo, was back on the farm. Not because he had healed the rift between himself and his father, but because his father had died. To the young man's surprise and elation, he inherited the whole property.

So he was a farmer on a big scale and he knew what to do about it. Go bigger. Mug was a man of his time. He took a bank manager's advice to modernize the plant and equipment, completely making over the place to meet the standards of a model enterprise. His two-million-dollar loan was issued at the Basic Keystone Rate, 25%.

The following year, financiers negotiated a Free Interest Scale with Roscoe Plenty's successor in Treasury. This Free Interest Scale was subject to the sole regulation that firms charging more than 50% would be required to lodge the excess above 35% in government Bullion Bonds. To offset this they introduced second division loans known affectionately as Key Money, splitting the existing loan into two, one loan at 35% and the other at 70%. Neat. Legal. And lethal.

On his two-million-dollar loan, Greg Sullivan was required to pay compound interest computed daily. He lived in penury on that splendid property, his modern equipment working overtime in a desperate and doomed attempt to catch up with the bank's legitimate demands.

Because the despised Standards Commission of former days had been stopped from hampering business growth and reviled as a hangover from a century of socialist woolly thinking, the equipment itself was soon found to be shoddy and in need of costly maintenance.

Greg Sullivan arranged a large life-insurance policy in case he might accidentally commit suicide.

34

Dorina took up her pen: she knew just what she needed to say to her son at the end of his first posting away from home.

I suppose I cannot claim innocence. All that I understand of your generation, your life and your hopes, is nothing better than a projection of *my* hopes for you. You do not need to tax me with this, my dear, but while I acknowledge the fact, I would also say it is not a base motive, Rory.

How could I fail to be worried? Haven't we seen our hopes, the fresh perspectives of independence, the claim to speak for ourselves and stand by our own decisions, fester, grow sickly and finally bring us down, for all our strength? I, more than others, should take it to heart, since in my view the whole shameful collapse can justifiably be called a betrayal. I need not say more. At this moment I wonder how it strikes you? When it all started you were too young to make distinctions. But our style had a kindly, clumsy barbarism then which I loved. We did not deserve our present fate.

What amazes me is the wholesale collapse of the political system, the proliferation of factions, the inadequacy of our formulae when the time came to adapt to new challenges.

These new *challenges* as I have called them were, and I confess this, being too much the coward, too much bound to my own comfort to broadcast it for the common good. . . these challenges were, right from the beginning, capitulations to foreign pressure. We have never tried exercising our own integrity. That is the sum total of your father's achievement. Yet, what hopes people had when they put him in power!

We ought to have learned a lesson from New Zealand. But instead of supporting her in her outrage, we smirked behind our hands, reminded of sundry abusive but harmless prejudices we had harboured right back to the early years of last century. What was inexcusable was our smugness, the way we thought so much the better of ourselves over the whole business.

You and I, dear, are the ones who must feel this most acutely.

It is beyond any doubt now that the whole edifice has collapsed to bankruptcy; though over the years since this depression began we have refused to give it so doom-filled a name. At first it hit only the poor; and who cared about them? The rest of the community closed ranks against the onset of misgivings. That was the beginning. We have hardened ourselves not to feel shame.

I write these things, Rory, because I have no one else to tell. Also because I believe you think a great deal. And I do care about what conclusions you may reach.

Look at the vocabulary of our capitulation, the common abuse we still heap on others, calling them cosmopolitan, weak, muddled, lacking push, when what we refer to might be better called tolerance, gentleness, subtlety and self-confidence.

In my own defence, let me assure you, I am equally outspoken to your father, although he seems beyond reach. I suppose I am writing, as much as anything, to put myself in your hands.

You too, I fear, have never been allowed to make your own decisions, or given the least power with which to buy independence. Here you have it, then, in these few subversive thoughts.

From your loving mother

35

Bernard Buchanan's eight bearers had to carry not only his natural weight, plus the weight of his accumulated power, but also his conscience. Over the cold oil-smelling tarmac they shuffled, among wisps of night clinging to the ground as thin and grey as on a beast with its hair half gone. Dank air clogged round their legs in clumps as they went. Warming jet engines haunted the great man with memories of a locust plague while he was raised to the cabin by hydraulic lift and from there taken in hand again by his bearers. They strapped him to a seat and dusted him down. His personal photographer took a photograph before wishing him *bon voyage* and departing. Thus he set out, followed by a fleet of aircraft loaded with his night-weary entourage.

— Lou, Buchanan spoke eventually as they hurtled along the runway. You are the only one I can truly say I have never liked.

— Is that so unique? Squarcia asked in surprise, packed comfortably tight in his years of success, totally at home on planes and already bored.

— Unique. Especially because you have never pretended to like me either.

And now they were airborne together, just the pair of them, plus a crew of perfectionists tinkering with dials and buttons, cabin staff to offer whatever luxuries could be fitted on a tray, and, concealed behind a screen, his bearers exchanging the muffled clichés of their collective celibacy.

At last, Buchanan believed, he would meet the men whom he had used to put him where he was.

That night, flying west, a fugitive from the sun, he found one novelty he was able to perform for himself; setting his watch back an hour at a time. Then a most surprising thing happened. He fell asleep. Yes, though it was not yet fully day. And he dreamed of a bus. He had not been in a bus for twenty-two years, yet that's what he dreamed. He is there, right inside. Even so, he is not one of the bus's occupants. By that alchemy of mind when the body has been shed, he is part of what is happening while not being a participant. The last bus, this one, becomes a refugee fleeing through suburban streets. The president has declared a curfew. This is the only bus which ever switches on its yellow lights. By the time the driver has it safely back at a depot the curfew will have brought on darkness.

Inside, the air smells of cheap cigarettes and the fear of three people: a man once young with hair still yellow as the lights; a woman who remembers changing her vote in those evil times when you thought you could be happy at no cost to anyone; and the driver screeching along his nerves, cheeks trembling more than the dangling straps, for he is running two and a half minutes late.

The roadways outside stretch empty shafts into a coal-black labyrinth. Only the footprints of recent passers-by carry the trace of human warmth. One unregistered dog cruises gateways. A hand reaches from a dark room to an open window and slams it shut on the sound of the bus. Bats begin to wheel round the streetlamps, crowding in from roosting places in wild gullies of loungerooms ruined to slums.

Through evening rain the bus tyres sigh and its headlights pick out needles of brilliance in the dusk. Suburbs roar to the despair of passengers without a future who find themselves trapped in a juddering Daumier world of resignation. The woman is contributing to the cigarette-smoked air and the interior lights burn on the gas of fear. The bus is late. This never happens to the last bus.

— They say, says the woman out of the hopefulness of her kind. That it's ordinary people has done this to us. She glances at her hearers, immediately apologetic, not meaning to put too great a load on them, especially the driver hunched under a stress of rules enshrined as the universal truth that the last bus always runs on time. But I say they don't know what they're talking about. She sniffs stoutly.

Another dead suburb lies behind them, cold with the president's benignity since he curtailed dole payments in favour of a meal ticket system to ensure minimum standards of nourishment among the poor and to keep, as it were, in personal touch with them through the requirement that they report to their designated kitchen in person.

— I used to be able to shut my door, she dreams. And close

the curtains of a winter night like this and switch on the heater for I don't know how long and simply bask.

The driver pushes the bus faster so the motor whines. Like a dog in pain, the motor. Windscreen wipers cut rigid arcs of clarity which are instantly corroded by the world. The man who was once young leans forward to speak to her.

— That's the point, he says in a gentle manner of one who has proved his strength. They've got as many clues as we have. And no more.

The driver's skin is terrified by this kind of talk.

The skin listens harder and the sweat of desperation keeps on coming, so his hand wipes his forehead several times.

The woman rings the bell for the light to die. She stands rocking in the bus, hearing neighbours whisper betrayals. She thanks the driver as she steps out and then, holding up her skirt, not caring about the rain or the age of her knees, she runs. Out into the watching evening she runs for the heater she cannot afford to switch on tonight.

President Buchanan woke and accepted a tray of delicacies. He did not smile at Squarcia, who joined him for the meal. When asked whether he would like an in-flight movie and which one, he declined to answer. He opened his mouth only to shovel in more truffles. He had something to think about. Home.

Here he was, a man of sixty and gone ruinously to fat, thinking of home, home being a whole country, the country he acknowledged he knew so little of that what he did know could justly be called next to nothing. Apart from one trip by train up the coast to Gladstone and another, nearly fatal, by car in a failed attempt to reach Paringa, he had never ventured beyond Canberra, plus that strip of closely settled and highly saleable land from Newcastle in the north down to Wollongong in the south, the two industrial ports shipping coal and steel abroad, and between them the colossus of Sydney spreading so wide that it almost linked them with wall-to-wall suburbia. He thought of the country as singular, like a great house he in the splendour of ambition had built to amaze succeeding generations while he lodged in one tiny out-building watching the place mellow and then turn shabby, watching paint peel from gutters, timbers warp, its dignity crack at a single rock thrown by some neighbourly child, watching at sunset when the masonry glowed warm as a woman's breast and at midday when the roof's overhang dropped a dark veil down all the walls he had so lovingly and lustfully seen rise and weather, and at dawn with the cool cleanness of insight picking out the substance of his airy nightmare, etching the unsafe mortar, shafting ruthlessly in through windows without curtains or blinds and showing him the sensational debacle of seven years' life in isolation speaking by telephone to builders, joking with a labourer lugging a ladder which he would leave propped against the east wall till it sagged crooked from waiting for a cyclone to blow it flat where it could lie under a mat of weeds and disintegrate in comfort, as the martins' nest disintegrated to an ooze of phosphorus leaking through virgin plaster of a reception room ceiling, as the water in all fourteen lavatories evaporated, letting the stench of his nation's shit hoot free and out at last from the rushing butting suppression of underground, as the mice finally succeeded in their enterprise of digesting enough insulation from the entire grid of wiring for seventy-two chandeliers to burst simultaneously into flame, and show the world that the whole place had not one saving secret to recommend it, beautiful in a dying flash unredeemed by human affection, not even any furniture to be at risk because the committee of interior decorators had fought themselves to a stalemate and while rival crates of Swedish-contemporary, mock-Sheraton and Bauhaus-clinical lay stacked on wharves round the country till the matter of priorities could be disentangled and, anyway, doomed to stay there by a decimation of wharf labour, chronic unemployment resulting in loss of faith, so even those who were still in work tended never to do any.

A mere seven years had been enough, Bernard Buchanan admitted in his dream as he never would under the guardianship of flashing steel insomnia. And, yes, he fell asleep again. The best he could hope of this foreign place called home was that the ruins might interest tourists, that the preconceptions of archeologists would one day furnish his memorial with all expectable luxuries, even to fornication, and crown his failure with an accolade of extravagance to rival Tiberius or Henri Cristophe, King of Haiti. He woke (perhaps he did wake) to find himself in conversation with the most dangerous of friends and saying humbly, yes Lou, no Lou, read me the news Lou while they bring us some coffee.

— Here's an item you will appreciate, Squarcia suggested putting that face of his, which was still recognizably handsome from the right angles, close enough to the page to bring it into focus. In 1991, he quoted. We reported a remarkable patriotic project undertaken by the East Penrith Boy Scouts. Using only regulation penknives, they carved a woollybutt tree-stump to a lifesized effigy of our beloved leader. This reporter humorously commented at the time that the seated figure had something of a Buddha about him. President Buchanan himself, on being shown photographs, agreed wittily, saying he was delighted and proud to have been made to look so much like a serene antheap. One year later, the scouts celebrated the award of a special presidential medal presented to them as further encouragement to expressions of loyalty. Many of them have since graduated to the president's loyal Watchdogs. . . Now, an even more remarkable development promises to raise their initiative to the status of a miracle. Are you listening to this, Bernard? In the intervening years, termites were found to have infested the tree-stump sculpture and the scouts, fearing that this might have unintentional political overtones, built a fence to screen it from the public. Seven months ago, troop leader O'Rourke reports: When we decided there was no saving the statue, we put it under wraps for fear the story might be misreported! But now he and his scouts need have no fear. A recent inspection showed that the termites have rebuilt the stump as a nest, the wood-fibres mixed with clay and hardened like earthenware. The amazing fact is that, having completely destroyed the scouts' tribute to our leader, the termites rebuilt it exactly as it was. There is now a termite nest in the form of a life-size seated President Buchanan. . . What do you think of that, Bernard? That's enough to gladden your heart, Squarcia said offering the page so the great man could see for himself. A senior ranger of the National Parks Authority, Dr Emmanuel Goldberg, has announced that he is applying to have this remarkable phenomenon certified by the Pope.

— The Pope?

— It's in the paper.

— Another miracle then, Lou? the president yawned, still haunted by some hollowness, the fleeing dark suburbs, the gas-fed lights of fear. Dr Emmanuel Goldberg, eh?

36

The man who had once been young stood in the railway station's concrete emptiness, gazing across at the entrance to subways where, until recent times, youths inspired by high spirits had leapt to try touching the ceiling. A tomb of air big enough for all the families of the family. He was breathing heavily though he had done nothing but sit in a bus and step out of it at the wrong time. Even now the driver might be reporting him to persons in authority.

He used to run screaming across this polished floor when a tiny boy and his father, the bald vulture, swooped to catch him; then, pretending to eat him up, ate him. The rain outside called urgently for silence. He remembered the dog without a collar and hoped it had not been caught. The nervy engine of the bus still whined in his ear. He stood dramatically alone where, an hour before, the great concourse of his fellows hurried for their bolt holes with averted faces. In that tomb of air he was breathing heavily though all he had achieved was to sit in the yellow light of a final bus.

The cleaner turned to stone at the sight of him, opened her mouth though saying nothing but what its openness told on her behalf. She was the last that evening and buttoned into her responsibilities. She might have been preparing an altar, so quiet and absorbed she was. Yet she ignored the solitary intruder and plodded away on the echoes of her heels. For all he knew her stone mouth might still be gaping with shock as she went. When out of sight, her heels continued to be heard. A few moments later the lights switched off. This was part of her commission, switching off lights, first one rank and then the next and the next. The last were left a little later. For a moment she delayed switching them, clear as a spoken warning. He could no longer see or hear the cleaner. Her face, with all feeling shocked from it by human error, lingered as a memory of gaping air. She left the lights in the last rank, inviting him to move away. But when he stood where he was in a space empty of the people it had been built for, these went off too, marooning him in alien silence. The air smelt of prison. Windows showed wet and black with the sky outside except where arc lamps blazed across the street. No heels could be heard. Emptiness sang in his ears as a remote menace approaching. Hollow spaces, big enough for there to be no escape sang with a stridulation he recognized. An armoured vehicle was driving his way; the tone peculiar to its kind, a growl overridden by harmonics like a kettle singing. Closer. Now it circled the carpark, tyres skimming and chuckling on wet asphalt, and slowed for a soldier to shout two syllables along the rainy roadway, then revved away.

This shocked him. Though he did not catch what the voice shouted, its accent was unmistakable: Australian words in a vacancy they had created, sinister as high buildings, cold steel words. We are doing this to ourselves. He pictured the vehicle rain-varnished, headlights sweeping the radius of a circle and picking out lamp posts, marking off their desolate regularity.

We thought of everything but this.

From the men's toilet deep within the station an automatic flush hissed and expired.

The cleaner had said no word. Standing on her reflection, she made a decision and kept it to herself. She knew the law. Everybody knew the law. With her official pass clipped to a pocket, she was accustomed to the empty station and perhaps enjoyed the privilege of inspecting its emptiness. Maybe she loved the litter, tickets and crumpled pie bags, cigarette butts, the abandoned drink cans. And loved the clean arcs of mopping them away. Yet, although her emptiness had been invaded, she breathed the same sterile air as himself, looked him in the eye and said nothing. Then, as if simply reading the time of the next morning's train in his face, walked away on her echoes. The lofty walls built to contain thousands found it too much to hold only him.

A chill rose through his feet. Silence set hard, heavy with the death of public announcements. His pale skin and pale hair reminders of the past, he stood beyond the hour of standing. He was not waiting, he was just tired of moving. Not even rebelling against the curfew, he was sick of having to think of somewhere to go for shelter. He was committing a crime in not thinking of anywhere. Light lay as slabs of white stone let into the floor forever.

The bus driver had been frightened when his passenger refused to get off.

— This is the last stop before we're back in the central city area, he pleaded and peered into rain-darkened streets at the verge of an industrial sector where the poorest people lived in hutches looking across to factory walls and high wire fences displaying private army notices: *Armed Guardians. City Security Enforcement Co. Watchdogs.* Beyond these prohibitions lay yards gravelled with smashed clinkers. The man who had once been young did not get out. He sat where he was in the bus-light with the trembling of the driver's cheeks, the squeal of nerves and the safe world fragile as reflections in a window.

— The next stop is the railway and that'll be closed, the driver objected. Then I knock off for the day.

— I'll get off there, the passenger agreed.

— It'll be shut mate, I tell you, the last train has gone. When I arrive they lock up. Routine.

The coordinated transport service earned much praise, each Rationalization program another proof of efficient planning. This driver in no way out of the ordinary, a simple man whose crime was being two and a half minutes late, a man of basic information with no time to argue, was not an enemy of the state. No one could accuse him of original thought, breathing dead cigarette smoke because unable to afford his own, but firm about the station closing as soon as he arrived. Closure had become ritual and the station was his terminus. He breathed the fear of others, but could not smell his own.

— That's where I'm going, the passenger said in words no more amazing, which amazed them both.

He had stepped from the yellowed smoke into the station's morgue-glow where tall green signboards listed stops no trains would travel to that evening. He stood till his feet drew the cold from the concrete, knees locked. He had faced the cleaner, he had stood in the last chance of a delayed light switch, he had heard an armoured vehicle clashing its steel gears while stone light lay embedded in the floor. But did he learn the lesson his leaders were trying to teach him? No, he was imagining how he might greet other fugitives, the legions of nightdwellers who lived in tunnels. What if the station, already mysterious and enormous with emptiness, turned out to be a common hiding place? Maybe hundreds of grey comrades rustled together for comfort, whispering treasonous plans; even an embryo army, ragged shadows drilling with real firearms. He could not be the only one. His head felt remarkably clear.

But he was the only one. The time had come and gone when people turned their faces to the hills and help had not come. He'd once been young and now he grew cold with knowing that ordinary people out there in tanks shouted Australian words across the wet road.

He thought of bodies falling from helicopters, machinegun bullets smashing into watermelons, radios exploding. He thought of today's badges and premature medals, sub-ranks of citizens not frightened by empty buildings, of vice-deputies above the acting assistants giving orders to the probationary Watchdogs and their squad of temporaries. The man who had once been young was young again, a child shouting for the sake of the multiplying echoes, for love of his own voice, his power to begin a sound and end it. This is my will. Even while the vulture's shadow swooped to gather him into its pain.

The resentment of hiding still keen, his limbs knew better than his head what he must do, so he moved round the lofty emptiness, trying doors. In the morning he'd use a lavatory for concealment, and from there anyone might walk out among the subdued crowds on their way to work. But the night must offer somewhere his pride would allow him to lie down. The doors were locked. Like a remote priestly figure skirting the corners of a cathedral, he applied to the shadows, perhaps kissing images, and backed away from each encounter to hasten to the next; something ceremonial, something purposeful, moving in a clock-wise direction as if his progress were one of meanings.

He came to a cross painted on a door with a brass knob. The first-aid room suggested memories of comfort. He tried the bright squeaking handle and the door swung in on a darkness of human breath. Wary, he whispered: Who is it? He strained to make sense of such thick-smelling silence. His powerful body, alive with emergency, took a step farther. Somebody shut the door behind him. His nerves thrummed in total darkness.

— Hullo? he whispered excitedly.

The dark exploded as a match held close to his face. The bitter chemical stench of it sharp in his nostrils, even the tiny intense heat causing him to recoil. But not far. Some man's body stood right behind. Hands grasped his wrists to pin them against his sides. He let it happen. He measured the strength of that grip and knew he could fell the bloke. In the momentary brilliance, grimy mechanic's fingers held the frail matchstick, raised it to a single ovoid flash beyond: spectacles. The match burned out to a hesitant spark surviving in the charcoal heart, then guttered. But the pressure on his wrists did not slacken at what the light had shown. He stood inert, playing for his future by lack of resistance. Someone slapped his cheek lightly, neatly. With a thrilling flash of anger he knew himself capable of killing. There seemed so little effort the slap might have been gentle, but it stung. He had not experienced such vitality in himself for months. The hands round his wrists, maybe sensing he could break their grip at will, could scarcely help but feel the sinews thicken.

— He's not one of us, a scornful voice hissed.

— Nor one of them, growled the man whose glasses he had glimpsed.

The warm breathing room seemed no part of the chill station.

Indecision gnawed at the dark. Some cold object touched his neck. He started, but it remained steady, rigidly shocking as a knife.

— Shit no, swore the rough voice.

— Okay, from the hissing one. Okay? half-laughing now in contemptuous snorts.

Assent came from a third at the other side of the room. Still the dying spark of a match travelled deep in his mind, crawling into the wood to be buried there. Okay, they said, belonging together but still needing to decide what their policy was to be. Yet they agreed about the information the matchlight showed them: they knew who was to hold his wrists, who to hit his face, who to say nothing but okay and still be a force he must reckon with.

— Lie down where you are. Don't move. Don't make a sound. You're in our way. And we don't like it.

— Fuck you, he thought he replied.

Until the guest worker scheme, the hated Friends of Privilege, he had been employed as a labourer dismantling chemical plants and oil refineries, then replacing the whole system once the installations has been cleaned. At a thousand dollars per seven-day week, he did well at this dangerous and exhausting work, putting in a month at a time and surfing for the next two. A good life. All finished.

— Face down. Shut your eyes. Shut your ears. Move and you're done for. We can't take the risk.

Perhaps they hadn't heard him. Perhaps they thought he said Thank you. Filled with curiosity about himself, released from the ennui of appeasement, he obeyed, a man's breath on his neck smelling smoke-sour, the tiny rub of clothing right beside him. He could have laughed: we did all this when we were kids (diminished jellyfish-faced delinquents in the night of a police trap and himself the only one to break free, the only one to think with fists and heels, lashing out, sprinting and leaping the thicket of broken bottles). He did not even bother to steal a glimpse when dim brown circles on his closed eyelids showed him they were using a torch. Nor when two thuds and a splintering blow were heard, followed by quiet exclamations, almost innocent in their surprise and satisfaction at what had been found. It was part of the game not to look. In the dark of his home city he lay, unafraid of anything.

Glass clinked. Small bottles.

Petty as such criminal offences were, the state, of course, took them seriously. Joy mounted in his heart: first the cleaner, now this. His excitement was such that he had to stifle actual laughter while another thud came and more of the simple wood splintered. Good on you, boys. Just aim a bit higher up the system. His breath came silent and composed.

Did they guess a leader had arrived among them?

The wildness of Australians begins with the land itself. Out where his father came from, you heard blood-stopping snarls at night, huge slaverings. Though you were taught to fear only snakes and spiders, farmers at the foot of the mountain found a bull with its head torn off. What predator tears bulls' heads off? Nothing ought to be taken for granted in so wide and mysterious a terrain. Minutes later, the dim brown light through his eyelids flipped to black.

— The longer you stay there sport, the voice hissed. The safer you'll be.

A doorhandle squealed faintly. He'd known the feel of it in his own hand. Emptiness from the station hall swamped the room. He played by the rules, obedient as a tiger waiting to see if this was a game or dinner. The latch clicked shut, leaving him no other sound than a swish of dragon-wings and a whisper of toothless grannies concocting moral tales. He woke momentarily to the knowledge that this city, not his any longer, had become the stronghold of an enemy who spoke with the voice of neighbours and spied from every street corner. His body settled gratefully again to the shapes of sleep.

He dreamed he was aboard a VIP jet and burdened with the frightful weariness of having his own way, suffering the fear that tomorrow he would, somehow, be seen through, that the world leaders he was soon to meet would sniff him out as an interloper, sneering because he had been born of such parents, the school inspector and the dumplings-cook, because he perched his sandbag elegance on a rusty bicycle and went skimming downhill all the way with half a mind to kill himself by crashing at the bottom.

He opened his eyes, snapped awake by a dull grey crack under the door. He got up to open it on future risks. Pre-dawn light swamped the station hall. He could read names of destinations. The air smelt like damp ashes. He glanced back at the smashed medicine chests and their rifled shelves, then stepped out and closed the door behind him, scorning to wipe his fingerprints off the handle in deference to the times. He was hungry. Desertion could be felt on the skin, and fungus spores swarmed in the air. Piles of defunct services, station names and times stacked in backrooms leaked again into the world as dust. The elation of the previous night crumbled at the edges. He walked towards the toilet he'd heard flushing in the dark. A dictatorship worth its salt, he thought, would surely have troops patrolling such key points twenty-four hours a day. He despaired, in a sense, because there was nobody here to arrest him. Even a fullscale villain seemed beyond us.

The stone slabs of light from the arc lamps remained unchanged in shape but now lay thin as milk on the terrazzo. He walked to the spot, still warm, where the cleaner had stood, her courage mingled with his. He crossed a barren space to the doorway marked *MEN*.

Plagued since childhood with fastidiousness, he inspected all twenty cubicles before choosing the least filthy. Everything was on a decline. He shut himself in and settled to wait, perhaps for hours. The chipped walls were daubed with shit. The back of the door bore witness to new urgencies: those crude sexual messages from a few years ago almost entirely supplanted by impotence of another kind, covert anger. References to the president of the republic ranged from sly to murderous. On one wall were the words *I want to die.*

He remembered lying on his back in grass watching clouds beyond the trees, their lightness floated gorgeously ripe and unlikely in a dark blue sky. He remembered the dog he owned as a child, teaching him lessons in trust. He heard memory-waves crashing against a cliff and wild cackling from a pair of sea eagles gliding high above him. Youth's unbearable fullness cheapened the rest of his life. He clenched his fist to punch the wall at the exact moment he heard shuffling footsteps enter. And stop. A metal bucket clanked. The footsteps retreated, leaving the bucket where it stood. A husky voice explained that some bloke was in there because I saw his boots under the door. Not to be trapped in a lavatory, on the defensive, the man with yellow hair pressed the flush and flung open the door with a resounding bang. As he reached the washbasins the entrance filled with a giant wearing a humble uniform and cap who opened his mouth but was given no time to speak.

— Were you sent to help with the ladders? the intruder asked sharply, flicking his wet hands.

— When was that? the giant fumbled nervously.

— When do you think!

— I haven't heard.

Then a rat person behind the large man sidled from hiding long enough to say.

— Ladders? They was speaking about ladders, I seem to remember.

— You stay here, the uniform ordered the suspect, thoroughly uncertain. I'll go and ask.

— Stay in the shithouse? Wrong man, mate. I've got a job to do. Unless you want to wear the consequences, you'd better let me get on with it. If I get caught in here I'm going to use your name. What is your name?

And he walked straight at them so they had no choice but move to one side.

— If some guy comes asking about ladders I'll be out at the enquiries office.

— Righto then, said the rat picking up his bucket and sloshing hot water over the floor.

— There's a warrant out for coves caught writing on lavatory walls, the giant informed the mirror, baring his teeth and admiring them.

37

— If I think of anything, said Bernard Buchanan. Then it is true. Even a whole country.

— All systems set? the senior scientist asked, his flat tone itself exciting the staff on duty.

— All systems set.

The director stood a moment longer at one window knowing their eyes were on him now. He gazed out across moonlit desert from which a sea had receded ten million years previously: a strangely comforting thought. He swung on his heel, white coat flapping open a moment. and smiled tensely around the big control room. These were his friends, these colleagues.

— When you are ready, then, he decided.

The Pacific Ocean rose from the night, calm and colossal, shouldering against the rotation of earth. Wind and current drove in conflict with the great westward-moving wave till it broke into separate heads of water travelling as a coronet. According to plan, the arc widened till its separate parts reached land, one wave targeted to the north on the tiny island of

Tuavaleva, and one to the north-west among reefs and atolls. Heading south-west, another passed between Tasmania and the Australian mainland. One struck Eden. One narrowly, and with fine accuracy, missed Port George, to sweep in across paddocks and thunder among forest trees, cutting the road from town to Vengeance Harbour prison. Bright dark waters lapped the cliff like a huge placid beast that cannot imagine what terror it brings, reaching up to clasp weatherboard dwellings and bundle together a clutter of old cars. In a fisherman's cottage (the man out at sea on his trawler riding that freak fullness of tide) his wife lay sleeping, up to her eyebrows in migraine. Children banged on the door with the fun of having seen once-in-a-lifetime waves lap the headland in moonlight and break at the foot of their own front steps. As the mother heard screams and bangs through her swathe of pain, slushing down the passage fully armed with energy to fix a whole clan of malingerers, she explained to her soaking brood: The sea's getting up a bit! And led them clear just when her house caved and floated away on the smooth muscular current. She had no time to be pleased with discovering a cure for migraine.

In the bay at Eden the devastation was far more serious. Ships at anchor rode high and drifted shorewards to the limit of their hawsers, swinging across wharves despite the nightwatch yelling hoarse helpless bellows of alarm, swinging far enough inland to clout the top off a church steeple. Town drunks told later how they stuck their heads out from under tables just in time to gag on a harbourful of brine and watch stiff black oiltanker and woodchip freighter shadows sweep above them, clashing together in a cloud of moonlit bubbles. The shockwaves belled so deafeningly that sharks, being animals unadapted for surviving shocks, keeled over, instantly struck dead. Powerlines spat sizzling bolts along the ripples; treetops still clear of the tide exploded in fire. The great beast, indifferent, engrossed, beached itself. The swell of humped back glittered silver, curve of clean spine rolling majestically.

Bernard Buchanan, under a pale blanket, turned in the recliner provided on his aircraft, sleepless now as usual, but still plagued with dreams.

Bodies in dead earnest could be seen cartwheeling through ecstatic clarities; and deep down, the rigid alignment of fences wavered. A lighthouse rotated underwater to scan crowds of fish dumb with admiration, the beam dodging among seaweed, while ships hovered like dirigibles round a television tower blipping hectic red warnings.

At this moment, IFID directors sat amid the New York feast of lunch, satisfied that a new element of their world armaments strategy, and a key element at that, should be in place by now, the puppet ruler safely airborne on the longest possible route out of the way and unable to interfere. So, indeed, Bernard Buchanan's plane floated along, jet engines idling. He need only imagine a catastrophe, he assured himself, and persons in Canberra must summon the courage for putting through a call to confess what had begun happening back home.

Once released to catch up with the drag of the moon and resume its normal cycle, the wave boiled down the re-emergent land. Ocean-going vessels which had peacefully drifted in over those warehouses and clouted that church, plunged and whirled, turning turtle, disgorging bellyloads of crude oil and shredded wood, shrugging off crates of luxury cars while thundering across the new naval dockyard, bulldozing it clear of every usable scrap of heavy equipment. Visiting stingrays flapped, caught in an aquarium of Council Chambers. The town's only suburb trundled out to sea. And a lonely crabber in the bay with paltry sail and oar whom, the poet says, poverty drives out to sea and cyclones drive ashore, found himself driven ashore in a place where they hung leis round his neck beneath the shade of palmtrees and serenaded him with ersatz music till they found he hadn't a cracker to spend and threw him in jail to reconsider his priorities.

— Mr President? the most famous voice in the world brayed personally out of Bernard Buchanan's airborne videophone. This is Mr President speaking, har har, old son, we *love* you.

The tiny screen showed a shot of the White House with Stars and Stripes fluttering, and then that household face, little quivers making the chin vulnerable, eyes bovine with kindliness, teeth distressingly too young.

— We love you, the voice droned, facial muscles out of sync. Don't try to thank us. Leave it till you feel less emotional, we understand unspoken gratitude. Isn't this show just something! But I have to put in my word for your Eden (is it?) folk who are giving their lives for the Free World. Bernie, I shall offer a posthumous citation for each and every one of them. Tell it to the nation as a comfort to the families, we love the families of those courageous pioneers, won't you, so just for the present let's leave it at that because we shall see each other in the Maldives tomorrow, we love you all. Click.

Out through a porthole the moon appeared groggy after its first serious upset in 4,500,000,000 years.

Searchplanes flew low through a grey dawn over the New South Wales coast, alert for flares, scanning smudged angry waters punctuated by still-glowing trees. Yes, and this very scene now flashed on Buchanan's video as Roscoe Plenty checked in with the details, sounding argumentative, blustering about compensation, some public outcry, loss of faith, a whole gamut of commonplaces, plus demanding to know what those Yanks had to say for themselves.

— Citations for the dead! the thin wolf shouted though he rarely ventured to raise his voice these days of his coming to power, and to all appearances enjoyed seducing himself with the glory of it. Are their families to make do with citations in place of a settlement?

— I don't see, an immobile Luigi Squarcia purred from his bedside chair while the Chief Minister was left hanging, awaiting a reply. How Roscoe can fail to rejoice. Obviously our own Paringa base has countered a Soviet experiment.

— This is a triumph, Buchanan roared back. A triumph you owe to me. We shall accord them a state funeral. Please arrange the ceremony at the national crematorium.

Roscoe Plenty glowered black and grey, bloating and shrivelling with bellicose fear, raging as courage and caution ran along parallel tracks.

— What I mean is that the Cultural Centre disaster complicates matters.

Silence.

— Tell me, the president invited quietly. About the Cultural Centre disaster.

— The whole place collapsed during the gala opening. Last night. Some hours before the wave hit Eden. I have summoned Penhallurick to explain.

— You've no need to hang about on the line, Buchanan sighed, breathing one of the heavier of the ten million breaths he would commit in a year. You may report to the nation that my flight is proceeding uneventfully, that I am safe and as comfortable as can be expected away from responsibilities so dear to my heart. You may also quote me as expressing grief over these tragedies, though on no account are they to be mentioned in the same bulletin. Keep them well apart, Roscoe. I won't have inferences drawn to mislead gullible people. Is that clear? You must see to this matter personally, just as I would if I were there.

— Why. . . ?

— God damn it, you idiot, do as you're told for once without holding an inquisition!

Bernard Buchanan slammed the phone down.

The Buchanan Cultural Centre, that marvel of structural engineering, occupied most of a city block, where once the Imperial Indoor Baths & Hygiene Facilities had stood, plus a miscellany of small businesses. The main feature of the building was a river which flowed through the lobby, small as rivers go, but far from ordinary. This one was computerized. The technique, explained to agog visitors clamping portable guide sets to their ears, used a remarkable advance in molecular science pioneered at Paringa to program the river so it would flow in reverse. Yes, like a film wound back, water climbed majestically, dream water yearning for a lost paradise, water rippling with the serene song of the phoenix up from its grand circuit of the ground floor, through ducts cast in bronze like Antonio Gaudi fishgills to the level above, thence in serpentine solemnity to the level above that. And so through all nine floors the spiralling flood defied nature, lifting its head as a paean to the new age, a mystery inexplicable in any but the most abstruse equations. When the mounting water reached the roofgarden it swirled, lifelike, between embankments thick with plants, and foamed along a tumble of channels constituting a work of art labelled Social Nature, which also featured ride-them-yourself motorcycles and piano-smashing facilities, to cascade through an avenue of treeferns (high above where a stainedglass rose once grew from the rottenness of 1901) and eventually gush into a capacious cistern from whence the waterfall was to drive built-in generators and provide power for airconditioning the Centre. The president knew this from the beginning; he had seen plans. The river, leaving behind that semblance of nature humanized with Kawasakis and dismembered Bösendorfers, drained down a conduit system to operate sewerage treatment works for the entire locality, and so eventually to the sea. Buchanan had declined an invitation to declare the complex open. He refused to let them re-schedule the ceremony just for his convenience because, he replied, if once you begin saying yes to the buttering of your ego where will it end?

In the two theatres the artloving public mingled with publicityloving artists to relax on plush seats, all the more satisfied for knowing that a dangerously large body of water slid forever uphill out there in the lobby and above their heads, a paradigm for man's Godlike quest to control the natural order, to part the Red Sea, to quell the storm, to survive death. Only those visitors who dared the final climb to the roofgarden had any idea that the sole hope of escape might be by motorcycle, the bravest of them revving machines and speeding round the track provided (could the great man believe what he saw?) then out across a glassy chasm down which they might observe, nine levels beneath, interval crowds at the bar never thinking to look up for a flying Cassandra, so buried were they by illusions of pleasure. *Remember me remember me* sang Dido in those unforgettable phrases to Audience One seated again and soggy with tears for their own domesticity, not hearing Purcell shift the cosmos a degree on its axis (much less the director of Paringa Research Facility), any more than Audience Two in Medea's kitchen saw the final curtain as a beginning of life: how the small boys got up from their bloody bier and raced for the shower without the least haunting of murder, how they dressed in the ordinary clothes of real dying, combed their hair neat as a corpse's and called Goodnight goodnight! to stray backstage crew, two boys in jeans at the stagedoor horsing around while waiting for a taxi to take them home to the anonymity of the absolute motel, unaware that, above, water bubbled upward as if this were its natural dignity and the flying motorcyclists looked down to catch a snapshot of danger among echoing *remember me*s from the twin theatres, plus another myth welling in the tears of suburban regrets. Once across the chasm that might otherwise be thought a skylight and back on the solid concrete roof, daring tricksters followed the contours of the building to its peak where they launched out, the only logic being a ride down the thermals, a hairfreezing descent on solid air as slippery as ice, out to where an unlettered populace hammered and bolted the world together, harvested and waxed it, dressed it in the ridiculous innocence of fashions, casting nets to catch the risen sun and pushing the cogs by hand to guarantee the advent of winter. The inevitable catastrophe of transparent intentions sped down from the tower and those with a gift for hazard felt the firmness of their way into reality and the joy of it, while the river inside the palace of art accumulated at the top, awaiting its release. The audience, already hanging bright pictures of their misunderstandings, colour-coordinated grief for the bedroom, Dido in matching purple, would have been frankly incredulous of the motorcyclists except as stunt riders, or the unpaid tumbling from the sky on machines more valuable than themselves and promising a bonanza of re-usable parts, they would have said but what's the pay-off? they would have said this is not reasonable, they would have said I don't see the comfort or there's no future in it if you ask me. Out across a Perugino sky the daring made their escape, and of course a few did weaken and look down, did see nothing beneath them, turned turtle in the madness of doubt, certain now to crash among applauding crowds, their loss of nerve surviving as the foolish smiles of those who wish to be acceptable again among the unenlightened. Meanwhile the lovely show drew to its close. Aeneas would never come back to show his muscular thighs, Dido had no more top notes left, and Belinda the eternal neatener was left to cope. Lights switched on in the galleries only to be switched off later; conversations animated the meretricious glitter of jewels. The motorcyclists flew unnoticed through the darkness outside, accelerating down their impossible quest. In the suffocating spaciousness of foyers mouths glued with chocolate smirked sticky marshes of opinion, exchanging discouragements in the matter of string tone and a flaw across the cyclorama would you believe. Dido's message had missed the heart and was talked about as A-flats by persons with an ear for gossip and little else, even the photograph of hell opposite the box office came in for a few appreciative lectures on tonality. Who cared that, outside, happy fruitpickers slept exhausted as factoryworkers from the cannery, that firemen keeping awake with a hand of poker thought Henry Purcell was most probably that arsonist facing committal to trial in the morning. The palace of art burbled stock exchange nonsense while silverfoxes and martens moved with their vicious teeth among huge moths whose wings floated from brassieres and waistcoated slugs bald as a slug, milling in their gilded cage, for a children's book illustrator of horrors to show them for what they were.

Such was the first fling in the Buchanan Cultural Centre, that astounding waterworks, a twentieth-century Wilhelmshöhe, when technicians and scientists out in the desert clapped at the success of their own exclusive show. Within a few moments the monitors had recorded all the data needed to prove their calculations had been correct. Till the switches were thrown again and they let out a collective sigh of accomplishment.

During that hiccup in the solar system when the ocean itself hesitated, pushed out a tidalwave, and sank back to its customary rhythm, natural rivers were left flowing downhill without a worry. But the delicate equations lifting the river of art scattered frantically on control screens. Operators at the Buchanan Centre juggled with scrambled formulae while the waterflow died and the rising river trailed a lingering trickle behind it from the eighth to the ninth floor, leaving its bronze and concrete ducts forlorn as public fountains switched off at night to save wastage.

While schoolboy actors escaped in the taxi with a smudge of greasepaint behind their ears and a last slick of carmine where their throats were slit, some troubled employee phoned the construction engineer in person and put the question.

— Well if you wish to interrogate me on a professional matter, Sir William answered crossly, sitting up in bed and glaring at the phone as he spoke into it. Make sure you have your facts right. And ring me back in office hours.

He hung up on the caller while lofty foyers filled with torn-ticket holders debouched from comfortable illusions to assess what they had purchased for the price, while a river not yet acknowledged as being up there still in that reservoir designed to carry a passing flow but now gushing full of too much inverted water, churned as a solid mass.

The motorcyclists landed in a puff of rubbersmoke and, bumping across town with *escape* branded on their brows, survivors of air made solid, missed the spectacle of flying water. High at the top of the building concrete floors gave way. The colossal jackhammer exhaled a gasp of release audible a kilometre away and shot down the shaft, demolishing intermediate levels, knocking all obstructions before it, to leave the shell clean and glossy. Even while a freak wave rippled across the Pacific towards Eden, the Cultural Centre's computerized river smashed through floors in descending numbers, each going off with a detonation which ought to have been heard through the trumpeted opinions below, but somehow was not. And even the screams of those who felt an inexplicable thunder from the ground could not alarm the majority who knew no possibility of disaster, who brayed reassurances and reminisced at the top of their range about a similar mystery at Monte Carlo in '89, or was it in '93? till the compacted debris of luxuries squashed them flat at a single blow, driven by a violent second day of creation when indeed the waters were divided from the waters, those which were under the firmament from those which were above the firmament. So it was that, while the president flew on towards the Maldives as yet unaware of the tragedy, Sir William Penhallurick also, tucked in bed by the loving Alice, enjoyed a peaceful night's sleep, never guessing he would wake in the morning to the delightful surprise of a new contract to build the same place all over again.

The First Convocation of World Leaders, bringing together seventy-one heads of state, was to be held in the Maldive Islands. After this, a summit had been arranged for the eight IFID-owned, or at least IFID-dominated, nations. Then Buchanan was faced with a third engagement, on his way home, a stop-over to sample the hospitality of Prince Haupoupou of Tuavaleva, a fraternal courtesy. Squarcia thought that on this one occasion Dorina, with her childhood memories of murdered school-friends, might enjoy the function and agree to join him, flying out from Sydney as the president left the Maldives and meeting him there. Dorina, for her own reasons, said she would.

At the enquiry counter the clerk put down the phone to terminate a call from the lowest rank of railway worker, an unspeakably earnest illiterate call, a whining call to demand approval, begging for notice to be taken.

— Are you the fellow waiting for the ladders? he asked an approaching stranger. You've taken your time haven't you? Just stand aside and I'll phone round when I can spare a moment.

The station hall had come alive with employees, exclusive as a club. The man who defied the curfew was struck by a ticket-seller's artificial manner of counting and checking her new ticket stock; she might do nothing else all day perhaps, just count and check and enjoy being seen at this important privilege. A porter pushed his baggage trolley which, when it had been unloaded, he would push the other way with the same unction. The upper ranks at their desks constantly snatched up and cast down their telephones in a theatre of urgency, pausing only to consume mugs of tea that filmed their watery eyes with steam. Each person was one of an elite and his busy-ness a condition beyond moral evaluation. Outside in the street, screened off by glass, crowds craned necks to look in. Faces washed grey by still-falling rain breathed cold fog. Chests pushed against the doors, not impatiently, not even willingly, but as a result of the slow anonymous crush behind. These citizens lacked the railway staff's easy manner, being a class who knew preferment at work depended upon feeding regular morsels of betrayal to an

Internal Security agent; a class familiar also with the problem of deciding who might be such an agent, and accepting the answer: Whoever behaves as if he knows something about you which you would rather hide. These were people already guilty of promulgating so many lies about one another to individuals who never dared dispel the suspicion they were the right ones to receive such intelligence that all integrity had long since been sold for seldom-eventuating favours or to avoid the implementation of unauthorized threats. They had become, as perhaps never before, interdependent.

Then the man who had once been young glimpsed a face he recognized and would not forget: the woman from the last bus, her features moulded by worry. He saw her, but she could not yet see him. Had something in his fatalism and his ready agreement that ordinary people had done this to us told her he would see the journey through, right to the terminus? Had she been sure of all but his survival while she'd smoked two cigarettes and gossiped about her heater? She could not know he stood at the enquiry desk waiting to join the crowd again and shuffle away to another curfew crisis. Or what if she had come to denounce him? What if this balancing on tiptoe were eagerness, the thrill of a hunter armed with authentic evidence that he had criticized the state?

Military police arrived from inside the station and marched in pairs across the echoing hall, metal caps on their boots clicking reminders of folk dances. They synchronized the unlocking of doors, then stepped back to supervise the workers who walked forward as a society, dense, sober, no longer wishing to get in.

— I shall phone round when I can spare a moment, the clerk repeated. He tapped his pen irritably to show he wasn't accustomed to inefficiency.

She spotted the fugitive immediately. She remembered him clearly in the yellow bus light. She heard again her heresy that they say it's ordinary people has done this to us. He could be an agent, with that hair of his. (He smiled.) At this moment she saw he had not informed on her and that he knew she had not informed on him. The day swarmed round. She was not bothered by the jostling. Her shoulders drooped and she turned to push against the tide till she was back on the street. She walked away in the rain, not caring any more than before, when she ran bare-kneed.

A railway official in cap and brass buttons, such as Bernard Buchanan remembered porters wearing when he was a child and therefore obligatory in the country of his nostalgia, approached and asked Are you the chap who wants to see me? He replied that he was, his pride hurt by his own voice. He needed to remind himself this was the daytime: that the night had been survived, the night of having his face slapped awake. And now he felt a tremendous disappointment at what patience had brought.

— So you haven't the money to buy a ticket for your train to work? the official enjoyed being patronizing as he led him away. Naturally we have a service available to suit your needs. Why else are we here? It's no trouble, he added as he installed himself behind a desk. All I need is your signature and citizenship number. Show me your ID card. Thank you.

So, a chit signed for and himself back under the wing of benevolent authority, he took possession of as much liberty as he was allowed and walked away along the platform to await a train bound for anywhere, it didn't matter. He saw, in a familiar flash of disgust, how reduced he was by the Depression. We have all begun to look the same, he realized in a fury of cold wind: men with shorn hair and simple clothes, women in skirts too long and dirt-green. From the darkening gloom he recalled the fancydress hats and beads of so few years ago, men with hair in tresses and girls puffing theirs to fluffy balls, a jostle of mixed races, the ostentatious hedonism, thunderous music, juveniles kissing in the street (himself among them) and sitting on public steps for the casual pleasure of belonging. He looked up. Sky, between the awning of this and the next platform, waned the colour of an aged sick body.

— Lost your job have you? wheezed a neighbouring skeleton, rattling with laughter in an undertone. He pointed to the chit. Had plenty of them in my time; and never paid for a one, he confided, having first looked about in case he might be overheard.

— Well I've got a collection, I've got thousands, the man who had cheated the curfew retorted sarcastically, so repelled was he by the skeleton's cringing manner. I'm going to build a house of them. Go and play golf.

With this, he turned his attention to the far platform where a train hummed ready to depart amid whistleblasts and attended by clanking motor trolleys; the carriages silent and shut. Boy soldiers stood in line facing outwards, barely strong enough to hold up their men's weapons. He could see past them to rows of faces sealed behind glass, the faces of Friends of Privilege being sent to a housing camp. One fellow stared back at him, black eyes burning, black face contorted with an unheard shout. Between them, rain streaked down and disappeared among the ballast stones; grubby streaks dribbled on the side of the cars. This was a daily sight. The soldiers were there to protect them from public abuse.

— See him! rattled the skeleton. Won't settle down, will he? He won't, he snuffled, merry with racial supremacy.

The man who had once been young wished he could cover his mud-blond hair and unlive the life of acceptable blood.

Has a single shot been fired? President Buchanan had asked in his first telecast to the nation after the state of emergency was declared. This is not, he boasted, any South American free-for-all, or a North American shoot-out, this is not cold communism with ice-bound concentration camps, or any Asian riot or African headhunt. This is calm rational acceptance of a necessity we regret having forced on us by the world crisis reflected as an economic plateau at home. My government doesn't like imposing the state of emergency any more than you enjoy being restricted by it. These are tough decisions we are taking. But we know you want us to take them. We have faced emergencies of this scale before. We've suffered. We suffered in 1894, in 1915, in 1929, in 1942. It is not uncommon. We stuck together and we won through. The Labor leader in parliament has called it a backyard operation. All right, Mr Robinson, go ahead. I don't mind that. Let's accept it. I'm not ashamed of that. Let's keep it in the backyard, then we are sure of controlling our destiny.

— Have you got a smoke for an old digger? the skeleton begged with another wheezing snigger. And tugged at his sleeve.

He did not reply. He scarcely heard through his fascination for knowing what it might be like inside that train, to have come among people who hate you for coming. Strangers like this had taken over his job on the shut-downs. He owed them his present destitution. Here they were again. Not their fault. Strange country. He felt like calling, to incite the shouting one to break out, the black man who that minute began forcing a passage away from his window, through the carriage full of packed foreigners brought in because, unlike Australians, they might be expected to accept their pay and not spy on the work they were given to do. For them, there was no advantage to be milked from such knowledge. A laser installation, nuclear weapons, a torture centre, a chocolate factory... what would it matter?

The Friends of Privilege were guarded by highschool recruits preoccupied with the silky beginnings of moustaches and with anxiety that their voices might not be as deep as their fathers', who either did not hear the muffled shouts from inside the train or paid no heed for fear of breaking ranks, for fear of some crisis plunging at them, diving down the safe burrow of simulated manhood, routing them, whelp-like and frantic-eyed. They must stand at attention until they fainted if need be. Fainting was the only escape from fear. And fear assailed them on all sides. They feared the crowds staring across with that homicidal desperation of the unemployed. They feared the automatic rifles and their own imperfect training. They feared the power to kill, as they lusted to try it out.

The train resolved this problem by lurching forward and tackling the rheumatic difficulties of its task. Squeaking and growling, it crawled along the line. The silently crying rebel, now at the door, beat his head against the glass when he found no handle on the inside.

The man who had cheated the curfew forgot his chit. Forgot even why he was here and not over there. As the locomotive collected tired forces and dragged its muffled morose freight, rolling out to a destiny of sorts, he ran. But nobody ran in those days. Running is something we have rediscovered since. The skeleton caught at his sleeve to save him, but he could not be stopped. His coat flapped open, he ran. Commuters stared. Newspapers were folded away and spectacles put on not to miss the sight. He leaped down to the rails, sprang across and up on the next platform, down again at the far side and up. He poised, confronting the soldiers who trembled between him and the creeping train. They recognized him: he was what they had been waiting for.

A woman let out a penetrating scream. Grief and anger hung in the huge cavern of the station among dancing motes of forgotten destinations, after a moment's lapse echoing back from underpasses to the suburban lines, the tunnels mouthing anguish.

38

Bars of golden sunlight shone horizontally through the cabin of his aircraft as the president of Australia awoke. At last he had emerged from that extended night. He looked down at the dim infinite opal of the Indian Ocean. He felt better already. Quite as if the worst of something ill-defined had passed.

— We will be landing in two hours Your Excellency, the captain came, deferentially, to inform him. Our flight has progressed very well, we're making perfect time. We've had a tailwind.

— Don't tell me, Buchanan retorted. What height we're flying at. I don't wish to know.

The president laughed and the captain laughed with him.

— Takes a special quality in a man to fly these things, he explained to Squarcia as soon as the fellow had gone back to his cockpit. Lack of imagination.

Then the steward arrived with velvet tread to suggest serving breakfast.

— Lou, Buchanan asked a long while later, not looking at him, looking instead out of the window, down to the grey film of air not yet touched by the warmth bathing him. What is the score on Tuavaleva?

Squarcia understood when to tell what he knew and when he could get away with evasions. Now was a moment for telling.

— Prince Haupoupou, he munched the last of his toast which allowed him generous pauses for chewing and swallowing. Is making a serious mistake. He has declined to attend the IFID meeting.

— So I'm to twist his arm while I tell him what went on, am I?

— Bernard you underestimate your greatness as usual. Modesty is your sole vice. So powerful an effect will your presence have, all you need do is arrive. You don't need to say anything. You will be a sign.

— The prince has been made an offer by IFID, is that it? And he might jump the wrong way?

— He will understand what your visit means.

— And you think it is acceptable that I don't?

— It is essential for your sake that you don't. We have to protect your impartiality. As it is, you haven't any ulterior motive of your own. You can be seen to arrive in the spirit of pure friendship. Nobody doubts your skill at diplomacy, nor your ability as an actor: our greatest actor, our pre-eminent diplomat. But your genius lies beyond those things. Beyond and above them. Any man might negotiate a deal. But you are, in yourself, a presence, a declaration. . .

— Bullshit, the president murmured, gratified nonetheless. Answer me one thing, he continued staring far down at the world in its own shadow. What may the consequences be if I change my mind. I mean the consequences for us, for Australia?

— That I can answer, Squarcia admitted, taking a last bitter mouthful of coffee. A first-strike weapons base on our soil, probably the north-west coast up past Broome. Would you like me to show you specifications?

— Don't bother.

— But you are so far in, would it make much difference if things came to that?

Buchanan glanced at the eleven-thousand-metre drop beneath him. The aircraft sailed on, held aloft by nothing but its own momentum.

— I shall look forward, he answered eventually. To seeing Dorina, in any case, at Tuavaleva.

Someone had screamed. Was it to Dorina's despairing insight that the vault of the railway station rang? Had she known all along where this would end? But no, surely the woman he glimpsed was younger, yes, as she struggled against a ticket collector, wrestling, wriggling, finally being forced to the ground and sat on.

Squarcia got up, obligingly, seeing the master wished to be left with his thoughts.

— Do you remember Lavinia Manciewicz, Bernard? Well her sister, not the fat one who came to Roscoe's dinnerparty, but the nosey little journalist for the *Sydney Courier*, went to the station to report on a Friends of Privilege train setting off for Vengeance Harbour. Just a hunch of hers that something was going to happen. It did. As the train was moving out, she realized her husband was one of the elect. She had no idea. They arrested him minutes after she left home. I remember, when I first caught sight of her once at the races, she looked rather pretty.

— Why was he arrested? Buchanan asked hollowly from the sink of knowing everything.

— All Aborigines have been. On your orders. Those, that is, who have failed to take advantage of free transport to Alice Springs and the new Arabana Homeland.

Squarcia made, now, a more definite move to leave the president in peace. A pudgy hand restrained him.

— She screamed, did she, and created a scene?

— I shall never fathom the depths of your insight, Your Excellency.

— Court! Stephanie fired the threat back at them, livid and fearless. Court, what for?

— We shall have to lay a charge, the employees in their sweaty uniforms explained as they held her down. Everything must be done by the book, or where would we be?

— Where you are now, she retaliated. Whatever you do you'll be hopeless. Her struggles erupted afresh.

Half-watching crowds, drawn by the magnet of rebellion, felt the rekindling of an intoxication they had all but forgotten. Rain rained out there on the lines, wet footprints muddied the platforms. Then came the alarm of a running man running their way; yet with his giant breaths their own blood stirred and a past reopened more brightly still, a hillside's bleached grass, a procession of monumental sunny clouds floating silently overhead, gumleaf smoke stung eyes acrid with yearning, they heard forgetfulness clatter in antique oily machinery and joyful explosions bang from a quarry as doors banged in a breeze because the house was not locked even at night and lights were left burning in every room so you could walk where you pleased as good as day. Long silences had calloused the inner ear since they last heard a woman courageous enough to scream aloud.

— Now then Miss, a senior ticket collector advised. He produced a notepad. He knelt to speak to her with that confidential treachery of his ilk. Calm down.

— Put this in your report, she dared. Still she wriggled (while the young lad felt wild spasms of lust as he defeated her), and spat in his face.

The man who had rediscovered running knew, if his courage equalled hers, the rashest of risks would pay off.

— You've got her, he yelled, charging on them, huge with encouragement. I've been chasing her for two hours. She gave me the slip again. Come along Mary, I said I'd catch up with you. And reached for her, taking her by the wrist, his gesture so possessive the younger assailant sprang clear, fists clenched and racing blood diverted to another kind of antagonism. Reached for her and took hold of her. Stand back please, he requested quietly. How would you like to be stared at? Mary, everything is organized at the hospital. I don't want any more trouble. With his free arm he swept the bystanders aside.

The ticket collector helped himself up by pushing with spread hands against his thighs. He wiped the spittle off his face, flushed as it was. He recognized authority in the stranger's manner but knew he ought to challenge him. And would have done so had he not been a man of his time. Was he to commit himself to a decision? Was he to ignore the fact that this person had all the earmarks of a police agent? Hierarchies existed, he knew, with strictly graded privileges of taking no action. Was there more to this than met the eye? Yes, apparently so, because the spitting woman did not behave like a rescued person in that she resisted the new arrival more hysterically than ever, making her rescue as difficult as possible.

She was furious because everybody stared.

The life of the great terminus stilled, witnesses cast in steely light, crystalline runnels of rain frozen on faces, a child's tongue numb against its icecream, porters arrested mid-stride, a newspaper's headlines stamped on air between the vendor and a lady passing up her bright Buchanan coins, the memory of a black man's face contorted with desperation, and the traditional four-sided clock having uttered its famous *chack* was heard to withhold the anticipated *chunk.*

The moment wavered.

The young woman's rescuer lifted her to her feet and, in case her resistance might give station staff the break they needed to collect their wits, half-carried, half-frogmarched her away, stretching the isolation of their walk together to a pretence of casualness, looking down at her and not seeing the amazed loathing of her expression, only her eyes as liquid gold and the bold arch of eyebrows. Then fresh awareness of danger and how urgent their situation had become, of his own vulnerability as well as hers, inspired him to repeat himself.

— I don't want any more trouble, Mary.

So the crowd sighed with knowing for sure that her name was Mary. Mary became a reassurance solid enough to send them on their way to work, to release the famous *chunk,* to acknowledge the coins as adequate payment for predictable blandishments, to muffle a black man's cry, to allow tears their way of falling. Nearby fringes of the crowd, having edged closer to eavesdrop, blocking the way while making certain to face various random directions so they could not be implicated as part of the disturbance, now shuffled off to the platform gate, gleaning what was said there.

— She spat at him, the bitch, the junior still gasped with excitement from the tussle, retrieving his fallen cap.

— She shouldn't be on the loose, the ticket collector confirmed, shutting his notepad at last.

— She shouldn't, the junior agreed.

— Who's going to answer for her next outburst? the ticket collector grumbled, dusting his knees, banging the dust off, to punish himself for not doing better than he had. He then retired to his post to resume his duties, while the young bloke, cap tilted, swaggered to check when their next train might be due. Grey air swirled around the station, the fragments of enlightened ideas reduced to drizzle drifting in across platforms and compelling passengers to cower for shelter: except for a woman of sixty-five or ninety-five wearing bright scarves and chunky jewellery of oriental design. Quite at ease in her gaudy outfit, she watched the one referred to as Mary resisting help, watched the public fade back to routine safety, commuting once more from dreary lodgings to dreary labour, the uniforms busy putting finishing touches to their demonstration of ineptitude, plus, all the more strikingly for these things, new life giving a spring to that one receding man's step, watched the couple walk away past the four-faced clock, among cheap raincoats dripping and crackling, past military police. She watched them till they were safely clear, through the main doors. Then she began her own, hardly less sensational, passage in their wake.

The traffic was almost as intense as during the symphonic days before the Emergency. He and she walked in their electrical fields of attraction and repulsion without speaking. They crossed the street where, the previous night, an armoured car had been heard stopping and some soldier shouted in Australian. Reaching the other kerb they shared the urge to walk faster, the horror of how close they had each come to falling into the state's clutches now chilling them; the face of the city ahead, for all its disfigurement, still a kindly face. Then huge pounding steps were running in pursuit. They heard the thud thud thud as a strange drum, the beat of boots solid with righteousness and timed to the asthmatic breaths of a racehorse at full tilt: another person who ran when running had been forgotten. No fugitive would achieve this even rhythm. The hunter was heard to run on his heels not his toes, confident with the importance of his mission. This was the run of a man in uniform who need not fear being mistaken for quarry. This was an accuser. This was the giant from the lavatories, refreshed by news.

— Hold on sport, he demanded, charging past, hoisting his body round and barring their way.

Involuntarily the woman's hand went out to her rescuer.

— Them ladders, the giant announced with satisfaction. We found the bloke supposed to help you. You had better come back right away. Raindrops pearled the hairs of his woollen jacket, beautiful enough for a Van Eyck grandee. He hunched his immense shoulders with childlike pleasure.

Light rain rained. Traffic cruised reluctantly past. A policeman watched from outside the station in case an opportunity arose for him to intervene.

— How do you keep your job? the man who had broken the curfew asked compassionately. They took me off the ladders a quarter of an hour ago. They put me on this escort job.

The giant stood nonplussed. Then, as if he really did understand, nodded briefly. He looked down at the welts of his sodden boots for what he must do next and finally, without meeting their eyes, let them pass. He headed home to his sepulchre. Even as he crossed the street, raising one paw aloft to arrest the flow of business and glancing back over a pearly shoulder, a further question finally having formulated in his mind, he found he had lost sight of the couple. Well before he reached shelter, the shadow of a smile lurked beneath the worry of whether he had done the right thing by his duty.

They walked, and where they walked was neither near nor far. They had nothing to do with destinations, they moved in order to keep moving, two strangers all the more estranged for having to be together to escape notice. It rained. It stopped raining. It rained.

She felt alone as possible dangers rushed at them from unseen corners. She did not look at him for fear this might communicate falsehoods she would have to answer for. Being a journalist, Stephanie soon recovered her air of capable control. She was used to living on the fringe of risks. She examined his look, his daring to gaze into her eyes as a man with rights. She had never seen him before; yet even while determined she never would again, she began to be intrigued. Once, the back of her hand accidentally touched his and she recoiled, regretting that she'd previously reached out for him. If only she'd had a sense of humour they might have become friends.

She thought of her darling Luke. Arrested.

Their shoes slapped against the ill-kept footpath: hers unequally and fast, his equally and slower. The sheer weight of his heat pressed against her among dank crowds and puzzled motives. Was he a police agent? A rapist? A plainclothes priest? What he looked like, she saw by the sudden clarity of her training, was a bushranger.

He, too, felt alone. Her anger jammed between them, her unforgiving scorn, the burden of an aggressive independence enough to drag her crooked, bending her body away from him as if she carried a heavy suitcase, the free arm occasionally fending him off. He worried at the plan. If he proposed they stop and talk, what reason could he give? And wherever he might suggest would be too near, reached too soon.

Porous faces on sad figures shambled past, offering no comfort. His breaths, such fleeting gestures of warmth, hung forlorn in fish-cold air, then dissolved. Lonely. Dissolve. His face thrust on. But the forlornness had a hidden motive positively glowing with jubilation. Yes, because he was love-prone. That was it. And still in there with a chance, still with a right to speak and have those golden eyes challenge his own, though he could think of nothing interesting to offer. His shoes said all that seemed possible: ponderous beat, wet slapping. Pathetic, laughable.

The farther they left the station behind, the farther away they drew from their reason for being together at all. They might have been two persons accidentally walking at the same pace, about to look up in surprise.

Fine rain darkened the tips of her hair. He yearned to tease her for the drip of water hanging from her nose. Perhaps, had he done so, the aloneness might have fallen from between them.

She brushed the chance away with her sleeve. What was he up to? In all likelihood he had betrayed her by appearing to take her part. Didn't this draw attention to her? Didn't it risk police interrogation? And had he, in truth, anything to offer? Did he expect she might allow him to take her home? And then? In any case, home had long since lost its warmth; what the television did not freeze to blue-edged death got screwed up with empty takeaway food cartons. Nobody called in unless to pry. Among non-pryers, the habit of calling had died of delicacy. Even supposing he had a home in mind to offer.

He had no home. The only records of his claim to belong mouldered in a biscuit tin in the lumber room at his aunt's place: detritus salvaged from schooldays and his first year at work. . . a couple of exercise books filled with botched homework to be kept with his reports so he could prove to a son, maybe, how he, too, had played up in class and only just scraped through (*Indolent*, a geography teacher wrote, *the boy has ability but no application*); the box also held registration papers for a car long since towed to the wrecking yard; bills and savings bank books, the archives of adulthood and self-sufficiency; plus one forgotten item (he would be ashamed of what it told if he saw it now, ashamed enough to laugh) his first razor still with hairs glued under the blade. Besides, having lain so long unwanted, the whole lot had probably been burnt by his aunt, supposing she was still alive.

The man who bore reminders of youth recollected those years once spent on beaches, body sated with heat, dazzling tides advancing, tireless, sensuous. Time lost, flat on its back watching the young moon's white arc slice though an autumn day. A layabout, his father raged. I learnt to be easy with nature, he answered. But did I put myself to any real test? he objected. I tried meditation to escape the shit they filled my head with. Tell us about the action!

How curious are the tangents between strangers brought together, strangers not yet familiar with the rhythm of each other's walking on a wet morning, who hear the perfect originality of an unknown voice, aware this is somebody not even met in dreams, no hint of promised interests in common, mutual acquaintances, nor even the same city being carried around in mind though using the one name for it.

— They might be following us still, he warned her. Act natural. I've got enough cash for a coffee each. He dived ahead into a cheap café. He was burning with the foolish elation of a man who cannot help falling in love. She lugged her anger in, grateful nonetheless, and sat watching him intently as he joined the queue. She was puzzled. It did not occur to her that she had behaved so very extraordinarily at the station, but she was quite certain he had.

— Milk and sugar, were her first words to him and, because this was the new Australia, she added. If there's still such a thing as sugar.

So she'd left him standing. She'd had to leave him because that lighthearted sarcasm transformed her whole body, fleetingly, and she feared giving herself away, falsely, as a woman capable of tenderness.

If he could hold her, he knew, he would be healed of pain. But her defence returned in the manner of marching off and letting him serve her. He carried their drinks to the place she chose, set them on a ledge, and perched on the stool next to hers.

— Who do I have to thank? she challenged him crossly.

— I'm nameless and homeless as a wild dog.

Stephanie sipped the scalding brew, cupping it in both hands to make the most of it, thawing her fingers. This anonymity suited her. She fixed him with a gaze till he felt ashamed of his scraggy moustache as bearing the signature of a man who has given up caring for himself but has not surrendered his vanity.

— Alright, she agreed, reading his face for gentleness. The Wild Dog. Okay. And I mean thanks. I've had a shock that's all.

— Spitting in the bastard's face! he grinned at last, finding refuge in the truth.

— I suppose they only let me go, she replied after a reflective pause. Because of your quick thinking.

He knew she was no longer angry with him. And though aching to accept this much credit, offered her a self-sufficient man's generosity.

— They let you go because you scared them.

— They didn't look too scared when they sat on me.

— If they weren't scared they wouldn't have needed to.

She liked the idea and, in a volatile shift of mood, became confidential.

— My husband was shut in that train.

Perhaps she also intended the mention of a husband to fling him into despair; and her success proved him less harmful than transparent.

— We expected *something*, she explained to make conversation. With racial persecution out in the open at last.

Now she had put herself wholly beyond reach, weakness invaded him. He not only wanted her but could not do without her.

— I went to the station, she added almost lightheartedly, so clear was her victory. To write an article on wives who choose life in exile for the sake of love. That's my job, I'm a journalist, she informed the exile from her own love.

He drew heat to his hands for a minute.

— Years ago, he began again in a voice exhausted with calling from one mountain across a valley to another. I should have done something.

But he did not say what, or how this related to his present distress.

A sharp downpour sheeted the road in glamorous black and a

silver wind gusted the drops so they clustered along as giant's-boot shadows.

The door opened to admit a slice of noise while three men came in: two together and one alone. The two, being business types and rather out of place in such cheap surroundings, made a point of politely holding the noise open for the workman following them. This workman took the Wild Dog's eye, by the graceful way he handled his large body, by his thinning hair, his fleshy face scored with the worries of a person of principle, and by his ovoid spectacles.

The businessmen, stamping water from polished shoes, hung dripping umbrellas on the ledge right beside the Wild Dog to reserve stools for them while they queued at the counter. The umbrellas nodded sociably as actors. The workman, in a momentary confusion about whether he or they had the right to be served first, shaking his head gently and, one might have guessed in perplexity, glanced round the room. His eyes locked with eyes he had looked into before.

At such connections wars may happen, daring flights of imagination, heroes hesitate for that fatal margin.

The coffee machine hissed, plates clattered, the hushed roadway outside glittered wet. The spectacles turned aside, flashing miniature pictures of the same forgettable silhouettes perched on stools but made gorgeous by rain-light.

The workman walked out slowly, leaving whatever he came for untouched. Another scamper of rain and traffic noise escaped into the café. Then the door closed on a probable pursuer. Watched (as he could feel by pressure in the small of his back), he crossed the road, careful to show none of the panic fluttering, arrowing ahead of him as a flock of startled birds.

In single file, the businessmen bore their drinks toward those ceremonious umbrellas, dumped cups on the ledge and settled to unbuttoning their suitcoats. One, then the other, grunted with achievement. They perched. And gulped at the simulated coffee, exchanging grimaces of delighted horror. They might have been father and son.

— Shit! the Wild Dog swore, caught between two pursuits and not willing to let either quarry escape. I've got to catch that guy. Don't go away, he pleaded, hesitating even so. I'll be back in a minute. I've got a story you'll never believe.

— Merasaloa, said the father, solemn as an oracle.

The Wild Dog pushed his stool back. But he sat again before taking a single step because a squad of Watchdogs burst in.

Watchdogs, the apple of Buchanan's eye, his commercial police force, could go anywhere, how and when it suited their whim. As the great man's favourite example for justifying the sale of public services to the private sector, they filled the café with the heat of habitual cruelty, counting the patrons' missed heart-beats. Their badges glittered codes. Even the businessmen felt a jolt of alarm though they, being of the right class, had little as yet to fear; the one who spoke the name Merasaloa shrank under an onset of senility, even to groping for departure in the form of his umbrella and poking the floor with it.

The Wild Dog, victim of feral passions, kept watch out through the window while his quarry strode away past an elderly lady dressed in garish scarves and too much jewellery. A sudden storm of anger broke in his mind. It's *us* you are doing this to! he raged. Lightning forked through his veins, shocking his neglected body taut in a flash of fear, fear such as he had not known since childhood. He was afraid for this young woman.

The Watchdogs stood, perhaps with orders to arrest her, elbows bent by muscles too thick to be pulled straight, feet apart to leave room for their swollen members swelling yet further with the enthusiasm of power. They took note of faces, of spilt salt, of two puddles and one shaky umbrella. Conceit sang in the crater they had brought with them. Identical as to their helmets, boots, holsters, and heavy bulges, the four of them looked like different positions of the one Grendel. They took plenty of time. Customers trembled, though such intrusions were becoming routine.

The Wild Dog met their eyes without panic, coldly measuring their strength against his own. The woman twisted round to see what was the matter, though she knew as everybody had to know, and turned back again, her movement breathtakingly natural. In the bleak lull and she acknowledged each other's courage. Steam leaked from the boiling machine, the stewed coffee-substitute smelt ranker than before, the umbrella ferrule probed a puddle, a feminist behind the counter closed the shutters on her accusing looks, a daft old crone in scarves smiled in from outside at the accumulating minutes.

Abruptly as they had burst through the door, the Watchdogs trooped away on iron heels, still surrounded by a chasm of untouchability, to check the next shop. They trooped on to the footpath, past that crazed smile, ducking their hard heads to meet the driving rain, as if about to gather speed and trundle off as a battering ram.

This adventure into tenderness had become too audacious for such sombre times. In the end the man who was once young would have to slouch off and sniff out some hole to sleep in, where he could lie like an idiot teasing his loneliness with memories of her scent.

He was on his feet again. A few steps and he was over at the door, though not before he caught sight of that waitress staring right at him. Her all-night face, leached of hope, accused him of upsetting his woman. Her look judged him, yes, but also sympathized with him. Curious. And how wrong she was. He wondered about this even as he stood aside for a granny in bright wet frippery whose lips, plastered with rouge, mouthed unuttered thanks, then laughed silently in his face as she stepped past. He was out: she was in.

He had not even caught the gist of that laughter which she now transferred to the whole panorama of shocked backsliders. This old crone didn't bother pretending to be a customer. Without preamble, she marched over and addressed herself to Stephanie Head.

— Where I come from, she cackled with a humorous shrug. A stickybeak neighbour of my sister's used to have a saying. History, her saying was, is not the load of things we've done. History is what we are and what we have been. Also, she arched her eyebrows (fantastically pencilled and surmounted by wrinkles echoing the one curve many times over, with the astonishment of a pool that has had a rock thrown into it). What we choose to become, it goes without saying. Now you, she conceded. May not have *done* anything, aside from spitting in some fool's face because he took himself too seriously, but what you're to become is another article. I would have thought the answer might be. . . useful. And if you're nice to me I shall tell you how.

She plonked herself where the Wild Dog had sat. She wagged a claw at the Father & Son Pty Ltd now both grasping their umbrellas. Complete with all the experience needed, she was ready to oblige.

The Authorized History of Australia dated from one night, in his sleepless energy, when Bernard Buchanan realized that to write a new history was to create a new nation. Had other men been enjoying privileges as far-reaching as his own? Tucked away in universities, hiding behind the forbidding boredoms of the intellect, had they too been wallowing in fun? He began to notice how, when he suffered a headache, fruit on the fruittrees refused to ripen. Naturally he ordered a scientific investigation and was gratified to be told that since he had installed himself in Canberra the weather pattern of the region had improved substantially. Okay then, he decided, we shall get it down on paper.

All kinds of fascinating data fell into place when viewed from this perspective, even to a stock market slump the day Dorina announced her refusal to move with him to the mansion. And the stock market as he knew, though not much more dignified than a vegetable market, was as predictable as a volcano. That day was stamped hot on his conscience like a wax seal. Possibly because of the place. He had never gone back there. He had no other memories of it to confuse that first impression.

He had taken Dorina to the house chosen by Squarcia as their retreat, which, unlike their previous place, had no luxuriant garden to invite one in. The approach was clinical. At street level you entered across a terrace. This was actually the roof to the main house which hung down over the side of a cliff. A door in the wall at the far side led directly into the lobby and then downstairs to an entrance hall. The house opened in both directions, a massive structure of clean concrete surfaces and crisp edges. The cliff it had been built against fell sheer to the water. Each room faced the same stunning view of the harbour and Harbour Bridge. Down below lay a miniature dock where a retired tugboat, propped on piles, gathered years of neglect while creepers festooned the deck.

Even here music befell Dorina. The moment she had opened her elegant steel-framed window, a pleasurecraft making the Viennese luncheon cruise passed. Held by some magnetism, the skipper had put his vessel about, circling the cove to the strains of *Wiener Blut* while diners enjoyed observing the really rich, who lived up there on the cliff.

Rory was sent to explore the tugboat, being, as he now was, expert on all things nautical.

— Bloody bridge, she'd decided eventually.

And Bernard had laughed with her.

— The surfeit of riches, Dorina had sighed by way of further explanation and added, to her husband's inexpressible surprise: I long for a Spartan life, a few stark possessions, those black iron pans, a wood-burning stove, a simple table, simple food. Things bought by other generations of people belonging to the same place, things that would expect to be left there for our children and grandchildren. The only luxuries I need are a garden and a piano. You think I'm joking, she fired at him. No, she corrected herself. Worse, you think it is horrible for a wealthy kept woman to beg for the stringent ways of the poor.

He had not denied this, pacing the empty room with the concentration of a bowler at a cricket match, about to pivot on the spot and come charging towards her, flinging down a hard ball with a deadly spin to it. The luncheon cruise drifted away out of earshot, round the point and into a neighbouring cove to see how more rich people lived.

— I suppose, she'd explained. I mean that I long to be tested, to show I can tell the difference between what matters and what does not. Then she was the one to pivot sharply, to search him with her gaze, dress rustling expensively. Do you believe that?

— One day, he'd admitted. You'll surprise everybody by coming out in your true colours.

(He recalled the phrase clearly, though it was years ago, now.)

Perhaps, regarding this as one of his more sensible insights, she'd merely smiled and returned to contemplating the tugboat.

— Once I settle in, I shall take your advice Buchanan, she then declared gaily. I shall find a hobby. Nothing to do with politics or good causes. I might, she proposed on a fatal spur of the moment. Have that little ship restored.

Bernard had dismissed this folly, cancelling the view with his nose: from north on the left to south on the right, then south-north, as he lumbered to join her at the window.

— The maritime museum might offer advice, she had protested. To see it put back in the water. The *idea* of the ship is there; it only has to be made so it won't sink. If I could do that, I should like to.

Such composure Bernard had taken in even worse part. So she did intend remaining in Sydney while he moved to Canberra, to the old Governor-General's residence, Yarralumla. He saw Squarcia's point: electorally, it looked unsettled.

— I regret to say, Dorina, that we are no longer private citizens able to please ourselves with foibles.

— I was not consulted about our going public, she'd burst out. I'm losing my lovely garden and my friends.

— Land ahoy! the child's voice had come, querulous with the kind of joy he expects may be taken from him at any moment. Land ahoy, Dad!

Buchanan had made circles of his fingers held to his eyes like binoculars. He'd scanned the sky and the harbour, focusing in all the wrong places while the child exploded with laughter.

— Land. . . land. . . , Rory had managed to snort again before falling helpless on deck, lost among the weeds.

Dorina, the enthusiastic shore party, waved and turned fondly to her husband.

— I will make you this promise, she had said. When you have a state occasion at which the respectable ornament of a wife is mandatory, send me a plane. But I shall return here the following day.

— It's because I'm fat that you've grown to hate me, he remembered admitting.

And remembered her look of disbelief, half expecting that he was still playing games. He was not. Steadying herself against the windowledge, she had added the first intentionally hurtful thing he ever remembered her saying.

— When you take over complete power, who will be nanny?

But how wrong she had been! The opposite turned out to be the truth: he was the one who fussed over everybody else's welfare. He cared for each individual in his flock. No case of obedience was too self-effacing for his praise, no transgression too trivial for him to punish. He took them all personally.

— Every single one, he murmured while the plane purred through the high-flying sunshine of foreign parts and night still clung to the world below.

— Did you say something Your Excellency? Squarcia's voice came from behind, sounding harsh with suspicion.

— I was simply remarking to myself, the president replied settling his massive head against the headrest. That wherever we fly it appears to be night down there still. Doesn't that strike you as curious? Almost as if the dark is waiting to swallow us when we lose height.

— Flying, replied the IFID man who could on no account be touched. Does involve a certain risk.

— Those are my very own words of comfort to Mr Owen Powell, said the president cunningly as he closed his eyes. When he talks to me about you.

Now it was Squarcia's turn to be lost in thought.

39

The Wild Dog had followed, right into an abandoned high-school of a design he knew: body-oils and grime leaving the wall polished between the shoulder heights of the shortest and tallest children who had malingered here; stained concrete stairways echoing, smashed windows, greenboards with chalk clouds smeared across them during some hasty expungement of knowledge. He knew the dark corridors and classrooms, each with a narrow window let into the door just above the handle. He knew how the cubic capacity of such rooms equalled resentment times bafflement times punishment. And yet light streamed in and the days seemed to have accumulated as an approximation of workable information, enough anyway to pass for education.

He followed, because he was not alone, down into the basement among boilers. Lagged pipes were slung from the low ceiling. At the back of a partly dismantled heating system they came upon the smell of blankets lived in only last night. The man who led the way swung round to face his visitor. Stood for a moment in the uncertainty of risking everything. Then slumped in one corner and waved a hospitable hand.

The Wild Dog declined. He remained standing.

The host's gaze dropped, a humble gesture offered with dignity.

— We're simple guys, he admitted. I know.

The Wild Dog did not need to say anything to this. He just went on standing on his two legs while the open doorway boxed him in light. His not moving told the whole story, both of uncertainties and trust.

— We're not young any more, the simple man added by way of finally laying bare how hopeless his case had become.

Part of the central heating system gave out a periodic clucking sound, meaningless in its irregularity, some vent or valve worked loose enough for the faint flow of reverse air from the cold city to set it flapping.

— There's clever ones out there, not like us. Solicitors and technicians, they're the ones you belong with.

The Wild Dog did not smile encouragement. He listened soberly as if listening and considering were one thing, as if the information made him more solid for the having. Immovably heavy on his two legs, he looked in at this fugitive who by leading him here had granted him power over liberty and life.

— You're the ones I found, he replied at last.

He thought about the lagged pipes and the cold classrooms overhead.

— If this is to be any good, he added. It's not because we might win (because we might not), but because we'd stick together.

The host, sitting on his blankets, looked doubtful. Doubt was altogether up to him and his responsibility.

— The economists and them, the Wild Dog pursued an idea, looking very carefully indeed at those pipes and listening to the flap of that fault in the system. Have tried all they know. They've tried to work the bastards over. Sabotage, computer failures, those things. Where has it got us? Deeper in.

— The fellows call me Spinebasher, the host volunteered eventually, taking off his glasses and revealing a face suddenly naked.

The Wild Dog laughed.

Spinebasher, not wounded, put his glasses back on again.

Far away, above them, the empty school took a lesson of laughter through its multiplication tables.

Still boxed in the doorframe, the Wild Dog squatted, haunches sprung ready to move fast.

— My idea, he explained slowly. Is to let people know they've had enough.

— You'd need to get on television.

— If I did that, they'd think it was part of the usual bullshit.

Spinebasher considered the truth of this difficulty.

— Okay, he decided (meaning now I understand, now my respect for you is complete, now I begin to see how I fit in; meaning, also, this makes our job bloody impossible).

— Those smart ones, said the Wild Dog by way of closing negotiations. Are the guys they have tabs on. If I went to one of them like I've come to you, I'd be marked already.

Also he measured his pride by the people he chose to work with. But he did not mention what this might imply.

There were others to be convinced. So it was arranged. They met in the school workshop garage: Spinebasher flat on his back underneath a vehicle, occasionally rolling clear to wipe mist from his spectacles; Nelson perched on a bench gouged with childish blunders, then slipping off it to pace the confines of the floor among motor parts laid out as a bazaar, picking through his repertoire of anxieties refined during a bank-breaking jail-breaking apprenticeship; and Nick. Nick, punishing himself with a heavy spanner, offered a quality not so easily defined: a thin hard body equal to the exhausting demands he put it through, yes, and a brutal scorn for sentiment, yes, but at the man's core lay some quality so dense it might be mistaken for emptiness. This was what might be called his purity. He held no beliefs, obeyed no principles, had no pretences. And measured each action, his own as well, by the unflinching independence of its moment. He rose to danger with the ferocious daring of a nihilist.

The Wild Dog, once again not quite inside, leaned against a greasy doorpost.

— Then all we've got to do is keep moving, he suggested. The idea will catch on. The Watchdogs can't crack the plan because there isn't one.

This was talking Nick's language. He finished whacking his thigh, hung the spanner on the wall where its place had been designated by a painted silhouette, glanced impatiently at the others, and then explained.

— If enough people won't go along with it, the system's fucked.

And sure enough, once they went into action the nights were filled with voices calling quietly, hands leading them into cool kitchens among smiling men and serious wives who shared their rations and were stimulated by rumours of a dissident network just waiting for some sign to join forces in a true republic. A whole directory of the disaffected fell open to their use to be learned by heart.

— How did you three come to team up in the first place? the Wild Dog asked.

— We're what's left of the Australian All-Star Circus, Greatest Show on Earth, Nelson confessed.

— A quarter of the Human Pyramid, Nick laughed. And half the Rogers Brothers. Balancing acts. Card tricks. You name it. Small beer.

They ranged right across the country finding in most places the same welcome, the same forgiveness for their failure to attempt an assassination or behave like heroes, the same encouragement from people downtrodden too long and eloquent with rebellious folktales. Where they were not welcome, at least they found the opportunity to build a reputation for staging virtuoso getaways.

Owen Powell (and it was the mere mention of Owen Powell's name which caused Luigi Squarcia to ruminate in the presidential plane) began to hear reports. He waited in his office for news of violence, knowing that then he would have the troublemakers cold. But none came, only a persistent ripple just beneath the surface of public submissiveness. It was a worry, he being Minister for Internal Security.

The Wild Dog explained it this way.

— I shouldn't want to have to go to the wife of a bloke I'd shot and tell her what I'd done. I shouldn't want to face his children either.

The others knew that, astonishingly, this is what he would do.

So, when he groaned in his sleep, it was as a love-prone man who let opportunities pass which he would have taken in his stride before, and not because he was dedicated to an unarmed revolution against Buchanan, only because his heart was fixed on one woman, already lost to him, no longer so young but all the more fascinating for that. She had disappeared from the café when he got back. He groaned with pain at her memory, tormented because the only way to find out was a way no man of honour could possibly take. Until the day the pain grew too intense and he took it. He went to the housing camp at Vengeance Harbour, rocking his shame on the train to Port George, numbing his disgrace while walking in a trance out to the convict jail, and presenting himself to the black husband of that blond woman.

— I'm going to get you out of here, he promised, body held stiff with ferocity while he added a regretful admission of helplessness. I'm in love with your wife.

Luke Head already knew. He had seen this before either Stephanie or her rescuer, he had seen it in the spring of the man's step bounding along that wet platform, had caught one last glimpse of him stooping to help her up from her assailants: and pounced at the wire screen. The Wild Dog, in his misery, might have surrendered all effort to defend himself simply for the satisfaction of contact with her by proxy (this possessive fury of the husband proving that she was as intensely desirable as he remembered). The wire netting held, shuddering and shackling the whole width of the yard, while warders ran to the rescue and ordered the visitor out under threat of arrest.

— I don't care who you are, the commandant yelled in a

frenzy. This is an orderly camp. No trouble till now. Don't intend to permit it. Dr Head has behaved well. Good report. Quiet as a gentleman. Friends of Privilege, do you understand? Blockhead. Complete and utter. His skinny shanks rattled as he sat down indignantly and dismissed the interloper. Fellow won't be fit to see patients for days. Accidents! Have you thought of accidents? Blundering in. Show your face here again and you're a goner. I'll see to it. Port George police just minutes away. Wouldn't surprise me, he addressed the ceiling from under a gothic arch of hands clasped on his head. If they have you on their records already. But the troublemaker had gone by then.

The Wild Dog walked out as a suit of armour might walk, hinge-jointed and hollow inside. If he passed through a crowd of jeering women gathered at the gate, he scarcely knew. The sea's detonations, smashing against the rocks below, pounded in his blood. Once before, he had felt an abjectness as crushing as this. He was a visitor then too, an outsider at the university; not exactly visiting, but attending a protest rally against the government for sending troops to New Guinea. The genial crowd, gathered on serious business, talked football as usual, some even laying bets on the unlikelihood of getting arrested. Well two there were who would never pay up, linked by the frail courage of ideals, voices pitched to a deaf press of the president's preferred journalists (known as Honourables), demonstrating long after the alarm, long after motorcycles cut jags across precious lawns, after an armoured car was driven in by a sound nobody would forget, that roar with something in it of a kettle singing, long after a loudspeaker gave avuncular advice, after troops lined up and advanced as a clockwork wall, left monotony right monotony left monotony right. The man who was still young then, feeling the fine morning tighten his sinews, feeling, as a man among these youths, he should set an example, shouted *Stand firm*. That was what he must live with, having taken the entire morning into himself. Because when the army outriders screamed away, the clockwork wall of a platoon knelt down and fired the most God-deafening blast above our heads. Into the square sky framed in gothic turrets a flight of bullets emitted bat cries. And two students fell on the grass: a lad with an extra hole in his face and a woman-child grabbing her stomach to prevent the evidence getting away before the inquest, while he, who was watching them act their deaths, sucked in his breath to take back the words, to take back the red letter day of *Stand firm*. The officer commanding spun round and searched among his men, searched with hot amazement for two who had disobeyed: those guilty of having judged and sentenced to their personal satisfaction and who had executed the sentence. What could he do? So the art of confrontation, decades of ritual, the greatest street-theatre since the Rum Rebellion, died there. In its place were thousands of gasping youths, the near ones thrown prostrate, weeping and cowering behind new white faces; those at the outer rim, hearing the future burst through their old canvas scenery, crept away among buildings where they dissected animals, analyzed explosions and deduced theories of mathematics to supercede everyday nuclear fission. Nobody mentioned football again that morning. Peace, like a collective orgasm, smoothed the furrows from every soldier's face; they were none of them to blame. Then that one workman strode away, in the open, striding boldly through the main gate to where he would tell the world. And the officer let him go, allowing himself no second's respite, in case he might miss a faltering gaze that would betray the guilty ones. What could the world be told, anyway, which it would not come to know officially? The soldiers holding hot empty barrels closed ranks on their innocence. By the time a television helicopter hung threshing the air for the last grain of sensationalism, the taleteller had left City Road, threading his way through a traffic jam, carrying his shock and guilt to the backstreets of Chippendale where they were deposited in the gutter with the vomit of a premature glass of beer. That was all.

The man with hair as pale as bus-light or youth faced the eight-kilometre walk back to Port George as an athlete might, taking refuge in action. His humiliation rankled. Only for the commandant letting slip the name Dr Head, he would be coming away altogether worse off than when he arrived. He followed the road along a cliff, the angry chatter of women, still unheeded, dissolved in distance. Below, the sea slapped down ultimatum upon ultimatum. He walked and the land walked with him, determined not to let him out of sight. Soon the road dipped and came alive with the laughter of children. Yes, this he did hear. And there they were, jumping into a rockpool, clambering out wet and slicked with sunshine. As each child went under, his shout went under. The water that made them so happy swallowed their happiness, till up they bobbed, mouths still open and the same penetrating shout released once more into the air. With them was a dog who would not give in, a dog who hated getting wet, you could see it, barking crazily as part of the fun, but although the children called and coaxed and threw sticks in the pool, the dog stayed dry, dodging when they flicked water up to its safe vantagepoint. Joyfully the children sprang into the pool. And when one rushed out, running wet, the dog shook itself in sympathy, so they all laughed more deliriously and chased the wagging tail in a futile effort to capture the animal and throw it in. Such happiness lifted his spirits. This mesmeric game went on as an inexhaustible continuum. At the sheer effort of shouting, bloodvessels stood out along skinny necks. Every so often one child would call, plaintive accusatory hectoring begging calls of Luke. Luke!

The man who had once been young himself and remembered it formed his lips for a whistle to call them over to him. In the dusty secrecy of his pocket his fingers closed on a twenty-cent piece which he turned in its cradle of lint. The whistle never came. But the children saw him anyway. They danced over rocks and ran up to the road, their laughter grown hungry. The churned surface of the pool immediately settled to the limits of its glassy perfection. The dog stood where he was, not sure what to do now nobody was egging him on.

— Man, man, screamed the children with Asian faces and fair hair, with African hair and freckled noses, fearless ravenous bodies eager for adventure. They stormed up to the road, pushing each other and exploding in giggles. A small girl took his hand and laid her wet cheek against it. He felt the cold smooth flesh. He felt her jaw move as she spoke.

— Give me money man, she crooned and caressed him with precocious sensuality. Money money, she crooned with her invulnerable softness.

He took out the twenty-cent piece.

— That's the lot. He gave it.

Like bloodthirsty seagulls they pounced on her, elbows and fingers gouging. The bright coin dropped and they scrambled murderously for it, teeth bared, so that the dog scented a hunt and began howling. The children's bright clean eyes glinted dangerously. Their jungle voices were hisses and snarls.

Cloud cast a dark shape on the sea, alien as the bulk of some island-sized creature surfacing.

The Wild Dog, with the gentleness of great strength, parted the combatants and set them on their feet. He bent down to take back his money. I am being taught by children, he thought. They tugged his clothes, went at him with little dartings and tweaks, a pinch here and a scratch there, wet mouths leered bestially. Beside and behind him they flickered out of reach. They found their voices again, voices to taunt him. They infested him with loathsome pricklings. As he walked forward he carried the weight of children clinging to his jacket, belt, pockets, their wildness speaking to his own, to the hunger gnawing at his guts. They molested him, fingering him with grim wriggling carnality. But was this mobbing any more savage or uncivilized than his mission of calling on an imprisoned husband to announce his lust for the wife? He took hold of a child by her clawing hands and swung her in a circle, the parasites swinging, too, behind him. He set her down, giddy and air-struck. He swung another. Up she went so the land swung with her and the sea swung, lifted and sank. And the noise of the sea rushed alternately at her left ear and then her right. Left. Right left. He whirled them round higher and faster. Arms held out, they each clamoured for a turn mister. So, suddenly they were friends in a simple game. The dog on the rock chased his tail. And the tide howled away to caves in the south.

A car pulled up and the children surrounded it, begging hands thrust in at the open window. It was a tiny car of obscure origin. The driver signalled to him to get in.

— Children children, she called. Don't pester grannie. My goodness, she laughed. If you all end up in the fighting forces we shall be able to take on the world, no worries.

He thanked her while he settled on a seat too small for him, knees hunched and head pressing against the roof. She met his eyes as they took off with a jerk and careered downhill on the wrong side of the road.

— I shall take you to her.

That was all. He stared in wonder at her profile. A woman of perhaps seventy or one hundred and ten, with the features of an Indian or was it a Turk or perhaps a Russian, and the white white skin of a Spanish countess who tests the colour of her veins against the sky. She wore a twist of silk scarves round her head brilliant as a turban, though decidedly more scatty, and another long scarf swathed under her chin to hide her lizard neck. She could be described as nothing other than beautiful. Ostentatious jewels on her fingers flashed while she steered. And well they might, because her steering was a busy occupation, swerving erractically to, as she put it, feel for the best of the bitumen and not wear out the old jalopy.

— Who is she, that you're taking me to?

She darted him a mischievous look, pursed her lips and opened her nostrils like a sphinx.

— I hope I haven't picked up just anyone, she murmured. If you are not Mr Dog, heaven knows what embarrassment I have let myself in for and I shall have to ask you to leave my car the moment I find a level spot to pull up.

— So that's it, he breathed, absolutely stoked, then shouted with laughter.

She reached out, putting their lives at peril, to press a glittering finger on his lips. In a flash he realized he had seen her before but paid not enough attention to remember when or where. She felt his recognition and renewed the pressure of her finger.

— I like you Mr Dog; you're an accepter. You go out and meet life head-on. It gives us a bond.

They reached the city through wealthy suburbs closed off with Area Gates. Attendants checked ID and reminded non-resident drivers to keep to the highway and not diverge from it. Cross streets sloped down to road barriers where armed Watchdogs confronted the tiresome routine of holding back a silent wilful crowd of scavengers awaiting permission to pass into the ambit of privilege, the hour before curfew, to beg at kitchen doors where food was known to be eaten, and clear off by dusk.

The old lady clicked her tongue and assumed a tart concentration on the road, which previously she had ignored.

40

Churchill barked once. He was of an age when a single bark seemed sufficient to fulfil his duties. Someone was coming. Rory made a face, an ugly childish gesture for a nineteen year old.

— I'm going down to the *Felice*, he said petulantly. Since you are entertaining.

— Will it matter if your uniform isn't perfect? his mother asked, stopping midway through her Schumann Opus 20 which she would never master, and watching him with that worried alertness of a heroin addict's parent probing for renewed proof of what she hoped never to find in the first place. She glanced at her treble hand; the white knob of her wrist showed, more prominent than it used to be.

The house phone rang. Rory, grumpily extending her this courtesy, went to answer it. Even in his fastidious but slightly lopsided way of turning on one heel, she saw he was still lost to her. The languid exaggeration of so simple a movement dreadful for them both to bear. He bowed to her to acknowledge that he had saved her getting up from the piano, listened a moment and then, without replying, slapped the receiver back too hard.

— The worst! he replied to her unspoken query. You are being called on. I'm definitely out. He regained the door with that same languid unevenness. Take a deep breath, he advised without looking back at her. The Chief Minister is here, together with Mr Big.

— What can you mean by that? she asked sharply and took a quick glance at the phone as if she might be able to see the security guard as well as hear again what he had said to her son and judge for herself what was true and what was not.

— Dad's dear friend Sir Bill Penhallurick. Didn't you know? Everybody knows, Rory sneered, but still did not turn to face her. The guys talk about it openly. Him with his international connections. There's no doubt he's the top boy. Millions he makes on a single deal. Imagine that. Defiantly he fired his words straight at her. Those of us who take the stuff are the mugs.

— I'm surprised, she said quietly. You haven't been thrown out of naval college.

— They'd have to throw half the others out too, he laughed. Don't worry, the navy itself is high most of the time. We're just in training.

Ah now, now he had something to really wound her with. He smiled the rueful smile, failing at the edges, losing composure, slipping to an agony, an appeal, that tore her heart.

— Darling, she cried in anguish. Don't.

He sorted through his own pain for a response tough enough to stop her getting at him.

— Don't what? he said, suddenly harsh, as the upper door opened and several men were admitted.

— Don't smile like that, she pleaded in an undertone (not to betray him as he left her). She noticed, irrelevantly, how nice and flat the pleats sat at the back of his jacket. Were all officer cadets so well fitted, or had poor Rory been singled out yet again? Was everybody laughing behind their hands at Bernard?

The upper door shut and Roscoe Plenty appeared on Dorina's stairs, descending slowly, each footfall heavy with self-esteem.

— Dorina, he began. How are you?

Behind him Sir William capered down in a fraction of the time.

Before either of them actually set foot in the room, the house phone rang again. She crossed the sunny parquet floor to pick it up.

— Judge Mack is here, Your Excellency.

So the door opened again.

— We've no time for drinks, Roscoe Plenty warned her though none had been offered. We've come to enlist your support, I'll be blunt about it.

— Please sit down won't you?

Penhallurick did, perching on the brink of his chair, but Plenty remained standing, so great was his agitation.

The Chief Justice of the High Court appeared now, grown distinguished enough to have lost all trace of individuality.

— My dear, he announced as he descended even more portentously than Roscoe Plenty. We are so worried.

Churchill, who had settled himself under the grand piano where he liked to be, let his chin fall on his paws thoughtfully. Dorina closed the lid of the keyboard, as she might shut a door on the privacy of her life.

— I'd hoped, Roscoe Plenty persevered with the impression he was making, you might have accepted my invitation to come to Kirribilli House. Then we needn't have invaded you here.

— I don't mind being invaded Roscoe, Dorina answered. I love visitors. I have no friends left.

Does she, Penhallurick wondered shrewdly, already know? She's no beauty but she's smart. She's keeping us at arm's length. He threw himself back into the armchair he'd chosen and stared at her unblinkingly.

No I don't know, replied her expectant look, but I am beyond being touched by any of you.

— What a magnificent view, the judge took a turn at delivering a verdict.

— I'd hoped, Roscoe Plenty repeated.

This filly, Sir William decided, is damned if she is going to be the least use to us.

Not necessarily anything so positive, Dorina's hands demurred as she placed them in her lap the way she had been taught at her ill-fated boarding school.

Roscoe Plenty sat down, scowling his grey wolverine scowl of a man who has tried everything he ever wanted and been satisfied by none of it.

— Whatever we have to say, he assured her. You may repeat

to Bernard when he returns. I don't want you to think we'd do anything behind his back.

The fine spring morning spread cards on the floor between them, but they couldn't be read.

— It's only a pity you don't see the Opera House from here, the judge commiserated.

— I shall make a speech to the nation tonight, the Chief Minister said. In the president's absence.

— Will he have arrived yet, Judge Mack wondered aloud. In the Maldives? One hears the islands are extremely pretty.

— Not yet I think, Dorina replied, recalling how she and Squarcia had entertained the judge eight years before on the appalling occasion of Buchanan's drunkenness, a disgrace he had never offered to explain to her. She'd said nothing at the time, knowing it would not happen again. And it never had.

Rory's hammer could be heard that moment tapping a distant jaunty rhythm. Churchill hummed in his sleep.

— A speech mainly about the Cultural Centre disaster. But we do not yet know the true cause. The police are looking into it. The most likely explanation is a technical failure.

Dorina wrapped herself in a terrible seriousness.

She does know, Penhallurick observed, she's getting herself ready.

— Meanwhile we feel, Roscoe Plenty continued. That I am not necessarily the right person to represent the president at the crematorium. I wouldn't wish to presume. Oh, I shall be there to honour the heroes of the tidal wave, he added. In my own capacity, as leader of the parliament.

Had he scented failure? Was he distancing himself from Buchanan in the interests of his own future?

— My wife will be representing *me*, Sir William piped up, eyelids drooping coyly, watchful for what this hint might provoke.

— I think that is the correct way, Judge Mack decided, nodding fifteen times to fill the gap till someone thought of making further headway with the business.

— There is a delicate balance, Roscoe Plenty supplied another clue, waiting to see if she might surmise the rest and save him actually speaking of it.

But she turned toward him again, challenging him to meet her eyes, eyes having something in them to make a man forget whether she was plain or beautiful, or confuse him as to the difference. They had a provocative brightness, filled with knowing and that quality of wit which is closer to kindness than to laughter, closer to action than to mockery.

— Bernard has never been away before, he inched the bait closer to her.

But still she was not tempted to help him in his difficulty.

— It's a question of strong feelings, the judge said and, reconsidering, nodded his head some more while he added. Also stability.

— I really don't see, Dorina decided at last. How this involves me at all. My husband told me quite clearly only yesterday evening that he had placed everything in Mr Powell's hands. Everything, I mean, that would otherwise have involved him officially, outside the parliament.

Oh, this filly was cutting up rough. Sir William scratched his ear, dislodging flakes of skin and sending them to flutter down on the chair arm. She wasn't born yesterday.

At the mention of Owen Powell, the judge converted his nods to shakes, as acknowledgment that the issues raised were of so responsible a kind they demanded no less than the scrupulous examination of a tradition ancient, grave and subtle. She ought not, his gentle negation signified, to try forcing the matter with combative measures. Some weighty issue was gathering shape behind the words, not directly touched by them, and yet dependent upon their suggestiveness.

— I'd already written out my speech to the nation about the Cultural Centre tragedy, the Chief Minister explained, watching to read what effect his words were having on her. Before anybody began to imagine there might be more to it. He paused, sorting for the right nonchalance. But now with the tidalwave too, we must be careful to distinguish between them, since otherwise we run the danger of inferring some link there. His Excellency insists that we must speak of the Eden affair as having affected only Eden people.

Affected! Dorina thought.

— If we are placed in the position of giving explanations, the Chief Justice explained. We might find ourselves out of our depth.

But it was altogether unclear who would be out of their depth and what the explanations might refer to. This was like Dorina's Schumann: she had all the notes under her hand; what eluded her was the completeness of how it might hang together. She could achieve passages of the most scintillating clarity, but then the thread was lost. Rory's hammer began again, nailing down her sharp refusals to cooperate. Dorina thought of him and prayed he would not make an appearance in his present state. The hammer stopped. Then a shaft of fire flashed through her, so hot she clenched her fists and clamped her jaws to withstand the agony. That she, his mother, should be ashamed of him in front of this ogre Penhallurick, who may have wrecked thousands of young lives and been insulated from guilt by his power! More victims died of drugs than ever died of tidal waves or collapsed buildings. And they died in squalor, a longdrawn death of petty crime. She knew. She supported Rory's habit, though it tortured her, to save him from turning to criminal means. Who was this. . . creature, this. . . enemy, to look her in the face even. Dorina flung open the window.

— Rory, she called with the rich voice of her courage. Rory!

She watched him look up, sitting on deck as he was, with long legs stretched out straight in front of him, the hammer in one hand idly whacking the timbers. He held it aloft. And suddenly he smiled. He rolled on to his side to push himself to a kneeling position, moving like a dreamy old man.

— Coming, he answered remotely.

— A national day of mourning will have to be declared, the wolf spelt it out, irritated by how wilfully she complicated matters. He glanced around the room at its stark yet tasteful modernity, arrested by a fleetingly attractive glimpse of himself in a mirror. He was reminded of a miniature version of Lavinia Manciewicz's painting. But looking again, he could not recapture the surprise.

— We would wish to avoid any unseemly dispute over precedence, the Chief Justice put it to her at last, squinting into the brilliant day laid out at his feet.

— Such an image will be unforgettable, Roscoe Plenty grunted. Once seen, impossible to cancel.

— Put it this way, Sir William proposed. For Bernie's sake we don't want people getting the idea just anybody can fill his place.

You know this already, he accused her silently, meanwhile classifying her as too tall, too bony and, with her lowheeled shoes, too lacking in chic, to be any European's mistress: you guessed the minute we came in the door. Women are not such stupid cattle they can't see round corners.

— For the first time ever, Chief Minister Wolf pointed out. Somebody will have to stand in for him. With the whole country watching.

— I can see that, the patient Dorina replied, though finally brought to the point (How petty! her mind screamed. There's my son in the grip of a terrible vice and all your blather amounts to this!) But I am not a public figure. So why don't we ring Mr Powell and see if he'll do it?

The side door opened to admit Rory, dazed with sunlight and holding his hand to his aching head. He had forgotten why he was here. The real world slipped beyond his grasp and he was stranded among the unbearable rigours of other people's routines. He remembered leaving the room more clearly than he remembered coming back; in any case he had seemed younger then and far less saddened with effort. He remembered, finally, the closing chords of the Schumann *Humoresque*.

— That piece of music, he spoke to his mother, tears me up. But I beg your pardon, he cried immediately afterwards in his baritone voice, unable to stop a grin forming on his face. I didn't know I was interrupting a meeting with the top brass. Did you want me to take Churchill for his walk?

Churchill's sleeping head went up at the mention of his name. He peered at Rory blearily, enquiringly, and then gathered himself for the effort of being obliging. Dorina was piercingly reminded of Rory himself a few moments earlier. The three visitors exchanged glances which she intercepted, so quick and protective she was. She went to her son and touched his arm affectionately.

— Thank you dear, the president's wife said.

Sir William Penhallurick resented this as the snub it was: Dorina owned the boy to convince them that, in their company, she was not ashamed. He wasn't going to let her get away with anything.

— Well Rory, he squawked so familiarly the young man's mother could not possibly miss his point. It's a long time since we went sailing together. You got a taste for it then, didn't you? he paused to allow the ambiguity to sink in. McKinley still sails her. We ought to have you back for more good times. What do you say?

No, not then, not when he was only eleven, Dorina begged silently, as if begging now could undo what had been done. Was Rory to be no more than a tool in their hands against Buchanan? Had they been so busy planning everything when that car broke down in the desert? She could never have foreseen such depravity.

— If, Rory himself replied, breaking through the mica screen of unfeeling. I were still interested. . . He hesitated at the over-powering nakedness of what was being laid open in public and then added with the heroic mildness of an adult who has learned there can be no end to suffering or the need to be counted as the enemy's enemy. . . I would have joined the yacht club, not the navy.

— With your privileges, Roscoe Plenty agreed sourly. You could have done anything.

— I wonder, Dorina said, returning to her piano stool and putting the great instrument between her and them. What the inquest will turn up? She opened the keyboard lid, adding. It looks rather suspicious, I'd have thought, for a brand-new building to fall down, so completely fall down, like something already rotten.

She dismissed them with a scatter of notes. The Schumann took shape and quite sudenly, of its own accord, made perfect sense. Dorina Buchanan, who had once been Dorina Lambert escaping the knives of a people desperate to be rid of foreign exploiters, played and played while her visitors mumbled uncomfortably, not knowing whether she expected them to listen right through and applaud at the end. After ten minutes, they made their farewells, surrendering to the inevitability that any decision must rest with Bernard. The *Humoresque*, oddly named for so large and complex a piece, chimed and sang. Rory stood to attention at the window, long after the petitioners had mounted the stairs and gone, long after the final chord sounded its triumphant bells, faded and escaped out to sea, staring through his tears at the *Felice*, the earthbound boat, tied down by a tangle of creepers, and waiting to be rescued.

— You mean to say, President Buchanan wrenched himself away from his fear of falling to a world still in partial darkness. That you knew this had happened and said nothing to me?

— Not at all Your Excellency, Luigi Squarcia replied. I learnt of it just this moment from the pilot, who had a message relayed from your wife.

— How long before we land? Buchanan snapped though he knew the answer to be twenty minutes.

— Twenty minutes, Squarcia said as he pulled his immaculate cuff down over his wrist again.

— It's a godsend, then, Lou?

— An absolute godsend, Bernie.

Buchanan grew instantly tragic at things going so well, at this compounding of fatal accidents allowing him to play them against each other, to confuse the issue, and to obtain leverage over Sir William Penhallurick while he was about it. He was visited by an ambiguous fleeting chaotic irreversible and ungraspable discontentment which was nothing less than life itself: and then lost the feeling for it.

— Everyone is so bloody obliging, he grumbled. I no longer notice that I am even here. You know that, Squarcia? If you left me to the mercies of the Owen Powells of this world, I believe I would disappear into thin air, big as I am. A man has to have something to make him angry before he knows there's a world going on at all. He leered. I'll tell you a secret. No I shan't, he recoiled winsomely. Unless. . . why not? I have taken to dreaming enemies. What do you make of that? He laughed suddenly a monstrous bellow of cleverness and pain. I'll soon be as addicted to my enemies as young Rory is to his *gear*, as he calls it.

— Or addicted, Squarcia asked after a decent pause, not to seem too astute. To the power you hope they will define for you?

— Why I should need to invent enemies, the president marvelled delightedly, when I have you with me, I shall never know!

A question nibbled away at his gut, small and sharp as a mouse: had he simply been Squarcia's dupe, taking the risks up there in the public eye? He glanced across to catch his companion out. He knows my limitations, the president admitted, ticking off points, my failings, my comfortable crudity perhaps, and apparently my serviceability.

Squarcia settled for a rest, not a wrinkle in his suit, not a wrinkle on his skin. Age simply left him, from some angles, a trifle puffy.

Just suppose, the great man supposed, I am his dupe. Does it show? Does everyone see through me?

Bernard Buchanan did not need to stare down at the dim world to learn the topography of shame. He had been a boy in school, hadn't he? He knew what it was to look aside at the critical moment and appear not to notice who nudged whom, not to hear insulting remarks, while hate and fear sent out taproots to fix him in range till such time as the tormentors grew bored with their own limited ingenuity. He knew what it was to shamble off dragging his soggy feet to the chance of a renewed attack round every corner. He did not even find refuge at home, enduring the caustic tolerance of his father, the frustration he provoked in his mother, and now, living alone, his wife's loyal kindly yet most belittling correction when she came to visit.

The president, surrendering once more to the tide of excitement, wondered how it would be, meeting world leaders and being part of the biggest game of all, the club, the most stupendous and wasteful crew of gamblers and con-men. He drifted closer, carried by that weird lunar floating of a big plane.

— Squarcia, he called imperiously to spoil the fellow's rest.

— Don't worry, Squarcia replied without opening his eyes. The people love you.

41

The arts the Wild Dog was taught by his new colleagues included balancing, juggling (at which he did not make good progress), contortionism, sleight of hand (another failure), quick costume changes, rope techniques, and controlled errors (the very heart of clowning). They had been trained in all these disciplines by a Chinese master called Ping when they first joined the All-star Circus.

The new team was soon to tour. Passengers in a Richmond tram saw, to their astonishment, a tableau set up at the roadside between stops: a gross Buchanan figure sitting on the backs of three working-men, inexorably squashing them down to the ground, helpless. . . but once the tram had passed and the commuters dared look back for a second glimpse, rejuvenated by the silent laughter of shock and anger, no sign of the tableau or the artists remained, only a few ordinary blokes crossing the road to catch a return tram to town or buying newspapers. The same act had been witnessed in places as far apart as Darwin and Tamworth. The peak-hour traffic along Parramatta Road was treated to a vision of fat lips (no head, no body) and colossal teeth chomping up a supply of babies in nappies. The babies were being fed in by a couple of respectable chaps in business suits. A patrol car happened to be travelling in the flow; the driver flicked his hazard switch and slammed on the brakes (causing a truck to run into the back of him), doors flying open and police leaping out on the spot only to find. . . nobody, or more precisely, everybody. Too many pedestrians were stopped and searched, while a traffic snarl compounded. Too many businessmen in three-piece suits resented being questioned. Nothing. Just a clean *Save the Children* pamphlet blowing about on the pavement all by itself.

Amazed citizens in Perth looked up at the Old Town Hall clock one morning to find a hideous object, a hideously funny object, leaning against the tower: a giant inflatable turd, rather more pear-shaped than cylindrical, with a little wreath of grey hair on its bald top. Another such object was seen floating up the Derwent River, and a photograph of this one appeared in an unguarded early edition of the Hobart *Mercury* before the paper found itself hastily withdrawn from circulation.

Three circus clowns and a strongman put on an impromptu act in the refectory at Adelaide University, never suspected of subversion until stamping cheering students let out a collective shout of derision and then fell silent, totally silent. Campus Watchdogs, vigilant as ever, converged on all exits. They found the place full of the usual callow youths cramming greasy chips in and slurping instant tea, heads down and eyes on their food, but no interloper anywhere to be seen, not one clown with chaotic eyes, not a single overdeveloped trapesius.

Even the national capital was not sacrosanct.

— How does a fellow become a human being? asked a wolf looking decidedly bedraggled.

— Come again? said a Buddha.

The laughter heard on the concourse leading up to Parliament House itself could not be caught even with a fine-mesh butterfly net. Guards were unable to report an arrest because by the time they had enough suspects the suspects were found to be outnumbered by their own alibis. These alibis had to be listened to, the offences having clearly become a case of guilt or innocence.

At long last there was somebody who deserved to be caught and put a stop to.

42

Most people at the time, quite mistakenly, imagined Bernard Buchanan to be a devoted and resolute eater, a gourmand spending his finest hours relieving tables of their freight, swilling jugs of ale while staff trundled in a whole pig roasted on the spit (to a turn, as they say) and presented on a bed of parsley with a fresh apple blocking its objections, flanked by tureens of sauce; and pickled mushrooms glazed with sour cream, leading the procession of vegetable dishes, while the aroma of soups already devoured, replenished and devoured twice, hung haloes around the heads of those serving and the entrée and fish courses left mammoth holes in the air, air thick with promise; and his mind filled by visions of zabaglione to come, plus Russian chocolates with the *caffè Galliano*. They imagined him casting aside tubsful of greasy dishes for the kitchen staff to labour over while cooks snored on divans with the exhaustion of Argonauts. But nothing of the kind. The president was not that ilk of fat man. He ate neither more nor less than the average male citizen of his age. He didn't care for the fine points of cooking; indeed, he judged the delicacy of certain classical flavours insipid, and masticated without the least sensual enjoyment. I do like a good feed, he'd say, patting his belly. But those who had dined with him knew this meant, ideally, an over-cooked steak with chips and a spoonful of stewed cabbage. Admittedly, he appreciated some port to top it off, but could never distinguish between tawny, vintage, and liqueur.

Food was no explanation for his prodigious dignity.

To imagine him aboard his aircraft, assembling the courage needed to disembark into the sweltering heat of a Maldive morning, one must begin by considering his girth, which was about as impressive as a cart-horse's, though apt to wobble gelatinously. Journalists attempting a description of this prodigy among world leaders were confounded by the extraordinary way his body changed shape. When held in a standing posture it was quite unlike his shape sitting. Once upright, masses of fat slipped and sagged, huge flaps sliding gradually off his shoulders which were left gaunt and exposed, pulling his various chins down almost to his chest and stretching the facial skin so he appeared twenty years younger at a stroke. As a sensible precaution against the unforeseen, President Buchanan did not attempt to walk, each leg being thicker than a normal fat man's trunk; he simply stood long enough for his bearers to efface themselves by a technique acquired over the years and known in its rudimentary form to many a security man, of not focusing on anything while remaining alert to everything and therefore not being seen.

When Buchanan sat he reinvented his more usual shape, the voluminous rolls of his thighs buoying up his belly, belly manfully supporting shoulders (he had no chest until he lay flat on his back and then not much), arms jutting straight out from the trunk at a fixed angle, as if not meant to be jointed at all, and neck puffed to its full splendour of four complete chins plus a nice cushion of fat at the back for him to rest his head against. Fortunately, his was a face able to sustain such majestic foundations, from the broad mouth full of crooked teeth to the huge Colleoni nose, big wild eyes bulging with all they'd seen, thick coarse eyebrows and a bald head. Even his ears, sprouting bushes of hair and touched a hectic pink, were characters by right of their independent thickness.

When he lay down, an intimacy few people were privileged to witness, the transformation was even more dramatic. Apart from the dominant pile of that gargantuan gut, blankets thrown over it folding to handsome fans of Fujiyama ridges, he was discovered to have feet and knees. His lower and upper body spread to prodigious breadth, evened out as if he were a sack of beans, revealing his talent for those innocent shapes seen in babies. His nose jutted up and his face took on an aspect of oriental knowingness. With arms and legs stretched wide, he filled the bed which had been made specially for him, two metres long and two and a half metres wide, on one narrow cliff-edge of which Dorina perched for the occasional night of matrimony. Alone, he lay as bulky as the bed itself, giving the impression of one bed stacked on top of another, a lumpy one on a smooth one.

This bed, unoccupied, stood in the rear compartment of the aircraft, which had landed and taken its place in a queue, behind the royal standard of Hannover and a Malawi Airlines Boeing. They rolled gradually, sedately, closer to the welcoming dais outside the terminal.

The sky exploded rain. Sheets of water slashed and pounded across the wings, wiping out all sign of the smiling dignitaries plus a band about to sound the G. Then, having shown it could do that, the weather cleared in an instant. The President of Malawi, sparkling with medals for hypothetical campaigns and resplendent in an army bishop's parade collar, stepped out into the scorching sun, far more at home than the Queen of Hannover and Great Britain wading through rococo curlicues of steam swirling up off the tarmac, each with hand outstretched (one bare, one gloved) and grisly determination stamped on their features.

Bernard, already enthroned in his litter, instructed the bearers to stop fussing around like overdeveloped aunts, because this was simply the world watching them and therefore nothing to be scared of.

At the press conference an interviewer observed that he was the biggest of all seventy-one participants and asked if he would agree to being photographed standing between the tiny lady Prime Minister of the new Federated Sovereign States of Indo-China and the President of the Pygmy Republic. *Well*, the caption quoted him as saying, *I come from a big country, so what else is new!*

— My one priority at the convocation, he told them amid loud laughter of which his own was the loudest. Is not to split my pants doing anything rash because I'd never get another pair made before the week is out.

No mention was made of the IFID summit scheduled to follow. Instead, the correspondents entertained themselves with speculating on the likely fright he would give any local sharks if His Australian Excellency were to lower himself into the warm Sri Lankan waters for a swim.

— I dare say you find the heat debilitating, sir? one porky British reporter suggested fraternally as the session closed.

— On the contrary. It makes me randy.

He had been a huge success.

And all the way to his hotel, Bernard Buchanan was haunted, not by a plague of locusts nibbling him in the dark, not by the tidalwave victims, nor by his many acquaintances crushed under the culture of the times, nor even by Dorina who, he had insisted, must represent him at the impending state funeral, but by Lavinia Manciewicz.

43

It could be said that when Lavinia Manciewicz first decided, if deciding is what painters do, to paint her portrait of Bernard Buchanan nude on a field of broken glass, she was as much excited by personal risk as by the professional challenge. She had an intuition he was destined for power.

The brevity and, she admitted, discomfort of her sexual adventure with him did rouse her to compassion, though perversely this took the form of mockery. Perhaps she, like so many others, could not compass a vocabulary for her feelings and, rather than deny them altogether, expressed them by the opposite. But there is no doubt the mockery in her case served the other motive even more effectively: she had had her say, defining her powerlessness as one who needs to comment on power.

Just once, they had played an elephantine comedy together. She inwardly wept with shame throughout while something remarkably simple, a fat man's longing to be undressed and not to mind, cheered him. This was in the picture also. The bravura style invested his supine figure with energy.

She made her sketch in the morning. By then he was dressed once more in his suit, of course. He approved the project. He hoped others would be scandalized, though this hope stopped short of Dorina. Dorina must never know. With that sole caution to qualify his agreement, he sanctioned the work.

The power Lavinia sensed latent within him had no business, though, to grow so gross itself. This was ridiculous: Bernard as candidate, then as the most unlikely president, and soon an autocrat with ambitions to become dictator. She felt, though the idea verged on the grotesque, her painting had been betrayed. Because, yes, she had shown him something in himself he'd not been conscious of. She had, in a way, created the monster all society now suffered. Once her skill planted the idea in mind that he did have the capacity, he was an instant convert, she saw this clearly. Who is to say what might have happened had his doubts remained dominant? Sheer insecurity may have stopped him in his tracks before he'd accepted he had it in him to make a ruler. Lavinia found ample time to reflect on such matters and tease herself with reminiscences about her own moments of power, because when Buchanan completed his third year in office he celebrated by purging society, as he put it, of known enemies, thus helping to ensure a future of smooth progress. She was one of the enemies. The Watchdogs invaded her studio at four in the morning.

By then she had come to see, and with a shadow of bitterness, how much an artist's stock-in-trade is simply memory and nothing more inspired than that. Her images of love and anger were recaptured moments of being abandoned by her mother and of Greta accepting crushing responsibilities (with what bigotry and courage Lavinia could only now begin to assess out of the detritus of involvement), moments also of her little sister Stephanie, a sandcastle, a green umbrella. So the door, when she opened it on grey faces and hard grey hands, on the reading aloud of treachery dressed in the lofty sentiments of law, presented also an enigma. Urgent as the present was, she found she had lost the power of the non-artist to respond directly. She could almost amuse herself with observing how detached she felt, treating this catastrophe as material to provide her with invaluable experience for working through someday. They waited quite politely, shouldering the air out of her studio, while she packed a few essentials in a cheap case. Essentials! Hadn't she heard that the only essentials in Buchanan's jails were heart and lungs and a skin to hold the messy parts in? They did not look at the paintings, not even the nude fat man; they had eyes only for her, serious questioning eyes that weighed her, measured her, tasted her, speculated on her private parts and her likely promiscuity. Eyes also which would spot the impulse to escape before it had even been signalled to her own muscles. They were the eyes of action, eyes never sparked alive by ideas and maybe not by emotions either. Expert eyes, eyes which saw her more knowledgeably, within their discipline, than she saw herself.

The pathetic truth was that she could not believe in the jail. And even if put there, Lavinia's acceptance might lack seriousness. She would, she was positive, be let out again as soon as the error became known. This had to be an error. She was guilty of no offence she could call to mind. With fatal naivety she comforted herself that Luigi Squarcia would speak up for her, their love affair having ended free from theatricals. She still had some influence. She had connections. She had, in short, no conscience. Where were the signals to jolt her back to the inescapable world? She lived her arrest as she imagined she might relive it one day for her nieces and nephews (Stephanie's children; she would have none of her own) or in some scumble of varnish on a grim canvas, some touch of living grey indescribably stopping your heart.

The years of poverty had come back bringing the situation of her being, as she called it, sub-employed. Part-time casual work enough to amount to drudgery and the fatigue of always encountering filth, but not enough to yield an income on which she might rise beyond the escape into her passion for painting. In these times she longed for the simple pleasures of a car ride, a picnic, an evening at the theatre. And nothing, nothing would have persuaded her to paint what she saw: the greasy scullery of a fish-and-chips café, ranks of ancient sewing machines in the shirt factory, the hopeful exhausted faces of her fellow workers.

No, she splashed canvases with carefree parrot colours and shapes more joyful than she ever imagined faith might be.

They waited, the grey men. Impassively they waited, demonstrating by their lack of haste the true hopelessness of her situation, telling her by their spokesman's considerate tone how far beneath them she had sunk in committing offences, whatever these were, punishable by the state.

Non-artists, to apply a term she had not thought out at the time, panicked naturally or faced arrest with dignity, screamed or fought. In whatever way, a non-artist could be relied upon to respond directly and perhaps betray quite clear insights into his or her character. But not the artist. At least, not Lavinia. She packed her few things, and rather too many even so, walking out among the shoulders as if they were her audience, as if what she did and the observation of it were the whole point of their coming along at this inconvenient hour. However, she did not manage the stairs with this beatific state unshaken. First her neighbour and sometime lover, Tim, threw open his door just as she passed and tried dragging her inside to safety. So foolish he was in his alarm. Please, she begged him as if he were the molester and the serious-eyed guards her benefactors. But she meant, please Tim don't get yourself hurt. He could not be expected to know, and had to be thrown to the ground, crushed by whoever could be spared from watching her to prevent any escape, and slung back in his untidy quarters as a mere object lucky enough to be bypassed in the case of this particular party's destination. Naturally he took her *please* to mean he must rescue her at all costs. So, gathering his bruised and never-too-well-coordinated limbs, he charged down the stairs at their departing backs, crashing laughably against the wall, having his head jerked up by a uniformed arm and his legs swept from under him by a uniformed leg and suffering a couple of stunning blows to the midriff. This time he presented the extra trouble of needing to be carted back before being punched about the face to keep him quiet and once again slung in his deplorably untidy room, and his slammed door acquiring a sentry to remain there till the prisoner might safely be locked in the vehicle waiting outside.

As if that were not upsetting enough and sufficient to shock Lavinia into the present, yet another Watchdog emerged from Mrs Connor's room, closing the door behind him on his parting words, *and thanks to you*. And thanks to her for what, an hour before daybreak? For Tim's sake, Lavinia had been torn between struggling to reach him and struggling to control her fury and terror. Her sole objective was to save him from more beatings, to save him being arrested in his own right. But no such complication held her in check at this second interruption. She shrieked: You bitch, you lousy treacherous spying bitch. Shoulders boxed her in and moved her, now not at all politely, out to the front door and into the wagon with its barred glass and warm motor pulsing in an arena of anonymous windows with the parted curtains being let fall into place.

Lavinia Manciewicz was jailed without trial.

She appealed to the High Court but her lawyer received a most courteous note from the Chief Justice laying out reasons why the appeal could not be heard. And she had remained in jail, without being told why, ever since. Tim, when he visited her, promised he would abandon his monumental investigation of drug smuggling and begin exposing the corruption of the law. Following her instructions, he wrote on her behalf to Luigi Squarcia and to the president himself, but neither replied. After this she just smiled tiredly every time he came with a fresh plan of action, another hopeless enthusiasm. She lost her fire. He saw how fragile her highspirits had been, how close to panic her joy in life. Occasionally Stephanie went with him straight from the newspaper office, but she had her own burden now Luke was conscripted to work at an assimilation camp. Failure and hopelessness settled around them. They lived a twilight life, futile as the unemployed, prodded and mocked by memorabilia of something to be done.

One night Tim had not dared go home. Even from the bus stop he saw his street flickering blue with strobe lights, police cars blocking it off, and a small huddle of citizens impounded on the footpath. He turned off along the back lane, putting up his umbrella for further concealment, though the drizzle had really stopped. Among the garbage cans he made his escape. But when he reached the end of the lane, on the corner of a neighbouring street, he could not resist the call to glance back, to look up at his own window. There was, of course, no one there. Lavinia's studio, however, which had been locked and sealed off by the Department of Internal Security, blazed with light. A bald tubby man stood looking down at him, peering from that bright electric glare into the gloom of a backyard evening. Tim ducked under the umbrella and hurried round the corner. He kept walking. He had quarter of an hour left before curfew. The risks were tremendous. He took a taxi to Darling

Harbour and walked some more, not knowing, in his fear, where to turn without implicating some friend or another. On a deserted wharf of the once busy port, among towering frames of a rusting development project, he came upon a shack. There, among the rats, he took refuge, certain he was too cold and miserable to sleep.

He woke, easing independent pains along each of his limbs in turn, trying out his cramped neck and letting the boulder of his head clunk back against the concrete wall. From the water came an intoxicating stench of diluted refuse. As he stumbled out into early morning, three youngsters approached along the wharf, pulling homemade carts. One had his head flung high with the joy of producing a penetrating out-of-tune whistle. He walked barefoot, as sure of his tread as a bushman. Dust collected in the cracked scabs on his knees and ankles. This lad might have been ten and bore the mark of a leader. The whistle stopped mid-note. Laughter gagged in the wide-gapped teeth of the boy behind. But the girl, defiant of the hopeless contemptible thing men were, urged them on.

— Goodday, said Tim wiping his mouth with the back of one hand as if he had been eating breakfast.

— Come on, the defiant girl insisted irritably. Or we'll miss out altogether.

They heaved at the carts again.

— Did you sleep in there? the youngest asked, peering past into the ruin.

Tim nodded.

— Bloody draughty-looking place, the child suggested.

— Come on, the girl yelled, tugging savagely at the rope of her cart so it thrummed and the wood stacked inside slid and slapped.

— You've made a pretty good job of finding firewood, Tim commented hoping to win her approval.

— I've got bottles, the little boy announced and surveyed his scroungings, hands on hips.

Tim took a couple of paces forward to see for himself. But the leader growled warily and threatened him with a length of lead pipe. This was all they had to keep hunger away.

— Peace, said the man remembering a game he played as a child. But they didn't appear to recognize the word.

The harbour glimmered quietly.

The little boy had socks as well as shoes. He pulled them up for the sake of his dignity, but the one which was far too big for him immediately sank to a heap of disreputable wrinkles. The leader's face, blithe and airy so little time ago, now appeared whittled from wood. He kept the weapon in one hand and dragged his cart with the other. The girl, keeping close, tugged her shame behind her, that old box fitted on pram wheels. Perhaps she was his sister.

— Tomorrow, the little boy confided to Tim. I'm going out after a load of horses' shit.

— Is that right? In the city?

— I found the paddock myself. They've got a pony club and all, those rich kids.

— That's one good thing about them then, isn't it?

— Their horses, the child called over his shoulder as he jerked the clinking load of bottles into motion. Are shitting all the bloody time.

Tim watched them. They slowed down when they found he wasn't following. The leader held his head high and let out that razor-edged whistle, moving the note up and down to approximate a popular tune. The girl who collected shameful rubbish kicked her ankles while her dress took on the angular stiffness of her back. The little boy turned and raised one hand. Tim saluted him.

44

— I can't tell you, Dorina Buchanan explained in an unsteady voice as her heels crunched the white gravel drive. How appalled I am. And she suddenly turned to her companion compelling her, really, to meet the gesture. So they stood face to face allowing the degree of Dorina's distress to be gauged.

— Darling, Lady Penhallurick wailed. It's very sad, all this. Sir William couldn't make it though he'd set his heart on being here. He was too ill this morning, truly. He has had a terrible blow, of course. He's ninety-six this year you know. He even wept a little. And that I have never seen before.

Side by side they resumed walking. Hundreds of others proceeded the same way in knots, many with that assumed gravity of people who know more about how to behave than how to feel, along the sterile approaches to the National Crematorium. And they regarded the building ahead (in those single swoops of vision we use to check our direction when choosing to contemplate the ground while walking uphill) without the least shudder at its squat functional design. Hearses were already waiting in line to deliver bodies, the first of so many.

— These people died, Dorina went on, plainly speaking of corpses other than the ones parked up ahead. For the same reason, I'm convinced of it, and we are ignoring the decencies. We have to because we have been told to.

The less fuss the better, had been Squarcia's phrase.

— Well dear, it's because we were saved, Alice Penhallurick explained, a little surprised that Dorina of all people should need to hear this from her. We were saved, she repeated fiddling with her rings, twisting them round while she stretched her fingers out straight. And these were the heroes.

— You can't be serious! the president's wife retorted almost rudely, her heels digging at the pebbles, a handbag dangling from her forearm to pat her dully on the thigh. You don't mean to tell me you swallowed that hypocrisy about the Russians? I have always been so much against experiments interfering with nature. Test-tube babies make me shudder. If the mothers are sterile let them do something else with their lives. Even worse are these scientists tinkering around finding out how to upset the balance of earth.

— Well I don't hold with test-tube babies either, Lady Penhallurick agreed doubtfully, choosing this as the safer of the two examples by a long chalk. That I will say.

— And now here we are, look at us, the collective hierarchy of the land, parading this public display for people who died because somebody made a cynical decision that they should die, that a few guineapigs dead would be all right. We ought to rise up in anger. At very least we ought to demand an enquiry and not, she waved her gloved hand. Wallow in a media jamboree.

— Your husband, the other lady dared suggest with her incomplete sentence.

— Oh he can't be reasoned with, Dorina risked exclaiming. But whatever he says, this won't look right in the eyes of the people. How can they be expected to believe the two tragedies were not connected?

— Both with water. . . ?

— Both with gravity!

Suddenly Lady Penhallurick, despite the clutter of her inherited millions, the respected family name and chain of newspapers she brought her husband as dowry, saw beyond the expedient just for a moment, saw Dorina Buchanan not as wife of the president, not even as a woman she had never liked or understood, but as incorruptible. Tinged perhaps with envy, this insight caused her to reach out and touch the arm the handbag hung from.

— You have such a good heart, she said surprised, then delved in her own bag for a tissue and blew her nose to cover the embarrassment of having committed a *faux pas*, but hastily tucked it away again because the television cameras were right that minute panning across the broad array of mourners and must, of necessity, linger on herself, even if only because of whom she was with. As an afterthought, she extracted the tissue again, not without a telltale surreptitiousness, and applied it once more to her nose, which this time, however, she did not blow in that hearty punishing manner so characteristic of her. The decorous gesture of a held handkerchief brought added reassurance: she would not be shown to the nation twiddling her diamonds, as happened a few days ago during a tour of the very building responsible for the other tragedy. This, she decided, must succeed in being both ladylike and noble in sentiment. She allowed herself a sniff too, now and again.

Marching up beside them, a file of pencil pines cut into the sullen sky, severe as railings, the arrested air chill and so dry it crumbled on their hats. The place smelled of quartz, that subtle but intensely mineral smell which nothing can permeate.

Dorina gave her up. What was the point, she lectured her goodwill despairingly, of trying to lodge any idea whatsoever in that empty cranium; let alone bold doubts suggesting that the merely private funerals of the Cultural Centre victims labelled their deaths accidental, that the silly woman's husband would undoubtedly be put before a commission of enquiry for negligence and probably a criminal court as well? Buchanan had always wanted some leverage over the old man; she sensed it and it made her suspect that till now the boot had been on the other foot. My dear, he had rumbled at the conclusion to her protest on the phone, your feelings do you credit and I'm grateful you've called all this way to tell me. The point is that a freak accident is a freak, even if it is a tragedy also. But I cannot ignore the special claims of victims of a war of nerves: they are as clearly war casualties as your uncle was in Crete. If I were in better health I would fly back in person. No one but you can represent me adequately. (Owen. . . she had begun to object.) Owen Powell will not do. And anyway that would set a danger-ous precedent. I can't have my lieutenants jockeying for posi-tions of seniority. I will not let any of them stand up there in my place. So I shall rely on you to attend. Who else could convey an expression of my deep condolences? All I ask is that you respect the fact that the public is highly impressionable, not to say gullible. Let's stick to one memorial service at a time. Diplomacy is the word, darling. And thank you.

She had calmed herself then, because a tearful woman was quite the wrong one to say what she needed to tell him. Bernard, she replied knowing that the rare use of his first name would announce the seriousness of this moment. I have stood by you over the years, even while not being at the mansion. I have watched you do things I confess I could never condone, and all through the trauma of being the president's wife I have held my counsel. I have given your enemies nothing, not one shred they can use against you, though it has cost me my peace of mind, my happiness, to do so. But this Paringa affair goes beyond that. It goes beyond me and even beyond you. I am an Australian before anything. I will not see my country die. You cannot fool me with lies. I know how the state works. I know about international diplomacy. I have only this to say: If I ever have to face the anguish of intervening to save you from IFID I shan't flinch. You may take what action you please now you have been told. But I will not live that particular lie because I have no right to do so.

— How very sad, Lady Penhallurick moaned as they drew near the first hearse and a microphone on a boom came swinging towards them. My dear, she sighed and once again laid her fat little hand on the lean arm with its dangling handbag. The poor people, she whispered emphatically.

Dorina, representing her husband, spared the cameras a single neutral glance. Her composure perfect, she couldn't have carried off the occasion with more dignity or courage, as commentators murmured appreciatively into the public ear. And so to the foyer of the crematorium. Morgues, Dorina recollected, were once called Dead Houses. This is the true Dead House of the modern city: barren brick and sound-baffling glass, the impersonal design, even of the pews, making a virtue of avoiding the least stylishness, even avoiding any special quality in the materials. An electric organ mooed its hideous mechanical vibrato, amplified and plugged through to all five chapels in the building. The further these banalities unfolded, the more she came to realize how heartlessly melodramatic it was for the state to have flown the bodies up from Eden and flown the mourners too, just for the record, just for the sake of a reported occasion.

She employed her full willpower to prevent showing the distaste she felt. Not even grief could be private these days, but
must be turned to political account. Then came a stir at the rear
of the chapel. Sir William Penhallurick had arrived after all. So
ancient was he and so sick he needed to be driven to the door
like another corpse. The Master of Protocol of the Presidential
Household ushered him personally to that empty seat between
the two women, which Dorina had been led to believe was to
remain symbolically unoccupied as a gesture of presidential
sympathy. There sat the old man for all the nation to witness,
shaken and fragile.

Only then did Dorina see how she had been trapped, how the
judge and Roscoe Plenty set this up not just to save themselves
but to protect the odious Penhallurick. She'd supposed they
were keeping Owen Powell from deputizing for her husband. By
playing on her wellknown independence of mind, they led her
to think the Chief Minister wished to make use of her, when all
the time it was the old man. Far from trapping Sir William in a
charge of personal culpability, here she was, by her very presence as First Lady, exonerating him from yet another crime,
being seen to accept him as still among the president's inner
circle and therefore beyond reach of the law. She was in purgatory at the thought of Rory watching his corrupter beside her.
She could not possibly make a fuss or leave in protest. Whichever alternative power-play the planners had in mind, they
engineered the effect scrupulously.

Once, she caught Kékszakállú's implacable tearful eye, raw-
rimmed and cold as a seagull's. She shivered at his closeness. So
when the time came for her to walk alone in front of the
congregation and place an official wreath at the centre of the
platform where it could be seen to grace the obsequies for each
successive coffin committed to the furnace in that two-day-long
procession, she did so with the relief of escaping contamination.

— My husband and I, she announced to the microphone in
her steady diplomatist's voice and well aware of historic ironies.
Offer our sincere sympathy to the loved ones of each victim of
this. . . tragedy.

No, she was not going to call them victims of a war of nerves
for anyone's sake. And if the occasion bound her to go through
with the proprieties, it also put power in her hands. So, when
she had delivered the speech prepared for her, she added a
personal message.

— At this time, too, we extend the same deep sympathy to

the families of those other victims who died in the collapse of our new Cultural Centre. The president sends personal condolences to you all.

Among the bowed heads, the Right Honourable Roscoe Plenty looked up sharply, playing his part for when the president would scrutinize this film, frame by frame. What was the bitch doing? his look asked. Didn't she understand my strict instructions?

Dorina placed her wreath exactly where it had to be placed and led the nation in a ceremonial two minutes' silence. Then returned to her seat to witness the first coffin sinking, the stage-machinery grotesquely slick and noiseless, the effect so vulgar nothing short of her reticence could have saved the service lapsing into complete unreality. Even her diplomat father would have admitted she performed flawlessly.

Sir William Penhallurick, though jubilant at the success of outwitting her, could now be certain she shunned him for worse offences than his scrofula, being, after all and obsessively, sensitive to the least slight. He knew he was not mistaken. So when they parted company outside the chapel, he into the limousine with his wife and she to walk with the other mourners back down the hill in contemplation of the departed, he thanked her for speaking with such emotion, just to get a good look. Her eyes, which had not met his until that instant, darkened with loathing and stared deeply among secrets. Once she fixed him in her sights she did not let him go. She would have it, her look insisted, that he escape. She stared him down with that haughty courage of hers. If the contemptible creature, she thought, wishes to provoke me in public, he can bear the consequences.

Bernard, viewing the ceremony later on video and observing this for himself, shook his head in admiration. She's a remarkable woman, he said, impossible as she is. Lady Alice also caught that look, even if only the corner of it, which at once sent colour flooding to her cheeks on behalf of her dear Willy who would never learn to cope with an Anglo-Saxon like Dorina. Fearful on his behalf, especially concerning his many previous wives and what, to herself, she called their fatal deaths, her blush was a blush of shame and too late to be hidden.

— She's not a very nice person, Lady Penhallurick confided to him that night in bed. To have so high up. You know, she told me the most shocking things. She said it was all hypocrisy about the Russians and a tidalwave. She said those other people ought to have been given the same state funeral. She said sterile women shouldn't be allowed to have test-tube babies. She's against the Paringa thing. She said her husband (Alice could no longer bring herself to call him Bernard, let alone dear Bernard, as she used to) was not to be reasoned with. I remember it exactly, I was so frightened by it, and all those cameras on us showing us to deaf people who can lip-read. It wasn't proper for conversation at a funeral, Lady Penhallurick justified her objection finally. Then added because he seemed unimpressed: And I dare say they made a film of all that to keep for the archives.

Sir William, already lying on his back, simply closed his eyes behind their painful lids, locking the precious information away in the safety of his dark dungeon. He supposed he had all he might ever want.

45

In the Maldives, Bernard Buchanan charmed a good many of his fellow heads of state by giving convincing proof of being as vulgar as they. He sat through sessions during which prime ministers and presidents-general recited statements cautiously phrased by public servants to give nothing away. A few of these sessions he enlivened with fruity jokes, or by delivering himself of abuse against anyone who began to look shaky. He stayed back for the IFID summit and complained that this was a lot less enjoyable. Even so, waiting to re-board his aircraft and roll out along the runway, destined not only to leave last but to be further delayed by a bomb scare entailing the usual scrupulous security check, he could only agree with Squarcia that he had scored an enviable notoriety. He put it in the form of a complaint.

— Hell on earth, these tropical islands! he declared in hearing of their hosts. This is my first taste, of course. I never went overseas at all before and I don't see much fun in it. They can't cook a decent steak, the beer is warm, the weather a furnace, while the real people rush off and hide when they see you coming. I used to plan to travel. Oh yes, as a young bloke, I made lists of the places I'd go, even mapping the exact routes through this town and that. Central America, Scandinavia, you name it, I went there in imagination. But never actually made it. You know how it is. . . you intend doing something and you're just about to do it when life hits you to leg and you never get the chance back. Well, this junket makes me one of the lucky ones, I've had a second chance. But I shan't say yes to a third crack at making a fool of myself, I can tell you.

The hosts smiled and nodded and sat forward attentively on their chairs.

This is how things were in the private departure lounge when Sir George Gipps turned up. He took notice neither of Squarcia nor the Sri Lankans, but launched right into a new line of hectoring: I understand what it is to cope with an antagonistic administration and a strict taskmaster on the far side of the world, he began in his band-saw voice of an English gentleman. But there the similarity ends. I certainly do not wish to mislead you into thinking we have anything else in common. (Buchanan cast his eyes to heaven or the clock.) I merely accept that these things drain one's energy and account for a certain abruptness. I myself was accused of being inhospitable in my dealings with those bumpkin-squires determined to make off with the Crown's legitimate revenue. They called me overbearing. You see, I know about that reputation and I acknowledge it. You should take a leaf from my book, because you are considered overbearing too (Buchanan looked to Squarcia this time, who looked back, noting how the president's eyes bulged), but the rift between myself and my Executive Council lay in the fact that they, like the squatters they represented, were opportunists, whilst I insisted on the rule of law.

Gipps crossed his short thick thighs tight as a couple of sausages in their immaculate nankeen breeches, stuck his nose in the air at a comfortable angle for looking down, and further entertained the furious Buchanan: By contrast, it's your parliament calling for thrift and the rule of law while you represent the opportunists!

Squarcia rescued the situation by producing a pocket video and suggesting they watch the funeral via IFID satellite.

There trod Dorina with her stately crispness, and the gushing Alice Penhallurick beside her. A line of hearses queued out of sight beyond the crematorium wall, chauffeurs standing at attention beside them, caps held against their bellies. Here was the Master of Protocol of the Presidential Household seating his official party and leaving a place vacant between the two ladies.

— Doing him this favour after his building fell down, Buchanan threw some gold riskily into the ring. I owe Sir Bill Penhallurick nothing.

Naturally he made no mention of the other side of the coin,

the criminal charges of negligence and manslaughter he might one day allow to be aired in court.

— Think of me, Squarcia said giving a skilful impression of not knowing what was meant. Stuck here for another four days. The food is so exquisite and plentiful I shall lose my waistline. He bowed, though sitting, to the Sri Lankan civil servants.

They wagged appreciative faces like competition kites.

— If your IFID meeting is as scintillating as ours was, Lou, the great man roared. You're in for a fiasco. You should have warned me this was no more than a PR stunt. Who wants to cop their propaganda? We have enough of our own for a good dose of indigestion. I didn't see the point of it. (His flight was called.) As for stopping off at Tuavaleva to oblige them further, I'd have half a mind to give it a miss if it weren't for my word I'd meet Dorina there. Dorina, he mused as he floated out on his litter to the renewed admiration of those for whom this was still a novelty. Keeps me up to the mark. She is never a disappointment. She always drives me mad! and he bellowed a cluster of laughs in different keys.

— *Buon viaggio* Your Excellency, Squarcia called as they shook hands.

Harvey, Noel, Craig, Scott & Company, all with brand-new tropical suntans, carried the presidential litter, garlanded and glittering, out in a blaze of spotlights between whirring cameras where Buchanan's trumpeted farewells boomed among batteries of microphones.

The night suddenly crashed about him as rain, sweeping him away in diamond veils while the exhausted band played *Advance, Australia Fair* at a gallop.

— One day, my dear, Dorina promised as servants settled them side by side in the places of honour. You'll come out in your true colours.

This was a saying of his own and a threat he had used against her.

— What day? Buchanan replied from the paralysis of discomfort.

They watched palmtrees swish and toss and crowds debating passionate pleasantries at forty tables less prominent than their own. Shaded by flapping canvas awnings (Buchanan suffered a flashback to a towel doing similar service), guests dotted the lawns of a great garden. (Now this, Dorina exclaimed, is a truly noble garden.) Squabbling birds populated the shrubbery, while a detachment of peacocks stalked along the grassy aisle, trailing capes like thin matadors and pointing their matador toes as they paused to consult silently, crests trembling, and then pricked a stage closer to the high terrace where the officials sat ready to be fed.

— Which colours? he asked from his sweaty folds of fat, pleased that the Tuavalevans had hailed his bulk as the mark of a king.

She could almost be deceived into thinking him humble.

There was nothing to be done for half an hour at least but wait to be served and watch the peacocks, which, despite their finery, had rapacious eyes. For all that gorgeous plumage, they were no more civilized than carrion crows when it came to the point.

— You'll be shown up for a man capable of madness, she ventured, nervily bright. With age her angularity had grown stringy, neck and arms stippled by moles as well as freckles, her whimsical determination to confront the truth more than ever a case of morality.

— You cannot appreciate how hard Roscoe is working, the Australian president rebuked his wife tenderly, bringing her back to the point. To save people from knowing how wide-spread the casualties were from that tidalwave. We are perfecting a technique Squarcia has invented a name for, Delayed Pacification. What do you think of that? Does it fit? I believe in having the right label.

— Don't try to tell me, Dorina held up her glass as a shield. That the times call for special sacrifices.

— I wonder do I have true colours anyhow? You know that, Dorina? I really can't be sure.

— Special *indulgence* is more like it, she pursued without attending to his digression. If more people had an ounce of commonsense, they'd read the signs and begin defying your crew as often as they could.

— Thank goodness, he joked. I have got you in my team. Then he reverted to her earlier accusation: I might say that all sane men are capable of madness. Only those already mad are safe from that. He grew confidential. In the interests of longterm security and international diplomacy we shouldn't jump to conclusions.

— You have not listened to what I just told you.

They thought this over for some minutes. The truth was that the babble of foreign voices oppressed them both. Dorina had begun by being excited; nostalgia surprised her back into childhood so that despite the heat she exclaimed at every compliment, at the vivacious crowd, the sound and solidity of things, knotted sarongs and their hosts' sweet attentiveness. But suddenly the magnitude of the gathering alarmed her. She stared at those hundreds of guests, plus perhaps thousands of dark faces respectfully looking on as a surrounding hedge of humanity, and knew her life to be in danger: she being so foreign and the past clotted with angry blood. The prescribed formality of such an occasion only made her the more vulnerable, stuck her up as a perfect target where any assassin could see her perfectly. What if some fanatic recognized her? Had she injured anybody or slighted them? How had she and Bernard been rash enough to walk into this set-up of their own free will? From one moment to the next might be the measure of her life. His too. Dorina learned this when young. As they paraded through the mass of welcoming islanders, somebody presented her with a flower, and a child offered a mangosteen. She nearly fainted at the touch of it. She had not seen or tasted the fruit since that day they found her sandwiched between concertina leaves of a folding screen and she'd scrambled out, running for the safety of her father's cold embrace, stumbling and falling, tripped by a human foot, she had screamed as she expected her attacker to hold her back; and then realized Miss Gardiner was stuck to the floor by her own blood and the nauseating stench making her father cover his nose came from the pit of Miss Gardiner's stomach where she had been opened up from side to side in a deep smiling clean line. Dorina, being Dorina, held on to the gift mangosteen and gritted her teeth. She said thank you and thank you thank you. She clutched that mangosteen till it grew warm and sickening, before a table presented itself on which she could place the fruit, singular as a trophy.

— I feel suffocated by ignorance of what they are saying, she whispered. Suffocated.

Music, at last, caught up with her. A thin jaunty reed-piping from the entertainers' pavilion. Oh, she had set out from Sydney with such romantic hopes.

But here sat Buchanan, mountainous on his throne, his mounds of flesh unnatural as a miracle, disgusting as a freak, opening confidential lips.

— I thought you spoke the language? You've told me over and over about your diplomatic childhood in Tuavaleva.

— It wasn't like this then, she replied distantly. I've forgotten, she corrected herself.

The garlands of flowers they wore smelled of wet earth. Too far away to be seen properly, a troupe of young women performed, with Islamic modesty, traditional dances. Their modesty got in the way like a thicket to be fought through, absorbed as they were with denying any sensualist the least hint of what interested him. Their sweet faces doubtless blushed at the temptations of so public an event; and this it was which left them breathless with animation as they were presented afterwards to the guests of honour, who were then able to verify for themselves the sweetness of the faces and the thicket of modesty.

— I do love your fabrics, Dorina said to the dignitary on her left, who grinned. So sudden and vivacious he was, she felt taken aback. An elderly man, he reacted with too much energy, an almost childlike willingness to please. Then she faced the more disquieting truth that he wasn't childlike in the slightest, but enviable in still having the gift of spontaneity though old enough, she realized in a further shift of mood, to have been one of the killers running amok through the school she attended. That school building, only twenty kilometres away if it still stood, had been the one place she considered revisiting when she agreed to come on this trip. Now the idea repelled her. How morbid. The man grinned in all his wrinkles and made light conversation about having studied, many years before, the novels of Charles Dickens. If, she thought, I could only catch sight of his ankle, I would recognize him perhaps. And yet Dorina did not shrink. It cheered her enormously to think that even a mob with knives could mellow to cultured and considerate old gentlemen.

— How much longer? Bernard groaned privately to her. And if it gets another degree hotter I shall melt altogether. You'll have to take me home in a giant bottle.

She felt the ache of her love for him.

— Buchanan, she whispered in his hairy ear. You are such a comfort.

— Even in my true colours? He looked at her for the first time in ages.

— You've always been in your true colours for me. I was only speaking of how surprised other people would be.

— This banquet, he remarked. Is going to outlast me. And we

haven't yet begun on the food. What I want to know is who among these individuals has been sent to report on me.

She acknowledged a new burst of cheering as entertainers with loud wind instruments swayed between the tables to blow a tribute especially for her.

— If only, she confided as though sharing her delight. You hadn't been so successful we might be having tea and lamingtons at Orange instead.

— Orange! He laughed his overfed laugh and the officials at the table looked on with mild interest. How exotic that must sound, a town called Orange. Who could imagine anything so. . .

— Domestic? she supplied.

Prince Haupoupou had welcomed the Buchanans, but then retired indoors, leaving them in the care of his ministers who offered the entertainment of some lively facts about the island, such as the population being 56% Malay, 9% Indian, 7% Chinese and 28% Islander, which was to say Polynesian. One minister laughed at the idea that there might be discontent among the races. No, another explained, we all eat crabs and durian so why should we quarrel? Promptly they kissed each other, the Malay and the Polynesian, to prove their accord. Bernard glanced at his wife, as much as to say: So much for your nightmares! We were once to become the capital, a third minister contributed as he guided them to their seats, of the whole Pacific, we had a British naval base here, then an American naval base, do you believe, and so many people coming and going. We had embassies, we had consulates. It's very quiet now. Even your own country sent a consul, I'm thinking.

— Did we? Bernard grumbled.

— Oh yes indeed, an Indian minister chipped in.

— Until we closed the port to all warships.

— That, the first explained, standing back interested while the bearers settled Buchanan on his seat, which had been installed earlier in the afternoon. Was Prince Haupoupou's doing. Thirty years ago.

The food eventually arrived from the prince's kitchen. Delicate flavours steeped in coconut milk, bowls of turtle eggs to be dipped in hot water and sucked from their elastic shells raw but warm. Poor Buchanan, Dorina thought as she watched him feign enthusiasm (she could guess how he would poke fun at the food later), he has no fear to live down. In life, he still expects something better to happen. She straightened her tingling back. Knowledge of the wild side of mankind gave her disadvantages she would not dare be without. A waiter bent over to serve her. She told him how much she loved the food piled, as so much of it was, on banana leaves. Suddenly she smelt again the odour of soap she associated with the dormitory, with her revulsion at that echoing bathroom and its violations of privacy. Then the memory was gone again, overpowered by the garland round her neck.

So dusk came to the palace garden and the swiftly flying night. Lanterns were lit. Tireless musicians flickered in and out of the dark. The tossing palmtrees wrestled desperately against something up there which had come down on them, some threshing presence the guests took no heed of. Shadow-puppets illustrated moralities by the harsh light of pressure lamps. The town crowd, having advanced through the gates, squatted mutely absorbed by the marvel of such festivities and checked that the foreigners were impressed too, for everyone's happiness hung on the happiness of the visitors. Outside, trishaw riders stood on the seats of their vehicles and, resting brown arms comfortably along the warm stone wall, smoked and exchanged views on poetry and fidelity.

The prince himself, gracing the banquet briefly in its later stages, congratulated the Honourable Buchanan for having a flower of a wife and retired again to appreciative clapping. Despite the tribute to Dorina, this was, Buchanan knew, an absolute snub. He recalled Squarcia's account of the price of failure: the new weapons stockpile might end up in Western Australia instead.

— Orange, Dorina resurrected their game to distract him from the insult. Or Come by Chance, NSW.

— Noggerup WA, Bernard rallied. Humpty Doo.

All this, Dorina comforted herself, will soon be forgotten. And at least it shows Buchanan is not invulnerable.

— Whitey's Fall, she helped him. And Banana, Queensland.

He is guilty, she perceived the truth, of not having grown up. He has the charm and the brutality of an innocent. She watched the frantic palmtrees and agitated canvas awnings, the shadows of the puppets crowded out by shadows of guests. The dancing had begun. Tables were moved and musicians took their place at the centre of the space. This, Dorina told herself, is unforgettable.

But later that evening her equanimity was shaken. Hour after hour the drums played. Dancers leaped and gyrated. The sense of life became so intense Dorina felt suffocated. Her flowers began to wilt. Her stimulation had no outlet. She yearned to go home to the villa where they were staying. One fellow thumped a gong which she found far more distressing than the drums. He struck it exactly on the beat every beat a hundred times a minute. He had been going like this for more than an hour and showed no sign of tiring. The pain, even at this distance, throbbed like an extracted tooth. Reed instruments squawked and a string sound whined. There were whirrings as a thousand birds circled the garden not to miss a note.

At last, departure was agreed upon. The hosts, delighted by their guests' good manners in having stayed late and enjoyed the food so openly, ushered them down wooden steps to the lawn. This really was rather fun, Dorina concluded. Gentlemen in sarongs stood aside for her as she led the way, towing her stupid handbag and regretting that she could not have taken a more active part. Buchanan's eight bearers stumped along in her wake, keeping step, each footfall shaking the ground with the immense importance of an invasion. A new thought came to her at this moment when she did not have the leisure to give it proper attention: Betrayal comes in the shape of those we trust and the hopes we most dearly hope, otherwise how can it be called betrayal?

Dorina strode among the tables, the perfect golfer, nodding to small groups of men (all men) who, still lingering over coloured drinks, chatted in gentle voices. One of the lanterns tossing in the wind caught fire as she approached, the paper shade bucking like a living creature in the grip of flames. Black patches were eaten away by the night. Young fellows rushed over, laughing while the smouldering relics fell and they could stamp them out. The dancers showed no sign of weakening. Dorina smiled once more and moved through the spectator fringe. So many unknown faces. Her heels turned on dewy grass. The pulsing rhythm screwed her nerves tight. The gong trembled with agony. Sweat jumped off the drummers. Then, immediately after the burning lamp omen, an event flared round her, highlighting her vulnerability. Dorina's gasp, the long fingers held to her mouth, were part of the drama, and for some the most memorable part. A young man who appeared drugged lurched from the dance, veered toward the crowd and then staggered across Buchanan's path, falling against a table. He writhed on the squeaky lawn, clutching his belly. The pain in his face shocked her more than anything.

Their interpreter hastened up and knelt beside the fellow,

whose teeth were grinding while clutches of muscle worked round his neck and jaws. Dorina watched his bare chest heave wildly above a rigid abdomen. She saw his eyes roll right back to white. He was howling and hissing at the same time, knotted into a tangle of tensed sinews. And now spectators formed a circle to surround not only the man in a fit but Bernard and herself too.

— Stop the gong! she shrieked. Can't you tell it's the gong doing it!

Their interpreter, wooing the man's reason back, cradled his head and clucked in a seductive voice. The stupid musicians played on as if nothing were happening. An old saint whom she recognized as one of the puppeteers stooped to assist, stroking the underside of the sufferer's arms and crooning also. Spectators exchanged comments in shopkeeper-voices, while the rest danced on oblivious and the band showed no sign of tiring.

— Make them stop the gong, Dorina pleaded, her fingertips digging at her lip. But they had switched off their power of comprehending English. Hysteria rose in her throat. Sickness swept through her. She would snatch the gong-stick out of the torturer's hand. The victim became a wild animal, face contorted, a white gluey substance trickled from his mouth and flecked his chin. Then his head lolled back, lips loose and swollen like somebody helpless under a lover's prolonged victory, nostrils stretched wide as a horse's and damp hair clinging in tassels. His pores exuded so much moisture he lay glazed in his own oils.

Still the gong beat its mechanical rhythm.

Dorina tried to look away, but her eyes wouldn't allow it. Her whole life had been marked by those hours when she watched for death through the slats of a venetian door. The natural angle of her vision had that same downward cast, whether supercilious or modest. And she could be both. Her memory of Australia, when she called herself to account to produce one, was a train journey across drought-baked plains, herself sitting at a window seat. Everyone along the sunny side of the carriage had pulled down wooden blinds against the glare. So she sat squinting at cracks, the land outside simplified to a few parallel streaks of blinding stubble, cross-sections of parched gulches, a sliced vision of sheep in the festering dust they had kicked up while scrounging for roots where grass once grew.

Now, through narrowed lids, she was forced to watch the sufferer gentled out of his trance. Though the gong still beat a hundred lacerations a minute, his eyes crawled back to confront life. His limbs were induced to surrender their grip on an ecstatic pain whose single promise of love was to die. An expression of the utmost bitterness appeared in his face as he submitted to having his twisted muscles massaged by the saint.

Dorina recollected a few particular words. Yes, all the years since she was eight they had hidden themselves in the folds of memory. One of the consulate servants who drove the car spoke the words to her father as they coughed Miss Gardiner's stench out and escaped from the carnage: You have done this to us, sir, you have turned kind people into beasts.

Only now did she put this to herself as a question.

— Perhaps, a voice advised in an undertone. He does not wish to be looked at.

— I'm so sorry, she ghosted.

As they reached their car, the interpreter caught up, wearing the bright clear colours of one who has saved a life, and presented Dorina with yet another garland of earth-scented flowers.

— If the gong stopped before we got him back, he said. He would be dead.

Bernard at that moment had the grace to pretend he couldn't hear. In addition to which, he had decided this interpreter was the most likely-looking spy.

When she thought back on it, the nightmare of that man in a fit comforted her. The journey through Tuavaleva, until this incident, offered nothing but delightful experiences, friendliness from people so natural and open, so animated and tender, the terror could more easily have been entirely in her own mind than here. Possibly she had invented it. Certainly, as her exclusive property, the bloodshed and hysteria shared nothing in common with the present. She wished, in her western innocence of rewards and punishments, she could surrender something precious as a gift for that man back there lying on the grass and racked with sobs.

— What was your famous Maldives meeting about, anyhow? Dorina enquired sounding snappish in the car. To read the newspapers one would think it was a Club Med for top-grade trash.

His look fractured for a moment as he took refuge in the perfect privacy between them.

— Those of us with heavy overseas commitments appear to be in the worst trouble.

— Oh, she sank back in her seat. Only another world economic collapse.

— This could be a big one.

— Well if it is, his wife sounded almost languid with disgust. There's always the remedy of war!

He turned away to stare into a night of people walking barefoot, the single naked lamp globe suspended above a food vendor's stall casting his customers' heads in bronze, and shanties with scabby stucco façades. A child bounding in front of the car, like a rabbit mesmerized by glamour, suddenly darted away to one side into a labyrinth of dark emergencies.

So the visiting presidential cavalcade proceeded in style.

Once home at the villa, Buchanan had himself installed beside the telephone for his nightly report from Squarcia, still in the Maldives. Meanwhile, Dorina strolled through the arcaded building, revelling in its space and coolness. Servants considerately disappeared into doorways and reappeared when she had passed. Then there was one who did not move, who waited for her to approach. The charm was broken. She halted well before reaching him and decided to go back. In a soft voice he called to her. So greatly surprised she was, she found her heart leapt with joy. Dorina believed she had been cherishing the solitude. But now discovered she longed for contact with these islanders. In the faintly rotting cinnamon-perfumed air, she hesitated while he stepped forward. As they met, she recognized his white hair and his hands. It was the saint.

— Do you know me then, he said delightedly, confidentially, Miss Lambert?

She was taken back more than thirty years, her maiden name sounding so extraordinarily wistful, so deeply familiar from lost rollcalls in high sportsmistress voices and presenting her with a gap in her life she had not fully known was there until this moment.

— Please, he said. Give my welcome to your father.

Now, by the way he touched his hands together so respectfully and tipped his head on one side to invite agreement, she did, at last, know him.

— Ahmad Zain Osman!

— I said you did not forget when you left us. I think of you, he dreamed watching the ceiling now, so tactful in giving her space to overcome her memories of carnage. You are playing the piano. You are so little and the piano is big. All those long things you played to God, he laughed softly as they stood without shaking hands.

Of course Dorina remembered. He it was, and not her father, who had dragged Miss Gardiner's corpse away from the folding screen to rescue her. He it was who had clasped her to him to soothe her convulsive sobs and protect her, before passing her into the consul's hands.

— My father died many years ago, she apologized.

He bowed his head in confirmation.

— I do not belong in this house, he explained. And I must go. You were my favourite. We had many consuls, many families. And you were the only one who loved me.

Tears sprang to Dorina's eyes.

— Tell me it is not true, Miss Lambert. That is why I have come. Tell me your husband is not the same as your father in the care of Allah?

— They could hardly be more different, she smiled her glinting fractured edges.

— You have been my daughter. And now you will be our mother, you will stand in his way, he persisted coyly. If he brings the power to destroy us.

— *Did* my father come to destroy you? she caught her breath at the impossibility she already knew to be true.

The old servant's white hair shivered. His fine hands sought each other's comfort.

— He talked to our Prince Haupoupou. To make him change his mind. Consul Lambert spoke for the British because we had sent them away. They wanted to bring their ships back to Tuavaleva and put their army at the port.

— I still play the piano, Dorina said, recollecting her position. And there is still no one to listen. But the things I play for God are a lot more complicated than they used to be when I was a girl.

Ahmad Zain Osman accepted her loyalty: to her father, to her husband, and to himself. He had said what he came to say. This loyalty of hers was a sign, also, of her power and a comfort already.

— Our life, he explained. Is simple. More simple than it was when you were here. Should we change because other countries change? he asked and she recognized the very touch he had used to gentle the dancer out of his fit.

— No, she answered simply and with all the emphasis of weighing her conflicting loyalties.

He did not say goodbye, this man who had shouted with
outrage against the vengeance of his own people, torn by a
desperation he shared with them. His hands shaped the word
instead. And he was gone.

Dorina returned to what she had made of her life, to the
bedroom which she reached in time to hear the close of Buchanan's overseas telephone call.

— . . .Lou. It failed. Just tell them that.

He put the phone down, not at all like a schemer but more
like a man who must think where tomorrow's dinner is coming
from. He faced his wife calmly. I keep dreaming, he told her. Of
a particular woman.

— But you never sleep, Buchanan.

— That doesn't stop me dreaming.

— I suppose, Dorina admitted tiredly. She is young and
beautiful and full of admiration for you?

He rolled his eyes, playing up to the image.

— No, he said afterwards. She is old and vulgar. She, he
pinpointed what it was that worried him. . . Is out to get me.

It seemed absolutely grotesque. How had Dorina come down
to this debauchery of pettiness?

— Well, she replied curtly. You have the whole state security
service to look after you.

46

One thing about flying, President Buchanan decided on the
journey back to Canberra. At least Gippso can't reach me here.
That would be an anachronism.

— Have you never heard of heaven? Sir George's voice
enquired.

The president thought about this and eventually answered.

— Not for a long time.

The excitement of an entourage assembling, the hustle and
clamour of public relations, the setting out, the arrival to a rainsoaked band giving off steam as if that was what drove them as
a life-sized mechanical toy, his triumph at entertaining the
world's press, the profound satisfaction of hearing for himself
the banal level of discussion between world leaders, such pampering and photographing (with his litter habitually set up right
at the centre for reasons of artistry), the diversions and extravagance, the loss of routine and a consequent sensation of floating

aimlessly but importantly through the day, fiddling with a neat little headset by which, at a flick of the thumb, he could hear himself back in simultaneous translation, giving out the old profundities in Swahili or Urdu, and even more pleasurably performing the same trick on other people's boring contributions, his rendezvous with Dorina; but the rich agglomeration of this whole experience balanced on a fragile foundation of imminent crisis, swiftly turned sour as a no-account princeling left a dozen ministers to cope with the grand incarnation of Buchanan as a sign, an IFID gesture, which Squarcia had promised would bring them to their knees. The turmoil mounted in mind on the journey home, churning, gestating while Dorina dozed and the aircraft whined a lullaby, at last beginning its descent. The captain ambled aft to present his compliments to Their Excellencies. Also to warn them that some turbulence might be experienced owing to a storm over Canberra.

— Don't bother me now, Buchanan snarled irritably and plunged back into the ruin of expectations.

For a moment, in the evening above the capital, the president glimpsed his city spread-eagled dimly among anthills. Ahead, awesome crags of cloud towered a hundred metres high. They cruised along sagging wet valleys and speared through blinding resistless cliffs to emerge into a weirdly illuminated space suspended over clotted vapour dense and dark as forested hills. Lightning switched on and off like a sheet of bright tin being turned. Colliding caves of blood dissolved into crevices and bastions. Dorina slept while the aircraft sang to her. One heliograph window far below signalled the day's end, glinting through veils of rain. The air was sucked from under them and they dropped into a pit, the wind down at the bottom rushing up to slam against the plane, solid as rock.

— Too late to change course, the president joked to himself. Having the fatalism of a novice, he supposed most flights went like this. He could have kept his cool nicely if he did not have such a lively mind. This is sheer madness.

Slanting waterfalls of light streamed from the storm as the jet dipped underneath it into an ochre dusk, set blindly on course, thumping against invisible obstacles, buoyed by the very air that assaulted it.

Sir George Gipps was heard having a quiet, mirthless chuckle, but declined to show himself.

Roscoe Plenty failed to show up at the airport to lead the

thanksgiving for Their Excellencies' safe landing; so it was Owen Powell who stepped forward into the limelight.

— Things were not the same without you, the Minister for Internal Security mooed lovingly.

— Naturally not.

Later, at the mansion, the president laughed the first laugh of his return.

— Mr Plenty I presume? I expected to be told you'd gone for a shit and a sniper got you. He stopped laughing. Are you aware that you missed the only opportunity you will ever have to be seen welcoming me home?

Not liking either alternative implied by this question, Roscoe Plenty, the worried wolf, fumed with the frustration of his late arrival.

— Engine trouble at Melbourne airport, would you believe? he excused himself. And I had to wait while they arranged a replacement flight. I was so angry and upset. . .

— Did you have yesterday? I mean here in Australia? Buchanan asked a solemn-faced Owen Powell.

— Yes Your Excellency, I remember it clearly, we certainly did have yesterday. Yesterday, he explained.

— Then why, the president accused Roscoe Plenty coldly. Did you not take advantage of yesterday to return? he held up one hand to halt the traffic-jam of excuses. There has been backsliding while I was overseas. I know it. I don't need to be told. I can smell it in the air. The moment we began our descent I felt it rush up to meet me. Well I'm back. So that's an end to the shenanigans. Don't try softsoaping me. I shall crack down as hard as I can. Let this be a warning.

And that was how he began his welcome home address on television.

— I will not tolerate backsliding. Some sectors of the community think they can freeload at the expense of the rest of us. This is not good enough, friends, as I'm sure you can see for yourselves. Someone always has to pay. Rumours are only rumours, I know, but there's generally a grain of truth in them. So let me say this with the utmost clarity: I will not accept any division of Australians into two classes, the wealthy and the workers. No, he thundered, suddenly in full swing. We are all truly one class. We are all wealthy. That is a fact. The person who denies it is a bloody stirrer, I'm telling you. Let any citizen who has ever been where I've just been, to Sri Lanka or Tuavaleva or to Europe for that matter, come and look me in the eye right here in front of you and tell me we have a poor class. I'd give him a thump on the nose for a liar. And you know what? If he got a thump from me he wouldn't come back for another, that's for sure. We are, as I say, all wealthy. We have different levels of wealth, I would be the last to deny that or wish it otherwise. There have to be opportunities to change places with somebody better off than yourself. Healthy competition. But don't let me hear any more of this two classes nonsense. I am going to come down very heavily on our friends the press if they indulge in this caper, the licence has gone far enough. From today I'm calling a halt. The reason will be clear to you; I'm not talking to a nation of nongs. We've all had free compulsory education to a very high basic standard by comparison with other countries, and we have had it since time was. Good Lord, we should surely be past that kind of mud-slinging. Naturally, again, there are more intelligent and less intelligent people, and the less intelligent have every opportunity of self-improvement to challenge the position they began from. If you, personally, feel in any way that you have not received a fair slice of the education cake, come forward right now. Don't go whingeing about it. Put your name where your mouth is. Write me a letter; you can all write, every man, woman and child can at least write, which is more than the majority of countries can boast. Write me a letter tonight. Dear President Buchanan, I have been deprived of my equal citizen's right to a full education in the following way. Then you explain what has happened and I shall see to it myself. You'll receive justice, no worries. And let that be an end to this snivelling pernicious talk of ignoramuses. What do they think we are? I mean, who do they think they are insulting? Whatever next, I would like to know! It's an impertinence that makes me boil.

He was back.

47

Owen Powell took a photograph of his sister when she was twelve and he was ten. He had screeched at her to pose on the steps of a ruined shearing shed overlooking the sea. Though they perpetually quarrelled she seemed, on this occasion, anxious to oblige. Perhaps she wanted him to succeed for once because there was something in it for her. Perhaps beneath the bickering she loved him. It is not impossible she had some intuition of a great career about to begin. As a photographer? No, she might have replied doubtfully, because you'd never imagine him actually *being* anything. And in this she would have been correct also.

Weeks after the holiday the little square photographs were picked up at the chemist's by Mr Powell senior. Owen and his sister argued over who should look first. Then she remembered there ought to be one of her and some premonition guided her. You took most of them, she said, so you can have first go. The source of the problem was their having been given the rudimentary box camera as a joint Christmas gift by an aunt who must have been a maiden aunt to know so little about children. The photographs, not so much black-and-white as grey-and-wash, showed impossibly small seagulls on a rock overlooking a tilting sea; the left side of their mother, including one arm one shoulder and half the face, laughing towards the right side of their father with a flower held in his only hand but the whole top of his head gone so his expression had to be gauged by his chin; the chin, thus isolated, appeared far rockier than the original surmounted by soft cheeks and cushioned on a fine round neck. There were a couple of pictures of the same car, small, undistinguished and empty, viewed from various angles. The snap of the holiday house came out really quite well with Owen and his parents on the porch, loaded with beach gear and sporting sunglasses, except that this time the photographer's aim had been rather too elevated, so the parents were presented as busts and Owen solely as sunglasses topped by a bush of unruly hair. Then came a perfect photograph in which the horizon was level, the image sharp, the black black, the figure correctly placed in the frame, her bare legs apart, hands on her hips, eyes intent on the photographer to make sure he was doing everything right. Young Owen gazed at what he had achieved and the whole future lay open before him. That's me, said his sister excitedly, that's really me. She looked closely at it. Then a note of resentment crept into her voice. That is really me. The awkward edge to the mouth, the demanding expression, a suggestion that under her toughness tears lurked, all this plus her knees, her ludicrous loveable dumpling knees, made her ashamed. She grabbed at the perfect photograph to destroy it. So unexpected was this vandalism, she accomplished the crime before he had a chance to protect his masterpiece. Streaming tears, she ripped it up and threw it in the garbage bin with the most terrible oaths available to a young lady who has never uttered an obscenity and won't. Mr Powell senior had, of course, a simple solution to Owen's grief. He took the negative back for another print to be made. Now came his turn to look into a photograph so interesting it could provoke violence. He saw straightaway what was the matter. Here was his own daughter summed up with all her faults. Here lay the truth. But not the whole truth, for where was her niceness, her generosity? He did not analyze his reaction to the point of saying it leaves her nowhere to go, but this was his feeling. What use were delusions or even hopes; she stood on the steps of a weather-worn shearing shed trapped for the world to recognize her limitations. Young Owen kept the new print and hid it. For years this provided the only hint of what might be in store for him, though he sensed already an insufficiency in the visual image, a contempt in himself for the manipulation of a medium so static.

Who could have guessed he would become the archivist of arranged photographs and master of modified tape recordings, all edited with exceptional ingenuity, and a man able to graft three bodies together in a single picture, or three conversations on a tape, so convincingly a court of law would swear by it?

At sixteen Owen was small and roundfaced, a lively child willing to please. His face lit up when he laughed. He had plenty of friends, though he entered into few of their interests. He was hopeless at sport and more interested in girls' clothes than the girls inside them. Several of his closest friends were girls. His voice had broken late and inconclusively. At nineteen he entered the public service and found his pedantic clarity in speech and handwriting hailed as a unique talent. Promotion went ahead at the usual annual rate, but superiors had their eye on him. Blessed with a modesty so complete it was mistaken for consummate deviousness, his career began developing without his seeming to do anything much towards it. Meanwhile he poured his energy and skill into hobbies. He spent his savings on miniature tape-recorders and stood innocently beside colleagues' desks with a machine running in his coat pocket while stories were swapped and libellous anecdotes told about the boss. Young Mr Powell had no thought of using these tapes. No, they were an artform, purely for his private entertainment. Being an adult now, he appreciated that one of his motives was the thrill of risk in doing what he did. But he left the matter there, while the dangerous truth gathered in rack upon rack of cassettes above his bed.

Once, he went back to that seaside town, the cliff where

paddocks fell suddenly to a shelly beach, grey post-and-rail fences bearing testimony to the hard labour of last century, to the very shearing shed on the steps of which he had taken his first true photograph, his initiation into all that truly mattered in life. He went in. The shed engulfed him in the eerie cavities of a skeleton, a space of latticed ribs and struts, a rich complexity of intersecting straight lines and crisp shadows.

He remembered none of this from his childhood. What he did remember were the worn wooden steps outside, their pale thick slabs cracked, the ghosts of Chinese shearers who built the place, plus his sister whom he hated for being better at sport than himself, standing in that masterful way of hers with feet splayed, wary as a wrestler, elbows akimbo, instructing him in a bossy voice to take his time, she had all day to look beautiful in. And his mother behind him tutting, look at that now, he takes her snap wearing those awful shorts when he could have got her yesterday in her rose dress. If only he had had a tape-recorder this would have made a character too.

As it was, his material tended away from such blameless vanity toward sensational disputes and revolutionary oaths. He had begun taking risks, habitually, to obtain his specimens. At first he wandered the streets of Adelaide, especially the brothel end of Hindley Street, loitering near enough to the pimps to catch a few words indistinctly, words he concentrated to decipher later in his room, words which acquired a symphonic quality, pure sound, each suggestive by its own character, compounded and magical with all that went on around it. He scoured the city for accidents, he knelt beside a woman dying after a bus had run her down, her husky voice repeated trivial complaints and then warded off bothersome attention. I'm comfortable, the tape said harshly. I'm comfortable. So she died giving him an appalling noise to listen back to, as if the body were a machine of some simple hollow structure collapsing from within. Owen Powell, then twenty-three, had never before seen anybody die. Nor even a dead body. He replayed this tape till he had learnt it and probed it for what it might mean in his own life. Comfortable. Yes, and then came the noise, wait, just six seconds later, the pause itself charged with meaning, six seconds during which a human being fought back the pull of death, mustered the sum total of her happiness to prove life worth living. Six seconds and she was finished. That's all, a life's enigma shaken down in a bin of loose wooden parts. He had recorded his first great piece, imperfect though it was in techni-

cal sophistication. A variety of arrests were also to be heard
among the treasures above his bed, but only one of these rose to
the heights he now knew himself capable of achieving. This he
had collected at a demonstration while on holiday with a cousin
in the north. Owen Innocent stationed his bland face among the
rebellious expressions of his contemporaries, bemused by their
passion over something as remote as abstract rights for certain
categories of person in South Africa, of all places. You would
mistake it for a personal levy deducted from their pay packet by
the fervent way they took it to heart. He recorded reel after reel
before nightfall. Then the Springboks, the visiting football team
which had triggered all this agitation, were due. Opposite stood
the hotel where they were to stay. Floodlights blazed on the
façade. The crowd shifted as a single excited creature. This was a
movie, a national occasion, themselves celebrities after a fashion.
The lights swept broad blinding swaths across them. At each
sweep, the prudent Owen concealed himself behind an obligingly large young man who had offered him some peanuts
earlier. Just as the coaches bringing the sportsmen swung into
view and demonstrators exhaled a sigh of suppressed violence,
squads of police poured from cars, from the adjoining buildings,
from a placid supervision of the footpath, to run with batons
flailing and drive the anti-apartheid demonstrators helter-skelter
back into the park behind them, the floodlights switched off,
creating a darker darkness. The morally outraged ran, tripping
over tree roots, crawling in the dirt, heard but unseen, being
belted about the shoulders and legs by bloodhungry police.
They screamed and a few cowered under streetlamps, some
fought back gamely, some swore, climbed trees, one youth
struggled far enough up a post to kick at a policeman's face. The
roadway had been swept clear of every last protestor in time for
the Springboks' arrival to be filmed, for the commentator to say
with a declaration of honesty there is no sign of a demonstration, for a welcoming committee of beer-gutted sport-lovers to
hustle them indoors while the visitors looked about, puzzled at
the absence of trouble but possibly hearing faint dwindling cries
from the pursued in the far darkness among unfamiliar trees. It
was over there that Owen, quick-witted as ever and running
before the first blows were struck, had stationed himself, taking
refuge in a bus shelter, stifling his panic breathing, straightening
his tie to show himself beyond suspicion while his microphone
picked up the desperate shouts of a woman pleading for mercy,
confessing that yes she had been at the rally, agreeing with

occasional off-mike interjections from a male companion possibly sprawled on the ground O my God-ing and Christ Almighty-ing with the amazement of real pain. And, professional as Owen had become, he did not flinch at playing through the part when the police accosted him.

— What the fuck are you doing snooper?

And his own voice coming so shakily he could never imitate the effect though he had tried often enough.

— Waiting for the 25.

— The twenty-fucking-five what?

— Bus, sir.

— Don't give me that crap. Belt him, Aub, to teach him manners. It's a policeman you're talking to, mug.

— I know sir. I'm waiting for my bus, he insisted, the tremolo increasing as his pitch went higher.

— Then why are you so shit-scared?

— I can see, he stammered having spectacular difficulty with his cs and ss. What's happening to them. He had indicated the writhing bodies. What have they done? he whispered in the most nearly authentic touch of innocence.

— Maybe he is waiting for a bus, another voice spoke. He looks wet enough.

— Leave him alone, said the woman's remote companion. He's nothing to do with us. I didn't see him back there.

A sample of an orchestrated pause followed this, giving the artist time to ponder the implications of being saved by the victims he was there to record.

— Here it comes, his voice said a moment later, bright with hope. Please may I catch it? Oh, in what contemptible baby tones that request was made.

— I shall keep my eye open for you, the policeman warned. And don't you forget it.

Shortly after this escape, Owen Powell decided his skill with the concealed recorder could be educational, that he might improve his knowledge of the world in those areas where he most needed information, taking his equipment with him to parties. He soon grew frustrated by the fact that when he carried the machine in his pocket the microphone picked up only what he could hear anyhow. He needed to get there in advance. Stage by stage he perfected his art of finding hiding-places for the gear and excuses for being early. With a couple of mishaps leading to the loss of one machine and its recording, he refined his technique, moving nonchalantly among unsuspecting acquaintances and hoarding the crop of tapes, filing them complete with annotations, date and location references, plus identification of speakers where possible. He knew Mark and Jenny MacGibbon were splitting up before anyone else did, he knew Jenny was already dating Philip by then, which even Mark did not know. He could have made this public. He knew the psychological soft spots of his entire circle, privy to the confessions of weak moments, cashing in on other listeners' talent for encouraging confidences. Inevitably some of this store of knowledge came to affect his behaviour. Friends began realizing he accepted their nervous disorders, their hang-ups and hopes. He was able to avoid inviting those who didn't like each other, and purposely bring together those who wanted to meet. By such judicious benevolence, never misusing his secret knowledge and certainly never hinting to anyone he had it, Owen became the centre of a group. People valued his intimacy, they paid court, they never refused his invitations, they began bringing troubles to him direct, sharing their hopes and plans. His reputation grew as his tape library grew.

In the department, he found favour with his seniors. Heart pounding fearfully, he planted tapes in the assistant director's livingroom one evening, risking everything at a reception. The gamble paid off. He scooped four hours of brilliant material. Everybody talked shop or exchanged confidences with other people's spouses. Scarcely a minute of the tapes had been wasted. Owen Powell now possessed the power to manipulate half the senior officers of his section. These tapes were so important that he spent night after night transcribing them, annotating the snippets of conversation and filling in gaps of identification. Here was the foundation of a spectacular career. Thanks to his judicious use of what he knew, Owen Powell was thought to be an officer of quite remarkable astuteness. And so he was. Just a hint on tape was enough for him to imagine the rest. Even the director took note, but didn't like the cut of the fellow with his pudgy face and high voice. Then came the day Owen presented himself at the office with a new hairstyle. Parted down the middle and very short at the sides, it changed the shape of his face slightly but categorically. The director, who wore a centre parting himself, smiled civilly and passed the time of day. A week later, some question of protocol was dismissed with the words: Don't bother me about that, ask young Powell, he knows the rule book back to front.

So there he was. At twenty-five this is what he had achieved.

Yet Owen Powell certainly did not have an obsession with work and promotion. No. He enjoyed the lighter side of taping too. The machines were his toys and not altogether serious. He transferred a good deal of material to big reels once he could afford superior equipment. He played about with splicing, mixing two separate conversations to make people say ridiculous things. With his fine ear he was even able to match the acoustical qualities of different fieldtrips (as he began calling his raids on privacy), so the possibilities grew endlessly amusing.

— What were you saying Geoffrey? a woman's voice asked.
— Am I squeezing too hard? a man's voice replied.
— Goodness, I can't think of anything more encouraging.
— Your husband keeps watching us.
— In my opinion we should take him to the vet to be fixed.

Then there were edited tapes using the one voice. Owen's favourite ploy was to doctor a political speech recorded off the radio, reorganizing it word by word to turn the argument into the exact opposite of what the speaker said.

Such was the stage he had reached when Mr Powell counted the score of possibilities his ethical restraint had earned him. Why shouldn't he, just once, take advantage of his skill and try out a sample creation on the right audience? Just one tape was supplied to a selected senior officer. The resultant empty desk fell to his own lot. He moved up. The success had proved so sublimely easy it carried a gloss of blamelessness. Still, our young hopeful did not rush matters; he waited a full year before trying another.

Much later, given the meticulous placement of an occasional sample, he was to ascend right out of the public service and into the elysium of parliament itself. During the second four-year term of republican government, his was the first such promotion to cabinet made independent of Squarcia's advice. In a subsequent Executive Council reshuffle (and the president discovered he could fabricate these with the frequent and scissile ease of authentic nightmares), the same reshuffle which saw Roscoe Plenty elevated to Chief Minister, Owen Powell inherited the portfolio of Internal Security, his old department.

He had learned too much to suffer the least residue of foolish reticence. No sooner was he lodged in high office with his nameplate stamped in steel on the door than he began moving against anyone he suspected might wish to replace him from below, as well as against those who stood between him and Buchanan above.

Out of loyalty to the president, who was by now going bald, Owen Powell's hair fell out with dramatic enthusiasm.

48

In the delirium of one hot day, Buchanan looked from his study window on to a desert of sparkling stones. Motes of light jumped off the unending floor of a sea lost for ten million years. He heard Dorina mock him: You were a proper Leichhardt, I gather. He swung on his swivelchair back to the familiar refuge of the study. . . only to find total blackness closing down on one last rift of stars. Blinding beams of light seethed alive with flickering wings, a chaos of fragmentary gleams and tiny masticating jaws. He reached for the car horn and pressed it. He would not let go.

The buzzer blared imperiously in an outer office.

— Send Powell, he croaked. Mr Powell, he went on immediately in a different voice and without looking up, so accustomed was he to instant attendance. I have a task for you.

— Of course BB, the minister replied as he came gliding in, aware that any crisis promised business. Though, to be fair, he accepted that one such summons might announce his own disgrace, his removal from office and his punishment. That there was no complaint out against him could itself be reason enough. Was he bribing critics to be silent and lulling the dear leader into a tactical error?

— Of course? the president questioned him softly. Of course?

— I can explain if you have time and patience.

— There is no of course about anything to do with me, I would have thought. Or am I to be told I am so predictable, so transparent that you already know what I'll ask before I ask it?

— No Your Excellency. I was using the phrase as a manner of speaking. *In* a manner of speaking, if you see what I mean, he smiled with polished clumsiness.

— Good Lord, man, pull yourself together. I'm the one who can't sleep either night or day. You ought to be more sympathetic, you ought to have your wits about you and no room for error in the service of the republic.

— I do agree Your Excellency. And I am here to obey your orders.

The great man looked back over his shoulder toward the dead heat of his mirage.

— Then listen carefully. I want somebody found. Not taken in, not interfered with, but found.

— At once.

— The task may be more complex than you expect. My mind, Owen, may be more devious than you give it credit for.

— Oh no, Your Excellency, it couldn't be, he protested and then struck his balding head in despair.

But this didn't even work as a fraternal joke.

— Listen, the great man switched to a muted tone, speaking fast and softly as if to get it all said before any could give him the slip. This woman is eighty perhaps, perhaps more. She visits me and I don't like it. I won't put up with her nagging. She pesters me because she is critical of what I do. Reason enough to put you on her track. Mr Powell, she is my Mama, no less. A woman filled with rebellion. She can't endure the idea that I have grown up, that I am no longer under her thumb. To be frank, she is jealous of my fame.

— But. . ., Powell interjected, now clearly driven by fear, though the source of his fear eluded definition; he had, after all, been scrupulously loyal. He knew there was nothing he could be charged with; empty as he was of ideas of his own, empty even of character. His career of spotting, as he called spying, and deducing, as he called informing, taught him that his relationship with Buchanan remained perfectly free from treachery. Yet now, perhaps for no other reason, he himself found this innocence hard to believe in. Mightn't his nature and habit have insinuated themselves somewhere along the line? Involuntary betrayal was what he began to fear.

— But. . . your mother!

— You know already? Buchanan asked sharply, whirling his huge back toward the mirage.

— Nothing, nothing but the most elementary, the least useful facts, in this case, Your Excellency.

— Listen, Buchanan roared so he need not have his nose rubbed in the likelihood that he had surrounded himself with nincompoops. His voice went quiet as he drifted slowly again to the salty wilderness of a private vision. While I tell you what I remember. I remember horsemen. This was a long while ago. I was very small. Also it happened in a primitive country. Horsemen encircled us, stinking of the blood and oil on their bare skin. They were moaning like a pack of dogs on heat. Round and round us went the moaning like a siren in the distance, you couldn't pinpoint where it was coming from or who started it. But this was what drew my Mama. Yes, she was there with me, that's the point, and looking grim, her black eyes burning. She was a tough one. You see bodybuilding females in magazines these days, with real muscles. She had muscles. And gold ornaments flickered at her earlobes. Also, as I remember, a string of gold coins across her forehead. That sounds wrong, but I'm sure it's right. This is the way I see it. Hands resting among the folds of her skirt. She had strong hands.

His mountainous flesh sagged immobile at the window, back turned on the hapless Powell who clutched a mint black notebook without knowing what he might be expected to record.

Warm grassbreath drifted in to refresh them.

Marvellous tale, the minister tripped on the cliff of saying, but he grabbed at saplings and hung there, gagging on those words which might connote fiction, might imply criticism, perhaps even sarcasm, no matter how carefully enunciated.

— Strong hands rest on her skirt, Buchanan repeated, moving the picture into the present tense and adopting the tone of a commentator describing a scene alive before him that moment. Her eyes are narrowed, nostrils white as a sliced pear. (*Sliced pear*, Powell scribbled.) Now their chief dismounts. He is showing Mama precious things. She has magnificent eyes, did I tell you that? And she turns them on him. Now she's moving, she begins pointing out the horsemen, choosing who will come to her and in what order, you understand me? (Powell nodded, his head tolling with the terror of calling the president's mother a whore.) Diplomatically putting him first, though I don't think she likes him much. Now she glides between the horses, inspecting their riders for breeding. She collects the treasure in advance and this is the key moment, this moment the world swoops like a giddy fairground. One of the barbarians has reached down to snatch me up, lifting me clear off the ground by the arms. I yelp and wriggle, I can tell you. He slings me, fat as I was even then, across the saddle in front of him. I hit out at his knobbly body, but no good, it's like hitting a lump of wood. The lion in Mama laughs, telling me they'll let me go all right when they see what she has to offer. I can smell the cape my captor is wearing, a cape woven of human hair, Owen, think of that.

The voice trailed off on a note of wonderment almost.

The two men sat silent: Buchanan lost in the retrospect;

Powell in agonized bafflement, hoping the president would suddenly swing round with a deafening bellylaugh and demand congratulations for his inventive skill. But then the voice resumed, to prolong the torture.

— Six months later I had grown from a child to an old man. We were in a hut and I woke to spy out of the door. A campfire flared, an enormous campfire this, tall column of flames, while men ran whirling round it, naked men, black bodies leaping in and out of shadow, passing from view behind the dazzling screen of flames. Flute music cried. The voices of the dead, Owen. Mama was out there, opening the front of her gown. That's what I saw. Imagine how I felt. The tribesmen around her beat a rhythm with their bare feet, all stamping together. The earth shook. A proper nightmare, I can tell you.

Owen Powell waited, hoping desperately that this fragile possibility would be his saviour, that everything might be explained as a dream, dispelled in a word.

— Another time we were nearly murdered. It happened in the Caribbean, but the French navy got us out, a frigate full of young bloods in short shorts and starched white shirts. Have you got that? They walked in pairs, everywhere in pairs, and all had identical little moustaches so I laughed at their vanity even then. Lean and athletic they were, those French sailors, but hopelessly vain, as if by parading in pairs they brought their own mirror along with them. They paid Mama more grudgingly than the primitives. What's more, they watched each other at their pittanceworth of sex, a coarseness those wild tribal fellows would have been ashamed to commit. Memories, Owen, such memories. (*Moustaches*, the minister noted.) Once we travelled with the Australian army, somewhere hot we were. I can remember the heat clearly but not the cause. So many wars were fought in hot countries when I was a child. At ten I'd become a full member of the team. (Pimp, said a dangerous dissident in Owen Powell's brain.) I took care of the front of house, you know. It's just as well you're ugly, Mama joked with me, because that may protect you against impatient customers. (Buggery, the impudent brain explained but the trembling hand wisely wrote nothing.) She could have been right. She kept herself young as a result of making love with youths only. And now the duty of turning away the aged and ugly fell to me. I hated it. But I chose for her. The method was simple. First I approached the handsome ones, you see, and explained Mama's terms; that they get rid of the rest for a start, then they must pay 50% down and the balance afterwards. We never lost this way. It was my basic training in business methods really. Once, when her clients ganged up and, having had their pleasure, refused to come good with the 50% owing, she shouted to the men who had been rejected and were skulking the boundaries. They couldn't stand the insult of the lucky ones getting her cheap into the bargain, so they blocked every escape and forced them to pay double to see who looked bloody fools now. I took that lesson to heart, Owen, in my own way. You can keep people poor in this country by playing them off against the rich.

The president's massive back considered what he had already told, landscapes of grass-scent wafting in through the open window. Perhaps he had finished. The minister read the notes he had taken: *Sliced pear. Moustaches.* He could almost laugh with panic, while the words *pimp* and *whore* and even perhaps *traitor* clamoured for inclusion. Traitor, his dangerous dissident agreed, because we don't know which side had the benefit of Mama's services.

— Well this was her life, the president explained as if he knew these censorious thoughts. But it couldn't go on, as she was advised by an Antananarivo doctor, for ever. I remember her courage because she cracked a joke. It seems to, she said. Think of it! But heroism on that scale was beyond the doctor's understanding. (And beyond mine, said the dissident.) Nevertheless I watched her filling up with tiredness, one drip at a time, a bottle which cannot hold much more. Her skin changed, the liquid greyness soaking out through it and collecting at the base of her throat. She had been a beautiful woman once. She began to learn please and thank you. (*Please*, wrote the hand.) The wars of the modern world, she told me, have kept us in style. I can hear her voice as she said it and added: Some of them we've been to on both sides too. (Owen Powell's pen fell soundlessly to the carpet; he bent, praying his knees wouldn't crack, and retrieved it.)

Why was the great man saying this? What category of test did it constitute, the minister begged in silence, such appalling slander against the mother of His Sublime Excellency? The dissident was busy chewing shreds of carrion. Could there be some monitor of unspoken thoughts set to catch him out? His fear raced ahead, foreseeing disastrous consequences, himself trapped and interrogated, records of the story being used in evidence to condemn him. Surely he must speak up now, he must interrupt and refuse to accept what he had been told.

Even to the president, especially to the president (for who else mattered?), he should say: But your honoured mother was a Presbyterian who baked pumpkin scones every Saturday and did her hair up in a tight bun, never soiled her lips with make-up or swearing, your mother wore men's size seven shoes, and gloves couldn't be found big enough for her hands, she was completely faithful to your late father and that's why she grew so angry with life perhaps; but not this, never this bizarre tale of naked tribesmen and French sailors watching her coupling. Worse, his fatal humility warned him, worse will be to come. And worse did come.

— Months of blue uniforms, the great man continued after an emotional pause, still presenting his back to the notebook and the pen. Whole deserts of identical serge and buttons, he said. Anonymous tonnages of meat. And Mama lowered her standards. If they're young enough to serve, she said, they're young enough to serve me. Which put the age limit up to about forty-five at a single stroke. Her voice buzzed in my ears because by then I had this loud irritation I heard all the while. One morning she emerged with a favourite. He had smuggled himself in during the dark hours. Feed him the finest breakfast, she ordered, I kept him last night. That was that, you might say. But as for me, I shuddered at what she had become, this beautiful dark-eyed Mama of mine. Elevated beyond the category of a customer, he was her lover. She saw what I thought and spoke sharply and privately to me about how I must grow up to see the orthodox as trivial. This man's energy had fired her, there was no doubt about that. I imagined him enfolding her in his hideous limbs, powerful and malformed. The point was that he had not wanted equality. His heaven was sublimation, Owen. Do you follow?

Owen Powell grew cold with the certainty that at last he did follow.

— He expressed himself through the beauty of her body. He did not want beauty for himself. So he inspired her. She began to love herself again after all those years of emptiness. Her former life was finished.

The story was, perhaps, at an end. The Minister for Internal Security finally put his pen to coherent use. He noted *The desirability of sublimation. . . happiness through service.* He could think of nothing else safe to write, so left it at that. He felt more comfortable. He now had something to show he had been listening. And if the moral were solely to bring home to him that he must not covet his master's power, he knew it, joyfully, already. He felt strong again and ready to talk if questioned. Then the voice began once more, still speaking in that abstracted tone.

— Mama's travelling bedroom became a pilgrimage for grotesques. Men in half-man shapes spent their life's accumulation of virility in one sublime act. Think of that. Mama was still a lovely-looking woman, you should remember, and her preference was not a case of exploiting them, let alone degrading them. She had no taste for their deformity; it was nothing of that kind, only for the sincerity of their pent-up passion. (Owen Powell began to lose track of the analogy.) She loved them for what could not be seen. The quality of their loving took all her strength to survive. Her skin grew flimsy as a fly's wing, Owen. You can't imagine. Stick-insect people came; mushroom people came; people who, if they had two arms two legs two nostrils two nipples, displayed them so shockingly out of kilter they could scarcely be classified as pairs. And their fire made her turn in horror from the least taint of beauty. She explained to me: There's a deadness about a handsome young man which sends a chill through me so I could no more share his bed than his coffin. That's what she said. I'll never forget. Have I ever before, he added in a perfectly conversational tone. Mentioned Mama to you, Owen?

— No, squeaked Owen Powell who knew the whole Buchanan family history, his school inspector father and dour mother stirring her protestant angers tirelessly.

— Strange, the fat man murmured into the hot salty silence of the death he found before him. A beautiful man, she told me, deadens the air about him. I agreed, I agreed. Envy probably. Not my problem. Well she even grew affectionate towards me. My sweet fatness, she smiled (she seldom laughed), was my one attraction. The backs of your knees, she explained during this period, those tender pink creases, are almost good enough to touch. She didn't touch them though. What could you expect but our business took on a missionary tone? Mama was out there doing good. Naturally, she was even more hated for this than when she had been wicked. Parents accused her of wrecking the lives of their freaks, came wailing round to the police station because this one had taken to having opinions, this one had found a beard growing if you please, that one burst into song in a public street. They hailed curses in the form of bricks so she'd understand their objections were solid. In some countries they burnt the houses we stayed in. At New Orleans they even dug a channel all through the night to divert the Mississippi so we'd be swept away in a flood by morning when Mama was due for a rest from her mission.

Owen Powell, who had found nothing else in all this which could safely be written down, re-read the words on his page time and again while he listened to the long preamble now more certain than ever to culminate in his downfall. *The desirability of sublimation. . . happiness through service. . . sliced pear. . . moustaches*, he read.

— Aren't you interested in what happened next? Bernard Buchanan enquired in his everyday voice.

— Of course Excellency, I am hardly daring to breathe, it has become so. . . so. . . absorbing.

— Well, the president's back continued, appeased. The flood came down at dawn just as they planned. But our hut was stout wood and the waters carried us straight to the Gulf on a stinking hot summer's day past St Petersburg, Florida, past the Dry Tortugas and into Havana where the state took us up in the hope that Mama could cure a camp full of deviates. But she explained in triplicate that they were so distressingly beautiful, do you see the point, they turned her blood cold. She was awarded a medal for approved morality and deported with a garland of wilting flowers for luck, which must have worked because in Santo Domingo where we landed next we found half the men had some part of themselves shot away. They were lopsided monopeds, flaps of meat sewn together round the hole left by good American steel. So although they might not have been born with magnetism, they had acquired it.

Powell's pen trembled at the words *American steel*, but he knew he must never put this on paper. What if (he made to smite his bald head but stopped short of the noise of it) the president were trying him out with his very own trick! What if a simple tape recorder were spooling this away, his failure to demur despite all the opportunities offered? He must make a stand soon. He must, without offence, decline to believe any of it.

— Well? asked Buchanan propelling himself round slowly to face his minister. Well?

— I am am, Powell stammered. Astonished by what you've been telling me.

— Of course you are astonished. Because you don't bother to look beyond your nose, Mr Powell. Just the same, I have a task for you. With all your faults I trust you still. I want that woman found.

Cold water circulated through the security chief's veins. He was completely bamboozled. He had lost all confidence that he knew how to respond for the right effect.

— No, the great man added looking keenly at his prey. She was not my mother. Why didn't you correct me? Don't you know my mother was a Presbyterian who baked pumpkin scones on a Saturday and tied her hair back in a tight bun? Do I have to tell you every least thing personally?

— Naturally Your Excellency I understood immediately this was not your own dear mother, such an example to others! Yes, but I had no doubt your story would reveal some moral if I could only be patient enough to wait.

— You were bored?

— Certainly not, never, not bored Your Excellency, quite the reverse, fascinated beyond measure, listening, taking it all in, the wonderful details, not wishing to interrupt, before presuming to. . .

— Stop crawling up my arse, Buchanan bellowed. I can't endure another hour of your crawling. This is beyond anything. You disgust me. Stand up like a man. Good God, Owen, this is a simple enough task for a minister with a whole department full of experts and layabouts. I want the woman found. Do you follow me? Of course she wasn't ever my mother, my mother had a Scottish soul, you could pick her a mile away by that. No, she's nothing at all like my natural mother. And the little fat boy was not me, was he?

— No, no.

— No. Nor even you. I don't know who he was. If I did I wouldn't need to ask. It stands to reason.

— That's right Your Excellency.

— Yet I am asking. So don't waste my time with red herrings. She is out there and no mistake about it. Find her. That's an order. I must know. I keep seeing them and dreaming about them, those two. You won't have any trouble tracking the old lady down. She'd be ninety now, I should think. Wears flashy make-up and a red scarf round her head. An old trouper. Darling of the forces. Distinguished service at the front in several wars. Always wars, mark you. That's how you'll find out. Singing, acting, and more. Hence the darling. You know the kind of thing. Remember what I've told you.

— Is that the commission? Owen Powell checked in dismay. Can't you tell me more?

— What! the president exploded. You've stood here for ten minutes taking notes, listening to a detailed briefing, and you dare ask for more. Your reputation is in this, Mr Powell. I don't mind warning you. Your job is on the line.

That evening the great man smiled at Chief Minister Plenty and asked him how he had been feeling lately.

When Squarcia arrived home in an IFID executive jet, the president's own car was sent to collect him.

— Don't tell me what they said, Buchanan ordered imperiously. I do not wish to know. But they will want a quick answer. You can offer this much. I refuse to be pushed for more. I shall sanction the immediate completion of Project 31. The second stage at Port George can get under way the moment they give the word. You should point out that we already have the Friends of Privilege stationed there right near the site, available to begin on the major building component tomorrow. But, mark what I say Squarcia, I will not on any account countenance a weapons stockpile in Western Australia.

— I'm afraid it may be too late. I ought to. . .

— I will not. Buchanan repeated quietly. Countenance a weapons stockpile. Not at any price.

— May I remind you, Your Excellency, of the contract you signed with the consortium before coming to office?

— At any price. Either to myself or to Australia. I am beyond being threatened by some document signed when I was a nonentity. You won't change my mind. This is my sticking point. I have done everything to be obliging, I performed like a circus monkey, I sweltered on that blasted island for their sake, I swallowed an insult from a ten-cent potentate. I lied to the world's press, God knows what I did not do. None of it was for me or my own country. All to oblige IFID. Enough is enough.

— Tuavaleva. . .

— To hell with Tuavaleva, Squarcia. If the Tuavalevans knocked back the proposal that's their funeral, they can fend for themselves. Haven't I got my plate full without being nursemaid to Prince Poo Poo? Now, for Christ's sake leave me in peace to enjoy my headache.

49

Stephanie Head woke to a disturbing aroma. The bedroom smelt of perfumes long since out of production, lilies of the valley mingled with a strange grape-green sharpness, allurements of an earlier generation, harder to resist than our own self-congratulatory sensuousness. Her body, muffled and sunken in eiderdowns and silk, swallowed by the mattress, moved, setting the covers rustling. The air hung heavy with men's sweat and the gratified sigh of actresses paid by the job. She rolled to the edge of the strange bed like a person fighting free of quicksand, and got up feeling ill and shaky. She went to the window, parting stiff curtains, but recoiled from a stab of light. She then tried the wardrobe for clues. Inside were men's dress-suits ranged in sizes from gnome to monster. Interleaved among them hung stiff dicky shirts to match, each with detached wing-collar dangling down in front.

Stephanie, already cursed as the youngest of three sisters and the victim of her ancestors, heard footsteps. Somebody must have seen the curtains move. She felt not just appallingly ill but frightened of the unknown. And flung herself back in bed. Although she had spirit enough to resent the subterfuge, she was in no fit state to invite trouble. The door opened on the odd old lady she had met before she. . . what? before she passed out?

Mama, seen as a brilliant green costume topped by vermilion headscarves, advanced with the stiff-hipped waddle of a parrot, which might have been comical were it not for her eyes embedded in sinister wrinkles and her beak so thick and sharp. She brought breakfast set out on a tray unused since the bombing of her favourite Hotel Grande Bretagne at Nice. She bore every appearance of friendliness. Stephanie made to get up as an apology.

— Enjoy it while you can, Mama advised. I don't suppose the service at Yarralumla Mansion is better than this.

— Real coffee, Stephanie exclaimed despite her intention to remain defensive.

— But if you don't mind I shall sit with you and have a chat. Are you strong enough?

— You mentioned Luke, she recollected. And then she

remembered escaping from the railway station with a man who might have been a police agent.

— Before we can do anything about Luke, you must get your strength back. You took foolish risks for a sick person. We do not spit in the faces of officials these days, oh dear no, however petty their position. There was a time when I myself was proud as you please, she dreamed. I'd have spat at anybody I felt like. Still, I gave those puppies a piece of my mind when they came to get my Gita. I am Mama, she reminded Stephanie. And my son is obliged to do State Service, as they call it, brainwashing poor devils brought into the country simply to be squeezed dry and thrown out again. Disposable humans. That's what we're up to. My son is with your Luke. Yes, dear Luke is on State Service too, as a doctor. His other choice was a boomerang and a cave a couple of thousand miles away in the desert and no airconditioning either.

— You know Luke?

— Not yet but I shall. The point is, I saw you trying to get to the train and I said that girl has pluck. I have never had a woman friend, she mused. Only these eternal men. But maybe, I thought, there she is, flat on her back on Platform Three. That's the way life happens. And I watched a certain fellow make off with you, yes indeed. Okay boyo, I said at that café, time for you to leave the lady to someone of refinement.

— What is happening to me? the patient asked weakly and then, because her mind was racing, enlarged the question to encompass the whole of society. To us all?

— Well what is happening to you is simple, Mama declared. You are getting better. What is happening to us all is not so simple; we're getting worse. We're giving away everything in our own backyard. We're watching the greedy ones grab what they can. And because a helpless fat man says the rulebook allows it, we sit back and let them do as they please. Have some more coffee, I shall be mortified if you don't. What is the point of my adventuring into the blackmarket if you refuse to enjoy the benefits?

— Thank you. But a whole society doesn't suddenly turn vicious, Stephanie protested from the purple splendour of her surroundings and the scepticism of her journalist experience.

— Do you want a bet! Mama collected the tray and made ready to depart. To go by the record, we lust after inequality, lovely inequality, such a rich mulch for growing poisonous weeds and burying the corpses we've hacked up. Give us the super-wealthy, our own famous few, give us envy, give us our share of nuclear danger. Let us have the thrill of guilt, oh yes. Don't deny us that. Mama decided against leaving, now her enthusiasm had been aroused, so she put the tray down again as she continued. In the middle of it all, up popped silly Whitlam with programs of enlightened independence to be financed on a legend that the boom goes on booming. Of course they got rid of him and we barracked from the sidelines. Silly big-mouth, bashing our ears with that cheery future waving the flag. Give us squalor, we cried, something to get our teeth into. And I was as much a mug as anybody. I was in Japan when I first saw him on television and I said to Yanagita, you've got another homeland, I'm going to take you home where I belong and proud to do so since you don't seem as if you'll ever get married here. That's what happened. But Whitlam went and we began selling our bodies off in lumps. Careful of the blood on the carpet, love. Have a thigh, why don't you? A tit'll go well in your cold winter weather. Watch me waving my arms while I've still got them. That was us in those days. And we let them do it to us. So at last we did see who we were: we were the ones who came and pinched a goldmine and then gave it away in exchange for a curfew, rationing, and the privilege of being a bomb target. She picked up the tray again for emphasis.

— How do I know I can trust you?

— I am the one, Mama said with simple dignity. Who has made a place for a stranger in her own house.

So began the recovery, a time unaccountably protracted by visions and nightmares. Stephanie Head sank in luxury and woke, palpitating, out of some half-graspable crisis of court proceedings to face food so corruptingly delicious she suspected she was being poisoned. She was tortured by uniformed beasts and left cold on a concrete platform, lying there all night till she came to her senses. She was licking the spit back off a man's coat, feeling the furry material against her tongue. She was awarded a medal that made her laugh when she thought about it. Women sewed buttons on rag dolls' faces to let them see. Men on all fours played at huffing and puffing and blowing her house down. She cried a lot. And then one night or one dark day, whichever, she heard Luke call her name. His voice unmistakable. *Steph*, he called, *Stephanie*. She wanted, how she wanted, to answer. But lying on the purple silk bed in a room draped with the odours of labouring males and perfumes as sweet as the 1920s, she was fully aware the voice called only inside her head. *Stephanie, can you hear me?* She covered her ears in anguish. This was too cruel. Yes, oh yes, she whispered. Then she felt a silence, as expectant as the telephone when you know the other person is listening. Luke? she asked after a while, but the line had gone dead. She lay in the ruins of her hallucination, not knowing how long she had been like this, or why her body was too weak to obey her command to get up and walk away.

— We *are* coming along, aren't we, Mama commented cheerily as she provided more meals lavish with commodities not available on ration cards.

Left to herself again, a maze of questions hedged Stephanie with frustration. She wanted to know what connected with what. She demanded to understand as she peered down a gun barrel. The brokers of power were her uncles and bound to her by blood. Why did this rubber jacket cling so tightly her sweat collected at the small of her back and her fingers felt cold and airy? Then she was all right and quite normal in a clean bathroom and emerging from the steam to find her tray with a note on it in Mama's flowery hand saying: Do pardon me for going Away today. You'll be Quite safe if you stay Indoors. And when I come Home tonight, I hope to bring News.

Stephanie didn't bother with breakfast. Fresh from the shower, she dressed in clothes thoughtfully laid out ready. She walked unsteadily to the top of the stairs and helped herself down, taking a rest on each one. She made an effort to breathe evenly. She reached the hallway and saw herself passing, undoubtedly passing, the hat-rack mirror. The doorknob felt so cold she withdrew her hand for a startled moment. Then she mustered the courage of the shower and normal clothes. She put behind her those asphyxiating corridors of her dream, those suspicions of poison, the languorous scent and glossy folds of bedding; she opened the way back into time, and stepped out through a dense patch of garden. Matted with fallen bark and leaves, the path stifled her footsteps. Then to the gate and, now more like a dream than the dreams, into petrol fumes and dusty scraps blowing along an ordinary Sydney suburban street with people walking in her direction and away, some seeing her without noticing. She sat on a bench at the bus stop to collect the necessary nerve. Her ancestors came back and clamoured round, tormenting her with their usual mockery. Many times she told herself to get up and catch a bus, to lose herself among the city's three million unknown faces. Yet she sat there while the leaves from exotic trees turned yellow and brown and fell in her freshly shampooed hair and her lap, while an east wind raked them and piled them round her ankles till they engulfed her knees and a southerly buster was needed to gust them away at a single blast back up among the branches where they belonged, growing green again and tight as buds. The shop along the road evicted a last customer and pulled down its blinds for the blackout while an ambulatory public suddenly looked anxiously at watches and hurried away into holes with a flapping of gabardine, a scarf trailing out on the breeze, an exciting accelerando-diminuendo of clocking heels. It came to her that she was about to break the famous curfew, that if she sat here a little longer she need not worry about taking the initiative to escape Mama; the police would help her into their warm wagon and drive her home to a fully self-contained cell without a skerrick of silk or a whiff of the 1920s, a cell perfumed only with the despair of the downtrodden, a hint of beer vomit, walls damp with ineffectual curses. She did not mind. She had grown familiar with jail before, when questioning people on her court rounds. In the distance she heard the wail of their approach and listened intently to be sure it was coming her way and not escaping. Yes, she relaxed on the uncomfortable slatted bench. I am not feeling well, she explained to her feet.

Luke's voice called *Steph, Steph*, with all the longing she knew him capable of. Oh yes, she replied as a cold wind swarmed round her knees, I'm here. *Why don't you come?* I've been ill, she said breathlessly. *We're by the sea and it's warm.* But his voice faltered as she looked around her. Am I really talking to you? she pleaded. *You're my only hope.* Then the horror of realizing all this was happening inside her head was shown to be a triumph.

— Tell me something to prove it by, she whispered out loud.

I had a visit, Luke reproached her. *From a guy who wants to take you off me.*

— I've been ill, she said again because she could make no sense of this message. Or poisoned.

Her wonderful release was cut short by a car, at last a car, buzzing round the corner.

— Hullo, Mama called from the open window, drawing near. Still waiting? It took longer than I thought. But such a lovely drive. Help her in, Mr Dog. That's the style.

They turned home at Mama's gate, skidding a little on the mulched leaves, the very moment a flashing blue light appeared at the far end of the street illuminating a flicker of evening scenarios framed with foliage.

— Now I want you two to meet properly, Mama announced.

And Stephanie looked at the man who had rescued her, knowing in a flash where he had been and what it was he wanted.

— Why, Stephanie asked when they were safely indoors. Do my memories seem to be only of hot days?

— When one is young, the sage explained. All days are hot. But you are being polite. We're back and you want news, of course you do, you want to know if I met your wonderful Luke and what I thought of him and how he is and what he said and are they feeding him and please tell me he isn't being punished. Am I right? Of course I am. So sit down, my dear, and I shall describe the whole adventure.

The silk cushions whispered.

— You saw him too, didn't you? Stephanie challenged the Wild Dog, her first words to him.

He nodded glumly.

— By what right? she shrieked.

— By my own right.

Mama offered whisky all round, but neither of her guests wanted any. She took a generous glass for herself to compensate.

— There, that's better, she began her odyssey to cut short their conflict. Well, I reached Port George with only two break-downs. The NRMA men are really so very obliging, nothing too serious, a new battery and a new waterpump. But darling, I said, I could have sworn the car ran on petrol, with the price I pay to fill her up! She drowned her snort of laughter in the seriousness of alcohol. To the point! she promised. Vengeance Harbour. What a place! The walls reek of blood, I'm telling you. I'll remember the last detail of this, I said to myself, so as to be a comfort to Stephanie. There it was, then, grim and dark even on a beautiful day, the sea down below dashing against rocks and gulls screaming all round my head. If you aren't the spirits of the poor dead, I declared, I'm not Mama. I'll stake my life on it, I will.

— He's there. He's okay, your husband, said the Wild Dog pale with his fatality. You didn't wait for me, he added giving a helpless gesture. I couldn't find you.

— You see, it all tied in perfectly, Mama sang.

Stephanie felt the illness slip away, out through her fingertips.

— So you have been in touch with him, have you? Mama

asked her shrewdly. I wondered how long you would take to get the hang of things. I know, she turned to the man prone to falling in love. All about your gang and your debonair failures. What you need in the twenty-first century is an agent.

He had a dangerous look in his eye, laughing suddenly all the same, and all the same passionate.

— Well now, she concluded gulping down the whisky. With Luke in contact and the Wild Dog among us, we are ready to begin!

50

Bernard Buchanan had not slept in four years, except for that night of disasters on his way to the Maldives. But now, having at last defied his masters, he found himself drifting off, his wakefulness already on a glassy slope: the flight of a brandless bicycle, suicidal release. During the years of power he had forgotten the heady pleasure of giving in.

Dorina, still with him in Canberra, lay on the same bed, awake. Ahmad Zain Osman had shown her ghosts she could not shake off. But there was, as she repeatedly told herself, this second chance. Through her husband she might redeem her father's error. Was error the right word, though, or did she have to admit it had been treachery? She must not fail her islanders, she must not fail Prince Haupoupou who snubbed her, nor the gong-player and lantern-dousers, nor those placid thousands for whom the feasting of the chosen was a diversion and a night out, for whom the murder of children told how far they had once been pushed. Her father exclaimed: They have forgotten themselves this time! But he was wrong, he who had been busy selling them to foreign interests; they had *remembered* themselves. Now she knew what must be said to Buchanan. But when she switched on the light and sat up in bed to signal how agitated she felt, Dorina realized he was dead. Drenched with shock and, to her own surprise, grief, tears sprang to her eyes.

— No, she gasped; and this was all, this tender denying of fate and its injustices.

Buchanan groaned.

Dorina bent over him like a scientist who discovers a new species, and at the same time examines the marvel of knowing a unique form of life will bear her name in its Latin label so that no specialist in future can ever see it without acknowledging her part as discoverer. Far stranger than death was his sleep. What did it mean? She put out the light and lay a long time thinking. But if this really were to be the beginning of the end, Dorina would need her faculties in their fullest clarity. Tomorrow, everything might be made new. She reached out in the dark and took hold of the mogodon and cool glass of water set ready, gulped down the pill and then, on considering the importance of the case, groped for another. Lying back, she sank into a deep sleep.

Waking is an ending as well as a beginning. It is a renewal, but it is also a condition of exposure and defencelessness, of fleetingly restored virginity. The president knew nothing about his wife's resolution, let alone about Stephanie Head's new consciousness the previous morning, nor what this brought each of them in restored hope. He himself was disturbed in a totally unexpected manner.

He woke from his first sleep in that gigantic bed, which was all the more sumptuous for its travels in the tropics and contact with oriental cultures of libidinousness and chastity, to a dream of underground roars. He listened. The noise was an outrage. He cast around for what it might be. Like all men reducing the inconceivable possibilities of experience to a few manageable and therefore contemptibly safe categories, he strove to relate the fading edges of this roar to something mundane. Maybe, he canvassed a description, a tank regiment heard by an ear pressed close to the ground. . . But his ear was not to the ground, it was on a pillow as huge as the average armchair. The total blackness of night disoriented him. He had a frightening absurdity to resolve: which way was he facing? On which side was the door? He had to force the room to conform to the pattern in his mind, actively rotate it to believe it was right. And he had no more idea of time than direction. A rat must hear such sounds in a lost wooden warship turned turtle and becoming under the waves a bell of airpockets shuddering tunefully as it shrieked down a reef on the way to final disintegration. He was dreaming a nightmare left over by Captain Cook. Or was he still aboard his aircraft tossed in a storm? Once before, at the approach of a locust plague, he had suffered such dislocating fear, a roar more vast than loud.

Then the mansion rocked. The floors heaved up and the whole alarmed building groaned in all its sprawling staterooms and guest apartments, in kitchens and chimneys. Suddenly it was no longer a summary of the safe inconveniences of everyday, the creaky functions of a small palace, disappointments of uninspired architecture, but a test of materials, witness to the skill of craftsmen. So the mansion lived as a heritage of trades, took breath with the ordinary air of workmen and braced against the tremor. Another underground wave approached, grumbling past. Again the floor lurched. Terrified, the president shook his wife who happened to be there still. But, though she moaned, her sleeping tablets proved too powerful to combat. What if they had to evacuate the ruins? He dreamed the romance of carrying her angular body and its promise of comforts, he who could not even carry his own body unaided. Far from his rescuing her, he needed her to help rescue him. Doesn't the brain's alarm system overcome drugs in a case of life or death? Have we become too clever to survive? Invisibly, Dorina slept on her cliff-edge. The alarmclock's tiny light of three-twenty went out. He stared wildly at the blackness where figures glowed a second ago, their green ghost faded. Once more the thunder which was not thunder, of a bombardment which might *be* a bombardment, spoke from the deep earth. It could be war because this was how wars had come to be expected: nighttime strikes against the undefended. He flung off his bedclothes and reached up to snap the light on. There was no light. This was the wrong era for air-raid warnings, this strategy of lasers shot from our own Paringa and reflected back by our own IFID satellite. The president groped at the button to send electricity jangling along the eight bed frames where his bearers slept. But no emergency bell rang. The total past of knowledge plus that immeasurable past of instinct slid out from under him, sands fluid in the undertow. This was fear as an absolute; fear without an object to be feared and without discernible relationship to any other experience of fear, unless skydivers free-fall through this state during their first suicidal jump from an aircraft. Buchanan was, himself, the only shape he could put to such terror, every cell of his body enlivened by it. He fought to free his mind at least, to set himself outside the sensation, to be able to look at it and name it, even classify it in rudimentary terms. Spies had betrayed IFID's masterplan, the great work which could make Australia the key to all world military operations. That was it. They are blasting us out of existence, his mind told his mind. No question. Missiles were streaking through the upper atmosphere, some aimed for the major population centres, others for the tracking-station sites. The vision of failing in flames wasted itself against his panic. He tried to stand. But his legs, more weak than ever from disuse, gave way and sat him back on the bed. He struggled to his feet again. Again collapsed. What was the use of anything if he were to be killed in the process? Surely the anti-nuclear cranks were not going to be proved right? Unthinkable. Dorina! he thought he shouted. But she would not stir. She was not going to be the one to save him now. She was not even going to be the one to hold his hand. Yet again he forced himself up, his courage teetering on frail ankles. . . and crashed full-length to the soft floor. Now he crawled on hands and knees, as once he had crawled when a baby with stern parents to look forward to, and much later had crawled bruising himself against hard stones. Suddenly angry, he set off for the door. Where the hell was everybody? How dare they abandon him!

The earthquake thundered. Vast rings of shock, arriving simultaneously at Adelaide, Albury and Rockhampton, linked farmers and wharf labourers, Aborigines exiled in the Arabana Homeland and poets exiled in tall apartment blocks. Insomniacs a thousand kilometres apart were joined at that moment and startled out of their misery. Junkies doubted anything unusual was happening. The president froze with fear. He once owned a boys' adventure omnibus with a cover illustrating a small boat at sea. Under this boat loomed a manta ray so enormous its dark flat lozenge extended ahead and behind and far beyond on either side. As the keel rested on the monster's back, the boat already tipped at a helpless angle. The adventurers, leaning back against the tilt, hung over the gunwale with expressions of anguish and horror. The manta ray subsided and let the presidential residence settle on its foundation of sandstone.

Dorina had been left behind to sleep the sleep she was longing for. Bernard could already imagine her sceptical smile as she brushed daylight though her hair, a hundred strokes on the left, a hundred strokes on the right, watching him guardedly in the glass, exclaiming: an earthquake Buchanan, but we so seldom have earthquakes in Australia, are you perfectly certain it was not gastric? And of course the bitter admission was that gastric it might have been. All his ambition, his knowledge of powers in himself still untried, met its measure of worthlessness. He was afraid for his life. Again a relentless tide of thunder passed deep beneath the city, roadways cracking and houses tilting momentarily towards each other. His body still locked on itself with chronic humiliating constipation, he crawled toward escape.

—Dorina! he shouted amazed to find his voice at last.

The door swung open and a blaze of flashlights flicked round the bedroom, over the flat form of a drugged wife, the thrown-back covers, scanning the room's tame luxury, glancing with dazzling flashes in a mirror, then discovering him helpless, his great bald baby head flung up, eyes bulbous with fury. Since the first tremor, forty-five seconds had elapsed.

INTERLUDE
An Old Voice

51

— Who then is free? the poet Horace asked, and answered: The wise man who is lord over himself, whom neither poverty nor death nor bonds affright, who bravely defies his passions, and scorns ambition, who in himself is whole, smoothed and rounded.

The moon floated, whole smooth round and free. Four people sat below at a table, deep and impenetrable in its clarity as a table cut from solid emerald. At one end sat the father who was in his same body the son. At the other end sat the mother who was in her same body the daughter. On the far side sat a man being also a woman. While on the near side, with her back turned, sat a woman being also a man.

The floating moon unfolded wings. It swooped as a bird of prey down to the brilliant morning, down on to this emerald table, glory of the world. The white sea-eagle plunged to a lake where it trapped its reflection in cruel talons and tore off its own pure feathers to devour them.

Then the moon rose from the lake, back to its fiery origin.

—Without great pains, said the poet. This work is not perfected.

No more than that. Here stands my vision complete. The investigator loses himself in his own watching eye. Through seeing, he creates the world by transforming himself into the world and dies of its simplicity.

— What did you say? Rory called from his nest in the weeds on the tugboat's deck. He looked up with that abstract indifference he cultivated and met the contemptuous gaze of Detective-sergeant O'Brien, who had not, in fact, spoken but merely stood there observing and then strode away.

— Am I allowed to read my book? Rory called with mirthless gaiety. Do you need to know the author? Izumi. Yanagita Izumi. Hang on, I'll quote you the ISBN number.

PART THREE

Paradoxy

52

Sydney, New South Wales, 11th July 1846.

Such is the excitement of the whole colony I can scarce overstate it. I imagine you back there at home (my home that was), I hear some crickets sounding gently from the reeds where I played as a child down by the folly, and a cuckoo calling in the warm darkness of Somerset, though I am sensible of the fact that it is too late in the year for cuckoos; and at such moments wonder if I might not be truly damned as you had promised me I should be. I have this to thank you for, Father, that, as revenge against your own blood, you chose Botany Bay in preference to Bedlam. You will have heard that I am a free man now and doubtless fear my return.

The worst I shall say upon this head is that I shall not yet say what my intentions are in the matter.

Sir George Gipps be praised (there being no God left living for any man who has been through the hell I have endured) my sufferings were mitigated by the single circumstance of not having met even one fellow convict of my own class. Here lies a moral in its own right.

I mention the folly to you because it is the only building on the estate not tainted with use. You will take my point, I am sure.

Since my release in such tatters of self-respect as were left me after my health and good name were wrecked, I have found employ as one among a staff of secretaries. You shall not know the name I have adopted.

To enable me to say to you what I need to say, I must begin by saying something about the Governor who is, in any case, worthy of study. His Excellency owns to about as much natural grace as yourself, which is to say he treats all petitioners with the arrogance of a voluptuary interrupted in the pursuit of pleasure. Unlike yourself, however, he is no such voluptuary and his impatience is to get on with tackling issues of policy. Policy is his passion, whether we are speaking of Crown land sales or education, of reforming the juridicature or curbing the powers of the token Legislative Council.

He is of the middle height and disagreeable visage. He wears his nose rather too high in the air and is given to turning his back upon persons attempting to be pleasant to him. Beyond doubt one day, a knife will be found buried in it. His vanity consists in Lord Wellington's having mentioned him in dispatches after Waterloo. He knows nobody of any consequence outside the Whitehall administration, but affects to be the most perfect autocrat. He has perpetrated outrage beyond outrage upon the little marooned community of squalid self-interest already entrenched here, and I love him for it.

I aid him by every means within my power, which is chiefly to say, by not stinting my secretarial labours, and by exercising my imagination on furthering his unpopular obstinacy. I discovered myself able to effect this quite by chance; the power had been put into my hands by the experience of witnessing how a respectable man behaves to those whom he does not care to impress. Then, only, his mask falls aside and the true character is shown.

Two years before my pardon, when I was still an assigned felon, beaten and driven by a certain English gentleman whose name would so amaze you I doubt you might not suffer heart failure (the which, could I only be certain of its effect, nothing might prevent my saying outright and unmistakably), who did not know me, so greatly am I changed and so nauseating was the filth of my condition at that time under his benign care, I was witness to a scene quite properly considered by the Governor to exemplify the very worst in our British temperament: which is to say, the capacity to look upon men who are plainly men and yet, by some miraculous skill at transmogrification, perceive them either as obstacles or as articles of furniture. This incident, the murder of twenty-eight natives, I shall return to a little later, when I have done describing a few of those who have grown immensely wealthy here in a single generation; those, in other words, who perpetually have one foot in the door at Government House, begging favours.

The place stinks with petitioners, the scum of the earth in both their guises; whining murderers picking their scabs, who, while awaiting the Governor's pleasure, rehearse their litany of grievances and boastfulness; and, not less obnoxious, the soapy virtue and hot-ironed linen of nonentities from Stoke Newington or Bradford-on-Avon sullen under the necessity of showing him deference while, as anybody can see, writhing in the grip of greed. Greed has its hot pincers dug deep in their flesh and no matter which way they twist there is no help for it, but the basest of all passions will be master. Neither class of rogue has the least notion of how the Governor thinks. I once amused myself by explaining the truth of the matter to a certain Mr William Macarthur whose father John Macarthur had enthusiastically exchanged life as a nobody in Devonshire for life as chief bully in the colony. William, a fifth son, as I understand, and notable only for his book upon the culture of the vine, and for being vintner of a most excellent claret, took me aside. Holding my sleeve, by which I deduced that he cannot have known about my recent convict past, he asked me as man to man, or rather as patron to patronized, what is the tyrant's porridge? (his own expression) His Excellency, I replied with as much malice as my smile would allow, is indifferent to wealth, contemptuous of flattery, dead to neighbourliness, and a proper fanatic for the book of rules; he has no sense of humour, no time to enjoy comfort and no patience for either fools or knaves. The crows may eat your eyes out, Mr Macarthur, here on the lawns of Government House, I told him for his own good, and Sir George would not even notice. All he would do is inform me an hour or so later: There was a fellow lying in an irregular manner on Crown property, please see that he is induced to leave with as little scandal as possible. That would be you, sir, led off by a couple of strapping Highlanders and turned to face in the general direction of the hazards of town whilst being advised to keep walking in a straight line not to be mistaken for a drunkard. He is a great man, sir, and if he could bring himself to laugh he would set the bells ringing from here to Parramatta; and did you know, Mr Macarthur, that Parramatta in Sanskrit means Great Mother?

It is a pleasure to deal with such genteel rogues, all the more because the scars on my back remember another side to them. Oh, they tell me, the Governor is an unfeeling man. As I said once to Mr Boyd: Do you think, sir, your convict labourers would give a better account of you? He rushed right into Sir George's office raging that I must be dismissed forthwith. My dear fellow, the Governor said to me after the wind had settled down and the tatters of his window curtains hung straight as new, if I knew how to do what you just did, I would clear my office of clutter in half the time.

Mr Benjamin Boyd was, of all settlers, Sir George's least favourite. He brought with him the odour of stale blood and foul gases exploding from the bellies of whales whose carcases his crews tow into Eden to be hacked by flensers into bleeding lumps and boiled down over furnaces: Eden indeed! Wealth is no prettier in the colony than back there behind the screen of England's

> . . .flow'ring May, who from her green lap throws
> The yellow cowslip and the pale primrose.

Ah, the lies of your English poetry! Only Blake sees what is truly satanic. Mr Boyd wears a sprig of heather growing from his heart while he trades in human flesh. Don't look too deep into his affairs. Great beasts lie dead, staining the sea, and men rot in misery to feed such glory as Mr Boyd's. He trades in the flesh of simple folk. Sir George Gipps, who always expressed the utmost abhorrence of the convict system, as much for its corruption of the free as for its brutality against the captive, found in him so prime a specimen of coarseness he offered me the unprecedented familiarity of coining a nickname for Boyd which we had between ourselves: the Flogger. Word of honour, *the Flogger is in the habit of saying,* Word of honour, Your Excellency, that fellow of yours in there is not what you think. I can smell a certain something about him. *Overhearing this, my blood hesitated and I could feel, under my cambric shirt, the knobbly welts of scars across my back, knotting and swelling. Only now as I write do I see a double meaning in the Governor's reply on that occasion:* You may be surprised Mr Boyd how little of what goes on in this colony escapes my notice.

His Excellency's manner to me in no way changed. I need not say more than that you, my own father, could learn enough from this to save yourself certain damnation.

Why am I writing such a letter, you may ask? The answer is, to be quite sure you cannot escape your conscience through ignorance of what you have done to me. For, of course, I may never leave this place now. Do you believe me? Do you breathe more easy? There is no way I could look at England again, but through the eyes of a man who has been beaten like an animal, a man who has saved his manhood only by holding on to hate, a man who has survived for one reason alone: to live to fulfil a promise of revenge against his father.

Mr Boyd it was who brought a strange visitor to Government House, the consequences of whose coming heralded the end of the house itself. He presented a Mr Bernard Buchanan, newly arrived at the colony; and in walked a man so fat he had to ease himself round the doorposts to enter the office from the vestibule. He took Sir George's hand with such uncalled-for enthusiasm, even clasping it in both his own, that the iciness of the Governor's voice showed quite plainly he regarded his two visitors as deserving one another. They had arrived, of course, to present a catalogue of complaints, which the Governor cut short, saying: Why do you think the transportation of felons ceased? We are, are we not, in the new posture which you yourselves so vociferously canvass? Free Trade? How much more do you want? You are granted land for nothing, you* *default on your taxes and now you enjoy an open market. Upon what grounds do you insist you should, given these circumstances, continue not to pay for your labour either? To which of the vices, my dear sirs, shall I ascribe such demands, Avarice or Sloth?*

This was in 1844. The South Island of New Zealand had, for the previous four years, been annexed as a dependency of New South Wales and came under our jurisdiction. Mr Buchanan and Mr Boyd disclosed plans for establishing themselves as major landholders there too (as had a certain Mr W. C. Wentworth who irritated Sir George only two days earlier with his petition for a massive grant of land in South Island). I was called to take notes, so I heard His Excellency say: *Great as would be my pleasure to see you both a thousand miles distant across a cold and turbulent sea, I have no intention of modifying the system or conditions of Crown land occupancy to oblige you.*

Buchanan, who had not even been invited to sit (because, I suspect, Sir George feared for his furniture and had nothing to lose in the line of a reputation for hospitality), suddenly suffered a seizure. His fat arms clamped to his chest, he leaned in defiance of gravity and kept on leaning further till he toppled, crashing against the great desk as he went, and rolling on the carpet, the floor beneath him giving an ominous splintering sound. Mr Boyd let out a laugh before he could prevent it in the interests of decency. Sir George remained sitting where he was, not even caring to stand and see if the fellow had died altogether. I, having sought permission, called for the Governor's own surgeon who pronounced the patient alive but too ill to be moved from the house. Two stalwarts of the 78th Highlanders dragged him off, squeezing him out through the door and across to the informal parlour on the far side of the vestibule, which the housekeeper was obliged to convert into a sickroom.

When the carpet was rolled back to ascertain the cause of that splintering, several floorboards were discovered to have rotted. The house, which had been begun in 1788, the year the colony was founded, for Governor Arthur Phillip, was discovered to have been completely eaten away by termites. What we had thought so solid it would last a long time yet was no more than an appearance of solidity. Indeed, the flooring where Mr Buchanan fell was shown to be the soundest remaining section of the entire structure.

The following year, Sir George ordered the whole building demolished as too rotten for saving. . .

53

A scream penetrated the wall from outside, so ragged it struck a savage note in the blood. The work of the prison staggered, wounded by that voice; the hammerstrokes of carpenters repairing the roof amid shrill electric wires faltered in their rhythm. The scream, with its jangle of red and white harmonics, ended as a sob, and then the guest workers knew for sure it was one of those women who hated them, camped outside, driven to desperation by the hopelessness of protesting against anything in these times, least of all against injustice.

On top of the wall an eagle had alighted, smelling slaughter about the place, feeling at home and quite cock of the walk, to amuse itself with tearing apart a rabbit's remains. Delicious morsels dangled. The beak cracked bone while a survey was made of the panorama, out to sea and inland. Cold beneath its plumage as a dinosaur, the real eagle showed in its slovenly demeanour, the scaly legs. It bent again and tugged another gobbet free. Only its eyes appeared to belong to a sentient animal; the claws and shaggy feathers might equally seem stuck together of stone and seaweed hideously animate.

Men straggled from the village of huts inside the wall because a whistle had shrilled, louder than the scream but thin and mechanical by comparison, a whistle coarse with routine resentments. They lined up while the commandant addressed them through his beloved loud-hailer. He waggled it against his lips and set his angular pelvis at a posture to provide his announcement with the right prurient éclat. This was the recital of names, summoning those who were being called on by the few people to know and maybe love them.

Penned in the wire enclosure, these lucky ones waited to receive visitors; among them, one Aborigine surviving that intense hubbub of Brazilians, Vietnamese and Ethiopians. He chatted with his companions because there was always a statutory delay while Commandant Curtis had the fun of personally reviewing the visitors and giving them a burst of his regulations plus assurances that they were welcome provided no trouble developed due to the excitability of the men. The lone Aborigine's eyes never left the outer door, eager for it to open. This was unfamiliar to him. He had never had a visit. Bone dust lay on the stones and on the stone faces around him.

A gobbet of flesh still dangled from the hooked beak.

The prison had been built by the first convicts early in the nineteenth century. Once they completed the outer wall they fitted the gate themselves. Redcoats closed in, keeping tight formation, flintlocks loaded and occasionally going off unintentionally with a puff of smoke as was normal with their erratic kind. So the builders found they had created their own ring of hell. Any who felt pride in the quality of their work were mocked by knowing it. The gate clanged loud as that cracked Russian bell huge enough to live in and listed wherever the largest and fastest are the measure of human happiness. Afterwards the only buildings erected inside the wall were huts which blew down each time a cyclone season hit, plus instruments of torture, chiefly triangles big enough to strap the biggest man spreadeagled for the lash. And there were birds of prey, then, who had no need of memories to induce them to perch along the wall, eyes everywhere, shaggy tails twitching with murderous excitement. So through the long reign of the cat the wind learnt to sing the nine tones of leather thongs by heart for another hundred and ninety years and the blood of those oxhearted illiterates wet the earth floor and packed it hard as concrete and richly coloured as cedar. The waiting of men known only by a number corroded the wall. Fists beating the ground moulded it pot-smooth while the tribe of Koories living as refugees in their own sacred territory watched with horror the whiteman's game of mutilating his fellows, heard the laughter of oppressors for the first time, witnessed a frockcoated governor of the jail on hands and knees late at night, believing himself unseen, tasting bodysalt on the floor where he flogged the best men under his care. The Koories wove this fact into a history they sang through generations, wandering the wilderness of alien tales; the stink of a new vice strong on the air as a dead beast in the claws of something mightier than itself.

When the convicts were set free to ravage the country in company with their masters, the huts were burnt by an unknown arsonist and a flame rose up in the form of an open hand. Chinese market gardeners moved to the vicinity and dug the soil outside the wall rich with rotten bones for growing pumpkins big as midnight. Saplings, over this long time, planted in the spittle of petty despots, germinated and blossomed as fig and appletrees till the broken prison became a haunt of children picking green fruit to defy parental warnings and afterwards returned as young lovers with memories of pains in the belly to slick the ground with sperm. Derelicts sheltered here from the moral indignation of the town which had happened two miles away. Seabirds swooped past, deflected back to the waves by the stench of floggings.

In the first Great War since the Great War lost by the Koories, troops of interned aliens were quartered in the jail, new huts built and German footsteps shuffled through the evenings when the restored gates were bolted and armed guards patrolled the compound. Again in the Second Great War since the Great War lost by the Koories, German civilians baked schwartzbrot, split logs, and mounted an amateur production of *Der Ring des Nibelungen* for an audience of backblocks Australians who appreciated its costume comedy and slapped their muscular thighs with ingenuous enthusiasm. Abandoned to wild wasps, butterflies and the migratory unemployed, the prison mellowed in a thousand family photograph albums. Through the prosperous years of good rain and mindless government the fruit trees thickened and the wall grew a pelt of moss, sleeping like an animal with its snout on its own tail. Then came the next awakening.

Trucks rolled in through the gateway bringing builder's supplies to be stacked under tarpaulin, a field kitchen in full battle order spouted steam to announce its hours. The army delivered hinge-oil plus two readymade gates, which they hung on the original iron seating and clashed together with a flourish of padlocks big enough to ballast a yacht. Into this newly secured keep guest workers of alien race filed on the appointed morning, to be issued with tools and plans for a village of huts such as they'd not dreamed of living in, and were told to get to work or they'd have no shelter this or any other night. So on that cold July day began the new freedom from poverty they had been promised.

Leaving Sydney they travelled without knowledge of direction. Although the train set off north, the track twisted so frequently that after nightfall no one could tell. It stopped often for an hour or more and rolled backwards, clattering across points and apparently being re-routed by amateurs, then picked up speed, heading flat-out for an unseen future. The track veered east at dawn; and when the signalman switched them on to a once-only branch line to the prison, they knew by the sound of the sea they were creeping south. So the government's intention took shape as a weathered stone wall. They climbed out as if their carriage had broken down in a desert.

Cursing the hole they were landed in, these Friends of Privilege did their best to remain cheerful, growing healthy on manual work and unpolluted air. The cancer of aimlessness dropped away. Ulcers healed and innocent anger brought freshness to their complexions. While armed officers all round the nation rifled the homes of the powerless and suburban clubs assumed the dignity of inquisition courts, internees at this old prison re-learnt the basic crafts. They roofed their huts, wove nets and moulded pots ripe as bellies. Outside the wall too, in the following months, a new settlement began, a few wives having arrived and then departed to find work in Port George; a second, much larger wave of women came but did not go away again, the whole point of their coming being to stay and demonstrate against those inside. So in a brief flush of hope, real estate dealers sold them tiny pockets of land around the wall on the usual system of minimum deposit and extortionate interest for life, till in time a slum was created, overcrowded with mothers, loud with brats, and host to a horde of trinket sellers, plus peddlers of softdrinks and soft porn for sightseers because there are always folk with time to gawk at the less fortunate or the more courageous. Periodically a truck delivered the smell of tyranny, disgorging more Friends of Privilege crouched in the back. But only one other intake (during Buchanan's second four-year term) warranted a whole train and entailed reopening a branch line down rusty rails, over splintered sleepers right to the housing camp gate while the driver, easing his locomotive there and back along straight and narrow prayers, lost so much body fluid they mistook him at the depot for his dead father.

This second train brought Luke Head, the lone Australian there with a thousand generations of belonging. His university studies, his dream of a professional life, simply an interlude to teach the doctor the cost of forgetting his place and stepping so far out of line as to love a white woman. He would be offered the chance of a few years' State Service, they told him, during which he might expect every encouragement to practise his skill. (Naturally, the interviewer smiled, we value the knowledge we have taught you!) His status and pay would be the same as for other inmates, but professional freedom was guaranteed. Any further questions? With four hundred workmen and an above-average industrial accident rate, could any reasonable patriot ask for more? His life still had the purpose he had chosen for it. Such was democracy in action.

Within and around Dr Head loomed a greater purpose he had not chosen, which nobody can choose, and which he might have run from had he realized it would be thrust on him. Two hundred years, more or less, after the British invasion, the protest ballad came round to the inevitable same old chorus: there would seem no end to how long the folk of one's own land can be persecuted.

Luke Head's ancestors once passed this very district, floating downriver in bark canoes, each with a fire laid amidships and freshcaught fish cooking in smoke while they drifted harmless waters, free of time, coming upon cousins crouched still as sticks in overhanging trees who signalled greetings without giving any visible sign or shifting their eyes from the spear point they held ready for prey swimming below. They fought the white men once they realized the inconceivable truth that these spirit beings intended to violate all tribal manners, all territorial sanctity, and settle. When scattered, they submitted to chains, the beauty of which entranced them during those critical moments before they deduced the function of such a marvel. They hung round the fringes of the town, as Bedouins might have watched the combined armies of the Upper and Lower Kingdoms kept from each other's throats by the great project of building pyramids. Besotted with magic tools that could cut stone, and loud bangs able to kill any doubters, they threw their wisdom on the streets for horses to trample among the shit. The keen edge of their intellect they blunted on an alien language. And rolled dry flakes of their dignity into cheroots for smoking. They offered their strength to the mystery of the straight line, bowed among rows of plants grown to succour oppressors, harvested what they were told to pick, and were paid in coin by earth-metal portraits of the witchwoman Queen in the island of the dead. They knew her fat face and pointed nose. They knew the front of her head which was tied to the back of it by a knot of hair. They knew she was the bodiless one, her neat neck sliced clean through and the head afloat in air. They knew she would never look at her victims, face always turned aside from their anguish. And when you flipped her over she had already flown into the distance, stealing the body of a woman warrior with a spear and a shield who sat guarding the great canoe of life and wore on her head a corroboree mask to deceive the kookaburra clan spirits who might be flying overhead to catch her by surprise. They spoke her name, Bicturia or Big Turria, in the quiet of early morning after the wail for the dead and when the gunjes of their own family had hidden in crevices and waterholes and disguised themselves as a moth's wing. Until an uncle put Big

Turria in his mouth, to the nervous cheers of his followers, and bit her so hard she broke his tooth. When he took her out there was no mark on her face. The story was told in a dance, so that night the uncle showed what Big Turria was like, and the roundness of her powerful symbol; he danced his own defeat and made an art of it. After this the victory of Big Turria became a favourite at the gathering of tribes for the feast of nuts when the moon grows warm on the first child of two children.

Art accumulated rituals until the acting of it lasted as long as a neck-thick log takes to burn, while generations of brown-eyed youngsters leaned against their mothers' breasts in the deepening night and dreamed of dancing this themselves in the place of the carpetsnake and the place of the moon-face-in-water. They would be named in chants to be kept for the life of the people.

One of these boys who did dance famously grew to have a famous son, famous for fighting in the spirit folk's way, bunching his hands to batter the faces of men he had no quarrel with. The more brutally he battered them the more excited the pale watchers grew, so they shouted till they turned red as a snake and peeled off their outer skin in the heat. Now this famous one was shut in a cave on wheels, it was said, and driven so fast he heard the wind of nightmare whistling and they put him into bed with a ghostwoman; she painted blood on her lips and her breath smelt of the corpses she devoured. She stroked his arms and belly, invited him to mate with her damp womanparts, but he sprang from the bed and ran through the rubbleheap of all their promises, out into the land where fifty-seven months later he staggered from the valley of the shadow of malignant gods into his homeland and the arms of the woman who would be his wife. But the magnet of evil would not leave him in peace and when she gave birth to a boy he took her to see where he had been, strutted in the footsteps of a fame long forgotten by the demons. He subjected her to the humiliation of life on the fringe of a city among derelicts. But he had not altogether forgotten the enticements of the past. He had been clever with his fists and now was clever with his head when he gave it a rest from methylated spirits. He even called himself Head. He ordered his wife to see the boy went off to school. And she, with inflammable shame enough to fuel an ocean liner, said you can be sure I will so he won't turn out a drunk like his fucking bugger of a father. She watched over that boy, she nourished and scrubbed him. She polished his skin with a towel. She recited his lessons with him till she knew them herself. She sang the twelve-times table over the ironing as beautiful as *Alleluia* and under her breath she repeated the principal products of Mozambique when she walked to the shop. She took a broomstick to her husband and drove him out to work, and though with one arm he could have cracked her spine, true to his sheepish nature off he went to pay for the boy's first pair of shoes and for a kerosene lamp he could do his homework by. To her joy the child understood what she had no language to explain. He let his father go and let go all the pain of that long catalogue of disasters. He turned his energies to winning a place in the football team, a place at the top of the mathematics class, a reputation for intelligence and hard work that shook the headmaster's faith in the teachings of European superiority. Look at this one boy, the headmaster harangued the school in a yellow fire of frustration, if you put in half the effort he does, heaven knows how far ahead you'd be. But clever as the boy Luke was and named for the Beloved Physician among Christ's disciples, he was spared the knives of seeing what this logic meant. Master Head, the headmaster called on prize day, first prize for mathematics. Master Head the prize for English. And Master Head, as captain of the football fifteen, the one to proudly hold a silver cup and see his grinning face drown in it upside down. Not till he had graduated Doctor Luke Head, his dad long since dead of alcoholic poisoning, did he stop to count one thing he'd never thought could be counted. He wept then over his mother's ravaged body, her exhausted eyes and swollen fingers, her string of younger children. He set her up for a year of torture in a sleek suburban villa which none of her kin dared visit unless two carloads of nephews went along for protection and then not after dark. Eventually he had mercy and took her back among her kind and she told him straight, she had paid the price of owning him in return for his success, and if he didn't go on in the whiteman's world to make his way as a free citizen, her sacrifice was wasted. No protestation that he valued love beyond the benefits of science made the least dint. She would not be happy, his mother said, till she saw him with a new car, his own general practice and an enemy girl for his doting wife. But fast though she had run, the world moved faster.

He longed for his roots just when the festival of Whitlamite tolerance began to be broken down. The few brief years of hope, the first in two centuries, died completely in the New Depression. The poorer the poor became, the more viciously they lashed out at those who had risen to live among them when the times were good. She and her kin were allotted land in Central Australia and police arrived by convoy with drawn revolvers to be sure they took advantage of this generosity. Only her doctor son in church a thousand kilometres away getting married to Stephanie Grierson escaped the round-up. Not till months later when he arrived at work, put on his white gown and pocketed his stethoscope was he confronted with the offence of blood by an officer in Owen Powell's security department and taken aside to have the problem explained, but since there was no help for it would he please get ready to leave immediately, though the Division Comptroller has decided it will not be necessary to send you all the way to the new Arabana Territory for Indigenes; since you went to university with his son, the nearest camp of alien guest workers will do and they need a medico. When Dr Head joked that, in his terms, the officer himself was the alien, he got hit in the mouth to teach him manners, herded that very morning aboard a train and told he should think himself lucky because other local blacks had a worse time of it than this.

He had sat among hopeful Chileans and Kampucheans, his mind afire with defiance, when from the window he saw his darling Stephanie. So she had found him already, by her clever journalist sense; she had known where to come. Hopes rising, he watched her argue with some fool in a cap who blocked her way, then in a half-seen crisis she was the body wriggling on the ground among people's feet. Luke rushed to the carriage exit, trampling men down, to be confronted by a door without a handle. In despair he banged against the window. He saw automatic rifles tremble in those young hands. He beat the glass with his head. The window, too, was sealed. The train lurched. He could not even call out to her. A workman leapt on to the platform from the other tracks, glancing his way, curious as a spectator, and then sprinted off to the scene of Stephanie's crisis. And reached to help her up. The hatred which shook Luke would not have stopped at murder.

Ever since this camp had been established in the ruined convict prison, angry women gathered outside, protesting on behalf of the unemployed. They dragged their children along too and hurled rocks at the foreigners inside. Concealed among them were wives of Friends of Privilege appearing to join the protest but showering their men with money disguised as anger. Commandant Curtis, though he remonstrated, took no action to have them removed. A few lucky husbands, amid the spatterings of blood and dodging rocks aimed to wound, unwrapped photos, loveletters, and read rumours of living in houses someday. More and more protesting women and children arrived to squat, till the secret wives could no longer support their allegiance there and moved to the nearby town to set up a fifth column of the faithful, penning tearsodden pleas and taking up petitions to the Minister. Still the demonstrators assembled and the tuneless blows of their amateur hammers clittered beyond the wall. Those who had no money for wood built cardboard homes and nests of chocolate-egg wrappings for baby. At night whoops of womanly laughter raced through the blood of the ostracized men locked inside. The women began to tell stories which they were destined to repeat and repeat as the first women's history of the world. They sang two-part inventions. Work began on the great macramé assault ladder they would one night throw over the wall, long enough to reach the ground on both sides and carry twenty armed amazons at a time. They brewed the record non-stop pot of tea to last one thousand nine hundred and fifteen days, which turned out to be only a week short of the full duration of their squatting there. They converted treadle sewingmachines to generate power for a community radio station to broadcast maledictions. So desperate were their curses against those who would not help that, one historic day, the Strike Force Airwing, mistaking the call for stranded bushwalkers, flew in to drop emergency food supplies. Yellow parachutes wafted the packages spot on target. The wild women broached these gift supplies and caroused all night on the unfamiliar salty rations men prepared for men. This was a holiday and the hardship nothing compared to life in a suburban kitchen. Winter frosts stiffened brassieres hung from their washinglines and yet they stayed, warming that aged wall and drinking their tea and singing their history, felt and heard by the men who found themselves imprisoned despite the recruitment promises given them in far homelands.

The rules inside the camp were strict but not brutally enforced. These fellows were, after all, state guests. Once the shelters had been built, the commandant called his wards together and assured them they were welcome, that any animosity they may have sensed was ignorance rather than malice. He himself felt absolutely no personal dislike, far from it. No, he alternately bleated and barked. No. Previous governments had made a serious mistake in allowing aliens to apply for citizenship and this confused the issue. The public misunderstood the present policy of guest labour. All would be calm in time and they could look forward to a far warmer acceptance and more comfortable lodgings.

This was not, and by no means should be thought of as a prison in any respect, he bleated. The government, while apologizing for the ignorance of the common people, had to take sensible measures. Protective measures, he barked, against violence. Beyond question, some unemployment had occurred among native Australians who could not grasp that this was a transition stage heralding a better society for them. Better for everyone, he shouted. Better for you because we can offer you work you cannot get in your own countries, better for us because we increase our leisure and standard of living by being hosts to so many visiting workers. Some among you, he added, have Australian wives whom you married here or overseas. These marriages, though they are acknowledged as valid, cannot be indulged by the state. Until a general improvement in the public welcome of the scheme, you will have to bear with the problem, accept protection along with your single comrades and look forward to the day when you can safely be reunited with your loved ones. Regrettable, he confessed shaking his head in the manner of a very silly person acknowledging his silliness. I welcome you, he concluded, as guests and I hope we can develop an amicable relationship during the time history has thrown us together. He wanted no trouble, he bleated. He foresaw none, he barked, as long as you cooperate with my staff and make no unauthorized attempt to leave. He pointed out that provision was not yet practical for them to have access to the outside world, beyond organized travel to and from their allotted place of work. If any do slip out, he warned, they automatically fall into the category of aliens at large and lose their special privileges. They will be committing an offence punishable by law.

We cannot be responsible for your safety beyond these walls. Your status as temporarily resident alien citizens is a complex one and subject to inter-governmental agreements well beyond your understanding or mine. The simplest thing, then, is to obey orders. You will find, he bleated, we provide assistance in learning the ways of this new country by employing instructors. These instructors, originally from your own countries and fluent in your languages, have lived for years in the Australian community under the misapprehension that previous administrations had the power to grant them citizenship beyond the duration of such regimes. Their misfortune, you will agree, he barked, is more lasting than your own. They will advise you. Also we have doctors, dentists, and vocational guidance officers living among you on the same basis. Please avail yourselves of their services, which the state pays for on your behalf. You have been granted the title Friend of Privilege, he smiled. Let us pray we shall not be cooped up here together for too long, that this inconvenience will have a happy solution. In our recruitment campaigns you were promised jobs. And jobs you shall have. We are not able to offer a choice at the moment, but 100% employment is guaranteed by the republic. Finally, I would suggest you elect a committee of spokesmen so that where matters arise which need discussion we can do business in a swift efficient and democratic style, good morning.

They were fed on silverbeet and sour milk, as there was a regional glut of these products at the time. Every day the interned cooks devised something new; partisanship for their national cuisines drove them to compete with a virtuosity of steaming, baking, frying, shredding and rolling, pulverizing, fermenting, pickling, reducing, brewing. In a fever of pride they served silverbeet with silverbeet sauce, glacé silverbeet fashioned into a giant rose, and silverbeet flambé on a bed of curds. The guards with their diet of steak and pork held envious protest meetings against the seductive aromas of the camp kitchen, so eventually the internees broke the spirit of their protectors to such a degree that they were permitted potatoes and flour as well.

— Luke! came a distant treble voice one night.

The cooks in the converted prison sang jungle songs in languages they had never spoken. Meanwhile, gardeners using the knowledge of bonsai wore their spectacles back to front and grew cauliflowers a metre across and solid as rock. They weighed and calibrated the sunshine so their passionfruit vines clustered thickly against the wall while those of the nearby town died from frost. The labouring jobs were hard. So the men began to see they had interests in common and while at work spoke of the prison camp as home. They banked their pay (compulsorily) and took home their tiredness. Some also took plumstones gathered from rubbish bins and nursed them into trees. They wove a net of their hair and caught seeds blown on the wind. Each night they dug the polished blood-and-clay ground of the yard till the sufferings of the convicts flowered their sesquicentenary and were eaten. With shreds of leather they tied up vines to the ghost of a triangle where stubborn flesh had split the cat-o'-nine-tails. At night they grew drunk on the commandant's jealousy.

— Luke. Luke.

Digging the soil they uncovered a dozen Portuguese gold ducats from 1528 in a drawstring bag, the suede mulched to cardboard. So the dirt they had been reduced to yielded not only friendship among the alien but riches of other kinds. The discoverer of the coins held them in his black hand and said these are a memorial to our grief, they are how the war began in my country. And those same ducats jingled strange music in his pocket as he heard his name called for the visitors' parade.

A whistle screamed, a sated eagle flapped away on blood-fed feathers suddenly seen to be magnificent in flight, and waiting workers were penned in the enclosure. The man wearing a doctor's clean white shirt stood unfamiliarly among them, eager with excitement at seeing his darling Stephanie again, blaming her for having taken so long to come, forgiving her in his tumult of tenderness and betrayal. The late afternoon sun burnt hot with lust. Jeers from the encamped women outside soon announced that the faithful had emerged from Commandant Curtis's admonitions and had duly signed in at the office. Dr Head said he knew all along Stephanie would not give up till she found him. Hearing a woman call his name the previous night had been no more than he expected. He'd lain aching with love.

An orderly began the ritual of naming each guest worker to take his place at the wire fence where the visitor on the other side could meet him. The mesh was large enough for them to hold hands and even kiss, which is how some spent the entire time. But, for the present, the Friends of Privilege had to be protected from surprise attack, so the fence remained.

As the hinges squealed and the gate clashed shut on screeching protestors outside, he heard the time coming when crops would rot in the most perfect climate and lips crack with secrecy and daylight be darkened by the lies of those in power and the nice plump limbs of a girl student be served at dinner to excite the juices of those who endured comfort without variety. The hubbub of universal languages had died totally. Abusive songs drifted over the wall. Remote gongings of large pots came from the kitchen bringing with them a bouquet, still, of silverbeet and milk curd. The opposite gate opened and in came wives, a few scared children, a well-known consul thought to be an enemy, plus one strange man among them.

Dr Head clung to the wire, expectancy pulling his face into a painful mask. But this was wrong: the visitors' gate shut. The wives presenting husbands with smiles already and no Stephanie. Children spoke in hoarse voices to their intimate foreigners. The odd person out approached. In a flash of rage, Luke Head recognized his enemy from weeks ago: relived his murderous desperation when a porter grappled with Stephanie on the ground, and a yellowhaired workman stared from the far platform at that exhibition of freaks. This same yellowhaired enemy.

The guard on the wall (yet again a guard whose duty was facing outwards) glanced back over his shoulder into the visitors' yard: the air excited by the usual jabbering of adults, their children as always withdrawn to the fear of facing more threats when the time came to leave. But across by the north block he witnessed a scene. That Aborigine doctor he sometimes nodded to, the one who had been employed here to save being sent to Arabana, had a visitor. What's more, they stood apart, away from the wire mesh, stiff and bristling, an antagonism between them such that even he, up at his patrol station, felt its electricity.

Tension cut through a butter of soft accents.

Shattering the block of solid air, without warning, the doctor lunged for the wire. Its meshes instantly held him, stretched flat as he was, white shirt trembling, immobilized.

The visitor, still beyond reach and hot with scorn of so futile a gesture, did not flinch. He said something. He watched the helpless man strung up by disillusionment. He turned his back.

Everyone else in the yard stopped to watch doors open and staff running from all sides to march the intruder out through the gate.

The guard up top sucked his teeth with disappointment and resumed his beat. He stared down at savage women besieging the place and marvelled, during a momentary lapse into independent thought, that they seemed never to tire of protesting. He watched yellowhair stride out among them; an invisible riot-shield of untouchability which could have been anger or frustration pushed them back to either side; he might as well have been unaware of their taunts and insults. Out he forged, past a bunch of children hatching tortures for the kids with their foreign fathers inside; round the outskirts of that shantytown leaning ever more flimsily under a haze of smoke from cooking fires, till he was lost from view on the road. So he had no car.

Back in the yard the black man still hung from the wire, a solitary embroidered figure stitched on a buckram frame while an elderly lady, somebody else's visitor apparently, waddled across to console him and pick at the threads binding him there.

54

At the parade ground's far horizon, a fence closed off Rory Buchanan's view: life as a barren square. Now in his final year at naval college, he stood to attention enduring heat and frost, marched the length and identical breadth of the prospect, performed about-turns, wheeled left and wheeled right as instructed, slow-marched in preparation for state funerals or celebrations, he dressed by the right, fell in and fell out. He thanked God he was not in the Land Force, whose officer cadets put in twice the time training on the square. Orders rasped, dust rose, rain poured, even (during one surprise night-drill) the moon shone. . . Until the passing-out parade, during inspection, when something different happened. Vice-Admiral Todd himself, instead of pacing steadily along past the front rank, contemplating his dinner as was proper for an admiral, stopped. His body ready to move on again, he turned his face sidelong, one eye cocked up to look into Rory's own eye (which stood a few centimetres higher and therefore vaguer). The band went on playing a traditional waltz and Rory had the laughable expectation that the admiral was going to invite him to dance. This delicious possibility soared around inside his head while his consciousness of duty plus his training in fear fought to suppress a smile.

— Good man, said Vice-Admiral Todd quietly as if they were old acquaintances and both taking the same view of some public stupidity.

Rory was frightened by this because he did not know what it meant. His cadetship had not prepared him. Besides which, even in those few seconds of their eyes meeting, Rory had seen down through clear depths, past the ice-grey ring of an outer expression, to that region of darkness never reached by warmth. There, it seemed, lay a question, the simple question an ogre always asks his victims while still in disguise as a king, a priest, a horse or a saint tied to his post: Don't you recognize me? while beyond this question a second question swims dimly into view: Are we not kin then, you and I?

— Now that the harbourfront is nearly finished, Bernard Buchanan instructed Roscoe Plenty. I want you to have the workers moved. The timing is perfect: Paringa ready and waiting. We can link them up as soon as the installation is built. I have cleared permission for whatever you need. It'll be plain sailing. Just get on with it. Now, here is your file of details for the contractor. The tender has gone to Penhallurick. No need to publish that. When the crunch comes you can answer any noseyparker questions in parliament under immunity if necessary. The finance consortium's own engineers can pay us a visit any time you like. They have some guys called electronics architects, I'm told, Buchanan laughed hugely. All clear?

— Before I go, Chief Minister Plenty cavilled. There's that query I promised I would raise with you about lapses in security since Owen. . .

— Are we still discussing Project 31?

— Not exactly, Bernard.

— Then it can wait.

— The trouble is. . .

— It can wait.

. . . *meanwhile, which is to say between Mr Bernard Buchanan's seizure and the complete demolishment of the old Government House, we had the pleasure of this gentleman's convalescence. He lay, supine and mountainous with complaints, upward of two months in the informal parlour, demanding attention, always with the preface: Now I shalln't be any trouble to you if I request some. . . shall I? Messrs Boyd, Wentworth and Cowper all took occasion to frequent the house on the excuse of visiting the sick man but naturally not wishing to seem discourteous to the Governor by failing to pay their respects to him each time too. They were after New Zealand. I sometimes wondered about the surgeon's diagnosis, Buchanan took so long to mend and provided his cronies with such profligate opportunities for aggravating His Excellency's already shortened temper. If so, they mistook him entirely. Gipps was not a man to explode with rage but rather grow colder and more steely. I understand your proposition perfectly, he once told Wentworth: You wish me, item, to confirm your illegitimate use of crown land for no compensation to Her Majesty whatever, item, to further relieve you of the payment of the taxes that every other gentleman discharges, item, to grant you as much as* possible of the South Island in New Zealand without conditions upon it, item, to rescind my opposition to the convict system and to plead your case in this matter with Earl Grey in Whitehall on the grounds of free convict labour's being inimical to your own prosperity or, failing this, item, to condone your Coolie Association's proposal to replace slave labour from the British prisons with slave labour from the ignorant and under-nourished of India and China. My answer to all these issues is, as ever, Mr Wentworth, no. The Masters and Servants Amendment Act you attempted to foist on me through the Legislative Council is a dead issue, the additional charges levied on pastoral licences for squatters to continue grazing crown land in New South Wales will be paid, and New Zealand will be spared the troublesomeness of your presence. I welcome your vexatious petitions as providing me with a measure of my own capacities to govern. Good morning to you.

The house went down to the hammer earlier this year. I see something of a warning in it. Gipps feared a Whig victory in the elections at home and the impossibility of his serving under Russell. The place is rotten, he remarked, the termites have been busy ever since 1788, working away in secret; blind, obsessive little fellows, soft-bodied and methodical. All those nights I lay here thinking I heard, from every direction around me, the grinding of tiny jaws, he told me, I believed it was nothing but the joists settling after rain. This was a good house, simple and usable, airy and cool, plain to look at but comfortable in all weathers. Well, it is gone now. . .

55

Stephanie Grierson lived with an enigma. For years she had felt the energy sapped from her. At certain words, apparently harmless in themselves, a flush of wrath would consume her, or lank self-effacing shame, or else she might recoil as if caught in disguise and unexpectedly recognized, or hit her own face and breasts for no better reason than that some box-office clerk insisted the stars could not be interviewed because they were recovering from jetlag.

She refused treatment. She refused even to consult anyone competent, the very force which sapped her refusing on her behalf. She needed these inexplicable outbursts to feel in contact with life at all. Certainly, when she bruised both hands during one such attack which had involved her rather more violently than usual, the thought did come: so the world can be solid. What did she expect? She expected to be haunted, to feel the pressure of unseen busybodies shoving her over a precipice. Darkness might congeal stiflingly round her at any moment, triggered by the unexpected, as she knew from desperate escapes on the beach, in the middle of *The Marriage of Figaro*, at the top of a ferriswheel's arc thirty metres above the carnival crowds. She lost her friends to this strangeness. They found it too demanding to cope. Periodically she acquired a specimen of amateur therapist; but even these meddlers gave up, as terrified by her fits as she was by her persecution.

Stephanie's two sisters were both much older. Greta, the eldest, had been inclined to regard her devils as a wildness which, given dedication, could be beaten out of her, or as no more than the poisonous vapours of sloth. Lavinia, on the other hand, simply was not interested. Lavinia had her head down like a steer at the rodeo who will not be ridden; she needed the full concentration of her energy to keep a grip on the fantasy of living as an artist. Both sisters, in their way, showed Stephanie spasmodic tenderness. But neither the corrective concern of the one nor the accidental affection of the other came anywhere near fulfilling her needs. Her father, in any case, had not been their father. Her father, so rumour explained her fair hair, was a nordic bum, twenty years younger than their mother, who declined even to stay the night once he had repaid a one-thousand-kilometre lift from Sydney to Brisbane in a matter of minutes only. But enough to ruin the woman's life, for her to say this is what I have been denied, skin greedy for him, for the easy clothes slipping off his body to the performance of an exercise simple as a cartwheel, no doubts. Free from hesitation, wasting no time on preamble, simple. Neatly accomplished and strong, the consummate tradesman slicing a plank in two and saying there you see the beauty of wood, a perfect edge. Her mother went, quite understandably, off the air.

Stephanie was brought up by her sisters. Greta dressed her in warm woollies and lumpish shoes, smacked her and kissed her and smacked again. Dear Greta, how much I owe. Why can't I be nice or even look at her without feeling a petrol rag thrust down my throat so the thanks come out as blue and yellow flame? Lavinia, save me. The world is not composed of paint in balanced masses of viridian and cobalt. The world is my blood which, look, I can claw out of my own face. The world, Lavinia, is this saucepan wishing through the air to strike the side of your head in a famous scene that ended with hospital for both of us. And then I was only nine, but already I knew. The engima found its way into the links of a gold chain, homemade pastry, and clapping hands. There seemed no way out of it. She explained the horror of life by saying, I suppose that's how I am. Meanwhile, smoothed into her mother's fine skin, glorying in her father's hair and golden eyes, she grew as beautiful as she was unpredictable.

This was how young Dr Head saw her when she flung herself from that ferriswheel, having mercifully taken long enough to fight free of the safety bar for the ground to swing upwards and reduce her fall to the cost of a broken leg. I know what that is, Dr Head told her clinically, I've been through that. What what is? she groaned, refusing to believe he might mean anything she hoped. My ancestors have done that and worse to me, he explained. But yours are pretty violent, he added admiringly, they pulled you about plenty. Suddenly she saw them, dozens around her. Whatever she did they mimicked or commented on. They helped her up and pushed her down, they encouraged her and they put the boot in, they moved so fast she could not pinpoint them, there was never a whole face she might memorize, but flickering hints of ear and nose, the flash of an eye, a gesturing hand, the neck on which a head turned to see over its shoulder, a silhouette that was gone as soon as looked at. Smells evoked violence among this uninvited rabble, and quite incidental trivia triggered the most debasing displays. I never thought, Dr Head explained, you gubbers had ancestors. So began their friendship. And now, Greta accused her of the final ignominy, you've been seen going out with a black man. He's a doctor, she had replied. Next I suppose, Greta stormed, I shall be told he's a witchdoctor as if that's all right too! Stephanie repeated this to Luke Head to observe how he would react. Tell your family, he replied, that language is every bit as much a warehouse of ignorance as of knowledge. She kissed him then. She saw past his being handsome to being a person she needed. Afterwards, she realized he had not necessarily kissed her in return.

All Sunday Stephanie wandered through hot bare Brisbane streets, just out of the town centre, not another person in sight apart from the fleeting passage of a fat little boy on a bicycle in the distance. Dusty frangipani trees collected apathy on their broad leaves. House after house squatted, overseeing a conventional garden patch where succulent roots lifted concrete paving stones, the moribund imagination of their builders improved by outbreaks of convolvulus. Her own footsteps sounded measurements as if in an enclosure of life as chosen by the many, while family ill-wishers gallivanted around her, gabbling a mixture of Swedish English French and much else, watching for the opportunity to push her under a car (but none came) or for a dog which might be provoked into biting her, preferably with a case of rabies. The spooky thing, Luke had suggested tenderly, is that these may not be just ancestors, they may be descendants as well. What nonsense! she cried. But then she thought how other people would consider the ancestors nonsense. That is spooky, she added in a changed voice. Sly too, she accused him and they both laughed joyfully. Still he allowed her to kiss him without quite positively kissing her. In this hot empty street she turned on her enemies, she swung round and tried to stare them out, she lashed at those within reach. The fat child on his bicycle who whizzed, once again, across the road ahead and away along a side lane caught a photograph in his mind of a madwoman flailing thin air, her mouth open for screaming. He paused, he stopped the bike, propping it with one foot, to listen. No sound came. Perhaps, he told himself, there's mozzies attacking the silly bitch. Normality restored by this simple explanation, he pedalled off to beat the world speed record. Indeed, mosquitoes did attack her; as soon as the thought was at large, they whined in from the unseen river, thirsting for blood. Why, she asked Luke, are they so aggressive? If these are ancestors surely there must be some to love me? We expect love, he answered, so we take it without noticing. At best we absorb it into ourselves, at worst we simply forget. But injuries and guilts fester; we can't forgive them. We rub our own noses in the muck. She glanced round at the dozen, no, hundreds now, of her misbehaving progenitors. You mean to say I want them! He'd laughed and put his arm about her waist. What if our sense of justice is so powerful almost nothing can live up to it, he asked, and that way we accumulate a whole stack of grievances? You flatterer, she smiled. A bus swung into the Sunday street, a loutish machine, bowling along with fat tyres squelching on the melted tar. She watched it approach, seductive as a steamroller, the wheels so big she could not miss (now, now was her chance), and pass harmlessly, empty, along a road quite innocent of blood, a forgettable passing, driver on the lookout in case she might signal him to stop.

Once she watched two dolphins mating. They had swum close in to the bay and begun circling. Their dorsal fins bobbed and ducked in tight circles, working the tide to remain at one spot for an hour. Their glossy grey backs rose, rubbing together

in perfect unison, to dip under the surface where they could still
be seen, hinted at, shifting shadows private as lovers behind a
frosted bathroom window. Up they came, one after another,
hovered, sticking their snouts out in a delicate game of imitation. Tirelessly they swam till she felt the communication of the
flesh had never been made more vivid to her, nor more
untouchably remote. They repeated themselves so often one
could almost believe they were showing her how. What they
did underwater Stephanie might only guess, but they kept
coming up refreshed so she eventually grew tired of watching. I
could always drown myself, she promised.

Much later, and humbled by Luke's patience, she asked: And
you, do your ancestors hang on, tormenting you too? They crop
up, he replied, they don't trail me, but I'm never out of their
sight. I see them when I am not expecting to. They are everywhere. It's natural. We've got a few million more ancestors in
this land than you people have. Afterwards she asked if any of
them were dolphins, recalling the glisten of sun on wet backs.
Bound to be, he said. And this time he kissed her. It seemed to
Stephanie that if only she could catch his ancestors waylaying
them with signs, she would know what she needed to know
about him.

How simple he is, Lavinia declared when she met him, you'd
never think he was a doctor. But his body, she added to do
credit to her art, is a most mysterious colour, do you notice how
the shadows go almost green, he has skin a mile deep, he's the
colour of a Bruckner symphony. Bring him round any time
Steph, though now I've had to give up work and look for a job
I'm not so easy to find at home. He's a dish.

Lavinia did not ask how does he cope with your fits, nor did
she advise against having babies as Greta did, Greta who would
never countenance a baby herself of course, and probably had
not been given the option.

Stephanie suggested to Luke that they give a party for the
deceased. You bring yours along and I'll bring mine and maybe
we can slip out on the quiet. I am feeling quite well these days
doctor, she added, thanks. The deceased will be a piece of cake,
he said, it's our living families we might strike trouble with. She
did not confess the latest opinions of her sisters. So he guessed.
And his relatives might be equally difficult.

Luke's mother said, this gubber girl is the thing for a doctor
like you. She's got class and arse! She honked with laughter. I'll
never think of another like that, she said regretfully. You got to

take a chance, is what I say. Whole country's gearin' up for another go at the sufferers. Got a mind to go bush with the kids. Class and arse she got. When was I wrong ever? What I like about her, she explained more seriously, is she doesn't look down on us fellas. Her, she speaks to me straight and simple. She has a cup of tea without lookin' at the cup. That you notice. For a gubber, she's not bad.

The passing bus left a smell of gasoline trailing behind it to sully the virtuous air of this street where Protestants and Catholics lived side by side without either risking damnation. The smell, common though it was, took her straight back to her first experience of hitchhiking, sitting disconsolately at the road-side leaning against her bag. The past seemed intolerably desirable. How young I was, this young woman thought as she strolled under the frangipanis with their freight of apathy, crossed the lane where the boy had sped out looking neither left nor right for traffic, intent on his world record. And thinking of youth she regretted the present so bare, so reduced in its meanings. She could still hear the noise of the bus dwindling far down the straight dead road, roaring between parallels which would never meet, justifying a timetable although nobody, it seemed, had the least interest in travel on a day like this.

56

The four men were gathered in a silence periodically orchestrated by the clink of metal on metal from inside the open motor and a sigh escaping the mechanic to echo in the school's defunct airconditioner.

Nelson, being a sentimentalist, called to mind their months of travel together, the quiet words and worried smiles of people drawn into their net by something as simple as refusing to report them to the authorities. He knew well enough that informing lay at the heart of Buchanan's power to rule. This was the point. This was their treason, which he felt as a painful spasm of love.

Spinebasher, head still stuck in the motor, converted any doubts he might have to problems solvable with a spanner.

The air was suddenly shocked by words.

— Are you getting ambitious?

Nick, having spoken them, rested his head back against the

wall, exposing a strong neck, and closed his eyes. He pursued his attack.

— Are you going to convert us to a cause?

The Wild Dog himself remembered peering out to sea through inadequate fieldglasses. Both sea and sky at that time were sealed in the one grey pearl of calm silence gliding toward them. The water heaved slightly, hugely. A gunboat drifted with the ice-coloured silence, a thrill of light scrolled under its bows. Turrets swivelled slowly. Gunbarrels levelled straight at them. In his mind, the Wild Dog re-ran another old movie. The cleaning lady at a railway station who turned to look with exactly this engineered directness, her stocky figure in its grim uniform reflected on the floor, then sailed away about her business at the dumb reaches of a national curfew. The sea heaved. The gunboat came and went like a premonition.

— Jesus! Nick swore once the Wild Dog told them of his meeting with Mama and Stephanie. Bloody women! he protested incredulously from behind closed eyes. If you get caught up with women we all know what's going on down. The Watchdogs'll have us cold. We know your gig. You can't mix it, he ordered.

The others agreed, not speaking, their own lives at stake.

— The rest of us have kept clear of females, Nick went on as the garage set hard around them, confining them within the need to resolve this unexpected conflict.

Still not speaking, Nelson and Spinebasher confirmed, regretfully, that they had.

— You can't help yourself, I suppose! Nick sneered with the freedom of a comrade-in-arms, only now opening his eyes to a slit, but still leaving his head lolling back.

When the Wild Dog had first taken command, it was as if command were a huge silhouette traced on a white wall once seen when he was a kid, and there and then he discovered he could grow big enough to fit it.

— We've done okay, he conceded, knowing whenever they'd been sold out he was the one to hold the enemy at bay while his men escaped. But we've got to keep moving. Otherwise we're looking at more of the same. It's time to hurt them higher up the scale, he chopped a brick of air with one hand in the only betrayal of impatience he allowed to show.

The dead airconditioner sighed through stale ducts. The floor became a map they might study for the meaning of oil spots dried black into the concrete.

His chopping hand rigid at the point of impact, the Wild Dog turned his explanation on Nick in particular.

Nick Clayton had been the larrikin of his platoon when called up for National Service. Okay guys, he yelled the first day they arrived, scanning those other nervous nineteen year olds who sorted through army issue and stripped off their civvies, putting the world of responsibilities behind them. The hut smelt of wool and size and, beneath that, of their predecessors' jungle limbs; stifled in mattress padding lay the heartbeats of those who had suffered before, pillows stiff with secret tears. Small square mirrors on the cupboards stored a horror of pimples and coarse intentions. Okay, Nick yelled to those who had just met in the line outside the Q-store, I'm offering you 5 to 1. How's that for odds? They looked up from where they bent over beds and open suitcases. He stood in his ridiculously baggy army trousers. The ranks of cupboards hung gaping and alert. You get one punch each, he offered, a fair punch to the belly, you put down a dollar and anyone who winds me takes home five. Queue up. Some of the young men, untried as they were, sniggered embarrassedly. Three or four became particularly busy unfolding shirts, but there were braggarts too, and one of these, encouraged by the challenger's slight build, threw his dollar on the floor. You ready? he said. The other laughed and locked his muscles to receive the impact. Smack, the fist hit him hard, leaving a red patch. But the man doing the punching was the one who grunted. He walked away shaking his head respectfully and with a touch of shame. That was some punch, he claimed examining his knuckles. Next! called the larrikin pocketing his dollar. A gorilla with combed hair stepped forward, his loose boots clomping on the floorboards. He leered as he drew back his arm, halted by a protest. Hold on, I'm not ready! The lads in the hut roared with laughter, the sound boisterous with male braying, and in that moment of enjoying a joke in common they all felt like having a go. Okay, he said. Whack. The blow staggered him momentarily but he regained his balance with a grin and collected this dollar also. They lined up: this was turning out to be a hell of a lot of fun. Next will be the wanking race, he promised them encouragingly as he took one punch after another. Roll up! All but three of his thirty-one fellow conscripts tried their luck, but not one could beat him. That's it for the day folks, he announced slipping a singlet over his raw bruised skin. Fucking skite, somebody grumbled. Skite is it? the skite blustered, can you stand on one hand? He shaped up to them playfully. Put your hand flat on the floor and I'll show you how. He laughed and they laughed with him. He organized poker games, practised back-somersaults, smuggled whisky, set up a lonely hearts dating service, offered himself as their leader and for a brief period savoured the satisfactions of an autocrat, but Nick grew bored with his rules and despised his own decisions. At that stage he already guessed he would opt out of it all by training for something purely physical. Now after the long accretion of cynicism, he did not care about pleasing anybody. He closed his eyes again. The way they were going about it, putting on small shows, fitted his contempt for the world and the status of his self-esteem.

Spinebasher shifted weight to reach farther into the engine. The broad cushions of his bottom, hardening, stretched his overalls. Down there in the dark, he muttered something incoherent.

— Till now, the Wild Dog said suddenly, fatefully, and with an irritability which brought them up short. Where have we got to? It's been nothing but crap. Kids' stuff.

They did not like it, having trained him in their own skills.

— And your old dame can show us a better way?

Then the Wild Dog himself doubted. Mama had said he needed an agent, an ideas person. But what did she know? Weren't they amazingly successful at their spoofs and at spreading the subversion that people could begin to trust one another again?

— It's this thing everybody seems to have got a hold of, Nick accused. Linking up all round Australia, like a bloody army.

Spinebasher emerged, but only to lie down on a mechanic's trolley and wheel himself underneath the Citroën.

— She's up to her neck. She's already in, the Wild Dog offered somewhat lamely. She's some sort of organizer. She's been with Maclean's cell in Melbourne, I know that for sure. She's hot property.

— Yeah, Nick simpered dangerously. And I suppose you've read this? he slapped a newspaper on the car roof between them.

Spinebasher trundled out to watch. He stood up. He wiped one cheek with the back of his hand, smearing more grease on it. He saw the news was bad and loyally stuck his face back in the motor. Bright spanner at work.

The Wild Dog refolded the paper and put it back where he had picked it up from. So it lay there. Now being nobody's.

— Something happen? Nelson asked from where he perched on a workbench in the corner of the garage, smoking a butt depleted and puckered with saliva till it seemed he must scorch his lips at the next draw.

Nick offered nothing, letting his weight roll slightly from side to side, limber even at rest.

— Um? Spinebasher enquired and twisted his neck to look up from under his armpit, spectacles glinting among the impeccable complications of power to remind the Wild Dog of that night-dark first-aid room at the station.

— Maclean, shot dead on the spot.

— Shot dead on the spot? Nelson echoed, his head suddenly full of holes: eyes, nose, mouth.

Spinebasher heaved himself upright and weighed his words for neutrality:

— This looks bad.

— Can you fix it though? Nick asked pleasantly, knowing how simple it was to take a rise out of him.

— Maclean, Spinebasher retorted, ruminating. Poor bastard, he added.

— They got him cornered. They say he fell on his knees (the Wild Dog could hear how pathetic this sounded as he went on). And begged for Buchanan's mercy. Offered a full confession.

— One of his men crept back and shot the bastard, Nick supplied the rest.

— But we don't know what that means, the Wild Dog cautioned. Anyone might have done it. We've only got the official version. He was forty-five.

— Maclean was a pain in the arse, Nick suggested from the dark of the open doorway. Him and his flagwaving garbage!

But Nelson, still perfoming the feat of sucking a nourishment of smoke from the stub, felt sorry for Maclean. Sitting high on the workbench among pliers, hacksaws and vices he knew despair as Maclean must have known it, but because he could never be clear about just what he did feel he said nothing. He only felt sad with a big sadness filling him, as he had when Barbara left and broke off their engagement. The others laughed heartless laughter about the engagement in the first place, because Nelson and Barbara had lived together for three years. Yes, but this is something more important, he'd said, striving to get his tongue round the sentiment, the beauty of the unnecessary. It was because they lived together already that the engagement meant so much to him. There he perched, uncomfortable now, remembering the absence of Barbara and feeling sad for Maclean's hopelessness. Maclean was a teacher and the wrong person to go round blowing up factories. He must have known he was the wrong person too, yet he stuck to it for the sake of bravado or his need to contribute to history. Maclean taught history, among other things including Bible Studies. This was the sadness: this unlikely wimp, giving the bastards a run-around, getting out with guns and explosives, who caved the moment he was caught. He had shown himself to be childish. And, like a child caught out, thought it would be enough to say he was sorry, to beg forgiveness on his actual knees, as Nelson had begged Barbara to come home and pleaded with her, cried in front of her despite being twice her size and a rough man with men.

— He was nothing but a pain in the arse, Nick repeated, disgust in his voice.

Nelson sat feeling sadder than ever. Because Nick and he had faced danger together they could say anything to each other without offence. They put their lives in each other's hands so often what could a difference of opinion, let alone a difference of feeling, mean by comparison? Besides which Nelson agreed about the pain in the arse. But this did not stop him sharing the sadness or liking Maclean more for his cowardice than for his cleverness. Nelson understood cowards, suddenly saw what the bloke had been controlling beneath his gangster disguise, whereas he never understood the intellectual stuff about historicism and constitutional reform.

— Poor bloody Maclean, the walrus said and shook his bespectacled head before offering it back to the engine.

— You're a fucking perfectionist mate, Nelson accused him, his voice choked with gratitude that Spinebasher had stood up for him and his feelings, given support to the imperfect Maclean, to amateurism and spontaneous nationalism, to the grieving for Barbara who would never now return.

Spinebasher grunted in among the sparkplugs.

— I reckon, the Wild Dog commented at last. He did a bloody amazing job of blowing things up, considering he had no guts at all. Bloody amazing.

Nelson leapt down off his perch, great with the love he felt for this man, and needing action.

— When do we get going? he demanded.

— When I say, Spinebasher's voice came upside-down from the Citroën's innards.

— Jesus, Nick spat. You guys'll fall for any bullshit. That little rat begging for mercy, ready to kiss Buchanan's arse. Enough to make a man puke.

To his own surprise, Nelson found he had swung a punch at the scoffer. Missed. And took the sharp smack of a return blow to the side of his head. Suddenly his brain presented him with perfectly clear understanding.

— You never cared about anybody did you? he growled, delivering another well-aimed swing, which also connected with nothing. Again he received a crisp punch to the same side of his head.

Nick smiled collectedly, ready for the next round, but the Wild Dog intervened.

— Save it, he suggested. Powell's boys have got their teeth into the job now. They've tasted blood. And they just might come our way next.

— So we put our heads in the same noose? (Nick)

— I'm not Maclean. And that's why we need Mama. She knows more than us. And we want to know what she knows. Buchanan's back from overseas, right? Something new is going to break. It'll be in the Port George area, I reckon.

— Port bloody George! (Nick, laughing louder)

— My sister lives near Port George. (Nelson) There's nothing there.

Mama saw at a glance the men did not want her. She knew there was no time to waste on niceties, she must come up with the goods straight away.

— Why, these are *my* people! she cried out in delight. Circus folk. I'd recognize you anywhere. Come along in, boys, and make yourselves comfortable. Oh but (her face fell) I don't know that I can afford you, that's the trouble.

She led the way, making one swift backward check to be sure she had them bamboozled. Straight into the livingroom she marched and then hit them with her second tactic.

— You wish to know what you should do next? Well I can tell you, she proposed in a voice accustomed to bossing the male sex. The answer is the one I gave poor Maclean only he would not listen, oh no, being too clever by half to accept advice from an elderly person. Your trouble is that your ideas are hopelessly romantic.

The remnants of the Human Pyramid were surprised into showing their surprise.

— All you need is a mob of horses and you could double for Ben Hall. Except that once he'd had his fun with a three-day spree for the whole population of Canowindra while he held the town to ransom, he shot real bullets at those troopers. He didn't kid himself the police could be brought to their knees without messing his hands in blood. That's history for you. You're a hundred years out of date if you haven't learned this lesson. And you've got the gall to take on Owen Powell? Let me tell you, he is as modern as next year, that little wet sponge of a turkey. How do you expect to get anywhere with quick costume changes or your silly French car, only ever half a jump ahead of the Watchdogs? All very clever, darlings, but does it hurt? I mean, sticks and stones and so forth. There's many a truth to be found in nursery rhymes. He has satellites and lasers and computers. There's millions of dollars' worth of technology whizzing round detecting what you're doing and telling him how to catch you at it. And when he gets you, because he will get you in the end, he isn't going to make do with holding you up to public derision, oh no.

Nick narrowed his eyes and sat down instead of hovering near the exit.

— I can see what is coming, she explained. Because I know what went before. There's no soft option for the country. You mark my words. We shall see fighting in the street before we're able to call ourselves free. We'd like to be our own masters? Then we have to grab it with both hands. The same goes for you, Mr Dog, you must decide what you want to hit and why. Then you go for it and hit hard. Just one thing at a time. Show the public what you're made of. Once they catch on, they'll be waiting for the next strike and they'll see how it *connects*. Are you with me? Let me ask you what, in your opinion, is your greatest strength? No, on second thoughts, don't answer, you'll get it wrong and I shall begin to think I am on the losing side, which I could never bear. Your strength is the disillusionment of those people out there. Okay so you've been making them laugh and that's good. Now you have to follow through with some real damage.

The quilted comforts of afternoon rolled apart. Mama had woven her spell.

— Do we have the next move planned? she asked, blandly including herself.

— I've got a hunch I'm on to something big.

— We require more than hunches, Mr Dog. It is no use

risking our hides for a rumour. Well! the lady announced pertly, shedding a couple of decades of wear. You may tell me about it over dinner. We do still have time for culture, busy as we are going to be. Mum's the word for the moment, are we agreed? And now I'd recommend you get to know our computer expert. I am a great believer in specialists. We happen to have the very man we need.

She fetched him.

— This is Colin, she introduced the teenage whizkid from her neighbourhood highschool.

— He's the *man*? Nick sneered.

— He's weaker than a girl, Nelson complained with open alarm, not worrying about the lads's feelings. Look at his arms: thin as cigarettes. He couldn't fight his way out of a paperbag.

— Brown paper, the Man (as he was dubbed from that day on) reproved him, unruffled. Withstands a pressure of up to four thousand kilograms per cubic centimetre!

Nick fell about, laughing.

— You see, Mama declared jubilantly. It's easy. That's the ticket. But I do have this to say in all seriousness; while we make plans we must never lose sight of the central fact: nothing will modify the greed of the greedy but a bullet through the head.

57

One morning Dorina Buchanan got up and, having no one home for whom she might care to maintain standards, wandered through the bunker with the cord of her housecoat trailing behind her. She wandered, fighting to survive suffocation for another day. And suddenly came upon a man in her music room, a strongly built man whose silhouette made her start momentarily in recognition. But whose back, when she came to look more calmly, was wholly and inexcusably unfamiliar.

— What are you doing in here? she demanded, one hand protectively at her throat, feeling the words echo through sensitive fingertips. How did you get in?

He faced her and then tactfully looked down at the parquet floor to save her feeling embarrassed by her state of undress.

— This is my new duty.

Dorina might have returned to the bedroom, or gone to brew

herself some coffee; she might have rushed to the house telephone and screamed into it to have the intruder removed, but
the whim of loneliness led her gently astray.

— How long are you supposed to stay with me?

— For the whole watch, madam.

She pursed her lips coquettishly.

— And, when you leave?

— Kosta will take over.

The president's wife let her glance escape now he met her
eyes. She reviewed the harbour. The weather itself had become
a stranger, the farther shore of Sydney a precinct for lives with
which she, in the interests of her own safety, must not be
allowed contact.

— But won't Kosta's watch extend beyond my bedtime?

He smiled at her simplicity, a smile without humour, without
malice, without interest even.

— We've been trained in what to do.

— Are you never to have a turn at the night watch? she
mused.

— There is no question of turns, Your Excellency.

Tugging the cord tight round her waist, Dorina sat and
considered what she might do. Here, out of the blue, came the
gift of an event. There were alternatives open to her. She could
choose.

58

. . .While I was in irons at Vengeance Harbour I promised myself I would
sail for England the day of my release, confront you with your crime
against me and murder you. You can have no idea how easy this would
be, as you can have no idea of my strength after six years of forced labour.
Sometimes I would denounce you in the village church, sometimes in
parliament, sometimes I would be content to drag you off your horse and
humiliate you in private. But now I know I shall do none of these things.
I am part of a society still in the making. I have given my work and my
youth and a good deal of my blood to help make this colony what it is. I
should rather set out with Mr Sturt or Mr Leichhardt across the desert, if
the reports of a desert are true, than sail again for the home I have been
denied. I can hardly remember your face.

I have begun to tell you all this for two reasons: to bring alive
something of the real concerns among which I am discovering a life that
still has room for moral robustness; and to show by what I observe

*around me that the years of humiliation and torture have not wholly
destroyed my capacity for refinement nor my hope for society, a point
which, as it affords me pride in my manhood, ought in equal measure to
strike you with shame.*

*You will never have heard of Mr Sturt, I suppose, nor Mr Leichhardt.
Sturt is a splendid fellow and in my view our ablest explorer.*

*The land itself is a land in the mind. We make up the idea of it as we
go. The explorers are our poets. The Governor needs an inland sea and
vast grazing areas such as America offers for cattle, so he encourages men
to travel out in search of these things. Sometimes they come back with
good news. Sometimes they tell only of deserts, landscapes of stone over
which the killing heat licks like the sun's tongue; and we adjust the place
in our mind accordingly. The great rivers Mr Sturt found fifteen years
ago, the Darling, the Murray, the Bogan, all flowing one into another,
lead nowhere, it appears. They run west out across trackless land to who
knows where? Logic would say they should run east to the Pacific Ocean.
It is so, too, with our laws. The dreadful question still hangs over us: Did
this land belong to the natives before we arrived? Most colonials would
argue the case for the negative by pointing out that there were no signs of
ownership to be found, no fences, no buildings, no crops, no grazing
herds; we walked wherever we pleased and hammered in our pegs; how
can such land be thought to be owned? We are not invaders but peaceful
settlers, in fine. On the other hand, as we penetrate the flatlands, peering
in at a swinging compass-needle, there is something haunting the continent, a presence not to be doubted. The bravest explorers observe one fact
in common, whether heading across forests or desert, the sense of being
watched, marked and judged, not merely by nomadic tribes but by the
place itself. There have been times in the quarries where I worked, or out at
the boundaries of Sydney on horseback with His Excellency, when I have
said: This place with its old wrinkled bony flanks is surely an animal
with eyes a thousand miles distant watching us and thinking, Shall I
squash these impudent bugs or let them live a little longer?*

*Sir George will have none of such nonsense. We have raised the Union
Jack, he says, the territory belongs legitimately to Her Majesty Queen
Victoria and must be protected in her interests. But at night, camped, I
have heard the land howl and grumble underfoot, uttering weird calls and
twitters in the dark, subterranean repudiations of our intrusion; and,
above in the trees, frogs singing out like birds, while birds in the daytime
cackle the laughter of maniacs. The young leap full-grown from a
kangaroo's womb. This is a continent not to be believed in but to be
possessed by. It is a paradox of impossibilities, which will never conform
to your England nor your England's narrow rules of how a land must be.
Cliffs made of sand, two thousand miles inland, withstand a sea of stones*

that ring like iron under a horse's hooves. Natives disappear as soon as they stop moving. Petty tyrants, adrift from your fixed system of English-ness in England, which is a question of manners rather than justice, turn to beasts whose beastliness is called enterprise.

The day Ludwig Leichhardt returned from the far north (he had ridden north-west from Moreton Bay to the shores of the Indian Ocean and back, and then taken ship for Sydney), the whole town went wild with the holiday. It was not the news he brought which excited people so much as his survival. You see how tired we are of your Empire? It is the individual man and the individual in ourselves we care about. The real issue that day, 25th March 1846, four months ago, was that when his ship berthed it brought the breath of survival. We went to the quay to look at Leichhardt because he had become ourselves. Vast wastelands and vast hungers were in that man, he breathed spaces in our midst. When he thanked the Governor for having supplied camels at the huge expense of £75 a beast, he thanked him in syllables of sun-drenched ranges and the waving crown of a forest his mind alone had stretched wide enough to imagine. For months his party had been lost to us. The newspapers speculated on how they might have perished; so when they returned, they returned from the dead. The unknown is surely death, indeed? This curious man-woman with his lingering eyes and vanity of ugliness is among us now, not as our most famous citizen but as a saviour, the stammering grinning proof that here in Australia one may defy death and live to drink Mr Macarthur's wine.

Do you see what I am telling you, Father? Can you feel death creaking around your bones? Did you take your skeleton for a walk through the grounds this morning, towards the orchard, was it, and glancing at the lion sundial on the way? Perhaps you are carrying this letter, reading as you walk, purple with fury at my impertinence, close enough by now to the stables to hear the horses stamping in their stalls. They have been stamping there for three hundred years and they need to stamp only a few more, one or two, to find you have become a puff of dust in the leaves of a book being put back on the shelf by one of your young men of the future. I can see him yawning, already infected with the lassitude of a rigid Empire in which the young are sapped by refinement while the old eke out the rituals of their futility until an arrangement of teacake on a tray is served up to them in place of dangers worthy of being faced. The ideas have all been used up. Fungus had already begun to take over during the reign of Charles I.

I have a wife and child. My wife's story is somewhat like my own, except for the honest origins of her family in Ireland. The baby will not be told he has a grandfather. As soon as he is old enough I shall teach him that he is his mother's son and his father's son and beyond that may lie all the possibilities of a world in which none but two mortal sins need be feared: to surrender one's own free will and to rob any other person of his. . .

59

A cold wind whipped among the huts inside the prison wall. Dr Luke Head imagined it must also be blowing in the city, saw in his mind crowds being driven indoors and flags on public buildings struggling against restraint. At such times, when he had walked the empty streets, he felt he was intruding on an alien shrine, unable to avoid trespassing in the sanctuary because he could not make sense of the place. Where were you allowed? As an Aborigine, he did not quite belong in his own land. He had developed the habit of watching shop windows to check his appearance in the reflection, not from vanity but (in a distant way like Roscoe Plenty) because by this means he might be surprised into seeing himself as others saw him. Often enough he hated what he saw. He was frightened by his insistent differences. No matter how he dressed them, they set him apart and declared him to be the intruder he, as one of his people, had become.

Luke Head took a turn about the windy yard. No one else was up. Just a guard on the wall who caught his eye and nodded with a proper country boy's gesture. A baby wailed remotely from somewhere in the lean-to shantytown that warmed the outside wall.

His mother had seen clearly enough to say to his father, Luke wants a city. You understand that? To be a leader. And we need them leaders too. That means joining the gubbers. Means bein' better than them at their things. Not a better shit carrier. I mean a better advertisin' man. I mean a better doctor. She was right in her way. What's more, she possessed the courage. But he had been left behind, somewhere back in his childhood, clinging to the tailboard of Uncle Archie's truck (or to be precise, the truck Uncle Archie drove), swinging with the other kids, running in pursuit, and shouting words of a language he could not now translate.

Circling the yard packed smooth with convicts' blood, he looked up at the guard again and nodded to him as they paced in time. This is what has been done to me, he said. If I met myself as a kid right now, we'd hardly know a word in common. One of the hut doors creaked. Every trace of that child had to be exterminated for the making of Dr Head, right down to the ghost of a gesture. (The guard took a break, standing with legs wide apart, the brightening sky beginning to flatten him to an outline.) I accept this as a crime.

Then his friend Yanagita joined him. They took a stroll round the yard, blowing frail puffs of steam. For a long time neither said anything. The guard watched till he grew bored.

Yanagita Izumi was a discovery.

During the weeks of resentment, the calendar marked by cycles of Luke Head's concern for himself and his desperate worry about Stephanie, very little of his attention could be spared for the men he had been thrown among and whose health he was to look after. Nor was he interested in the active jungle sprouting within this same prison's walls, densely growing plants watered by the tears of hungers jostling among that community of men without women. An obscure genital smell leaked from the living quarters to the yard. Frustration hung about the place as pollen. Fights broke out.

Amid this activity, a cool centre of restraint could be found: despite the wars between Kampucheans and Vietnamese, Ghanaians and Nigerians, Greeks and Turks, despite daylong accusations and counter-accusations of Indonesians and Timorese, even despite the cheerful Chinese, one small man carried within himself so deep a stillness he could stop the wind blowing or cut short the complaints of retired brothel-keepers and, even more impressively, exiled professors of jurisprudence. Luke avoided him, sensing a challenge too original, aware that this person did not waste energy, nor did he put the least effort into making an impression.

— It's as if God said certain animals must desire the unattainable and I shall call them humans! Dr Head burst out at reveille one morning when he was tormented by such a passion of disgust with himself he needed a confessor.

— You are not satisfied with life in camp? the Japanese (for this is what he proved to be) suggested in perfectly idiomatic English, which he spoke as if digging clay.

— Worse. I'm not even thinking about camp. It's the same at home, even while I am enjoying my work, dining out, music.

— Frustrated libido? Yanagita Izumi asked as they took a turn round the dusty yard.

— Here, maybe. But not there. I'm crazy about sex. Even at the moments of degrading one another, even when we're down to shit, I feel a purity in myself, the profoundest I know. Now you despise me.

Izumi drew this confession into the stillness of his philosophy. Much later he spoke again.

— My mother taught me the beauty of deformity.

So Luke found a friend.

Another day Luke asked: How did you get to where you are? They paused to look each other in the eye. Then Yanagita put the flat of his birdboned hand on a wall built of convict logic, square shapes in rigid ranks, and slapped it. They sauntered on past a grove of competitive vegetables, past sockets in masonry where the squeal of shackles could still be heard.

— I believe death to be the true test of honour. I can die any time. The dark excites me. We have a code of life. Put it this way, suicide is meaningless in Australia. Though I am half Australian myself, the knowledge of how to die I have from Japan alone. People in this country do not appreciate the glamour of death.

— Is murder glamorous too?

— Difficult. A man shoots his wife. What chance is there that they both accept the act as a gift? Even in Japan a glamorous murder is headline news. Like the death of Mishima and his disciple. But here it is all messy, the bullet is messy, the terror of the victim, the terror of the murderer, the hiding, the lying, all messy.

— And you have no concern for the woman?

— Women are our teachers. They carry new life inside them. We can never be told what their blood knows. How else do you explain suttee? For centuries, Hindu widows climbed on their husbands' funeral fires to die there, till the British interfered and stopped it by law. Why? Because they could not comprehend. Those women knew an ecstasy which life had failed to give, and could not give, until such a moment.

— I reckon the Poms were right, Dr Head declared though he sensed that the desire for the unattainable might just be the same thing as a refusal to accept death.

The cloud cover gaped open and dawn poured red fire over the prison complex. Right-angles stood forward as lucid and unlikely as an opera set. That guard on the wall glowed in a baleful blush.

— I've thought of murder too, Luke confessed a moment later. Only the other day. But there was no salvation in it, he added.

— Anger might be the truest salvation.

Outside the wall the protesting women stirred, while their babies wriggled on crackling beds of chocolate-wrappings. Wattle birds repeated eternal questions, filling the morning with uncertainty. One magpie dipped to rinse its wings in cool prison silence, the feathers creaked and hushed.

— The man I'd like to murder, Dr Head explained. Came to offer me freedom.

Yanagita smiled with a thousand years' experience.

— He also told me my wife escaped arrest.

A whole flock of silvereyes now flittered into the bare-branched fruit trees and darted about on the soil below, filling the bell of the yard with crystalline chirruping. In a mad scatter of highspirits, they were gone again, swooping over the wall, the ghost of a tidalwave, and away among Australians of authenticated stock.

— Belief, said the Japanese. Matters more than truth.

— When I am ready to escape, I told him, I'll do it my way.

As for my dead body, Luke imagined it: the clouds go floating above me still. That's all I need to know. He turned to his companion. On this occasion they occupied a sunny corner, enjoying the change of weather as spring lay beast-warm in the soil, its spirit hovering already through the forest above, a forest luscious with dark foliage and inhabited by women dancing with women; the one person having the gift of speech speaking flowers, while a messenger of the gods reached among leaves to pluck an orange perfect as the sun itself.

— Tell me, Luke's voice proposed. Why you didn't get out of the country before they came for you.

— My life, you want? replied Yanagita the weaver of tales.

They laughed into undergrowth budding blades of foliage, some tortured memories opening to huge pale lilies adrift on secret waters.

— Why else is suicide *le vice japonais*?

— I will have to begin with Mama. She was a camp-follower with class. She went to the wars. Perhaps you have no experience of this. I was a fat child when I was small and she took me everywhere. At the start we had an apartment furnished with silk, silk pictures, silk covers on the bed. You see it? She would entertain no one except handsome officers, young men. She inspected them before agreeing to anything. She asked them many questions; were they of clean family, had they wives, children, did they eat meat three times a week? Many questions. She was very particular. And everything she did had the shape of a ritual. Maybe she learned this from my father. But then she began to slip. The silk went first. She made do with any temporary apartment as long as it was near the battle and ventilated. She began to take lower ranks. Next we travelled, even to Cuba and Malawi. I grew up knowing about the things other boys are kept from knowing, and nothing of what they do know. In erotica and demography, I was a prodigy. All the same I was lost and nobody could help because nobody guessed my ignorance, not even me.

— How did you come to Australia?

— This was the only place on earth not likely to have a war, or so Mama said when she was disillusioned with her years of success.

— So you came as a child?

— I came as a pimp.

Luke rocked on his hams, listening delightedly.

— Now, he invited. Tell me the truth.

— You're right, Yanagita confessed. I wrote it in a book, that story. But it is the truth all the same. My father was an aviator, though I don't remember him. An amateur. In the 1930s he flew sporty monoplanes in races for the rich. But he was not rich. He should have been because he felt no nausea whatsoever with the baubles of luxury. He had no objection to driving a Railton Special and wearing sealskin coats. He'd live on sturgeon and marrons glacés. He paid more for a haircut than the average person spends on a week's food for a family of five, and did not go mad. Mama went mad instead. She told him if he imported another cursed Percival Gull she would sabotage it for him in the interests of moderation. Poor Mama, she never heard what his lips said to that. But an oath is a promise, and this he could not get his Bollinger-pickled brain to work on. The tragedy was that he found enough dupes to back him. He financed the aeroplane and helped take it out of packing crates himself in all its heroic newness. For seven weeks and three days she didn't see him while the Percival Gull was made ready for its glorious maiden parabola from one holy city to another, from Kyoto to Osaka as so often was the case with frogs in fairytales, except they were green. Mama said just you remember what I said when the engine of that big toy dies of bronchitis. But he had his earmuffs on and his eyes, lost behind goggles, were fleeting brightnesses of shared excitement. The best I can hope, Mama concluded, is that you'll dig a deep enough hole with the nose of that folly to save the cost of a regular burial. Already far away in his leather helmet, Papa waved at her as at a cheering crowd. Up he flew in his gull, and no sooner had it reached a truly lethal height than down it came a good deal quicker for the help of gravitation. But true to form, Papa cost us money on an American scale even then. He crashed into an aviary and three million yen worth of exotic parrots escaped to lament the lost Orinoco. They carried their cries to the hearts of accountants and fisherfolk. Admiral Togo himself spent half a life's savings in the failed attempt to teach one macaw to pronounce the Japanese *r*. Papa didn't even bury himself. The Percival Gull behaved as impeccably as the manufacturers promised and refused to explode or fall to pieces. It crashed as arranged by Mama but, apart from the injuries inflicted on it by the disintegrating birdhouse, delivered its dead pilot in perfect condition, complete with identification papers for the owners of the escaping parrots to use when claiming compensation in the courts, plus the cost of removing the aircraft, also the return hearse fare from Kyoto, a round trip of sixty kilometres. It was at this point that Mama preferred the risks of war, claimed she no longer existed, sank her savings in silks, and took her apartment in the name of a Shikoku princess of the thirteenth century.

— When did she die? Luke Head asked, amused, patting the warm ground.

— Mama dead? That's not likely. She has even been here on a visit. They have allowed her to remain living in state at home. She interrogated the policemen arresting me. How many generations of your lot have we had to tolerate? she said. If it's a miserable hovel we must come down to, so what, we came of miserable stock. But I'll have you know my family own this land and we have been here since 1817, when it was a spacious farm before the city of Sydney ate it away to a garden. They founded the Bank of New South Wales the very day my ancestor hammered his first tent peg into the soil here. And I don't doubt the tent leaked. Yanagita smiled deprecatingly to acknowledge the infinitely longer claims of Luke's own ancestors. The tent leaked later in Whitey's Fall, she went on, so it was a good thing we hung on to this place. When the police mumbled some kind of answer, she flew at them. You have the impertinence to suggest my Yanagita can't be mine? Of course he is Japanese, his father was Japanese and the whole shebang of relatives on that side. The state! Don't mention the rotten state to me. Does the state presume I had no part in the birth? Should I instruct your precious president in the ABC of getting a child? No. Take the boy. Welcome. Teach him better manners than I have, if you can. But when you find yourselves clapped in your own jail it will be too late to regret crossing swords with me. I've seen your faces and every eyelash is safe in my memory. Men, she said. I never make a mistake. I've got you catalogued, never you fear. And I shall have you curried for dinner. As for you, boy, ring me the moment they let you out so I can tell you what to do next. If they ask questions give nothing but the truth, then they will be sure not to believe you to avoid being poisoned with shame. Dry between your toes when your feet get wet. And never translate anything for anybody. That's all you need to remember.

Luke laughed incredulously.

— Okay, his friend agreed. You can laugh, till you meet her. But when you do, you owe me a forfeit.

— My life has been so ordinary, he replied. Perhaps I resent all these fireworks.

— Boy, she called me. She'll never change. That's why she doesn't go senile. I'm over sixty.

Doors banged open. Guards rushed into the exercise yard and around the huts yelling: Out, out, all out! Come on, you lazy swine, do you think the country can afford to feed you like parasites with nothing to do? Guest workers, you are, not guests. On your feet! The Friends of Privilege stirred, rolled off creaking bunks and stumped about the shaky floors they themselves had built of their inexperience. They shivered and exchanged brief courtesies from remote homelands.

Martin Place, as Luke, sitting in the sun, pictured it, was full of people who belonged, looking for entertainment and paying no heed to the delicate evening rain which he imagined hanging among the trees outside the General Post Office. He did not want to tear himself away from this vision, lightglobes flashing occasionally as gusts scattered the screen of leaves, nor from the anticipation of what his friend might be going to say, now he had a friend. So they were left only a few free minutes while the others got dressed and assembled.

— I was in the electronics business on a big scale, Yanagita explained. That's my training. Once I met a wise man who told me there is beauty in accepting responsibility regardless of the work one is doing. I tried to live by that. I tried to make electronics my hope. But the financial side tended to take over and money can offer so little in the way of beauty. My success outgrew my technical ability. In the end, routine made me a dull man. My inner self, I suppose it was, told me this is not the world, this is not the scene I have dreamed of, the deepest part of me is alienated.

Men hurried past to line up on the blood-polished yard, men whose homes had been in dusty villages of thatched huts, in hanging slums that broke off by chunks and slid into some river during typhoons, even a few in expensive clubs and gambling dens. Most had at least been used to extensive families gathering for the festival of daily food, or in the throes of starvation. Here they were given orders, and the democracy outside would pay them for having come.

— Then they brought me to this camp Luke, the Japanese added gazing away and up at the guard on the wall, who in turn stared out over Buchanan's domains. I asked a civil question the moment I arrived. Instead of an answer, I was punched. You see the result for yourself. One hit in the face and I am young again. Wonderful country. Wonderful system.

That was it. In a curious way, the converted prison seemed more honest, to Dr Head, than society outside. Here, he certainly did not feel he was trespassing on anyone else's sanctuary. He knew how to fight simple harassment.

They got up together and dawdled across to join the ranks.

— This morning, the commandant announced, climbing on some steps outside the guardroom to be seen from all corners of the yard, disarmed by the act of doing so because he showed his weak back to the assembled foreigners and the arthritic curl of his little finger on which he wore a ring. This morning, he repeated. We switch to a different work site. Also in the local area. You are to be congratulated on your success at the port. Good show. This new job is even bigger. We shall be employed as sub-contracted labour. Clear? Highly respected firm: orders from me, work for them. Understood? Big changes in the wind, he added shaking his head. All very exciting. Attention. Dismiss.

60

Once inside the make-up room, the bearers deposited Bernard Buchanan to confront his image in a mirror brilliant with lights. The woman pinned a bib round where she thought his neck might be, her gestures intimate, fingers not at all nervous of touching him. She even patted the hillock of his shoulder.

At the president's right hand sat his Personal Deputy, a new position created specially for Owen Powell who might be Judas, observing the whole performance with respectful attention. Why was he the one to mimic every attitude? Why was he the next to stroke a cat if his master stroked it first? These were questions which must one day be answered with favours or punishment.

— As you say, said Deputy Powell. As you say.

The president caught Squarcia's eye, one black coal that gave away no expression but missed nothing, hot as his cigarette. Behind him a security guard stood against the wall, an awkward cove also noting every least thing but in quite another spirit, sly and apparently working strictly by the book: Wilson, he replied when interviewed four years ago. At the president's left, his press officer Margaret Talbot perched on a table corner. Could be a militant feminist with nothing against him but his sex, though that was serious enough an offence in some people's eyes, God knows how high her ambitions might run. Sufficient dubious quotes, sufficient public occasions less than perfectly prepared for, to put her neck very close to the block.

— This'll be good, she declared brightly.

Whatever that might mean.

Another security guard supervised the far side of the room, but had not been privileged with a goodmorning handshake. And wouldn't be, because Bernard Buchanan sensed an attitude. One thing he would not tolerate was subordinates smirking at the difficulty his eight bearers had in lowering his chair without a bump: Harvey, Craig, Scott, somebody, somebody, somebody, somebody and Noel. This continued to be an aggravating issue, because as he took more powers to himself he became still fatter. He was considering ten bearers. Why had his guard been changed today anyhow? And why without consulting him? He did not like it. He wished he might sleep again as he slept during his overseas tour, the sleep of those who forget to be grateful, the profound oblivion of the unworthy.

— Rest your head, the make-up lady prepared him, having slipped the usual pillow in place. And close your eyes.

Yes, like a bitter parody of sleep. There was no relief in this. Quite the reverse, he felt on edge. Now would be the time for an assassin. The knife plunging silently in while his loyal staff stood back to watch, not to miss the least twist of his agony. Or a needle inserted in his arm, a strangler's cord feeling for his sweaty neck, the blast of a revolver slamming its deafening door shut on his life. To die without ever having known why. Who was it advised him to continue with this make-up treatment before appearing on camera anyway? What was wrong with the way he looked? Whose hands were touching him? More security guards muttered possible betrayals to the bearers outside in the corridor. No, eight were enough, he already found them confusingly numerous, four of the team spending their lives behind his back. Those low voices were what had been bought in return for selling out the state police force, with its traditions of service to old ladies crossing the road, and corruptibility to the right bidder. These unknown operatives. Pink blindness cradled him. His eyelids were tinted. Firm fingers took hold of his features, nose, ear (could somebody be heard smiling?), dewlap. He tensed and then, as always, surrendered. The make-up artist overcame his unease, conquered him with his desire to appear good, to be loved. She smoothed and smurlicated him, she made love with her sponge, her powderpuff. She patted and dusted him, she toyed with his hair and perfumed his cheeks.

— It's easy these days, she explained so the conspirators outside could not be overheard. When I began training we had to do a full job on men as well; eyeliner, lipstick, the works.

— I have had it done, he capitulated thinking back on his past life of simply making money. I looked a sight. He opened one eye to glare in the mirror, but the smirkers had cleverly averted their impudence.

— Eyes shut, she admonished. Nearly finished.

Was this a lovely treat, or a second chance for the gunman? She brushed his lids with her butterfly and declared him fit to live.

— There now, Your Excellency.

Declared him finished. For what that meant. He took it easy, making a show of indifference; slowly scorched the room with a collected stare. (Why did you tell me I'm beautiful, the young Dorina had accused him many years ago, now you have spoiled it all.) Squarcia's cigarette glowed red and then died to ash. Wilson shifted his weight to the other foot. Margaret Talbot's hand hid inside the pocket of her woollen dress and declined to withdraw under scrutiny.

— I'm so used to doing Your Excellency's face, the make-up lady prattled. We're twice as quick as with anybody else.

The producer presented his report that, respectfully, everything was of course ready in the studio, full facilities having been made available to the visiting BBC crew, and please come this way.

Come this way! In his own mansion, to the studio he himself had had built for convenience! Buchanan snorted. As if I'm going to walk it. As if I don't use the stuffy hole every morning anyhow. No sooner have you rebuilt a great house, no sooner are you ready to enjoy the glory, than you find decay has been working as fast as you have.

— Owen, the president explained to his deputy. I shall need you in the control room to be my eyes and ears. The Poms don't know it but they're on trial. A whim of mine. You're familiar with the image I've grown to expect. Saying which he navigated the way for his bearers as Wilson held the door open. A bit to the right, Harvey old fellow. Don't jolt me. Thank you Wilson, he added. I never forget anyone.

Andy Fortescue had left London with a very precise brief as leader of a BBC news team. Of course we want the *truth*, the producer explained ticking off his points in italics. As usual. But, you know, the Empire *had* much to be said for it which hasn't *been* said, for all its *horridnesses* and so forth. Are we unsympathetic then, Andy asked, to the republic? Quite the contrary my dear, quite the *contrary*, but I *do* want us to ask the *central* questions: *what* are the benefits of independence, what do they *say* has happened and what really *has* happened, that kind of thing. It goes without saying.

Andy strode off the plane in his brogues and corduroys, simmering with enthusiasm and overheated as this was a warm spring midday. The BBC had arranged the centrepiece of his program, a personal interview with President Buchanan, for a week's time. Meanwhile, he would begin in Sydney and get to know the place again, having been here in years gone by, naturally. As he rode down the escalator (musing that all escalators ought perhaps, linguistically, to travel upwards) to customs, he was surprised to observe a squad of military personnel standing at the bottom looking up. Despite its French affiliations, the escalator bore him inexorably down towards them, and by the gradual lowering of their sights in perfect accord with his own position, he deduced they must have mistaken him for somebody else.

— Mr Fortescue? a pleasant major asked. Please follow me.

And that is how he came to be marched out of the building, past the queues where his own team awaited examination by customs officials dressed in shortsleeved shirts, shorts and long white socks. Out to a waiting vehicle, they steered him, then away across soulless flats, riskily in front of jumbo jets howling on the tarmac, to a cluster of dark green combat aircraft undergoing constant mechanical pampering. Up the steps to one of these he was ushered ever so urbanely. The moment he and his escort were safely strapped in their seats and the doors sealed shut, the machine roared out on to a reserved runway, picked up speed in that spectacular rush so loved by Luigi Squarcia, and off. He was treated now to the obverse view of Sydney, the harbour slipping away to his left, where it had shafted in from the right as he landed.

— Here, the major explained. Is your schedule. You are to be ready to speak to His Excellency in fifty-six minutes from (he consulted his watch and paused a touching few seconds so that his information on the time should be exact for the overseas guest) now.

— But my cameramen, my staff?

— Will arrive by a separate flight. Within minutes, the smiling officer assured him. Cigarette? Drink?

— No thank you all the same, Andy Fortescue retorted primly with that beautiful disguise of a newshound caught in the thrill of action.

So when the make-up lady had released Bernard Buchanan from her ministrations and his bearers positioned him at the microphone, he sized up the enemy as last-minute staff flitted around with glasses and fresh jugs of iced water, feather dusters whisking at the perennial imperfection breeding on shiny surfaces, closing doors with the air of we did our best at short notice. They packaged him more firmly into his chair with superfluous comforts. A vase of rosebuds opened as soon as he was settled. His interviewer was there already, and waiting of course, sportscoat unbuttoned dashingly but his Oxbridge manner striking a perfect blend of the deferential and the independent. He stood, acknowledging the president's welcome with an ever-so-slight bow and, watching his hand disappear into the president's huge mitt, left it there obediently until it was disgorged. The floor manager attended to what his earphones were telling him, one hand rising very slowly with the accumulating tension of the created moment, signalling for silence. The interview began. Buchanan, so impatient to shine with an untried audience, took the lead the instant he had been introduced.

— The first point, as you will have observed Mr Fortescue, is that we are efficient. The second is that regrettably we can no longer await the pleasure of the BBC. So, this is where you must begin.

— Your Excellency, you are most kind, Andy responded without the benefit of his meticulous notes.

— What would you like to ask me? the president invited the camera.

— Granted, Andy proposed moving smoothly into an improvised routine. That you achieved an impressively trouble-free transfer to republican government, would it be reasonable to suppose your greatest support came from Australians of some generations' standing and from non-British immigrants? Originally, that is?

— Andrew, the president beamed in all his hugeness, his shoulders and even his knees rising to accentuate his benevolence. We love Britain and our British migrants. You'll find no anti-British sentiment here. A successful eight years of the republic simply means we did not need you to hold our hand any longer.

— Should I put it this way: there has been speculation that as we moved out the Americans moved in.

— Quite right, and that happened in 1908 after you had signed a treaty passing the Pacific region on a plate to Japan. I am very pleased, Andrew, to have this opportunity of addressing the British public directly. Many of you have relatives here and longstanding bloodties. I would like to reassure you that we have not changed. We still play cricket with you, don't we? And we still win! He laughed a trembling cake of laughter.

— The unease, the interviewer slipped in neatly. Became inevitable, right from the beginning, when her Majesty. . .

— Was shamefully abducted. As I said all that long time ago, we were being used by outsiders. This was not an Australian abduction, such a thing is unthinkable, but a foreign abduction carried out on our soil because we were too trusting. That has all changed. We've woken up since. And I believe we have already responded as contritely as can be expected of one nation to another. We all thanked God Her Majesty was safe. There never had been abductions in the past and there have been none since. Now may we have your next question, perhaps about something a little closer to the present.

Andy observed the flowers critically, playing an expert game of hesitancy.

— My next question, he extemporized. Concerns yourself personally, if I may venture.

The president sanctioned the venture with a wave of his paw.

— There have been suggestions, Your Excellency, that during your years in office rather too much of the burden of state may have fallen directly to your lot.

— Am I a dictator, you mean? Bernard Buchanan shook with jollity. Do we hang people and oppress them, do we imprison them? Do they go without food? Without liberty of speech?

— There are those who would answer yes to all five questions.

— As there are those who would sell us to the Soviets despite their Oxford doctorates of gentility.

— You do not wish to say something about the reported state of emergency and curfews in the cities.

— Yes indeed. Thank you for raising the matter. Buchanan, astounding as a monument, crossed his legs at the ankle. A lot of nonsense has been circulating on this subject. The state of emergency is not the product of my administration but a measure taken in all conscience to halt any further slide into the quagmire left us as a legacy by our predecessors.

— You say *us* as if you belonged, merely, to a political party.

— Do you object to the Queen opening the Westminster parliament with a speech about My government?

— But Mr President, it is surely too long since your predecessors were in power for them to be blamed?

— You see how patient we have been.

The great man reached forward and touched the roses between them, perhaps appreciatively, disarranging them in the process.

— Having been so kind as to answer a question about yourself, Andy said. May I ask one about me? Since this interview is being recorded, in your studio, will I have the full video to take back with me?

— We thought, the president quipped delightedly. You would so fall in love with our stable society compared to the turmoils of England, plus our splendid climate, you would consider settling here permanently.

The ice stung in his veins. This was the moment of genuine shock Andy Fortescue took away in the military aircraft that flew him, strapped beside the affable major and refusing cigarettes and drinks, to where he had started at Sydney. Of all that followed during the interview (the forestalling of racial conflict, exclusive trade agreements, the rumours of a new wave of lampooning), his impression that a trapdoor had opened under him persisted. Far too well trained to allow a sinking heart to show, he joked with the fat man and finally relented far enough to play a little to his vanity with questions beginning, now you are acknowledged as one of the world's great statesmen. . . and, having retained your sense of proportion despite the enormous esteem in which you are evidently held here. . . to round things off with, how do you view future relationships with other countries of the South Pacific region?

— Listen, Buchanan replied. We are cooperating on joint projects for contributions to stability in the area and therefore world peace. We are party to the World Jet just as we have been for many years to the World Car and the World Satellite. You know about this? Components made here, components made in Taiwan, others in the Filipines, in Korea, and so forth. Close and cordial relations.

— But I mean. . .

— And this is a perfect model for our political interdependence. We do not kid ourselves that we are part of them nor part of their aspirations. Our geographic position is purely accidental. What's geography anyway in the age of nuclear missiles? Our satellite links with Britain, or Norway for that matter, are no less instantaneous than those with Indonesia. Don't give me that old stuff. We are no longer frigging around in sailing ships, Andrew. This is a modern nation you are asking about. We produced the world's first test-tube baby, you seem to forget.

— You are not concerned by reports that rebels in Tuavaleva have been found to be using U.S. armaments?

— Here, we mind our own business, the great man said pointedly.

— But you were in Tuavaleva so recently.

— All we saw of Tuavaleva, Buchanan replied, dismissing the question with a bellow of derision. Was the art of eating turtle eggs, which you're obliged to be enthusiastic about though they're raw, and a demonstration of how to drive a man into a fit by beating a gong non-stop for an hour or two.

And so they played at wanting information and not having it to give, the interviewer's surprises meeting a bluff cheeriness which had in it more than a trace of wilful ignorance. And, on the other hand, the suggestion by the president that poor Mr Fortescue was missing the point, that Australia could not be so tidily summed up as he appeared to suppose, neither in her foreign liaisons nor in her private aspirations.

— Aspirations for what?

— To be left to our own freedom. You see, you have a certain style of boxed-in mentality typical of a European. You want to package everything in neat little questions and answers: are things like this or are they like that, where do we draw the limits, and so forth. It doesn't seem to occur to you that we revel in this lack of definitions, we love it. One reason we had to cut ourselves free of that British colonial past was because we couldn't stomach another minute of being asked to account for ourselves at every turn and be able to point to just which pigeonhole we belonged in. We've never belonged in any pigeonhole. Have a look at a few of our outback towns when you're travelling around. You'll find a straight street, so wide it's more like an invasion from the surrounding land than a street. And on either side are shops and buildings as if they've simply stood there for the present because they heard there was a road passing by. And there's that road zooming out across thousands of kilometres of nowhere under a sky so pure and blue it gives a new meaning to heaven. We don't *want* a little vista at the end of a modest lane of human proportions with dinky little kerb-stones and gutters and everybody's place snug behind a clipped hedge. We'd suffocate in that world. We love the daring fling of space, the whole huge rush to be at the horizon and find that still, blissfully, there's nothing there to measure it by.

— Do people feel that way about government too?

— They have big broad government, if that's what you mean, a government able to stand a bit of knocking about.

— Who is the Wild Dog, Your Excellency?

— I shall let you into a secret, the president offered without hesitation. Every leader needs some kind of barometer for indicating and anticipating public reaction. I call my barometer the Wild Dog. He appears here and there, always at points sensitive to policy. He crystallizes possible kinds of dissent. If ever his pranks elicit public support, we shall know we must act.

— Take decisive action against him?

— Of course not, he is our barometer. We don't blame the barometer for the weather in this country, Andrew. When the time comes, if the time ever does come, we shall look hard at our policies and also the possibility that propaganda by the malcontents might be taking hold. To date, I am gratified to assure you, we have been given no cause for alarm.

— Thank you for your time and your frank hospitality, President Buchanan.

The cameras were switched off, the lights dimmed, the visiting producer fulsome with gratitude, and Mr Fortescue found himself invited for coffee with Margaret Talbot (my press secretary, who knows more than I do about what I know).

— And now Owen, Buchanan ordered when the pleasantries were over. We shall have a little chat in private, shall we?

The bearers set off with him, through corridors and staterooms to the far end of the mansion, where he had his office.

— Very very good that was, Bernie, the Minister for Internal Security and Personal Deputy to the President exclaimed as the door shut on the soundproof bearers.

— Don't call me Bernie.

— Your Excellency, you were superb. He thought he had you, but each time you got out of it with absolute ease.

— I got out of nothing, Mr Powell. Are you suggesting I told less than the truth?

— Good God no, what I mean, as you see, as you *saw*, were the traps he thought, just thought, he had laid, was what I was going on to say.

— What traps?

— That business, well, about the Pacific neighbours, and. . .

— I am reminded, Minister, that it is a long time since we made an example of our predecessors. This state of emergency is entirely their legacy. It was under their rule that the populace grew spineless and unproductive. One cannot cure decades of rot overnight, and it's too bad if people are allowed to forget it. People do forget. They need reminding, Mr Powell.

— I shall attend to it. How many guilty parties do you feel would suffice?

— How many, Buchanan shouted at the deaf room. By what right do you dare ask a question like that, as if I dreamed this up to suit myself? As many as are legitimately guilty. I leave that to you to find out. Go and consult with Squarcia if need be.

— Of course, Your Excellency.

— And make things a bit tough for Little Lord Fortescue while he is visiting the country. He is too smart to fall for a luxury holiday on the Barrier Reef. Let him survive a few minor jolts so he feels good about himself and I'll bet he will come out of it on our side. As for those BBC cameramen he brought with him, they might be better off spending the next few weeks in Sydney on an exchange basis. You tell me they amused themselves at my expense, is that it? Very well. Unfortunate camera angles, was that your phrase? A sudden look at my hands for a betrayal of agitation, you say? We know the kind of thing. We were brought up on it. Fortescue can have a local team to travel with, which should include a couple of your men. What he can do to me on the screen I shall not have him doing to my country. I'm good for a laugh and I can take it. There's no cultureshock in that for me. I've been fat all my life. By the way, I believe he requested permission to interview Dorina. I shan't prevent it. And on that occasion alone I will not have him watched, do you understand. That's an order, because I will not have *her* watched, not in any circumstances. As long as he doesn't get a whiff of poor bloody Rory, he shall talk to her, though I don't give him a chance in Hades of persuading her to appear in his film. She'd think this was altogether too vulgar. Give him permission to see her tomorrow. Leave him alone for a day. Oh, and one more thing, Mr Powell, your Wild Dog idiocy. I have had enough of it. I am a very patient man and kindly to a fault, but I will not be put in a position of wasting my time on questions about some self-seeking hoodlum with a nickname. I want him crucified. But don't implicate me. I can't even be seen to admit he's a nuisance. I have no weaknesses. Just catch the mongrel and keep him out of my hair.

— I shall put my best men on to him immediately. It'll be a simple job.

— Why have you waited to be asked then, if it is to be so bloody simple?

— Simple, as I would put it, now that measures have already been taken, as I understand. Simple from here on, Your Excellency. Though whether our agents can be said to be actually on his track I couldn't say.

— Listen Owen, the president let one hand fall on his deputy's arm as his tone switched from the fuming to the confidential. I know there is nothing beyond your talents when you set your mind to it.

— Your. . .

— Bernard. To you, I am always Bernard. Remember that.

Casting off the irritation of the television interview, the great man threw back his head, opened his huge gullet, and trumpeted with laughter, quadruple chins clustering up and down excitedly. He had forgotten already. That's how much harm the interview had done him. Andrew Fortescue was consigned to the past. The past was a thing which Buchanan, in the fatness of his appetite for power, merely waved away. Likewise, the future served simply to make him irritable. The present was his. He drank the present in gargantuan draughts, he sucked it into his gorge, smacked his fleshy lips, his eyes rolling frenziedly, while he sighed Ahh and Ohh and Good. Then what could be seen of his neck, with no adam's apple to it, let the events of the moment stream down unimpeded. Glorious! he would declare for no reason.

He dispensed with Owen Powell's soft arm.

— There's nothing beyond your talents, he repeated in the sudden gloom of ominous expectations.

61

The following afternoon three meetings took place which were eventually to have their effect, each upon the others. One in the presidential mansion, one in Dorina Buchanan's bunker and one, well, who can tell where such a meeting does take place?

That is to say, Stephanie and Luke Head made contact again.

Mama had been talking. She sat flushed with the success of her tirade, hair dishevelled and slipping free from the loose French roll she wore it in. She panted with the excitement of giving orders to so dangerous and dominant a man: the three of them, Mama, Stephanie and the Wild Dog, a group on the back porch, which must have been the side porch of the original house, with a view over the hectic profusion of Mama's garden. Rare plants held out black leaves, and vines bloomed pink as waterlogged fleshwounds; towering bamboo, like insect-parts under a magnifying glass, knocked their jointed limbs together while swaying in the wind; spine-covered tendrils and disorderly mops of leafage tossed and clawed at a tattered relic of sky.

— Okay so we are to work together, Mama was saying. I provide you with a base, all the fancy electronics, weapons, foodstocks, money and publicity. I've got the lot. But I haven't told you what is in it for me yet. You must make me a promise: bring my boy back safe from their clutches. I carted him round the world while I provided my services to the fighting men of nineteen nations, and a proper brat he was. I didn't put myself through those hoops, faithfulness and duty and I don't know what else, for some christmas pudding of a politician to shut him away. So his father was Japanese? What about his mother? Aren't I Australian? I'm that close to the lags of the First Fleet, I could have come over with them in chains and I wouldn't know the difference. And now I am going to tell you how to go about your business. You are a good lad and I was following your career before we ever met, but, if you don't mind my saying so, you haven't got much of a clue. You've done everything wrong except choosing your name. (Here Stephanie smiled a slight, strained smile.) The Wild Dog has got a popular ring about it. I like it, I buy it, we'll keep it. The donkeys out there, she waved one arm at the world beyond the garden, setting her bangles clattering and clocking. Have bought it. But whatever we plan, you must get this straight: those bullyboys are in it for money and kicks. They love being rich, yes they love it and love it, it's their whole world; and they love having power, ordering this one his cut of the graft and that one a medal and you a bullet in your balls. Love it. There's fools around who think the corrupt don't know they're corrupt. Tell me a new joke next time, why not? They are having a fantastic lot of fun propping up their cronies and their floosies in positions of power, doing deals, fixing everything and getting away with it. So if we're to make out against them, we have got to enjoy it too, are you kidding or have you gone troppo? Darling, you can tell the dumb ones by the questions they ask. You need to be tearing across the screen with your red scarf flying, flashing your smile at the ladies, alley-oop and away. Get me? No need to push a point, I say. The public cottons on pretty quick too. The public gets treated like morons and it is such a mistake; they're only idiots. So we're sure to be called terrorists, what the hell? she leaned comfortably close. A true terrorist does not ask for lots of dead bodies, but lots of attention. Hijackers are the perfect example: how often do they actually blow up a plane? No, they're there to publicize a cause and they believe it's only a matter of time before the whole world comes to see the light. For all that, the terrorist is an unpleasant cut of a character. I'm sorry to report, she explained cheerfully. You fit the bill. Handsome as you are, there's something unsavoury about you, something I don't understand, something not quite human, rescued only by your sense of humour. You know, one thing you never hear in a lunatic asylum is laughter. I should know. The mad don't laugh, life being too deadly serious in there. Your danger is love, that's obvious. She glanced accusingly at Stephanie and continued. If you don't get over this love-struck nonsense, you may lose a laugh that will save your life. First, you have to see the enemy the way they are: players in a play.

Mama took a break for a moment, leaving her garden filled with the promise of further heresies. She tugged at the tube of a Turkish water-pipe she was smoking. She puffed. The primitive device made gobbling sounds which pleased her immensely.

— How I love a politician, she resumed. Firm-fleshed, grey at the temples, the appearance of rank and all that, while inside. . . nothing. Have a piece of Delight, children. She passed the box, her fingers already white and sticky. She looked down at the Wild Dog, at this powerful animal, its simple face quizzical with the desire to please, but to please Stephanie not herself.

— As for the parliamentary women, she resumed in a voice richer for its rose-petal jelly and water-cooled smoke. Leathery and tireless, putting every statement through a pencil-sharpener, alternating between mother-of-two and Medea. What a performance! Ladies who have seen everything and survived, bursting a bloodvessel over the price of nappy pins in Wangaratta, lovely.

Here Mama, gasping and excited by her own eloquence, snatched another puff of her hookah.

— You reckon the hookah's overdone, you lot out there, she called through the glinting leaves and black tendrils of the garden as if to an audience in hiding. As sure as my name's Mama you're missing the point while you worry about that. There's hookahs around, right? There's people who smoke them? So let's call it quits, she lapsed into confidentiality again. This is what comes of being paid in kind when you are a traveller!

The Wild Dog waited, eyes calm but head filled with the past he had put behind him, months spent living in jobless squalor, memories of meal-ticket queues, of being arrested by fisheries inspectors for catching his own food, driven from the coast by police and hounded back to the city, his survival among derelicts in condemned houses, his determination to hold on to the sentimental ideals of youth still too strong to stoop to hurting the weak. He fanned smoke from his face with a hand which might, even so, have killed.

— You think you are in Ireland shooting at your cousin? her voice hectored him. This is a government you are up against. And not the Australian Government either. Is that news, Mr Dog? Of course not. Well, there's hope for you yet, she conceded, perverse enough to be grudging. Then Mama turned to Stephanie. Your part will come very soon, my dear.

But Mama had not got over her coolness to the younger woman whom she saw watching the Wild Dog's every reaction and reading this lecture back, as it were, through his responses. She raised her dimpled arms to re-do her hair, extracting a hairpin and plunging it back more securely.

Stephanie did not mean to let any such interest show. In her heart she was loyal to Luke. Yet she did watch while humorous lines played at the corners of the man's mouth, animating his stern cheeks. Dressed in jeans and a singlet, he had been squatting on the deck. But now he moved to settle down and stretch his legs, resting his spine against the doorpost. As he changed position, she saw, disguising her fascination by keeping her head low, an arch of muscle ride up the inner arm near the armpit, a prodigious hollowing and swelling. He was so utterly lacking vanity she felt her glance had passed unnoticed. Only herself to hold in check, teased at the centre of a flickering pack of ancestors, being winked at and pinched, bewildered by tatters of clothing and lewd gestures, what she felt was not lust as such, but a profound curiosity. His neck had the chiselled lines of something meant never to change.

Without a word, she scrambled up and left them. What she proposed doing once she retreated to her room, Stephanie had no idea. She shut herself in and then flung open the wardrobe on all those dress suits, each an envelope for its matching dicky-shirt and bowtie. Enraged by the care with which they had been hung in order of size, she grabbed a couple of hangers, thinking to dump them in a mess on the carpet. But once the heavy garments were in her power, she found she had pushed a cluster of suits further along, as she might shove a queue of lechers, her hand on the nearest chest, and re-hung them in the wrong order.

— So he is a gentleman, she hissed as she lunged at these mementos of a vanished ballroom era, lashing out at them idiotically, and stumbling, falling among graded shoes, men's patent leather pumps, each held stiff and creaseless by a shoe-tree. So he loves me? Tell me something I don't know! But familiarity had little to do with this annoyance, her despairing tone an admission of a far more serious offence, an offence of her own: that she had ceased to be angry. Stephanie was lost and knew it. She could never again fabricate a feeling. Now she detected why she had so instinctively rushed indoors and flung open the wardrobe; not for privacy, not to violate Mama's functional fantasies, but to pack the few trifling things she stored there. To get out while she could.

Desperately she threw her bag on the bed. And threw herself after it. Lay; the sheeny silk outlining her body with an aura, a light-catching depression in the dark mood. Like an insect on the skin of water. Waited for a chance wind to blow her to where she might get some purchase on life and struggle free from the treachery of misfortune. The covers whispered her name repeatedly, lingering on sibilants and fricatives. Oh she had behaved hatefully, she accepted the fact. She had joined in the plans just for the conceit of feeling she might actually do something. She had made no effort to escape the Wild Dog. Quite the opposite, she had become his colleague. The silk rustled again. Stephanie rolled on her back, aflame with the stigma of having been thrown to the ground by that spotty-faced lout at the railway station.

— News for Mama, the silk whispered.

Her blood raced and she found she had been crying. Her cheeks were soggy. Her nose was running. She felt washed out. Darling Luke, she thought passionately. My one darling. There is nobody but you.

— You with me? asked the silk.

Always. Always. She bit her lip at the upsurge of hope, her last glimpse of his fury, his distorted face being swept away down the track; a fury felt more for her, she knew, than for himself.

— Tell Mama the men have been switched. New job. Something big.

I love you Luke. I love you.

Blank. She had lost him and surrendered to the unsalvageable mess she made of things.

— So helpless here. So angry, Steph. Angry with wanting you, the voice said close and clearly.

I've been too ill to come. I must see you soon. It won't be long, I promise.

— Mustn't be long.

— It can't be long, Stephanie murmured, filled with fear that she could not hold out. She clutched at the silk bedspread, drawing it in rapids around her.

Downstairs on the porch Mama was still holding court.

— If you ask me, Mr Dog, she's getting a message I have been expecting any day.

Her bangles clattered conspiratorially as she reached out to pat him, for a moment stirred to old memories by the handsome arm under her hand. Keep calm, the bangles suggested.

— There's going to be a connection between Paringa and Port George, he said at last, now they were alone. But he did not offer to explain how he came by the information.

She smiled and the spring day twinkled from one gold tooth.

— Now I know you trust me. Good. And I would have sworn, she added reproachfully. You were far too dangerous with your hands, Mr Dog, to be smart as well.

She puffed her hookah. The Delights, being finished, left nothing but little cubic depressions in the tray of icing sugar.

— What do you suppose we have felt like, being Australians, Mr Fortescue? Especially during those years when we were simply the farthest outpost of your British Empire. But then, you are not quite English, are you? Don't look surprised, it is your attitude not your accent that gives you away.

Dorina Buchanan sat back and, in her kindly way, allowed him time to venture a reply. But he did not take the opportunity. Apart from acknowledging the pleasure of her company, he was controlling the ludicrous impulse to sing a tune he found running in his head. She went on. What do you suppose we grew up with? Inside us it was dark. We were nothing but eyes looking out at the bright land, the familiar world of suburbs and the bush waiting over there just beyond the houses. And beyond that, we looked to the glamour of foreign events which made up our history of how we came here in the first place. We could see everything, but not into ourselves. We were in agony if some confident Englishman turned up and said: but just what is an Australian? How to answer? her hands described a swift flight out the window. Worse still, if he had the bad manners to accuse us of being hollow (which I'm sure you would never do); shells, a tough exterior and nothing inside, beautiful and soulless, without religion, philosophy or history. It has been said. Oh yes? merely a solid darkness, we thought, with our blood on the boil. At that time, Mr Fortescue (and have I yet said how much I admire the BBC, so you mustn't take it as a judgment that I've refused to be interviewed for your program), being an Australian was to conceal a benign demon, because we wanted to be asked but had no words for an answer. We put ourselves in the way of being asked, always with the hope that the crisis of embarrassment would one day trigger the very answer we'd felt all along but never been able to express. We thought you might help us to it. Our first question for a newcomer was: how do you like us? Don't you see, this is why I won't say such things in public, because they still cannot be said and expect to be understood properly. We still don't have the words for what we are inside. We have the feelings, yes, and they might split us apart with frustration, but not the words. Because we'd never lived in this landscape before having a language at all. That's the point. You can hear it in Aboriginal words: now *they* had the knowledge before they tried to put a name to it. Woomera. Murwillumbah. Wooloomooloo. Billinudgel. The landscape is there, in all its weatherworn age-old delicacy. So here you have our true inner war. You could do worse than make it the theme of your program.

Andy Fortescue glanced down the passageway to see right into a room at the end. The door stood open on a shaft of sunlight striking the far wall and the chest of drawers placed against it. On this chest of drawers lay a heroin addict's kit, the syringe and burnt spoon unmistakable. He allowed himself only a micro-second to take in the information before returning his grave neutrality to meet his hostess's suggestion.

— The fate of Australia in the longterm may well depend on how this issue is resolved, she continued.

He sought to make sense of what she was saying. He could not escape the suspicion that she might have seated him there with just that view along the passage, knowing he was bound, at some stage, to look.

— Unless we are blown to bits as surrogates for the superpowers when their tempers get the upper hand. And do you know, I believe there are people insane enough to believe a global war would be the neatest means of deciding once and for all who will go to heaven and who to hell! The Dark Ages are still with us. The immediate question here is whether the land can change us fast enough to prevent our mutilating it beyond recognition. And to tell the truth, I can't pretend I have ever known anyone whose feeling for it was so deep they could truly say it had never presented them with a threat.

The harbour view composed a likeness of every Sydney postcard he had ever seen. The calm voice of this distinguished lady announced that his interview was over. And he felt, how should he put it, regret. He felt it would be better to be a poet than a television reporter.

— I do apologize for not being more use. No, no, you may be

sure my husband had no objection to your proposed interview, otherwise you would never have been let in. But he also knew I would not agree to it. Good afternoon, Mr Fortescue, and good luck.

As he rose to go, he contrived to glance once more down the passage at the specimen in its illuminated showcase.

— That's right, she encouraged him. Straight up the stairs. I suppose you have already arranged to interview the young man who saved my husband's life in the desert? Now *he* had strength to measure up to the land. I take back what I said. He wasn't threatened by it at all. You didn't hear about this? Wait right there. Peter Taverner, his name was. He left an address with me, though that was nearly nine years ago, I warn you. I always keep such things in the one book. Of course I can find it. Though the address, as I recall, was not his own, even then, but some parent or relative. Written on a scrap of paper. Here, keep it. We have no need of it now. We are quite cut off from everybody.

She was pleading with him. He could not mistake her intention. Those eyes, so tranquil and expressive, even the suggestion of music perpetually impending as if her thoughts themselves were melodic and one might tune in to them, pleaded with him to hear what she, as the president's wife, could not say out loud, and would not say, in any case, from loyalty to her husband. Who was the addict? Could his television program be a weapon? A weapon which she wanted him to use deftly and courageously? Was he to be her voice to the outside world? He accepted.

Dorina watched him slip the piece of paper in his wallet as he climbed the stairs.

— I so look forward to seeing what you make of us, she called in a microphone voice.

With this double meaning uppermost in mind, he strode out across the terrace, past the guardhouse, and into his waiting car. He did not miss a fleeting awkwardness as the driver, caught unawares, reached surreptitiously to switch something on or switch something off while asking:

— Where to next then?

The day the news broke, Sir William Penhallurick was, providentially, at the president's mansion. He and the Americans having completed their preliminary consultation, plans were rolled up, figures fed through calculators, jottings made and collected for shredding, and the tables left bare except for warm patches where participants had rested their forearms. The doors opened and closed. Buchanan sat on his litter, hedged by a semi-circle of armchairs where various departmental advisors had perched ready to be called upon for specialist feedback during the less secret parts of the meeting. A cliché of smoke lingered in the old-fashioned air.

— Are you being bought out? Buchanan demanded bluntly. I won't have you bought out. You've grown too big. We can't afford it now.

— I grow sad, Sir William rolled his eyes under painfully crusted lids and simulated a child's pout of grief, the ancient Kékszakállú. To think how few people can truly say they have a friend. The way I have you, he explained.

The president glared uncomfortably, uncooperatively, from his past of so much remaining too long unspoken. Wrong: they were not friends, they were collaborators. That was why the cost never need be counted. Thanks to a buffer of doubt, a murky no-man's-land between them, they were able to continue, as a reflex almost, putting favours each other's way, as one might put out a saucer of milk for a prowling yowie, that wild creature never yet seen by white man but known for its periodic forays into tearing the heads off bulls, gratified enough to see the saucer licked clean next morning without feeling the least desire to hide with spotlights ready and a museum curator's acquisitive eye for what may be observed emerging from the night, unsuspecting but cautious all the same, docile enough to make straight for the milk but savage when cornered, and against whom no net in the world could be guaranteed secure. Buchanan thought they shared this mutual respect. Might it, he now wondered with chagrin, have been respect he felt for the old man but which had never been reciprocated? The instant the suspicion arose, he knew it for the truth. Each generation must face the fact that those who were already powerful when we were young cannot accept us as anything but beginners, interlopers.

— This was a good deed you did, Sir William explained, darting him a crafty look before resuming an unwanted, sentimental tale. And you are right to be concerned. I have to keep control in my hands. I'm sure you know the international boys have been after me. Stock market raiders. Getting the Tuavaleva contract will mean I can stave them off. I plan to live another twenty years, at least twenty, and then you'll see an empire! (It shone in his merciless eyes.) You have been a great success, he added proudly. For us.

In one respect they were alike: pleasure and displeasure being, for both men, simple and absolute states.

— There is no Tuavaleva contract, Buchanan retorted in a dead tone of just such displeasure. Unless and until Haupoupou changes his tune.

The incorrigible Penhallurick turned impish. He had grown as perfectly at ease with his knighthood as with his anglicized name. He wagged one finger, the dear little rogue.

— What if I know something you don't? he tittered, then switched back to the maudlin manner of his choice. Will you ever forget? he asked.

The tone made the president glance sidelong and watchfully, surprised to find the other man looking him straight in the eye with a directness that had in it some presumption of a deeper unspoken understanding which now, after a long time, might need to be called to account.

Momentarily, Buchanan was sick of his life. He longed to give all this away. How he would relish being one of the kitchen staff due any minute with trolleys to remove teacups stained with emptiness, to open windows and let out the words spoken in confidence, calm words in rich male voices. Words, nevertheless, of betrayal. Yes, to rush at them with dusters and chase them out to where a flock of magpies might swoop down and clean them up like so many grubs wriggling, white and lively. Servants do not have to make up their minds. They obey, on the one hand, and are bound by bonds stronger than submission on the other. As individuals, they are contemptible because incomplete. But marshal them together in a gang or a union or even a pub and you have something else entirely. Only after the question had been fully put and a transparent protective coat of silence hardened round it did Buchanan realize exactly what had been said.

— Will you ever forget that courtroom, Bernie?

— What courtroom? Sir George Gipps fired at his victim. And there he was, dressed for a blustering gale, in a black hat and a greatcoat with a collar so huge it spread cape-wise right to his shoulders.

— *I* never will, Sir William affirmed in that same sugary tone and unaware of the intruder. It lives with me in here, he tapped his head, knocking a few flakes of skin free. And here, he placed his other hand caressingly where his heart should be and held it there while smiling the Danube smile of a fiddler who accepts applause for his *Zigeunerweisen* during the goulash. You had my life in your power. I remember you, how you stood, a fine solid specimen, and spoke for that jury of saints.

Gipps took off his hat and dropped it on a chair warmed by an American bottom; Buchanan watched him while retorting to his other guest (because if the unspoken was to be violated he could do some violating of his own).

— You wouldn't think them saints if you had heard what they said about you.

— Ah, I know what you are waiting for, Penhallurick simpered, tender and spiteful and so very foreign. You want I should thank you and you alone. All these years I have known that. He tapped his head again with the fingers still held up there. But you see they *must* have been saints to let you talk them round. They were all against me, were they?

Gipps unfastened his coat. And this was a sizeable enterprise, involving some thirty buttons.

— Are you making a confession, Bill?

— Oh no. You won't catch me surrendering, not even for the truth.

Gipps bent double to reach those buttons down near the hem. The material, stiff with saltspray, made his task harder.

— But you'd like to know, wouldn't you, the industrialist added, provoked by an unwelcome memory of Dorina Buchanan treating him with icy condescension. If you knew the answer to that, how simple your life. What do you say? In any case, I have done all I could to help you along.

Gipps now threw open the coat flaps, shrugging his shoulders free, one after the other, in a gesture the president had never seen before. He swung quickly to catch the heavy garment as it fell from him, shook it straight and tossed it on the back of the chair.

— Not for any reason, Bernie, but because I like you. Because you are a son to me.

Gipps did not look up. He began unwinding his white cravat. It came away in a broad bandage, still bearing creases where it had pressed against his neck and, when he dropped it on the seat, the material curled again around the neck of air, hideous as a living thing missing its master.

— I never had a son of my own. You mustn't feel compromised, really, my men will make a first-rate job of this contract when it becomes available. All those wives I had and not one of them bred me a son. You wouldn't want to bet on the odds of that, would you? What do you say?

Having removed his waistcoat, another article of clothing rich in buttons, Gipps bent to unbuckle his boots.

— Just an only daughter. And she married that headshrinker McKinley. Hell of a lot of good he must do his patients! He can't make me out for a start. He told me so. Quite humble about it he was. Don't ask my advice Papa, he said, I can't make head nor tail of you or what keeps you ticking.

Gipps sat on the chair arm to tug his boots free. One. And then, with some difficulty of rheumatism, the other. They clunked on the floor, but Penhallurick was too absorbed with plucking harpstrings to notice. He continued.

— If it wasn't for sailing, McKinley and I would have nothing in common except those brats of theirs.

Now Gipps rolled down his hose, revealing white white legs infested with black black hairs. In a trice he had crossed arms over his chest and whipped off his shirt over his head. He threw it down as a gauntlet on the floor between them. Now he removed his breeches and his undershirt. He stood defiantly nude, his figure so grossly private he might never have looked at it himself, let alone made so obscene a gesture in public. Splodges of damp fur stuck to his chest, belly and groin.

— This is sickening, Buchanan shouted violent as a bomb belatedly exploding. Keep it to yourself.

— Excuse, Sir William Penhallurick stood nervy but obstreperous still, fuelled by reserves of self-flattering resentment. I talk too much about things of the heart.

He made moves to leave.

— But there is one other matter, he added, little terrier that he was. My sources tell me you are planning to rationalize public utilities along American lines. Don't answer, I should not consider asking for an answer. I have never been that kind of man have I? What do you say? You know me and the Americans know me. Simply to put your mind at rest: you do not need to worry about finding a taker for the defence forces. Is this all right? You needn't doubt it. You have my word. With my empire and Alice's together, we can assure you of very favourable leasing arrangements. What do you say? Say nothing. And still Australian-owned!

— Yes, *nothing* is exactly what I am saying, Buchanan responded dully, assessing the confusion caused by his outburst. On such a hypothetical subject.

Gipps smiled his nasty humourless smile.

Of course the president had Penhallurick over a barrel since the Cultural Centre collapsed. But only, in a sense, morally. And this carried more weight with him than with the old man. How much simpler life would be if he had never allowed himself to fall into such a person's clutches. Why had he let it happen? The question surprised him, indeed offended him. But I am the one with power, he objected tetchily. Despite this, an undercurrent pursued its own logic as the man who had called him a son shuffled documents together and stacked them in a briefcase. There was a moment, he might have admitted, when he took the plunge and challenged the other jurors: were they able to swear they felt no prejudice against the accused because he was a foreigner, because, and here the deepest motives are often the least reasonable and those which appear too superficial to be considered, he was ugly, small, weak and scrofulous? Could they be sure they were not punishing him for having had an Australian wife in the first place? Yes, that was the moment. From then on the rest fell into place, acting itself through with little more than a nudge or a pat on the back from him. I am in his power, Buchanan saw the fact plainly, as the old man clipped his briefcase shut, because I did him a favour. Because, unasked and unknown, I put myself on the line for him. He thought briefly of Peter Taverner. Was Peter Taverner in *his* power as a consequence of having saved his life? But the old man had turned on him with rueful malice.

— The whispers are out against me, he was saying. And against you too.

— Pettiness.

Gipps, sensing he had lost control of the situation, began floating in the air and drifting across the office, his body's slackness all the more positively obscene.

— Whispers of corruption.

— What do you want? Buchanan bawled, looking up and around him, his eyes everywhere but on his informant. I'm sick to death of this nonsense.

— You, Penhallurick conceded. Are the president.

Buchanan, staring this way and that, did not call him back as he began to leave, and did not apologize. At that moment, Margaret Talbot looked in, excused herself for interrupting, and made an announcement, breathless with implications.

— There has been a *coup d'état* in Tuavaleva, she explained, not noticing the pallor of anger or shock creeping down from the master's cheeks to his chins, nor the darkening red of his hands. Prince Haupoupou was murdered in his bed just before dawn this morning, sir.

Buchanan recalled the palace so clearly at that moment, the delicious cool of marble corridors after the blazing heat outside, punkahs stirring the perfumed air, barefoot servants discreetly padding about, the whole place furnished with the leftovers of colonial grandeur.

— The new leader, she added before withdrawing. Says he is for progress and a closer alliance with the west. Merasaloa, he's called. General Merasaloa.

Sir William Penhallurick made his way out after her, treading on a thick carpet of smugness. He did not need to look round to score his point.

Gipps, as if he had nevertheless accomplished something at long last, levitated back to the chair, where he began taking up his clothes and, item by item, covered that mid-nineteenth-century nakedness, the skin having both cringed and gaped at exposure to so much air. Last of all he heaved his salt-rimed coat on his back and, by custom patient, set about the task of fastening the column of ascending buttons. Taking his hat in his hand, he could not resist the tone of I-told-you-so in his *Good morning,* and walked straight through the wall into the garden, casual as a man who sets out for a brisk stroll home.

. . . So, Father, by this you may judge how little any thought of inheritance means to me.

A house, an establishment, as we saw so recently, is a calamity of dust, gone from the hilltop in a single gust of our mild north-easterly. Mr Buchanan's fall had led to a lesson we shall not forget. A friend of mine, Conrad Martens, is making some drawings. Martens is a Londoner, a most engaging man and a gifted one. He says a friend of his named Charles Darwin is brewing ideas which could turn all Christendom on its head: and the sooner the better, I told him.

Even while Government House was being pulled down, men levering the rafters loose, watching the riddled timbers fall and crash to a powdering of soft splinters like an under-sea explosion, two of the gardeners were still tugging heavy rollers along the gravel drive. I asked them what they thought they were doing, considering the house itself stood only as a broken wreck, the roof part-gone and sky-bitten. They replied respectfully that they had not been given orders to abandon their routine! Little Britishers in their exhausting doldrums waiting to be told what to do by someone higher up, meanwhile tugging at the growling metal, trundling it up and down through a daydream of Lancashire or Lanark, I suppose, and a cottage in its muff of hollyhocks, with a paling fence proof against the armies of chance.

In this, Mr Buchanan, rogue though he is, could see further than Sir George. Even Mr Buchanan's supposed seizure and lengthy recuperation with the connivance of the surgeon were a stroke of imagination beyond the Governor's suspecting. This fat man knows the world of facts from the world of dreams. He is, in short, a dangerous fellow.

Although I speak of Gipps as having the old Government House demolished, in truth the termites had already accomplished most of the work, even to carting away the solid weight of timbers for their nests and leaving instead a joist-shaped idea of joists, bearer-shaped ideas of bearers, a house more air than fibre, an idea of respectability, an ideal of power, ready to buckle under the body-weight of a single man who had difficulty mustering the strength to mount the four steps to the front door. The glass in the windows was found to have held the window-frames in place, and when the chimneys were demolished, each had to be chipped from a solid core of soot. The roof-tiles, which the workmen stacked ready for re-use on the new house, His Excellency ordered sold. Put them on the market, he instructed me, there are plenty of doctors with ambitions to buy me out of my shelter, the new Government House shall not carry any taint of the old; but in this he reckoned without the cunning or the indolence of our contracting workmen, who saw no virtue in fashioning afresh what had already been adequately cut and dressed.

The house, when it was gone, stood clear as air. The driveway rose in a curve to the entrance, leading the eye up stone-shaped air steps into the cubes of used argument, the smoke-cured corners and the solid rectangles of sunshine cut at regular intervals into the walls. The ashes of decisions lay in the office hearth, where I alone knew what they might have amounted to, while turbulent clouds in the upper storey sighed damp with Sir George's longings through his eight years of solitary confinement in the service of mistrustful masters. Even this, however, is finer than the theft of self-respect known in New South Wales as being a gentleman, to say nothing of the murder of the conscience. . .

President Buchanan, when he made his evening telecast to the nation, remembered Penhallurick's accusation and rumoured whispers.

— Let me tell you, friends, it is pettiness to doubt my ministers. What is corruption? he bellowed. If not cleverness? Are tried and trusted colleagues to be sacked because they are too clever? No doubt the Opposition parties would feel safe from being accused of the same offence. Let me tell you, corruption is a word invented by those not smart enough to get out of the way in time.

Consequences became another word famous for the sarcasm with which he pronounced it.

— Do I realize the *consequences* of this thing or another? I'll tell you what I realize: I realize when I am face to face with cowardice. Go easy, back down, get scared, that's what is meant by consequences. The consequences, I am told, of allowing commercial security operators to prosper is to invite them to grow into private armies which might one day threaten the state. Do I look threatened? Do I look as if I am about to give up being the state?

Around this period certain disaffected individuals began a rumour that the president had become so imprisoned in his palace at the vastly extended Yarralumla Mansion, so removed from contact, that he ruled an imagined Australia while Watchdogs, flaunting their narcissism, took him at his word and mocked the weak, obliging the police, shamefaced and powerless, to look the other way.

— What if I were to tell you, Roscoe Plenty once stormed in the days when storming was still an option. That you are alone in your ignorance? That you only think you're governing the country? That we have a separate budget to finance your illusions? What then? How could you prove me wrong?

By way of answer, Buchanan touched the emergency button with his knee and Wilson's security men poured in through both doors. Others stood, guns ready, outside the windows. Although on this occasion the president had the satisfaction of seeing Roscoe Plenty turn white and complain of being put at risk when he'd only asked a playful question (because some fool could easily let fly with a real bullet), the fact was that the jibe nagged Buchanan. His Australia out there was indeed a land of memories and fantasies. Even as he invented its history to suit his purposes, he lost a grip on what had been true before and which facts were his improvements.

— I mean, he might say plaintively to (perhaps) Owen Powell. What was my last word on surf carnivals?

— In your wisdom, the answer would come back from whomever. You have expressed yourself both against and in favour of surf carnivals, allowing your administration valuable discretionary powers in enforcing the law.

— If novelists, he shouted one evening in public. Cannot refrain from meddling with matters which are none of their concern, such as morals and politics, then I'll close them down altogether. Do they think we can't be without new novels? What arrogance, as if there aren't more than enough in circulation already. They'll have to apply to me for a licence and the publication of unlicensed books will, I assure you, be prosecuted. I mean, we all enjoy a good read, don't we? Nothing nicer. Why should a few selfish smart-alecs wreck it for the rest? There's nothing subversive about a bit of blood-and-guts, a mystery, or a Western, there's nothing wrong with Mills and Boon, for that matter. If you've got a story to tell, tell it and good luck to you. But if you're out to bend minds and pervert the innocent with ideas they never would have thought of left to themselves, then watch out for me and my hatchet men.

— I don't want our international sporting personalities, he stormed on another occasion. Dictating to me how we should respond to a case of race relations. They'd better get on with their training, catching balls and jumping higher, and leave decisions concerning who they will compete against to those of us able to give such important matters our undivided attention plus the benefit of a broad political understanding. Have I made myself clear?

— Science, he smiled into the camera. Is a truly wonderful aid to technology. So why do some fellows spoil it by whingeing about funds? If they wish to fritter away their lives on fanciful research into microscopic thingumajigs that probably don't even exist, then let them. I don't object, provided they aren't milking the public purse to do so. Once we are talking about budgets funded by government resources, then they can do something useful with their time or get out and earn an honest crust digging roads.

Even so, the jibe rankled. Scarcely a working night passed without his hearing again Roscoe Plenty's voice saying, what if I were to tell you you are alone in your ignorance, that we have a separate budget to finance your illusions? And Gipps was not to be let off either.

— One last point, the president thundered darkly. I hear that nudity has become alarmingly rife on our beaches and perhaps even in the home. Men displaying their ugly hairy bodies. I won't have it. Henceforth, nudity in any public place is to be considered a punishable offence, a blatant imposition on those who do not wish to see such things. This way, at the very least, we'll save a lot of donkeys making asses of themselves.

He did think the better, though, of putting a similar ban on levitation.

The loss of his television team could not stop Andrew Fortescue, survivor of an education into the divine right of his élite. After all, one of his ancestors was the author of a book, *The Difference Between an Absolute and a Limited Monarchy*, which, despite its having been written four hundred years earlier, came to be famous at the time Australia was first proposed as a colony. Andy knew about such things. The family memory went back a long way further too. It is not to be supposed that the great-grandson of the author of *De Laudibus Legum Angliae* would knuckle under to bullying from such a simpleton autocrat as B Buchanan.

Or perhaps this had nothing to do with it. Perhaps he was not just a know-all Pommie trailing his past like a peacock, ready at any moment to heave it up as a collapsible backdrop to dazzle any chance passing peahen, but a person quite simply charmed by the power of incipient music.

Why could it not be both at the one time? He had, certainly, at the front of his mind, a desire to repay Buchanan for treating him with such arrogance; but equally, he was aware of Dorina's unspoken plea. I so look forward, she had called as he left, to seeing what you make of us.

Well, Andy pursued his own enquiries, and took expert precautions against bugging devices. After a week's harmless filming of city scenes, he granted his crew the weekend off, that Australian crew foisted upon him, who went home without suspecting a thing. No one from Internal Security had thought to instruct them properly. Taking a trainee, the only member of his original team left, the BBC's Mr Fortescue kept a clandestine appointment which took him first to Greg Sullivan's outback property and then on to the desert beyond.

He thought about his thoughts: This convenient national image has been overdone. . . the emptiness etcetera to be found at the heart of Australian society too. But my impressions may be superficial. The emptiness may only seem empty because I do not know what to look for.

He glanced at his new companions: Nelson, the earnest unionist; the practical goodhearted Spinebasher; the boy brimming over with highschool marvels and passionate enthusiasm for modernity. Where did the empty heart theory fit any of them? Possibly it said something about Nick? But no, not him either, because in Nick he felt a dense core of fury which was not at all vacuous, nor even disillusioned (having perhaps never known illusions), a despairing fury, a lust to tear down the whole social order, a man tormented by the mere appearance of anything permanent. This led, inevitably, to the most challenging enigma, the Wild Dog. All very well for me, Fortescue accused himself, bringing my fixed English appreciation of manners and privacy, the shared reassurance implicit in a courteous offhandedness, and the importance of the Way Things are done, but mightn't a man like the Wild Dog see this as game-playing, *this* as hollow. And hollow indeed. He, one would guess, had never found himself inadequate to life. Not from want of imagination, which he had, nor want of sensitivity because, surprisingly, he had that too, but because he knew what mattered. Yes, in questions of courage and love. Big issues: survival and the spirit. His charisma went far beyond good looks. Among Andy's notes he had jotted a line from an Australian war poem which now came forcibly to mind. *And fight the better because he knew he was as good as dead.*

— Do you feel this land is sacred, he said suddenly, quietly, to the Wild Dog. That it *can't* be sold?

In reply he received a smile, warm and open and more eloquent than thanks.

— How come you are the first to say it? the terrorist asked.

— I never had a country of my own, he replied promptly. I was born in India and brought up in Kenya. The last days of the Empire. I didn't land in my father's country till I was thirteen. So you see, I could never take anything for granted.

62

The Wild Dog was in.

A reduced version of the Human Pyramid unlocked itself and one man leapt noiselessly to the ground while the other two straightened up, stretching their necks and shoulders. A vaultingpole was slipped in through the wire mesh to the Wild Dog, who took it and propped it against a wall for when it would be needed. Steadying its jumpiness, he felt it tremble under his firm hand.

So now the danger began. He sprinted into that cube of artificial fluorescence.

Paringa floated, improbable as a space station in orbit: its surfaces sterile, its angles perfect, and the six golfball domes glowing white against a clear midnight sky. A million light-years deep, the darkness up there appeared no vaster or more mysterious than the surrounding desert.

The Man had put the electronic scanners out of action. . . this was the promise the Wild Dog carried in his head as he ran, a star-shaped shadow rising through the concrete to meet each step.

Rectangular administrative offices and service units stood widely separated, each one isolated on the yard, mournful and diminished in the dazzling glare. People with their backs to a second-floor window were busy at the twenty-four hour dedication to being first to throw the world off balance. Nothing less would do. A faint cacophony of pop music, issuing from various sources, leaked away into infinity.

Beyond the fence encircling the compound, Nick and the others held their breath as the Wild Dog raced across an open space. Floodlit from all sides, he appeared less than substantial, bigger than lifesize. He flung himself flat against Block Six and launched out again immediately. Before him lay the front courtyard, bare as a parade ground, cold as only the desert can be, with a keen airless corrosive cold. Ahead, Block One rested at the edge of that expanse, more like a container ready to be picked up than a permanent installation.

Guards at the gate were smoking: American servicemen, no doubt highly trained, but bored from years of never sighting a single unauthorized person, of clashing the gates open and shut for staff cars and trucks. A frail puff of luminous cigarette haze hung over their sentrybox, inexpressibly lonely and nostalgic for Chicago. One soldier stepped outside into the starlit wilderness and stood just beyond the arc-lamp's cone of light. What did he intend doing there? Perhaps urinating? Was smoking on duty forbidden? Come on, come on, the Wild Dog whispered, get out of the fucking road, I don't want to have to jump you.

— Funny thing but. . . , a second soldier called from within so that the smoker swiftly snatched a last draw, put out his cigarette between thumb and finger, tucked the butt in a pocket and stepped back while his colleague finished what he'd been about to say. Those three words remained marooned in space. The Wild Dog knew the rest of the sentence: my screen hasn't been showing a thing for a whole minute, no interference, none of the usual insects, nothing, it's just gone blank, but it's not a power failure, it's still alive. (This was how the Man rehearsed the drama.)

Again the Wild Dog darted out, he ran right up to the white wall of Block One. From now on, speed was all that mattered. He had to take the risk of being caught. There was no longer any room for caution.

Outside, his colleagues held their breath. Through the wire mesh they could see him in a slice of perspective between two buildings, his right arm describing huge signals. Wide flowing meanings carried him along the whole front of the block on dancing feet, out of sight and back again. They watched a seated guard behind bulletproof glass snatch his telephone with one hand and gesticulate impatiently with the other.

Sterile floodlights blazed over everything. Faint, bland music pulsed confusedly.

Then, as the Wild Dog began sprinting back, the guard-houses suddenly came alive with feverish questions. People peered at video-display units for advice, tinkered on keyboards, looking in instead of out, wasting irrecoverable seconds, tapping urgent requests and facing each other with failure, with the shock of being forsaken by the equipment. Careless of being seen now, elated with his own strength, the Wild Dog came belting across the open yard, his gym shoes scarcely raising dust, grabbed the pole from where he had propped it against the wall, balanced it, giving a skip and beginning to lope with a springy rhythm, judging the distance, then piling on speed. He planted the pole and floated up, one trailing hand gored by wire as he cleared the top where, on the other side, the pyramid reassembled itself. Feet first, the Wild Dog dropped and slid neatly down Nick's back, Nelson's and Spinebasher's, to land unhurt. He reached in for the pole which had fallen against the fence as rehearsed and pulled it clear. The four of them ducked away to a drainage ditch where the Man was waiting with his portable equipment. They peered up over the rim.

Seems they've made contact again, Nick's look reported.

Seems they have, Nelson's look replied.

The little screens are in business, Nick confirmed with a calm glance. They don't seem to know what went wrong. He grinned: The Man is a genius.

The Man, crouched over his electronic box, blushed in the dark. Three minutes, his nod said. On the dot.

Sentries were observed telephoning each other from two posts. When one man took off his cap to cool the sweat under the band and put it back on, his companion slapped it tight down on his forehead for him, horseplay eloquent with relief.

The night's silent emptiness swept past the floating space station and away.

This is the crunch. The Wild Dog smiled tensely: If they see what I've done it will all have been for nothing.

They're not going to look, the Man trembled.

The Wild Dog kissed the wind.

Bert admitted he felt nervous because he was inexperienced and only an assistant.

— What a cunt of a job, he swore.

— He loves it really, Andy Fortescue interpreted this for the others.

As the sky grew light, guards outside the administrative offices and service blocks of the IFID base witnessed an astonishing scene: a police van, appearing along the horizon of iron stones, pulled up about a kilometre distant from the gate, blue light flashing on the roof just as if it were at home in a city and some erring citizen to be pulled over to the kerb, the doors opened and three officers in uniform emerged, accompanied by a couple of civilians.

— What the hell? one guard asked.

The other, with binoculars trained on the scene, spelled out the printing on the side of the van.

— *Republican Police. National Unit.* Hey, he lowered the glasses and then clipped them back to his eyes. They're setting up a movie camera. Ring emergency. Aussie cops, plus a television crew by the looks of it. Get on the PA and tell those guys out there not to move till I get a ruling on this.

In the excitement of coping with a crisis at last, minutes passed and sirens wailed before either man turned to see what the camera might be trained on. Huge spray-can letters defaced the front of Block One, impossible letters incriminating the whole squad, letters that defied all faith in the electronic miracle.

NEXT LAUGH — PORT GEORGE

Out there in the peaceful morning a couple of pioneer insects warmed their lovecalls. Bert the cameraman filmed the information needed, zooming in from a wide shot, so the cluster of dice and marbles on a bare table jumped forward as windowless domes and administration buildings where doors opened behind a high fence and office workers poured into the compound, mingling with white-coated technicians and insomniac scientists taking off and putting on their halfmoon spectacles. Leaning into the curve like motorcyclists, a posse of guards sprinted round a corner of one building. The desolate yard became instantly populated. Even in the compound beyond, where the top-secret domes clustered behind formidable barriers, uniformed functionaries could be observed through the lens trying to make out what was going on, enlivened by the possibility of a break from boredom. A moment later, and promptly at that, army vehicles left the adjoining airfield to roar along foreshortened perspectives.

Bert recorded all this, remembering his training, hands steady and cheeks pinched tight with concentration. He filmed a lone face at an upper window looking down on the dispute raging in the gatehouse, and he filmed two maintenance men spraying white paint (not a second wasted, as Mama observed later, you have to hand it to them, they know about organization) to obliterate the graffiti, working back through the letters from last to first, unsaying them.

Bert packed his gear, which he lugged aboard the van while the Americans, having dwindled again to miniature figures in the distance, regrouped in ant-scale huddles, passing on the director's order to take no action which might lead to an international incident. Keep cool. Discipline. And watchful. Training counts. The police vehicle started up and drove away. Immediately an IFID army security squad set off in pursuit, keeping a respectful if puzzled distance, till they reached the old civilian airstrip used by the construction contractors. Here a jet without markings was waiting, engines hot. The intruders abandoned their van, climbed into the plane and took off, flying out over the stony wilderness where a single rusted automobile body stood, with its dingy hubcaps placed on the ground around it.

The director of the installation radioed orders for a cordon to be thrown round the van until further notice.

— Their own people can deal with this, he said as he picked up the phone on which President Buchanan waited grumpily to hear why he was being disturbed at this inconvenient hour, just as he had got to bed, imagining, almost, that they could see him supine at that moment, huge as one bed on top of another and his feet and knees being discovered.

The small jet aircraft was never seen again. Admittedly, thirty-five minutes elapsed, owing to human fallibility (later identified as a game of poker) before a tracker satellite was alerted to the job. But by then it appeared to be no longer in the air. Andy Fortescue and Bert turned up for a Melbourne appointment at 10 am on the dot and, although a police check was made, no film or any other evidence could be found to connect them with the Paringa raid. They were allowed to go about their business, observed but unmolested. So the matter remained until the day Fortescue, reunited with his original team, flew out on a Lufthansa flight via Singapore.

The sensation broke in Great Britain. Euro-television bought the program in defiance of the CIA. The Australian ambassador lodged a bitter complaint in Brussels. Cautious reports appeared on page 9 of a Melbourne newspaper, implying that a foreign broadcasting organization had abused our hospitality. Pirate stills of the graffiti flooded into the country despite customs surveillance. The laughter began in whispers, but soon the whispers grew so numerous people took courage. Boxers, clinched under the floodlights threatening a knockout blow, hissed *Port George next!* Drunken ladies in a powder room shook their heads after vomiting, rinsed their mouths and delicately dabbed the corners, smiling wanly in bright mirrors and remarking to their neighbours at the hand basins, *It'll be Port George next, I suppose!*

Mama laughed till her eyes bulged tears.

— Brilliant, darlings, she greeted them. Let's talk about it. We have to hit them again while they are still reeling. This time we'll do some actual damage. Yanagita sent a message through Luke. All visiting hours at Vengeance Harbour have been cancelled indefinitely. No contact between the public and the Friends of Privilege to be permitted. So, she added eyeing the Wild Dog confidentially. I find we were right. Their new project is connected with Paringa.

The Wild Dog looked past her, hoping to catch a glimpse of Stephanie.

Roscoe Plenty woke to the certain knowledge that his efforts fell short of favour because six policemen wished him good afternoon, helped him off with his pyjamas and buttoned him snugly into a garment bearing the odour of his own good. In that state, he was paraded before the president and instructed to listen to this. . . his own voice saying things he could categorically swear he had never said, because they were what he really thought.

— The botch-up at Paringa, his voice spoke from Owen
Powell's neat little machine. Is nothing special. No need to make
a fuss about it. My advice is simply to keep calm. He is
vindictive, as we all know. He is narrow and childlike and
vindictive. And not content with driving the whole population
to desperation with his crazy fiscal policies. He scarcely seems
aware the economy itself is on the point of ruin. Don't be fooled
by the upturn in the money market. That is symptomatic of a
sell-out. It can't last. Any more than Buchanan can last. We just
made a damn fool error of judgment. No good can be done by
stirring the soup at the moment. And what good does it do for
us to go blaming the Americans? So, the whole. . .

The great man himself had reached over and switched off the
machine.

— Your Excellency, Owen Powell, protested, waiting for his
consummate stroke of artistry implicating Squarcia, anxious not
to waste the chance of demolishing both his worst enemies at a
single blow.

— No more, the president murmured.

Quiet drifted round them cold and unstoppable as snow.

— Is that your voice, Mr Plenty?

Where was the point in answering? The Chief Minister submitted to what followed because he could no longer move.
Everything would be taken care of by hospital staff, including
the burden of thinking. A needle in his arm, a private room, and
the consideration of the medical profession, psychiatric branch,
were enough to persuade him he was better off there than he
had ever been in his life. One day he was before the public eye,
right at the top, smiling sinister smiles, the next he vanished,
and that was that. Only the trained staff heard more from him.
And they had the skill to interpret it.

— I want to die. I want to die.

Electrode wires stood up from Roscoe Plenty's head, quiver-
ing each time a shock jolted his genitals. He would not be
making any more sexual offers to the painter Lavinia Manciewicz who was in jail anyhow. So soon, within a few hours of the
treatment beginning, his mind detached itself from the body
and witnessed raw shouts, observed the nervous system going
into spasms. I understand, was what his mind assured the
torturers, though throat and tongue had no connection with
ideas any longer. He was already in a position to refute certain
linguistic philosophers on one of their basic precepts. I under-

stand you, I see you as overgrown children doing what you are told. And doing it also because it fulfils a need. Jolt.

His body jiggled on strings. He heard his voice shriek boldly as an animal to whom the concept of shame can never occur. He watched the eyes of those professionals and knew they would take their young to the zoo tomorrow, or to gasp at a horror movie. Why not bring them here? This out-zoos the zoo, out-horrors any movie. The kids would ask, how can anybody do this? Jolt. Though even kids might not find words to ask, how can Daddy do it? And here came the daddies again. Close, loving, the ultimate intimacy. Sex was never so free of pretences or complications. Roscoe Plenty's detached mind floated in reach of inescapable sights, watching adult men assault a helpless body. He recognized the frenzy, the climax of it. Coffee break.

The professionals mopped sweating faces, apparently well pleased with the product of their labours. This was tough work but always a challenge to the ingenuity. They had become precious to him. They had become his last intelligent contact with humankind.

Later that day, the Minister for Internal Security called in person. Too late. His esteemed colleague had given them the slip, though heart and lungs still functioned in first-class order. There was nothing for it but to continue straight on to the presidential broadcast studio, where he was expected.

Owen Powell appeared on national television: his head as round as Buchanan's though a few sizes smaller, a pursed mouth above a fleshy chin, the spooks of long-ago laughter. Yet his skin was not tough like the leader's, it looked colourless and tender. And his eyes in the albino mask shone soft and dark as those of a young woman still expecting happiness. He expressed gratification at his appointment to Acting Vice-President. Using Buchanan gestures, he reiterated chunks of Buchanan speeches. He couldn't have been more pleased, he said, or more honoured to speak on the great statesman's behalf in public. And Buchanan was there too, clasping the fellow's beloved hands between his own.

Already plump, Powell grew fatter with loyalty. So, staying back after another conference on the increase of public laughter, he dared pursue, just to keep his hand in, a second vendetta.

— But, Your Excellency, I took it from your generous manner that you were delegating this decision to Margaret Talbot to test her integrity.

Bernard Buchanan radiated satisfaction.

— Now you understand why I chose you, he cried out. Then pounded the desk with his fist, again and again, thumping it and shaking with rage. I shall test her, I shall, I cannot live without knowing who to trust. Trust is the cornerstone of my policy. How dare she cross me when I made her what she is? Do you know I saw her at that make-up session before Fortescue interviewed me, I saw her smirking. She didn't think I noticed, but I did. Now why did she smirk? Could it be that she knew what was going to happen, that that little twister planned to doublecross me and try to make me a laughingstock all round the world? She didn't think I noticed. But where would I be today if I missed seeing all that goes on around me?

— You are too unsparing of yourself, BB.

— What more do I need to know? the president said, restored to goodhumour. How I wish I could stand. More than anything I'd like to take a walk round the grounds. Wouldn't that be nice? But it'll never happen while I carry so much responsibility. Rub my ankles Owen, he added plaintively. Like a good fellow. That's better. I hate calling the doctor. I will not be lectured. And he has bad breath too. Ring for my bearers, will you? That banquet to welcome the Ugandan Ambassador the day after tomorrow, Owen, you attend in my stead, all right?

— Shouldn't I go simply as myself? Nobody can replace you. If I were to try, I'd look a fool.

Buchanan shot him a look full of chaos. But in his innocence Powell did not notice.

— As you choose, the president decided. Come in, men. Hoist me up. We're on the move again. My ankles are aching as if I'd walked a mile, God curse them. That's the style. I feel like Father Christmas. Mush mush! Up there, Dasher. Get along, you bloody reindeer, let's see a bit of action. Hup, Dancer! All I need is the sack of presents and a chimney as wide as a room. He laughed as he went.

Then the Minister for Internal Security and Acting Vice-President, being one of those dear little men who completely close their eyes when they laugh, took the risk and laughed too.

— Come on Owen, no hanging back in my office, playing make-believe!

63

Dorina remained in the kitchen where no maid had ever worked. She watched coffee grounds sinking in the glass jug. Then she poured herself a drink. But what imparted peculiar concentration to her movements was, paradoxically, the fact that her attention was focused elsewhere. Dorina listened, her highstrung nerves fluttering. There could no longer be any doubt: at least two men were in the livingroom. Their discreet voices exchanged information, casual untroubled strategic and lethally personal information, about her hiding in the kitchen, about the aroma of fresh coffee despite import restrictions, about the certainty that soon she would sit at her piano and practise for a concert she knew no one would invite her to perform.

She did not call to them in her schoolmistress voice. She knew, after all, what had happened to Miss Gardiner. She did not compromise her pride by admitting they had the least power to unsettle her. She must wait until she next saw Buchanan in private. . . and then Master Owen Powell with his tighter security arrangements might find himself with red ears.

Dorina sipped some coffee.

— Are you still there? she called, scarcely raising her voice but giving it a cheerful note. Looking after my safety?

The oven sang out that her croissants were ready.

64

Greta Grierson was being wooed. What is more, wooed by an exceptionally handsome man of twenty-eight. At least, she had the impression he was wooing her. Yet when she came to consider carefully, she could not be sure. To go to the beginning of this business, they worked in the same department at the university, she as secretary to the professor and he as a tutor.

Greta could not claim to be a popular secretary, which is why she kept her job. Her professor, head of the geography department and one time Dean of the Faculty of Arts, was a crochetty old maid from Edinburgh, Percy Murray. Professor Murray's ideal academe consisted of wood-panelled offices, librarians wearing green tennis eyeshades, quiet commonrooms where a glass of sherry might be sipped in the evening without interruption, plus a squadron of lecturers, heads down, organizing the diurnal output of the department without bothering him. His idea of a good time was strolling along a shelly beach with his trousers rolled up to the knee and a warm briar pipe between his teeth, or an acquiescent partner at chess. He contemplated the hazards of geography from a peaceful height and this was how things were going to remain. Like so many meek personalities, his pursuance of small ends showed savage singlemindedness. Professor Murray's idea of a secretary was a fleshy shy loyal woman with a tendency to be stubborn perhaps, a woman who held his erudition in awe, who owned some skill at correcting his dreadful spelling combined with the tact to disavow taking any such liberty, also a respectful attitude to Scotland appreciated. As this made up the entire breadth of Greta Grierson's character, it was only a matter of time before they found each other and separation became unthinkable. If the professor did not wish to be disturbed by people, nor by students, as was the usual state of affairs, absolutely nobody got past her desk to disturb the stagnant air of his sanctum. She developed a particular skill with the telephone too, answering yes to everything but with so delayed a delivery, so dubious a tone, a whole range of possibilities might be understood by it, from *no* to *I cannot make sense of your peculiar accent*. But almost never *yes*. The phone rang. Yes, she spoke into it, having allowed her characteristic silence to elapse. Is Professor Murray in? Yes (meaning perhaps not). This is Dr Inigo Jones here. Yes (meaning so what?) I would like to speak to him. Yes (meaning I'll take a message). Unless he is otherwise engaged. Silence. In which case I could always phone back I suppose. Yes (meaning yes). He knows my extension: Jones, Architecture.

The geography department staff found Miss Grierson categorically impossible. She regarded them as wasters of her professor's time and possibly as debauchers of the students into the bargain. All the more astonishing when one of them, the American, began making a spectacle of himself by being pleasant to her, hanging round her door with the time of day. His libidinous designs, which could scarcely be doubted any longer, carried over into the street. She was posting a letter to her estranged mother at the General Post Office in full view of the law; standing hesitantly while the slot waited to receive unwise confessions of loneliness and regret. Perhaps she ought to think again. Write, yes, but a different letter altogether. When what should happen but an unknown intruder approached, withholding a letter of his own, offering it to the slot and then snatching it back. Finally he dropped it in and spoke directly to her: That's the way it's done Miss Grierson, let go, take the risk, flit, down among a hundred others and never to be gotten back, there's a fatal beauty in letting go. She gripped her umbrella ready to defend her honour and faced the hoodlum. . . only to discover herself confronting a smiling Ganymede. Mr Sikorski! she exclaimed with relief, which he plainly misinterpreted as joy. He really was most wretchedly good-looking. Her feelings safely hidden inside a woollen cardigan and pinned down by her amethyst thistle, Greta retracted with a slightly sour apology: I thought you were someone I didn't know. You *don't* know me, he protested. You are looking very flushed, she accused disapprovingly. He explained that he had been playing cricket. As this seemed respectable enough, she favoured him with a confidence that she herself had played cricko, a ladies' game of the same kind, she explained, at school. Also tennis for years after that: C-grade fixtures. Did your team, he accused her delightedly, ever win the championship? Almost, she admitted and popped her letter in. Why not? Her mother couldn't eat her.

Young Sikorski escorted her to the carpark, where skulking figures scattered hugging their petty thefts and melting out of sight. This simple courtesy on his part ought not to have entailed serious consequences, except that he then invited her to offer him a lift home. She clammed up. You, she accused him silently, are what's known as a gigolo. But he was not a gigolo. The truth lay many layers more dreadful than that naive naughtiness. Whatever the case, she had the presence of mind to say she was heading in the opposite direction. He would see her Monday, he supposed, and flashed her his irresistible smile. Oh I don't trust you I don't, she told herself. And in these times one had to be especially careful. Packs of unemployed labourers wandered the streets morosely, watched by packs of Watchdogs. The stories of neighbours spying on one another became so commonplace you had to believe at least some of them. She tried not to know. It wasn't a pie she should stick her nose into, she insisted. But the general wariness proved contagious. You'll learn soon enough and you'll have to, one of the typists screeched at her the day this woman brought disgrace on the university in the form of two policemen furnished with a warrant for her arrest. But Greta Grierson stayed out of the way. When the curfew began she said, how tiresome. But she rather liked it. She liked the sudden hush in the streets, a religious simplicity of respectful streetlamps. She liked it because now she could be home by nightfall, legitimately alone, and not feel the social world of city evenings out there mocking her for a killjoy. Nobody was having a good time, so what was she supposed to be missing?

The poor professor had been most distressed by that scene with the warrant. Politics, he said, is none of our business, our business is knowledge, pure and simple, anybody who lets themselves become mixed up with undesirable elements has no one to blame when they are found out. The occasion was one of their rare departmental staff meetings. Shall I record this in the minutes sir? Greta asked, interrupting proceedings for the first time in seven years. To record it, Mr Sikorski spoke from the unfavoured end of the room, would constitute political action. Quite correct, Professor Murray wailed through his pipe, er, Ganymede. We shall not record it Miss Grierson, we shall simply agree to emblazon it in mind. I would recommend you each one, and this shall also remain outside the scope of the official record, to keep a clear head on the subject of the university itself. As academics you need nobody to tell you the academy is paramount. But I am telling you. Let us retain a fine focus on the reason for our employment here, the researching and teaching of factual information upon the subject of geography. Nothing more than that. Any inept application of ideas simply confounds the ideas themselves. There are serious complexities being defined in society at large, as you must be aware. We are the privileged few, a little community with important work to accomplish, work which is satisfying and keeps us in comfort. Not that comfort is at all our objective or even among the priorities we would consider serious. But let us be grateful and get on with the task. He opened the flap of his soft tobacco pouch, probed inside it with thumb and finger, producing a small wad of tobacco which he kneaded on his palm and fed into the pipe while he awaited approbation, perhaps even an expression of respect. He savoured his moment of personal power with a pout of satisfaction and tamped down the tobacco, struck a match with uncharacteristic vigour, and puffed a sudden welter of smoke.

For a moment I thought he was going to give us a surprise, Ganymede Sikorski told her confidentially that afternoon. But she decided that, pleasant as this game might be in its way, she had to call a halt before misunderstandings developed. Mr Sikorski, she explained, you are new to our department, you'll soon learn that Professor never gives us surprises. Then, he responded, in case your life becomes unbearably dull, perhaps I had better give you one. And, oh dear, this was what she dreaded, perhaps even some species of proposition. I want to meet your sister Lavinia Manciewicz.

Nothing prepared Greta. Weeks of silly speculation brought her down. The names Manciewicz and Sikorski suggested to her clannish mind the wide terror of a plot.

— I have not seen her for years, she gabbled recalling that shameful dinner party, her gorge rising at the memory of foodsmells, at the thought of Lavinia painting gross men naked, plus her most obsessively repressed fear: the knowledge that she had once met and dined with the president of the republic and had walked out on him and his friends. This insult nagged her so she became convinced she was a marked woman with her phone tapped, men's footsteps on the roof at night, the heavy breathing of spies outside her bedroom window, informers with stopwatches recording her observance of curfew. Mention of Lavinia brought it all to the surface with a rush. The invincible Grierson spun on her typist's chair to hide her face from Ganymede Sikorski. She was deluded in thinking so glamorous a creature might be lusting after her (though she had no intention of allowing him to have his way). She was stripped of her anonymity. The hateful Lavinia would ruin her in the end. And that conciliatory note to her mother, too late to take it back.

Lavinia, as Greta well knew, had been jailed for some offence against the state and was still locked up.

— Why do you people persecute me? she whispered into a panicking handkerchief. I am not responsible for anybody else. I have done nothing wrong, ever, nothing.

Mr Sikorski listened with amazement. He quite liked the old stick and was sorry to have upset her. But his needs were ruthless, nonetheless. So he pursued his point.

— Just tell me where she is, please. That is all.

— I don't know, whined Greta because, of course, he wanted her to confess the shame of having a traitor for a sister.

— She must have a studio.

Behind his words she heard the steely state. He would surely know the address already. He was testing her loyalty to the law. What had Lavinia to lose?

— Will you leave me alone? she begged.

His cold eyes watched the back of her head, the fat neck with its powdered helpless creases, tender hairs nestling behind her ears.

— All right, she whispered and wrote the address.

Her phone rang.

— Yes professor, she answered in a tiny voice. Yes professor, of course. She hung up, stood, adjusted herself to appear in public, pushed past Sikorski shooting him a watery plea to get out of her life, and entered the sanctum of the divine Percy, who noticed nothing wrong.

— Oh indeed, Marcia Connor told Ganymede Sikorski. Lavinia is a neighbour. They say she was arrested, but I wouldn't know.

She memorized every detail of the caller's appearance in case she might need to report him. Marcia Connor could make mincemeat of babies like this, good enough to eat. She straightened her back and treated the American to her special brand of friendliness.

— May I offer you a drink? Have you come far? Such a pity to find your way here and then only be disappointed.

He stared at her insolently, as if they knew each other already, as if his calculating eyes were totting up her successful prosecutions and weighing them against the frustration which drove her to more. Could he see, then, how she despised herself, how she revered talent and beauty, loathed her lumpish body and lumpish imagination? An early recognition of grace seduced her into expecting she must grow to satisfy her hankering to be spoken of in one breath with Pavlova. Her childhood ambitions left her abilities woefully behind. Could he see so much, with his girlish face prettier than her own had ever been? Though she despised him already, she could not stare him down.

— Do they notify informers, he asked with academic detachment. When they have been successful in persecuting someone, I wonder? And do they notify them to beware when the victims are released, if they ever are released? Interesting to know just how loyal the establishment is to its agents.

Mrs Connor's blood rose and she bounced back.

— Lavinia is a friend of mine, she retorted hotly. You can ask Tim when he gets home if you feel so army-smarmy. With that capacity for responding to imaginative creations already remarked upon, she now believed her own fiction, believed herself insulted. We don't need a lecture from you, she declared.

He shrugged as she stormed away. Very well, he would ask Tim (Mr Manciewicz presumably). He sat on the step and took out a book. Marcia Connor, who had banged downstairs and slammed herself indoors, kept a keen ear cocked for evidence and wasted the entire afternoon sitting at her window, notebook and clock at the ready.

Once when she went to her Captain Lonigan, Australian Strike Force, Intelligence (Civilian Security Section), to report some serious news about young Anderson across the road worrying his mother to death with the friends he kept and her positively seeing him smuggle in a sheaf of leaflets, she pleaded with the captain on the family's behalf. They're good people, she said, and worried about the lad. Meg Anderson wouldn't have a bad bone in her body, she's the soul of loyalty. All it needs, she explained, is to give the boy a scare and show him what the consequences might be if he doesn't stop running his parents ragged. And although the captain listened politely, he was determined not to let the Watchdogs beat him to this arrest. His squad arrived that night, blinding the house with mobile searchlights, belting at the door with rifle butts, flinging poor Meg Anderson and her worries back against the wall, dragging her dear pride Danny, at fifteen, out to their paddywagon, passing a wad of printed sheets to the officer in charge. Marcia Connor had watched the great lights snap out and die back into their reflectors, heard the crisp orders, even the sob of a child, before the little convoy roared brazenly at high speed through streets guaranteed empty by law. Next morning, first thing, she went to comfort Meg and share her fears.

Old Mr Stubbs came in, coughing as always. He lived in a ground-floor flat and spat on the path whenever he went out. First thing he did was to hawk and spit. She watched him.

Sister Bennett arrived sooner than she ought, ran to her room and immediately came scurrying back on her little legs of an excitable mouse and skipped into a waiting taxi with quite unfashionable lightheartedness. Of course, there will always be sick people, so those who batten on them for employment need never be short of a job.

Then Tim arrived home.

With no time to lose if her emergence were to appear accidental, Mrs Connor flung open her door just as he passed on the stairs. She went down to the porch carrying a couple of milk-bottles warm from waiting by the sunny window. She began writing the milkman a note, standing just inside the porch to be able to hear.

Ganymede Sikorski could see her highheeled shoes, her thick legs in fine stockings and the hem of her floral dress at the brilliant doorway past the dark silhouette of, presumably, Tim mounting the stairs. Her emergence had identified him. Ganymede stood, placing one finger on his lips. Tim looked up in alarm, seeing a stranger. Then despite the tension tugging his face painfully stiff, he spoke in a wonderfully ordinary voice.

— Hi there. Long time no see.

65

. . . So the Governor is going home. Sitting in my room, not knowing what my future might be under Sir Maurice O'Connell, watching the sails of the ship being set and the sheets hauled in, my mind turns more and more to Mr Leichhardt's plan of returning to the inland, and to Charles Sturt out there, of whom no news has been heard for more than a year now.

At the quay I encountered Mr Wentworth who once again had Mr Buchanan with him. This is a day of rejoicing, ay, my boy, Buchanan said to me (though he cannot be above five years older than I am), to see the back of the worst Governor the colony ever had. Indeed, the rejoicing among the crowds around us had grown shamelessly rowdy. Quite the contrary, my boy, I replied, he is a great man in his narrowness and one who will be missed. Mr Wentworth offered to beat me with his walking-stick. To give him his due, he was not to know I had survived the lash, as I stood before them and smiled at their furious impotence. Wentworth then bellowed: History will prove me right. History, I replied with an outward show of calm, if it has any more sense than a spiteful child, will forget Sir George Gipps's trivial faults and honour him for the many good things he achieved, not least among them the recognition that the natives have a right to be considered human beings. Had the walking-stick been a gun I believe I would be a dead man by now, for the murders at Myall Creek muddied more sinister depths of savagery among our landholders even than Gipps's outrageous claim that they ought to pay for the use of land they have not purchased. I felt this all the more keenly for having been present, as I have already intimated, during the whole of the massacre.

Permit me to tell you more of your world.

My master (can you conceive how such a term sits with me?) at that time ordered us to bring the dogs and two spare guns, though he would never entrust me or any other of his convict labourers with shot and powder, you may be sure, to accompany him, joining several neighbours of like intentions. They were to take revenge, it transpired, on some impertinent Aborigines said to believe the creek where they camped was still theirs, though how this intelligence had been gained from the tribe I know not. A whole party of us went on horseback. As convicts, thought not worthy of the pleasure of taking part in the actual killing, we were spared the necessity of refusing, and ordered to stand-by in case of need or emergency. The gentlemen began tying up victims and stringing them on a long rope. This set the poor creatures wailing in their own tongue, sharp warning cries, especially from the women who had difficulty managing the net shoulder-baskets in which they carried their babies while they themselves were trussed, bobbing along ahead of us, brown shoulders the same dusty hue as the rocks, and wild hair tormented to a procession of bushes. I noticed their feet, and how they knew precisely where to place them for the easiest way among sharp stones. This was their land, beyond any doubt. Men, women, grandmothers, babes at the breast, they were led to the execution place, as countless Indians and Arabians, Hottentots and Chinese have been before in the same interests of civilization.

At the execution place, our men slaughtered them, using service swords and knives. In many instances, the heads were hewn off. One young gentleman sheep-farmer repeatedly shouted as he hacked through necks: the savages, the savages! throwing heads aside with every sign of disgust at having come in contact with such vermin, but he was too close to his voice, in all probability, to have heard himself. Throughout the terrible artificiality of the massacre there was no chaos, none of the proper and excusable fury, the lashing out and turmoil of a human occasion however disgusting, the fleeting moments of mouths open to receive the host, of excrement and limbs at their most lustrous in the moments of hope. None of this. Instead, I witnessed a clumsy catalogue of amateurism, the humiliating failure to kill cleanly, desperation and cowardice among killers not knowing where to cut to kill, soaked in the blood of their victims, bruised and winded by desperate buttings, boots slipping, legs staggering under the strength of their own ill-judged thrusts.

To the amazement of the entire colony (and Sydney alone has now some twenty-five thousand inhabitants) Gipps put the eleven settlers on trial for murder. This was simply unheard of and the whirlwind of alarm rattling sheep-station doors all night was disbelieved except by cynics whose most general opinion was that such lawlessness on the part of the administration would lead to anarchy. The jury, comprising settlers who lived in similar (if generally less fortunate) circumstances to the defendants, took a quarter of an hour to acquit them, all eleven. The public went wild with the relief of fifty years exonerated. But the Monitor, against all expectation, launched a campaign, and twelve days later His Excellency ordered a fresh trial, new red-scrubbed faces, new collars and collar studs, new vestments for the beadle and the clerk, and a new head under the judge's wig. This time seven of the eleven were found guilty and sentenced to death. In the public houses a judgement was passed on the judge and *his jury, for how can one murder a thing, an object, an animal? people asked. If it is murder, then the natives must have to be declared human beings like ourselves. An appeal against the court's finding went to Governor Gipps who quietly and irrevocably refused it. On 28th December 1838 they were hanged. All were free men, men with land. The Governor had already been here two years at this stage; but thus it was that a final rift opened between him and the gentry who doubtless felt at any moment they might vomit fire. They have not forgiven him and never will.*

I was a convict still, so the freedom of news seldom reached me then, but I and my kind had begun to feel a dramatic change in the way our masters were allowed to treat us; we could no longer be beaten as had formerly been the case, we were offered conditional liberties and encouraged to believe there would be a respectable place for us in New South Wales if we stayed clear of crime upon the expiration of our term of penal servitude. Here I might comment upon a general matter by pointing out that the colony has been built not by the governors or their architects, nor by merchants or pastoralists, but by slaves like myself. We built the quays and the churches, the barracks and government houses. What has happened since is not our doing, but we it was who cut the timber and dressed the stone, we baked the bricks, burnt lime, drew water, and carted everything where it was needed. Did you ever imagine that your callousness and your lies might reap such a harvest of utility? . . .

66

Owen Powell found Mama. Naturally he did. In this period the nation had grown nerves; wherever you were, you could be certain some delicate mechanism reverberated with information about you, what you said, who you were with and for how long. From the unlikely soil of a community of narcissists (such as we had been, in various modes, at least since 1914) this new puritanism blossomed once Buchanan came to power: nobody had eyes for themselves. We watched each other.

The diviners of messages were outnumbered only by interpreters of them. Interpretation grew to be so essential to daily survival that sharp operators opened interpretation clinics and ran interpreter academies. No keyhole was thought complete without its spying device. Overlord of all such divination loomed the Panjandrum of Innuendo, Owen Powell himself.

So of course he found Mama. How else could the country hold up its head? What use would it be for Australian freestyle swimmers to set new world records, as they did, while one octogenarian woman eluded our battalion of snoops. Where would be the pride in that? A nation has to have priorities. Powell's top agents had been selected for the assignment and told their jobs were on the line. Forty-eight hours later his assistant, Jack Cohen, received the new file and brought it straight to the master. There it lay on the desk: MAMA (otherwise: IZUMI, Bernardette; née McALOON). Widow. Height 155 cm, weight 83 kg, age (est.) 82.

— Thank you, he dismissed young Jack, apple of his eye.

Yet, as he picked up the file once the door shut, his hand shook. This fear had little to do with stupidity. It was the vacillation of a prudent man, and a fair indicator of his ruthlessness. In such a game he knew whom he was playing against. He was a tactician. Suppose he were simply to open the file and begin reading: would he not sacrifice his precious ignorance of the information inside, information which could never be expunged from mind? Yes, if he elected to read it, he must also choose never to be free from knowledge which could be compromising, knowledge about which he might need to feign ignorance when the president changed his mind and recalled the order to track this Mama person. And then where would he be? He'd be living on the perilous edge of admissions, harbouring incriminating slanders about her. . . even, perhaps, about the great man himself. Powell had trained his own interrogators in the art of patience, in letting a victim talk, listening to catalogues of lies, peeling them off, knowing that eventually, if from no other cause than failure of inventiveness, they would lay bare a core of truth. Certainly the file ought to answer tempting questions as to why Buchanan wanted her found in the first place. Yet this alone constituted a matter of some delicacy.

He would read it later. Maybe. Meanwhile, the information was safe nowhere but here in his possession. So began the period of Owen Powell's carrying an unopened file on Mama everywhere he went, oozing sweat when he feared it had been mislaid, suffering heart murmurs at the thought of a bag-snatcher wrenching it from his grasp at the airport, breaking out in a nervous rash if he needed to broach the briefcase for any other item and risk the terror of its falling out, scattering deadly information on the floor in full view of agents. The first product of this secrecy was a perfect paranoia that it would be discovered to *be* secret.

Clearly, all information must be kept out of the system or this

Mama-Izumi-McAloon woman might be molested. She must not be troubled in any way, neither watched, nor followed, nor, categorically, bugged. She had to be left to enjoy her privacy under the president's personal, if indirect, protection. Only one other person in the country commanded such favour, the leader's wife, Dorina.

Nevertheless, alert to the fact that His Excellency would wish to be shown evidence of his request being satisfied, a surrogate file was appointed to stand in. The minister recalled the case of a woman investigated and found completely in the clear, a woman with the right connections, known to have moved once in the president's own circle. And quite fortuitously, that enquiry had been requested by the lamented Roscoe Plenty, now beyond caring any more about it.

Owen Powell himself opened these two files, MAMA-IZUMI-McALOON and GRIERSON GRETA, to extract their contents. His plump capable hands, busy and deft, switched the covers. He made a brief note on the Grierson papers about Mama as a nickname and returned this to the system under its new heading. He locked the other in his briefcase and comforted himself that this minor crisis was unlikely to last long, also that he could not be at fault for protecting His Excellency's peace of mind.

If Owen Powell already bore some resemblance to the leader prior to being named as his deputy, this was insignificant beside the transformation which took place immediately afterwards. From that day, he began stacking on weight, his hair fell out and the remaining wreath of it he combed the way Buchanan combed his. With gratification he discovered he too grew a fourth chin once he had enough condition on him, and his walk suggested a hint of difficulty. He smiled, with synchronized goodhumour, as and when the president smiled.

It must not be thought for a moment that these two notables really looked alike. No. Bernard Buchanan had become a matchless giant of a man, whereas Owen Powell was simply nouveau gross; Buchanan's hair was grey, Powell's that peculiar brown of a bad apple; Buchanan's prominent nose and bulging eyes miraculously married camel with toad, whereas the Powell nose remained little more distinguished than a boil, and his eyes sank smaller with every increase in bodyweight. The point of his success was a consonance of style. In this more subtle matter of appealing to the essence of his master's choice, Mr Powell (or Dr Powell, Professor Powell, call him what you will; all titles were his eventually) succeeded beyond praise. It was an identical question of essences which made that photograph of his sister so distressing she felt impelled to tear it up and guided his father, in obtaining a fresh print, to deliver it disguised as a page in a picturebook of Bluebeard.

67

Dr Luke Head invented the great idea. His idea was culture. The inspiration came casually enough. One of those mornings, sitting in the sun with his back to the wall, being surprised by Yanagita's stories, he came up with his own surprise.

— You know that stuff they print on the back of breakfast cereal packets?

— Keep fit the easy way? Great Explorers?

— Well, couldn't we do our own? We'd call it World Wide Wisdom, or Culture Cut-outs.

— You and me? Yanagita asked lazily, not much amused.

— All of us. We could write them and illustrate them and print them. There is a whole generation of kids out there who don't even know other people are human, they don't know how to grow into men and women. After eight years of the fat man, they are brainwashed. They don't know who they are or what they are or how they came to be here or how to get themselves out of the mess they're in.

— We've got Hottentots among us, they must know a thing or two, and Chinese, Yanagita admitted, beginning to perceive the charm of the idea. There's the wisdom of the honourable ancestors to start with, apart from some pretty hardnosed political know-how.

— Samoans, Finns, everybody.

— Venezuelans. They'd bring a world of experience about big power interference. And Afghans the same from the other side, Yanagita conceded, warming to the subject. All different, all connected.

— All brought here to use their hands, Dr Head pointed out. To build buildings and no questions asked. But in this prison our brains run hot with memories.

— A monumental series of cornflake packets on How to be Human by Those who Know, the older man agreed. And then smiled, not at all mockingly.

— We can do it ourselves. There are sure to be tradesmen printers among us, put out of business by electronics.

— Your Australian Buchanan, Yanagita Izumi told the silver-eyes flocking into the yard and picking among memories of human bones. Imports untold treasures which he is happy to waste. Even our commandant, not the most powerful intellect among men, has learnt to count to twenty-seven; he told us yesterday there are twenty-seven nationalities under his care. Think of that.

— The poor buggers, Luke offered dreamily now his invention had begun to take flight.

— Twenty-seven languages for a start, give or take a few. And a language, doctor, is the store of wisdom from all its centuries of use; each one an encyclopedia of inherited knowledge. Multiply the art, religion, medicine. Multiply the science and craft, Yanagita Izumi the convert cried out, clarifying the prospect with a single phrase. This camp is a world university.

The silvereyes whirring back and forth between the walls were noisy with gossip of blood, though blood had not been spilt here for a hundred and fifty years. Tiny excited beaks and cold eyes flickered in the dancing greengrey foliage of their own feathers. But perhaps these same birds had been alive all that time ago and longer. Perhaps the convicts' sufferings were remembered as a brief fruiting of the place. Or maybe the gossip was not so much crystalline catalogues of lost glory as rumours of another harvest. With sudden collective impatience, the tiny birds sheered away over the wall. They left the twigs of those budding fruit trees trembling.

— How should we begin? Luke asked, fully awake.

— We need an organizer with the right training. Luckily we have me.

When the commandant was approached he sighed with gratification. He was already aware of the plan and had thought it through. Such matters could be trusted to no one but himself. Being used to a prison community with compulsory workshops producing mailbags, furniture and hand-stitched shoes, he had a good nodding acquaintance with productivity as a virtue and knew how to handle it. He opposed the idea of Friends of Privilege buying their own machinery, because there was a printing press already on the premises, installed during the First World War to print *Welt am Montag*, a news-sheet for the German civilian internees. A fine old claptrap, he called it. And his satisfaction in this was not at all simple. Commandant Curtis began to rediscover an almost forgotten tradition, that of the enlightened administrator. He did not see it as dangerous. No. He was an opportunist willing to follow his instinct that this far-out plan could be made to reflect credit on himself and might even, in the longer perspective of achieved cornflakes and rice bubbles packets, be cited as a turningpoint, clear proof of the survival of humanism among state officials. He smiled. He grew serious.

— Considering the step of offering myself, he added. As business manager, needs somebody on the telephone, booking orders, general admin, all that, leading cereal manufacturers to be sold the idea. Have to deal with paper and cardboard merchants, box factories.

The seed had been sown. Like those pumpkins plump as midnight, the proposition was found to have sent out tendrils blossoming furry gold and weighing the mind with fairytales. At Yanagita's touch, the ripe shell fell open and a jungle of fruiting vines proliferated. That prison of free guests, that welcome of armed guards facing out to ward off grateful hosts, became a treasurehouse of the unexpected. Folk philosophies, a harvest of knowledge for survival, the power to evoke a collective consciousness, legacy of uncounted millions who thought and spoke what they thought; all this now lay within their ambit.

Yanagita divided the material they acquired into forty-seven categories, such as Knowing Your Own Strength, Knowing Your Own Mind, Knowing the Electro-magnetic Forces of Earth, Knowing How Animals Think, Knowing When to Fall in Love. Luke suggested fifty categories would look more saleable as a number. Though they pondered together, trying to hunt out the missing ones, neither man could come up with an acceptable suggestion.

Meanwhile, each night when they arrived home exhausted from work at the IFID construction site, translators sat down to the task of converting the garnered knowledge into English; others were appointed editors and tackled the challenge of cutting thirty-thousand-word anecdotes to the couple of paragraphs allowed by the format; artists, refreshed by visions, pored over drawingboards; and tradesmen topped up the ink tanks of the ancient printing press and set its rollers turning till the metal parts clattered and chuckled rhythmically. Production began.

The nights grew joyous with flare-lit ceremonies of their hopelessly outdated notions about society and what mattered. Symbolic reindeer locked horns in a wild dance from the north and a ring of black voices chanted the mountains of Zimbabwe to this place so the listeners might look up and identify the peaks.

Those angry women encircling the prison wall, themselves unemployed and wives of unemployed husbands, heard their own voices falter for the first time in years. They listened to the new turn the world had taken. And recognized the hateful affability of men, that enclosure of clubbishness which needs no wall to keep women out. Naturally they recognized what they so bitterly knew. A change had happened in there, they could tell when the ground shook with big feet stamping and shrill men-cries igniting the darkness while basses sighed resonant as the sea.

Each evening after work and after their meal, men gathered in the central yard, gulping the lees of silverbeet tea to be first in the best positions. Offers to contribute came so prodigally Luke Head declared a list and supervised it. By virtue of being the healer they all knew and having ancient origins in that place, he became master of ceremonies. Each evening the blood-packed yard with its exuberant gardens resurrected a heritage of what was precious to them. Yodelling Austrians in lederhosen slapped their knees and rumps to a rhythm both virile and sentimental, warcries sounded down the gulches of the Andes, and giant Borneo masks swayed drowning in flute music and improvised gamelans.

This the angry women heard and it fomented their anger. But then came a silence which they were unable to interpret. Shushing children, they leaned toward the wall and, as a lone gull might be glimpsed flying through the night, caught rising fragments of a man's speech, the context forever fading away and eluding them.

Within the circle an elderly Japanese from the teaching staff told this story: My brother fought against Australia and it was because of him I came, in answer to the spirit. He was a kamikaze pilot during the Second World War. I was a member of his ground crew. The squadron flew out that day. He said to me, I know what to do. You will move heaven, brother, I told him, because I understood his plan, you will call up the Divine Wind. This day he would honour us by becoming one of the inspired suicides. He took out a piece of paper. And this, friends, is the picture I still carry living in my mind. He spread the paper on the wing of his Zero, stroking it flat. His goggles were worn high up on the cowl of a leather helmet. At his sixteenth birthday three years before, he had been so proud of the black fountain pen with its gold clip and lever. He held it now in those fine fingers I admired as he grew. Because, although he had surpassed me in strength and fame, he was my younger brother. And wrote a letter to our mother. Once, wind flipped the page and it almost escaped him. But his reflexes were swift. He was decisive. He bowed his head as he wrote, bowed it with pride for his mother's loss (the women outside caught this phrase), chin nestling on the clean white scarf knotted inside his flight-jacket. As he signed his name he confirmed our fate. I saw his mouth tighten. We always got on well, he and I, but at this moment he was already dedicated. With the remote look of a monk, he gave me the letter to deliver. Our hands did not touch. He put his pen away carefully in an inside pocket, buttoned his collar tight round the scarf, and pulled the goggles over his eyes. He climbed into his Zero as if there would be a next time. By such men we defined our greatness. But not only ours. By such men we also helped to define the greatness of those enemies who were set against us.

— How can I hold up my head? Yanagita confessed afterwards. It seems impossible that I did not think of it. There is our forty-eighth category, Knowing How to Die. My sole consolation is that the reminder came from one of my own countrymen.

That very night, artists set to work on representing this enemy of Australia in all his fineness and virtue.

— We shall learn the human face of those who are against us, Luke promised.

— Does it, his friend asked gently. Help you see the human face of Buchanan?

— First, the Aborigine burst out spiritedly. I have to be shown the human face of the white invaders in general.

— Why not start with the man you wish to kill?

But this was more than Dr Head had been prepared for.

The catalogues grew. And men, having something now to share, began to understand each other. They laughed in many languages on being taught the ancient word *Xoxouhqui-yollotl.* Xoxouhqui-yollotl. Xoxouhqui-yollotl! they greeted people who had no other word in common. Xoxouhqui-yollotl! came answering back, sounding like a Dutchman laughing into an empty bottle. But in every one of thirty-two languages they learnt its meaning also: Free Man. The literal translation as Green-heart or Fresh-heart they understood too, embowered in plants they had raised to burgeon against all probability, sustained by a harvest of their own foresight. So they greeted each other with Free Man! as the Greeks greet each other with Rejoice!

Tales were told, not just of war, though the kamikaze pilot left recollections of slaughter, stoicism and vengeance still burning their minds the morning after. Tales were told of the quest for knowledge and for peace. But most of the stories recounted on quiet nights, while the protesting women were shut out, concerned love and told of longings the gathered wives could not hear, the loneliness of being forgotten by your children, of one man who relished his wife's easygoing devotion, their dancing together, swimming together, acting the fool during carnival, and the perplexing inventiveness of their lovemaking. Another told of himself and how he set out early one morning, you must imagine, from his cottage. Across snow-crusted ground he plodded, realizing, after nineteen years of living in the one village, he could still feel estranged there; and did, as each intimate familiar detail recurred for the first time. Somebody had walked that track before him, but he could not identify the foot. Every winter of his life he had known the soles of his family's boots and his neighbours' boots, heels worn crooked as a signature, the old smooth tread, the new; he had learnt the length of their stride and would read their haste or indolence when such rarities occurred. But this day the dawn rolled out its carpet of clean snow already printed with doubt. The air smelt of the kitchen fire burning birch-logs he had cut and stacked last summer. He did a thing so unusual it shook his faith: he stopped and turned round to see if he still recognized the house he had been born in. And no, he did not. Every characteristic of the walls, the capped chimney, were as he knew them to be. And yet he found them stamped against a landscape as troublingly foreign as those footprints. The bare appletree he climbed as a child, stubby and gnarled by too much fertility, grown gross as an old woman who must keep giving life and life; this tree stood firmly in the ground, an unknowable intruder. Until then, the taleteller said, I thought I was in love, that I must dig the field in spring or the world would not go on forever. So instead of starting work, I turned about and I stamped along, treading in those outlander's tracks, crushing them as I went, blotting them with my own which were a bigger size, until they led me to my fiancée's house. Even when I spoke her name, it came as a puff of white and blew away. I knew the letters to spell it with because I went to school to learn. But when I looked at the letters standing clear in my mind, they were shapes as strange as Egypt. I spoke my fiancée's name again. And another puff of white escaped me. Even my lips, don't laugh please, my lips felt strangers against each other. What was there to make me hesitate longer? What was there to make me hesitate at all? I threw open the kitchen door. The room was warm with steam and the fire smoking, from the mantelpiece a pair of stockings hung wavering in the heat. The mother stood unmoved as oak. But the girl who had been promised to me covered her face with her hands. Tears began dripping from her fingers. Into the cold air they dripped, the cold air I had brought with me.

The narrator sat down quietly and became one of the audience while translators finished retelling his story, taking longer in some languages than others, so the hushed groups listened after their own version finished, while various speakers spun out the same tone of voice in alien tongues, diminishing one by one, until finally silence bloomed dark flowers while those tears leaked on between the young woman's fingers and the stranger, who had come through the snow and departed, continued free, striding away, leaving a frozen landscape where he had been.

The story seemed as remote historically as geographically, a fable of long-lost innocence. This became the first entry in the forty-ninth category, Knowing Your Own Ignorance. In each category ten different stories were planned. Delighted at the cheap attractive format, cereal manufacturers hit the market with their new packets; and thousands of families began to read the art of recovering the life they had lost.

Izumi and Head were called to the office.

Commandant Curtis was one of those gangly persons who make a habit of folding their elbows and knees at improbable angles while fixing you with a penetrating stare magnified to superhuman brilliance by spectacles, who pat their flawlessly parted hair, paying you the deference of wishing to appear neat in your presence, and then cancelling the impression by some blunt impertinence.

— Interests of frankness, he began. Shan't ask you to sit down. Won't be here long enough. Claiming modest percentage of takings. Balance the books. Agreed? Our facilities, after all. That'll be that, then. Good luck, men. And well done. Fall out.

Still there were only forty-nine categories, though fifty had been advertised, when, straight after hearing of paleontologists in the tundra dining on steaks cut from prehistoric mammoths preserved in ice, a sad little black man from no known country came privately to Luke. They sat together, night after night, hearing complex tales of angels carrying favourites across wide seas to escape persecution; of the curative effect of smelling donkey-shit; of the king who could not be heard to utter a word without his divinity falling from him, who must respond to petitioners by signalling one of six traditional judgments or find knives in his lustful heart, and his craving to be human rewarded with its final proof in mortality; of tractors clearing aside a jungle of drudgery; of laser beams reading fingerprints; of a journey regularly made each thousand years on logs that navigate themselves among the island relics of a sunken continent; of binary mathematics; of the power to teach your heart to pump so slowly you can lie three days in a coffin underground and still be brought out alive. Then the sad man from nowhere in particular provided the last link of the program. The story he told, which took almost till dawn in the telling, made its first appearance on a line of Oat Crispies in this format, with tasteful illustrations of two key scenes.

Series 50

KNOWING THE VALUE OF OBEDIENCE

No.1: Josiah Henson

Josiah Henson ought not to be forgotten. He was born a slave in Maryland. One day a white foreman raped his mother. All he remembered of his father was how he came home and attacked the foreman, and how they punished him by cutting off his ear, whipping his back raw and breaking his head. Young Josiah was sold by one master to another and another. He grew up to be tough. He was a born leader. Eventually he managed his master's plantation.

Then came a time when the owner drank all his profits and had to sell up. A brother, living 800 km away in Kentucky, wanted his slaves. Josiah Henson was entrusted with the job of taking them there, all eighteen. He drove them in a cart, he walked with them on foot. And along the way they met many other slaves. When they came to a big river, he hired a boat to take them across. Here they were greeted by some free black men who said, "Come away with us. You've got souls, man, you've got no chains. There's nothing in God's world to stop you being whole men and women." But Josiah Henson took pride in obedience. Out of his vainglory he spoke up, "You take your hands off my folk." He pushed the boat out into mid-stream and they drifted away from the insults of the free people. He was so strong in his mind and his body, all eighteen followed him right back into slavery.

Josiah Henson suffered as much as his people at the hands of the cruel master he took them to. His only comfort was that he had done no worse to them than he had done to himself.

Many years later, he was written about under the name Uncle Tom.

The Wild Dog and Stephanie sat at the table in that uneasy truce of a new situation still being learned. Because she had stopped hating him and become defenceless, he felt constrained by honour not to presume or make use of his opportunity. Mama, in her slippers, her voice of a cracked china canary trilling away, supervised the joyous activity of the kitchen, eggs bouncing in boiling water, toast popping out of a toaster, sausages sizzling in the pan, and the coffee percolator bubbling a humorous burlesque of the hookah. She was jubilant.

— Help yourselves, darlings, she warbled. Plenty of milk and honey here.

The cereal packet stood like a wall between her two guests, presenting the man who was perpetually a victim of passion with *Series 4. Knowing When to Fall in Love. No. 3.*

— Aren't they clever, Mama added, noticing the barrier. At last they have done something truly wicked.

68

Roscoe Plenty hung, the air about him white and immaculate as plaster. Marvellously, he was found to be savable. His reason returned, so the exquisite refinement of medical science might then be employed to carve it away again, paring it delicately and measuring the effects at each stage.

A new class of torturer gathered round, wearing grateful expressions and commiserating with him among the echoes of his chronic anxiety. You are a benefactor of science, they promised. So he came to see that knowledge is the mockery of the sacred, these probings a violation of all that may be called godly in man. This was the day on which Roscoe Plenty could truly be said to have risen above himself and achieved that noble stature of mind we find characteristic of a statesman. He heard his doctors exchanging data and analyzing their research as they went, ready to present papers at an international congress of their kind, the earnest tone unmistakable, the absolute dedication to accuracy. One is never told how specialized such a career must be, what intelligence it demands, what imagination for choosing which technique to try next.

Then the line went dead.

The experts conferred in subdued excitement. They took readings of the strong heartbeat. They annotated a chaotic brain scan. They set about systematically checking the nervous system. No detail was left to conjecture. Roscoe Plenty had done all he could in the interests of progress. They got the picture.

. . . An old lag's face may be read as a register of what he has lived through: the mouth perpetually open seeking food to stuff the cracks of past starvation; eyes dim from only daring to look inward; the wrinkles of a puzzlement cut short by the sting of fire; ears bashed crooked by some fellow citizen of the new Athens; nose flattened on the lustrous squalor of an eternal blood-stench.

There comes a time when his strength and endurance are only sufficient to keep him on his feet still, though staggering and bloody and without energy to spare for masking what he has become under the heel of gentility.

During the year we completed building the model prison at Vengeance Harbour, of 238 men held captive there, 202 were flogged to the extent of 100 lashes each. Try to imagine 20,000 cuts. The work of flogging became so heavy the staff could not be expected to perform it. We were driven to flog one another while soldiers stood over us with loaded muskets. The man I refused to flog was given the job of flogging me for my insurrection; and did it. . .

69

— You think I am afraid to take, when I feel like taking? Bernard Buchanan boomed in his rich lovable comforting voice. Taking, he exulted. Is a divine power. Do you suppose you'd ever catch me asking please?

Gipps, as he departed, tilted his chin and made little explosions of impatience with his open mouth.

— I am the one to draw the line across people's lives and add up what they have amounted to, said the president.

Yet, left with an undercurrent of discontent, he sorted round till he isolated this twinge as the risk of appearing ridiculous. He had been successfully mocked by a hooligan spraying graffiti on a wall. And such a wall; in a place where even he would not be allowed entry. That was the point. Also by the simple subterfuges of a television interviewer.

From time to time, and this was one of them, he wondered if

his image had come adrift from reality. He saw himself terrified and despairing in a cloud of nibbling insects, harmless little things made nightmarish by darkness and infantile fears. Neither was Bernard Buchanan spared seeing that helpless hulk, naked and unprotected, rolling on a field of broken glass in Lavinia's portrait.

He picked up the telephone.

Granted that it must have taken Silverwater Jail half an hour to clean Lavinia up, plus another hour to rush her to the airport, her arrival in Canberra within three hours was a credit to state efficiency.

— How nice it would be to walk together round the garden, he greeted her as she was ushered in. Arm in arm. I always think a walk is the very best aid to reminiscence.

She knew in that moment how truly irresponsible he was, that he had no concept of what she was going through, or what he had done to her and so many others.

— Well how shall we begin? she challenged him, not at all chastened. Shall I ask why I have been brought here like an animal on display? Or why you shut me away in the first place?

— But sadly my walking days are over, to be realistic. And I have a philosophical commitment to pragmatism, as the world knows. It wouldn't be the same with those beefy blokes carting me along, perving on us, would it?

She stood at a distance from him. The room, as cared for as a museum of comforts, derided her. Yet momentarily, despite herself, she heard in his words a reminder of the Bernard she had once, though briefly, known.

— Then I shall begin by asking your reason for bringing me here.

— Sentiment.

Lavinia gaped at him. He sat in a padded leather seat, jacket unbuttoned to display a vast breadth of stomach stretching the fabric of his waistcoat. She had known him as a fat man and often pathetic in his clumsiness. But now each movement, far from being clumsy, suggested a miracle. His leaning forward and placing his arms on the desk, thus, took one's breath away. He smiled a voluptuary's deep secret inward smile.

— Do sit down Lavinia. It seems an unspeakably long time since we were together. Help yourself to some brandy.

She chose a settee forbidding in its boxy shape and spotless linen covers.

— Are we to grow mawkish? she snapped though the prospect seemed unlikely in such impersonal surroundings, comfortable as the settee turned out to be.

— This is my bedtime, he remarked, offering her the compliment of an intimacy.

What could she say? She thought about her imprisonment, the waste of years, angry that he should have power to rob her while here he was, incapable even of standing on his own feet.

— I am no longer who you think I am, he added.

Lavinia could believe it, as she did pour a drink, indeed she could not doubt it. His presence was astounding. Set among sterile comforts, he exuded magnetic power. She sipped the fiery drink and sought release in a small painting on the wall nearby. She tasted a sensation rather than a flavour. The artist had chosen a Melbourne street scene in rain, people balanced on their reflections, and dim misty buildings painted with faith in the gospel according to Turner.

— My favourite, he exclaimed softly.

— Is it my painting of you that you want?

— How stark the room looks, the way I see you judging it. Yes, you do me good, Lavinia. I've no business living in ordinary surroundings. That's what you are thinking, isn't it? My advisors are so respectable. Don't imagine the blame can be put on Dorina either. Dorina seldom comes here. And when she does, she wears the same expression as you.

— Is it my painting of you?

He spread his fat hands, revealing another miracle: that he too had ten fingers. To show their uses, he then linked them over his stomach. She responded tactically, crossing her legs, exaggerating her comfort. And turned with possible impertinence to stare at his litter, that highbacked wooden seat mounted on long carrying poles, which might have been an uncomfortable relic of some ritual soon to be forgotten. The door opened, admitting no one, and then silently closed. But Buchanan was too quick to let the intruder escape.

— Owen, he called. Come in, come in. You haven't met our delightful Lavinia Manciewicz, I think.

The door reopened, hinges smoother and more silent than when she had used it. A pale cherub hurried in, his dainty steps silenced by the carpet. Lavinia deflated with relief: it was not Luigi Squarcia, whom she dreaded meeting in these circumstances.

— *There* you are, he responded as if surprised to come upon them. I had no intention of interrupting Your Excellency, he simpered. Charmed, he said to the woman, throwing the small jagged rock of his acknowledgement at her. I thought I might not catch you before you retired to bed.

— Quite right Owen. This is the indispensable Owen Powell. Sit down, man.

— I'm sure I have no wish. . .

— Sit.

Powell swept a distressed hand across his balding head as he obeyed; the gesture startled Lavinia who recognized it as one of Buchanan's mannerisms. She watched shrewdly. In her estimation, this diminished them both.

— Does the odour of prison offend your sensibilities old fellow? the fat man enquired, brutal with joviality. Don't be put off. Mrs Manciewicz wasn't cut out to be a criminal, he became earnest. She is as respectable as you are, he beamed maliciously. And it will do you good to meet your victims once in a while. You should be interested, he lowered his eyelids momentarily. To be frank you could find yourself in the same disgrace one day, couldn't you? Anybody with your power is automatically under suspicion. Only the clods are really safe, he held up his hand taking an oath. To be serious though, how do you think you'd cope with prison? The dirt, the confinement, lack of privacy, sexual assaults, those things?

— Well I. . . if I deserved. . . by, for example, failing you. . .

— Damn it man, take me seriously. Don't come this lapdog bullshit. Mightn't you even squeeze out a little anger against me if I did that to you after all your loyalty?

— Oh I'd be angry, yes. . .

— So. By putting you in prison I am in the wrong, am I? The atmosphere of the room was lowered ten degrees by the terrible present tense. Powell, in his alarm, became more cherubic than ever.

— I assumed you meant my private feelings, not my public loyalty.

— There we are, Lavinia. Now you might begin to understand why I have brought you here at such expense to the nation, so my righthand man can confess that his private feelings do not accord with his public loyalty.

Owen Powell hesitated nervously. Then his clever little eyes of a soft woman turned to look at her for the first time. He smiled.

— I see! he announced.

— Perhaps you don't, she retorted nettled.

The room crackled with tension. Fiery alcohol churned in her blood.

— This is so much fun we must do it more often, the president laughed till his chins bobbed around. But the noise and the physical action seemingly had no connection, were simply coincidental separate phenomena.

— To hell with the consequences Lavinia, he announced. Let's have that walk after all, bearers or no bearers. He rang a bell. Owen can run the ship while I am taking my pleasure. We won't collapse into the chaos of anarchy during the next quarter of an hour, will we, Minister?

Harvey Noel & Co arrived. Without waiting for instructions, they heaved him out of his leather chair and supported him. Like an infant holding his parents' hands who suddenly lifts his feet off the ground for the delicious sensation of hanging, he swanned round to the litter.

— We are going for a tour of the grounds, he explained to them. Come along Lavinia. You may talk freely, he invited as they moved out into sunshine. The fellows won't mind.

He and she set off, carrying nakedly such memories as they had in common, over lawns by the acre, toward a copse of European trees.

— You have changed, he began in a new voice stimulated by the breeze in his hair.

She felt the insolence of this and declined to comment.

— Did we ever wander in a park? he asked, knowing they had not, while his bearers walked before and behind with practised even steps (minding their own business, wearing the sombre but impersonal mien of undertakers who avoid disturbing the solemnity of a funeral, on one hand, or presuming to have a part in the grief on the other). How long were we together? Was it only that single night? Ludicrous in relation to a whole lifetime, for one night to have any importance at all. It wasn't two, was it? According to Squarcia you had been with him six months by then. The wheel turns, Lavinia, whether we like it or not. I always meant to ask you, now neither of us has anything at stake, what you thought of going to bed with a fat man. Is it really so bad? You have to understand: with the question of state protocol and all that, my personal life is over. I am a public citizen and a full professional. I don't even think of women. But I do wonder from time to time how to evaluate the past.

The oddity of Lavinia's sensations struck her forcibly. Having woken up, still in jail, still subject to the humiliations of a prisoner with lower status than a criminal, only to be issued her clothes back, flown out privately, and invited now to stroll in the gardens of the presidential mansion, with the president himself gliding beside her, his head at just the usual height, as if he had no lower limbs but floated up to the waist in some lubricating element. She felt overcome by vertigo. The powerful scent of a daphne bush perhaps going to her head. Sudden hungers sucked the strength from her. She could not feel her own legs. Possibly she, too, floated legless through a paradise of no beatings and bewilderingly beautiful foliage. Sunshine poured between the trees in a dazzle of patterns tantalizing her artist's eye. Was he holding her hand to steady her? reaching out from his highbacked wooden chair to recover the innocence of those days when he simply made money for a living? Brandy burned inside her. She breathed the intolerable joy of freedom. The angry words she had spoken since arriving here flew twittering away, lightwinged and elusive. What had she said, indeed? Somewhere out in the world stinking piles of laundry bowled down chutes to be pulled apart and fed into machines, gates would be clashing, somewhere out in the world battered-faced women cooked stews of vengeance sitting on the very seat she had warmed while they defined the limitations of each other's power. Somewhere Tim took a telephone in gentle hands which had not been held for four years and spoke briskly into it, reporting reporting, while colleagues watched, listened, waited for him to make the mistake that would put him with her behind bars. But rising sap in the trees fountained to exultant limits, dancing in the light high above. There was no word for such anger becoming an exuberant celebration of release.

— Why am I here? she asked, and it seemed that he had already allayed her fears.

— Because, on the spur of the moment, I took it into my head to ask your advice.

Then she knew she was ill. The jet flight, so sudden a rush of speed, a closed car from the airport, the fierce spirits cutting her open all the way down to the hollow of her hunger, garden perfumes, so much brilliant sunlight. She would be sick, for sure.

— Any time I want your painting, he added. It is mine. How foolish of you to imagine I would take the trouble to bring you here if my needs were a simple portable object.

Even so, his voice came to her gently after the flat plastered voices of prison with their buff-painted rigidity and harsh corners, came to her garnished with birdcalls she had forgotten. Of course she'd never liked him.

At night stupid rabbits, mesmerized by the beauty of car headlamps, stay on the road a second too late: a second being enough. He took her hand, drifting along effortlessly, tugging her lightly as a tide. She had to adjust the length of her stride to be comfortable. And this when she, possibly, could not even stand. A bed of flowers blazed at her. Naturally she had known he was married. How could he ever get the idea she had taken him seriously as a lover? Call it desperation at least. Herself of an age when she could well believe in failure and Luigi saying, to make them both laugh, this fat man will soon be the fairy at the top of the Christmas tree. Till the puffy doll patted her with hands strange as warm fish, drunk though he was. Can you, Luigi added with an apology which she correctly interpreted as suggesting she should make use of her opportunities, keep him till tomorrow morning? I'll come for him then, he had added in case his message was not already perfectly unavoidable. Later that night the visitor sobered up enough to see this for himself. Lavinia had undressed without the least shame. What shame should she feel? It was her future she must look after. As long as my fingers don't touch him, she promised, I shall be all right. Sure enough, he did all the touching needed by his gratitude, big brachycephalic skull travelling shortsightedly over her body before coming to rest between her breasts. Then the hideous contortion of his lust; reared up on stiff arms, back strained while he drove himself to couple with her; the belly, prodigious even then, an obstruction hard and unfeeling, making any intimacy a quest, a valiant labour. Finally his excitable coming, erratic and brief as a schoolboy's, evidently all he could manage because he collapsed to one side so slicked with sweat and reeking she feared he might have a heartattack. Flowers, too blurred for her to identify, glared red beside the path. She had said to herself, now I know what falling from grace means. This was immoral. Once done, the act became inexcusable. She lay tense and calculating while his open palm (curled back-to-front like a stage villain sidling up for money) crept towards her thigh, pudgy fingers waggling in an effort of playfulness. Her jaw locked. She hung on to her nerve. Give him a few moments so he won't be too hurt, she decided, and escape. Mustering her reserves of courtesy she lasted long enough for him to tire, even of this minimal effort. Released from his attentions, she slipped out of bed into the bathroom. She ran a bath, never mind the hour, and emptied two sachets of bathsalts. She heard him call conceitedly. Are you all right darling? and plunged her legs into the too-hot water. She watched a bright red waterline appear across her thigh. This was good. She sat gasping as the bath cleansed her. Saved. She found strength to soap herself and then lay in the water until the heat evaporated. I did it, she said triumphantly, I did it. And what she meant was immediately clear: she had sacrificed the last stronghold of personality to her art. As an experience, the fat man completed her initiation into carnality. He might also one day, incidentally, lift her to fame. Oh yes, much as she might regret it, art was not enough unless fame followed. Now, she told herself, I shall go and stretch out beside him and be nice. She feared he would be offended, feel unclean. So she went to reassure him. How could she have so mistaken the impact of her washing? Glowing and exuding perfume, hair damp as a sensualist's, she brought with her an irresistible melting headiness. He grabbed her wildly. This time it was his hairiness more than his fatness which repelled her. With odious salivations and a shocking indifference to hurting her, he wrestled on the bed and heaved himself on top, his hands devouring her hot skin and his lips among her privacies. She fetched desperate breaths and dug her nails into his shoulder. This, this was what his life had lacked; this was the love filmstars simulated in suntanned narcissism on the screen. Again, he was quick in the discharge of his duty. But his exhaustion achieved an air of conquest. Previously he had tried to suppress his heavy breathing in case he sounded unfit, but now he wheezed and rumbled theatrically, so confident was he of having proved himself.

Lavinia reached for a flushed pink treetrunk: steadied herself against it, the smooth wood warm in her grip. The bearers stopped and brought Buchanan swaying in more gracefully and purposefully than he might have managed by himself. But they could not rescue him from self-importance, from plonking his hand on her arm with blatant faith that this would heal all anguish. She shook him off, not caring who saw. She set the aircraft motors whining in reverse, unwound the sickening rush of speed, she escaped from the stuffy car into green grass, she quelled her stomach's rebellion.

— Lavinia, he murmured.

— You have denied me the sight of trees for six years, she

hissed savagely refusing to relax her grip on the least particle of stored-up rage.

The hurt in his eyes was genuine. *Had* he denied her? When he agreed to her arrest there was no mention of never letting her see a tree. Merely accepting Owen's advice. She must understand this, surely? The safety of the nation had to come before all else.

— Has it occurred to you, he asked. That I too am imprisoned? That the private Bernard Buchanan is shut away and never let out. That I am only ever and always public property? This moment together is my first release too and I've been locked in for eight years. I can't act or talk as a private man. I am even denied the human necessity of sleep. This moment my loyal bearers are closing their ears, just as they close their eyes when they lift me on the toilet. But I don't ask for your pity, do I? I don't load you with my resentments.

Again he took her arm between finger and thumb, sliding his hold down to her wrist. She tried to shake him off but he held her more firmly. Lavinia struggled to break free. He pulled her towards him, the bearers bracing themselves as they stared stonily in the other direction. Desperate, she lifted her arm towards her face and bit his hand.

— Aah, he sighed with pleasure but did not let go.

In the distance they heard a telephone ringing across the lawn. It stopped. He released the arm as if giving her something she might not know how to use, something perhaps a little too fine for her, and raised the bitten hand to his mouth. His eyes smiled at her above bared teeth, the old yellow teeth of a hippopotamus. Then he sucked the bite marks, lips wet and red. Perfectly anticipating his wishes, the bearers began to move forward again. He swayed in his chair ruminatively. She surrendered to inescapable duty and walked beside him.

— What do you really think happened between us? Lavinia asked her shoes she had not seen for years and which felt like somebody else's. Thinking: my feet have changed shape.

— It's never the same thing, he replied obliquely, defensively. Some firetail finches caught them up and fluttered bossily into a flowering shrub, picked among the twigs, and flew out again in confused unanimity. If I have precious illusions, he cried of a sudden. Why should I need the truth?

— You must be the only person left with illusions, she responded watching the lead bearer step forward on to a gravel path without betraying the least sign of comprehending what was passing between them.

Buchanan wanted to know, naturally, what life was like out there under his thumb. He had not thought to discover. Perhaps he was too powerful to expect the privilege of being able to be told. Lavinia, uniquely, had power over him. She had indeed. This gave her the strength to risk honesty. He regretted his outburst and acknowledged her rebuke by leaning back in the uncomfortable chair made to his specifications. He watched treetops pass. Her walking became a little more companionable, which the bearers observed without looking and took into account. So Buchanan swung along at her pace. She must be made to see his need.

— I only ever wish I was thinner, he began again. When I feel the urge to pretend to be someone else. Being unique is a pain in the neck. How can I go into the street and say I am an Eskimo or a Spaniard? I'm restricted that way. I'd like to stand helpless at the corner of Pitt Street and jabber a bit of Urdu and see how people would look after me. If I came that caper as myself, they'd run a mile, you know it's true. But of course, he shot her a sidelong glance. The fate of foreigners is not my real interest. It's what a foreigner's experience would reveal about life in ordinary Australia.

— We are on the brink, she replied. She could see a payoff for her sacrifice. She went to bed with him as the ultimate surrender to her art. Now, quite properly, even inevitably, the essential interdependence of art and life, art and politics, was being demonstrated. She'd thought she would bind him to her as a patron with power to give, and discovered he was bound to her as a petitioner with needs she might possibly turn to the benefit of the whole country. Even imprisonment seemed, momentarily, a justifiable price for such power. Buchanan was not merely a despot, he was her despot.

He made as if to pet her arm again, but the distance between them had grown in an instant too great to reach across. He converted the gesture to a public display of his wound and then carried her teeth marks once more to his thick moist mouth. Besides, kissing his own hand did not displease him. Instantly the moment was deep with threat, the carrying chair smooth as a camel ride developed a hypnotic motion he must fight against. Were they doing this to him deliberately? The plunge out of sunshine into dense shadows of a transplanted Europe, the nine pairs of feet working gravel between jaws. Back in the mansion the nation might be falling; that missed phone call a signal, or a last-minute warning. Buchanan glanced over his shoulder, as if to set eyes on the telephone, unintentionally meeting the glazed look of bearer Malcolm (the name came to him unexpectedly clearly). Glazed with what possible hatreds? A look denying all personal contact, the stare of a being whose function depends on the absence of independent thought. What was to prevent Lavinia, berserk with revenge, drawing a knife and stabbing him to death? Even if the bearers were loyal, their hands were full. Had she been searched when she was admitted? Possibly not, on the feeble excuse of prison security being too tight for her to have armed herself. But what of the aircraft crew, car drivers, guards at the front gate, his own personal private secretary half dead with the all-night hours. . . any number of suspects to equip her for the satisfaction of an undeniable motive. Why, indeed, was Harvey heading for so dense a clump of bushes? Assassins with guns could easily hide there. Or (and again he glanced back to see, also partly fascinated by a second look into those blank eyes to impress upon himself their blankness) a sniper on the house roof, steadying, himself quartered in the telescopic sight. This time the eyes were not blank in that sweaty red face. They were looking right at him, not presuming to smile or reassure him, but surprised into an interrogation which might equally mean: Am I jolting Your Excellency, or Are we carrying you too far beyond bedtime?

— The brink? he said as he swung back to confront Lavinia with her unfinished reply.

— Yes, she seized the opportunity. The anger against you, the frustrations of poverty, unemployment and lost pride have driven us to the brink.

Assassins watched him from behind leaves, dense angers. His gauze skin kept nothing out. They were moving him along so fast he froze in the breeze of their going.

— Us?

Courageously she nodded. This time it was she who reached out to him, reached out with her honesty, her hope that maybe he was not fully to blame. She dared to think of him as the man she knew and not as the politician he had become.

— Bernie, she said past the obstacle of her sufferings, the nausea at glimpsing his lambkin incontinence. It's all going wrong.

— The people love me.

— They used to.

— They love me.

— How could they? You can't know what life is like out there, the heyday of thugs in uniform, a whole new economy based on informers and bribes. You began it. You have to stop it.

She waited for him to explode with anger, that anger so well known, the towering incoherence of his phrases making perfectly clear how he felt.

— This sounds like Dorina without the piano accompaniment, he joked lamely, coldly, discovering he did not wish to know what he might have learned disguised as an Eskimo on a Pitt Street corner. I never grant favours, that only makes enemies. There's no mistake about it, he added a few moments later following a private line of thought. The American space program is a cultural event. All military events, he considered further. Are cultural when you come to think about them.

— People sell information, have you been told that? Sell each other? Dirty information. Innuendo. The whole tragedy.

Still the bearers rocked him smooth as a camel, their camel eyelids drooping, broad camel feet placed fastidiously flat, one then another on the gravel, damp smells seeping from their clothing, necks swollen in the painful grip of respectable collars, huge shoulders bulging submissively. Why, thought Lavinia, don't they simply dump him and leave him here, helpless as he is? What crazy pride is this that measures its achievement in terms of surrender?

— Did you ever think, he proposed in a richly presidential voice. Of appealing to me for a pardon?

She thought: What if there were an assassin hidden in these bushes, or a sniper on the roof of the mansion? Then he'd get the truth, straight through his brain.

— No, she replied.

The bearers' shoulders grew huge with budding wings, the swanwings of medieval angels.

— Why, you ask, did I take it into my head to want you here? Once, years ago, he explained. You invited me to lie on my back on your studio floor. Remember? Being an engaging chap, I obliged, even though my suit had been recently dry-cleaned and your floor was none too hygienic. I obliged. This is how I want you for your portrait, you said. But is that how I appeared in the portrait when you painted it? No Lavinia, it is not.

Buchanan shot a look at the back of Harvey's head to be sure he was not listening, as if one glance at his ear and the evidence would be there. Lavinia had become impatient for the crisis: where could such a ponderous preamble be leading?

— You painted me naked and looking out over a field of smashed glass. Point one. Let me also remind you that Luigi covered up for you at Roscoe Plenty's morgue of a dinnerparty by saying this was your prophecy for the future. Point two. With Bill Penhallurick there I wasn't admitting a thing at the time, naturally. Even though you were upset by your sister's protest, you made no attempt to deny this. Point three. Are we clear so far? Ah-ha, now you begin to understand who you are playing with? Let us proceed to the next step. I put you in jail. No one else was to blame, no one else had anything to do with it. Owen Powell is a puppy when it comes to real life, let me tell you. He does what he is told. And so he is as close to me as a son. An obedient son, he added fleetingly thrown off his point by a recollection that he did in fact have a natural son, wherever the dope might be. Since you forecast a future in which all that is fragile and precious has been trampled underfoot by a man without anything of his own to offer in return, a naked man, a man lacking even the gift of energy, a recumbent figure smiling his slothful smile. . . you see how closely I looked into your work, how I appreciated your skill, Lavinia. You were quite wrong to dismiss me as a philistine. Please do not trouble to deny anything. So now. . .

Stepping between avenues of flowering exotics, breathing the perfume of loving care, Lavinia understood helplessness as a symbol of power; saw how potent his impotence was, brought out in public like this; how in secret his crippling disability would be pathetic, whereas such bragadoccio obesity, such monumental fragility appeared so stupendous even enemies were dumb with admiration on seeing him lifted and carried by his slaves.

— So, he continued still sonorously presidential. Tell me what comes next.

— There seems no way to be rid of you, she flashed at him with the anger of rehearsal. Our one hope is that you'll fall ill and die.

— Even that wouldn't kill me.

He laughed. The more he re-presented this cleverness to his mind and presented it again, the wittier it seemed. Even that won't kill me, he said a second time, tweaking the third of his four chins flirtatiously.

Now she could see what he was up to! The more powerful a man grew, apparently, the more he hoped to be pitied as well.

Noticing how aged she was, he took something like satisfaction in having a preview of her future. Incredible that the eager young painter of ten years ago should become so worn a woman. This was his own doing, as he was not too squeamish to acknowledge. But the coarse skin, slack features and ruined hands, these he had not expected. Were his jails factories of change, laboratories of epidermal decrepitude? He played a moment or two with the diverting insight, successful experiments, a pending Nobel Prize for Medicine.

Again without signal, Harvey Noel & Co responded. They sensed the woman had fully supplied the insight he craved, a glimpse behind the façade, a new image to silence all trace of sniggering, so the angels took him floating across lawns back toward the safety of telephone crises, back from the wild margins of Kythera, ripe (as if he were the female and she the male impregnating him with the seed of her experience) with new purpose. She had reassured him by restoring his roots in mediocrity. But the truly mediocre, as his intuition comforted him, do not see themselves as mediocre at all. Only an exceptional mediocrity like himself can accept his nature despite adulation, despite having millions upon millions of citizens under his rule. The rocking camel-gait gave place to flight, an intoxicating instability, the sensation of riding thermals with a chance of suddenly being dropped. He did not look back to watch his mistress of that one night's redemption plodding in their wake, still bowed under the volume of anger she thought to crush him with.

Lavinia stopped. They had gone, the nine of them, vanished into a shady porch. The glow of sunlight on the dictator's bald head had been put out. And was she the fool, she asked, for hurrying after them? Being alone. Yes she found, here, that haven longed for so desperately; no one to harass her; no one even watching or apparently caring where she was; no one shouting, judging, or hitting her. Alone, for the first time in years, and sunlight to be breathed, great distances of sky to be looked into, the patterns of leaf-shade to dazzle her. Sure, there were sentries patrolling the far small end of the drive, plus a secretarial woman upstairs in the mansion with her back to the window, leaning against the glass so her brown dress stuck to it like a slug: but they ignored her. Yet at this longed-for moment

Lavinia's pleasure was undermined by a nagging dissatisfaction that freedom was only the outward show of her irrelevance.

Never mind, she shrugged, enjoy it.

. . . Gipps is gone. That stiff little man pushing his cart-load of parsimony everywhere he went, seeming to be perpetually battling up-hill, his empty hands held just before him. But in his view, reward for no work was as immoral for himself as for anybody else.

Count Paul de Strzelecki, a Polish adventurer who has made several useful journeys of exploration beyond the land already staked out for sheep, brought mirages of plenty to the Governor's office in the first months of my employment there. Gipps insisted I should be present. He hated and feared private meetings and always made sure to have at least one independent witness at every interview. I, with my flayed back still erupting in sores and my mind a clock of whip-strokes, had been privy to the true barbarity of European civilization because no man hesitated to shed his carapace of moderation in front of a convict, no one hesitated to show the raging beast he kept hidden from his peers. Who was I to be trusted with the Count's secret?

Strzelecki, after much prevarication and show of nervous excitation as well as disapproval of my presence, announced that he had discovered a gold-field in the Bathurst district.

Governor Gipps (who was not my father and owed me no loyalty whatsoever) asked me what, in his shoes, I would do. I confess that, being brought so close to surprise tears by his trust, I replied I would be lost, because in anyone else's shoes I should implicitly follow the advice of the Governor. He did not smile. He shot me a suspicious look. Even so, he turned my reply upon the explorer as his authority and voiced the request that this discovery be kept secret. Kindly pledge me your word of honour as a gentleman, he said, otherwise I fear the serious consequences which, considering the conditions and population of the colony, are to be apprehended from such a discovery.

Sir George could not understand greed any more than he could understand generosity. . .

Lavinia strolled along one side of the house, each step an assertion. She luxuriated in the sponginess of the lawn underfoot, the smell of crushed grass. At the quiet sounds about her, her eyes filled. But what if some security guard were to catch her, as he might put it, prowling? This would undoubtedly be a serious offence. She glanced at the rooftop, realizing any sniper there would more likely aim at her than at Buchanan. She walked slowly now. Soon she would have to return the way she had come. If she *had* been released from jail, let them say so officially, let her not live in hiding, plagued by doubts.

Abruptly, as an afterwake of the president's swift departure, she swung round to hasten indoors toward whatever fate awaited her, even if (as she half-expected) it was the fate of being forgotten. And found herself confronting Luigi Squarcia. How long he had been standing soundless, observing her from a distance, she could not tell. Lavinia expressed her shock as action: she marched toward him.

— You, she accused. Are here to escort me back to the car I suppose? Do you wave goodbye to enemies of the state when you put them away? Do you even bother to ask if they are enemies of the state at all?

— You and I, he replied remotely, not moving to approach her. Live in different worlds now. I would never presume to speak as a person with rights to your confidence. Let us accept that that is all past. You are not the woman you were. Nor am I, he added gallantly. The same man.

As she drew near, he suited himself to her pace and they walked together. Lavinia remembered his height and the feel of having him there, his manner of tossing up an open hand of fingers like a sudden spring flower to express some thought he did not care to put into words. He was ostentatiously suntanned, exuded a hint of scent and, as always, had left one flaw in his shaving, a small patch just under the jawline near his right ear, the only evidence of his defective eyesight. That scrubby patch gave her daily, though she had never let him know she noticed it, an intimate compact with his body, endearingly independent of his vanity. The effect of his immaculately tailored clothes was spoilt by a touch of sensual vulgarity so many women, herself included, found challenging.

In a flash, Lavinia knew something so clearly terrible her tear ducts shrivelled and her eyes hardened in a fixed stare which the least movement might crack like stone: she had been jailed to spite Luigi Squarcia, to prevent his being able to enjoy living with her. The reason Bernard seemed unable to grasp how grievously he had injured her was that *her* feelings never crossed his mind. . . and all he saw was that through her he had been able to score over Squarcia just for once.

70

Tim grew older and brittler, simply and uselessly older, preserved from serious trouble by prudence and ingenuousness. He had been no more able to keep from visiting Lavinia in prison than to commit a crime serious enough to warrant being locked up himself. Where his articles were too outspoken against the system, a kindly sub-editor toned them down. Always at the one desk, he ceased to be noticeable. The accountant who was Owen Powell's informant on the payroll regretfully extracted a file from the Active Suspects disc and transferred it to Inactive Suspects. Tim's entry on the dossier in the main Ministry for Internal Security memory bank ended with the comment: Thought to be concealing detailed background data on drug dealing implicating well-known individuals, however several searches (refs: 22917853 B and 25896473 Gii) have not yielded concrete evidence.

One morning, when Tim arrived at work just after ten-thirty as usual, he was amazed to find the newspaper's owner, Lady Penhallurick, last of the Neilson family who had founded it, standing beside his desk, idly glancing through the work in his In-tray. She habitually trailed her plumpness and nose-blowings round the building, addicted to the atmosphere of news-gathering and deadlines, the cigarette smoke, the beer-desperate eyes glazing as faces exhausted of responsibility peered at visual display units with a mixture of cynicism and creative pride. But she confined her friendliness to the executives and senior editorial staff. She was rather afraid of reporters. She had never spoken to Tim directly in all his years as her employee. Yet now she glanced up at him with the fractured familiarity of a hostess whose guest has risen late for breakfast.

— Where's that pretty young woman who sits next to you?

— She has been ill for weeks, Lady Penhallurick.

— It's serious then, is it? I ought to send flowers maybe? She has been with us quite a long time.

In her agitation, she spoke rather too fast, distressing herself by not seeming able to finish her words properly.

So, Tim thought, you have been eyeing off our Stephanie, have you? And there could be little doubt, observing the old woman's vivid colouring at this moment, that she had more than business interests in mind.

— Do you see her, ever? Lady Penhallurick added, turning

away as if this too-long contact with the lower ranks might count against her in some future managerial decision. Give her my best wishes. What's her name, she asked, but was unable to stop giving herself away by blurting out. Miss Grierson?

— Not any longer, Tim said with a tinge of malice. She married a Dr Head. She is Stephanie Head these days.

— At least, the owner rallied enough to comment faintly and wholly without humour. She has a doctor in the house.

Tim thought it wiser to say nothing of Luke's arrest. Instead, he plunged into a course of action he'd despaired of ever finding courage to pursue.

— Lady Penhallurick, he declared suddenly, hoarsely. I have been hoping for a chance to tell you something confidential. May I take just a moment of your time?

— Certainly not, she retorted, one hand reaching anxiously for the other and then submitting to the comfort of having its rings checked and twisted round. The Chief of Staff would be most put out if I allowed him to be bypassed. I have people paid to deal with your problems.

— This is not my problem, but yours. It has nothing to do with the *Sydney Courier*.

— What can it be to do with then? her querulous tone forbade any further intrusion on her goodwill; but she had so little self-control, she added. My husband?

The fear she had dreaded ever since she married her dear rogue got its claws into her and shook her. She could not, like Dorina Buchanan, call on resources of pride and courage sufficient to meet a catastrophe. She wasn't that stamp of woman. Alice often said of herself she was too warm for her own good.

— Not here, she whispered pleadingly. Come to my office in half an hour. She produced a handkerchief and blew her nose peremptorily to conceal any nervousness. Then, trembling in all her pudgy excesses, hastened adrift, fingers fluttering after elusive solace, imagination afire with horrors she had not even known she knew: court cases, gambling crimes, faulty buildings.

71

Whispers solid and sinuous as reptiles coiled round Dorina's ankles, tripped her, and slinked their cold chainmail around her throat. The grand piano itself opened a threatening cave. Needles of poison glittered and danced in her eye from the black harbour outside. She banged her head dully against the bullet-proof glass. Rory was away as usual, this time at some camp or other. But no, she, Dorina Lambert, would not, was never going to, so far forget herself as to submit, nor ever be seen taking leave, to use a common misconception, of her senses.

The security man on night watch in his plain grey suit took root near the stairway, concentrating on seeming not to be there at all. Haberfield, he said his name was, Lionel Haberfield.

— Mr Haberfield, she began, voice emerging at a silly pitch and feebly. Will you consent to be my audience? I am to give a concert of Franz Schubert. Not the songs, though, she apologized. Unless you. .? Perhaps?

72

The day arrived when Luigi Squarcia was informed that if he wanted a private audience, bath time was all the leader could afford. He was, it seemed, to be spared nothing. But his suavity being in no way diminished by experience, Squarcia took this in his stride, arriving promptly and strolling round the large room with its square sunken tub. For security reasons there were no windows, but the bright morning plunged down through a skylight, to remind him, vaguely, of somewhere. He had been sent ahead to make himself comfortable in the deckchair set ready.

— Good God, Lou, the president cried jubilantly as he sailed into view. You've suddenly become middle-aged.

— We can't all escape reality, he responded casually.

The team of bearers, having deposited their precious load near the edge of the bath, began the ritual of undressing him while he so revelled in obeying their instructions, lifting one arm after the other as he was told, Squarcia's barb passed unnoticed. He leaned back for buttons to be undone and forward for garments to be hauled free. He squealed with babyish abandon. Plainly he looked forward to this. And every so often shot his guest a glance calculating enough for Sir William Penhallurick.

— You know something, Lou? he mooed tragically. My problem arose the day I realized I could unsay anything I'd said and it would make not one jot of difference.

Item by item the supports were peeled away, his tailor being in large degree responsible for the near-human shape he wore in public. Anarchic flesh flapped loose.

— I could declare myself a revolutionary against my own state, he explained with impulsive delight at the discovery. And the entire herd would about-face to follow the new official line.

They stripped him from the top down. His collar being removed, dewlaps sagged to his chins, and these in turn spread to bury his neck. Waistcoat and shirt gone, his special zip-up underwear, stiff as a corset, was unfastened in panels and taken away as shopkeepers during his childhood had unhooked clattering wooden shutters at this very hour of the morning to reveal goods displayed behind. The task completed, four bearers supported him in a standing posture while Harvey, as their senior, wrapped a tent of bathrobe round his shoulders to prevent him catching a chill despite the suffocating heat.

— I always behave as if there is no one out there, came his cossetted voice. And quite right too. Until they have the gumption to make me feel something.

Petulantly, the president shuffled forward, toes scraping the tiles in a parody of walking.

His gorgeous ballooning form wobbled and dimpled to the brink.

— Unless there's a reaction from people, he seduced the company. Like a boot in the pants or a kiss on the arse, I shall continue to believe they are not there.

The robe hung open, so Squarcia found himself an unwilling witness to that sulky member lost in the scrubby neglect of a cave overhung with calamities. The soft ponderous mass of thighs and calves were pinched painfully at the ankles tottering down broad steps into the bathwater.

— I know, Squarcia observed. When I am made unwelcome. Though it does not happen often.

Buchanan was concentrating too intensely on his exploratory immersion to reply. Down he went as they lowered him, one caution at a time, till fully in, the bathrobe having been expertly slipped free to hang from a waiting stand for when it might be needed again. In the hothouse light his skin took on an unearthly pallor, heightened by ghostish foreshortenings underwater. The bath had been equipped not only with rails all round, but with a suspended harness on which he rested the back of his head. He was ready to enjoy himself.

— You are mistaken, his voice boomed up from the depths of

gratification. The fact that you have not been here before is a sign that for some time I have been rather disappointed in you.

— Then I am back in favour?

— I decided you should come today, Squarcia. Because too often I have had the feeling that you do not see me as I am. That you see me, perhaps, as an imperfect substitute for the man you thought you had created. Am I wrong? Oh, you have always known the difference between a bullet and a metaphor. Of course you have, and so I treat you with greater respect than anyone else. You are charming and casual. You've never embarrassed me once since that first meeting when you proposed a diet and an acceptable tailor. I recall your exact phrase, an acceptable tailor. This was the one thing I liked you for. You gave me an occasion to respond naturally. The moment I screwed up your tactless suggestions and gave them into your hands I gave myself into your hands also, for the duration of the campaign. But how is it that even now you hide your feelings? You're looking at me as if you feel no disgust at all. What must I do to bring you back to me if my poor sinking shapeless body is not enough to arouse pity, or shock you out of treating me as an object? his voice had developed that rich edginess of a lover's.

— I came to report progress at Port George, Squarcia responded with icy composure, sitting once again in the deck-chair (he had risen from obligatory respect) and crossing his legs elegantly. You are to be congratulated, Your Excellency, on the efficiency of the whole concept. Having the labourers housed right on the spot, so to speak, and men eager for work. The foundations are already complete. It looks as big as a city. I was astonished quite frankly. The American engineer is all praise for the way we get things done. Some of the equipment itself is to be built into the structure as it goes up. And this is the reason for my report today: they are requesting an army escort. A couple of cylinders arrive from Germany next month.

— From Germany? Why from Germany? Can't we manufacture them ourselves?

— Not since you closed down our steel mills. The point is that, being so huge though at the same time high precision stuff, the nearest port facilities capable of off-loading them safely are at Newcastle. So we've been asked to guarantee transport by road.

Abruptly the president raised a wet hand for silence. Without trying to screw his head round to see, he ordered the bearers to leave. Out of loyalty they hesitated, then obeyed.

— They were right to be worried, the great man observed. They know a thing or two about this carcase of mine. Now, what are the cylinders for, did you find that out?

The question came hollowly.

— The most I know is that IFID is thought to have broken away from the main thrust of US and Soviet thinking on defence, the so-called Space Vigilance Systems.

— So, they're going on the offensive again?

— Whatever this is, it's something altogether new.

— We've had a taste already with the tidal wave, the president sloshed his bathwater playfully. More tidal waves? he proposed.

— Not now they have a base of their own right on the coast, Squarcia joked.

Buchanan boomed magnified jollity. His body sank to the bottom of the bath and spread even into the corners. Only his laughing head, held up by the harness, remained dry, neck stretched to show he did have one after all.

— We'll cooperate, he said, suddenly weary.

Hovering steam began to clear from the water and the walls glistened damply. Buchanan gave thought to IFID, wondering, as many dependent third world leaders did, what life would be like without a hungry superpower to satisfy before looking to the needs of his own people. He habitually used that phrase, the needs of my people, without the least idea of elderly women who could not afford to heat their rooms on a winter night or citizens fully occupied in voluntary spy networks throughout the suburbs, to mean his own free hand at pleasing himself.

— I can't float like other men, you know, he admitted.

Silence.

— So, if anyone wished you dead, Luigi Squarcia measured his words. Now would be a heaven-sent occasion?

— Try it, the leader tempted him with a wicked smile.

Promptly, Squarcia slipped off his shoes and socks and rolled his immaculate trousers to the knee. He descended the steps till he stood right behind the cradled head.

— Are you there? the question gonged between tiled walls as the swishing was heard to stop.

Fresh daylight poured down through traces of evaporating fragrance and into the water. Squarcia placed his hands one each side of the untouchable face. Warm dry capable hands, hands which had once captured a foolish old woman, packed her collapsible limbs, and bundled her aboard an ocean liner for her homecoming to a ridicule she, in her happiness, despised. He took that solid head filled with raging dissatisfactions. His fingers communicated calm. At length, when their heartbeats grew less agitated, he lifted the weight gently from its supporting halter, frazzled ends of coarse hair scratching at his wrists. Very gradually, Luigi Squarcia did as he had been invited and lowered the object to the water. Neither participant uttered so much as a sigh. Their concentration on what they were doing together was absolute. The tide of warmth crept up Buchanan's nape and flooded inlets behind his thick ears. The perfectly level line of it was an advance of rising comfort drawn in an elipse round his cranium, a reminder of Physical Geography and a teacher whose chalkdusted knuckles passed in loops across the blackboard, filling it with God's-eye views of hypothetical mountains and then translating the contour lines to a horizontal elevation, a case of theory made marvellously manifest; the power of recording converted back from mystical circles to a mundane drama of slopes a man could fall off.

Luigi Squarcia felt the jaw under his hand begin to move. With that palpable silence cellists use before launching into the complex sensualities of a Bach suite, the voice prepared to speak and then spoke.

— In most countries people grow rich by producing something.

The opening theme hung, complete as a remembered icon.

— But in this wonderful Australia of ours it is not necessary, nor even usual.

Already the counter-theme suggested impressive ramifications. Squarcia held the head. He kept the words themselves from drowning. The moving jaw had set myriads of tiny ripples playing over the cooling bath, fluttering against the rim with remote gossip of their own.

— Foreigners think the quintessential Australian business is sheep farming.

Even the unshakeable Squarcia felt a shiver down his spine at the whisper of that quintessential across the already trembling liquid.

— Not true, the cellist touched his C string. Nor uranium mining. It is real estate. And I was good at it. I have an eye for land and an eye for houses. I made a lot of money. But I never produced a damned thing. You know that? You may have wondered about my crazy inland trip. What possessed me to dream of driving to Paringa? You never asked, though you once told me to learn my lesson from it. Yet this shows the difference between a businessman and a politician as clearly as anything can; I couldn't bring myself to sell a block of land I hadn't put my own value on. Does that sound too simple? It was a habit of mind I was powerless to shake off. So, if you ask what made a politician of me, I have to answer: the fact that I've grown too fat to go and see for myself.

The instrument gathered momentum, his words flowing together, rhythmically persuasive, melodically seductive.

— If I have had one guiding principle during these two terms in office it has been that in the management of money, business and politics share no common ground. Politically, money is nothing more than promises. That's a fact. It's not paper money, nor bank transfers. It's not even computer print-outs.

Water touched Squarcia's fingertips as he held the shaggy head.

— Whereas business is nothing but money; and promises don't mean a thing. Always buying and selling, always on the move. You see; take real estate again, there's no limit to our lust for this land, with buyers and sellers suffering the one fate. They cannot stay put for more than a couple of years at a stretch before they've got a craving for something nearer the beach or up in the mountains or closer to the shops or farther from the airport, somewhere with a warmer climate or somewhere they can escape the heat. The real estate market is the best image I know for business in general. And when you come to the point, people are not looking for a place to live so much as a place to die. It's like musical chairs, pure lottery. Another of our addictions. That is why they're so jumpy. Because when they find what they're looking for, they don't really want to rush into that final test of suitability.

Squarcia, who had survived innumerable traps in his time, simply offered a polite snort of amusement. He listened to echoes, again reminded of a past not quite graspable. Therefore he grasped the head more firmly. This being a signal in itself, the president spoke again.

— I had an eye, he boomed quietly. For land and an eye for houses, as I said, but I also had an eye for people: another talent useless to the politician. Politics has nothing to do with people.

The morning sun strengthened, the skylight lay printed as a golden rhomboid high on the western wall.

— If, he began afresh. Some agent, perhaps of a rival or even a foreign power, had it in mind to assassinate me, this would be the cleanest way. No joke, he convulsed with a shocking bellow of laughter. Suppose my head slipped out of the halter accidentally, due to a quarrel, nothing more lethal than a disagreement, what do you think, how could any man hope to haul my weight up out of the water? He'd get splashed, he'd get soaked, he might climb right in, but he'd be excused for failing to rescue me. Hard to get a foothold in a slippery bathtub.

— Were you, Squarcia offered at last, and soothingly. Offended that I never showed an interest in your background? Though naturally I found out about your father the school inspector and your Presbyterian mother.

— Dorina came to me as a clause in a deal. Imagine that. A deal I did with her father. You could say I acquired her as part of the property. Oh, I wanted her, don't get the wrong idea. I was crazy about her and I still am. Would you believe it, I only have to mention her name and my old fellow under there begins to perk up. I can't see a thing down that far but I can feel it. Clarence Lambert was sick to death of toting her around, as I understood the situation. But he had no sooner got rid of her on me than he died of a stroke. He set out to have his big fling, the fun he'd hankered after all his life, careful diplomat that he was, safely retired, free of encumbrances, and bingo! he was down for the count. Kicked over the traces and kicked the bucket into the bargain. I laughed like a drain when I heard. Plus all that money I'd paid him falling straight back into my hands via the lovely daughter.

— I came to tell you, Squarcia said quietly. That IFID cannot promise to support you at next year's election.

— She had tone. Still has. She's a lady, Dorina is. Through and through.

— You've been very lucky the coup in Tuavaleva was successful. That lets you off the hook as far as the Pacific weapons base is concerned. Also, I am authorized to tell you they're satisfied you are giving Project 31 appropriate priority. But, to be frank, they do not endorse your trade policy, they want to see much freer speculation on the dollar and closer consultation in areas where our two countries are competing for the same market.

— Freer speculation, the president spoke in a bright clear voice. Being, I suppose, a mealy-mouthed way of saying they are demanding to buy further into the country on crippling terms, giving them yet more fingers in our economic pie? As for the election, that can only present problems if I permit one to be held at all. The day any election presents me with an inconvenience I shall do away with it. Temporarily, I need hardly add, nothing to deny people their democratic illusions for too long.

— General Merasaloa, Squarcia explained, still holding the head steady and forcing the man to listen. Having done you such a good turn, finds himself in an embarrassing predicament.

— No bastard will speak to him.

— The White House would like to back IFID, but America is too big to take the plunge first. That might do more harm than good.

— Say no more. I shall not disturb my bath worrying about tomorrow. When I come to a decision you'll hear from me.

The vast submerged body heaved and settled again.

— What a fascinating story about your wife. Did she resent being sold with the property?

— You don't imagine she knew! her purchaser's derisive harrumph thundered round the steamy walls. She'd die of boiling blood.

— It was a deal between gentlemen, said Squarcia who understood such matters perfectly.

The rhomboid blazed above, enigmatic as a symbol from another culture.

— Lou, Buchanan began again, this time wooingly. What if I asked you a favour. . . as an old and trusted colleague?

The emptiness made no promises.

— Be a good fellow and push me under.

— Am I allowed to *hold* you under?

— I don't like you to sound amused.

— How else should I sound? Squarcia asked of the echoes, knowing this must be a test if not a trap, because he discounted any possibility that the leader might suffer from either a tortured conscience or lack of nerve.

Without further warning President Buchanan convulsed, wrenching his head free of the sustaining hands and sliding deeper into the bath. Scarcely a splash. His face went under, those wild eyes still staring at chaos even through a wavering lens, cheeks floating wide. Bubbles poured from his mouth and nose, to burst at the surface with spooky chuckling. Squarcia reached down in his own good time, grabbed a fistful of hair at the temples, and yanked it up again. He was not unduly rough, but he made no effort of respect either. He frowned, more from annoyance, or perhaps disappointment, than alarm. With the efficiency of a person trained to this duty daily, he lodged the streaming head on to the halter. Buchanan gasped and choked, retching perfumed water, his eyes now closed under lids laced with tiny creases of pain. Water leaked from his nose and ears, hair lay plastered sideways across his scalp, like one of those sad old men who cultivate the naivety that they can save themselves so simply from decay.

Fists banged against the doors and muffled voices outside conferred in alarm. Squarcia listened as he dried his feet and legs (had some emergency system been triggered?) and sat in the deckchair to pull his socks on. Michelangelo knew a thing or two about the difficulty with damp skin. Or was it Raphael? Some countryman of his anyhow. Those bathing soldiers caught naked and vulnerable in the exertion of struggling back into their equipment.

Simultaneously three entrances were flung open. From two of them, squads of bearers and Watchdogs rushed in. At the third, Owen Powell, not yet decided whether it was advantageous to be seen, stood framed.

Without opening his eyes, stricken and waterlogged, President Bernard Buchanan spoke.

— He meant to drown me.

Harvey and Noel raised him gently and, as others joined them to support the vast torso cascading suds, swathed him in folds of bathrobe. Sleek and purified, he surveyed his subjects from the almost standing position with a dignity possibly not seen since the first *homo erectus* discovered such tottering nobility to be his true mark.

Owen Powell, unable to conceal how he exulted in the fall of Squarcia, stepped forward to be counted, a sophisticated private recorder whirring in his pocket and arms outstretched as if for an embrace. Then, because he knew he never could expect permission, turned his gesture on the traitor instead, merely switching his hands from welcome to repulsion.

— Do not attempt to escape, he warned with memorable impressiveness. I have suspected you all along.

Squarcia mopped at the wet sleeve which appeared his chief concern as he replied coolly.

— Then how is it possible, Minister, that you had not guarded against this contingency?

— Exactly! the drowned Buchanan fired, snapping his eyes open and baring yellow teeth, huge visage glazed on its plinth of crimson towelling with a particularly barbaric effect. Exactly, Minister.

The curious fact was that no one yet thought to restrain Squarcia. He stood apart and at ease.

—What would you say, Lou, the president boomed in the room grown cold despite a warm rhomboid morning slipping down one wall. If I pardoned you?

The space filled with draughts and flutters, with hands, empty hands suddenly itching to lay hold of a victim, while starchy clothes rustled protests and boots betrayed the clocker-hoof evidence of shifting balance.

— You have nothing to pardon me for, except refusing your foolish request to push you under, and for cracking an even more foolish joke about holding you there.

Buchanan, victor of two elections, scorer of a brilliant six in his only adult attempt at cricket, the man whom Prince Haupoupou had been so unwise as to snub, shouted with merriment. Broad paps rose and shook, arms swelled and his whole flesh hardened, slipping as a mammoth cake of soap, so that his helpers had the devil's own job keeping hold of him and preventing him keeling over in what might have ended as a fatal accident indeed. The wet wan face flushed bright as the gown, droplets spun off his hair, and his fingers clawed impotently to gain a purchase on emptiness.

It was Owen Powell's turn to be stricklen deathly pale. He had given himself away and made a most dangerous enemy. How was he never able to keep pace with the mercurial moods of the leader he idolized?

— Clear off, Lou, the president conceded with a truly grandiose flourish of one arm. I shall call you when I am ready to continue our fascinating discussion. Now, he snapped at his loyal subjects. Get me out of this humiliating gear and dry my head while I think what to do with you all.

73

Sir George Gipps did not always find himself trailing after the tiresome Buchanan, he had family duties as well as public. Often enough he joined the crowd clubbing together round a most receptive subject, a journalist woman said to have made a hazardous marriage. He kept circumspectly to the fringes, being punctilious even in his indiscretions: for this was not a legitimate descendant but one of the blood nonetheless. He made a few surprise acquaintances there too and looked forward to the occasional attendance of the balloonist Joseph Montgolfier, from another branch of the family, with whom he played courteous games of paying back the Frenchman's broken English with his broken French.

— When asked if Australian history can be summed up in a single sentence, he said flatteringly. I have often answered yes, it falls wholly within the era of human flight, thanks to *les frères Montgolfier*.

— You make not mention, Montgolfier objected on one such occasion. Of the families we are to be allied wiz in the presaunt generation. Soon will come to us the Aborigines and we must learn how we speak to them as we speak to one anozair.

— I have the honour, Sir George Gipps admitted later when his modesty had been somewhat whittled away. Of having been first to bring colonists to trial for shooting natives. From that day, only, did they officially become human beings according to the law. The outrage against me was diverting, you have no idea.

— Then I am thinking you will be a hero and a famous man among us when it is their time to come.

— *Non*, Gipps replied. *Heureusement, mon vieux, je suis oublié*.

By this time they had drifted well behind the other stragglers and could only just pick the blond head of their descendant on the far side of the street. A phalanx of cars and buses roaring between, she hesitated outside the *Sydney Courier* building, torn by doubt. Should she present herself for work once more, or go slipping home to the suffocation of Mama's padded silk house and her own obsessive curiosity about the Wild Dog?

She went in. But as she did so in that distracted frame of mind, she collided with Lady Penhallurick who was rushing blindly out, hand already raised to attract the attention of her driver dozing in the limousine parked by the opposite kerb. Gipps and Montgolfier had just begun rising up to float away (without needing the mechanism of a hot-air balloon these days), so they stamped on the car roof as they passed to startle him into service.

Stephanie Head and Lady Penhallurick did not recognize each other.

. . . *What a thing is public opinion! Public opinion would have it that you, Father, are a highly respectable, upright nobleman. Well, we know how deep that goes, you and I. Public opinion would brand Sir George Gipps the worst Governor this colony has ever had, too mean to offer his*

Legislative Councillors so much as a cup of tea when they call. Mr Buchanan, who is among the loudest in his vituperation upon this score, appears conveniently to forget the weeks of his recuperation in that stricken house, growing ever fatter on government stores and discommoding Sir George by occupying his private parlour.

The newspapers are scandal sheets for the most part. The Sydney Morning Herald *of today carries a disgracefully spiteful piece gloating over Gipps's ill-health and cheering his departure as the single welcome action he has taken during the entire eight years of his administration. I should not at all mind knocking a few heads together to teach them better manners, even if better sense is beyond them.*

I am neither dead, Father, nor dead to social values. Too cowardly to murder me, you used the power at your disposal to kill me by a long-drawn death in irons. Do you begin to see yourself? Do you enjoy what you got off me by these measures? Do you begin to see my life through my own eyes? I believe you will have every reason to fear death when you are called to account before Our Maker. . .

74

Luigi Squarcia, having changed his spoiled suit with the damp sleeve and trouser legs, roused his guest of the night before, asking her to be ready to leave in ten minutes. Then they drove together through streets where grey citizens stood dumbly in queues while helicopters rattled close overhead.

Next, he was observed at a certain rooming-house on an upstairs landing, a key on its ring dangling from one manicured finger while he hesitated for dramatic effect, knowing this could not go against him. Lower down the stairs were two security men in hats, who accepted that his hesitation had nothing to do with them, that the histrionics were entirely for the female's benefit because she showed no sign of weakening. If Squarcia expected her to break down or make a display of relief or even admit what power he had, the expectation would go begging. But the fact was, he did not expect any such thing, his taste in these matters being more subtle than rapacious. His gesture was to provoke her, simply, to participate. Her stolid waiting one pace behind him sufficed: he could feel the anger of it, the vulnerability, yes, the torture of her hopes. This was what he had come for.

Thus he was observed, mid-drama, not only by her and by the security men, but by a fourth person. From the next landing down, Mrs Marcia Connor, dedicated as ever to civic responsibilities, had them beautifully framed in her peephole. She calculated the handsome man's air of unlimited power, his face no older than when he was a regular here, a daily, not to say nightly, visitor. She took in the shady creature in her dated frock, lumpish and stubborn behind him, too. (Now *she had* aged.) The security men were out of her restricted sightline but she'd checked them on the way up and recognized why they might be needed.

— Will you do it? Squarcia turned to his companion, offering her the key.

She showed no sign of hearing except to shoot him a glance in which the full force of her complex personality concentrated to something like heat. Her hands hung passively at her sides. She might also have been listening, picking up some sound too high for his ears, a sound she already expected but he had never imagined existed. She made no move to close the gap between them, gave no indication of even recognizing where they were. He smiled very slightly, a smile his face appeared to resist, so she understood how deep was his satisfaction at this moment; she understood it was a drama she had come to take part in, his drama.

— Lavinia? he asked again on behalf of the key. And then, the lack of an answer deepening his pleasure, he himself thrust it into the lock briskly and flipped her studio door open.

The door swung inwards on a past so intense they felt it as a spasm, unequally shared. The room stood brilliant with daylight. She had dreamed of it just so, but not of having to look past Squarcia's tailored shoulder to see in. The quality of window-glass was what stopped your heart, faintest green at the edges, imperfect panes distorting the light along several lateral bulges so subtle only years of intense observation allowed one to see them there at all. The very frames too, so exactly known to her, startled her like living voices.

He saw the furniture: those shabby pieces he had lounged on, a chair in which he'd held her captive of his tenderness, forcing her head back against its cushion by the strength of his neck, the shoddy rug they'd used more than once on a hot night for their naked games. He had, of course, no distaste. Heavens, he'd been through genuine dangers in genuine slums to get where he was. Far from it, these objects were quaint toys dug out of a box stored under the house years after use. A grown man may acknowledge the childishness of his teddybear while declining to repudiate it, so Squarcia cherished the simplicity of those years before the republic. What a lad I was, his gesture said, as he waved her in before him; waved her in (it might be thought) impatiently, as though she ought to have more concern for his memories. And Mrs Marcia Connor down below, remarking this impatience slight as it was, squinted tighter, in full agreement.

— You lead the way, Lavinia said ambiguously, tartly, meaning this as a comment on how he viewed his whole life.

So he went in. He took a turn round the studio, glanced through open doors to the bathroom, the bedroom and an empty kitchen cupboard, the whole place laid bare for inspection, scrubbed clean as might reasonably be expected of paint-spotted floorboards and splodged walls. He smelt disinfectant and the cleaners' disapproval. The paintings hung where they always had, untouched; her student still-life, her industrial landscapes of Wollongong, inscribed drawings and prints presented her by fellow artists, also the portrait of Bernard Buchanan as a fat nude on a bed of shattered glass. Squarcia took a good look at this picture and once again his face resisted showing satisfaction. He squinted back to where Lavinia still stood at the top of the stairway, a drab woman whose angers were superfluous, still clutching her prison bag of the possessions restored to her.

— Do you imagine it means a damned thing for you to be considerate, Luigi? In jail, among all the brutalities of that rotten place, I was shown kindness more than once by people who know what kindness costs. Kindness from them was precious. And that is something you wouldn't even know about. One day, she ground her words in the mill of fury. Your past will catch up with you.

Squarcia gazed outside. Down below, the poky backyards appeared less cluttered than they used to, but even grubbier; rubbish littered the lane, a newspaper puffing to balloon shapes and collapsing with tormented shudders against a wall.

— I have changed, she concluded.

— Not a scrap of food in the place, he remarked over his shoulder, reaching out to place one ringed finger against the glass. Allowing a pause for effect, he swung round with a possible joke on his lips, to discover the doorway empty.

A terrific shriek ripped through the quiet building, a thumping on wood, a man's guttural shout, and the bang of a door loud as a gun going off. Squarcia was not in the habit of running but he moved fast. On the next landing down, he saw Lavinia, arm upraised holding that cheap bag transformed to a weapon, rectangular and solid, heavy with the weight of oddments inside, metal corners sharp. This arm had been pinned to its gesture by one of the security men embracing her from behind and smothering her objections with his other hand. While Squarcia watched, she fell forward against the door, borne down by the man's weight and letting out a sigh of hatred. Her case clattered on the floor and broke open, the contents so tightly packed they dropped out like a sandwich. The second security agent put them back with a remarkable show of delicacy and clipped it shut, while the first apologized and helped her up. When she saw Squarcia watching, her face still wore its loathing of Marcia Connor.

— The woman, the second security man reported touching his hat. Just opened her door to come out.

— Was it your business to interfere? Lavinia raged. And now she ran stumbling up towards Squarcia, straight past him, her bag clubbing the corner as she rushed inside and slammed herself into the bedroom.

With the very slightest nod he indicated to the guards that they were free to wait at the car for as long as it took him to reappear. He then entered and latched the studio door behind him.

In the privacy of loneliness, Marcia Connor sat, convulsive and jubilant, to recover her breath, not knowing whether to laugh or scream, really.

75

— A matter of grave concern. Utmost importance to us all in the, ah, long run, said the famous man now grown quite twiglike but keeping his toothbrush moustache trimmed as it always had been. He smiled deprecatingly; the moustache bristled. His famous eyebrows, bushier than ever though he was now bald, worked wildly at the problem of getting an uncomfortable truth in regimental order.

Delegates sat, row by well-padded row, silent with the effort of learning how to treat a serious matter which appeared to be beyond any question of immediate self-interest.

— No room for doubt, he quavered. Unfortunate fact of life. Trustworthy team.

He faded back from the microphone, feeling behind him for

his chair and guiding his body into it as if helping some dotard altogether more feeble than himself. No one applauded.

A spokesman for the firm of researchers came briskly to the lectern.

— I am tabling a draft analysis, he droned and, still talking, removed his spectacles to rub sore eyelids. It was not possible to have the edited material in your hands prior to the session, regrettably, he continued and, surprised at the authoritative sound of his own voice, opened little china eyes. But let me assure you of one thing: there can be no doubt about what is happening. Every take-over bid and every merger involving major stocks has now been put through our computer. This is to say, covering the past ten years. He replaced his spectacles. I give you just three sets of figures to consider: 52% and rising of the gross national product is currently paid out in interest on foreign investment. As of this moment 87% of all foreign holdings, this includes holdings in New Zealand of course, have been bought by companies which we can trace as subsidiaries or fronts for Interim Freeholdings Incorporated of Delaware. Industrially speaking, then, IFID holds an estimated 45% equity in the whole.

The famous man, the man whom Luigi Squarcia once chose as having spotless (*immacolato*) respectability and distinction (*potenza*), groped for the microphone again. But, having anchored himself to it, he in fact said nothing further. He would have spoken except that he was struck dumb by the hammerblow of wondering whether he might not have been gullible in his beliefs all his life.

— How much constitutes actual ownership of Australia? came a voice from the body of the hall.

This triggered a barrage of questions,

— Does it need to be 50%?

— For effective control?

— Won't everything depend on how the position is used?

— Would it be 35%?

— Have they got us already?

— It depends on the international exchange rate.

— Exactly. And they are the ones keeping our dollar down.

— Didn't we put the economy on the market? Why are we squealing?

— Can you supply evidence of how they are using this power?

— Does it need to be 50%? Could it be 35%, for instance?

— I don't know, the researchers' spokesman came to the rescue after his own cautious fashion. Control might have changed hands already. Many factors would need to be examined.

— But with 50%, one questioner persisted. They must have absolute and effective ownership, surely?

— We don't know, the researcher replied. Frankly we don't. I suppose there may be *political* tactics left open: trying to take the dollar off the open market, tariffs, restoration of powers to the Reserve Bank, constitutional gambits, nationalization, I can't say without conducting an adequate study.

Inconspicuous among the delegates, Sir William Penhallurick, whose own companies remained notably untouched by the stock market raiders, offered nothing. He darted a few sharp glances at the speakers as their hands went up, and took refuge in extreme old age to appear dead already.

76

— Insomnia? Dorina repeated quite abstractedly. I know you suffer, Buchanan. Also that, in this respect at least, I don't. I'm not unsympathetic, but I do deplore having my nose rubbed in it. She looked up sharply, meeting herself in the mirror. And tried the speech out again. Insomnia? I could care more for your sufferings Buchanan if you showed the least concern for everybody else's. Do you not realize we're in a depression, with the whole nation collapsing about our ears? The mirror indicated this version would never do. Dorina sighed and stared round the empty room. An empty room, as she described it, full of junk accumulated by the Governors-General and their wives in a desperate bid to find out what was nice, after all. The poor dears had Buckingham Palace breathing down their necks and setting an unbeatable standard of vulgar opulence. She knew the rumours, rumours of her eccentricity, her lapses of memory, queer behaviour, rumours of her going mad. Yes.

— Your insomnia Buchanan? she tried the mirror again. Have you ever thought it might be a moral rather than a medical condition? That there might be no cure other than for you to change your ways? It's little use my saying I know the good you have in you. Isolated as I am in my house, I cannot help but hear things have gone wrong. The mirror seemed to approve of this a little more, though still not enthusiastically.

— I blame IFID entirely, she began again but acknowledged the impossibility of such an opening and dropped it.

— I blame myself entirely, she said and the mirror gave her the go-ahead, she was on the right track at last. Your insomnia is plainly the result of sensitivity. Yes, the mirror agreed, yes. Not until the people are secure once more and prosperous as they used to be will you sleep easy. Isolated as I am in my bunker, I still find out a good deal of what goes on. And this is why I've come, to suggest something rather daring to you. Right, the mirror agreed, you are going well. A reconciliation with your political enemies as a fresh start, an effort to cooperate to rescue the economy. Umm, the mirror doubted.

The door swung open and in floated her husband on his litter. Dorina had not finished with her hair but she left it, dangling across one shoulder, to rise and kiss him. Sometimes she was genuinely pleased to be back in his familiar ambit and this was one such occasion. He chuckled delightedly.

— Insomnia! she declared. You look indestructible to me, and flashed a victorious glance at the mirror. But I have to say I am worried about you all the same.

He looked at her enquiringly, surprised, affable. And this so took her off-balance she could not recover the harsh truth she meant to tax him with, could not find it in herself to assume the role of an advisor requiring him to change course. Dorina, had she seen the truth of it, had lost some spark. Her style survived, but not its focus.

— I want to ask you seriously, she went on. If you have given thought to St Swithin? It never rains but it pours Buchanan, she explained twisting her escaped hair and pinning it on top of her head with unthinking expertise.

For a long moment he considered introducing the subject of her mental health, or, as perhaps he would call it in his kindness, the evidence that she appeared to be suffering nervous strain. But her eyes met his in so alert a manner he retreated to a safe commonplace.

— Shall we see you at lunch in half an hour then? he asked, not only disappointed at having been fobbed off with one of her esoteric conundrums but perhaps also genuinely stimulated by the great occasion before him, the distinction of being used again as an IFID front-man to help carry their empire a stage further, and in more comfortable circumstances than last time.

— That will depend, she replied returning to her mirror of

memories, to the hard sheen of truths she'd not been able to utter. On whether I can bring myself to stomach the show.

— You never let me down Dorina, he granted warmly.

— Then clear those snoops out of my house, she retaliated grasping her meanings while she could. Isn't it enough to have them infesting the terrace? Must they watch me go to bed as well? And believe me, there is a great deal of pain beyond these. . . unforgivable walls.

She watched him in the mirror, floating among the impassive bodies of his bearers, huge head raw as a sculptor's maquette, the clay slapped on in profligate dollops awaiting the refinement of a shaping touch. Their unenquiring rows of faces, ranged just above his, concentrated on some intuited signal which would soon grant them leave to escape witnessing a possibly embarrassing scene. Certainly such dangerous doubts about the stability of the regime must cause them qualms if they ever gave thought to the likelihood of being closely questioned by some interrogator intent on learning what they knew but kept hidden beneath their professional discretion. His nose changed colour several times: no other evidence of reaction was granted her. She watched his wordless mouth. The chaos in his eyes she knew well and had known all their married life. Then, abruptly, at no visible sign, the bearers received their permission and swung him round to float out the door. She observed his immense back, appearing as a pile, a remainder of some event, the dense inutility of form built of rubble fallen from the space round the head, much as mountain slopes may be built of landslides rather than rock strata massing upward. He had no neck. His head sat in a rancid cushion of flesh. You could even imagine the skull to be quite average once extracted, cleaned, and measured.

A faint odour of male sweat reached her.

I remembered! she told herself, gathering strength for the impending ordeal. I warned him clearly this time, so he can never say there wasn't a single person with courage to speak the truth. And his silence proves that the truth hit home. He knew already but he dared not face it.

77

. . . *Mr Buchanan, the Governor said acerbically. Had you been in the colony a mere two and one half years ago, you would appreciate more fully how ill-informed your own statements are. His Excellency went on to point out that far from being a stay against the independence of landed settlers, his had been the administration under which the Act of Government came into effect, allowing a degree of elected representation. What is it you want, Mr Buchanan? he demanded crossly only yesterday. The complete overthrow of order for the sole sake of gratifying your appetite for power?*

Meanwhile I, Father, listening from the side, recognized something I had known since childhood without ever realizing I knew it. This Buchanan who haunts Government House is the very type of an oppressor, though an oppressor as yet without power. He has not grown up. The mark of the school bully is still upon him. He can never be satisfied because he does not know what adult satisfaction is; the more he gets, the more spoilt and agitated his behaviour. He has no vision; without vision there is nothing by which he may measure satisfaction. Whatever might be done for him he accepts as his due and immediately takes up the next complaint.

Sir George, crusty with correctness as a seahorse, is absolutely a man. When he talks of tradition, he speaks from the authority of independent vision concerning matters he acknowledges as far greater than himself. Whereas, when Mr Buchanan speaks of tradition, he sneers with the fearfulness of a child who truly believes he is the centre of the world and the absolute lodestar of interest throughout all his acquaintance.

At this moment I am looking out upon the gravel drive of the new Government House commissioned and completed by Gipps. Beyond, the great harbour of Sydney lies like a dish of bright coins. The welcoming garden-party has already begun despite the previous Governor's ship being not well clear of the Heads yet. Lieutenant-Governor O'Connell is here by the oval lawn distributing greyness. I cannot doubt but that he has already written to Whitehall, a letter being carried in the same vessel as his predecessor, urging the new Colonial Secretary to take advantage of such unforeseen good fortune and secure his inestimable services by removing the Lieutenant from his commission. At present he is receiving Messrs Wentwroth (let that slip of the pen stand) and Boyd, but they are too ecstatic to be greyed, and there Mr Buchanan joins them, laughing like a cow in pain, which puts a strain on the buttons of his Sunday waistcoat.

What on earth is this to do with me? you will be asking, as another who must be at the centre of everything. It is to do with you precisely because this is what you will be thinking.

I grant you that, unlike Citizen Buchanan, you would not hover on any fringe. Unthinkable in a man whose family has been chronicled for eight hundred years, but the hollowness is the same. The moment the

Governor's visitor fell through the floor and lounged for inconsiderate weeks haunting the place, I knew him in a flash. His behaviour was as familiar to me as my old hobbyhorse and bells. Sir George once said: I can't make that fellow out. Thus I was able to reply: I understand him thoroughly.

I have one further item to add.

This morning, when I took my leave of His Excellency, he treated me quite coldly. Thank you for your loyalty, he snapped, seeming unwilling to find the least merit in my service. You and La Trobe, in your different ways, are the only two men who have never let me down. He did not bother to shake my hand; but when he reached the outer door, he realized some gesture was still lacking, I suppose, for he turned just long enough to say in the same forbidding tone: Your entire history, so far as it goes, has always been known to me.

There you have it.

The ship has cleared the Heads. The signal has come back to the quay. I know this, without looking, by the cheers of the cretins down there. Even at this distance their jubilation may be heard all too clearly.

I shall not correspond with you again. My manhood has been restored to me. I am no longer your son, not even in name. I owed you this only: the chance to be shown yourself as you are and what you, among others, have had done in your name in this innocent country, filling it with blood and the suppuration of needless misery, spawning Macarthurs of greed and Buchanans of emptiness, transplanting so successfully, after a mere fifty-eight years, barbarisms never known here before.

The crime, Father, lies not so much in the barbarisms themselves as in what they exemplify: a failure to live up to the great and humane richnesses of which European civilization is capable. For a beast to behave like a beast is scarce worth comment, but for a man to behave like a beast is unpardonable. I leave you with one more article of information: another little happening, another twist of the knife.

Upstairs in the music room above the office where I am writing this missive, Mlle Clorinda Lambert, a visiting concert artiste, is practising the pianoforte. She is not a guest in the house; she comes purely for the instrument we have here. I asked her this morning about the composition she has been finding so great a challenge that she cannot leave it alone but must perpetually petition for extra time at this, one of the few good pianofortes available in Sydney, to battle it out with the notes. The music, a long piece, has for days sounded formless to my ear. Notwithstanding delicious fragments, it is turgid and sporadic; the product, Mlle Lambert tells me, of a new German musician named Robert Schumann, who is at present 36 years old. The same age as myself.

Thus, listening to what he has achieved, I cannot help but indulge in contrasting our lives, his and mine, the productive and the enslaved, he from the middle classes and I from the aristocracy. Until this hour the music puzzled me, but while I have been setting down, at last, what I long wished to write to you, the harmonies convey a perfect good sense. In its awkwardness and its clarity, its hesitant rhythms and surges of passion, this music is a journey. Not, as I began to think, a journey through some narrative poem or landscape, but a journey through Herr Schumann's understanding of how a man may love and may face death.

I, too, hold my head up, for I have faced death and I have been blessed by love.

There, even as I put this to paper, the music stops. I am left with my thoughts: one might comprehend how an ancient culture could perpetrate atrocities in the colonies if it were not also capable of continuing to be fruitful and produce such music. But this Schumann, whose father is of a generation with my father, shows the atrocities for what they are. He has understood that silence is no longer to be endured: evil must be called evil to its face.

So I have written to you, at last, and so I end.

78

At 12.30 pm Owen Powell was ushered into the presidential study wearing a uniform specially designed for the occasion, clinking with metallic importances, the stiff cloth inducing a swagger, cap clapped under one arm in approved officer fashion (he had just passed inspection by a military attaché), and bearing a missive from the US ambassador. At this period, as Bernard Buchanan well knew, practically all essential functions of state in America had been sold by tender to commercial enterprise. Such missives, then, inclined toward advertiser's jargon.

— Stand there Mr Powell, the president bellowed genially because, having grouched his way through a morning of disagreements brought on by the upset to his routine, he'd decided the compensations of a sumptuously inventive banquet must count for a good deal and that he should begin cranking up an appropriate cheerfulness to do the occasion justice. *What* a sight, he enthused. What dignity. The proud Aussie peacock, is it? Never thought you had it in you. Come closer. Yes. Belt polished; is it a bit tight? Nice solid belly to hold in though, don't be ashamed of that, that least of all. Put your cap on, put it on, Owen, so I can admire the whole ensemble. No no. I mean seriously, I won't be out there at the airbase so I'll miss the best part. Put it on, man, and turn round while I take a look from all advantages. That's the show. My goodness, I wish it was me in the finery. Why haven't I ever thought of a uniform? I mean, they've done a first-rate job on you. Measurements perfection, just the right amount of braid, lavish colour, stars, medals, sash, lanyards, piping, studs and bits of glitter everywhere, sword. By God it's perfect. What *are* you then? What have I made you? A colonel, is it? Brigadier Powell? Must be a general for all that business on the epaulettes, red tabs and black mounting, the works. What is it you've become for the occasion?

— Marshal, Your Excellency.

— Marshal, that's the ticket. I remember. We didn't want the little general thinking he'd come among a mob of dills who'd jump at his first word, we wanted to pull rank on him. And the Armed Forces Chief of Staff objected to field marshal because you've never been on the field, never even been a private soldier, I hear. Tut tut Owen, even I was a private once a thousand years ago and wearing a khaki jacket I wouldn't be able to button up round one leg these days. Laugh, man, this is a great occasion. This is your triumph as much as mine or General Meraslalopa's, whatever his name is.

— General Merasaloa, the tyro marshal said syllable by syllable.

— No worries, I've got an hour and a half with nothing better to do than learn it off. Wog name, would you say Owen? Sounds good though. Sounds like a dessert with ice cream and pineapple liqueur in it. Waiter, two cream merasaloas please!

— He's a Pacific Islander.

— So am I. Now how are we going to greet him, this neighbour of ours? Here, pretend I'm the little fellow in person. The US bomber's door has opened, see me up on the gangway, pause, my nod of the head looks good on the screen, I'm coming down, Owen, by God I'm making a beautiful job of coming down, short legs but nifty, war-dancing develops the calves you know. Righto, we've hit the tarmac, I'm coming for you. Got it? Good, that's good Owen, I like the way you move, a bloody clockwork statue, lovely. Smile, Owen, quick, fire off a smile before he does, then the little fellow can't go away thinking they're a surly lot of drunks those Australians; steal his initiative, he doesn't know where he is or what's likely to hit him, he's fazed as hell and the Yanks have primed him up with a whole lot of indigestible statistics about us plus a pint of

whisky-sour and there's been a few bumpy passages of disturbance in the upper air, he's had to weather that, you must
remember. So where are we? Safely on the ground in a friendly
haven with a homely plump (you don't mind that, Owen, do
you?) military-looking man, positively oozing dignity, in a uniform richer and more tasteful than the old Prince Consort's, plus
a slight sway (see it?) to his tread betokening a history of
horseback escapades in the outback, holding out his hand (hand
out, out, Owen) and, miracle of sweetness, smiling hospitably
(smile!). Here, shake. You'll do me. That's the ticket. Nice firm
shake. Let's try it through again.

— With respect, Your Excellency, the Master of Protocol of
the Presidential Household has already rehearsed me over and
over again.

— Did he tell you to smile before the other fellow can get one
in?

— Not exactly.

— There you are! I might sack him tomorrow for incompe-
tence and then who will he be? I'm the one you've got to
please, not my flunkeys, right? We shall try it through again,
because next time will be for real.

— Before I forget, said the marshal making an effort to
salvage the situation by fumbling for the missive he had
brought and delivering it into Buchanan's own hand.

— What is it going to tell me?

Owen Powell stalled. If he said he knew, would that bring
him under suspicion of spying on diplomatic matters? Or would
it demonstrate alertness and the efficiency of his department?
He was not to know his blunder in the presidential bathroom
reassured the great man, who feared coups might prove contagious among cleverdicks.

— It, he risked. Apologizes for his inability, at the last
moment, to attend. You see, Bernard (he became endearingly
familiar sometimes when rattled), the general is expected to sign
both agreements, for the strategic base and perpetuating their
mining rights, for safety's sake, here in Canberra, tomorrow.
Nothing to implicate us, he hastened to explain. All quite secret
at the US embassy. Meanwhile the ambassador feels he should
appear aloof.

The president weighed the envelope in his hand, gazing at
the eagle crest. Then passed it back unopened.

— I shall take your word Owen, he said portentously. So you
may begin to realize how deeply I trust you. Now; once more

for the smiling handshake, then after lunch I'll slip in an hour's nap to freshen me up for the browsing and sluicing tonight. Though really, he confided. It's for gathering strength to face Dorina's disapproval.

This intimate scene, rather than Powell's unctuous performance filmed at the airport, was what he recollected that evening when he floated out into the reception room, his bearers wearing felt overshoes as they always did on the best parquetry. Here he would meet the general himself and conduct him into the banquet hall. Dorina stood to one side, looking magnificent as only she could, her long dress discreetly gorgeous enough for a royal wardrobe, strangled by jewels so that her natural awkwardness seemed a product of fortune. And General Merasaloa stepped into the vestibule, his briskness itself a proclamation of confidence.

Then they faced one another and the visitor saw for himself how grossly his host outweighed all descriptions of him: the immovable thighs on which his belly piled mountainous slopes to support the upper bags of a body seeming perpetually to slip back towards what lap was left, the full yet drooping forms not just of a fat man at his peak but a man who has been overcome by fat, the fat as a victorious parasite clinging to him, a human equivalent of rainforest sagging under the burden of prolific growths, even his face threatened by the fungoid rolls framing it, and wrists similarly weighed down by encroaching excesses so lush as to enfold hands which, though large, appeared in their setting positively dainty.

Buchanan in his turn surveyed the boy he must play host to, the boy with power not only to grant IFID rights to rare minerals but to let Australia off the hook. He knew why Paringa had been referred to as a provisional agreement pending expansion of possible arms installations. He knew also that this was the point at which he would have to stick or, to use a Squarcia-type pun, come unstuck with his own electorate. A mere slip of a Merasaloa, probably not above getting out there with a machinegun of his own and blasting into families of the slow-witted just to show his mercenaries what true fanaticism looks like, the boy doubtless ranked senior to himself in terms of the world arms race. At that instant, he saw something else, something he'd never thought to guard against. The general, eyes darting quick assessments, plainly discounted the posturing Marshal Powell and now, though with far more deference, discounted himself. He knew it as one does know such things, with a flash of recognition. Unmistakably the visitor looked elsewhere for the real power, the man he might have to contend with over rival interests, to Luigi Squarcia. So, the president's fear demanded to know, has Squarcia framed me, taken me unawares from obscurity and set me up as fall-guy among international thugs? Too late to mask the alarm that might have shown in his eyes, there to be recognized by the visitor as clearly as the visitor's own perception of who mattered and for what reason.

In the event, however, neither man cared to judge the other too harshly just yet. They were playing parts in a game far transcending this paltry arena. They looked upon each other with the special interest of two exhibits allowed into the one cage. They had not met before because Merasaloa's counter-revolution brought him to power since that unreported meeting of IFID heads of state in the Maldive Islands. Then at Tuavaleva it was his predecessor who had exchanged measured glances of this kind with Buchanan, who had snubbed him at the banquet, though outranked in the world stakes by Paringa, apparently content to let his islanders sink back into pre-microchip primitivism.

As for Dorina, she made up her own mind. She was introduced by Owen Powell, his ribbons aflutter, puffing away like a carnival train impelled by an irrepressible head of steam. She graciously acknowledged General Merasaloa, seeing him as an oaf with youthful delicate skin and killer's eyes. She had learnt the lesson of blood splashes on a sinewy ankle and knew what to expect from the likes of him. She detested him on sight and in the name of his defeated people. In that sneering vanity she saw the slow death of Ahmad Zain Osman and all his gentle kin, as well as the noble Prince Haupoupou. She recollected her first arrival on Tuavaleva as a child, how very surprised she was that the dignitaries embraced her and threw their welcoming arms around her father who had no notion how to respond. People untutored in nuclear power games, on a tiny hummock of land regarded for many years now as offering little an empire could wish to take from them. And she (standing to one side on that occasion also) had seen for herself their sweet disposition. They were the generation to stand in Merasaloa's path, no doubt. She detested him, yes, and was afraid of his bloodguilt too. This much she would grant, for what it was worth: he carried his power convincingly.

There was another aspect to her revulsion that evening. An

hour previously she had seen the dinner menu sanctioned by Bernard. So shocked was she, she called for the Master of the Table. I have become a vegetarian, she informed him, a convert to vegetarianism in fact. I know the change is sudden, but that is the nature of conversions. The point is, I shall require the same consideration as the Indian ambassador. To accommodate your staff, as well as helping me feel more at ease, I should be obliged if you would adjust the seating arrangements and place us together. Vegetarianism will, she joked tensely, give us a subject for light conversation. But seniority, he objected, the IFID representative, madam, he demurred. May sit, she retorted sharply, on my other side. She regretted it now, that asperity of tone, but the reason was simply desperation. She'd had to protect herself as far as was possible at this late stage. Why, why, she harangued her husband, why agree to such a travesty? Why, she dogged him, allow me to arrive from Sydney without any choice but to condone it by being present? You don't imagine, she demanded, I could stomach a single bite of such food? Bernard was all for placating her but, finally provoked, pointed out that she might have supervised every detail of the arrangements to her satisfaction had she agreed to give up her stubborn insistence on living a separate life. So it was left. And so, in an agitated state, she had dressed in her splendid gown and wound the strangling jewels round her throat. She blamed herself. Buchanan was such a child when it came to novelties. She would rise to the occasion as always. She was, the Master of Protocol murmured yet again, the only one you could completely rely upon never to put a foot wrong. Adding hastily, except His Excellency himself of course.

Dorina, making smalltalk with the distinguished visitor, answered a question in his own language, dropped it so carelessly and easily he darted alert glints this way and that. Really, she thought, he has the eyes of a disobedient pig always looking for a way out. I had the pleasure, she explained frostily, of visiting your beautiful island when life was less complicated than I suppose it is now.

The general recognized an enemy, face to face. He bowed gracefully from the waist, the bow itself extravagant enough for her to get the point, and when the time came for him to escort Dorina in to the banquet hall he performed this duty with dissembled charm every bit as credible as the charm of her response. They were to sit, fortunately, on opposite sides of the table.

Beyond the window, moonbright lawns padded softly among the trees: that huge ugly garden, so imitative, so (as she put it privately) Australian. Formless as if some naif had begun by throwing handfuls of potatoes to decide where the saplings should be planted. So much like peering into my own mind, she admitted, except that there I've grown just the potatoes and not trees. At the end of the drive, the lesser drive from a side gate, she glimpsed diminutive sentries crossing, their automatic rifles photographed in her mind at the instant they formed an X, a bomb target on somebody's map.

The thought of the banquet nauseated her. Lyrebird-tongue pâté and sautéed koala ears. (We are not normally so excessive, she had found herself explaining to a Filipino cultural attaché, in our nationalism.) Even the bland food she was eating in company with her neighbour toiled in her stomach at what she could see and smell. She caught Sir William Penhallurick's saurian eye, which blinked. She observed his scaly hand select a glass to sip from. The little band of virtuosi installed for the occasion finished a bracket of sugar-coated snippets from the semi-classics and took a break.

A treefrog positioned itself outside the window and, having been lured to the spot by Dorina's need for some real music, obliged with a serenade of penetrating chirrups. She smiled the only smile of pleasure to visit her all evening. But even this was tinged with distress at recalling another frog, of quite different species, offering her E-flats just too rapid for her favourite Mozart symphony, squatting as it had on the rim of her goldfish pond at the house where she was happy. Squatting, that is, before Rory came round the kitchen corner and threw a stone at it. The same pond was once squinted into by Peter Taverner's blue eyes while the pulse ticked in his neck.

Each setting, replete with five crystal glasses plus a private cruet surmounted by wattle sprays of enamelled leaves and yellow sapphire flowers, sat islanded in a shifting pageant. The tumult of real flowers could only be permitted a fleeting grace to display their dying for the occasion, replaced and replaced again by others with perfumes to complement the food flavours. Tamarillos and golden chrysanthemums added a dusty pungency to the budgerigar soup. And then were gone. In this ballet of the senses, the champagne sorbet was announced by vases of that dark brown boronia whose fragrance is known to carry far out to sea from the wildernesses where it grows so profusely.

Apricots, seductively downy in blown-glass bowls, witnessed yabbie claws demolished among cracking consonants and declarations of bipartisan goodwill; and so to the infamous lyrebird-tongue paté. Hardly had Lady Penhallurick settled to the task of checking her rings and giving her nose a cursory blast than down the immense length of the table frail delphiniums shimmered blue in the heat rising from the koala ears, each of which cupped a disc of pickled cumquat (Oh this, squawked the IFID representative sitting the other side of the Japanese ambassador but leaning forward to address his enthusiasm to her, is something else!) accompanied by the filling of fresh glasses with white wine tinted an elusive eucalyptus green. *What* else? Dorina raged in silence. Memories of the E-flat frog offered her a means of refuge. So she glozed the horrors of the evening with Schubert's last Mass, which she felt certain was also in E-flat major, the very well-springs of serenity, a declaration that guilt and conflict need not underlie faith. Her training brought its rewards as she relived a fragment of the *Benedictus*, where soloists emerge from the chorus to affirm how blessed is he who comes in the name of the Lord. How I wish, she said to her impassive neighbour on the Indian side, I could believe as a Christian. Then she conversed graciously of music to the IFID executive and the Japanese ambassador between them. Were they, she enquired, familiar with Igor Stravinsky's judgment of Schubert? The IFID man was, he thought, not. Stravinsky had been asked, she explained, could he honestly deny that Schubert's works sent him to sleep? Her listeners nodded heads filled with ambitions and marginal percentages. To which the genius replied: What does it matter, if, when I wake, it seems to me I am in paradise? Teeth cracked the crisp koala ears. Tongues smacked at the tart cumquat. Do you have conservation laws and wildlife protection? came a brave voice from among the guests to Dorina's right. Obviously we do, an enthroned Buchanan roared delightedly, as a civilized nation, of course. How else, he demanded, do you suppose we keep enough stock to supply a feast like this? His big-bellied laughter caught fire among the gourmands as the illusion of delphiniums clotted darkest red with roses to honour a course of wombat steaks in kangaroo-kidney relish. Dorina suppressed her gorge by memories of a Himalayan summer trek on small horses lavished with bells, their hanging heads too heavy from the weight of rose-petal perfume... even, the delicate coconut-steeped flavours of Prince Haupoupou's banquet in honour of the same world pressures. At this juncture the IFID man found himself so moved by the occasion he stood and improvised an unscheduled eulogy on the hospitality. Dorina shot him a glare of such hatred it penetrated even his sentimentality. He sat, uncertain how foreign this familiar country might really be. He put the rebuke down to an offence against protocol and Aussies more British than they liked to admit.

Caged birds were carried into the musicians' alcove to cry melodiously for help.

During the dessert, a delicacy of platypus eggs whipped with honey and sprouting crytallized petals of a rare tree-orchid, clouds of wildflowers tumbled from the ceiling to dangle by the frailest threads just above the table; they hung there, stirred by the delighted gasps of the assembly, settling finally to form a map of Australia. The lights went off and each flower was seen to cradle a fleck of phosphorus. Momentarily the magic country hovered in mind, so fragile no one dared breathe. And then in tiny irregularities its light went out. The particles of phosphorus died individually and in clusters. Darkness closed over it, black flowers (or, as Dorina saw, rampant cancers) opening, followed by applause and a blaze of electric chandeliers.

— This is National Pragmatism in practice, bellowed President Buchanan. Bring on the chef, bring on the designer, the gardener and the Master of the Table.

All four were paraded to take their bow, but were not allowed to retire in becoming modesty, no.

— Sit down, Buchanan ordered. Pull up those chairs and sit near me. We don't stand on ceremony, he instructed his guests and the astonished foreigners in particular. These people are every bit as good as us and a long shot cleverer than most. Have a drink, he ordered. Waiter! Bring drinks. Make yourselves at ease, he told them as they perched on the edge of their seats anxious to escape. And now, he blared with the energy of a man so perfectly in his stride he cannot put a foot wrong. A surprise. I have here a reward for each of you, the Medal of the Republic. Velvet-covered boxes were brought in and opened. One after another the creators of the dinner ducked their heads for the scarlet band to be slipped over, then stood upright displaying a simple gold disc: an image of the president stamped on one side and that of a nearly extinct marsupial on the other.

Dorina would never forgive. She recollected the feast as a form of torture, as childishness too horrible to overlook. And yet, and yet, some corrupting refinement, some appetite for the unique, some covert fascination with wastefulness on a freakish scale, kept her from castigating him that night. She never blamed others unless she could pronounce herself innocent. She, who so scorned acquisitiveness, who classed the collector as among the barbarous mental types, had to concede that such profligacy squandered on fleeting effects redeemed the torture with a dash of style.

79

Dr Luke Head was summoned to the central pillar-crane. The cranedriver had apparently collapsed up there in his cabin. Its turning arm stopped, a huge concrete module hung suspended above the jigsaw of foundations as a reminder of the fragility of man and man's heart.

Crushed into a tiny open elevator, the doctor, the site manager and a relief driver swept up the tower through hypnotic rhythms, blunt guillotines rattling by, through cold bands of panic sickness, beyond the fear barrier, to a terrifying jolt at the top and a job of work who waited sprawled in the cabin eighty metres above ground. They clung to a handrail, not to be swept off by wind, while their clothes flapped and tormented them with vertigo. A bullying gale pressed against their bodies. The tower swayed and flexed so the whole extended buildingsite loomed and sank fractionally and loomed again. One by one, the manager first and the black doctor last, they swung into the cockpit with its bank of controls. A computer console blinked coloured lights and sketched fugitive graphs across the screen while no one was looking. Luke swiftly checked the patient and nodded. The site manager jabbed one finger on the radio switch.

— Okay Joe, he shouted to make himself heard. Doc says he's alive.

The relief driver took the controls. The computer graphs settled to being watched. But when the concrete module began again to move, gliding across the panorama, something precious had been diminished, some power in the symbol itself, and some expectancy.

Childlike anxieties rumpled the stricken man's forehead. He was the colour of moist mouldy bread. The site manager, having once glanced that way, took refuge in the view: clay roadways being packed down by cyclopean tyres looped among the foundations, linking embryonic buildings and the separately fenced stores of construction materials; acreages of red plastic sheeting flapped in a sea breeze which was also busy rusting thickets of projecting steel reinforcement rods; vehicles on all sides dug, smoothed, carted loads of waste or slow-moiling cement for the smaller cranes to deliver into waiting formwork that one day might house a time-reversed lightwave generator or an executive urinal.

— Call for the ambulance please, Dr Head requested from where he knelt on the ribbed steel floor.

— Not a chance, mate, the site manager muttered in despair, still at the window. This means trouble.

Plainly he saw his own absence from the office as a dereliction which would require more substantial excuses than saving a dying man or securing a seventy-three-ton missile. The doctor now stood also, slender and taller than the free man he was appealing to. He looked out across Project 31 which spread below like an ancient fortified city just being uncovered and scoured clean, while earthmoving equipment at the perimeter banked and ramped soil and sliced through ridges of solid rock. Far beyond a fleet of empty buses ready to take the workmen home from Port George to Vengeance Harbour when they had finished, lay that scarcely touched land of Luke's ancestors. Viewing the construction site whole, as he never had before, the doctor saw in it a breathtaking statement of power. Despite himself, he felt admiration.

Down at the gate, a party of visitors had entered. Flanked by police, they trailed their restless crew of men in uniform with weapons ready, observing everything, gazing up at him too, remote as he was. They advanced between the massive incomplete walls towering here and there, past the stub of two round towers, towards an inner keep with five radiating fins of austere concrete joined at the base of a ziggurat to comprise a structure so large it already reshaped the landscape. The visiting party formed a wedge proceeding slowly along their inspection route, penetrating to the heart of the project, the white hardhats (temporary issue for visitors) distinguishing them from the yellow worn by labourers whom they were driving out of their path as they went. Even from so lofty an observation point, the three men, and possibly the sick one too, heard the hubbub of progress gradually dwindle: tools switched off and put aside, trucks, front-end loaders, and the clusters of smaller cranes slowed to a standstill. The workers themselves became spectators once the inspection party took over the show. Some important person had come among them. Luke felt it as a threat, confirmed by the site manager's next comment.

— One false move and they'll pick us off, no worries.

The new driver concentrated on his task. The concrete module, having floated above the drama, was set down on the exact spot designated.

— Who are they? asked the doctor, suddenly exhausted.

— You're better off not knowing. But I'll tell you this, there's no way an ambulance or any other bloody thing'll be let in while *he*'s here.

Down below, submitting to being escorted through the warm spring day by one of Buchanan's functionaries, General Merasaloa stopped now and again for architects and consulting engineers to be introduced. As he walked he looked his greedy look. The moment was sweet and he relished it. Soon he would see all this happen in his own backyard, just such a majestic cliff-face of concrete with one tiny person standing on top raising a gloved hand to signal a workmate, the sun right overhead glinting on the peak of his hardhat, and across the way, a facing wall already beautiful as a waterfall. Blocks of shadow, more solid than the building itself, leaned down at the slight angle of buttresses. This was the future.

His host, Sir William Penhallurick, reputedly popular for his vulgar touch, lived up to this fame by calling on a specimen labourer to be presented, a Lithuanian giant certain to have no language in common with the general, plus a local police sergeant to whom credit was due for clearing all bystanders from the Port George streets as well as from the route to the site. The Lithuanian clicked his heels admirably. And the sergeant, thanks to some youthful experience canecutting, knew how to relax, as he liked to say, with wogs.

— Quite correct, sir, but they've got to do as they are told. This is not a bad town, he explained as he shook hands with the little chap and smiled his frank Aussie smile of a good sport who's a bit of a rogue on the sly, marred only by the dead side of his lip recalling a scuffle with someone once who wouldn't have his fingerprints taken, a wild young fellow loaded with cash supposed to have been earned tuna fishing.

— You have beautiful country, the general continued graciously but not without envy. I am surprise to see some broke houses on the road we come.

— A tidal wave did that, several months ago. A freak, it was. Never seen the like.

— I understand. Also us. We have tide wave. When people say our Gods are anger. I show them: here is path to freedom.

Merasaloa turned again to the decrepit contractor.

— I am much much impress. So work. Such fast. So. . . his gesture measured its magnitude. I like ask, he went on a moment later when he had selected the appropriate English. Is your company to us in Tuavaleva? You come, Sir Penhallurick (pronounced Serpent Alaric)?

— We would be honoured, the old villain bowed, his sugar crust cracking. Yes indeed. And shot him a calculating glance. What do you say? he added cheekily, capering beside the young conqueror.

They stopped at the foot of the great pillar-crane in time to watch an elevator deliver two passengers on the last stage of their journey down. Jarred and jounced at the bottom, the site manager unclipped the safety bar and hurried apologetically toward Sir William who, instead of scowling, received him with a cheery greeting and paused to listen considerately to his excuses.

— Put your report in the logbook. Don't bother us now. You're doing an excellent job.

General Merasaloa walked off on steel springs.

Penhallurick took the hint and dismissed the site manager to the back of his party; but the unthinkable had already occurred. There being no end to the rot if once you allow just any riffraff free access to a man of power, that second individual from the elevator, a mere black, caught up with them. The contractor waved lizard arms dumbly; and, a minute later, knotted with rage, shouted.

— Get out. Get, he reached back to some memory of impulsiveness, some murdering fury against the asphyxiation of having to *suffer* a person. Out! he concluded as he might cough up a hunk of his own bleeding meat.

The doctor recoiled from this frenzy. He had to get help. Driven by what he knew of the crisis, he switched his appeal to the most influential of them all, to the foreign visitor, now moving some way off. Eyes afire with outrage at the callousness of his first rebuff, he sprang hopefully in front of General Merasaloa, who at least wasn't a white man.

Three shots were fired, so nearly perfectly timed that one barked on the rebound from the others. Islander commandos mused over their weapons lovingly. The doctor dropped as the strings within him were cut. Half-built walls grew blank at what had happened. Rumours of murder snaked down untried drains and ducts to hide among sweepings of cement dust. No one touched the corpse.

The touring party, shocked speechless, gathered more closely together and began shuffling forward, a wedge of accomplices, to put the deed clearly behind them. What was the point of checking a couple of holes in the head?

— You must do this, you must do that! Sir William got his explanation out at last, muttering to his senior staff. He actually threatened me: all for an ambulance. Why an ambulance, I ask you? Madness! Get out, I told him.

Although his skin was shocked thick with memories, he squeezed a decayed smile to placate his guest, darling of IFID and bearer of a multi-million dollar construction contract for himself.

— Lively lads, he approved cautiously of the commandos. Quick.

Only the Port George police sergeant stayed behind as, at last, having business on his own account with somebody.

— Shit, he swore softly. Can they do this?

And a Chimbu labourer sank on muscular haunches to cover a dead black hand with a living one.

The official party strolled through a second set of security gates, the only entrance to the inner structures, and round one side of the ziggurat. Behind them the cry went up, long ululations that stretched back to the New Guinea highlands, an unearthly grieving angry challenge, the cry of a man who knows his fate.

Guest workers from all quarters came running by hundreds, in overalls and blunt boots, men with their hair in topknots and turbans, men built like gazelles and gorillas, men with boils and bandaged elbows, escapees from ceremonies of being pierced by wooden nails, all came; but only a few knew how it felt to be treated with respect, among them warriors, warpaint still behind their ears; others as they ran remembered promises, mothers, and vowing to be true to the eightfold path of righteousness, or dreamed about the paper crown they would one day wear for having carried home the wealth of exiles; spearthrowers and ice-dancers came, fire-mountain men and devil-worshippers, they ran down the walls, they skimmed along ramps, out from among the five radiating fins of concrete, out from the steplike platforms of the ziggurat, from the diggings beyond and the city of spaces already near completion underground. Men running like men. The cluttering boots and the horror of hands. Eyewitnesses likening the tragedy to home and sombre ones accepting a return to the law by vendetta. All of them gathered round the doctor who had become their leader in camp. A sea wind moaned against the crane's latticed steel. From deep in an electrical conduit system of one round tower, Yanagita Izumi's slight figure emerged. He stumbled a moment under the dazzling impact of sunlight or bereavement and then approached through the crowd. In silence he stood gazing at the dislocated body. Whether he thought of silvereyes busy about their early morning scrimmage for survival, or of a Zero pilot braving fate calmly as a monk and defining his enemies' greatness by his own style in death, could not be guessed from that hardening mouth. He said nothing. He simply went to the security gate and stood there, waiting for the general's entourage to return.

The entire workforce went with him, all four hundred. The killers had no other gate to leave by and now not even this.

Meanwhile, the relief-driver high up in his wavering crane had been radioing desperate calls for help, reports of his mate struggling to hang on, reduced to a thing, of strange noises happening from its throat, of serious relapses, and what was the Doc doing about that bloody ambulance?

The touring party returned.

First came bodyguards and then the homicidal smile of the little conqueror whose head, only, could be seen wagging politely in admiration. Senior consultants were answering his questions with quickfire formulae he appeared to enjoy more than the architects' highflown jargon of ten minutes before. Merasaloa did not stop when he saw the blockade, but his commandos moved ahead and closed ranks in front of him. The Australian security men, deeply uneasy in a new situation, tended away from one another, as if they might argue about what to expect next and how best to confront it.

The world flew from west to east.

Sir William Penhallurick, careless of his life as only the very old or the very young are, with that complete disbelief in dying, darted forward to prevent further bloodshed on his construction site.

— You fellows get out of the way, he raged. If you know what's good for you.

They appeared not to comprehend. The giant earthmoving machines stood round the perimeter, still as the rocks they had been pushing aside. A Sunday-graveyard silence stood up clear while dust settled back where it belonged. The mildly spoken Japanese replied.

— We need an ambulance urgently. And we demand the arrest of Dr Head's murderers.

— You demand, do you? We'll shoot the lot of you if you don't see sense. Have a good look, man, and say if this isn't open rebellion? Ask those other fellows behind you, they'll know what it's like to be shot at. I'm not joking. What do you say?

The words, shrill as they were, fluttered in the emptiness of a place designed for housing ideas to shake the balance of world power.

— An ambulance. And the murderers.

If the gap between the opposed forces held firm, that classic confrontation of armed coterie and unarmed mob, it was because these two men, individually, kept it that way by sheer force of unremitting fury. Then, to Yanagita's wonder, he watched the ninety-six-year-old contractor start to smile. Versed in such complexities, he observed a flush of blood brought to those ancient lips and light to the eyes. And he saw what Sir William could not see; high above them, the giant crane had begun to lift.

Automatic rifles remained locked on target. The hero of Tua-valeva arrested their fire with an upraised hand, the very hand so recently and so bloodily raised against Prince Haupoupou. The commandos, because they were armed and for this reason only, could not back down; victory being the right of those who have nothing else to gain. Confronting them, four hundred workmen stood firm in a tradition old as clans, committed to their cause of honour without ever having the freedom to choose it. Stubbornly, they blocked the gateway.

In the madness of standing, both sides stood, all thoughts erased by recognition, everything emptied from mind to clear the way for the rule of alert reflexes. The tension reached that climax of calm wellknown to fighters but which only the Span-ish have a word for, that *querencia* of the bull and the bullfighter, bonded by the same stench and the same ruthless gaze, beyond combat, searching deep to discover the essential animal each confronted: a rapierpoint held steady between the beast's shoulderblades ready to drive down to the heart while the beast, collecting its desperation of knowledge, bears up under the weight of fatalism, all four feet planted solidly.

Rigid shadows set, silent as the walls they buttressed.

The giant crane lifted its arm. The cable thrummed taut. The concrete module, not yet unhooked, rumbled where it rested, tilted slightly on one side. . . and rose clear of the ground. Up it drifted, above vaults, above projections of solid obscurity. A weapon.

The crane rotated with excruciating slowness. The module, checked in its rise, travelled horizontally to sweep past the point where that lone workman in a hardhat had signalled with gloved hand, on past the end of the ziggurat steps, past the round tower and the conduit system opening near it, smoothly gliding until it came to a stop right above the gap holding commandos and Friends of Privilege at bay. There, over the no-man's-land between declared hostilities, the seventy-three-ton cube hung by a thread, drawing all eyes but those of the men with cocked weapons. Too massive to be swayed, even by such a gale, it turned and turned slowly, hypnotically turning, with the ease of a body in clear blue oil.

This very morning the police sergeant had read on an Oat Crispies packet the story of Josiah Henson leading his kinsfolk back into slavery. This very morning, not so many hours later, he had patrolled Port George, clearing local shoppers from the streets as a precautionary measure to prevent any assassination attempt against the little general. And now witnessed the amazed logic of someone else being murdered instead, with those whom he had been protecting shown up as the aggressors. Against all regulations a person had been killed. He could not clear from his mind the neat snick of bullets, the killers at their trim parade-ground drill, the total absence of moral difficulty. All, like a single high voice singing in the hushed chapel of his communion, put him in direct touch with powers beyond personal frailty. Perhaps not even aware of the suspended module, but knowing what he had to do and that arrests must be made, he stepped between the antagonists, into the module's tower of shadow.

The sergeant neither looked at the Tuavalevan visitor, nor caught his expression of indifference tinged with curiosity at such fuss being made over a single death. American engineers, introduced so little time ago amid friendly gestures, remained out of focus, as did those commandos inflexibly dedicated to the magnetism and flawless power of American armaments. He addressed himself to the bloke with a title.

— Take me to a telephone, sir, and let's get this show on the road.

The module, rotating, presented one face. Another face. Shade switched from this side (wait) to that to (wait) the next (wait), exhibiting crisp corners. While its shadow down below, big as the floor of a room, flat as paper, mobile as mercury, twirled; a simple organism flexing stretching clenching, a constant area restlessly mutating from hexagon to rhomboid to square. And back again: rhomboid, hexagon, rhomboid, square. Sides and angles cast with immaculate geometrics but fascinatingly fluid. A dark supernatural sign.

From the mesmerism of watching elusive edges, the eye, like the analytical mind, sought the deep focus of a common heart within the flux. And there, alone in the charged silence between enemy forces, stood the policeman, an individual making history, the first man to wield the state's authority against the state's own masters.

PART FOUR

The Blows of a Friend

80

The crisis, though expected by the Executive Council, emerged startlingly all the same, the room awhirl with President Buchanan's steel-edged words.

— This evening it was discovered that I weigh 274.7 kilograms.

He let the information sink in.

— Yesterday, he continued. I weighed in at exactly 276. The loss of 1.3 kilograms, gentlemen and ladies, is too substantial to be an error or passing dehydration. For the first time in eight years I am diminishing. What's more, this has occurred the very day we are to discuss a date for the coming presidential election.

He salvaged some satisfaction from seeing how the news scared them, how weak they were, these privileged few whom he kept in power.

— Allow me to develop my point with an example, the president proposed sweetly. In my maiden speech to the nation as first incumbent of this high office, I promised that if the Coca-Cola Corporation wished to go on trading here they'd have to toe the line and rename the product Coca-Koala. Now that was a witticism, an inspiration on the spur of the moment. I was only half serious. But look what happened; they took it as a directive, complied, and trebled their profit within two years. The public bought the name. Just the name; it was the identical softdrink in the bottle. But today the name is the very thing we cannot sell. Today it is not good enough, apparently, to be called Buchanan.

Again he took stock of each councillor in turn, including Sir

George Gipps representing the ghost of moral reform, confronting them with the hellish dissatisfactions of his silence.

— Our attitude to Your Excellency, Luigi Squarcia replied eventually in that harsh languid voice of the only one with nothing to fear. Is similar to your own attitude to the United States of America. (He was enjoying this.) Our loyalty to your cause is unshaken. Do I speak for everybody? As the Americans have made light of losing a few yacht races to us because we are Little Brother, so we have been pleased to observe your indulgence of our small incursions into the exercise of power. But we have no thought of claiming such power on our own behalf. You remain undiminished, at least in our eyes.

— I should think so. I give each of you my absolute trust, having accepted a promissory note for your absolute loyalty in return for it. But the time has come when I might need to call in those promissory notes.

It is one matter to inherit laws too severe for the conscience to permit you to enforce them, Sir George Gipps warned Bernard Buchanan. But to condone the passing of such laws oneself, to actually push them through parliament with the purpose of denying people's rights, is to take upon oneself so crushing a moral burden as I doubt any individual could rightly sustain. In short, sir, I see quite well where this latest caper is leading. My opinion is that you are behaving like an hypocrite, loud with piety while willing to let justice and humanity go begging.

Buchanan reached forward to slam his hand on the table.

Owen Powell seized the opportunity. Opening his briefcase, careful not to reveal the truant file concealed inside, he extracted a neatly bound wad of papers.

— May I at this point, Your Excellency, move a Revised Emergency Special Powers Bill? I have had sufficient copies made to pass round.

— What does it propose? Now be brief Marshal Powell. In one sentence, what does your bill propose?

— To abolish the forthcoming election, or at least, insofar as that goes to. . .

— One sentence.

— To postpone the election, then.

— Indefinitely, the president confirmed. Are we in a position to vote? We have a quorum and I am prepared to second the motion from the chair. Any objections? I believe we may trust the Minister to have considered all the issues.

Rather than using your powers of government to suppress

criticism, Gipps interjected drily while no one else dared commit themselves, might you not be well advised to look to your debts for an explanation of it? No electorate can be expected to remain faithful to an administration which allows speculators to contract such an overburden of foreign loans that more than half the gross national income from products of all kinds is paid out annually to financial houses with no real stake in the country other than making a profit out of it.

— God damn you! the president roared tetchily from the dumbness of shuffled papers, staring at the unseen figure in a frockcoat who sauntered round the table peering over shoulders to read what his councillors were writing on ballot slips they had helped themselves to. Have you all lost your tongues? Is this a charade or do we mean to get on with the overburden of government? he bit back Gipps's word, overburden, but his faithful ministers took it for a joke to leaven the crisis, chuckling.

It is a charade, Sir George answered promptly.

Had Buchanan been able to stand, he might possibly have had a heartattack to compound the problems of his weight loss. The trouble was that wherever he turned, he could see only the present, the marvel of a moment diminished by the impossibility of grasping it whole.

This was supposed to be it: he had reached the top. He could pick up his glory and handle it like a precious handpainted dish, too precious to be used for anything, but empty of itself, which must simply languish on display, or at best wait to be smashed; the very catastrophe he moved right now to avert, though the shock of such a smash must be, he conceded, a great moment in its own right.

The irony was that, had the country not become a republic, he might be tempted to retire to some grand sinecure at the English court, some superannuated title with a castle and a couple of seaports attached, not to mention a seat in the Abbey during royal funerals. His own state funeral offered no consolation. He had little doubt his cortège would comprise enemies striding an inch above the ground with relief, alongside whom Dorina was a saint, and even the hopeless Rory not positively sickening.

The great ones of the land hunched over the decisions they recorded on tiny scraps of paper, like primary school pupils hoarding their guesses, masking what they wrote to prevent others from cheating.

Buchanan's second four-year term would be up in a matter of

months. The constitution set the final date for an election at 1
January 2001, exactly one hundred years to the day after Federation. While he waited for the vote to be taken, he pondered the
great issues of life: the unsettling fact that Luigi Squarcia had
not even mentioned any forthcoming campaign, for example,
the fact that he had been right to rely on Owen to work things
out for himself and come up with a postponement, the
unfeigned concern and personal shock his loyal bearers had
shown when weighing him and discovering his missing one and
a third kilograms. Say what she might, Dorina was wrong about
the boys. Still she insisted on remaining baffled that he showed
no disgust at the intimacy of being lifted from bed and
undressed. Well, this was because she had no general understanding of what it is to surrender. Actually, when lowered on
to his uniquely capacious lavatory seat, he felt. . . precious. Felt
that even these vulnerabilities since they were public, must be
important. His bearers were the most professional of his inner
circle and their demeanour was impeccable. Without so much as
a misunderstandable glance in the wrong place, they weighed
him each night when he arose, hoisting naked mounds of flesh
on the machine, piling him up by the fistful, proud of his
achievement, gathering to watch the precise needle advance
round the dial. The day he had reached 250 (on the way up), he
awarded them a bonus. If bloody Roscoe Plenty could have
learnt a thing or two from them he might have saved himself
going mad, for example. Even when they took their places back
against the toilet walls, he reported to them on the event. In the
case of constipation, they might expect to stand there upwards
of half an hour, being told progressively that it was no good, no,
it was hell and like squeezing a loan out of a New Zealander, it
was half a fart and a river jammed with logs, it was his
grandfather's complaint and Alexander the Great suffered too.
For, despite a modest food intake, digestion still gave him
regular trouble. Harvey or Noel often needed to oblige by
administering an enema while the great man gasped with
excruciating pleasure. Among the bearers he was able to joke
about his motions, while they responded with a few choice
sentiments of their own such as: Too right Your Excellency, or
You're quite a character sir, or The nation is hoping with you.
Dorina's failure to appreciate their value he put down to her
having never cared for common people. She lacked the gift of
belonging, witness the time she forgot to give those removalists
their beer even though he had taken the trouble to lay it in. If

they'd had their beer, he instructed her in the ways of men, they probably wouldn't have thrown your blasted piano down the stairs.

The Executive Councillors' votes were posted in a box which they passed round. A paralysis which, for minutes on end, had traumatized the starboard side of his face released him long enough for the president to smile and call his press secretary Margaret Talbot as returning officer. Constrained by the courtesy of the great, he watched the silly votes counted. But he had plenty to occupy him, even a new ambition. The idea came from Lavinia: he must conquer illness. Even dying of diseases will not kill me! he'd said. And no sooner was this brilliant riposte out of his mouth than pustules pushed up under the skin. As he flew home across the lawn to his office, a torment of itching already set in and he was engaged in a trial of endurance against a worthy adversary. He appeared on television, disfigured by erupting ailments and mopping dropsical eyelids with a hand-towel. The populace looked on in alarm. What would happen to them next? They clamoured for ways to show their support. Out of the misery of economic collapse for all but the very rich, the slump in morale, they rallied to his suffering. For special climactic effect when addressing the nation, he reclined fully clothed on a couch and waved one feeble hand, spruiking still, mountainous yet soft, ferocious eyes bulging, ceaselessly spruiking in bullying paragraphs five minutes long between breaths. The more afflicted he was with asthma, gout, tuberculosis, hepatitis, boils and softening of the bones, the more gorgeously contemptuous his speeches. He no longer cared about pleasing people and they no longer cared to be pleased: they wanted him as he was. The tougher life became, the more they welcomed hearing the worst. He gave it to them. If this, he thundered from a helpless pose flat on his back, if this is a dictatorship it is a dictatorship of genius. Don't ask me to explain my reasons and set them out like so many virgins to be knocked off by university cleverdicks. Reasons have nothing to do with it. Staring at the unseen ceiling of the studio, he presented his audience with the rare sight of his profile in that position, nose ballooning up towards the top righthand corner of the screen, one huge ear at the bottom directed purposely for its hollow mysterious spiral to overhear their petty seditions. Government, his sidelong mouth rumbled, is a question of energy and opportunity. A splatter of herpes, sensational as mud thrown in his face, disfigured his forehead from the eyelid right up to where the hairline had been before baldness set in, sticky nerves blossoming darkly. And when this cleared at a single swift bitter frown, so characteristic of him in his security, his chin was seen to thrust from within, extruding, while his features coarsened, lips gross, and the hidden tongue swelling against them, stretching his cheek to a deep stressed fold, and his raised hand itself enlarged with scaly flesh. Don't argue with me about the rights and wrongs of what I do. The fact is you can't possibly know what you are talking about. You voted me into office to run the country. So clear out of my hair while I get on with it. Little people obstruct the passage of world progress. It's happening everywhere, his recumbent head shook with bewilderment. Lunatics for the protection of trees! Lunatics against digging holes in the ground! Lunatics opposed to cheaper electricity! Lunatics for the abolition of roads, I dare say. How long can we suffer this, cluttered with malcontents who can't enjoy a good time? His eyes closed, knobbly eyeballs roving restlessly under the lids. He opened them again, but not to look at his audience, simply to stare once more at the ceiling. The visible eye underwent alarming changes, both lids retracting, shrinking away from what could be seen, baring a ball veined with tiredness in the nation's service and seeming ready to drop out altogether. His mouth regained control of its sense of proportion. But even as chin and tongue subsided, an immense thyroid growth welled over his collar, burst the button which could be heard skittering on the floor and bulldozed the tie through its own knot. I begin to feel too ill to stand up for your rights. I seriously consider retiring to make way for a younger fitter man, he once said. Beautiful, the way he could talk without the least contact between words and meaning. Then he did at last turn to confront those millions in the dark anxiously watching his side-slipped face on the screen: But who is there? His neck pushed on against the tie, collar standing agape. Nobody, he replied demonstrating his collapse of hope. Am I to live forever because you can't produce a successor for me? Nevertheless he did not lose weight, not just then, at any rate.

— Am I to live forever? was also the complaint he murmured at this Executive Council meeting, now looking, quite the contrary, as though he would not even last till morning.

Are you simple enough to believe you will escape personal culpability? Gipps commented tartly, his birdbright eyes fixed on the great man while those little slips of paper were tipped from the box and Margaret Talbot pinched the creases out of them with varnished fingernails. Small wonder you cannot sleep.

— Yes: eight, she announced. No: zero.

Bernard Buchanan's ailments cleared up instantly.

— So I shan't need my casting vote, he conceded. Ladies and gentlemen, we all wished to avoid this regrettable emergency, did we not? That can be truly reported to the people. But we know our duty and we won't be deflected from it now we have the necessary powers. Thank you for your patience and dedication. I think we may take the rest of the night off. But before you go, I have one other matter to raise. To be blunt, and despite this timely Revised Emergency Special Powers Bill, Owen is under suspicion. Suspected of being craftier than me.

The rest of the Council chortled as they kept their eyes on the president. But Buchanan did not laugh and nor did Powell. Gipps laughed immoderately.

— You are upset about the Wild Dog case? the marshal admitted, alert to his danger. I have not been idle in Adelaide. All this may turn to our advantage.

— So it is to our advantage that the mob has begun smirking behind closed doors! No doubt it is to our further advantage that my Washington hotline has become a one-way stream of interrogations and polite threats? People, Mr Powell, are losing confidence in us. And I am one of them. Isn't that true, Squarcia?

— Could we discuss this privately afterwards, Your Excellency? the Minister for Internal Security whispered.

— So you can comfort me in my naivety? So you can remind me what I owe you? So you can mimic me and look at me like I look at you? Am I to be confused by that? You are so compliant, Minister, I don't know where I am. No, afterwards in private will not do at all. Surely you aren't suggesting I alone run the country? Are you telling me I am a dictator? Why do I bother calling regular meetings in that case? Is it a game I'm amusing myself with? My goodness, you must think I'm short of entertainments. No, the point is that there comes a limit. What leads you to think I would dream of holding our colleagues in such contempt, keeping important matters for discussion afterwards in private?

Gipps said quite plainly that this was the regular procedure and everybody knew it. And the answer to Powell was that any man who heaps another with greatness should expect to be brought to ruin for having done so.

— How is it, Luigi Squarcia intervened mildly. We have not been shown what this Wild Dog looks like? Has anybody here seen a published picture?

— Only descriptions, Powell snapped pettishly. Medium height, solid build and blue eyes.

— Dammit Owen, I'm of medium height and solid build. I have blue eyes. Am I to be a suspect?

— The point is, Powell continued, that I do not believe this is just one individual, Your Excellency.

— The country's infested with wild dogs then? All my citizens are discontented and rebellious? What sort of comfort are you offering? Is this a circus we're running here? No, don't give me that bullshit. I know. The reason I was successful in business was that I understood people. And when I came to politics I saw one thing more clearly than any man of my time: I saw what a republic meant. A republic, gentlemen and ladies, for a small nation, does not mean independence; it means the right to choose your master. The dying years of the former commonwealth were riddled with disastrous indecision. Out we went in our nappies among bandits, spreading the good word of nonalignment. Who's this little chap, the bandits laughed. Shall we rape him or eat him for dinner?

The diseases subsided further, his thyroid shrank and the pustules cleared, his eye brightened.

— So between myself and the White House there has been perfect goodwill. Until now! he crackled with instant anger. Some lout breaks into the Paringa compound, God knows how, and plasters one wall with a slogan. Then, lo and behold, here we are, right on cue at Port George, with a disgraceful collision of interests. The civilian police have got their heads down and their blinkers on, pursuing their duty as they call it, obstructing Owen's Department of Snoops, thwarting every effort to get those fuzzywuzzies flown out of the country on the quiet.

Across a desert, prophets stumbled against the desiccating wind of accusations, shivering in animal skins, feeling their intestines shrink and casting about, mad-eyed, for some miracle of divine reprieve. That was the Executive Council.

— Only last week I approved Chief Justice Mack's speech, declaring the High Court free from all tincture of political interference. Too bad. He'll have to be demoted, for a start. A little dose of confusion never did the media any harm. It's the least face-saving we can afford. We cannot risk having a bench of sheep landing us with the wrong decision. He can go down to the Family Court, out of harm's way. Merasaloa's men have to be released. I'm authorizing a press visit to Project 31. We've got to move fast. Let just the one reporter in, Owen, one of our Honourables. There is *no* laugh to be got from Port George. That will be all.

Gipps bowed to each in turn as they filed out. When they had gone, he made himself comfortable.

I am here to explain to you, he said. How a governor may be both conservative and ethical. I am here to deny the assumption shared by you and your enemies that policies designed to advantage capital need necessarily outrage all standards of common decency and justice.

— Then you can save your breath, the president retorted.

81

Tim Davies had just happened to walk into the editor's empty office when a call came through from the Department of Internal Security. This job is strictly for an Honourable, the minister's personal assistant said. Yes of course, he replied with a gust of resentment against those compliant colleagues. Yes of course, he repeated, neither his anger nor his sarcasm quite discernible. Then in a flash of reckless inspiration he knew what to do: We shall need your letter of authority, of course, so please have your Sydney office deliver it direct to Mr T Davies.

Mr Cohen at the Canberra end of the line, instead of seeing through the bluff and gasping at such impertinence, simply agreed. He sounded earnest but, how shall it be put, preoccupied. Tim Davies, like so many nervous and possibly cowardly people, had trained himself to be sensitive to fine nuances. That was how he kept one jump ahead of trouble. The madness of what he had just done would hit him with full force later, no doubt, but for the moment, having begun, he must play his part and play it with perfect coolness or he was lost.

So the letter arrived authorizing his visit to the new construction site to watch the Friends of Privilege at work. So, also, he came to inspect the Vengeance Harbour camp. Came, indeed, by a further subterfuge, to look the sixty-year-old Yanagita Izumi in the eye and hold his attention. Only once before, when trying to defend Lavinia from arrest, had he done anything so foolhardy.

There was no evidence to be seen of trouble on the job or at the camp.

Inside the prison compound, insulated from the world, the aroma of silverbeet and milk-curd curry reached him as lingering traces of an extinct orient. Across the quiet bare yard, Commandant Curtis could be overheard remotely bleating and barking in the office, fatuous with autocracy. The Izumi interview was already developing along routine lines while Tim mustered courage to take the plunge he had come to take. He knew the consequences might reach as far as Owen Powell himself. But in his timidity he had the extraordinary strength of fatalism. He would surrender to the need for putting himself at risk. This was the way he felt, shutting his eyes, this was the means by which he cushioned himself against the hard jolt of taking irrevocable action. And he did it.

— Mama knows I'm visiting, Tim slipped the words in quietly so the supervising guard would neither hear, nor exactly not hear. He paused, denied breath by the celibacy of the camp and the chances of this elderly-youthful Japanese being a spy.

— We don't have much to cheer us up, Yanagita replied suavely, his tone ideally frank and at the right pitch to be heard but not heeded. You could say a few television sets would go a long way to helping us. It's the drug everyone outside uses, after all.

— Homesickness?

— We'd need women to cure that, he laughed though he seldom normally did laugh.

Till the guard convinced himself he too was at liberty to let a smirk show. Knowing women as he knew them. Tim's pen dug at the notepad with cryptic symbols in shorthand.

— I suppose you work hard. Enough to be pretty tired?

— Luke was murdered.

— Plus your enterprise. Yes, I heard about that from Mr Curtis who tells me you make quite a profit.

Tim's nerve gave out. His eyes faltered. He looked away from Izumi, away from the guard loitering nearby and the guard patrolling the top of the wall. He looked, descriptively, at the old earth floor packed hard with morose blood. At that fearful logic of walls. At the confined sunshine through which no one had called *Xoxouhqui-yollotl*, Free Man! since the day the doctor died. He felt there was something missing.

— The steel cylinders are due. Big things. Huge, Yanagita

laughed again and stopped laughing. Can't do without them, he added out loud.

Ah no, thought the guard, that's true enough. We can't, poor stupid sods that we are.

— Back to the cereal packets for a moment. Do you divide your takings among everyone equally?

— Equally.

— Not just those who put the artwork together.

— Equally. But some is taken by the commandant before it reaches us.

— I don't need to hear about that, Tim objected, biting into green fruit.

The guard, who had leaned forward, relaxed again and watched a flock of tiny birds swoop in over the wall, fluttering noisily round the garden beds.

— You work labouring, I take it?

Yanagita shook his head.

Tim had been told already that the rumours of an industrial accident were greatly exaggerated. He had stood beside the site supervisor who pointed complacently to where cranes nodded above sheer walls, to big machines reshaping the perimeter of vivid red soil, to the puzzling disfunction of structures already so diverse that only the base of two round towers seemed at all related. Now, as then, the air grew dangerous with questions he must not ask.

— I'm an electronics man, Yanagita Izumi offered in his excellent English.

The silvereyes whirred past them stirring ghosts among shadows of early evening.

— People out there think we are freaks? he added.

The guard was a man who, at moments of confiding in someone of his own kidney, was apt to describe himself as having had a fair dose, regardless of the subject under discussion, whether of worry or luck or matrimony. Even prospects were a temptation he had enjoyed a fair dose of. Freaks certainly, he'd had more than a fair dose of them when he worked in that lunatic asylum until the day came when they brought the Chief Minister of the Republic in a straitjacket and he said to his wife, this means trouble and, not to mince words, a dose is a dose so I'm clearing off for a quiet life. Here he was, then, with nothing more to grumble about than most others, nodding.

— They certainly see you as set apart. And with so much unemployment, I'm sure they wonder how you feel, having a protected job like this. Especially if you used to live as an ordinary Australian before.

— Well, we're in it for the money now. There's nothing else left.

Tim put his hand out to feel the wall, which was the temperature of blood. He recoiled, staring at the hand as if it had misbehaved.

— Let me ask you, the pen dug a few more impressions on the page. About your family.

— Well I'd like to send greetings to Mama. My old firm, Kawakoya Electronics, he dropped his voice. Is supplying the hardware. Uragami is the man.

— Back in Japan?

— Of course, when I am free to go.

— No political stuff, the guard snapped, suddenly awake. You were told that, Mr Davies. I have my orders. The workers came here by their own choice.

A door opened, the sign *Commandant* swung in as Commandant Curtis himself emerged to stand on the five stone steps of his glory. He signalled the guard. Yanagita was sent back to his quarters as they let an Ethiopian into the yard to be interviewed. This man approached in an arc, which immediately charmed Tim, himself not noted for directness.

— One Japanese, one Ethiopian you asked for, the Commandant called across the blood-hardened space. He spoke humorously, but like a man accustomed to having his subtler points missed. We've got everything.

This African was less wellknown to the guard, who felt it his duty, therefore, to step a little closer. Commandant Curtis watched for a moment, apparently satisfied with arrangements.

— I shall see you before you go, Mr Davies, he called again, as a reminder.

The man from Ethiopia had seen everything, so he was able to explain everything. He began, full-bore, eyes popping wide and excited hands helping sweep aside the entanglements of an inadequate language. He took as his text that Australia is paradise, which he pronounced para*dise* and repeated several times in order to review all dimensions of this divine marvel.

— So rich the rain, he explained and his fingers rained. And who is getting murdered? his neck clicked back as he died there and then, only to be resurrected immediately with his delighted grin cocked on one side to encourage agreement. Not us, all the time, I tell you! Paradise it is. Let us admit, dear brother, if God created such a land and put it on the earth, his hands scattered paradisal seeds which instantly sprouted, leafed, burgeoned and blossomed till the very trees broke out in perfume and the watcher's gaze rose to the profound possibilities of the sky. How would He stop His angels to grow jealous, do you see? God is more clever than many men think.

Asked if there was anything he missed since he had left home, the arc-walker smiled with pain, spread his fine calloused hands, hastily dusted the cement powder off them and presented them spread again.

— Courtesy, he confessed.

Afterwards, in the office, Commandant Curtis received the *Sydney Courier* fellow with a show of goodwill, sat him down and offered him a mug of instant coffee, but without the option of sugar, owing to a wellknown shortage since the industry collapsed.

— In the old days, he blared cheerily. Would have thrown you out on your ear.

— Well *then* of course, Tim fired back, clutching at his rags of courage in a high wind and wrapping them round him. We didn't have to submit our copy to state censorship.

— Ah, the times, the commandant agreed exhibiting limbs, pleased they were longer and thinner even than his visitor's. Do change. Kids grow up. Too smart by half. Find out anything interesting?

— Yes. That this is paradise, he smiled expecting a smile in return.

But the older man had packed away his portable bonhomie.

— There you are then! the commandant declared and held out a hand for Tim's notes which he inspected, peering at indecipherable marks.

There were the names, right in the open.

— Shorthand! Mr Curtis declared in the victorious tone of a man who gets things right.

So Tim's journey home became freighted with precious treason. Kawakoya Electronics and Uragami might be known to Yanagita's mother already or they might not, but the steel cylinders, those essential cylinders, must be news. He had discovered that the rumours of an industrial uprising were true and that poor Stephanie's Luke had been murdered. Alternately flushed with pride that he had dared carry out a dangerous mission despite the Wild Dog's obvious doubts and stabbed by a cold needle of fear for the same reason, Tim drove to Sydney.

Had he risen to the challenge simply to prove himself in the eyes of an outlaw? Perhaps he had. Tim drove well because he drove habitually, resting only once on the way, just south of Newcastle, where he turned along a sidetrack just off the highway and stopped to commit his notes to memory. He lit a shaky cigarette, which eluded his fingers until he clutched at the thing and bent it. He filled his lungs with gratitude. Then ripped page after page from his pad and got out. A constant traffic roar still reached him as he struck a match and watched heat shimmer from the page, flames invisible in sunlight. He let the frail black shell fall to the ground and tremble there before crushing it to dust under one fastidious shoe. A faint ugly stench of paper-smoke clung to his clothes for when a police-man might stop him and pick up a clue useful to the state security service.

He had a risky record already. No use now to struggle against the mesh of entanglement. Perhaps the maddest folly was speaking privately to Lady Penhallurick. But she misunderstood his motive and had intervened to have his salary raised, even insisting his articles carry a by-line again, though he had grown notorious for refusing to join the Honourables, snubbing the Allied agency, and even turning down public service hospitality at every one of their departmental Reporters' Clubs. In less treacherous times he might see the funny side.

Along the Pacific Highway Tim Davies drove, gliding through privileged North Shore suburbs, more prosperous than ever before. In Lindfield he stopped at a pedestrian crossing where children from a private school chanted rowdy games, one of which centred on a young man. What they were taunting him for, Tim, within the snapshot frame of a passing motorist, could not tell. But a glimpse of the man's face caused him to slew into the kerb. He did not sound the horn, because this quaint licence had now come under scrutiny of the law, but he leaned out.

— Ganymede! he called.

And that handsome head turned from the humiliations of some petty involvement to light up with a brilliant smile. He sprang across the road, alarming the oncoming traffic, skipped round to the passenger door, and flung himself in beside a friend.

They talked with relief all the way to town, pausing only to be inspected and allowed out through the Residential Area gates. Their trust in each other had been absolute from the moment they realized they belonged to the same subculture, the illegal world of homosexuals, condemned by Buchanan's laws and hounded by Buchanan's police. The daily survival of such people depended on discretion and loyalty.

At Mama's, Tim begged Ganymede to wait in the car. People walked dully past, footsteps muffled by their shadows. During these times it was taken for granted that one did not invite a friend into a strange house.

Five minutes later Mama herself, head filled with comfort at news of Yanagita, hearing Stephanie's remote howls escape the padded swathes of silk and somehow being irritated because this obliged her to show sympathy she could ill afford when action called, went to the window to take a gander at who it was Tim couldn't very well ask in. She recoiled in horror from catching sight of a perfect profile.

— He reminds me too much, she explained faintly as she warned Tim that however mild an article he wrote to help the government off the hook for Luke's murder and however he might offer a passable semblance of appearing to align himself with the Honourables (which was to be his excuse), he must make sure to sow the seed for revenge by mentioning the cylinders somewhere along the line. Just plant the idea in the public mind, dear. Goodbye then. I shall be in touch. Go to your friend. I cannot have faces hanging round in front of my house. What will the neighbours think! Also, she called after him through black daggers of overgrown foliage. You may be certain Mr Dog will be pleased with you when he gets home from pursuing his destiny.

She let the curtain fall so she would not have to suffer seeing that one out there smile.

— Now, she informed herself firmly and faced her duty to console Stephanie. At least she knows why she lost contact. At least she knows he wasn't faithless like my Izumi. Him dead and (she tutted as she tackled the stairs, keeping a critical eye on the brass rails holding the carpet down) poor Gita with no one to talk to of a morning. She paused for breath on the landing. Luke was a good man, she said seriously. It's a sadness.

82

Bernard Buchanan took it into his head to have himself carried around the garden, and why not? In fact, he made a circuit of the very route taken when he had accompanied Lavinia on her first walk back in the free air, a joyous occasion and worthy of celebration. But the intention, as so often in human affairs, was marred by the means. Once out among nostalgic perfumes, he found Harvey Noel & Co an intolerable intrusion, their broad camel feet placed one after one so conscientiously flat you could scarcely tell left from right. It was grotesque and comic. He hated them; he despised their anonymity. Stop! he commanded when they reached the flushed pink treetrunk against which Lavinia had steadied herself, still giving off a trace of her warmth and the heady aroma of daphne settling round him. Out of sight of all sentry posts and security beats, he felt a desire to be himself, Bernard Buchanan the private citizen, nostalgic, yes, for his lost fallibility.

— Put me down and take twenty minutes' break. No; more. I don't want to see you for half an hour, is that clear? He watched their dumb backs hump obediently, he watched their unison shuffling, the whole contemptible performance as a collective animal with sixteen feet shambling across grass, watched for the slightest hint of exchanged looks or murmurs. But they kept to their blank sobriety right out of sight in the direction of the kitchens and their private quarters. He heard their leather-shod feet crunch distantly on gravel, walking, would you believe, in step! Cretins. And they were his most intimate household staff.

A tearable length of blue sky tautened between the treetops. Buchanan's legs were assailed by pins and needles, if not by ants, but he had no way of checking or protecting himself. Without warning he was in the grip of helplessness, held there by positive, active inability. He could not move. The sky quivered tight. This was the moment for a shot to ring out.

— Help, he said quietly, almost in the tone of Good morning. But the stubborn word went nowhere. He waited, not being one to allow panic the upper hand. The still garden struck him as creepy. Why was there no wind, not even a breeze? It was as if somebody had stopped the projector, as if posterity were staring at a frozen frame of him, examining every detail for clues to his downfall, passing their judgment, cracking refined jokes, in a different time, an unreachable space. Help, he repeated into a gag. But he could do nothing other than sit on the chair he had designed for himself, weighed down by the proud burden of victories. This was his place, he had no option but to stay here. Nobody saw when he waved his arms. And he did wave them, laughably flightless arms. Nobody saw when he twisted round violently, as far as he could, lashing out against a murderer he sensed approaching and standing behind him. Nobody saw him clutch his own throat to be certain he actually shouted help and did not imagine it. A pillow of perfumes smothered his cry, sopped it up and squeezed the air out of it. He struggled against weakness. He managed to heave himself almost upright, neck and face crimson with strain, trunk still contorted so he might see behind him. . . and lost his balance. In a flash he knew he must fall. The knowledge struck him with the fullness of insight, also that no other person could be blamed unless there was, indeed, an assassin present. He underwent a vision of the fact before it happened: a head of state collapsing ignominiously in the dirt, gravel-rashes along the inner skin of his wrist and disfiguring his right cheek, pain seizing his body to clamp it in a ridiculous posture. This was the scene he began toppling towards. Then, miraculously, someone took his weight while he was still only just off balance, a steadying hand gripped his left arm before too late and hauled him back into the litter. So there had, indeed, been a murderer behind him. He crashed on the uncomfortable seat, bruising his fatty hip, but otherwise surviving, and turned shocked eyes on his rescuer and enemy.

— What are you doing? the president demanded querulously. Here?

— Saving Your Excellency from falling, said Luigi Squarcia modestly.

Foliage rustled, creeping closer round them.

— A man in your position, Buchanan challenged clutching at his heart with both hands. Must be prey to all manner of temptations.

— And, with respect, a man in your position too.

— There you are wrong. No temptations, that's the damned problem. I have set myself too high above them.

— This is true power, then. Squarcia picked a rosebud without asking permission, stripped the thorns with carefully tended nails, and fixed it in his buttonhole. Though it had seemed pure white on the bush, the rose showed creamy yellow against his whiter suit. Would you like one too? he offered apologetically as if this garden were his. Perhaps a red one?

— When last we were in private together, Buchanan declined morosely. You began telling me something and I promised the time would come to continue our fascinating chat.

Magpies carolled mocking Amens.

— I came to your bathhouse to warn you that IFID could not guarantee support for your campaign at another election.

— So I believe. And you did tell me, too.

There were no memories of Lavinia any longer. Her warmth had escaped the pink trunk. The whole idea of this journey into sentiment soured.

— Do you imagine I have not thought about the nature of power and what toll it takes of a man who enjoys it?

— Naturally you have, Squarcia agreed. If only from vanity.

Buchanan laughed and the laughter restored him.

— That's why I like you, you don't pull any punches. From you and you alone I can be sure of hearing the truth even when I don't want to. You once said something clever to me: you said politics is the delectable impertinence of spending other people's money. I memorized that word for word because I wrote it down at the time. This, I said to myself, is the key to our friend Lou Squarcia and I'd better not lose sight of the fact.

Squarcia inclined his head almost as gracefully as Her Majesty the Queen had when she accepted the loyal sentiments of the citizens of Hannover.

— I disagreed then and I disagree now, of course.

— Of course, Your Excellency.

— But that is only proper considering the gulf between us. You fit your role admirably, I may say. As for me, posterity will confirm how I have filled mine. The point I am making Lou is that true power is not manipulation but creation. All this riot of life and energy around us, this turmoil which we call society and the curbing of it which we call the Emergency, I have created. Yes, the bad as well as the good. The bad especially. I imagined it with such intensity, everything happened as if there were no other way.

— But we hear each hour of malcontents out there plotting to bring you down.

— The same goes on in here, the great man banged his forehead with his fist.

Squarcia perched on the carrying pole nearest him, straddling it, tweaked the impeccable crease of his white trousers, and put his next question.

— What about hegemony, then?

Buchanan chuckled delightedly, his giant stomach wobbling.

— There you go again. Another punch square on the point of the chin. Hegemony is a delusion by which people without power can be duped into believing the world is arsy-versy.

Hegemony would suggest that I am their invention instead of them being mine, right? The answer, Lou, is history. History won't have a bar of your tidy hegemony. History will say Buchanan did this and Buchanan said that. Incidentally, Buchanan says yes you have permission to sit there.

— You are speaking of the history book you yourself have written?

— You're a proper devil today. What other history is there? But, to come to the present, you are here, I suppose, to report IFID's reaction to the fact that I have cancelled the election and taken away their weapon against me?

— Why enquire about IFID's reactions? What about the voters?

— I rule the country, up here. (He tapped his head more gently this time.) On my own terms. I will not be castrated by mass hysteria. Nor, for that matter, by mass caution. The people exist as a reason for me to be in power. There you have it, Squarcia.

— When I told my IFID man the election was off indefinitely, he said: Is that right?

Far away, at the end of the drive, sentries with loaded weapons patrolled the gateway.

— What else could he say? My point entirely. You ought to have asked me before you rang him. You see, the leader explained kindly. IFID is just a convenient peg for us to hang our international coat on. No more than that. The world thinks in simple terms: hunger, spaceflights, boundaries, war, the calendar. That is how the world thinks. Big simple things. And big simple names: Jesus Christ, Buddha, Jehovah, IFID. All illusory. The British Empire was as simple as you can well imagine anything that stretched right across the world: take a map, colour as much pink as you can, and then sum it up in a single boast. . . the sun never sets on the Empire. There you have it. Beautiful. Nothing whatever to do with those hundreds of millions of Indians and Africans, Chinese and Lesbians. Forget them. No connection. Just a simple tag for simple people. Call it the British Empire for no other reason than that Jimmy Jones in Wagga Wagga collects stamps in two albums, one labelled British Empire and the other labelled Foreign; and in the first of these little Jimmy learns all sorts of comfortable facts, he learns the shape of Ceylon and the rig of a native prahu, he finds out what aloe plants look like and countless butterflies, he's got the names of historic ships and portraits of the orang-utan, all surmounted by the unsmiling heads of Kings Edward, George, Edward and George, or Queens Victoria and Elizabeth, with a couple of coronation pairs and a prince or princess for luck. Jimmy has got the point. The Empire was the British Jehovah. Now we're out of it, we can see how completely irrelevant it was. While they paid our debts and creamed off our profits and dictated who we should go to war against and how our institutions should be run, well okay. But, in truth, that wasn't the Empire, much less the British Commonwealth. That was money. Big money. Now in the case of IFID, IFID itself is as irrelevant as the Queen was. You don't trip me up with that. But as long as money people take a hand in our economy under the name of IFID, I say: Oho look out, this is power, this is not hegemony and nor is it dear old BB, not in a fit. This is power. This can't be stuck away in a stamp album. This goes beyond Jimmy Jones. Without money, IFID is merely an idea.

— Yours? Could we say you imagined IFID in order to acquire a backer with enough clout to put you on your presidential throne?

Bernard Buchanan turned to the charming Squarcia with a look every bit as frozen as King George V floating disembodied above the tea pluckers of the high plantations.

— Yes, he declared. Yes.

Squarcia thought this over, admiring his rosebud buttonhole and every so often gazing into the surrounding foliage.

— With respect, Your Excellency, may I now ask one further question? Do you believe the state itself exists?

King George grew fatter and rosier and his beard was really only a cluster of extra chins. (The Pope, he had once told an adoring crowd, has a triple crown; so what, I have a quadruple chin. And no one can take it off me.)

— The state, he said as he might say *Lavinia*, rolling the warm mulled word on his tongue. Modesty advises me to shy off the subject. Perhaps you should explain your motive for asking.

Squarcia stood, partly for dramatic effect and partly owing to the uncomfortable shape of the handle he sat on.

— No more than to learn your views and improve my mind.

— And then what?

— I have a job to do, Squarcia replied with dignity, each syllable perfumed.

The president, at last, relaxed in his amateur seat. He was not going to be murdered, he was not even going to be attacked. And any minute now those eight camel-footed galoots would tramp back in step, weighed down by their maddening endearing submissiveness.

— I may appear as a genius to you Squarcia, but I am not. You might be surprised to learn how naive I am at heart. (Squarcia looked absolutely unsurprisable.) How much a dabbler, how little changed since the days when we were on the road together and campaigning against huge odds. The cricket, remember? Those endless dinners with Rotarians? My answer is simple: the state is right where we are, in the garden of Yarralumla Mansion. After a few minutes, the state will return behind its desk again. That is National Pragmatism for you.

Squarcia stood poised, as he once had at the brink of an indoor swimming pool watching golden scales of light waver over a wall of vegetation, a place echoing lost joys, while some agent slipped him an envelope bearing the name of an unknown real estate developer. Such antiquated secrecy smacked of affectation, of Sir William Penhallurick's old-world schmalziness. Then the precise focus of memory switched to a date, yes, set in a stainedglass skylight where beards of lichen hung rooted to the accumulated muck of decades, himself contemplating a glass rose that sprouted from the decay of 1901 in an edifice since demolished to make way for the disaster of the Buchanan Cultural Centre. He reached among thorny branches and picked the most splendid fullblown specimen, a deep red rose in its final flush of brilliance. Wearing an expression hard to decipher, so swiftly did it change until the inner conflict resolved to impatience, he presented Buchanan with the flower.

— Tell me Lou, the recipient wheedled in the soft voice of a dying child. What happened when Lavinia went home? What were her feelings? The studio had been looked after, I hope.

Squarcia saw this coming: in any professional country, such a buffoon and his sentimentality would be dead long ago. The pink tree leaned over them.

— Did you take her back? the voice grew even more fragile. I mean you, personally?

— Everything had been kept exactly as it was.

There followed the possibility of satisfaction from the way the fat man's hands composed themselves, disclaiming any suggestion that the questions were interrogations, but rather some kind of elegant parlour game in which the words *yes* and *no* were never to be used on pain of a forfeit.

— Did you make love to her then or was it afterwards?

— Owen's men obeyed orders to the letter.

Leaves shifted as the breeze turned fitful. Their clustered bouquet of light blew dark like venetian blinds abruptly shut by an unseen hand.

— Prison, I suppose, has aged her body? Her face looked very lined to me and streaks of grey in her hair. She couldn't be more than thirty-five, though. You know we were lovers, don't you? Try as you might, you cannot avoid certain things you and I have shared. So what is she like now, naked?

— Your portrait still hung in its place. (Squarcia relished the perfection of his English.) Without doubt Owen has had it photographed though.

The moment deepened between them. In a flash of clearsightedness, the president wondered if he had achieved anything in his own right, anything at all, or was this odious Italian always there at the opportune moment to plant a suggestion you could scarcely refuse to act upon? His most secret self was that fat boy who found freedom to love life only when flying along on his nameless bicycle. And now he took refuge, ungenerously, in abuse of those most faithful to him.

— Here come the clones, he sighed. And catching me being presented with a flower. What next! The locals will hear about this in the pub, for sure.

83

Shortly after the journalist drove away, leaving his ministerial letter of authority, Commandant Curtis took delivery of a tape recording from one of the staff. He popped spectacles on to magnify the brilliance of staring and patted his oiled hair, having checked the straightness of the parting.

— Machine ready? he asked.
— Sir.
— Clean job?
— Sir.
— Piss off, then. Good work.

His long froggy fingers stabbed at the controls. He listened without much interest at first. The tape made at the worksite had been completely clean, after all. Then came a passage that clicked him into rigid angularity.

Mama knows I'm visiting.

We don't have much to cheer us up. You could say a few television sets

would go a long way to helping us. It's the drug everyone outside uses,
after all.

Homesickness?

We'd need women to cure that. (Laughter.)

I suppose you work hard enough to be pretty tired?

Luke was murdered.

Plus your enterprise. Yes, I heard about that from Mr Curtis who tells
me you make quite a profit.

The steel cylinders are due. Big things. Huge. (Laughter.) *Can't do*
without them.

Back to the cereal packets for a moment. Do you divide your takings
among everyone equally?

Equally.

Not just those who put the artwork together?

Equally. But some is taken by the commandant before it reaches us.

I don't need to hear about that.

(Curious squealing squeaking noises intruded like some complicated and fragile piece of clockwork needing oil on all its
multiplicity of moving parts.)

You work labouring, I take it?

I'm an electronics man.

(Long pause, with distant squeaking.)

People out there think we are freaks?

They certainly see you as set apart. And with so much unemployment,
I'm sure they wonder how you feel, having a protected job like this.
Especially if you used to live as an ordinary Australian before.

(That tiny yet clamorous clockwork, momentarily closer was,
of course, a flock of birds.)

Well we're in it for the money now. There's nothing else left.

Let me ask you about your family.

Well I'd like to send greetings to Mama. My old firm Kawakoya
Electronics is. . . the hard. . . is the. . .

(Words obscured by a sudden burst of loud twittering.)

Back. . .

. . . free to go.

No political stuff. (A voice from further off, with the twittering
still quite loud.) *You were told that Mr Davies. I have my orders. The*
workers came here by their own choice.

One Japanese (Commandant Curtis listened with special interest to how his own voice sounded, calling remotely), *one Ethio-*
pian you asked for. We've got everything. I shall see you before you go,
Mr Davies.

This Australia, it is paradise (a new voice almost singing), *paradise. Paradise. So rich the rain. And who is getting murdered? Not us, all the time, I tell you! Paradise it is. Let us admit, dear brother.*

That long froggy finger stabbed at the controls again. After a delay the tape blurted into renewed action.

Mama knows I'm visiting.

We don't have much to cheer us up. You could say a few television sets would go a long way to helping us. It's the drug everyone outside uses, after all.

Homesickness?

We'd need women to cure that. (Laughter.)

I suppose you work hard enough to be pretty tired?

Luke was murdered.

Again and again he tried the passage distorted by birdcries, but he could not make out the words.

— Had the blasted microphone in a tree! Curtis swore. Bad news.

The commandant was one of those officials who perpetually suspected his superiors of plotting to keep him down, convinced his acumen had never been given due reward. Someone up there stole his thunder and practised petty suppressions against outstanding ability. He would not notify his administrative officer, no, nor even his director. For the first time in his career, he had something in his hand powerful enough to go above their heads. Davies had gained entry by presenting a letter from the ministry, so this would be his own line of approach. Why not phone the Minister direct?

But Owen Powell was not available to just any caller. No matter how urgent the business.

— Then sir, I shall put you through to the Minister's personal assistant Mr Cohen.

— You can tell *me*, Jack Cohen's invitation crooned down the line. I have the Marshal's absolute confidence.

Cohen was, as he himself put it often, a tiger for hospitality.

But the commandant, who had prudently withheld his name, wanted a reward in honey from the man at the top. He knew more than enough about the Cohens of this world, assistants who think of nothing for themselves but latch on to anything they can, voraciously scavenging better men's insights. He'd have my grandmother as his if he stood to gain by it, Cornelius Curtis later explained the failure of the phonecall. A few hours' delay surely couldn't matter, anyhow. He had acted fast. The culprit not much farther away than Port George by now. Enough leeway to let a little time slip by without harm.

— I shall try again soon. Please inform the Minister I rang. Just say a responsible officer of his department, he replied, and replaced the phone as soundlessly as possible, knowing he had made an enemy in high places.

— But what else? he demanded to be told. Some puppy!

He got up and pranced to the door, which he flung open so he could surprise the yard and maybe catch it loitering or absent altogether. The traitor birds flurried away in a chattering flock, they whirred up from his own steps where they had been lurking and listening. He stared out, still with his reading-glasses on and his eyes big as a horse's. The guards at the wall-top smartened themselves.

A short delay meant he might be running one risk, he perceived this. . . depending how soon the cylinders were due.

The silvereyes swooped again, jeering at him with fragile excitable cries.

His progress back to the telephone was rather in the style of an amputee tripod and his sticky fingers tripped one another while dialling the Project 31 worksite. He got through eventually as darkness crept in across the Pacific Ocean.

— Confidential, he informed the phone curtly. Mandatory I get the site manager's number. What's that? Ay? No. His afterhours number, of course. Who's this? Speak up. Mandatory. Matter of the highest importance. I have the Minister's personal instruction. Ay? You blasted fool! he swore, but only after he had put back the receiver in that manner of a man on the run. In fact he quickly seized it again and then slammed it home in case the cursed thing was not cut off.

— It all depends, he said. When those things are due to arrive.

He phoned Owen Powell once more.

The Minister was working back, yes, but all enquiries were to be referred to his assistant. Oh. Well unless the gentleman identified himself and explained his business, how could any-body judge whether it warranted disturbing the Marshal?

A quarter of an hour later, he repeated the call. And a quarter of an hour after that. By now he was sitting in a pit of darkness, frantic with worry at how huge his responsibility had grown. If only those swine would allow him into the arena, he'd dazzle them with the power he had to show.

Then the receptionist explained with regret (which sounded more like relief) that the Minister had finally gone.

— Home?

— I'm afraid that is something I cannot divulge to the public, sir.

— Not the blasted public, you moron, he raged shrilly and threw her back to extinction while he prowled his office trailing the telltale odour of funk.

84

This time Dorina had been called to the presidential mansion for an unimaginable reason: her husband needed her. Not for any state function, but for herself. She dropped everything and went. As soon as she saw, her heart went out to him, ogre though he was and firmly as she promised she would take this opportunity of charging him with a new crime against decency. She would refuse to concede, she had decided during the flight, that an election could be stopped like that just to dodge the consequences of unpopularity. Who did he think had put him there in the first place? He must accept blame for the everlasting shortages and the curfew still in force.

But she had not expected this.

— You've lost weight Buchanan, she said, compassionately avoiding any comment on the dreadful ravages of disease, his skin pitted and etched and his features sagging crazily to one side.

Over the years, he being the only familiar object she could feel at ease with in the mansion, Dorina had developed the habit of standing behind him dusting his coat collar. She took refuge in doing this again. At least it would save having to face him with comforting lies that cost her her pride.

— Don't tell me I've caught the dandruff from Sir Bill Penhallurick?

— Not as far as I can see. It's just hairs. You are shedding hairs all over yourself.

It was quite as if, she put it to herself later, she were visiting a husband in jail.

Dorina presided from the foot of the table at a lavish vegetarian dinner, with a few diplomatic people invited specially to please her. And she was pleased. She remembered her French during a spirited debate on residual radioactivity in the Pacific region, and huddled together sufficient Chinese to enjoy some jolly reminiscences about Yellow Sea pirates with a Beijing trade commissioner. Afterwards, to make up to the French ambassador, she played them several luscious pieces by Debussy. The deep chords tolled with her frustration and her grief for Rory lost to his habit, while the melodies sang some terrible fate through their liquid top notes. One sleeve slid back from her wrist in a graceful gesture and her odd, distinguished features grew so alight with intelligence she was beyond question beautiful.

She grew in strength from dawn, when she woke to a swishing of trees like the sea, till she accused Buchanan over boiled eggs of losing touch with the times. He chuckled indulgently. He liked her to correct him. And mocked her gently.

— How can you tell? I never knew anyone so divorced from the times as yourself. You have hung on to your precious classics through thick and thin. You've never given a damn for what other folk enjoy. You turn up your nose at their food and switch stations to keep yourself uncontaminated by their music.

— Does anybody imagine one has to *swallow* all that to be part of it? she snorted with disgust and ground more pepper on to her egg. Really Buchanan, I believed such intellectual creationism had gone out with the cannibals. Of course I am a person of my time, I could not avoid it even if I chose to. By keeping my personal standards I have been challenged to test the words I use and the music I love in the fires of a new antagonism, a new society they were never intended for.

— Elitism.

— Of course it's élitism and I am proud of that, if élitism means the company of those few who think. But why worry your head about the few. What you have to worry about is the many.

— They daren't attack me, my dear, he buried her spoonhand under his own. That's the beauty of being head of state as well as head of government. Even if they don't like me, they know that attacking me would be like tearing down the flag.

When she left him to his work and took a turn in the grounds, he was happy to remind himself she managed her duties to perfection.

Better than you do, Sir George Gipps agreed.

The president made sure he failed to notice, even in his gratitude to Dorina for treating him as a person who could still be spoken to intelligently.

Gipps looked sourly out the window.

Watching Dorina head in just the direction he had taken with Lavinia, the president brooded on her refusal to live with him.

The fact was, he had begun to miss her. These fleeting visits unsettled him rather than helping. Even Luigi Squarcia declined to move into the mansion when invited, not because he had any such claims as Dorina to employing himself gainfully at the piano, but because as he said in his convincing excuse his lifestyle might fall short of the establishment's high tone. And besides, he pointed out, it would never do for IFID's hot-line to be connected here.

George Gipps, who had come to stay without being invited, of course, began winding himself up to dispense more free advice. At this point, the president, in a sudden fury, concentrated on getting rid of his tormentor. He stared right through the fellow, as Gipps was said to have stared through those petitioners who most irritated him in his day, until the filing cabinets beyond showed through his dapper coat, till the haunting melted along a slant of early light. He was alone again.

— Summon an Executive Council meeting for eleven o'clock tonight, he instructed his secretary. I've had my dose of daytime living. . . up to here.

— Mr Powell may not be able to attend, Your Excellency. With Mrs Buchanan here for another two days, he took the opportunity of flying to Adelaide on business last night.

— Tell him the main item on the agenda is his rumoured resignation. We'll see if he gets to the meeting or not.

— Very good, sir.

He sifted through some documents and began signing them, reading each one thoroughly. A few he cast aside. On some he crossed out paragraphs, others he screwed up and threw away. Nothing was to be delegated when it came to minor matters, otherwise he would lose the satisfaction of feeling how omnipotent he was.

— In business, he grumbled. I faced none of this trouble.

The only person left to confide in was Dorina. Roscoe Plenty had defected to the madhouse, Squarcia behaved as if everybody else had done the same, dear Owen Powell was getting too big for his boots and maudlin into the bargain, Margaret Talbot was a schemer because that's why he appointed her, Veronica O'Toole would sting you to death with arcane footnotes if she thought she'd found a vulnerable spot at last, and the clones said, You're a character sir, or Pull the other leg Your Excellency.

So it came about, over lunch in the private parlour, that he did venture a question on general, even philosophical, lines. He asked his wife what she thought of the power of conscience. Gracious goodness Buchanan, she replied disentangling a Spanish comb from her hair and digging it back in, next thing you'll be abdicating! But he insisted on a serious answer. Being Dorina, she respected this, her hair a little astray, eyes big with too much hazard. She supposed, she said, even a president may suffer guilt.

— Guilt! he echoed and urged her for an explanation. But how could she go further, victim as she was of unrelenting surveillance, oppressed by years of checking in and out of her own home, aware that every move she made put the security men at risk as well as herself, aware that, however strong she may remain, Rory rendered her helpless. Yet she mustered at least the manner of her old courage as she conjured it up.

— And you do rather stick your neck out.

— How do you mean? he enquired, pushing his soiled plate aside as he might reject her answer before she made it.

— Getting all those people to vote for you on the promise of good times, when what they have had is, can't you see, sheer hardship.

— Not all of them, he protested meekly.

— All but a few, she sighed, apprehensive at making her meaning so clear. The conscience, she explained, must be there *for* something, don't you suppose?

— Let me tell you the truth, her husband offered. I have considered the issue far more closely than you may imagine. If I were to lose an election now, I would kill myself.

— Oh Buchanan, never! Her voice dropped (perhaps fearing this may one day reflect upon her own conduct) as she added. How. . . cheap.

— It is quite trendy, my dear, among the really successful. I'd be given little choice. Where is there for me to go from here? What is there for me to do? How would I even move without my litter and my bearers? And even supposing they stayed with me, how could I tolerate their intimacy if I were just a man and not an establishment?

— I've never known how you can bear *that* as it is, she declared. You should have a wheelchair made.

— What! he shouted, angry at last. Am I to look like a common invalid!

— Roosevelt did, she recollected with composure, relieved to escape the subject of conscience, also noting how anger improved his condition, bringing colour to his complexion and lifting the droopy side of his face almost level with the other. He was, she perceived, as completely self-absorbed as Rory, as completely addicted to his vice. She no longer even wished to comfort him. She could barely conceal her distaste.

The bearers arrived at the prearranged hour to carry him to his study.

— The nation won't wait, he apologized.

Till then she had been unable to overcome the strangeness of their seeming friends and offering him the respect due to one who lays himself open to injury. But now he had handed her the very stone she found she was longing to use. The weight of it being so beautiful a temptation, and his temples so looming a target, she let fly.

— No, she agreed in a wild rich gipsy voice. It will not!

But he had gone already, effortlessly escaping though there were only six of the brutes lifting him this afternoon. Surely he had not lost that much weight? She could have wept at such an inane failure, she who spent her life in a wilderness, presented with the choice of going mad or seeming to go mad. There never was a day when she quit, after all, gave way or revelled in the fame she'd become so hated and envied for possessing.

Dorina once played through the solo part of a piece by Nigel Butterley called *Explorations*, which began with a strange chord and repeated it in a slow regular pulse one hundred and twelve times, always with the same D-flat as its upper note, a single element of the bass changing each time. The original chord seemed independent of harmonic theory, something found, just like that, and contemplated deeply, repeated and repeated but never twice the same, always discovering new emotions. And when she had finished, Dorina was not satisfied she'd even touched on its possibilities. So she went over it again, all one hundred and twelve strokes, and then again, absorbed in her search, fascinated not so much by the challenge of exploring the piece but by the piece exploring her, creating a stark world she knew too deeply to doubt, the percussive dissonance belling, belling, ribs of it, subtle as sand-dunes in their approach and drifting away, reiterations all alike, stretching behind and eventually ahead, but each one unique to its moment and in its character. She saw how Buchanan came to be marooned: he was not imaginative enough to believe anything worth doing twice.

Having understood this left her free to go on. And the deserts of her loneliness were not always voluntary.

Dorina had simply walked barefoot into a land of cactus. She kept her head high and gave the best possible impression of not caring. But privately her entire being concentrated on those tender soles, the brush and snicker of spines, till she developed a virtuoso cunning and swept lightfooted among them, immune, while the jungle of pricklypear turned harmless green cheeks her way where anyone else (and Master Squarcia in particular) would be in agony by now and absorbed with the business of picking hairfine tortures from his flesh.

Her project while she was at Yarralumla Mansion was, she said originally, to read the Bible straight through from end to end. Each time she arrived, her chief interest was to pick up where she had left off and foster the illusion of having some function in being there. She made one attempt to involve her husband by reading aloud some lines from the first chapter of Isaiah: Make the heart of this people fat, and make their ears heavy, and shut their eyes; lest they see with their eyes, and hear with their ears, and understand with their heart, and convert, and be healed. She read it with trepidation, fearing that it made her opposition to his rule rather too explicit. He looked up, interested as it turned out, in her tone.

— That takes me straight back to my schooldays, he rumbled with pleasure.

She vowed never to try again. And yet, now, her intermittent readings brought her to a passage she simply could not keep to herself. Dorina marked the place with her finger and looked up round the sumptuous sittingroom. A manservant hovered in one doorway, tray in hand, waiting for the inevitable drinks order. Is that all the diplomatic set do, she wondered, drink? She went straight to the study knowing he seldom moved from there, drawing the fascinating threads of power to his still centre, silking the day with visitors and telex messages, his six phones ringing, his squad of secretaries and assistants shuttling in and out. Sure enough, the bearers loafed outside idly chatting about their muscles, their diet and the elysium of a day off perhaps. They came to attention at her approach. This was not an occasion on which she had anything to gain by familiarity, so she failed to see them. She strode straight past the restraining hand of a security man without seeing him either, opened the door for herself and went in, bearing the Bible thicker than usual by one finger. Buchanan was, momentarily, alone.

— Remember this? she asked without preamble, disregarding his irate gesture. I knew I would find it for you someday. Such a surprise when I came upon it unawares: The blows of a friend are faithful, but the kisses of the enemy are treacherous. What do you think of that for bitter truth! Proverbs.

He motioned her to pass the book across and stared at it, remembering the cricket match, a pretty youth whisking away his champagne glass and fixing him with hard eyes. He remembered also the courteousness of ministers.

— Once again your reading has been a service to me, he intoned ponderously. May I borrow this for an hour, Dorina? Miss Colquhoun, he called the secretary on the intercom. Send me Mr Squarcia.

Without her Bible, Dorina faced the regimen of yet another stroll round the garden, which never failed to feed her frustration, or down to the lake to watch an empty tourist launch plough by. Instead however, in one of those inspired gestures so much her own, she elected to confront her foolish dislike and be fair to the brutes. They were not furniture, were they? Nor even to blame for accepting such odious chores, considering the publicity they got, plus the respect this must have brought them over the years. And if, she reasoned, their alternative was to be dogged by unemployment and hopelessness, did they have any choice?

— Good afternoon, she greeted them as the study door closed behind her. And because she felt awkwardly like the grande dame she tried not to be, gave them no chance to recover from their surprise. I do apologize, she hurried into what she must say. For upsetting your routine each time I come here. Do you find you get tired?

— Not us, Your Excellency, Harvey shook out a readymade reply. We have our work.

Oh dear. This was the thing she least wished to hear. Looking from one to another, the president's wife was reminded of an irregularity she'd noticed earlier.

— Are you only six today?

— We have a new rule, Your Excellency. One day every week designated as lighter duties.

— Heavier duties for those left, she joked riskily.

They were too well coached to smile.

— We take our leave two at a time so it gives us each a day off once a month. But there's always either me or Noel here as leader, he added to allay any concern she might be feeling.

— Well, Dorina gave up the attempt and, clasping hands on the loss of her Bible, offered them a nervous laugh. I must be off. Or I shall miss catching the steamer.

— Thank you, Your Excellency, Harvey spoke on behalf of them all, hoping like blazes he had passed whatever test she had been putting him through.

But one of the younger ones began humming a popular tune, quietly, contentedly.

— Catching the steamer! he murmured incredulously.

They soon snapped to attention when Luigi Squarcia arrived along the corridor. He made straight for them, driving a wedge of poisonous ill-will ahead of him, and vanished into the study. A trace of Paco Rabanne hung round for a few minutes while the bearers waited to hear raised voices. But all remained quiet. Then the tourist launch tooted as it rounded the point at the bottom of the mansion grounds, at the one time a warning and a salute.

— That is not possible sir, the telephone answered brightly. Marshal Powell is in Adelaide for the next few days.

Commandant Curtis had not slept, had not even left his office. He let his eyelids shriek down to close off his despair and placed a damp priestly thumb and a priestly finger, one on each, to hold them shut.

Pride would not allow him to cover his ears against the twittering of small birds outside his window.

— No dear, Mama refused. I don't believe it is good for your system to stay in the house all the time, breathing the fumes, if you see what I mean. Up guards and at 'em, as my uncle used to say. To work with you, girl! Widow or not, you must look after yourself. You have a profession, so you are one of the lucky ones and perish the thought that you may ever forget it or cease to be grateful. No, I won't hear any argument. Gracious me, what a mess the gentlemen's wardrobe is! There's no accounting for people. As soon as you've had your tea and toast I expect to see you dressed to go. Well I wish you wouldn't press me to a discourtesy, but I am afraid there is no choice, Stephanie. If you won't accept a hint I shall have to tell you outright: I need the room today. Saints preserve us from the simpleness being contagious. Put it this way, there is a special gentleman I am entertaining this afternoon, is that plain enough? You do try the patience, considering you are supposed to be the smart one.

85

Trees fountained black in the brilliant moonlight.

High on a forested hillside the men crouched behind the Wild Dog, whose glossy hair cast his face in shadow.

Nearby, a small creature shivered.

The hours they had waited moulded the air around them heavy and clear as liquid. The moon floated among bleached stars. Trees grew, unaware the sun no longer shone on them. The men crouched, blood easing along limbs licked cold by a breeze.

When next they looked up, surprised by the rich deep sky, blue as stormlight, the moon had stopped rising and stood on her tower of mild lustre. Even now, the scene might explode in violence. The roadway below, which they had come to watch, glowed white. Empty. An insistent wind shuffled among leaves. The Wild Dog's face, a mask of moon-shadow, turned and looked from this to that of his comrades; a movement which, by shifting the balance of his body, called attention to the weapon he leant against, an anti-tank gun lucid in the glittering night.

The Man prayed: let nothing happen.

The moon on its tower of silence inspected the road for innocence. Tongues were at their chilling duty. Storybook justice shivered in the shadows. The blood obeyed instincts.

Curious how trees and rocks come to know about human affairs, how insects gather for a chosen event, hovering in the interim not willing to miss a thing, how even grass stiffens as spiky ears. This was the night. Mosquitoes quietly sucked blood through little straws, all eyes for what might happen. Leaves stopped shuffling. Nothing. The men felt their skin grow thick with waiting and the boy prayed, please keep things like this please.

A single rifle shot broke the spell. An impossibility. The moon jerked into motion. Who would fire a rifle, for christ's sake, a puny rifle? And just one shot. Useless. But not far off. That unmistakable plop, a rent in the balloon of night, nothing dramatic, not loud at this distance, but enough for the whole huge wrinkling bag of night to collapse. The waiting men gauged the range at perhaps 800 metres to their right up the valley. Air drained away through that gap of a shot. They could scarcely breathe. Was this all; cold night baring the immense emptiness of a mistake? They expected mammoth trucks led by motorcycle escorts and gun-carriers, all travelling hastily, hoping to complete the journey before daybreak.

Or had they been spotted? Might that shot be a prelude to a barrage of small-arms fire? Or even some third party warning them? Air had drained away altogether. Their chests heaved under the effort of survival.

Ordinary as a drawingroom conversation, the initial statement was answered: a machinegun let out rapid denials with an upward inflexion, stopping at a question mark.

After a long pause during which the hillside rumbled gently and the whole countryside could be heard shifting ground, the rifle thought again and fired a further bullet.

The moon on its tower enjoyed a grandstand view of what remained hidden from the hidden men. The set stage lay patiently expecting action. The Wild Dog checked his anti-tank gun and glanced at Nick with his. Their shadowed faces held each other briefly and confidently.

The air rushed back with a dull roar, vast as a rising tide of deep water. Two machineguns snapped a peremptory retort. And that was that. The grinding earth changed gear at the brow of a rise, and far down the road a battery of headlights raked the corner, shredding the night.

The thundering convoy sailed majestically into view, seeming in its slowness too fast, as the Milky Way wheeled above too slow in its inconceivable flying asunder. A squad of motorcycles led the way, police stolidly astride saddles, gripping the machines between huge thighs and leather-clad calves for 100 kilometres at that exhausting deceleration. Either side of the road, half on the dusty shoulders and ditches, came eight armouredcars, four in line on each flank, with mobile search-lights slicing arcs through the bush, while two trucks in the middle occupied the crown of the roadway, crawling inexorably on a tidal roar.

Surmounting the combat vehicles, soldier outlines could be seen crouched close behind their weapons, ready to let fly. Searchlights, sideglow picking out the escort's bristling arma-ments, scorched the hillside, flooding the bush behind and in front of the hideout, sweeping from time to time across the watching men.

The trucks advanced to the top of the rise down there where the road turned on its moonshine plate and veered away toward sleep. The Man glanced behind him, suddenly suspect-ing troops encircled them with knowing grins.

Though Nick and the Wild Dog were marksmen and facing huge targets, their weapons felt unmanageably crude and cumbersome. Mama's arsenal consisted entirely of leftovers from forgotten wars. The convoy tugged the night in its wake through a tremendous thickness of noise: trucks and cycle motors pulsating and the mingled whining growl of armouredcars.

A searchlight from one of the rear vehicles passed across the head of the convoy picking out a line of three machinegunners on the turrets ahead, each with an offsider next to him wearing earphones. Tall whiplash aerials swayed.

The moon stood on its column as if it had always been there. The hard bright patch of road, thrilling to the approach of massive weights, lay empty and expectant, an innocent bend, a blameless arena.

Nick and the Wild Dog settled their weapons, feeling for perfect steadiness.

On came the motorcycle headlamps, cold trembling beams, the lights flashing above them cast miniature rocket-bursts on domed helmets. Plumes of dust billowed and milled in the guncarriers' wake, swirling high to either side. Into the moonlight. For a few seconds only, both transports presented their sides, clearly displayed, down there on the road.

The double detonation of anti-tank guns had already gone off and their missiles had either hit the mark or missed when the Wild Dog realized he had no means of telling. Still the convoy filled the valley with an oceanic roar. He and Nick lay motionless under the fury of heartbeats while they lowered the barrels. Searchlights raked back at the retrospective scrub around them. Nelson kept his machinegun ready to retaliate. But it was all over. The Man rediscovered breathing.

The last armouredcars whined, growling out into whatever darkness the future held. Red tail-lights glared as one vehicle after another swung north round the bend and hit the brakes momentarily. The two giant crates teetering tall in the reflected glare appeared ready to topple. The soundlevel sank gradually, leaving trees to glisten darkly.

The moon stood on its column.

Mosquitoes buzzed lazily, engorged.

Utterly dastardly disgraceful vandalism. The most shocking waste of public money and violation of my faith in the commonsense of the Australian people, was how President Buchanan described the incident the following morning. He loomed on every channel, mouth gaping for oxygen in this suffocating banana republic he was chained to by accident of birth and misplaced loyalty.

— These components, he roared at the stupid populace who might have been a grinning class of fifth-graders right in front of him and visible, were imported from West Germany. All the way they came, his voice acquired a wonderful preacherly nuance flaming at the edges. Without mishap, without hitch, without delay or trouble of any sort. Huge components, shipped safely to our shores. Imagine. And then. And then, he choked. We sent them by road to an installation where all the preparations had been completed spot on schedule, a tremendous feat of organization. Everything ready, he explained for the sake of the drongos. And what happens, for godsake, but some vile parasite of an agitator, some unprincipled delinquent bombards them with acid. Steel cylinders, milled to the finest measurements. How was it done, you ask? Well, I promise I shall find out how. No worries about that. Heads will roll, you may rest assured. Heads, he roared thumping the table. Will roll. Damage as big as that! he gesticulated with a single wild windmilling circle of his full armspan. Corroded. If we installed them now, every worker on the plant during its whole operational existence would be at risk. Did they think of this, these patriots? An outrageous waste of public money. Your money. Don't get the idea it's us up here who're suffering. Money out of your pocket, and so much of it you wouldn't have a clue. Replacements, you ask? Replacements cannot be a practical possiblity for months at the earliest. And what happens to the jobs of the Friends of Privilege out there at the construction site. Who thought of them? What about our world reputation? This is a strategic base, I'll have you know. Vital to the defence links of our allies. You haven't got the least idea, he yelled at the clods while Luigi Squarcia pursed his lips in the control room. What fools this makes us look. The criminals who perpetrate these outbreaks of sabotage (because this is not the first) can only remain at large because sentimental misguided citizens fail to report irregular or suspicious activities. You've been asked and asked again. Have you got the message this time? However insignificant you may think it is; if you notice anything out of the ordinary going on in your neighbourhood, report it immediately. We must unite to stop these vandals. They won't rest till they have the whole country in ruins. Turn them in, he raged. They are your enemies. They're robbing you of your money as surely as if they had their dirty hands in your pocket this moment.

Mama switched him off.

— Now, she declared with huge satisfaction. Who says the boy can't do it? What a brain. Acid bombs!

The Man grinned goofily.

The others just sat around, quiet as they sometimes could be. And this was the best part. He knew they accepted him. This was better than anything they could have said.

86

Stephanie was not there for the celebration. She had left without ever feeling she belonged, her strongest contact at Mama's, first by the resentment he stirred in her and then by his magnetism, being the Wild Dog. With Luke dead, her ancestors redoubled their taunts. Fragmentary presences tripped her and plagued her with the glitter of malignant glances. She seldom caught sight of more than a foot here or a lace cuff there, but even these she could never speak of to anyone but Luke.

First there had been the silence. And that was awful enough. Then the news: Tim's voice bringing him along the hallway with it, a funeral tone already escaping him. If she fell from the ferriswheel now, it would not be on a merciful downswing towards a black man who understood she was being pushed, but from the very top to make disaster certain. Her silence, although a hint Tim did not miss, failed to ward off his confession of what he knew. His voice, growing loud with terrible truths, led him to find her parked in the big dim kitchen of a woman who expects she may one day employ a cook again; parked, that is, in front of a mug of hot sweet liquid, she scarcely cared what, as long as it scalded her lips to cleanse them, plus a newspaper propped in front of her. *Her* newspaper, and his.

Stephanie allowed Tim to deposit one hand on her arm, where it caught fire, till by shaking the paper scornfully she tried to shrug off his gesture without hurting him. But he took a firmer hold and now she noticed nobody was with him. Even the ever-interfering Mama left them alone. There could be only one explanation. A blank bright light probed the back of her mind. She did not need words. Stephanie Head stood and sobbed once, an effort more like bronchitis than grief, a sound she had uttered before, when a child, on the day Greta told her their mother had left. She clutched at Tim because he was too tender to let anyone else break her trust of silence, and wept a mute brimming-over misery.

He was ashamed at having thought more of his own risk in going to Vengeance Harbour than her loss.

— Take me with you to your place, she begged. Or Lavinia's if you can't have me.

So Stephanie came to sit in the studio chair Roscoe Plenty once occupied while his wolf portrait was being painted. Tim and Ganymede had left. Lavinia, perched on her workbench, picked at a blob of dried pigment, chrome yellow; looking older, even, than forty-one.

Their eyes met briefly, each searching for the independent spirit they shared in common and which often bound them in league against Greta, but neither finding it.

— Prison, Lavinia observed sorrowfully and tossed her head to avert a blow. Makes one selfish.

To look out on the roofs below, Stephanie had to peer past her infuriating crowd of fragmentary bodies in fancydress, two of whom waved as they floated up past the window in a decorative basket.

— There's one thing I always regretted, Lavinia began again, dislodging the blob of paint and appraising it between her fingers like a gold coin, remembering. Though it seemed slight at the time.

— Yes, her younger sister agreed from knowing such things. You refused my simple request to meet your Mr Squarcia. Lavinia replaced the flake of light, wishing to restore its permanence.

— At the races.

— All because, Stephanie confirmed. I wanted to interview a fat man he was managing. Before he came to power. What a scoop it might have been, she mused. If I had seen through him.

— Nobody, Lavinia told the unheeding roofs of Paddington. Had the least idea.

— Far from it, Stephanie discovered in herself a spark of that lost fire.

And she pointed to the real estate agent's portrait still hanging where it always had, above the record-player and stacks of grimy discs, many of them never returned to their sleeves.

The two sisters considered him on his carpet of shattered

fragilities. The air of unused years had been entirely stripped of its linseed-oil smell.

— One thing you got wrong was his expression. You made him too. . . well, regretful. Why don't you take it down anyway?

— That would be admitting something I won't admit.

So the spark came to flicker again in Lavinia too.

87

— Fat is tough, the first president announced.

— Men! Veronica O'Toole commented scornfully, but in private.

— I love you, Ganymede told Tim, also in private.

— Never ask questions, said Squarcia. And don't quote me on that.

— Clear as day. Usual precautions. Full report, remember. Good work, men. Piss off then, Commandant Curtis said as he stuck the Minister's letter of authority on a spike.

— Why haven't they ever thanked me? Greta Grierson asked the photograph taken in 1972 by a neighbour.

— How's it going down there? This is the big one. When we tell you to move, you move.

— Life is measured by death, Yanagita explained. As we are measured by our enemies.

— What's cooking? the Wild Dog asked cheerfully, reaching for his gun.

Miss Gardiner sighed against the folding door.

88

To his amazement, Sir William Penhallurick was not shown straight in. He was kept waiting.

— Would you like a magazine? Ms Colquhoun offered. *Time? The Business Week? Fortune?*

He waved aside the feasibility of his being softsoaped, flapping a petulant hand.

— Does he know it's me?

— Of course he knows, Sir William.

He plunged his birdweight back against the cushions and punished his eyes by staring straight into a lamp on the side table. Beyond these funnels of warmth the immense darkness of the antipodes flew past, shot with silver threads of satellites. He had always liked the cosiness in here, that confidential bustle of the trusted who work all hours, each desk luminous and discrete. Here alone, in the whole country, one could believe people were not spying. But tonight the charm palled. He felt stifled, contemptuous of these ferrets digging in burrows to come up with nothing more glorious than a bedraggled rabbit or two. He waited on that comfortable settee in the discomfort of scratching his resentful skin and fitting his gritty eyelids to the disillusionment of eyes. When eventually he was shown through the presidential suite, past an alcove where the bearers played pontoon in their sleep, to the familiar door of the study, he was fairly raging. He realized no visitor had come out: so Bernard had sat there alone, had he, refusing to see him for that agonizing half hour? The door shut behind Sir William Penhallurick.

Neither man spoke.

The air clustering and madding with messages.

Such anger, probably, was not good for a ninety-six-year-old grandfather. Two Penhalluricks experienced the interview: one on fire, purple face popping open with fury to utter blasts of scorching invective; the other a skeletal creature who nervously picked at scabs on his knuckles exactly as he had done when a lad in the early months of 1919 smuggling arms for Béla Kun, once skating across a frozen river with his school satchel crammed full of live ammunition and the terrible weight of it stooping him as he flew over black ice leaving a telltale wake of white wounds; then after successfully carrying a message and its reply, being brought before the great Kun in person to be patted on the shoulder and told he was a hero of the people. Oh yes, he could see that fellow now, toad eyes and wide toad mouth, going bald on top, the pale skin pushing up from under scattered stubble he wore cropped short. (Buchanan was a great deal larger and further gone with power. But the type held good.) And only six months later this very lad had visited the same river, now flowing, to plant a bomb for the Whites in the hope of blowing Béla Kun and his compliments to hell, but the sly toad had changed plans so the boat sank with no one of any account aboard, only a couple of illiterates who manned her plus three peasant families and a cow.

— I have always, said the scab-picking Penhallurick while the fiery one suddenly understood that English expression: being beside oneself with rage. Had your interests at heart. You are like a son. What do you say? his lugubrious voice being swallowed by the big man's room.

The president, apparently, said nothing. But he produced a newsclipping which he passed across the desk, a piece from dear Alice's own paper, by some female reporter, about progress on the rebuilding of the Buchanan Cultural Centre ten months after the tragedy. Along one margin, in the president's own hand was a comment, *Another fatal upside-down river?*

— Well, Sir William brushed this irrelevance aside. We can't have that beautiful technology going to waste. The calculations are all complete. It's a spin-off from the Paringa research on gravitation. You have to move with the times.

He slapped the clipping back on the desk, his disdain measured by how far it lay beyond the president's reach. Buchanan still did not speak.

— The point is, I have been in touch with New York, he said twice, once pale, once in flames. Had he said that? He didn't mean to come out with it so soon.

— And Washington, he added as a gush of heat.

— More, his fading voice echoed. I have been thinking.

The flames took over again.

— You may not realize you are facing a crisis, Bernie.

— I'm too old to be kept waiting, whined the child.

— Tell me this new Act of yours was worded in haste, in the passion of the moment, one Penhallurick demanded and the other begged.

The study withdrew to its puddles of light while outside the night fled away and away, and stars skated across a lake which never froze.

— *I* can forgive you, the child sang its generous old *zigeunerweisen* but then, lost in a forest of moss and soft paw-treads and dark stalkings, with pine branches wheezing like wolves, added immediately afterwards: Watch out! Watch out though! and the wheezing crept all round, a thick pelt of fallen needles shifted underfoot while he nearly stumbled over the name of treachery. Bernie.

Hadn't he said what he'd come to say yet?

— I am on the verge, declared the irresistible Penhallurick who was really Zoltán Kékszakállú and none other. Of big things. . . my whole life.

— With this international corporation, snuffled his ailing voice.

At long last the presidential ogre cleared its throat, setting all four chins wobbling, and spoke:

— It needs licensing by me, if you are to continue operating in Australia. Unless you are thinking of permanently emigrating to Tuavaleva?

The décor sat back with satisfaction written all over its comfortable face; this was the appropriate voice for such a setting, neither gasping hot nor squeaking frail. A succulent voice leaving no room for rebuttal.

— What do you say? wailed the one near death.

— IFID, the furnace roared promptly. Insists.

Buchanan let out a couple of dogs of laughter.

— You are here, he enquired. To urge me to allow the election to go ahead?

— Exactly, don't you see? a grateful Penhallurick probably explained, though the other one stamped any suggestion of gratitude into the carpet.

— So, the president sneered. I give you your licence and you give me the arsehole. Is that the deal?

— I treat you like a son of my own, the little chap whined.

— You treat me, Bernard Buchanan doled out words he had been maturing for twenty years. More like you treated your wives!

So it had come to this.

Satellites threaded their reliable web while the night sky endlessly fled. Warmth breathed in the mansion and Dorina slept or did not sleep upstairs, alone.

For a long time after the champion of democracy had gone, President Buchanan savoured his first taste of true power.

89

— I have found us a navigator, Mama declared. He's not used to fieldwork though. I must apologize for that, Mr Dog, she added, staring a moment out of her window at the tired figures in the street, exhausted women sitting with backs against the fence, heads resting on folded arms, asleep maybe, and men presenting blank faces, empty of the past.

— Where has he been?

In the interests of optimism, Mama snapped the curtains shut.

— He navigates for the Sydney-Hobart yacht race every year: recommendation enough to a patriot like me (she announced the word *patriot* as a privilege, having nothing to do with any shallow nationalistic competitiveness). Better still, he knows Tuavaleva. But you'll have to hold your sides when you hear his name and promise not a one of you will laugh in his face. I say this specially for the benefit of the Man who's given to the weaknesses of the immature. Dr Ganymede Sikorski. Well you see, she explained. He's American. Polish-American to be precise.

— Shit, Nelson swore.

— No no my dear, Mama took him up on this. We really mustn't judge Americans by the foolishness of their rulers. They are lovely people, as we are ourselves. Many's the time I've been there and always felt like one of the family. Are you willing to meet him?

— What the hell, Nick agreed. Supposing we don't like him we can always put a bullet through his head before he squeals. Granny Corkscrew we'll call him for short if we keep him!

— Mama, the Wild Dog said ruminatively. Remember the day you picked me up in your car and you knew who I was? Well nothing has gone wrong yet, we're still alive and stirring.

The old lady accepted this as both praise and a challenge.

— I should warn you, her jewellery jingled theatrically as she signalled somebody outside. He has this sort of knowledge on a world scale. Makes you dizzy. Not like the geography we were taught at school by Mrs Ping, a Chinese lady teacher now deceased, God rest her. He knows the floor of the ocean like I know my backyard. I said, when I caught a glimpse of him in a certain person's car, this is just the man we need.

A door opened and the guest walked in to sit, sinking in quilted cushions, among his judges, the silk uttering little shrills of interest.

The Wild Dog turned away to speak to the youth beside him, but said nothing. Contempt printed itself deeply on Nelson's face. Oh yes, Mama had anticipated this. She didn't hatch out of the egg yesterday. She knew how the Wild Dog burned in his code of manliness and how it would eat at him to put his life in the hands of such a pretty creature.

Nick, seeing she intended to begin talking down their alarm, cut her short.

— Do you fight and fuck and all that crap? he enquired kindly.

Ganymede Sikorski rose to the challenge.

— No, he replied with a perfectly American intonation. Neither of those things.

Nick burst out with a delighted laugh directed at the Wild Dog, who made a point of honour of holding nothing against a man who had had no chance to prove himself.

— We get only one shot at this job, he warned.

Ganymede Sikorski nodded.

— The Man has been working at it, Mama burst out.

— Yes, said the Man, knowing these few minutes were his contribution because the Wild Dog had already forbidden him to take part in the action. Now he faced them, feeling the tears sting. Oh, he was a hopeless romantic, and science no defence against feelings. Yet he found within his isolation a reserve of calm; the brutal self-possession of a child who says, when I die they'll be sorry, which allowed him space for a mature gesture of resignation. . . preferably to be followed by a quick dose of strychnine or hara kiri for a person with the requisite training.

— This, the Man cleared his tender throat and began twice. This is the story I've nutted out. Some is old hat. Some we guessed. Some is news. Yesterday we got a report from Uragami. Very sophisticated hardware is on its way. You see, under top security. And when. It's due to leave Yokohama on the fifteenth. This month. To come on a ship. The *Sirius*. Registered in Panama. Okay? Built in Belfast, 1938. By Harland and Wolff. Now owned by Worldnet Industries.

— A subsidiary of Interim Freeholdings Incorporated of Delaware, Mama put in, in a loud whisper, not wishing to steal the boy's thunder, seeing how jealous he was of another intellectual arriving to take his place.

— Specifications? he referred to a scrap of paper. All still in the old scale: 15,600 tons, draws 17 feet 2 inches. So! Why such a small ship? Plenty of big containers coming from Yokohama. For a while I thought, just a while. . . secrecy. They could sneak in without anybody noticing. But if you look. My second idea. You come up with another. (The Man blushed excitedly in the rush to get it all said.) Can I go back a little way? Can I? Look. That first message from Luke. . . Port George harbour ready. You see! And when Tim stayed in the town he said the place is crawling with Watchdogs. The equipment they're bringing might even include stuff that's against the United Nations Outer Space Armaments Limitation Agreement. But it's a small port. And an old ship would be a good disguise. There is a catch though.

— Where can it refuel? Spinebasher asked suddenly alert.

— Just in time, the Man flashed them his triumph. IFID has a new base, see? Right on the way between Japan and Australia.

— Maybe so, Ganymede observed. But they can't bring that ship into Tuavaleva harbour. The channel won't take 17 feet 2 inches.

Nelson and Nick exchanged a swift glance.

— She'll be refuelled off-shore, the Man agreed reluctantly.

— That's tricky too, there are reefs out there.

— You see why we need you, the Wild Dog put in.

— Anyhow, the Man explained, offended. That is the end of my report. Except to say that when they take the fuel out to the ship, the fuel-carrier itself could be our weapon.

The silk cushions shrilled.

Mama made a mercy of her laced fingers.

90

Commandant Curtis seriously considered throwing his tape-recording into the prison furnace. Without doubt this was the best safeguard for personal interests now the cylinders had been damaged on their way to the construction site. Owen Powell, in the same situation, would not have hesitated, even if it had been one of his own works of art. But then, the Powells of this world are amateurs compared to the Curtises. Our commandant had been trained. He believed in outspokenness and integrity; his own above all others', even *despite* all others', if it came to the point. Duty demanded that he submit to the Cohen person, hand over the evidence he had held too long and then, as he put it, take his medicine. Which might be the finish of his career. Beyond question he had had it in his power to prevent that ambush. He chuckled bitterly when he thought how he'd promised himself this piece of vigilance would earn him promotion. He had been taught a stern lesson; he was not about to nullify the other information on the tape. Cohen it must be. Spine held straight, he put the phone to his ear as if it must burn him and listened attentively to the dial tone. But his long froggy fingers went to work independently: they flicked through the Canberra directory and dialled a number his regimental brain had never dared consider.

— Commandant Curtis here. Vengeance Harbour Friends of

Privilege camp. Matter of vital importance. State security. No one else will do. Sorry, can't explain to you.

He listened to a series of clicks. His line was being checked, naturally. Time enough to curse the idiocy of imagining so great a man would have time to speak to individuals of no importance.

— This had better not be a hoax or I'll have your balls, Bernard Buchanan's voice boomed into the good man's ear. Your call has been traced.

— Permission requested to read you the transcript of a recording made some days ago, sir.

The president listened as always to every detail. He had a touch with the common man. Nothing too small for his attention, everything being suspicious. He received the name Mama, he heard that somebody called Luke had been murdered, he accepted news of the cylinders without even a grunt escaping him. He jotted the name Kawakoya on his pad, all without involuntary reaction. But he did flinch at some imbecile chanting para*dise* about his internment camp in his Australia.

— My helicopter, Mr Curtis, he said gently when the report had run its course. Will call for you within the next two hours. Please be ready to come here as my guest. My office is arranging your leave clearance.

— But Your Excellency, Cornelius Curtis cried out, cut to the heart by such kindness. (He didn't consider the danger at this stage.) Must confess to you. Could have saved the cylinders from ambush. Tried to notify Marshal Powell the day before yesterday. Up the whole night phoning. His damned secretary wouldn't put me through.

— If I had a thousand Commandant Curtises at my side, the telephone spoke with that famous warmth known to all. No one on earth could hold me back.

Owen Powell, monitoring this conversation as part of the president's comprehensive security screen, called for Curtis's file which would now need his personal attention. He put it in his briefcase on top of the illicit information about Mama, clipped the lock shut, announced to his staff that he had been called away urgently, and left with the utmost nonchalant speed.

— How come, Ganymede protested increduously. There's no scandal over this?

As an American he was too foreign to be told. And too

intelligent. He would simply not understand if Tim explained that, in our press, even during its better years, scoops concern, essentially, domestic misbehaviour. He tried.

— A scoop is a woman pushed from her fourteenth-floor apartment who sprains her ankle, a father accused of sex with his sons, a boatload of politicians being photographed *in flagrante delicto* with a wellknown prostitute. Those are scoops.

— And the CIA interfering to have your government overthrown in. . . 1975, was it?

— Not a scoop. A scoop is a Russian spy, because that confirms what we already know. A Russian spy saves us having to think. He does us a good turn.

— A foreign corporation buying up the economy of the entire country?

— Certainly not a scoop. Print such a story and nobody would believe it. The shit-stirrers are at work, they'd say and turn to the next page. Look, as a nation we are proof against shocks. You can't catch us off balance. You can knock us to Kingdom Come and you won't have the satisfaction of seeing us flinch. We haven't even noticed what is happening. If a man's grandfather or his accountant suddenly gets a hefty sentence for drug smuggling, he has the satisfaction of wagging his head after the event. That's when he wags it. And he wags it with respect for the way the world hangs together: so now we know where the old devil got his money, he says. And he is *pleased*. Do you get it?

91

Dear Greta,

You have no right to victimize me with the past. That is all water under the bridge and such a long time ago. You were too young to judge. I have a new life and a husband. Why not let bygones be bygones, I should like to know? This is such a shock, you can't imagine. Why do you haunt me now that things are peaceful after years of struggle? Are you writing just to put me in your hands, then? Let me inform you. Notwithstanding the pleasure it gives me to know you are safe and sound, I wish you to understand that such a thing must not happen again. This is my last word to you.

My present husband, who is a good man, is on the shire

council, so he is not a man to be trifled with, you see. Keep out
of my life or I'll fetch the police. I will not have you ruining
everything when I have got it so nice at last.

Your loving mother,

Mrs Amanda Seward
(Grierson, as was)

92

It had been a disaster.

Ganymede, waiting till the loudspeaker blared another message across the night sea, started his motor. The retch and snarl
of their escape was lost in the throb from two idling ships. The
launch skimmed away far above a ridged and fractured seabed
he had once spent months mapping. He never thought he
would end up in a black wind on racing water as a fugitive,
jolted by the huge thud thud thud thud thud of a heart,
buffeting into obstructive waves.

He knew he was right not to wait for orders. This was the
style of a Wild Dog's man. The Wild Dog himself, streaming wet
and panting, invisible in the dark, within hand's reach but not
to be touched.

They watched the glimmers dwindle till it seemed impossible
that dead friends lay on a wet deck under twinkling lights.

The big man, his hair dripping, shivered at the memory: once
the lighter had drawn near, its blunt prow breaking waves to
slops and spurts, floodlamps were switched on along the larger
ship's rail to shine down on the water, creating golden ponds
and casting tremors of dull reflections up the freighter's black
flank, showing it as immense, frail from decades of overwork
and pieced together with rivets dribbling rust. The canvas hose
swung across on a boom, then pump motors banged into life,
generators whining to cope with the load and aboard the old
barge all but emergency lights switched off to conserve her
feeble power reserve. Both engines pulsed ponderously; churning screws kept the parallel craft from drifting too close or too
far apart. Among the deckhands there were also troops, each a
little Merasaloa, who helped secure the bayonet-fitting of the
giant hose, and then went stamping across the steel deck, back
to their posts, while the skipper engaged the pump. The motor

dipped to a bass note, the hose stiffened. Then the Wild Dog saw it fly off its housing, dancing from the boom as it whipped above the deck, casting a black sheet of diesel oil right from superstructure to rail, oil also fountaining from the pump outlet during the seconds the skipper took to slam it off. The entire deck swam, pungent with fuel illuminated by the few dank blobs of bulbs left burning. Lightermen came skidding over to ram the brass rim home again, locking it securely. The waiting freighter's flank towered close, leaning enough to topple right on them. Only to sigh away, a current sucking round weed-hung plates. The pump started again, hose standing stiff with cargo, and the job settled to a routine of keeping the vessels from colliding.

He watched that gush of oil sheeting the entire deck, mirror-perfect.

The skipper, as a silhouette, peered from his illuminated wheelhouse; while over on the freighter's bridge the American captain sat in conference, twisting astride his stool, now and again reaching for the PA microphone. One deckhand below leaned on the rail where a floodlamp, rusted to its mounting, gazed into a private pool of molten gold. Time for the Wild Dog and his acrobats to begin moving. Swift and stealthy they were, each going about his chosen task. . . till one Merasaloa snapped on a torch and brought the plan unstuck. The slicked deck mimicked its small sparkle, glittering sharp flashes from under-foot, just in time to catch glimpses of an unauthorized naked heel. Nick. The soldier leaping in pursuit. Slipping. Running a few crazed steps, letting loose a yell and staggering against the hydraulic hoist as the lighter lurched. Nick skimming back out of the night, sliding to the attack across the spillage. For an instant the Wild Dog lost their two dark shapes, then saw them again and a third and fourth figure converging. Nick went down and his corpse slewed flat, rotated headfirst under the rail, straight out to the churning channel between the vessels.

Nelson, large and bristly, was already in the wheelhouse struggling with the skipper, reaching up to disconnect the light, fumbling, fully visible, thumping at thick marine glass under a mesh of steel. He must have known he was a marked man by then. The fatal delay.

Spinebasher had showed briefly near the door to the engine room, no longer carrying explosives. That's when he was hit, staggering out into the open with a soldier lunging after him. The Wild Dog felt the barge reach the pit of its roll and launched out, gliding from cover into the tropical night, the oily deck hot underfoot. He remembered one shoulder being grazed along a redleaded wall and, that's right, an L-handle clouting his head.

He now touched the wound still wet with water or blood. The hectic thrill of speed was what he felt at the time, judging the tilt, easing his bare feet farther apart for balance as if riding a wave, he streaked down the slope just as it began to lift, heart singing with dark passion and fist ramming the soldier against the superstructure. He and Ganymede were escaping.

— Get out Peter, it's done, Spinebasher had gasped. Those were his last words.

The freighter loomed and leaned and sank past in a mutter of wet rust, righted herself and pulled away to the limit of the canvas hose, then recovered at a touch of the helm.

The soldier's head, when his fist hit it, smashed back with a crunch of bone. The Wild Dog swivelled clear as the vessel heaved, hearing the night come alive with shouting voices, Merasaloas flashing torches, weapons at the ready. Then, a dreadful surge of grief taught him what it meant to accept the challenge of violence. He escaped through a covered way, dizzy with suffocating fumes from the spillage, slid into the open and vaulted overboard. Nick was dead. So was Nelson. So was Spinebasher. The cost had been too great. He swam with an experienced surfer's tireless stroke.

Yet he missed his breath and spluttered, salt cutting at the back of his throat, for suddenly he was not swimming in the ocean but swimming in fear, swimming in a story he had heard of a submarine crippled by torpedoes during the Second World War. Greg Sullivan's father had told him how it felt to be there, enemy ships steaming nearby but refusing to hear the SOS. The entire crew escaped, some with flotation rings, some simply hanging on, bobbing around for two days before anyone came to pick them up: a two-day feast for sharks. The sharks circled, taking their pick in sudden flurries and foamings. A dwindling group of survivors huddled together, paddling about in the bloody sea: darkness more terrifying than day, and then the day in its turn more terrifying than night. Birds skimming the water for scraps.

He swam. He held on to his nerve. Swamped and robbed of strength, his head went under. But he pulled himself out of it. He knew that even this nightmare was simply an escape from feeling again what he had felt, knowledge of which would never give him peace, the splintering bone, that whack of a hard hollow ball, a man's skull against steel, a head filled with thoughts of love, with knowing how to cope in life and what to say, knowing a whole foreign language.

This was the first man the Wild Dog had killed. Well it was war. And he must escape.

He picked up his stroke again. Soon he would show his flashlight. He ploughed on. Immediately and without warning, his own head crashed, clunk, against a solid wall. The shock jolted a cry from him. He touched the sleek boat. What boat was it, though? His hair streamed wet. He floated in silence. Waiting.

Then Ganymede began asking unnecessary questions in a conspiratorial whisper, feeling round for an arm, sloshing the water with amateur groping hands, even beginning to murmur encouragements like a mother guiding some poor infant through the first terrors of hospital. Granny too, the Wild Dog knew by this, had lived through a frightening time.

— Nothing. Nothing's happened, he protested between gulps of salt breath and heaved himself up, twisting like a tuna to propel his sleek body heavily into the boat. Hell, he swore in an undertone. Spinebasher told me, his huge breaths could not be quieted. Told me he. Had blown it up. They're all dead, he added hoarsely.

Much later he offered an obituary: The others believed, but not Nick. He believed in nothing.

Ganymede, one hand on the throttle, stared at the strip of white water churned by slowly mincing screws, several kilometres distant now. He was looking for signs of any other motion. Who knew what fast light craft the *Sirius* might have aboard to give chase, what grid of radio communications with Merasaloa's coastguard? An aircraft with heat-sensors would pick the launch straightaway. He said nothing of these fears.

Black wind banged at them in patches. The mission had failed. The freighter would proceed under her Panamanian flag, refuelled and doubtless given air support, to Port George where the wharf crawled with Watchdogs. There were no second chances in this game. As for their escape, speed alone could save them. So it was that, without asking, Ganymede had started the motor. Twin plumes of spray shot astern, cascading in glassy fountains under the Milky Way.

Things had begun going wrong even before they left Australia. The men were uneasy because the plan involved killing. During their journey north from Darwin, Spinebasher grabbed Ganymede roughly and shouted at him for no reason, their faces six inches apart. Nick had pulled him away, saying: I reckon you need to be sure you are losing your temper, mate, and not your nerve. Spinebasher swung round on him, spectacles flashing, and landed a solid body punch. It simply bounced off. Nick made no move to strike back. The aggressor stopped in his tracks, looked down at his fist, turning it and examining it, and said in a remote voice as he ambled off: That didn't make much impression. When Ganymede tried to express his thanks, Nick advised him: You don't need to hit a man to win a fight.

Once the words were out, they sounded unmistakably like a criticism of the mission itself and of Mama's plan as a whole.

Was it to calm this tension that Nick then began on those army reminiscences, dreadful stories, till even the Wild Dog yelled furiously at him to shut up during an anecdote about being sent as riot-breakers to disperse a protest against Australia's involvement in New Guinea; how the order came to fire above the students' heads, but Nick, so he claimed, shot one guy clean between the eyes, a total stranger who couldn't have felt a thing? This was when the Wild Dog let out his cry of anger and shame. Nick just laughed: I wasn't the only one with the idea of bringing down the army, some other bloody hero scored a lady, quite a chick too, shot her in cold blood; I'd like to have asked if he was a true man or an animal, but I never found out who did it.

The memory of this confession made Ganymede shudder. And Nick's hand on him, kindly.

The dwarfed cluster of ships' lights dipped from view as the sea rose and poured past. Their ears grew numb to noise. Then, and then only, the Wild Dog and Ganymede looked at each other, face to face, confronting a dark mass, no more than a human-shaped silhouette. They knew they were watching and being watched. They gazed past the shield a face presents by day, complex with warnings even to friends, straight to the soul, transfixed by mankind's deepest need to recognize himself in another of his kind. With this impossible hope of revelation, as the launch thudded toward escape, dragging a pale scar through the sea, the Wild Dog and Ganymede exchanged knowledge of their needs, call this grief, call it desperation, call it passion or prayer, till their faces flamed with light and they stared nakedly, far into the open question of actual eyes, eyes glittering dark and intensely alive. The night blazed stupendously, darkness a flammable element, heat spouting so fast it appeared not to rise but to have always hung there. Above the blaze a dense roof of smoke massed, luridly floodlit from below. Then the detonations hit them, swiping across the Pacific, to slam against the launch. One. Another.

From high in the crest of the explosion, a plume of debris showered down through rings of sound expanding ever wider and sweeping out to envelop the ocean of whales, of Tuavaleva; rings wheeling to the Indonesian coast and Australia; then to New Zealand and Chile surely; at last arriving (though it might only be in the ears of migrating swallows shocked briefly off-course) in the United States of America.

— Who did that, then? Ganymede yelled excitedly, shocking his comrade almost as much as the explosion had.

The pillar of fire sank to burning rubble on the horizon.

After a long pause, during which their features were claimed back by darkness and the raw wound of wreckage subsided farther in the distance, and they listened to the engine purring, the slish and persistent hassle of waves against the hull, the Wild Dog corrected Nick's obituary, finding the one qualification he needed now the mission had succeeded.

— He believed in nothing but action.

93

Bernard Buchanan felt a sharp discomfort in his belly. Not enough to be called positive pain, but too much to ignore as indigestion. He was busy, as always, with documents and decisions, attending personally to an immense range of minutiae. Running the nation.

Yet he neglected the discomfort, resenting any interruption. He was reading the questionable case of an American rumoured to have left the country without the immigration authorities knowing; an acknowledged homosexual and intellectual (disastrous combination), suspected of sympathy with terrorists, observed visiting the studio of Lavinia Manciewicz. Buchanan now read with keen interest. Though the gnawing at his stomach persisted, he took no notice. Back among the early pages of the file, he found reports of this newcomer mixing with unsavoury company. The gnawing made the president squirm, but he read on. . . and reached a rivetting paragraph.

Candidate Buchanan, having successfully turned the occasion to his advantage, gave back the bat. But as he walked towards his car the waiter handed him a glass of champagne and said something I could not hear, but which caused the candidate to look up suddenly, the smile wiped off his face. I cannot tell what this message was.

Buchanan took a pen and wrote in the margin: *The kisses of the enemy are treacherous.* (BB)

The discomfort in his belly grew so urgent he slapped the file shut on his desk, rolled back his chair and did his best to see what the cause might be. The upper dome of this great anatomical feature spread magnificently visible, sheathed in a carapace of waistcoat with shirt and singlet as tender underwings, but the lower part, where he felt the pain (now it had indeed grown to be pain), remained as impossible to examine as the far side of the moon. He sat deliberating. Ought he to call for an adjustable mirror? How might such a request be explained? And although no subordinate would dare demand a reason, he knew that under pressure of his own reputation for mateship he'd find himself giving one even so. Then Buchanan caught sight of something wholly unprepared for. A mouse skittered along the skirtingboard of the study and, boldly, out across the carpet, tail switching, straight for the presidential boot, up the presidential trouser-leg, and out of sight in the region of his stomach. The twinge of pain came again.

That mouse must be in my clothes. No, the idea is preposterous, abominable. Or in my body.

The great man sat paralysed with nausea. True, there had been one night in his life when hundreds of locusts clustered on him, covering his face, his clothes, his hair, working at him with jaws so minute the action felt more like sandpaper than bites. True, also, that he had survived. The pain came again, too shocking to ignore. He bent forward to reach the spot, to cover the hole and protect himself. But his hands would not reach that far. The locusts were no preparation for this. On top of which, in those long-lost days he knew how to call for help, knew there was somebody even in the desert to come to his aid if only he could make the fellow hear; whereas now, in his own capital, power had elevated him above all recourse to human sympathy. Mightn't his staff simply watch him eaten alive? Or, if not, they would surely have an amusing tale to tell.

He imagined the way such news would be reported: A janitor was called into the presidential suite this morning to remove a nest of mice from among the president's intestines. In an exclusive interview afterwards, the janitor disclosed the fact that he had removed two mice and four young from the nest, which he described as very neatly kept.

Only Dorina could be trusted. She alone was able to boss him around lovingly: Now then, Buchanan, he'd hear her say, enough of this nonsense, ugh, mice, how disgusting, out with the lot of you, clear off with your fleas, it's a mystery to me Buchanan where you pick up your associates, hold still while I bathe your poor tummy, and you be sure you go straight to sleep when I tuck you in.

But Dorina was back in Sydney, 300 kilometres away, half crazed with rumour and martyred to that concrete bunker he had put her in.

Heart pounding, Bernard Buchanan threw his weight back in the chair. The wall mirrors were too far away for him to focus on. And a hand-mirror was impossible, of course. Whoever brought it would have to hold it in place for him, training it on the spot, kneeling down and keeping the angle steady. However loyal, they could scarcely avoid seeing directly what the mirror showed him at one remove. He panted, wild with the knowledge that he had risen beyond all help. He felt what it was to be himself; the I, remembering his father's funeral; the I, remembering how his mother watched him on the pot and assessed his future with critical eyes. He felt the I of all those inadequacies the human memory persists in allotting permanent space, among flowers merely vague and haunting perfumes of our successes and enjoyment. He felt as a sensibility shut in dungeons of fat, peering along corridors or out through a high window at the impossible drop of walls, over to a far sunbright city of alternative opportunity a mere bird-flight away. He had been seduced by power, as he once was by the skimming speed of his bicycle. He had taken the power as it came to him, heedless of consequences, made brave and handsome by sheer forgetting, discovered new graces in himself no one ever would have seen otherwise. But the price was now counted in this tremendous sandbagging of fat, the engulfing of the real Bernard by accretions of dross he could never put off. His skin performed the miracle of not giving way, not splitting under the strain, and it was with his skin alone he could lift parts of this grossness to look at it (as he now hoisted one arm), the hardened fat hanging trembling like a net full of squid.

To save drowning, he threw himself a line: who was the agent responsible for reporting that cricket match? Could it have been the car driver? No, as he recalled, the car had not come back at the moment of his accepting the champagne. Surely not Squarcia? Squarcia as cosmopolitan go-between had already been promoted well beyond the rank of peepers and whisperers. Was it, he wondered with distaste, one of those lesbians? Owen Powell must be put on the mat. Buchanan the Good wasn't going to have sexually sullied information left in his files, oh no.

The mice burrowed away. And he thought he could hear, through labyrinths of imprisonment, a man softly sobbing.

— Why are we interested in this Ganymede Sikorski now though? he asked aloud, rallying to divert himself with work because, apart from a munching sound, he recognized in the sobs the tone of his own voice. And there on the file's two last pages he found an answer.

The Tuavaleva water-police report an oceanographic survey launch missing. The launch belonging to the University of the South Pacific was taken to sea by Sikorski, an authorized geographer, with a group of Australian tourists aboard on 19th September, the day the *Sirius* and its fuel lighter exploded. Neither Sikorski nor his passengers, nor the launch have been seen again on Tuavaleva.

The very last report was brief:

Sikorski observed with male friend at Darwin Aero Club 21st September. Footnote: reference to this male friend also to be found in his own file, see under Peter Taverner.

Ah such ferocious pain in the great man's belly, such skittering of sharp feet, rub of flea-infested fur and ruthless grind of incisors, the busy necessities of housing and feeding a family!

94

A curt rap at the door so long after curfew meant the Watchdogs had come. Lavinia walked quickly to the vestibule, the fatalism of an old prisoner giving her courage. She snapped the lock back to see. Though she achieved this with quite some show of briskness, Lavinia then found difficulty managing the simpler business of standing in the opening to face what she discovered there, the most she could think to achieve being to block the way. A man loomed from the stairhead with outspread hands confessing to blood already shed; wild, mute and threatening. Completely unknown to her, he blundered forward to get past, and did, stepping in, legs stiff as if he had no knees, face daubed black, shoes soundless though he came on powerfully. Lavinia tried standing her ground. But he barged past and shut the door quietly behind them both. Crystalline blood around his mouth cracked as he spoke.

— Is Stephanie. . .?

She was too appalled with relief to rip the gag from her gaping mouth.

He tottered, facing her, eyes staring inconceivably blue from that smirched face. She did not know him but she reached out to steady him and turned aside to call into the studio. There was no need to call though. Stephanie had already come running noiselessly, and grabbed the man's arm with a violence that might lead to her hitting him next. The eyes winced because he did not resist. He had arrived safely. He took refuge in a domestic detail: battered hands clubbing at a zip, proving helpless to open his jacket. His own hands.

— It's him, Stephanie whispered.

Lavinia knew it. I'll heat some water, she suggested to allow them a moment alone. And went to switch on the power. Then slipped next-door for Tim. When they returned, Stephanie was steering the outlaw to the bathroom; their two figures, eroded by loneliness, paused like Antarctic explorers collecting enough stability in savage weather not to crumple on the wilderness of snow they must cross to get back to where all this began.

Tim took over, inspired with cheerfulness.

— You're a bloody mess, he observed. We'll tell you in a minute whether you'll survive.

A smile crept into the Wild Dog's expression.

— Sling your arm round me like this, Tim instructed. I've got you. Not much farther to go.

Stephanie went ahead to test the shower for warmth. They all understood this visit might cost them their freedom.

— You're a bit on the filthy side, Tim reported. But you smell much the same, becoming at last master of an idiom he had felt excluded from all his life. Must have your annual sluicing, can't see you fouling up a lady's studio. Florence Nightingale's fixing the tub, so get your gear off.

In the tiny bathroom, Tim propped the Wild Dog against one corner near the handbasin and, needing to steady himself too, unzipped the leather jacket. His intake of breath gave him away.

— Bad?

— Messy.

He peeled the leather back and tugged stubborn sleeves down over those wounded knuckles. Stephanie was there to ease the coat clear.

— The blood has stuck your shirt, she murmured. That's the trouble.

He grunted gratefully.

— The only way is to get you under the shower and soak everything off. The water won't be long.

They sat him on a white wooden chair and worked at his gym shoes which were stretched tight and caked with mud. Squatting on the floor they each rolled down a sock, revealing feet shockingly swollen, puffy white and bruised.

— Well that proves one thing, said Tim exploiting his new virtuosity. He has still got both feet.

Lavinia stood outside watching, as if by her presence she were able to muffle their voices.

— Will his trousers come off? Stephanie asked, desperate and restrained. Or shall we do that under the shower too?

They stood him against the wall again, brushing his useless paws aside, while Tim opened the zip, easing thick material from round the hollow pelvis. But narrow though his hips were, the trousers proved difficult to remove and everything must be done gently in case of a hidden injury. Lavinia returned from the kitchen with a knife to slit the seams. Flaps of cloth fell away. By now the rescuers expected anything except what they found: the unblemished limbs of a man at the height of his strength. His bloated feet appeared too grotesque to belong.

— I wish I'd known, Lavinia apologized. I would have booked enough water for you to soak in a bath.

Stephanie turned the shower on and they eased him into the cubicle. He hissed as liquid fire stung him. His body shuddered, but soon grew calm, and he shuffled round to face the flow.

— Good, he uttered breathlessly.

As a youth he was always first to jump into a cold pool and dare others to follow, or surmount the fear barrier in the face of some outsized wave. If it were a case of grabbing a snake he would; or, as happened once, dragging a victim from a fire. In his quiet way he acted impulsively and didn't bother thinking much of it afterwards. He hated the fuss people made, being perpetually wary of the insincere. Now, as water ran lava into his lacerations, he surrendered till he could float up to the

surface and break through, sloughing off the pain, arcing graceful as a dolphin into his dream behind closed lids.

— Okay, Tim proposed, planting the big feet of the lanky all
over Lavinia's bathroom floor. Let's have a go at that shirt.

They extricated him from his clothing while water pattered on
it. Breathing steam, they lifted stuck patches of singlet centimetre by centimetre, archaeologists with the heritage of millennia
to keep in one piece. The worst mess came from two bullet
wounds. Both had passed between his arm and body, one
tearing through the lateral muscle just below the armpit, the
other grazing the waist. There were numerous abrasions, too, on
his neck and arms.

— Soap him well, Lavinia instructed Tim, her whisper darkened to subversion owing to the innuendo of bullet wounds. I
have no antiseptics in the place, of course.

And the Wild Dog recollected a railway station and once
having come upon men robbing the first-aid cupboard for items
as basic and as scarce as iodine.

— Tell you what, Tim offered. With hands and feet knocked
about like this, plus a hole in your side, if you let your beard
grow a bit I'll guarantee to get you a part in a film as you can
guess who.

— Stephanie, the Wild Dog growled from the satisfaction of
suffering. Do you know this bastard?

— Little by little, she admitted while she turned off the
shower and wrapped him in towels.

— I'll make a bed for you in the studio, Lavinia promised. But
nobody must overhear your voice once Tim has gone.

No need to tell him, of all people, how to lie low and erase all
sign of his being, to restore the pile on rugs after each footfall
and breathe back his breathed-out air, to duck below the sightline of mirrors, to cut off the top of his boiled egg exactly as his
hostess did and pick loose hairs from the pillow, flushing them
down the toilet in a ball of paper. Even his shit must be
regulated to the colour of theirs if he were to stay. He had
survived so far because this he did know.

— Where's Ganymede? Tim asked hoarsely.

The women tore bandages from strips of sheeting and put
their patient to bed with the ritual ecstasy of priestesses at an
altar, hearing stony mountainslopes tremble echoing cries
against the gods, dipping their myrtle branches in a spring and
anointing his body of twisted gristle, ready for the old men with
knives.

— Bali. He'll write, the Wild Dog sighed from where he lay swathed in peace.

He had survived again. And he had severed his link with Mama by not taking refuge at her place. Since the death of his friends he wanted no more to do with her. He would never go back to that house of perfumes and silk, that portrait of a goggled pilot in the cockpit of his Percival Gull who waved goodbye without the least idea she knew it would be for ever.

The two sisters began mending clothes, washing them and ironing them dry, ready for the fugitive's escape. They mopped muddy footprints and wiped doorhandles. Once all such traces had been removed, his presence, powerfully there on the sofa surrounded by clothes draped across chairbacks, attained something of the miraculous, the body having reached where it lay without touching doors or walls or treading on the floor.

— Don't worry on my account, Lavinia said at length to Stephanie. Jail holds no fears for me. Not any more.

These days they neither struggled against one another nor exploited the dependence of the younger nor the irresponsibility of the elder. They stood at the still centre of a maelstrom raging withershins round the entire country. Heaven knows what Greta would have made of them.

Next morning the Wild Dog still slept so deeply they feared for their lives. Terrified he might be found, they shook him and stripped the blankets off till he lay with just a sheet to cover him. But he slept quietly on. They tried to carry him into the bedroom, Lavinia grappling with the solid shoulders and lolling head while Stephanie confronted those wrecked feet, but he was too heavy to move. Tim could not be called (that would provoke suspicion) and they were grateful when they heard him pass the door on his way to work instead of breaking with routine by dropping in. Lavinia had to leave. Though unemployed, this was her day for reporting to the police, a procedure required once each week. She was due there at nine o'clock, but they liked to keep her waiting till lunchtime before a senior officer condescended to receive the form she duly filled out. Stephanie must stay and cope alone, knowing the janitor of the building had master keys and that investigators could enter at any time without a warrant. Lavinia left.

In one corner of the studio a kettle sighed on a gas ring near the washbasin permanently caked with oilpaint dribbles. The workbenches and easels developed that asymmetry of disused objects. A small divan which had always been pleasantly threadbare now appeared tragically so. Some famous people had sat there at one time or another and, as Lavinia told her, some good people as well.

The kettle sighed. Matisse-blue curtains faded while the day strengthened. Near the window where the Minister for Internal Security once stood, when Tim had glanced up and seen him from the lane, was a shabby Chesterfield in which Stephanie sat looking everywhere but at the couch, denying the magnetism of that man asleep. She appraised Lavinia's canvases on the facing wall: an early portrait of their sister Greta which failed to win a scholarship; and a nude Bernard Buchanan lying on his back, his grand belly a landscape sloping down in the direction of forest-beleaguered nipples, the fat man's face twisted to look directly into the room, one side bullyingly vacuous, the other wistful. His knees and spade-shaped toes were hilarious.

A wind outside hooted warnings in gutters.

Too late to go to the office, even had she dared leave him. Her face pinched against the humiliation of inventing lies for missing yet another day's work. Tim would fill in for her. She had to stay; there was no choice. The kettle blew her a hot damp kiss.

Her ancestors were gathering round, teasing her, tweaking her, fluttering and evasive, trying to draw her attention to something. She could resist no longer. Her eyes found the man on the couch. And Stephanie knew she'd never dared really look at him till now. She observed the mouth she had thought vain that time he presumed to accompany her out of the railway station; it set more trenchantly now, carved fine as the lips of a marble Apollo. He was not rough, though she'd persuaded herself at Mama's he was. There could be only one word for his incurable maleness: beautiful. His bare arm, dangling to the floor, was the arm of a man accustomed to fighting for his life. Thick veins ticked at peace. The massive pad of shoulder fibrous with muscle quivered a moment, delicately. What had she allowed to happen? Safety slipped beyond her control.

She rescued the kettle and made tea in the absence of anything sensible to be done. She glanced out at the city where suicides were happening, people cricking their necks to see right into some back corner of an oven, people choosing which bullet to put through their brains, dining out on snail poison, converting themselves into etchings with a swill of acid and exhibiting in the daily press. Bodies like swollen prawns clogged storm-drains, and bodies fragrant as rose petals drowned in the sewer. She clanked her cup on its saucer, setting an entire mock tea-party of forebears clucking and tutting. Along the back lane below, an umbrella moved to the rhythm of walking, a green umbrella that by osmosis stopped her heart as it had stopped Lavinia's.

A knock came at the door. A knock impossible to interpret, clear and neutral. Not weak. Not urgent. Not soft enough to imply she must be nearby. Nor the prolonged knock that acknowledges an apartment is empty. She took a sip of tea and replaced the cup silently. Why should anybody call, when Lavinia claimed to have no friends left but Tim? She weighed one danger against another, the crime of concealment being worst because you began on the defensive. Once caught out, it was next to impossible to recover your balance. Stephanie stepped bravely, closing the studio behind her.

— Yes? she said before she had released the latch.

No answer from outside.

She bit back the question she most wanted to ask and swung the door wide. The enemy from downstairs stood there, craning to peer past, sure of her power over Lavinia and the little blonde, confident she need no longer fear being attacked.

— I saw your sister go out by herself and I thought of the trouble you'd be in if you were late for work. So I decided uh-uh she must be ill. I might be able to take her something. We've been neighbours such a long time, Lavinia and I. Though we've had our differences, I wouldn't let her down if it was in my power.

Had Stephanie said, how kind Mrs Connor, I'm hungry and lonely and we don't deserve your consideration after Lavinia's crime, the intruder might well have burst into tears. Or even if she had said, please come inside and let me tell you all about it. Instead, Stephanie spat her few words at the vile creature.

— I can manage perfectly well.

She shut the door in my face, Your Honour.

A tall woman with graceless limbs and ginger fringes, Marcia Connor narrowed her eyes and re-examined her motives; yes, entirely charitable, entirely concerned for the person's welfare, suspect journalist or not, who looked pale as the plague and might be on drugs for all a respectable woman knew. What right did she have to refuse help in that condition! Well she shan't refuse and expect to get away with it. She's a case for the Public Health Service. I shall put the nurses on to her. She might be committing suicide for all anybody knows, she needs protection from herself.

Stephanie sat on the end of the Wild Dog's sofa, shaken, her heartbeats painfully percussive. She's spying on me. What might she have noticed?

The body shifted in its sleep.

She touched her lips to stop them shuddering. She did not blame him for her present danger, though he was to blame. She watched him, even while she knew the risk too well. She surrendered to being swept along at delirious speed, his sinewy arm a pledge that she would never be safe again, not within the dictates of Buchanan's contemptible tyranny anyway. Love, she caught herself thinking, has become a luxury in our times of paring back to the hard winter core.

Stephanie went across to refill her cup and sipped some tepid tea as she looked over that backyard scenery she had come to like. Who can endure the boredom of nature, she asked, hills and trees going about their predictable decay? She was standing very close to the glass and peering down when she became alert to some presence behind her. The studio filled with threat. Out of the dark bathroom, from the leather sleeves of a discarded jacket, from clay-stained gym shoes, from the deep breathing of an inert figure, a shadow choked the whole space. Stephanie swung round, tea spilling bloodwarm on her wrist. She saw nothing alarming, since she could not see herself.

The studio was braced to hear another knock. None came. The place smelt of stiff dried clothes and an early memory, early enough to resist being recollected. Her sensation of being abandoned persisted. Then she saw that her ancestors had left. The whole gang. That was what made the morning so very clear. Those perpetual pryings and comments, the lewd suggestions and proddings, the traps, the ploys to push her out of windows or under buses, all were gone.

She managed a smile. And the body on the couch opened his eyes.

Naked under the sheet, he had been renewed by sleep. This was not the wreck of the previous night but a man ready to make light of pain. They neither of them shrank from the price demanded. The studio had not been filled by a threat, after all, but by a call of the blood pushing into slack chambers and filling out abandoned hopes.

Stephanie watched the sheet shifting and aching as he was aroused after having his proneness to love so long put off. Nude, she knew her power by the power she sparked in him, her firm smooth waist gliding to his intention. His shoulder and arm swung into a play of clefts and striations as he reached for her and plunged them both at the bed as if it were inexhaustible as deep space and the one flame flickered through their two bodies, exploding pent-up energy, towering over the sudden night which swallowed them, casting them wet and panting on the bedclothes, only to find they had swooped again into a flowering light even more intense the second time.

They did not hear the door open, Stephanie having forgotten to throw the latch.

One thing Marcia Connor could be sure of as she stood there: that she had a *right* to come back. She belonged, being part of Lavinia's household, a functionary of the stricter aspects of Lavinia's social conscience. So, pregnant with plausible explanations, she stood in the studio long enough to see a couple lying together at rest, the full length of the man as he lay on his back with his penis stirring and rising again, but not much of the woman who had propped herself on an elbow to watch the same thing, just one sleek shoulder showing and her golden hair ruffled lovably. Mrs Connor backed away silently. So absorbed were the lovers they still did not realize anyone else had been there when the door closed with a touch soft enough for Owen Powell himself.

Marcia Connor knew what she must do. Flying recklessly downstairs, she staggered into her own flat, wading through mire, entanglements catching at her hair and jerking her neck tight; she crawled, she sank, gasping, she heaved clumsy burdens of knowledge over rocks to where she could bleed for what she had noted the night before when she thought he was a derelict or a criminal calling, reached up. . . and ripped the pages out. She crushed them to a ball which she jammed in her mouth. She gnashed and chewed till the juices ran and her jaw ached love. Her police must never, she swore, catch *him*.

— This time will you listen, the Wild Dog murmured tenderly to Stephanie. While I tell you my name?

95

Bernard Buchanan had just intervened in a parliamentary debate, switching himself through. His image filled the big screen in the House. Members still simmered, furious and terrified, at his announcement that Question Time would be abolished as an outdated hangover from the Westminster system. Questions are a waste of time, he explained with naughty charm. If it's an answer you want, don't ask each other, just ask me. By this one stroke of imaginative thinking we shall reduce the number of sitting days, your job will be easier and we shall come out of it with at least an extra month's holiday a year.

When he caught the mumbles of dissatisfaction, he bellowed victoriously: To hell with caution. Fat is Tough! That's my motto.

But a matter of minutes after this enjoyable duty, he was seething over a letter brought in by Miss Colquhoun, a letter from the Hannoverian ambassador.

Your Excellency,

I am addressing this advice to you in reply to your recent request.

The Kingdom of Hannover, pursuant to its declared policy of seceding from the Federal Republic of Germany, has formally renounced any connection with NATO, to include all responsibilities and obligations which may previously have been entailed in such treaties as included the former Hannover as part of the Federal Republic.

Further, the Kingdom of Hannover, through its most gracious sovereign, gives notice that no Hannoverian co-operation will be permitted with any nation on any project involving nuclear weapons, space technology for purposes of offence, or any communications-based operation which has military application and therefore might be deemed to contribute to the purposes of offence.

I am charged to give notice, therefore, that the steel mills may no longer undertake any new contracts to provide components for such installations and that, with regret, your Government's request for urgent replacement of damaged cylinders cannot be met.

Respectfully yours.

96

Dorina loathed the bunker all the more now it was invaded by day, while a doubled squad of bodyguards aged with boredom in the glass watchhouse built on what used to be a terrace roof. Her neighbours moved away owing to constant harassment by the same surveillance and the repeated searching of their cars and guests. The devastation of the whole district attested to her importance and isolated her more cruelly. But at least she could still look out on water, she sighed, for solace; the morning harbour a dazzling dance of light, the evening harbour sweeping her away under the bridge toward deep blue times which she may now, probably, never know. This would always be preferable to the detested pretensions of Yarralumla Mansion. Though the mansion had a splendid music room, it was too splendid, the acoustics too glossy for the disturbed intimacies of her music. There she could derive no pleasure from playing, it always sounded like a concert the public had stayed away from.

Since the day of purchase, Buchanan had never returned to the bunker. Indeed, he would not now fit down the stairway even as far as the living room. Although he several times complained she had grown defiant in her refusal to sell the place and move into his presidential suite, he developed a taste for their arrangement, particularly since on some visits she managed, just by a look, to deflate his importance. And this last time had violated protocol by trying her smalltalk on his bearers, walking alongside while he was being carried, asking their opinion of the weather, asking, even, if they found it a strain to be separated from their families. Did she expect them to chat back on such homely subjects, panting as they were, and keeping their eyes where they were treading, cocking their carefully groomed heads to appear polite? They were not paid to be individuals when on duty, he had explained crossly, they were bearers. Off-duty they could be fathers or lovers or anything they liked, they could be philatelists if they chose, he would not oppose it, but while carrying him they had to show perfect respect for his dignity. Dorina wandered through state-rooms, putting the furniture out of alignment, off-centring pots of flowers which the housekeepers tracking her would have to correct surreptitiously. Making faces at lavish antiques bought for this showpiece cage by a grateful nation, she scuffed the rugs, left her impression on cushions, and distributed hairpins along the mantelpieces. Although he felt waves of affection for her and the birth of a new dependence, he soon tired of her criticisms. So Dorina was, one way or another, welcome to the bunker.

A domestic drift which suited the Buchanans did not necessarily meet with Luigi Squarcia's approval. The day the bad news came from Hannover, Squarcia was not in Canberra to report it to IFID. He had decided to visit Dorina.

Immediately after breakfast while her security men made their first inspection, she sauntered round, watering indoor plants, poor mutants she called them. Lying back on the settee for a read (she'd begun tackling Schopenhauer in the original now and took great draughts of silence after every paragraph to settle each idea in mind with the utmost clarity), she kicked off her shoes and hoisted her legs on to the seat, crossing them so her stockings whispered together. The ogres passed and repassed. She did not notice, being in another world. We shall do best, said Schopenhauer, to think of life as a *desengaño,* as a process of disillusionment: since this is, clearly enough, what everything that happens to us is calculated to produce. She closed the book. She tormented Schumann and gave him up till tomorrow. During all of which time, a cyclone bore down on her, whipping up the dust of scandal and publicity, spooling closer without a hint of warning, homing in on the bunker. No sooner had the inspection finished, leaving her alone in her room, than the intercom buzzed and spoke with an awed cough to clear the phlegm from so portentous an announcement.

— Detective-sergeant O'Brien, madam. Mr Luigi Squarcia is here wishing to see you.

Dorina thumped the last chord of a disgruntled Schumann, adding a couple of discords of her own. The odious Squarcia Bossy Boots. But why this unprecedented intrusion?

— What an ingenious house, he admired it as he descended the stairway Bernard would never fit down, holding out a ringed hand for her to shake.

— Here, I am able to pretend I am a nun in training for canonization, she responded sharply but with a cordial smile, gathering the stray threads of her madness.

— May I sit?

She wagged her head to grant him this courtesy. But she herself stood by the window, hands behind her back like a man.

— Dorina, I shall not waste time complimenting you on your taste in clothes and views. I am here as your friend and Bernard's friend. Possibly we two are the only friends Bernard has. I will come straight to the point. The matter is extremely serious. He has to be persuaded to change his mind.

— I am the last person on earth able to do that, as I have found out on many occasions.

— I myself believe you are our sole hope, he insisted.

She looked down over one shoulder to the little tugboat, restored but still on its rusted slipway. It will never float again, she realized at this moment. One may only enjoy it as a curiosity, something functional which has become useless.

— Bernard has stopped believing, Squarcia said solemnly. Do you see what this will lead to?

Creepers had grown under it and up its hull, working towards the deck. How enormously sad, she thought. A beached boat is as sad as a drowned cathedral.

— I should explain, Squarcia explained. You know that IFID absolutely insists on an election? And you know he would not be where he is today without IFID?

She gazed across the water, from which morning sparkles stabbed at her painfully. Something of her old strength had begun to return.

— It's ten o'clock, she said.

— You have no need to conceal your feelings from me Dorina. I shall go on: then you may judge this crisis for yourself. Bernard has done well over the years in a demanding job. IFID is basically satisfied. I could not put it more warmly than that, but satisfied is enough. I appreciate how hard they are to please. So he has this to his credit. But the moment they cease to be satisfied, he'll be out. Gone. Finito. They won't waste time. With an election he has a chance. Without, he has none. They will get rid of him. A coup. A bullet in the back. Who knows? Something subtle like that. Even the collapse of the stock market would do. Nothing is beyond them. The point is that he must be pulled away from the brink. Do I make myself clear?

— I should offer you tea.

— Damn it, Dorina, the country is about to fall and you offer me tea! My mother, he accused her. By now she would be wailing and tugging out her hair by the handful.

— I cannot afford that much hair, she protested turning to the water again.

— You've seen the television. What a clod Owen made of himself. A bunch of hoodlums out on some godforsaken island, and our international credit blown sky-high. But do you think he has a shred of useful evidence? They claim to be the same mob who painted that daub on the wall of the Paringa base. They know what they're doing. There has to be a security leak. The next laugh *was* at Port George. Now the whole nation of clods is whispering What's going on? Whispers these may be, Dorina, but we hear them. And when I say we, I mean IFID. You have stood apart from the whole catastrophe. Above it. Perhaps you already saw what Bernard was about to do with this new Emergency Special Powers Act?

Blinding jewels spread over the harbour right to her feet.

— Dorina, I trust your judgment. You have the background, a more subtle diplomacy than Bernard for all his genius. The second five-year bipartite agreement on American communications bases is up for renewal. Whatever happens, Bernard must push that through the formality of a parliamentary vote. And the moment he has safely done so, he must submit himself to the people. IFID requires nothing more, but nothing less either. If he goes along with this, they may not actually oppose him at an election. That's as far as they'll go. There is no further room for negotiation. They are patient of his eccentricities, they will even forgive his snub to their take-over bids in recent months, but they have him completely in their power. If he bends with the wind, he just might survive. It's up to us to help him.

Dorina turned sparkle-blinded eyes on him, disapproving of the hysteria hinted in his tone, not to mention the constant bullying: Bernard must, you must, we must; nor the presumptions he made about how much she did or did not understand.

— What are you proposing I should do? she asked eventually, feeling filled with vigour again.

— All rational argument has failed, he pleaded.

— Am I to persuade him to your confederacy by irrational means? she enquired coldly.

Squarcia stood and bowed to her. He had, of course, accepted the impossibility of this expedient before stepping out of his jet. She simply confirmed his assessment of the case. He started back up the stairs. At that moment the intercom buzzed again. Squarcia paused where he was.

— Detective-sergeant O'Brien, madam. A Mr Peter Taverner is being held at the door. He claims to be paying a personal visit.

She moved to the machine with surprising swiftness.

— Send him in.

— But Mr Squarcia's security men insist that. . .

— Mr Squarcia is my guest. I run my household as I please. I am waiting for him, she added to provoke the creatures.

After a significant delay, the door swung inwards and the man she would never forget came to the stairs, meeting Luigi Squarcia face to face. Ten years had given young Taverner a commanding air. It was with a thrill of, yes, pride that she saw how he met Squarcia's interrogating stare, a stare filled with that arrogance and impertinence the notorious and powerful reserve to themselves. He is worth my faith, she thought, my interest. Squarcia resumed his ascent as a procession of one, past the man whose face and name he had memorized. He reached the door.

— What is IFID by the way, Luigi? Dorina Buchanan called.

He stopped as if shot. Whatever else he expected, he had not expected this.

— I am sorry, he replied. Once again we must have misunderstood one another. Goodbye, Mrs Buchanan.

She waited to hear the lock slot home before holding out her hand to her visitor. The experience was just as she remembered. He accepted it firmly but considerately. Some disquieting recognition trembled through her. Of course, the BBC man must have told him she was the one who had brought them together. I cannot say, she told herself, to what heights of courage he has risen in coming here today.

— What happened, he asked remembering her very words. To the hideous paintings?

This time his presumption of intimacy lapped her with comforts. She returned to the view. A silent shout of relief surged through his body.

— With these huge windows, he said. I suppose they can listen to every breath you breathe.

She turned and faced him, questioningly, where he stood.

— That's how it is done these days, he explained. A long range microphone may be a couple of kilometres away across the harbour trained on this house. The glass acts as a membrane.

She recoiled from the window. Then what had Luigi Squarcia been playing at? What had he said that he wished to have overheard? What had he planted on her?

— May I offer you some tea?

— Do you have time to spare? he asked, knowing his own life was being counted now in seconds.

The polished floor glittered with window-shaped sunlight. She walked right into the centre of it, warming herself still, appearing to stand on a mirror in which her spirit lay revealed.

— You know I married Buchanan, she replied. To punish my father. The room trembled as the windows, perhaps, transmitted her words. That, she added, is why I never criticize the young. Are you still young? No, I suppose not really. But younger than I am.

His gaze escaped out to the Harbour Bridge and lost itself in a past too ugly and too sweet to be endured. A past in which he had redeemed himself, lost and found his manhood.

— Good to see your tugboat restored, he observed. I like that. That's really worth doing.

— Do you think? she could not bring herself to claim credit. I thought it might have been another symptom of madness. The workmen, she said, made an appalling racket for months, hammers going all day. Enough to drive one to distraction.

— Will it float? he asked, asking an unspoken question.

— I hope so or what would all the trouble have been for? The room grew restive.

— My father, she explained, making no effort to pursue the formality of tea. Laid such store by refinement. Everything was nuance. Not only did he read between the lines, this is all he read. He was genuinely hateful, I suppose, dabbing eau-de-Cologne on his temples and primping in front of younger women. She paced the mirror and stood with her back to him. If, she sustained the awful task. If he had an ambition other than his abominable sexual fantasies it was to be presented to the Queen. He once promised me I would marry into aristocracy because I was clever enough. Also, he added, cold.

— Do you mind if I smoke, Peter Taverner proposed.

A breeze escaped the waterfront and swept through the house. She hooked a few hairs behind her ear. He snapped his lighter shut and tucked it away. The cigarette sat perfectly unspoiled between his lips. Dorina turned away. She had been repelled by the cultivated sensuality of Squarcia's lips, too perfect and too grossly composed. These were slightly flaked, perhaps generous, but so masculine she felt at a loss. Her own lips grew fat with confessions.

— I married him, she repeated in a voice suddenly under strain. To punish my dear father. Don't doubt that I have enemies.

He sat calmly, willing to let her dictate the terms of what further risk she was prepared to run, though the nightmare was closing in on him.

— There has never been anyone in my life, she added ambiguously.

Every gesture became a theatre of portents. Her courage rose to meet his.

— But why bother with boring formalities, Mr Taverner? We ought to be enjoying ourselves. She hurried round the concrete house collecting essentials, her handbag, her woollen wrap and her Schopenhauer. I was planning to play for you, she said flushed with excitement as if she knew he would call. But that must wait, I cannot get my fingers round the Schumann Opus 23 I am working on, the spirit of the piece eludes me. Come, she ordered pertly and clattered upstairs, communicating in the piercing silences between one sentence and another, one footfall and the next, the unevenness of all she did, the impulsiveness, the reserve. And now this girlish vulnerability. She positively threw open the front door. Once he had followed her out she slammed it behind them, returning the detective's enquiring gaze with a look he could only describe (and did describe later) as brazen.

— We shall take your car, she decided. Mine is far too well known.

— Excuse me, madam, the detective showed signs of insisting on protocol.

— O'Brien, she said flattering him with intimacy. You are a man of the world aren't you, O'Brien?

Dumbfounded, he watched them drive away.

Peter Taverner swung up towards the highway and then cut through wealthy suburban backstreets. Neither spoke as he stopped at a harbourside park and got out. She remembered the slamming doors of the school that offered refuge to no one but herself. And something she had forgotten till this moment: Miss Gardiner's body, when thrown against the folding doors of her hidingplace, uttered the one word *duty* while a beast growled and an inexplicable kissing sound followed. She must have been dead already, that one word escaping as her legacy, outliving her.

— We'll take the ferry, he told her. I'm surprised they didn't blow the car up.

— They are hugging themselves with delight, Dorina explained quietly. The multinationals being ready to ditch Bernard, a domestic scandal would be right up their street. It cannot help but be useful. I dare say they enjoyed milking that little scene of every last detail they could get.

At the jetty he and she stood side by side waiting for a ferry to churn along in its own good time.

— Now, she addressed the mild wind blowing in their faces. Why did you come?

— You are my last resource.

— Twice in a single day! she seemed genuinely surprised.

What have you been doing these eight years, she asked suddenly numb with suspicion.

— I haven't been wasting my time giving in. And I guess that's made a name for me. He laughed deprecatingly as he spoke the words for the first time since the bitter description he gave Stephanie a year before: the Wild Dog.

Dorina swung towards him so impulsively he thought she might slap his face. Then she looked away to find her surroundings were living through her, the harbour treacherous, the ferry's engine her own pulse.

— I think I believe you.

A short-lived laugh sprang out uncertainly. Then she collected herself for a question.

— How can you be sure, Mr Taverner, I was play-acting back there? I might be serious about you.

— It's your life we have in our hands, too.

They boarded the vessel and set out, drumming, across sleeking escaping water. Around Dorina the solid land shifted and swayed.

— At all times be unpredictable, he advised her. Take no notice of anyone, whatever happens.

In the airport lounge she panicked.

— They'll recognize me.

She let her hair out loose as a gesture of disguise, throwing the Spanish comb into her handbag.

— They'll never believe their eyes, Mrs Hyde. Here is your ticket. They'll congratulate you on being a great woman's double. And I mean great.

— Mrs Hyde! she acknowledged the joke nervously. But why a plane?

— I thought of it as a treat.

Now Dorina knew she had not been mistaken in him. No, they were not meant for one another, being different in many ways, this music-prone woman and love-prone man. But he showed an exceptional delicacy of feeling to understand how she might hanker for the fearful coffee and biscuit of a routine airlines flight, services she could complain of, people to tread on her toes and push her out of the way, how she might yearn to pay simple money for simple things and have the small change slapped rudely on a counter, to weigh herself on a machine and miss a bus, to sit in a darkened cinema where anything at all might happen and laugh with a thousand ordinary people at what they could see in common. Quite the most plausible was the plane. The question arose: would she ever go back to the bunker or Buchanan? She thought of Rory and admitted her fate had become too complex to escape by such naive means. Poor Rory.

Airborne, and with the privacy of high-backed seats, they were able to converse quietly. He explained his failure at Paringa and again at Tuavaleva: Australians had not been woken up by laughter nor, as Mama expected, by shock.

— I think you may be too impatient, she replied. You have to allow them to be cautious, because they are. You may even have won a convert in my husband himself. So she explained Squarcia's visit, which he had interrupted, and the threatened withdrawal of American backing.

— Does Bernie realize he has been stooged? I had a feeling he'd lasted too long. We probably won't be able to protect him now. He must know they'll bring in someone else. If he'd just talk. He's the only one who can. Unless he does, it'll never get said, it'll be another trip on the merry-go-round. He's the only one with the chance of stopping it.

— I long to know, she asked with demure composure to disguise her tremor of excitement. Why you are risking your neck to give me this outing?

He scowled at a hostess who noticed Dorina and, with a large steel teapot to counterbalance her, leaned back and passed a remark to a companion bringing the tray of milk and lemon slices.

— What's in it for me, do you mean? Not much. I'd like the answer to a question. Some bloke stood trial for murder once. Your husband was on the jury.

— Where did you hear that? she instinctively played for time, the habit of protecting Bernard.

— *He* told me.

How this confession must have preyed on Buchanan's mind ever since, she thought, taking only a moment to reach her decision.

— Sir William Penhallurick, Dorina replied.

The Wild Dog reclined his seat and crossed his legs.

As Dorina saw him, Peter Taverner was a natural gentleman. What did she mean by a natural gentleman? Item: a man not afraid of getting hurt. Item: a man who can control any situation he lets himself in for. Conclusion: a man with strength to impose his will. Moral: but who chooses not to. This was the point, this was true courtesy.

Bodies tell as much about the character as faces, she observed. He is free of selfishness.

— Nobody else I have ever known, he droned. Got a piano downstairs as quick as that. He laughed impulsively. I need those guys!

Dorina laughed too, a long longing laugh, her eyes taking in the freckles on his hands, the one broken knuckle which had regrown with an enlarged knob, thick wrists. Simple facts like the length of his legs (not so very long after all) led her to say.

— I always wanted to believe we should try everything. Within reason, she cautioned.

He glanced at her with his clear look, failing to catch what she, in her forty-eighth year, was driving at. He flashed her the smile she dreaded, that tight jaw, lips gentle with his cigarette.

— I have a message for Bernard, he said and nothing could have surprised her more. Tell him I was walking across the stony desert because *my* car had been tampered with too. Exactly the same as his, the same salt water in my fuel cans. I went out there to look at Paringa before we swapped it for our independence.

— Have you ever thought, she whispered sedition as they began their descent and an indecipherable city smudge lay blighting a landscape so expansive great height could only enhance its grandeur. How trivial are the concerns of power?

He nodded. And she observed something she had not seen before. A private sorrow imprinted itself on his features, the sort of sorrow one recognizes as new, unprepared for, and incurable.

— I have lived with littleness for a long time, she sighed. On the way up, people expect some fine plateau of success to await them, with mountain air and discreet music, luxurious food; forget about the sweating cooks and farmers. They expect that somehow, without the least effort on their part, understanding of lofty ideas will come to them, that great men and women will gravitate their way for conversations which defy the mundane imagination. Once they get there they discover they had more direct power when they were torturing their wives in secret. Of course they can now say, Build a bridge here for me to cross the river, and it has a fair chance of being built. But they have to wait too long. By the time it is built they have forgotten they ordered it. Fetch me a book, they say, and when it comes they are no closer to understanding it than they were during their poverty. Show me something truly magnificent, they command their entertainers, and are rewarded with mountains of tinsel and half-naked floosies doing suggestive nothings with feathers. Hit me, they cry finally. But nobody dares hit them now. Hit me, they beg, becoming frantic (oh, she was enjoying this extravagant performance of hers and enjoying its undertone), and some flunkey gives them a tap as a daring gesture of trust. But that is worse than nothing. They want to suffer. They want to be hit. And they want it to hurt so they can believe they are still human at least. This is why, when illnesses come, they collapse in bed so gratefully. At long last something real has caught up with them. Thanks to a virus they are genuinely laid flat on their backs, terrified of dying, with the most skilful medical practitioners in attendance. Why do you think Bernard gets carried everywhere? His ankles obliged by giving out. Poor President Buchanan, the idiots write in their gossip columns, such bad luck, it must be glandular. He adores being carried. The impertinence of those oafs ogling at him while he performs the most disgusting intimacies is the best measure of power he has got. I'm not much use to him. What a symbol it is to be helpless, what vanity. You cannot imagine the pettiness of the powerful, nor how imprisoned they are by disillusion. Sooner or later the button will surely be pressed and a frightful war break loose for no better reason than some baby of a world leader can't get any satisfaction. He has to press the button because it is the only crime big enough to prove himself by.

This tirade, bottled up for years, she delivered in an undertone and, in doing so, found herself leaning across, intimately close to his ear. When suddenly he faced her, their lips almost touched.

— Please, he said. Memorize an address. He spelt it out to her and repeated it. In case we get separated. They are friends. I'm trusting you with their lives.

He need not have explained this. Of course she knew. She wished he had left it for her to acknowledge. She had never felt more in control of her faculties.

When the aircraft touched down and roared along sun-hot tarmac he gave her the address again.

— Once we get out, he explained. I'll split, for your safety. Please walk straight past the baggage area and wait for the car to collect you. He took her hand to shake it, a formal gesture, awkward because they were still seated, but achieved so frankly she knew nothing could be more perfect, more comradely or more perfectly correct.

This was the last she ever saw of him.

Dorina stood in the warmth of a Brisbane spring, nervous that she was bound to be recognized. She strolled the concourse, glancing at her watch with theatrical impatience, making public her exasperation at being kept waiting by someone. People stared. She waved away a taxi at the exit. She watched fellow passengers drive off in a coach. For twenty minutes she begged him to rescue her from this purgatory. Then she had a sensible idea, she would proceed to the address he had given her and wait for him there. Exactly. Confident of her memory, she marched to the taxi rank, sat herself in the back seat of a car and recited the number, street and suburb. The driver made no move.

— Well? she demanded.

He screwed round very slowly, to get a good look at her, helping himself with one meaty arm braced against the wheel, the other hooked round the seat back. He assessed her, his fat butcher's face with no eyelashes, and loaded his sarcasm with the malice her cultured accent called for.

— Are we drivin' all the way to Sydney then? he drawled.

Dorina blushed a furious scarlet. This was noxious. Mortifying. Of course it was a Sydney address, though she had not recognized the fact. How demeaning. She climbed out, her limbs temperamental and uncoordinated.

— I beg your pardon, she snapped and took refuge again inside the departure hall which boomed and echoed with an undersea voice announcing a departure for Sydney. What next! Who could have imagined such a fiasco? To be abandoned a thousand kilometres from home without even enough money to get back. Ordinarily she had no need to carry cash. She was out of the habit. She rifled through her handbag. No. Nothing but small change and the used airline ticket in that stupid pseudonym. Mrs Hyde felt the onset of nervous disorder and a sudden cold loss at what he might have meant by choosing such a name. She opened the ticket to witness the completeness of her despair. And then saw the return coupon. In a flash she noted the booking, consulted the clock, and hurried to the seat allocation desk to catch the flight he had arranged for her.

Why why, Dorina fumed inwardly, must he protect me? Aren't I to be allowed to share the risk? But even while resenting the let-down, she acknowledged a flood of relief that he had been so considerate.

On the plane she decided not to go home, perhaps never to go home, to the bunker.

97

— I do apologize Your Excellency, Owen Powell's personal assistant replied to the telephone. But the minister left the office on urgent business ten minutes ago. No sir, he did not say. But we do expect him back soon. Of course I shall ask him to ring you the moment he returns. I beg your pardon. . . you. . . yes. . . I see, in case you yourself are unavailable by then. I shall certainly give him the message without fail. May I repeat it back to you, Your Excellency? He is to apprehend Mama immediately. The arrest to be discreet but on no account delayed. You want her confined within the hour. Yes. Is that name sufficient? Very good sir. One M: M-A one-M-A. Immediately, Your Excellency.

The president, he thought afterwards, sounded overwrought, perhaps apprehensive. Or was it just that this was one among a hundred tasks he must see to in person. It was, really, no particular tone at all, unless exasperation that the minister was out. . . which could, in the long term, involve far-reaching implications for senior staff with the right flair and an ambition to work.

Owen Powell had chosen as his personal assistant Jack Cohen, intelligent, ruthless and impersonal. Jack brought a moral sternness to the operations of the Snoops and Powell reaped the credit. It is not to be supposed, though, that this meant the young man held so very high-principled a view of loyalty. Loyalty was relative. And his dynamism arose from ambition. Secondly, though his chief regarded him as a treasure, he regarded the chief as a dithering sentimentalist. Cohen, weedy and pale with a night-creature's skin, took it upon himself to be the most resolute and incorruptible member of the department. So now President Buchanan had spoken to him personally. This was a first. This was news. And he, the professional, coped by replying crisply without hesitancy, so the word had come that action was needed within the hour. Powell might well take longer drinking a cup of hot chocolate, let alone whatever business he was apparently conducting, business too secret to be disclosed, it would seem, to a trusted personal assistant. What would be the consequences if he did not get back in time? Cohen guessed the answer might be the chop. . . probably for both of them, he having been the one to take the message. This was a matter which could not wait. There must be a file. Plainly he had to act.

— M-A-one M-A. That's all.

When a file arrived on his desk almost immediately, Jack Cohen was grudgingly impressed. Old Powell had a few things organized, then. Opening the folder with his left hand, he already held the phone in his right and the Chief of Security Police waiting on the other end.

— Frank, said Jack Cohen because they had established an understanding which gave the reciprocal comfort of cutting out Owen Powell. Here are the details. Priority job. The boss is away and His Excellency wants word within the hour.

— Done, Frank assured him and hung up, well aware of how desirable it was to take action before the Minister's return, and by this means make the best of claiming the credit due.

Young Jack sat back, paler than ever with the glow of defiance, his meagre flesh clung to his skeleton; sailors on woolclippers isolated high up in a wild cold gale had felt like this, the world swaying at their feet, ears, nose and fingers bitten off, the heart exultant.

98

— I shall tell you what is wrong with us, the Labor Party leader offered. We are a nation of hopers.

Apart from the no-hopers! Buchanan considered interjecting but, for once and in response to a rare whim or a gaping crevass of doubt, refrained.

— We are putting up with shortages and indignity because we do not believe these conditions can last. After eight years, we are still hoping. That is what I mean. You see how gullible we have grown? Brought up to the definition of freedom as simply being Australian. That is the point, Mr Speaker, that is our weakness. We have never thought to test it. As much as to say: If *we* are not free, what chance is there for the world? Foolish, and blind to the fact that there can be more than one form of invasion. The reality of life in our cities, which is becoming a nightmare we could never have foreseen, is in my view a product of the hibernation of anger.

— *You're* doing all right, one backbencher sneered and wriggled in his seat to be noticed.

— You young fellows might not know what I am talking about. Let me say, I was a serviceman in Vietnam. I was among the very first intake of conscripts sent there by Menzies. I mention this, Mr Speaker, not to make any special claim for my patriotism (hoots of derision), but to point out that there was an uproar against conscription at the time. You could not just dictate to people then and have them meekly obey.

— Yet you went!

— And I shall tell you what I saw, Darryl Robinson darted his lizard-look around the chamber and his tongue flickered in that unfortunate speech defect he had. I saw one of our men stick a bayonet in a Vietnamese child. At the court-martial he defended this action by saying the child was a Viet Cong child. A Viet Cong *child*? What could that mean? Can one have terrorist children? And what did this say about our presence there, if even children took arms against us? Mr Speaker, I am haunted by that boy and the way he screamed in a woman's voice while he struggled against death. The soldier, one of our own, kicked at him to tug the blade free, you know, to get him off the point of the bayonet.

— Would the Honourable Member for Mooralbank please come to the point?

— Mr Speaker, this happened while we were, so they told us, at peace. Australia had not declared war on Vietnam and we never did. We were there simply to help whitewash the Americans so they wouldn't seem to be waging war alone. What haunts me is how this child knew what to do. It was his country and we were invading it. Even by the way he died he knew, screaming to shock us with the fact of his being a child. Beyond doubt he had fired the rifle, I know. He had wounded a corporal in our own section.

The House of Representatives suddenly became aware they were listening to Darryl Robinson, so long a personality in politics, making his last speech, that he knew it, and that this was what he intended, looking round at his colleagues of all thirteen parties, it might be thought affectionately. His voice had grown quiet. No one needed to stamp him off the blade.

— He was a Viet Cong child. A boy. Perhaps eight years old. Robinson began to sit but checked himself halfway.

— The court-martial's verdict, he added and bowed politely to the Speaker. Was not guilty.

99

Throughout the night, waves thudded and swished along the beach. A membrane of cloud stretched taut the whole length of the horizon, the rest of the sky spreading clear black and prickly with stars. Where Dorina sat, the sand had soon cooled after sunset. How could she go back home with what she now knew? Grey and purple breakers smashed, frothing almost to her feet. Like a beast chained just out of reach, water lunged to get her, slavering, again and tirelessly again. Then she saw the waves as infinitely gentle rises and falls of that vast ocean out there; to think the limitless Pacific could be safely confronted by one so helpless as herself, not even able to swim. I'd be like a giraffe swimming, she retorted when her cousins had urged her in, like a giraffe, all neck and bony knees; she laughed laughs quite unlike her cousins' snorting grampus noises from the deep basin of the creek where kingfishers darted bank to bank. It's not really cold, the taunters called again, once you are in. So pretty and so treacherous. Dorina shivered. A gentle tongue of water flecked with salt foam advanced from the night up the sand, pushing to within inches of her feet, and withdrew leaving a quilted mirror in which stars were reflected. She watched the mirror's brightness soak into the land and smelt shipwreck on its clean breath. She was driven farther up the beach by the incoming tide, but yielded only minor concessions, not wishing to surrender the intimacy, the engulfment of her senses which (yes, she realized) gave her relief. Still the rising sea moved in with those fortuitous rhythms so gratifying to a musician's ear. Not too cold, now the wind had dropped. The membrane of cloud knotted itself into a remote landscape, a flat snowstruck country with a few hilly knobs and one diagonal folded valley. As each wave swept back to draw itself up for a renewed push against her defensive position, hordes of moon-bright bubbles skimmed down the running wet sand, so frail she felt she might become a Christian. In recent years she had been, as she put it, *looking into* Buddhism. Lovely it was, but Buddhists have no equivalent for the fragility essential to her in all life's rewards, being too robust, too loving and warmly inclusive. She felt drawn again, and by surprise, to the tentative fable of Christianity, to the perception that anguish lies at the heart of salvation. Christianity, seen rationally, she now conceded, was truly ridiculous and relied on the pierced hands and attenuated pallor of a hanging cadaver to vouch for its credibility. A squat white city formed in the cloud landscape, thrusting up surly turrets and spilling down to the sea's edge. The Buddha, she decided, settling her handbag in her lap and tugging the woollen wrap tighter round her shoulders (she was sitting on Schopenhauer), is suitable for those who need to feel they belong to all this. Being engulfed by it is one thing but indistinguishable from it quite another. No, I like to make a garden out of nature. I don't want to be an atom among the minerals. I like to believe I have been chosen as someone special.

The millennia of adventures broke gently and gently broke on soft sand, occasionally leaving behind flecks of phosphorus, tiny unexpected lights personal to her darkness, random, and lasting a few seconds only. She breathed purity. She said, I can smell the element in this air. The name Christian Morgenstern crossed Dorina's mind. A culture which produces a poet called Morning Star is not to be dismissed as materialist, she affirmed. The cloud city of her horizon grew bigger, piling tower above dome, a candle flickered beneath it, from which the sea passed fleeting glimpses landward.

Do the laws of men in all their barbarity, she asked, serve God's purpose?

How bleak all this purity felt. Dorina stood and stamped her feet, her court shoes sticking clownishly, stockings shedding a crust of sand. She flailed her arms across her breast as she did when a child. In the clothes she had worn when she received Luigi Squarcia that morning, in which she sat on the back seat of a Brisbane taxi while the driver turned with his butcher's face to scoff at her, she shivered. Her joints creaked. She rescued her book and walked north along the beach. Then she returned south. Whichever direction she took, the world paced with her, changing its mind as she changed hers. The tide crept in and crept, savage under its mask of delicacy. Might fish, in their cold fire, be gazing up among storm-tossed night birds?

Lightning flashed way behind the cloud and low down along the sea, clean as a slice of light beneath little Dorina's bedroom door, making monstrosities of the floating city and letting loose a delayed rumble of thunder. Have I been too passive? she asked, and answered with a confession. Is this my form of vanity? Waves drew back as if sucking her out to sea, where she would thresh about for dear life against forces so vast one could justly call them meaningless. Not for her. She salvaged a few certainties from the past. The violence and sensuality of the crucifixion answered to her knowledge of life. My bedroom door banged loud as a gun, Dorina was reminded, at one of our apartments, but I cannot think who slammed it and whether they were coming in or going out.

I have been lucky in life, she decided as she sat once more hugging shreds of warmth, as a reward for being difficult to satisfy. Shush, warned the sea, in case she might mention Peter Taverner. Shush. Her confusion of recent months, her distracted clumsiness and unaccountable passions had fallen from her, leaving her cold and vulnerable. Rory was so upset when Churchill died. But I could not help him falling from the cliff. He'd grown old.

A gust of fine spray swept over her to announce wild weather out there. Have I always failed you, Rory? she wept suddenly. It began, oh perhaps it began right back when you were a baby and so painful to deliver. The nurse said, don't worry about how you believe you ought to be feeling, Mrs Buchanan, motherhood comes of its own accord, soon enough you will find you can't think of anything but dear little Rory and Rory suckling. Pain, all pain, she cried to the sea which responded with hisses. Even the love. There was a time when I thought, at the first intimacies with Buchanan, if I can stand this I can stand anything. But I reckoned without the child. The child used me, the child Rory reduced me. He bit and punished me and demanded my life, all at once, and never a scrap left over, not even as carrion. He loved me too possessively, I suppose.

The storm blossomed. Dorina thought of herself shrinking under Bernard's paw. I am so healthy, she called aloud in despair and a black creature flew at her head, flew into the voice as if this were comfort. She ducked as the bird flipped its wings and passed her face, so narrowly avoiding her she heard it utter an effort of despair and she smelt its warmth. Goosepimples proliferated in panic-stricken colonies all over her body. High above, the wings of companion birds creaked and wheeled.

Only now did she think of the suburban houses, just out of sight, set back from the sand on the far side of a road, in which obedient citizens slept lulled by the curfew and the promise that something was being done. She could walk up there any time she chose and terrify them by screaming or even knocking on their windows. She could violate the street's emptiness with her walking. She could defy the local dogs and wake the police. She could play at being the president's wife entitled to be addressed as Your Excellency and perhaps even entitled to disregard the curfew. She had never tested her power, after all. She had never been interested in it. She had no notion of her freedom. Dorina thought, momentarily, of Detective-sergeant O'Brien, young Haberfield and Kosta among others, frantically trying to trace her, or sitting tight hoping to cover her absence till she might return of her own free will. Never.

Rain began tapping her scalp and hands. I believe I fell in love the day we met, she whispered at last. It was so implausible. I cannot tell how unhappy I am. What is there to weigh it against? But unhappy enough to fail those people out there in their suburban houses. Do they know a truer misery? Have I fed on it? Dorina Buchanan gasped at the first chilling downpour. Am I to be hated as well as pitied?

Rain bearing a message from outer space swept darker brushes through the darkness. She stood to meet it, her morning clothes clinging to her skin (I shall not waste time complimenting you on your taste in clothes or views, Master Squarcia had presumed to say), her shoes waterlogged boats. She chose pure sensation and was not responsible; though enough of the habitual Dorina survived to tuck her Schopenhauer with her handbag under one arm, protecting them as well as she was able.

Her racked body shivered, legs cramped and hair shook off braids of coldness as she cried out.

— Now I know!

Dawn light had begun to filter in from New Zealand and the strip of scrubland behind her woke to a few piercing bird cries. The whole air stood stiff with sea haze, the early day shone red, a marvel of red mist riding in over the oily rolling of exhausted waves. This rosy light appeared less a diffusion of the risen sun than some spontaneous ignition. The subdued sea advanced and advanced when it was really retiring. Dorina, ill with cold, crouched on the beach; her handbag crouched beside her. She looked up into the new light and out across the Pacific Ocean.

Then the extraordinary event took place, the epiphany hinted at the night before.

As she looked at the slow-rolling backs of glinting waves, knowledge came to her that these were not waves at all but whales. She narrowed her eyes. Yes, whales circling closer and closer to land, there could be no doubt, dozens of them. Solid, intentional whales.

Dorina stood up, forgetting her handbag with its used airline ticket, forgetting her book of ideas, entranced at this gift of nature. But her elation turned to panic. The whales were coming in. They were not going to stop out there as a passing event, a lovely show. She was to be threatened by them. Of course. She had read of how they beach themselves despite the efforts of whale-saving societies who go out in boats to drive them back to their home element and, at a later stage of failure, wade in the shallows pushing them, manhandling the brute bodies for their own good. They become beached nonetheless. But you cannot deny them your last effort, because once on land there is no going back.

The red sea haze dimmed as it lifted and dissipated in mauves.

Her whales came rolling in to her beach. Dorina took only a moment to decide. She ran to where rocks reached out into the current. She removed her shoes and waded along the sandy shelf.

— No, she called because as mammals they could surely hear. Shoo! Go back, you silly creatures. She was up to her waist and feeling menaced by water warmer than air, water which lured the non-swimmer. It can only mean death up here, she shrilled hoping her inhospitable tone would communicate. Not paradise.

The colossal shapes slid smoothly through the sea just beyond reach. Dorina waded deeper.

— You must, she gasped with her father's intonation as a wave broke and splashed her to the neck. Do as you are told!

Petty undercurrents tugged at her feet to topple her. The narrow band of water between her and the drifting whales meant the same from either side: past this no-man's-land there would be no going back for them, nor any for her. Suddenly she felt so very angry with them for putting her at risk. She was able to look now at the very shape of death, to remain one step but only one step away from it. Had she read somewhere that they were once land creatures which survived, when the dinosaurs died, out by taking to the sea? Was this their return? It seemed an improbable theory. Or what if, Dorina then thought, whales have devised the theory of evolution; what if, out in the opaque waters they sing it as a symphony and these are the faithful, the committed few with courage to swim ashore, drawn by the rapture of enlightenment, to prove their destiny. These are the avant-garde, anticipating natural selection by millions of years, way ahead of fellow whales, claiming the right to their future on land. A cold wave slapped her face, but it had no effect. She took the necessary step. And a huge hard body slid by along the shelf where the sand and rock dropped away to deeper water. She leaned forward to ward it off. Repelled and jubilant, she slapped at the massive flank glistening black in the morning.

The mist vanished and the light grew cold.

— Go home you idiotic thing, she screamed for its own good. But the reasoning voice within her persisted: they have transcended the barrier of instinct, these inspired few.

And the approaching whale was not black at all, as she could now see, but rich with a patina of bronze and green and violet. The sidewash from its passing swept her legs from beneath her. She floundered, gasping, refusing to succumb, and sought a new footing on a ridge of rock. Her wrap dragged with the stupendous weight of wet wool. She let it go as she had let her philosophy go earlier, though this she had not realized, nor seen the pages clasping and unclasping like gills as they sank. Another whale approached. She was, she perceived, a curious and unexpected impediment to its faith. A skin of light now sheathed the water with polished steel. The dark looming shape cruised; perhaps, under the surface, singing its ecstasy.

— Please, she insisted tenderly as she might once have pleaded with the baby Rory to go to sleep, and this time placed hands flat on the cold body to push it, actually push it, away from suicide.

They must think: we are being opposed. She saw her actions clearly from their view, a land animal determined to keep them down, resisting their competition, trying with ruthless patience to ridicule their vision, employing the power of gentleness to thwart them at the very moment of achievement. Martyr whales, already exhausted with the trance, turned and turned again wearily to reach the promised land. She saw their introspective eyes glaze to help them concentrate on the inner vision. Dorina leaned her full weight against a stubborn whale, so bleak under her hand she felt in its flesh the unyielding cold of Antarctic loneliness.

— Please Buchanan, she begged, pushing with all her strength and the strength of her passionate belief in mercy.

With that push, she went under.

It was presumed that the president's wife had intended taking her own life. This was certainly Bernard's understanding. A surfer, arriving early at the beach hoping for waves, was disappointed to catch no more than a greying mat of hair, a waterlogged woman reduced to her last gasp, plus the handbag, which had given warning as it sat on the sand, waiting for her to come out. He pulled her up on the beach and resuscitated her. He yoked her arm over his neck and hoisted her back to life and all its joys, much as another young man once carried her husband. The reception clerk at Casualty put down her novel and the memory of when she last read it during the lazy days just before they demolished the old Imperial Baths, and recognized her straight away, having enjoyed an ardent involvement with the royal family and found the change to the presidential family surprisingly painless, having gloated over the luxury of Dorina's banquets at the mansion, criticized her hats and totted up her possessions. She had seen through that Rory, too, much though one wished for Prince Charming, and shared his mother's frustration with so unyielding a son. Wasn't she a mother herself, with problems? Women's magazines had shown her how it all felt and no mistake. This was, beyond doubt, Her Excellency in person despite being in an unforeseeable mess. The hospital superintendent drove in, doctors assembled out of hours thinking there might be some preferment in eagerness. Matron thanked her personally for showing presence of mind in an emergency. The VIP suicide was whisked off to a private room to be lavished with suffocating luxuries of nourishment and attention.

— Thank you, she groaned to the awakening agony of survival. Are the whales safe?

Her rescuer, on being produced and questioned, reported that he had not noticed any whales but he couldn't say if there might have been one in the bay or not. Whales do exist and have been seen.

— On the beach? she whispered.

This he could assert absolutely, positively, there was no sign of a whale on the beach. A whale could not be missed, especially by a man observant enough to see a handbag waiting, apparently fruitlessly, for its owner.

Dorina slept, and slept right through Bernard's state visit. He arrived complete with his nest of mice, a light blanket smothering his lap for privacy, floating round the hospital in a cage of eight large male bodies, his version of living caryatids, enjoying the novelty, yet frightened by the possibility of a trap and an assassin round the next polished corner. He was even more frightened at what would happen to him if Dorina died. He ogled a few nurses. The entire building swarmed with Watchdogs and police. A parade of surgeons and specialists trooped along at either side of his litter, listening devoutly as he recounted the fairytale of his love for this graceful woman who was his wife and laid down guidelines for keeping the whole disaster of her rescue secret from the press, rounding it out with his personal recommendations as to her treatment, thank you all deeply, this is a moment full of grief, we love each other dearly.

100

Passenger faces, presenting so many flat dishes lined on the shelf by tiers, lolled back against the head-rests. The thick gold light of late afternoon poured in the starboard windows striking horizontally across the cabin.

— Ladies and gentlemen we have now landed at Sydney airport, said the captain's voice. But we ask you to remain seated please, even after the aircraft has fully stopped. We have an emergency on board, but it is no cause for alarm. An ambulance is waiting for one of our passengers. After he has disembarked, we will proceed to the airport terminal. This should not cause more than five minutes' delay. Please remain seated to keep the gangway clear. Thank you.

The huge plane eased to a halt far out on wildernesses of tarmac, turning smoothly so light fanned the interior space. A passenger terminal building could be seen squatting oblong on the horizon, overlooked by a control tower with its oscillating dish. The man the hostess had spoken to just before landing looked up surprised, a chosen bar of light glowing in his gold hair. His surprise contained an element of challenge as an officer emerged from the cockpit and, passing ranks of dishes, approached him, bending to say something privately courteous. Other passengers came alive, their annoyance at any slightest delay switched to gratitude that this might provide some novelty. The man whose hair still glowed gold, for the bar of light became fixed now the aircraft had fully stopped, looked about him past the officer's bluecoated shoulder, at faces emerging from anonymity. He saw the woman across the aisle, remembering her complaint that she had requested a non-smoking seat. He saw the little girl beside her, a child with braces on her teeth and unhappy hands. He saw the elderly man between himself and the window who had confessed this was to be a holiday, a reunion with his sons and grandchildren, and had hinted at family feuds being laid aside. He blinked in his bar of light while the jet engines idled.

An ambulance drew alongside, light flashing.

The aircraft's forward door was opened and a set of steps dropped into place. The man with golden hair, who was a man once blessed by youth, smelled living air with a whiff of aircraft fuel. Passengers, chewing over their sympathy, stopped talking: an ambulance must mean sickness or accident or even death. They craned their necks to keep an eye on him, while wishing also to appear as if no such morbid concern could possibly interest them beyond the mere coincidence of happening to glance that way at the crucial moment. Far off across tarmac the dish on its tower oscillated, netting silent information. The two ambulance voices outside could be heard, but not what they said. Waiting, they looked up the gangway, it might be thought apprehensively. The officer spoke again in his confidential manner, so several observers supposed he might do for a convincing doctor at a bedside. Evening light struck in across the cabin. The motors purred and whined. The outside air smelt cooler than the inside air, yet the clear late sky looked like summer. The man who had twice been spoken to, once by a hostess and now by an officer, looked at his fellow passengers as though he might have something to say, and they looked back. But he knew why he was looking at them, and they did not. So they grew uncomfortable and their expressions developed a less neutral, less tactful tone. They were not to know he was indeed ill, ill with the knowledge that his friends had been killed because they believed in his leadership, ill with the relapsing memory of their bodies slumping, their fateful loyalty. If he considered hijacking the aircraft, he had cause to regret how lucklessly polite he'd been in divesting himself of weapons in order to call on a lady he must not risk failing. And a hijack was not beyond him. The officer straightened up, locked rigid by the bands of rank on his sleeve, to stand in attendance slightly behind the seat, indicating that now was the designated moment for the person in question to leave.

Those beside windows in a position to watch saw ambulance attendants take up their posts, apprehensive and silent, one either side of the steps. Jet engines purred and whined. The word SYDNEY spelt itself in huge letters on the passenger terminal they had been delayed reaching.

The person spoken to stood up. He stood surprisingly like a man at the barber's whose turn comes at last. Quite ready to pay when he has received some service. Not as if the ambulance held the least horror for him. His mouth in a smile that, casual though it was, said if I wanted to, I could make some flash gesture that would amaze you all.

Witnessing faces lolled back among comforts. The officer put on an expression which also meant something rather peculiar, being the stern look of a victim in such a fright he has no time to catch breath or assemble the right cheeks eyes brows lips and chin for anything less severe.

The ignorant felt their old warm air escape in fugitive eddies of expired breath.

The two standing men, among all the rest still strapped to their seats, could not now see the oscillating dish on the tower, but they alone knew what the air traffic control officers inside were expecting to monitor through their binoculars, what truth stood paralysed above their cooling mugs of tea.

In those few minutes the marooned plane's shadow spread out on the runway, large as a building, only to be swallowed in the vaster shadow of earth itself tilting away from the sun. The gold bars faded without warning, leaving a cold temporary light for closing down.

Then the man who had been spoken to, still wearing his smile, did a thing so improper his fellow passengers forgot all about the waiting ambulance and waiting attendants. He had begun to walk toward the exit but stopped halfway and leaned across to a gentleman who afterwards swore they had never set eyes on each other before (a gentleman making ready to rush off the plane first because of the superior importance of his appointments, who held a briefcase expectant on his knees, hat already on his head and an umbrella hooked over his wrist against the unlikelihood of rain) and lifted the hat off this gentleman's head. A quite ordinary hat, grey felt and not inexpensive, of a kind once mandatory for respectable males and now coming back into fashion in the irrational manner of the trade.

He took the hat with not a word, only that smile of someone who could make a flash gesture if he chose but would not, and put it on his head. Clean-shaven and jaunty, with his eyes he told the gentleman: You and I are enemies and always have been. He smiled around at his fellow citizens but not at them as enemies. And they saw he suited the hat much better than its rightful owner. The officer now appeared more terrified than grim, but also like a man whose duty might transcend him.

— Wearing that hat, said the mother of the child afterwards. You'd have thought we had to know who he was, even though we didn't have a clue.

When she heard this, the child with braces on her teeth watched her unhappy hands.

He walked to the front of the aircraft, drawing all eyes. Though not exactly tall, he stooped, he and his enemy's hat, to pass through the doorway into the open air of burnt jet fuel and too vast a distance for running in any direction.

The elderly healer of family feuds looked out on ambulance fellows who somehow did not fit their uniforms, having the wrong shape for helpers. His neighbour during the flight, not yet visible in person on the steps, was dramatically visible in their faces. A baby far back in one of the rear seats of the economy class began to cry tiny penetrating sustained cries that stood the hair up on the back of your neck.

Then the illicit hat, worn at an angle completely unfamiliar to it, appeared halfway down the steps, its wearer partly masked by the shiny arc of the plane's fusilage and seeming smaller out there. The ambulance people leaned in toward him as he approached, drawn by the heat of his presence. One of them spoke briefly, voiceless mouth mouthing the attempted firmness which expressed itself as simply a new kind of stupidity.

The man inclined his head to listen, an indescribable nobility in the restrained grandezza of his courtesy.

Then the elderly witness at the window saw somebody else, somebody central to the drama he could never have believed: a third hireling waiting on the far side of the ambulance who had doubtless been there all the time, now moving to a more advantageous position.

The hat looked up from considering what had been so briefly and quietly said. His face showed now, calm eyes resting on this third and central character whose shoes were to be seen from the window and even one trouser leg which flapped in the wind. The smile, lost on the way out, crept back. He grew large again. His hands hung relaxed with relief, this man who, on the subject of conscience, had once boasted he did not gag and that he saw things through once he had started them. He recognized who this was and what would happen. He rejoiced as the kamikaze pilot had so many years before. In his audacious strength, purloined headgear set rakishly, his smile broke into a laugh. He would at last assuage the horror of a man's skull shattering under his hand.

That loud laugh, heard even through the remote piercing grief of the baby, broke free. But not as loud as the exploding blood from his stomach. Belatedly, forgetfully, he clutched himself and spun round with the elegance of acrobatic training, to present the gunman with a three-quarter back view. More silent holes appeared in his light clothing, each as if something small had burst out of his body rather than a bullet pumping in.

The baby cried its voice black and empty of breath.

He faced his attacker again. The ambulance men closed in and gripped his arms; he threw them aside imperiously as having no share in this. They grabbed at him again. He felled them, one with each dying hand, swift savage impersonal blows, and walked forward, upright, bold flowers of blood blossoming on his shirt. Across the wilderness between him and his killer he strode by sheer force of dignity, by outrage at having his climax stolen, across a desert big as the whole country, in the half-hidden coward's direction.

So he, by all reason dead already and leaving behind him the writhing agonies of his two victims, stepped surely toward the third. More silent holes opened their urgent mystery in his clothing. His gymnast's body danced forward then feinted, sending the hat spinning aside, to execute a tumble that ought to have been performed with space below it for the full beauty to be shown, not slap up against hard ground, not cut short by grey bitumen shocking to his artistry. The body, spreadeagled on its back, did not even twitch. His dying had been done already and perhaps many times over.

Door still open, the aircraft began to roll smoothly forward. Some obstruction, caught under the bottom of the stairway, uttered the grating screech of a murdered animal, a moment later tumbling free as a metal box, crushed and scraped but bearing still a painted red cross. One vast wing sliced the scene from the world entirely; first the ambulance vanished under its diagonal blade, next the killer's protruding foot, his leg being wiped out up to the knee, then his gun hand holding the hot weapon, then the vivid corpse despite wind tugging at his shirt to urge him up. Gone in this clean diagonal wipe-out. Then the corpse's face no longer smiling, followed by those ambulance people, one as still as the man who knocked him down and the other last seen on his knees crouched over his pain. Lastly that fugitive hat passed under the great gliding silver shroud being drawn across a tragedy no one had yet put a name to, though bearing a name they would discover they all knew.

101

Greta Grierson's outrage stemmed from a knowledge of blamelessness solid as a treetrunk. She had done nothing, categorically nothing, as she protested to the police, to warrant arrest, or for that matter to warrant anything but gratitude. She was, she informed them, a perfect secretary, incorruptibly silent where her professor's business was concerned. But once she saw they were not to be reached by logic, she took refuge in Scottish good sense.

— Very well, she said frankly. So you are making a mistake which will surely prove embarrassing to you in the long run. But if you are determined to make it, I am not one to resist the law. I respect your uniform and many's the time I have blessed a policeman for his help and the comfort of knowing he was out there keeping society in order. May I fetch an extra cardigan? I expect it will be cold in that van of yours.

— Of course, madam, the inspector consented. Though I won't hear of you travelling in the back like a criminal. The constable will gladly give up his seat for you. And I shall drive.

— Oh, said Greta going to pieces at this show of gallantry. Still I might perhaps be glad of it at the station. Police stations are always said to be cold.

— Please yourself, the inspector agreed. But you aren't to be taken to any station. Not a special case like yourself, madam. Every comfort laid on.

— Really! Greta was almost as surprised by this as by noticing that she no longer felt the least bit afraid of what was happening.

In the van she admitted privately to cankers eating at the heart of her solid tree: Lavinia, always little Lavinia who never would understand what a burden it had been to cart her around and take responsibility for her, plus that disastrous dinner and walking out on such people, the host destined to be chief minister and another who had since become president. She knew she would have to be punished for this some day. So now the punishment had come, Greta accepted it with relief. And then there was that mortifying misunderstanding with Mr Sikorski, also to be put down to Lavinia's account, and the subsequent scandal in the geography department when it appeared he had not only failed to honour lecture commitments with his students, plus being absent from one of the professor's staff meetings, but had apparently taken himself for a holiday to Tuavaleva and lost, if you please, an oceanographic survey launch. Yes, she was guilty, guilty of harbouring shameful hopes about him. For this, too, she would accept punishment.

— My orders, the inspector was saying as he glanced back through the barred window into the van where his subordinate joggled in unrehearsed discomfort. Are to deliver you to the airport. A special plane is waiting to fly you to Canberra.

— Canberra, she exclaimed like the winner of a year's supply of washing powder who does not know how she will do justice to so much good luck.

— You are to be held in custody there, and I tell you this confidentially of course, in a private suite attached to the Ministry for Internal Security. That's what I have been told. Plus orders to treat you politely. Which I hope you will agree I have done.

— Indeed you have, Inspector. I shall speak highly of your courtesy if I am given the chance.

She smelt again that damp bark odour of untrodden mulch. The very day came to mind in a flash, exactly as it had been when she first walked out with a young man, yes, Desmond his name was, expecting that despite her life of drudgery caring for two sisters he would find her at least attractive enough, at least compliant enough, to kiss. He did try. But she, victim of some mindless antimagnetism, quite astounded and dismayed herself by repulsing his efforts. What could have brought so ancient a wound to mind? Something in the manner or voice of this pleasant police officer? His own odour perhaps? She recoiled from such intimacy. A mad idea possessed her: he was, being of an age, that same Desmond now grown and successful and quietly musing on the identical memory of their failure to kiss. She stole a look at him. Impossible. Not the same face. Or was it? People do change.

— If I'm to give your name, she said precipitately. I ought to be told it. And wondered at the asperity of her tone. Please, she added humbly.

— I beg your pardon, madam, Inspector Riley. Kevin Riley.

— That's not hard to remember, she replied with more relief than might be thought suitable.

His fingers were quite mauve around the knuckles. Is this, she asked herself the usual question, my real life, the only one I shall ever have on earth? No answer required. Then it doesn't make sense, she commented. Not any sense at all.

The crowds gathered at Sydney airport were in a state of excitement. As her escorts ushered her past flight attendants and security guards, through electronic weapons-detectors, out on to the tarmac, she observed, far over, a jet standing still on the ruled horizon, engines curdling the air while an ambulance with flashing red light waited parked beside it. Some drama appeared to be happening out there while rumours in this age of rumours agitated the passengers and visitors in departure lounges. At least, Greta Grierson put it in the most sensible perspective, giving them more to do than gawk at me between two policemen, I've that much to be thankful for.

102

Poor Rory received a telephone call from his mother in her saltwater voice. Now a graduate of the National Strike Force Academy, he had entered service as a sub-lieutenant. At the time, the press made a family occasion of the graduation and misconstrued his sullen resentment as manly reserve. His mother understood. Poor darling, she whispered privately, to see you in this claustrophobic uniform. You'll never forgive me enough to give up your addiction, I suppose.

So he was a naval officer. And although appointed to Vice-admiral Todd's personal staff, his superiors then behaved perfectly correctly in allowing no taint of family connections either to sour or sweeten their professional dealings. Rory began to construct a life from the mess of his upbringing. Simplistic as a game with building blocks, he manoeuvred the frustrating puzzle of his abilities and disappointments into some semblance of a shelter which was his own.

His father's power had been a lie he carried everywhere with him. Sycophants addressed it as they shook his hand, bullies kept a wary distance because of it, intellectuals conceded defeat in argument in deference to it. The more he protested, the more he was suspected of secreting special powers of insight, reserves of ambition under the guise of placidity or, failing any natural talent, at least sufficient inside information to give him the edge in any dispute. His self-respect was routed with every victory. He passed exams, even those he declined to attempt, earning credits for writing impotent abuse against questions on the private meanings of *The Waste Land* or common characteristics of communities living above the snowline. He wept with rage at his first goal in a junior football match because they let him score.

Poor Rory, all he salvaged from his miserable youth was a sardonic honesty expressing itself as indifference, and a commission. He didn't miss the manner of his appointment either, Vice-admiral Todd having apparently picked him with something in mind for the future.

His mother said little on the phone, yet her voice eroded his self-possession. He knew every nuance, as a lonely child longing to escape must.

— Darling, I thought we might have lunch somewhere. It is so long since you and I enjoyed a quiet chat.

He said a stiff thank you, which he regretted the moment it was out. But wondered afterwards had he really been injurious, or did his tone tell her as much as hers told him? He enjoyed the use of a navy vehicle with his new rank, so he would come for her. She had, of course, despite her decision, been sent back to the bunker once the hospital discharged her.

— And then we shall decide where to go, she agreed. Really this is very good of you, it solves a shocking poser.

He imagined the amusement of whoever was tapping the call. But despite her idiosyncratic slang, he considered her deeper and more dangerous than his father.

Didn't he, after all, still possess a letter she had written him, a letter calling the Buchanan regime a betrayal of the people? True, she ended by explaining that to put such subversion in his hands gave him power over her, but didn't it also keep him awake at night knowing the envelope was still there in his pocket and might one day be found by the security police? Didn't every lapsed day confirm and compound his crime of not reporting it and bind him closer to her? He could not guess her true motive for sending it, even to the risk of having it read by the navy censorship officers.

— Is this car for your personal use? his mother asked when they met.

— No, I simply got it from the car pool.

The information appeared to stimulate Dorina.

— Do you suppose we are alone?

— Unless we were to jump hand in hand from South Head, I should think this is just about our best chance. Where to, madam?

She recited the address she had been taught. He found it on the map and they set off.

— But if you have the least suspicion we are being followed, his mother added. Don't go there, we'll simply sit in a park rather than give Owen Powell the satisfaction. You're looking well dear, she added nervously. Considering.

— I am well, he replied. Considering.

Rory had turned out to be an ungainly young man, weak and large-boned, his black hair so fine it fitted his head like a felt cap. He had his mother's angularity without her grace, his father's bulging eyes without the fire. He was born to be a lifelong dependent.

Dorina offered no explanation of where they were going. All she said was: There may be nobody home when we get there.

But somebody was home. Rory stayed in the car as requested, craning his neck to catch sight of who opened the door of a large house overhung with trees and besieged by a garden of exotics gone wild. Not a glimpse. The door shut behind his mother as she went in. He consulted his watch, momentarily holding it to his ear.

Warm weather was returning, the day airy, light went flying through the street, one of those lovely Sydney streets with saw-toothed terrace houses stepping downhill dappled by an avenue of planetrees. He would, perhaps, stretch his legs, take a walk, despite his mother's injunction on no account to leave the car unattended for an instant. What did she expect? Someone to plant a bomb in it? Once again, her voice was what impressed him, so charged with excitement and fear. He had not asked why. In fact, he had not answered at all.

On a wall across the way a feminist accusation from the time when such matters were taken seriously had almost worn off: PHIL EVERLEIGH IS A MALE MOLE. Huge fresh lettering had been stencilled nearby: STOP THE ASIAN INVASION.

He found himself being watched by an elderly man who perched on the bench at the bus stop. He was surprised by glazed eyes, the saggy mottled skin and alcohol-preserved nose of a traditional Sydneysider, that air (no longer usual) of I'm-as-good-as-you, under which anyone who stood up to this pugnacity might be reasonably sure of finding a person simple with good heartedness.

Rory ran his finger inside his service collar.

The livingroom lay along one flank of the building and the moment she walked down the passage Dorina realized the house had been built to face that way. The street must have come later, a tacked-on entrance porch accommodating the new address. She was assailed by pungent sensations. The woman who led the way, clothes rustling her along busily, trailing a perfume Dorina had not smelt since she was a girl, looked back once with her glittering youthful air of a travelling goldmine, bangles a-clatter as she waved encouragement. A radio in one of the rooms advertised slimming biscuits and then collapsed in a welter of sickly music. She wanted to laugh with the thrill of risk.

— Let me look at you, the woman declared as if unwrapping some coveted new purchase, eager to reassure herself they had not given her the wrong one, and faced Dorina's excited trembling. It is you, she confirmed.

— It is, Dorina agreed, a tinge of hysteria giving her a high colour. Then, caught up in the whimsical extravagance of it all she added. And it is you?

In the green room her hostess laughed a hearty broad laugh of the kind that has stopped listening to itself and is purely in the service of merriment, setting her scarves aflutter and the jewels jumping at her neck.

— They never told me! she said complimenting her guest on her wit while inviting her to relax.

The careful respectability of the room, combined with its voluptuous ambitions, spoke to the president's wife as clearly as a confession. Among such plump cushions, such silks and velvets and silver photograph frames, the woman could only be a retired brothel keeper. The time had long passed when Dorina might have withdrawn among her sticklike virtues, tilted her long nose and frozen the creature with curtness. Life had taught her what such moralistic superiority was worth.

— I am Mrs Izumi and it is a wonderful comfort, Mama declared. To think we come from opposite ends of the spectrum, you from the golden heights and I from the deep secrecies, to meet in the middle at this green room.

In its quirky way her statement struck Dorina as gracious. She was, indeed, wearing yellow, as Mrs Izumi wore purple. The word my type uses about her type, she thought, is brassy. But to the credit of both ladies, she knew it could never fit.

— Have you heard of my reputation? the hostess enquired making a quick calculation.

— Apart from your name, which you have just told me, I don't even know who you are.

Mama was, as she put it later, most awfully let down.

— That is my late husband you're looking at, she nodded affably to the photograph of a person so swaddled in leather, goggled and helmeted one could scarcely tell he was Japanese. *Late* a long time ago, she confessed. He has been dead, oh, umpteen years, she laughed away the exact number coquettishly.

— I'm very nervous, Dorina said at last.

— It's Mrs Izumi you're speaking to, Mama nodded to emphasize the correctness of her information. Mrs Bernadette Izumi, nee McAloon, known to my intimates as Mama. We were all so very shocked, she went on immediately serious. By the loss of Mr Dog. A national loss if I'm not mistaken, Mrs Buchanan. But seeing you come here today he must be trilling on his harp like mad, I should think. He said to me: that Mrs Buchanan won't let us down or I'm no judge. The gist of the matter is this, my dear. Word has reached us that your husband's neck is on the chopping block, and without meaning offence I might say there's a powerful lot will thank God to see him go. But we also know who is doing it and why. I'm sure I don't need to waste your time with elementary information.

— Naturally not, Dorina answered, pride refusing to allow her to show her uncertainty.

— If they say he's out, he's out. Now, look at it from our point of view. This is the best opportunity we have ever had to expose them. We've got to get him to speak up before he is sacked. Frankly, my dear, we are asking if you could talk him into it. A national statement. A public confession.

— You think too highly of him, Dorina responded quietly. He is categorically incapable of saying he was wrong.

— Not even to save his bacon?

— He could never be persuaded to believe he is hated.

Mama slapped her knees in despair.

Dorina sat miserably on the green settee, contemplating the lugubrious respectability of the place and its bright parrot of an owner.

— I do not know who you are, Mrs Izumi, or what power

you may have. I am here because Mr Taverner gave me this
address. I want to ask you frankly to whom I should go to
discuss the plan I have in mind.

Mama jumped up from her armchair and rushed to squeeze
her guest's hands. Their rings clicked against each other, so that
Dorina thought for a bizarre moment how complex and competitive such a gesture would be if the recipient were Alice Penhallurick and not herself.

— I am the Wild Dog's agent and publicity planner, she
stated. I believe you could have confidence in telling me.

Dorina looked about desperately. She accepted the danger of
what they were doing, also the tension of knowing Rory would
be out there watching his clock, the possibility of their having
been traced, the inevitable bugging devices, the tightening net.
Although, she thought, they could never track down the Wild
Dog. This, of all places, must be safe. For a mad moment she
considered the alternative of telling everything in front of Rory
in that other safe place, his navy car.

— I want you to arrange for me to file a divorce suit, she said.
In one week from today I shall come again. No (she remembered
the Wild Dog's advice to be unpredictable), let's make it a
Tuesday. Tuesday I shall come to meet the solicitor and sign any
papers. Do you know a journalist?

— Of course, there's our Stephanie.

— I have to surprise my husband into agreeing to an open
court. He lays great store by his bravado. A journalist will be
essential for that.

— But what good will a divorce be? Mama pleaded from her
dashed hopes because, though she was fertile with ideas of her
own, she never had been perceptive about other people's. This
will take away your power.

— You must do as I say, Dorina ordered putting such power
to good use while she could and standing ready to leave. Just do
as I say.

And hurried out to hide her tears for Bernard. Out from the
bower of sinister plants to the dark blue car with its insignia and
uniformed driver.

The old Sydneysider who had been sitting on the bench had
already caught his bus and gone.

He drove, dear Rory, without asking a single question though
he smelt the perfume of obsolescence clinging to her and caught
the distraught fringes of her look.

— Now, he said when she calmed down. When do you need me and my clean car again?

At first this seemed the ultimate kindness, tactful and unquestioning. But such was the society Buchanan had created that Dorina was not to be spared the possibility of his knowing she had plotted his father's disgrace and was assisting her in every way he could. Tears filled her eyes.

He sensed what she needed. He sensed that anything anyone said was likely to sound wrong at a time like this; that words by their treacherous rationality were bound to hurt. So Rory, who never sang at home, began singing. He sang, softly, a song she had used all through his childhood to put him to sleep. A song from Eriskay in the Hebrides, sung to the selkie language of those whose true element is the sea and who must yearn to return home to it.

> *Ver mi hiu, ravo na lavo,*
> *Ver mi hiu, ravo hovo i,*
> *Ver mi hiu, ravo na lavo,*
> *Ancatal,*
> *Traum san yechar.*

103

Bernard Buchanan meanwhile began breathing heavily. Anchored in his seat he followed the visitor with his eyes, eyes full of pandemonium. Wrath swelled inside him, solid as a sentient brute. He turned purple, hands braced on chair-arms as if able to propel himself across the study and crush his impudent tormentor against the wall. Twisted with strain, a bloated bag of blood, the president concentrated his whole being on that spruce figure, the composed Sir George Gipps, fastidious with his dry righteous skin and Church of England fingernails, Gipps whom he had dismissed in *The Authorized History of Australia* as, quote, the least likeable and least significant of colonial governors, unquote, hoping to suppress whatever threat a knowledge of the past posed his own regime.

Then the master perceived what ought to have been clear long before: not Gipps as a haunting of history, nor Gipps as the voice of public doubts, but Gipps as embodying his own anger.

If I were a woman, his sigh of fury said, you would have to show me my grief.

He saw cloudlessly, he heard birds in the garden where so

much had happened even during the short walk with Lavinia, he gripped the chiselled shapes of chair-arms, he felt sweat stream off him and an exorbitance of mucous dislodge. His vast carcase's tortured shape, of course, he could not see, but heard his seized joints crack. The full force of such avengers as his imagination knew took all his concentration to muster. They were the avengers his mother had promised so long ago, archangels with glittering swords. While the president swelled yet more desperately plum-coloured, the flurry of white garments and swan feathers, the bloody hacking of weapons whirled in the far corner. Gipps had been sitting on a chair under the portraits of Captain James Cook and Governor Arthur Phillip. Desperate threshings of a dying man rose and sank in the shrouding rebuffed shapes of his attackers rearing back and plunging in again. Buchanan, taut with concentration, his fat heroically assembled to almost human shape, glared with wet red eyes at the scene, willing it to happen, urging the angels to make an end of his hallucination, and finally sinking back, shapeless and exhausted, hearing the phone ring which had been ringing for minutes. He tugged a handkerchief from his pocket, mopped some mess from nose and mouth, folded it and wiped his eyes. He checked the revolver in his top drawer and the cyanide capsules. He lifted the phone to shout a single word *No*, and slammed it back while glancing at that corner where the murder took place. His inspired dreamworld of sixty years' maturing dissipated into thin air. He found himself staring at the empty banality of a chair set against a wall beneath Cook and Phillip in their domesticated severity.

Dorina is, of course, he informed himself confidentially. Going mad by degrees.

— Send me Mr Owen Powell, he growled down the intercom.

The door opened almost immediately to admit a harried Minister for Internal Security, who insinuated himself across the carpet, bowed and smiled and stood awaiting instructions.

— Dear Owen, the president began promisingly, wearily, as his deputy noticed the sweat-soaked collar, the high flush in those weighty cheeks, the hard bright eyes. Is it true, what I hear? Have your agents finally tracked down the Wild Dog and his schoolboy adventurers? Was he responsible for everything: the ruined cylinders, the Paringa break-in, blowing up the *Sirius*?

— Everything, Your Excellency.

— And your men shot him at the airport. That is correct also?

— Well, Powell prevaricated. I wouldn't like to claim sole credit.

— Come on, man, don't mince around in that poncey manner. Out with it. Are you the one I have to thank or not?

— Well I suppose so, Your Excellency. But entirely as a routine service through the normal operation of my department.

— Owen, said the leader unaccountably looking to one side, looking in fact to an empty corner of the room with relief in his eyes. I am worried about our friend Roscoe. He's been gone a long time. I haven't heard a word of him since you had him admitted to that hospital. Be a friend and bring him here. Understood? How soon can you arrange it?

— I suppose in about an hour and a half, the minister replied, thoroughly on guard.

— Call it an hour for good measure. I do hate hurrying people. You can fix this for me. There is no one else I trust as I trust you. You realize that, don't you?

— I do what I can Bernard.

— Thank you Owen. Thank you for everything. Now leave me to have a few minutes' rest. This has been a day of great importance. He is to be here in an hour, remember.

No sooner had Owen Powell closed the door than a mouse, crouched under Sir George Gipps's empty chair, came skittering around the skirtingboard, across the carpet to the presidential boot, up the presidential trouser leg and out of sight. Buchanan felt the sharp twinge of pain with a sigh of reassurance.

Veronica O'Toole, on receiving permission, rushed in with her hair winging to either side like a spaniel's ears and her spaniel's face glittering. She made so comic a sight, this refrigerated academic surprised in a flurry of passion, that the president hooted. The hoot stung her, since, in common with many graceless people, she could not bear being thought less than soignée. Today, remarkably, she had at hand the means to knock the rudeness out of him.

— Have you heard? she squawked, still high on adrenaline. In my opinion Penhallurick is behind this.

Outside, it was already full daylight, though the lamps kept burning and the room remained warm with yesterday's warmth. Bernard Buchanan's derision was snatched from his open mouth by history. So the old man had dared hit back, had he?

Veronica O'Toole saw her news was, as she hoped, news.

— Fifteen notable citizens! All out in the open too! she declared disgustedly, keeping a sporty eye on his response.

He waited to be told what he had no desire to hear, a helpless mound of flesh with a head squeezed up through his collar.

— Read it for yourself, sir.

He accepted the *Sydney Courier* folded to display a boxed Open Letter on the front page.

As trusted friends of His Excellency the President of Australia, and as acknowledged leaders in public life, we, the undersigned, beg Mr Buchanan to reconsider his decision to suspend public elections under the Revised Emergency Special Powers Act. He, as our much loved leader, was put in his present high office by the free will of the people. Despite economic difficulties and the admittedly widespread disturbances, we believe the denial of franchise can only further exacerbate an already tense situation.

As a mark of loyalty to him and confidence in the public, we are declaring openly our conviction that he will be triumphantly voted into office for a third four-year term if the election is held by the due date. Also, that holding such an election will be the surest way to refute those cynics who claim that this has been his political strategy to cling to office against the wishes of the people.

In Australia we have a proud tradition of democracy which we have entrusted to his capable hands. We are confident that even the dissidents who provoked this emergency are *Australian* dissidents and therefore open to giving our leader a Fair Go.

The fifteen signatories, headed by Sir William Penhallurick, included three industrialists, two High Court judges, a bishop, a yachtsman, two football stars, plus the usual poets and media academics.

— I shall keep this, he promised, then suddenly snatched back the tail-end laughter he'd been robbed of before. Doesn't it tell its own story, he demanded of the bilked Dr O'Toole (one-time Professor of English). When the William Penhalluricks of this world become champions of democracy? I think, he concluded merrily to her further chagrin. I might have to admit I'd prefer me!

104

A motor mower, solemn as a tank, advanced across the lawn toward Buchanan's window, trailing a channel of almost imperceptibly shorter grass. The lawns were kept immaculate. The gardener sitting astride the machine drove with a maniac concentration on straight lines.

Indoors, the president rested on a couch, another item of custombuilt furniture of his own design bearing the personal stamp of the incurably unyielding. His feet were crossed, neat shoes highly polished, soles unmarked by contact with the ground, a carpet-salesman's shoes. His arms spread horizontally along the backrest, he glared out with the bulbous strain of ill-health and weight loss.

Suddenly the gardener's work assumed the character of a threat, motor clattering loud as machinegun fire, the inexorable progress menacing, the concentration on geometry monstrous. Beyond the work, dark green clouds of foliage were cogitating storms while armed sentries marched across the mouth of the drive far over but not out of rifle range. The president saw into the scene's demonic orderliness, its inevitable violence and tyranny of regulations. He would not spare himself, he would face it. . . because the moment had not yet come for turning to confront the other people in his room, people who stood near the desk trying to live up to this latest event. Although he had not looked at them he knew Luigi Squarcia wore a light suit with a rose on his lapel and Mediterranean justifications all ready in the play of his fingertips, that Owen Powell watched the master closely to adjust the angle of his own bald pate so he might catch the drift of posterity, and that Roscoe Plenty's ghost, corsetted into a straitjacket, was intent on employing one shoulder to wipe some dribble from his mouth. The mower, drumming, crawled malignantly nearer. The gardener wore a celebrant's downcast eyes. These elements composed themselves into a perfect crisis.

— Explain, came the president's voice from a long way out, from as far away through the window as those assassin-harbouring trees. Explain, he repeated without once having looked at them.

Squarcia watched the great shaggy head he had so recently hauled dripping from the bath. All right, he may as well play along with Buchanan's game and pretend to ignore giveaway signs of shakiness. A miserable Owen Powell contemplated the carpet-salesman's shoes, feeling his own would never stand inspection. Roscoe Plenty wooed that shoulder and stuck his lips out to reach it and taste the comfort of the other-self.

—The whole country is celebrating, Marshal Powell suggested hopefully.

— I am the whole country, said the distant voice of stormy trees. Do I look as if I'm celebrating?

— You see so much farther than we do Bernard, Owen objected.

— Your Excellency!

— Your Excellency, so much farther.

— I don't like that Mr Marshal, came the awful remote consonants lent a gravelly edge now the mower sliced tops off grass leaves just outside the window and swung to about-face with a whirr and gnash of blades.

The gardener's back looked even more ominous in its dedication than his approach, his going away a rejection, a declaration of contempt. Unpleasant fanaticism cut yet another straight line. The pitch of the motor had dropped a semi-tone, now being heard from behind. Buchanan lowered his own pitch accordingly.

— Welcome home Roscoe, he growled.

But neither Roscoe Plenty, ex-Chief Minister of the Republic, nor his lovely shoulder showed the least interest in anyone but each other, nor any matter but the safe collection of punishable spit. He gave a slurping snivel of piggy concentration, well-timed enough to do service for a reply and intelligible as many another answer heard in this same office.

— I think I speak for us all, said Squarcia relishing the

syllables as a man who has made foreignness his art. In saying that we rejoice at the death of the Wild Dog as the removal of an irritant to your presidential dignity.

Buchanan's anger flashed round on them, more terrible than the blades of the cutting machine. The mounds of his black-clothed greatness raging hot. Above his elegantly shod feet and inert legs the belly rolled to one side of the couch and hung there precarious as an exotic fruit. He confronted them with red eyes and red nose, his padded lips apart and the yellow teeth of a hippopotamus displayed.

— Don't give me that bullshit, he roared, the volume of sound a shock in itself. Who had him shot?

Roscoe Plenty, whimpering, stood stiff like the bundle of strapped bones he was. His head of a trapped animal willing itself into labyrinths of bolt-holes, eyes flush to the sides of his face as a rabbit's, big and glossy, luminous with the health no longer required for the rest of his functioning, unable to comprehend that escape could not be made without his body, and the body a numb lump in the trap's jaws. Owen Powell shuddered at his victim's proximity, such proof of the power of his skill with tape recordings; shuddered also because he suspected he himself might be on the mat for unguessable offences. Why else would the great man ask what he asked? Hadn't this already been settled? Hadn't Owen been thanked already for putting the Wild Dog out of the way? Wasn't he on to something else now, simply waiting for the chance to divulge the facts about Commandant Curtis?

— May I with respect, Squarcia spoke for them all. Suggest you consult your own files on the Paringa raid?

Buchanan hoisted the pendulous fruit back from the precipice. He had always known whom he had to deal with when it came to a showdown. He turned again to the window. The gardener's military back retreated along an uncorrupted strait. Dark trees toiled in a fresh wind.

— What do you anticipate I would find there?

— Your agreement that IFID's agents may legitimately protect their interests, Squarcia replied. Even against the state's own subjects.

— IFID, the president echoed from far fringes of the storm.

He knew in his bones the outlaw's death would be the end of him. Already, public shock had provided the occasion for that Open Letter. His waistcoat, which a mere two weeks ago would not button up, hung baggily on him today.

— Everyone wants to claim credit, is this it? First Owen, then IFID's agents. And what has been achieved? I've been shown as small enough to have a ruffian murdered. That's what. Disruptive, he was. As idiotically romantic as a bushranger. Even the cause of some international embarrassment, yes. But more than this: he was one of us. You hear me? What you forget is that he was a factor in my power. The evidence is clear. Just look at today's paper. The pariahs don't wait on niceties.

Given the emotional issue of postponing the elections, Buchanan could not afford to carry dead weight, apparently.

— Can't you comprehend that! he bellowed at his quailing deputy, at the trapped rabbit in the straitjacket, and at Squarcia, coldbloodedly cosmopolitan.

— No, Your Excellency, no, babbled Powell amazed into telling the truth and accepting that Commandant Curtis would have to wait.

Roscoe Plenty gave a gargling yelp of terror, shaking his head frantically on its bundle of sticks made ready for burial.

— Take him away Owen, the President requested calmly. Take him right back to the hospital. I should never have suspected him. Don't let it be said we treat him inhumanely. Take him yourself, please. Be there to deliver him home in case the reporters smell a rat. Get out of the van in person and support him by the arm. Will you do this for me?

— Of course, Your Excellency.

Owen Powell shot a triumphant glance at Squarcia and gratefully took charge of his light duties, guiding the ruin of an old boss across the carpet like a child wheeling out his Christmas bicycle for the thrill of a selfish ride.

The door shut.

Squarcia did not move. He did not need to.

The advancing mower tracked along a parallel to the left of the president's direct line of sight. Sentries at the distant gate crossed and recrossed, counting their monotonous drill essential to state security. A motor vehicle started up. The gardener did not raise his downcast eyes even for a second, harvesting orderliness. The mental hospital's shabby van swung out along the drive. Wearily Buchanan shifted his right hand a few degrees to lift the telephone.

— I am sending back two patients for you to keep, instead of one.

He dropped the instrument on its cradle. The inexpressive

blacksleeved cylinder of his arm sagged to express, unmistakably, regret.

— To begin with, he began a new conversation. It was just us, Lou. Do you remember?

The aroma of fresh-cut grass wafted in.

From different perspectives they watched the mower complete a line, about-face, and head away again, carrying with it the incorruptible eye of the gardener. Luigi Squarcia saw ahead to a whole new scenario with himself still at the centre. President Buchanan, by contrast, looked back. He relived the news, watching an announcer explain how the notorious criminal was lured into the open. The camera tracked out across airport tarmac. The plane had gone, leaving a great hole in the story's credibility. A first-aid box lay tipped on one crushed corner, empty. Two uniformed men stood over a corpse, one of them keeping the left side of his face from being seen. Another man in uniform lay, unexplained, nearby. Temporary floodlights on wavering stands supplemented the sunset. Wind tugged maddeningly at everything. So the camera, with the logic of its kind, moved in yet closer, swooping on the prey spread-eagled, face upward, his light clothing splotched by grotesque stains, face wiped clean of expression, familiar eyes staring out at Bernard. Older, somewhat gaunt, this was a face he would never forget. How was it possible nobody had warned him he knew the Wild Dog in person? Nor would he forget the young man's strength, who lifted him on his feet and supported him back to the stranded Mercedes, to the only shade in a merciless world, and provided water as well as companionship till rescue came. The screen filled with a flat, bare wilderness as the camera tracked back toward the departure lounges. The roaring in his ears was not the lawnmower with flurrying grass-chips stirred like living things in its passage, the roaring was that appalling plague more universal than loud, that stinging clatter of wings. The ambulance headlamps burned. Those very legs, when neither dead nor twisted against pain, had come striding through the beams while insects puffed around each step, legs setting wheelspokes of shadow moving across his cry for help and himself being hoisted to safety.

— Why did he try to visit me? Twice he came to my house.

Squarcia, who watched all this in the uncrossing and recrossing of presidential ankles and a momentary squirming on that cheerless couch, replied.

— Three times.

Bernard faced him very slowly, the cushions of fat under his chin changing expression. Regret, dwindling from his eyes, opened a gulf back into other memories. He said nothing. He allowed the silence to require an explanation.

— Yesterday as well.

In the lull a challenge was born. What had Peter Taverner known or needed to know? What might he have been going to offer by calling in private?

— I, too, Squarcia continued casually. Called on Dorina, to persuade her to talk you round to my way of thinking. He arrived as I left. We met on the stairs.

Buchanan resumed his contemplation of the garden, the tree-storm which would never break. Watched parading sentries complete and complete their routine, stamping inaudibly in the gravel. Watched that rowdy machine chewing everything in its path. Saw the tyre marks of the hospital van clearly etched along the drive.

— Loss of nerve, he spoke at last. I was waiting for him to show his hand or make a false move, something, anything. Through the years he was too perfect. He loved me.

Admiringly, Squarcia realized the president's confession referred to Owen Powell, who might as well be called the late Owen Powell. Without being invited to do so, he sat himself in a comfortable chair. The fat man, mesmerized by the rule of law being imposed on his lawn, gave no sign of noticing.

Either, thought Squarcia, he can tell I arranged everything or he has made a skilful move against IFID which we will have to counter.

Who, Buchanan racked his ingenuity for some comfort, had implicated Dorina? She was the very person of integrity. However necessary the freedoms of petty corruption to the economy, he sustained his sense of proportion by reference to her. At a state banquet she shone, her arrogance a virtue and impersonal in its absentmindedness, refreshing as her indifference to what people might think of her. The further their lives drifted apart, the less fault he could find with her. Really, she was the most interesting person he knew. How mistaken she had been all those years ago, chafing at his being the business executive and not her, his being the politician. She achieved a distinction far beyond either of these; and something that could not be taken away from her. In that moment Buchanan watched the deadly slow bobbin in this celestial loom threading another green strand of warp across the fabric lawn. He heard nothing.

And this nothing was fear on Dorina's behalf. What had she got herself mixed up with? He had never cared enough for her safety. Security at the bunker must be perfunctory. He seldom telephoned her: had he presumed she knew of his added and growing respect? No, he did not know it himself until this moment. From long habit of waging household wars for dominance, he had not offered the least hint of how he looked up to her, how her every sarcasm stimulated him.

Now the storm did break. . . that storm of dark green leaves down the drive, the dense foliage offering such opportunities to an assassin, exploded in a colossal fountain of branches, rocks and dirt, a rising burgeoning impossibility, the solid missiles at its extremities falling away while billowing dust umbrella'd to swallow them. Afterwards a thunderclap reached the two men looking out at the garden, an ear-shattering slam of sound to shake the mansion as once an earthquake had, so in retrospect there were those who thought of that earthquake as prophetic. The sash window dropped a guillotine within millimetres of Buchanan's hand and its glass fell to four continental shapes remaining in the mind as glittering promises long after they scattered knife-sharp trash across the floor. The lawnmower left an obscene wiggle before swerving toward the gravel path and riding over a border of annuals to massacre the famous Yarralumla irises. The machine stood at the far end of the iris bed, its blades threshing. The driver could nowhere be seen. Rich brown soil of a hundred years' loving mulch pattered round from the blast, the last drift of particles floating away across the eastern boundary. The air cleared from the top down as if the landscape beyond were a newly painted scene being winched up. With an unobstructed view the public road could now be seen, much closer than one might have imagined, where once a shrubbery created cunning illusions. The gates had vanished, also the sentryboxes and the sentries with them.

Rudely, the mansion jangled electric alarmbells.

— I don't think Owen could possibly be credited with having arranged a farewell, Squarcia commented, suave as you like.

— Did I invite you to sit?

Military personnel sprinted round the garden, apparently to forestall another such blast, their clumsy boots mutilating the perfect lawn. Officers barked commands. A helicopter approached, rotors banging away at thin air. Three telephones began ringing. Neither man made any attempt to answer them.

A moment later the telephones fell silent. Luigi Squarcia stood slowly, pale from the shock of the attack.

Do they want us, Bernard Buchanan enquired in that faraway voice he had used at the creation of the world. To give it to them, the entire country, on a plate, for nothing, just like that, and kiss their arse into the bargain?

He called his secretary What's-her-name and asked her to contact the mental hospital.

— I told them to keep the new patient, he said. But have them send Mr Plenty back to me here. We used to be friends, he explained quietly. A long time ago. He and I.

— Before I do, the forgotten secretary ventured. May I mention a minor matter? she relished her coolness while other office staff could be heard in the background screaming and tearing around in the panic of expecting worse to come. We have had another representation from your guest, Commandant Curtis, asking to know if there is anything you wish of him. He has been hoping for an interview for ten days now.

The president did enjoy dealing with details.

— I shall see him this evening at ten-thirty, Miss Colquhoun. All right?

One truth loomed above everything else, casting solid shadows and barriers: nothing could be done about Squarcia. What would be the point of liquidating him? His strength was his personal irrelevance. No one in IFID would spare a tear at Squarcia's funeral. They would all be too busy monitoring the success of whoever had taken over from him. Squarcia can beat me, Buchanan admitted, because I am unique and he is expendable.

105

The piano stood shut. Dorina saw herself as a fluid blackness reflected in the curved black lacquer, approaching, hesitant, on occasion wavering to one side, but never reaching it, never close enough to touch the lid, or allow her fingers the betrayal they ached for.

Exposure to such elements as Dorina had known, though briefly, could never be expunged from consciousness. While she'd remained in hospital a maid was employed to look after the bunker. Once, on her rounds of the room, Dorina regretted dismissing this maid who had seemed a harmless creature, because harmlessness was precisely what had become so rare. At another approach toward her reflection in the piano's side, she admitted Buchanan, too, might still be struggling to free himself from a vacuum of great distances singing in his brain.

The vulgarity of suburbs that crowded to the water's edge all round the harbour turned her away from the view everyone envied. Neither Debussy nor Schubert, nor even Schumann could tempt her now from the purpose growing clear to her imagination, a purpose looming out of motives so deep in her psyche she did not care to try identifying it, she simply felt a pregnancy, a solid autonomous approach, something beyond her power to refuse to nourish, something she could only abort by putting her safety in Squarcia's care. Like power itself, Dorina could not expect it to be gone in the morning when she woke up. It would only grow. Awful as it was and sick of herself as she felt, she gloried in what she had begun. This was not just a case of an action she could no longer stop, she wanted it to take over her life completely, literally to take that life perhaps, if necessary.

The guardhouse staff announced sub-lieutenant Rory Buchanan's arrival, madam. Dorina, ready for hours, hastened up the front stairs, the piano being left to reflect furniture doomed to stillness, glimmered only fleetingly with a chock of meaningless light as a door leading to the garden steps opened long enough for an agent to check whether she had left yet, and then shut again to the simple curve of black lacquer.

106

— Don't bother me with your tapes and your security, man, the president cried impatiently. I'm sickening to death of security. Can you imagine what it's like to live here as I do? Always being watched, no more free than a baby with a couple of dozen hairy nannies? That's not what we want you for, is it Roscoe? he referred the matter to a tortured figure hiding in one corner, arms tightly bound to his sides by a peculiar sleeve-like garment, and dribbling. No. Let me see you stand to attention, Mr Curtis. Yes. Yes, I think so. Very correct and scrupulous. What do you say, Chief Minister? the picture of a dependable man, eh? I like the cut of him, all those joints and shanks. Shall we make it official? Why not? Here, Mr Curtis, have a look at this. What do you make of it?

The commandant, being recalled from a horrified fascination with what he could only describe as a loony, stepped forward smartly to accept a sheet of paper.

— Design for a uniform, he deduced. Not any of the armed services. Could be the uniform Marshal Powell wears.

— It is the uniform Mr Powell *used* to wear. But now you have been appointed Marshal of the Internal Security Force, it will be yours. We have here, Marshal Curtis, the address of an acceptable tailor. That will be all.

— When. . .? Cornelius Curtis dared ask, catching sight of something not even his war experience could steel him against: a mouse, peeping out from under the flap of the president's waistcoat, *munching*.

— From this moment. Welcome to my staff and congratulations. As for your old job. Well, that will be for you to make a suitable appointment. You have a whole department to play with.

Buchanan winced at something painful and slapped his hand once on the desk. The mouse was shocked into running right out, down his leg and across the carpet, till it came to Roscoe Plenty's felt slippers. The mouse paused beside this piece of furniture, whiffled its whiskers and mustered courage to scamper back home, up the familiar billowing slopes of trouser legs and in under cover.

Roscoe Plenty snorted desperately, struggling to recoup some escaped saliva in time to avoid punishment.

— Privately I am worried, the president confided to his Chief Minister when they were alone again. By reports that lately my wife's behaviour has begun to appear bizarre.

Marshal Curtis was expected at the office. His assistant, Jack Cohen, welcomed him ceremonially with introductions all round.

— Cohen? the marshal repeated.

— Jack Cohen, his assistant affirmed with an ingratiating smile which told all that needed to be said of who really set the department's exemplary standard of efficiency.

Curtis was not one to forget. Cohen, though indirectly, had been responsible for his present elevation. Without Cohen's obstruction, he would never have been driven to the extreme of contacting the president personally.

— Just the man for the job, the new marshal decided. Report for duty 0800 hours tomorrow morning. Vengeance Harbour. Clear? You'll excuse me, Commandant Cohen. Busy man. New challenge. Lot to straighten out and so forth. Dismiss.

— Oh Marshal Curtis, quacked the telephone in Buchanan's voice. I have an urgent job for you. It's a missing person, really, I want him found. Do you have a pen handy? Good man. Gipps. Sir George. That's right. Treat the bastard with respect when you catch up with him, Corny. He was on my staff until recently. I might need him. Top priority. Let me say again how glad I am to have such a reliable man aboard.

What had been going on all this time? Cornelius Curtis looked at the name. Gipps, Sir George. Well, he told himself, there have been coincidences before.

107

Dark rocks lay on the surface while a flat shimmering sea was being stitched to the sky by diving gannets. Up looped the birds, and down they plummeted, emerging back out of their own splash (occasionally shaking small fish into their gullets) to flutter aloft once more. The sun, slung too low for summer, nonetheless burned with unseasonal heat.

Mama had plenty of time to notice these things, driving at her usual claptrap speed, erratically independent of the guidelines painted on the road and showing plenty of interest in looking around as she went. Vengeance Harbour spread beneath her its most benign aspect. She swung into the hairpins climbing to the old convict prison, northerly slabs of sunshine passing into the car and sweeping away to one side caused her eyes to squinch and flashed from her rings as she juggled with the steering-wheel. The little car's faithful nose then pointed to a fresh stage-set dragged in from the wings presenting shaded cliffwalls tufted with ferns, water dripping from a faultline in brown rock, or the prison on a solid plinth of rock blocked in against an impossibly solid blue sky, or the scintillant Pacific anchored by a couple of fishing boats out near its sharp-edged horizon. Observed from above, the gannets were seen to be looping through nothing, but they collected their reward just the same. Soon the vexatious sun nested among Mama's scarves and the prison veered into view as a buttress of corners topped by a catwalk. The car swerved at the last moment to avoid a wall coming for her at irresponsible speed and then braked suddenly, right at the prison entrance, the Car Park sign having sidestepped her too neatly to be noticed.

Only now did Mama see the huddle of hutches propped against the foot of the bastion, scores upon scores of lean-to shacks constructed by women protesters, so many more than the other time she graced the district with a visit. And once her operatic motor had been switched off (a process involving not just the ignition key, but quickly releasing the clutch to jam the temperamental machine into submission) she heard a hubbub of voices. The wives of the unemployed were a garrulous lot and bred children with preternaturally robust lungs. A horizontal veil of smoke, too heavy with the fragrance of recently cooked rabbit lunches to rise much above head height, screened their family intimacies from the strutting guards on the catwalk.

Mama felt hungry. She had been driving since dawn. But her mission would not wait. She teased her scarves more winningly before setting sensible feet on the gravel path bordered by whitewashed stones. A woman poked her head out of a nearby shack made of crates stencilled

THIS SIDE UP

calling to ask if she had come for the meeting. And there did appear to be some evidence of a crowd jostling at the far end of the settlement.

— Of course, Mama replied promptly. I am a person who never misses a meeting.

— You'll be late soon, the woman supposed.

— I suppose. Soon, Mama conceded.

— Mu-uum, wailed a child. And tugged its slave back inside.

— I don't care, Mama explained magnanimously a few minutes later to a pleasingly ugly youth in uniform. Who he may be, or whether he still hasn't finished his lunch, I may say I have not yet *begun* mine, I still require an interview.

— Your son, I regret to say, the commandant told her between chewing a pad of cheese sandwich and swilling it down with tepid tea. Has been arrested. No madam, he recovered his habitual polished manner. I fear I cannot let you see him because that is no longer in my power. He is not here. We haven't any lock-up facilities.

— What kind of prison is this? Mama baulked at so preposterous an oversight. I shall lodge a complaint.

— Well that is your right, of course, the commandant conceded, his polish wearing thin already. You'll find him at Port George police station.

— May I say, Mr Commandant, I am shocked. Marshal Powell shall hear from me, a sole parent and no long-distance driver.

— Owen Powell, Jack Cohen replied baring his incisors for an attack on those tasteless provisions. Is no more.

A resounding *Hurrah* drifted in from beyond the walls like the swift passing of an immense flock of birds.

Mama was, as she put it later to Tim on the eve of his departure for Bali, not at all impressed with the service. Even when she was back outside in the sunshine and making progress, fluttering towards the excitement of joining a crowd with a cause, she replayed her little scene and put names to the objections she would raise against the new man.

Protesting women had gathered by the east wall overlooking the warm ocean.

— The scabs are on strike! Our first breakthrough in years, said a handsome strapping virago.

The crowd swayed and gossiped. Unleashed brats shot off among legs. Smoke drifted, as a magic carpet, out to sea.

— But already the army has been called in to force them back to work. How long do you think they're going to hold out?

— Why don't we go and show them some solidarity? a raucous mother of at least the four hanging to her skirt yelled from the ranks. What do you say, Ruth? Let's go, ay?

Mama, by rights, ought to be on her way to visit her imprisoned son. But this was exciting. Here she felt in her element. Bother silly Yanagita. Trust him to get into trouble. She was tired to death of trying to teach the boy manners. He had waited till now; he could cool his heels an hour or two longer and no harm done. Excitement was working its effect on her. She grew no taller, but her loose bulk drew in on itself, compacted more firmly than had been the case at any time since she reported to the Cuban authorities that she found their camp of deviates too distressingly beautiful to be converted to heterosexuality, despite her credentials in the forty languages of fulfilled desire staining her cheeks with such dreadful glamour. Her legs grew young. The firming flesh above her elbows gave signals of impending action. Though itching to speak, she was a person decent enough to bide her time.

— There are many of you, Ruth said with an authority which marked her as one who was already unshakably popular. Claiming that we should leave them alone because they are the enemies we came to protest against and nothing can change this fact. Well, my husband lost his job just like yours. And there is no work for us ourselves. Women are always the first victims. How well we know. We share the same feelings. But I want to suggest something. Here (she brandished a sheaf of cards cut from cereal packets) are the full ten parts of How to Make Friends with Your Enemies. We could use these examples to put the men to their own test, see if they can make friends with us, because right now we are still their enemies. They offer half the story, the male half. I say it is up to us to provide the women's half. Perhaps now is the time for this and we should begin while they are bailed up at the site, them and the army boys. What do you say? And we can do a hell of a lot worse than take a leaf out of their book. (She shuffled the cards, picking a few samples.) I'm sure we wouldn't take long to give some personal equivalents of these from our viewpoint. Here's the surrender of Breda, quote, a simple anecdote; when Justin, governor of this Dutch city finally gave up the keys, the victorious Spanish general Spinola wept on his behalf and embraced him, because the defence of the city had been so heroic. (Ruth picked another.) Here's the tramp philosopher Diogenes ordering Alexander the Great to get out of his patch of sunlight and Alexander saying to some followers, If I were not Alexander I would choose to be Diogenes. Here's two hill-tribes who learned to laugh at their gods and put an end to a vendetta lasting fourteen generations. (She flipped through some more, and began reading from a card.) When the Mughal Emperor Akbar had beaten the Rajput princes, he appointed them to command his army. Though he was a Muslim and they were Hindus he showed them equal favour. He even married a Rajput princess. His court, possibly the most splendid the world has ever seen, was also the least oppressive; if Akbar's ideals of tolerance and incorruptibility had been followed since his death in 1605, in India alone many millions of lives might have been spared and much needless suffering.

She looked up at her listeners and found them listening; much as they had lived through and little as they had to show for it.

— There's a story about some people who painted themselves black and some people who painted themselves white and discovered how simple it was to believe in a lie. There's a goldsmith who kept a lump of gold for the whole of his working life but never found inspiration worthy of it. After many years he mustered courage to give the gold away. And the day he did, he received in return the knowledge of what he might have created if only he had learned sooner.

But the tenth card she did not read out, uncertain of whether it would be thought relevant and so moved was she by private meanings.

In building a maze there are three rules. First, the tip, but only the tip of the objective at the heart of the maze must always be visible. Second, at all times, if the person in the maze heads resolutely towards the objective, the passage must lead him away. Third, at all times, if the person in the maze turns his back on the objective and walks away from it, the passage must lead him towards it.
— Daedalus

There was no need for further persuasion anyway. These women, who had had the courage of their anger, soon found in themselves the courage to surmount it. Mama knew their mood, mingling among them, and that all they needed was one other person to speak up.

— I have a car, she announced bright as an angel and quite as strange. Small though it is, I can begin ferrying you over to the site.

So she went on to explain that with five passengers in the three available seats, plus two younger ones on the back bumper and one on the front (not to obscure the driver's view), she could take eight at a time of those who wished to travel in style.

— Now ladies, said she who had never really spoken to women before. I shall have you there in a trice.

Not till the ninth journey was her car, creeping along close to the road and proceeding right down the middle in the interest of avoiding accidents, stopped by police. But only then because the patrol van pulled across her path and she ran into it while a delicious young lass, windblown as a figurehead, kicked up her legs to avoid having them crushed, and rolled laughing on the bonnet, finally blocking Mama's view of furious officials struggling to get out of their vehicle fast enough to bundle her in behind them and drive her in a delirium of hunger to the Port George police station. What did she care? Her mind was filled with the afternoon's glorious events, the astonishment of those army boys (and what didn't she know about soldiers?) at being defied by women, and the even greater astonishment of the

Friends of Privilege. But beyond everything was the beautiful history Ruth and her friends began to tell there as soon as the first carload arrived, singing, acting, talking, dancing, the world from the other side of heroics, a women's tale, rich in detail. As she took a breather between each journey, Mama drank the truth in bitter honey. This long-rehearsed performance promised to continue all night, and already she knew they would end by incorporating her own arrest as it occurred, plus the strange contingency that although she was with them, the ones who knew her and cheered her as a heroine were guest workers on the other side of the security fence, she being the mother of Yanagita Izumi, the man whose stand for his dead friend Dr Luke and whose arrest after passing secret information had triggered the strike.

Despite all this, the highlight from Mama's point of view and the satisfaction which printed her features with a youthfulness enough to set officialdom's teeth on edge, was something wholly unexpected. As a woman who had lived her entire life among men and, from time to time, through men, Mama discovered women. Nothing she knew prepared her for the warmth, the sheer frankness of the experience. Neither she nor they tried using one another; these new friendships were free from innuendo, rich with the unspoken insights women have in common.

When the police sergeant treated her quite roughly considering she was at least sixty-five or ninety-five, was it because he sensed her change of allegiance? Men had always been polite, habitually, recognizing themselves as the centre of her world. Now at a single stroke this was gone. Just as Mama had once been converted overnight, literally, to her passion for the deformed, now she was converted again. She simply could not stand the male sex at any price and marvelled that she had survived so many years of them. She would not feel comfortable entertaining even her special friend Noel. The very thought of those continental birthmarks (Africa smothering his chest and Asia right across his back) no longer sufficed to license the real tenderness he showed her. Who cares anyhow? she told herself. Life never has been fair. Fairness is no part of it, as I very well know. This big slug of a cop could shove her about any time he liked, it simply confirmed her nostalgia for those history-singing ladies she had last glimpsed from the police wagon's rear window. And just as well such was the way she did feel because his impatience grew worse on the journey into town, while he grumbled to his offsider about some cranedriver, a black doctor, if you please, a whole bloody calamity of foreigners, a Yank invasion and a long-lost quiet life with nothing more than a couple of drunken uncles to be taken in of a night, plus the occasional hashish bust when a strange yacht berthed. His offsider concentrated on driving, never once presuming to respond, let alone commiserate. He knew something, that young constable.

Mama had no fear of the sergeant who took her by one jewelled wrist and pulled her into the police station, because she could laugh at him and the possibility that he may once have hoped to be loved. Even when he stood her in front of a machine and explained its use as an Eye-dentifier, the latest improvement on fingerprints, even when he instructed her to gaze into the lens and line up the circles like a gunsight while the microprocessor scanned the eye, even while he informed her that the system would now compare its findings with a data-bank, she felt she could scoff at his hopelessness and what he was missing.

— We shall soon see about you my girl, he declared, free to call her my girl from his lofty moral superiority as an enforcer of the law. He recognized in her the retired brothelkeeper Dorina had seen, plus an active troublemaker as well. If you have a previous record, we shall know the whole story inside half a minute.

The sergeant had already forgotten about reading Josiah Henson's story on an Oat Crispies packet and the lesson of it.

— This little box is foolproof, the eye-print can never be faked like fingerprints can, he explained, having come a long way since the time, nearly nine years previously, when a wild young fellow who wouldn't cooperate smeared ink all over his good uniform and left a visiting card in the form of two dinted filing cabinets plus that dead half-lip which only showed when the sergeant smiled, which he was not attempting right now, being indeed far from it, gaping and even unaware that a faint gargle of amazement escaped his throat.

— Impossible! he muttered, baffled at reading the computer screen. That is impossible!

President Buchanan woke with the alarm of a shipwrecked sailor who finds it is true he has been shipwrecked and must still cling to a raft superfluous on the bare ocean. By now he knew what this signified. I have lost more weight, he admitted. And I have slept through the best hours.

Sunshine piled thick in his room as an unwanted residue of the climate he himself was accountable for. The twinges in his belly lasted to qualify as real pains, long probing iron bars lodged elusively deep. His state of mind offered no refuge either, nor even diversion except as an even more uncomfortable alternative: he had seen a film in his sleep, the sort of thing insomnia once guarded him from. The film comprised fragments which were being pieced together and spliced by the skilful Owen Powell of recent memory. What began to emerge on these fragments nobody appeared able to explain, least of all the Eye-dentifier system he himself had inaugurated at Owen's invitation by glaring in at some gunsights and lining them up as, he urged the TV camera, all responsible citizens were required to do in the interests of state security, becoming eye-print number one in a national databank. This infallible computer had, at the beginning of the fragmented documentary, found some female's eye identical to his own. An officer declared the coincidence impossible and the databank agreed. . . The film clip jumped to a group of policemen bent over the equipment, tapping messages to make it behave and shaking their caps at its stubbornness. Meanwhile, something else was happening outside. Through the window, the focus sharpened on two civilians, a Japanese man and this gaudy harridan whose celebrated eye had guaranteed she would be neglected for long enough to escape, seen clambering into the gondola of a hot-air balloon; casting off moorings and throwing out buckets of ballast in the form of uneaten watchhouse meals (also, less desirably, eaten watchhouse meals); floating up past the window, trailing a wisp of smoke from the brazier they carried aboard, which they fed with straw from palliasses out of the cell. The balloon itself, a gimcrack patchwork of paper pasted together, as would subsequently become clear, from a print-out of the entire public records kept by the town's constabulary, rose. . . The scene cut to another humiliating fragment, this time showing troops supposed to be quelling a riot by Friends of Privilege at the IFID site, sitting round, commanderless, enjoying the company of hundreds of women, plus luxuriating in taking potshots at a balloon drifting high above them through the dusky air of approaching night. . . Then in the film he'd seen in his sleep some helicopters dispatched from an American camp in town roared over, only to be outflown by that bauble of paper which floated up with dizzy lightness while its occupants continued feeding the fire, using police-issue straw, till the brightness of it glowed on the underside of the sphere, so that it drifted up like the reflection of a setting sun.

Poor dreamer, he awoke to the fact that he had been made a laughing-stock again, his Presbyterian mother's disillusioned complaints in his ear: this is nothing short of lunacy, you shouldn't allow it! and his father noting down something remiss in a black book. But when Bernard Buchanan came to look closer, also to find he could sit up unaided, there, at the foot of the bed he now no longer so completely filled, stood Roscoe Plenty.

Roscoe Plenty had given away greeting people with quickfire interrogations in order to catch a glimpse of himself in their surprise reactions, he had forgotten he ever slapped a young niece just to watch the representation of his hand emerge on her bare thigh. The most he could manage was to balance upright, rigidly tottering and watchful, as misused in powerlessness as he had been in power, his crazed eyes of a cornered rabbit telling the president of a final catastrophe which the film did not show, that the armed forces had abandoned all respect for constitutional authority and wallowed towards anarchy, that senior officers seldom saw their men because they spent weeks on end saturated in boyish excitement plotting his overthrow, studying precedents in Argentina and Fiji, waiting only for the propitious time, the ungoverned swing in popular feeling, the momentary loss of grip.

Then the reason for these unsettling sensations came clear with wakefulness. The great man saw that his friend's expression was actually one of sympathy and he knew just what it meant. The mice gnawed ferociously at their dwindling meal.

— Today, he agreed. Is the day Dorina brings her case against me.

108

Why should the family law court hear this tawdry charade behind closed doors? President Buchanan had said when it became obvious the case could not be stopped. I know all about customary practice, but I believe I owe it to you, the people of Australia, for my wife to say her say in public. She and I are public citizens, no longer enjoying the rights of privacy you take for granted, he assured those millions who sat watching in darkened rooms with the curtains pinned closed against snooping neighbours. There is nothing to hide, no illicit love affairs, though many a fine female has given me to understand my fatness is not displeasing to her. He chuckled like an uncle. No, if Mrs Buchanan has so serious a grievance it justifies such sensational action, then let's hear it. With luck we may find out who is behind this. Because there can be no question the divorce case is calculated to strike a blow against me at a time when there is unrest among those who have prospered under my government, even to publishing Open Letters like a mob of cowards too chicken-livered to come to me personally when they know my door has always stood open for them any time they cared to call. Well, I can't think of any such grievance, unless devotion is a fault these days. (He raised his eyes quizzically.) It may very well be, for all I know about fashion. One thing I am confident of, and this I will say to you, my wife does not tell lies. Whatever her reason, or whoever may have put her up to bringing the action against me, she will be truthful in court. And that is a two-edged sword. Let me warn you, if there are any of you people out there who expect your names to be kept hidden, you have left it too late. When she is asked, she'll name you just like she's naming me. A good swift punch to the jaw, that's my dear wife's style and I respect her for it. You may be wondering by now why I am using my Address to the Nation to air these domestic matters. Well, it is to invite you as the public and the media to feel free, come and listen, come and report the case with perfect openness, I have nothing to hide and I want that known. Such is my confidence you will find the divorce suit a catalogue of petty complaints of a kind any husband or any wife could reel off, one against the other.

Now the day had come and he had Squarcia and Roscoe Plenty with him in the viewing room at the mansion, because naturally there was no possibility of protocol being so violated as to expect a president to appear before the court in person. He would be content, he said, to watch with the rest of the population, savouring the novelty of finding his ultimate security prove insecure after all. Squarcia sat a little behind him, with legs seigneurially crossed and head cupped in nonchalant hand. Roscoe Plenty wavered at attention, his raven eyes glazed television blue. Sir George Gipps did not put in an appearance and had not been seen for weeks now, though Cornelius Curtis let slip that he was on the right track. Dorina took the stand looking shockingly pale and emotional. She was going to make a goat of herself, Buchanan sighed, and for what purpose?

— My client, said her counsel. Is filing a case for annulment on the grounds of mental cruelty.

— Yes, Dorina admitted when asked if she would like to speak to the court. Please. She pulled herself together. In a composed distraught voice she explained her accusation. I claim mental cruelty in extraordinary cirumstances. When I married, I married a real estate agent, a comfortable situation and a private one. I did not marry into public life and there was no mention ever made of any intention to make it public. Public life has been thrust upon me, much against my will and without consultation. The nervous strain has been relentless, being surrounded by armed men, right from the beginning when my husband was made to sign some papers. And I had to pretend not to know that. There has been too much to list here for the court, but I do wish to mention my personal interests; this I can do without in any way betraying anyone's confidence.

Bernard relaxed. He squirmed round to check whether his bearers were in the anteroom, watching on their own set, and seemed satisfied that they were. This was going to be harmless and could, perhaps, even provide some advantage, a story about himself complete with human touches. He too, all said and done, had had to give up the privileges of privacy. Why should they not pity him when the time came?

— I would cite the matter of my garden, she explained. I am a keen gardener. While my husband was still in business I created a beautiful garden in the grounds of our house, created it out of wilderness, that's how the property was when we moved there. I should mention that some photographs will be presented in evidence by my counsel. House and garden were sold without the least warning or consideration for my feelings, let alone for the countless hours of manual labour I had put in. I found myself condemned to a concrete bunker of a place on the shores of Sydney Harbour. Enviable though the view is, this house with its courtyard and terraces completely fills the block. There is no place for a new garden with which I might console myself in the traditional manner of wives treated like articles of baggage. But this has not been the worst burden I have had to bear, and bear without the right to choose my lot.

Dorina stopped to look at the faces in court, bland faces with carnivore eyes, all concentrating on her; all willing her to go on, to break free of the polite trivia of digging her garden, to rise above complaining about her harbour view.

— We have one child, a grown man now, and we are proud of him, she began in a new voice of such determination the spectators (they could hardly be called less) leaned forward in their seats not to miss a syllable.

They were her judges also.

— In fact, I ought to have had two. I should explain: at the very time my husband returned home from a trip and informed me of my fate, that I was to become a politician's neglected wife, our doctor confirmed my second pregnancy. How. . . How can I tell this court, she murmured hoarsely and fought to control her voice. In that instant, they knew what she was about to confess. I could not. . . could not face it, at my age, another baby, another child to rear, so much responsibility and without a husband's support. She stopped to compose herself. Light flickered in her eyes, so she lifted her hand protectively to her brow and left it there. You might object, she rallied. That I was presuming, only presuming, Mr Buchanan's new career would take him away from home, away from me, away from sharing the joy as well as the care of a new baby, from supporting me during a pregnancy I had been warned not to incur and the likely chance of my health being seriously damaged; even, I don't believe I'm exaggerating, the possibility of my life being in danger. There is medical evidence to confirm this, Your Honour. But I should add, because it is so often not understood; joy needs to be shared. Sharing is an essential part. The lone mother has nobody with an equal stake in her joy, nobody to use as a sounding-board, an echo. . . Forgive me for expressing myself this way, I am limited by being a musician. Not just as an echo, perhaps also as a competitor. Well, the point is, I was not presuming. My husband had arrived home ill from an accident in the Central Australian desert. He was suffering exposure, but within days he had driven himself to his feet and was sufficiently fired with ambition not to hear me when I began telling him of my pregnancy. I knew then, and I had it thoroughly confirmed later, that I had lost him, he was already an article of public property though he hadn't been elected yet.

Buchanan stared at the screen. Poor woman, he thought as if he had never met her and her case bore no relation to his life. Poor woman; what she has hidden beneath that composed manner.

— I am, Your Honour, I believe I may say, a moral woman.

By this I mean that issues of moral judgment are important to me in my everyday life. I think a great deal. Well I thought a great deal then, I can assure the court. My aloneness became an agony. I felt the cold house was my prison. And I had grave doubts about how we were bringing up the child we already had, doubts I could not persuade my husband to discuss, though I raised the matter many times.

— She did, Buchanan acknowledged. She did, many times.

— Even, Dorina's voice dropped. To humbling myself to make him listen.

This, this is what the public wanted. Oh yes, political issues aside, here came the true drama, calling up the juices of their festering appetite.

— When I decided to seek an abortion, she resumed after a break, I bore the whole responsibility. I have come to think of it since as my crime.

The bland faces grew blander with sucking a familiar candy.

— I wish the court to know that my conscience has been tormented by what I did. At times I have felt this so intensely I wondered whether I might not be going mad.

Yes, yes, cried the mute faces and avid eyes, mad, give us more of the madness, the guilt, the bloody foetus, give us the crime again. Dorina saw them with inordinate clarity, as if some photographer had placed each one in an ideal light, displaying his or her particularity of wrinkles; and laying bare their generality of lapsed character. Her glance travelled round the room until once more she faced Judge Mack seated in his vanity of a low chair identical to the one she herself had been sitting on before being driven to her feet by agitation, his studied avoidance of any regalia, the plain lounge suit, tired hair combed flat across bald pate, eyelids sagging away from his eyes, hands pink from being chafed together; this judge whom she had once entertained to keep him from knowing of Buchanan's single drunken lapse while Squarcia came to the rescue, this scapegoat judge demoted from the High Court. He tried so hard to be ordinary, his success was absolute. Dorina felt saddened by the dependency of people, these elderly passive children, and glimpsed again through angled slats of a folding screen how the timber floor gleamed gold in brutal sunshine where a foot appeared; tasted again the sticky sweetness of mangosteen and heard her heart thump to get out of the trap it was in. On the assassin's sinewy ankle a small blot of blood sparkled brilliantly. Now *they* were not children, those people, not childlike in the least, small and delicate as their bones might be. They had not been willing to surrender their pride utterly, they fought. When the time came for saying this far and no further, they fought. And I have always called it murder (she considered her ignorance) though in fact it was liberty. Of course they killed children like me, the next generation of oppressors, for the love of their own children. Am I, she marvelled, the only revolutionary in this country since Peter died? Conservative me? Such a notable dry stick? Fastidious and, she granted herself, sensitive? The humour of it caused her to smile a very slight smile, sure to be misinterpreted by the watchers. They fixed her with unflinching ferocity. She held the rail in fingers rich from their store of Debussy. Rise up, she wanted to say, throw off our convict past, we have only to shout *No!* here and the whole nation will follow; but she knew in the marrow of her reticence she could not do this, any more than they could respond if she did. She had deluded herself, imagining she might beat Buchanan by creating a domestic scandal, beat him and save him, keeping to herself the one treasure of his unforgivable guilt. No, as Dorina saw those innocent weathered faces, she hated him for not having the breeding, as she put it, to decline exploiting the idiots. She hated them too for their intellectual spinelessness. She didn't doubt their courage, once roused, but knew the shackling unlikelihood of rousing them. If they were Tuavalevans, with an alive gift of honour, the streets would by now be running blood and the international pawnbrokers looking elsewhere for dupes, surely. Well, what these dear people of hers dared not do, she dared. They may cosset their lazy reluctance to think, but not Dorina Buchanan who was once Dorina Lambert and determined to be known as brilliant even if never liked. For the first time she faced the television cameras; she would address her worst to them rather than the poor old judge. She paused to control her agitation. Just when they thought she had achieved a workable climax and won her suit outright, she opened another matter. And plainly this involved something altogether different. Buchanan, who knew her so well, who had learnt her style even by neglecting her, watched with the coldness of a man who sights his enemy for the first time.

— I claim mental cruelty, she began again slowly, remembering that Peter Taverner had died on his way back from a journey made specially to ask her one question: to obtain one name from her.

— Yes? the judge coaxed her.

— Because not only have I had to suffer moral torture from my own actions, but I have had forced upon me the additional load of my husband's guilt over the method he used to gain a foothold on power in the first place.

— Stop this, the president roared and the anteroom burst into action.

— Have you a specific item in mind you could help us with?

— Yes. Many years ago an immigrant, Zoltán Kékszakállú, later known as William Penhallurick, stood trial for murder. My husband, then unknown to the public, was foreman of that jury.

A commotion broke out at the back of the courtroom. Police were seen struggling against police. A bewilderment of duties developed. Dorina glanced up and knew that she must not stop until the expected bullet stopped her. Training gave her wonderful presence. She lifted her chin and straightened her back. Now she knew she would, after all, save her Buchanan.

— He announced their verdict of not guilty, for which he had argued strenuously, though all circumstantial evidence pointed to guilt.

— Order in court. We cannot retry a case, Mrs Buchanan. Order!

A redoubled rumpus was heard from the doorway.

— I make no comment on the verdict. Only on the domestic consequences, the fact that my husband's spectacular rise to power followed it and that he himself was tortured with doubts.

A detachment of Watchdogs trooped clattering into the courtroom, weapons at the ready. The judge called for them to be ejected. Dorina cut him short. She had no time for niceties.

— My husband is a man of principle, she went on calmly. He suffered bad dreams. I suffered his dreams too. His presidency was financed by a foreign consortium known as IFID. Zoltán Kékszakállú was the chief operative of IFID in Australia. IFID right now, though my husband may not have realized it, has well-advanced plans to remove him from office to clear the way for buying up the country completely. If I could protect him I would. But no one can protect anybody any longer. It goes beyond that. We have been too deeply sold out. Doubtless these schoolboys with their murderous toys, she addressed the Watchdogs directly and with such courage that Bernard, furious and capricious, felt a stab of love for her. Doubtless they are prepared to shoot me. And they, Dorina declared scornfully. Are fellow Australians! Such is the shameful state we have sunk to.

Such is the burden of shared guilt I have to bear. Let them be the symbol of my case. But there is more. There is the hatred and dull resentment of ordinary people in the street who have been pushed down to their lowest limit of tolerance by curfews and shortages, inquisitorial police and amateur informers.

The profound terror and thrill in court spread a contagion of silence through the country. She had named the unnameable. People held their breath for her as never before for anyone else.

— From our proud hopes, she explained in words each bright with the perfect isolation of its meaning. We have come to this in so short a time. We are no longer free.

The nation dared not let out its breath.

— I cannot be seen in the street without going in fear of my life. (She realized the Wild Dog had planned it all so she should not betray herself in the shock of watching while he was gunned down, he knew she would do this to avenge his murder.) And for what end? The greed of a few individuals of mediocre intelligence, I can assure you. The threat we see nakedly displayed here in the precincts of a court of law is no more frightening than the covert anger of the housewives and the homeless I meet any day I set foot outside the prison of my house. That is why I shut myself in. They may shoot me now and relieve me of further shame.

No shot came.

— Last night, she resumed in a stony voice. We all heard my husband, in his Address to the Nation, accuse me of timing this blow to damage him. My intention, indeed, goes further than that. He keeps on without ever, apparently, seeing who it is that stands behind him. He has been used. And those who have used him to take over our country for their own interests will not let go now. They can't, can they? There is too much at stake.

— Are we wandering from the issue before the court? Judge Mack interposed gently, his face worn away to a limestone cliff.

— Yes, Your Honour, and on purpose. I am here to ask for my freedom back. Freedom within my own limitations. I am here to ask the same for everybody else. We want our freedom back.

So that was that. Even with their orders, the Watchdogs could hear it was too late, too late even for phonecalls to the television crews to stop the cameras or for the transmitters to jam transmission. And officers who might have acted had also, perhaps, consciences of their own not fully dead. The bland faces worried

their way free of blandness. But, Dorina saw instantly, she had
gone too far, for the ferocious eyes lost track of ferocity. No, she
needed them angry, not ashamed. So, although she had sat on
that modest chair, she leapt up again, fairly sizzling with energy.
Her voice rang through the courtroom.

— He did only what was expected of him, what *you* expected
of him, she accused them all and those watching at home too.
You did not just *allow* him to do this to us, these curfews and
secret bases, these lies, this hunger and despair: you made him
do it. That, she accused them to stir their anger. That was what I
wanted to say.

Dorina stood a moment longer in the blind certainty of her
triumph.

She had lost them altogether. And at home, others were
muttering about how she must have gone round the twist, poor
thing. But her counsel still kept a last card to play, though he
had not consulted his client about it, she being a shade too
unorthodox to be reasoned with:

— There is more evidence, Your Honour, which I ask your
indulgence to exhibit before the court.

— It is never a question of my indulgence, Mr Foote, Judge
Mack warned gravely. I am simply here to see justice done. The
law, he explained obscurely. Cannot itself be moved. If you have
evidence, it is not just your right to bring it before the court's
attention, but your duty.

The barrister signalled a woman to step forward. She brought
with her a large cardboard parcel, flat and oblong and almost
too big to manage. If Justice Mack trembled, fearing the kind of
bomb divorce courts had become famous for, he did not show it.
Dorina, still flashing hope, watched with the irritable surprise of
a virtuoso seeing some clown steal her audience. Two policemen
helped open the parcel, while baffled Watchdogs grumbled
around their indecision. It contained a painting. The woman
who held it before the court and cameras was that little reporter
person Mrs Izumi had brought in with the solicitor to leak the
news of Dorina's divorce proceedings. What was the girl up to,
displaying her loathsome object before the world, this disgrace
of Buchanan portrayed lying on his back naked as a newt, gross
tummy doming almost to the upper edge of the frame, and
broken glass all around him, not to mention the fatuous scowl
he wore?

The public rasped a collective gesture of alarm which it was
not their place to do.

Judge Mack, reviewing an occasion when he had escorted Dorina Lambert to some college dance, sated with the bitterness of demotion from the highest judicial post in the land, perused this exhibit while the eloquent Foote pointed to the humiliation of so refined a lady on discovering her husband had posed nude for a female artist.

The judge's face was a cliff, seamed with knowledge of its own grandeur, gritty and unapproachable, its impassiveness windworn by a thousand pleas for clemency. Such a face vouched for the solidity of the mountain behind it. And now, though the limestone nose and old chipped mouth remained immobile as ever, his eyes creaked and considered. The eyes (and the courtroom was crammed with a dense frog-spawn of softer more gelatinous eyes) sidled about the picture, pupils fading with effort. The rubble of hands which had collected in his lap stirred to tiny knockings. But no other warning showed. How could anybody have foreseen the landslide about to begin? In the thick of his terrific silence, fractures appeared: a tremor along one grey cheek, a cluster of cracks fanning out from the corner of an eyelid, nostrils gaping a pair of caves and the chin crumbling crystals. Then the shocking distress of collapse, clunks and clutters of laughter. Yes, there among the guns and camera lenses this cold stone face grew pink and blurred, all rage and all veneration for the law sacrificed in laughter. The faded eyes floated, drifted, sank. A groundswell rumbled through the court. The spectators' jollity bounded about, crazy with release. Lolloping squatting froggy laughter overtook police and Watchdogs too. Gun barrels wagged helplessly. Only the television cameras remained steady, panning the entire show as the system collapsed, sparing nothing.

For the second such panic in ten years, there were those who quietly packed their treasures, sometimes including their families, and drove to an international airport where they left luxury cars to gather parking fines and fled the country in a roar of burning gasoline while trusted secretaries kept vigil all night to sacrifice a decade of intensive enquiry in shredders before pocketing their severance pay and clicking the deadlocks shut on a life of patted bottoms and calculated décolletage.

Buchanan himself looked peaked and almost handsome in his large-featured way. Luigi Squarcia offered, with exquisite deference, to bring him some tea. To which he agreed, there being nothing more important to do. He did not bother switching the set off: he had switched his mind off instead. He ignored an announcer babbling the News, presenting world upheavals, in the fashion of these days, as entertainment. So he missed hearing that leftwing insurgents had recaptured the capital of Tuavaleva from the scattered forces of the late General Merasaloa and he missed seeing a film-clip of the new provisional leader, Ahmad Zain Osman, hair wild and blood clotted on his shirtsleeve, speaking, from the smoking ruins of the old principal palace, of love.

Squarcia had not yet come back when a visitor, known by sight to President Buchanan from his prominence on many ceremonial occasions, entered, even the bearers deferring to the uniform of the future. He did not salute, but he spoke pleasantly and without hectoring.

— Admiral Todd, sir, here to inform you that, with the assent of parliament, I am to relieve you of all responsibilities, pending a general election. The mansion, he explained regretfully. Is in my hands. By now my statement of interim power should be broadcast throughout the whole country.

And exactly on cue, there he was, the television showing a perfect replica of the man, punctilious and reserved, only his eyes firing with tiny eruptions of violence.

Bernard Buchanan who could not move did not try.

Roscoe Plenty began moaning and sucking at one shoulder, fearing a renewed bout of punishments.

109

FOLLOWING TELEX (CODED TOP SECURITY) RECEIVED FROM IFID HQ NEW YORK: BEGINS: DESPITE TUAVALEVA UPSET, EXECUTE PLAN AS ARRANGED. YOUR ACKNOWLEDGED STAKE IN TUAVALEVA WILL BE HONORED WHEN WE RECOVER THE ISLAND AFTER THEIR PRESENT TROUBLE SIMMERS DOWN. MEANWHILE AUSTRALIA FIRST. EVENTS DEVELOPING SMOOTHLY. SO FAR SATISFACTORY. OUR INTERESTS MUST BE SECURED BEFORE A NEW PARLIAMENT BEGINS SITTING. TODD CANNOT KNOW THE SCORE YET. KEEP BUCHANAN OUT OF SIGHT. TOMORROW WE BID FOR YOUR PENHALLURICK ENTERPRISES (GENERAL). THIS ONE YOU ACCEPT. EXCHANGE RATE GOOD. TIMING PERFECT.

110

Lavinia had come home, wet from the warm drizzle of a Sydney spring day, to find one of her paintings missing. Filled with rage and despair, she considered a shadowy oblong left on the wall where the Buchanan portrait hung for almost nine years, not even moved by Owen Powell's investigators, not even confiscated by the president himself. Now, just a blank darkness of its having been there. And then Lavinia was afraid.

She was not to know the court case had reached a point when Dorina looked at Judge Mack with that same incredulous distaste she had once, at Roscoe Plenty's dinner party, felt for Alice Penhallurick and her clumsy reduction of art to a category of buying and selling. Nor that waiting in the wings, as it were, stood her own sister Stephanie, ripe with vendettas for two murders, bringing a large flat parcel wrapped in cardboard.

A door banged downstairs. Lavinia heard footsteps mounting. The whole staircase creaked. Heavy people. And caught a couple of syllables flying loose when a man called something urgent. Then a voice she knew replied. Not Marcia Connor this time: the chill she felt clutch her entrails involved a deeper enmity than that. It was Greta, dear Greta whom, years ago, she had hoped to appease by sharing her new acquaintance with celebrities, Greta using the very voice she once and so habitually relished, that aggrieved exasperated tone which said clearer than words: I have had enough of you and now I am coming to get you.

The horror and the courage of her time in jail took command of Lavinia's body and huddled it into the bathroom, locking the door, opened the narrow window for it and forced it out, squeezing and scraping her hips, to dangle over the roof of Marcia's out-house kitchen, picked her fingers off the sill and let her drop, tumbled her jeans thundering down the iron slope, whipped her shoulders out from under her, rucking her jumper as she rolled skidding on a rust-rash and clutched for the gutter, wrenched the downpipe off its wall for her, and swung the little brick terrace up to meet her twisted ankles just as she needed it and not too painfully, though she slithered staggering in the wet.

Marcia, of course, was at the other end of the house, engrossed by the action around the front door (a confused flashing of blue lights as police cars banked up) and the emergence of a rival informer.

As her prison courage let her out the back gate, it also put into Lavinia's keeping a shabby umbrella found propped against a stack of flowerpots. She closed the gate with torn hands and walked briskly away along the back lane between garbage bins; skirting puddles; her identity concealed from above by the green light of the opened umbrella. When she reached the corner, she did not look back.

Lavinia turned up the hill, pushing on, stung by drizzle all the way to Oxford Street, and hailed a bus. She stepped in, collapsing the umbrella. What would she have said if she'd known that as the folding doors hissed shut, paper wrappings were being shuffled off her purloined portrait and the nation outside the bus clutched its belly with the indigestion of something painfully urging to get out?

— Wet ay? remarked the little woman she sat beside. And dislodged her smoker's cough. Still and all, you can't complain. At least we've seen the back of winter.

They looked down at their damp clothes and puddled footmarks, perhaps shyly.

— There was a time, the little woman mused. When I could go home of a cold night and shut my door, switch on the electric and simply bask. Long long ago. What a flock of dills we are, she rattled ruefully. Come to think of it.

And the bus was suddenly full of passengers who looked away from one another, out at the rain, out at the memories of places once the scene of happy times.

Down in the city, the grey streets they should have driven through were no longer grey. Decorous passers-by, not content with decorum, threw aside their worry. Masks gone: stamped to shards under stampeding feet. Youths blocked the bus's passage while some shocking effortful thing they did distorted their faces. There at the corner of Liverpool and Castlereagh Streets the bus stopped altogether, at a diagonal, motor switched off, and the driver, turning to his passengers, wore the same fierce horror of loudness as the lads thumping on the windscreen outside. He was laughing, blind butting stumbles of laughter. Now the bus doors wheezed open, people climbed in and out whether they held tickets or not, and yelled mythologies at the dullards whose minds were still back in their suburbs.

The city surged under chaos and more than just the chaos of celebration; the howls of the bereaved broke from silenced shells months after that tidal wave had struck the coast and the Buchanan Cultural Centre collapsed. Excitement pulsed through the city. Rumour, by sheer energy, became truth. People started clapping and weeping with relief. They clapped the blood back into motion. They remembered a life they had left in cold storage and the sweetness of voicing opinions, they woke up from the nightmare, conversations resumed from the semi-colon at which they had been interrupted by some informer. People with no natural ability at dancing danced. They raged with helplessness to express how great a release they felt. Car horns blared. Driven by whistles, thousands surged towards the Town Hall (as thousands of others towards other Town Halls throughout the country), they swirled centrifugally against an equal centripetal dispersal of those headed for home. Traffic locked other traffic at a standstill, overwhelmed by a fiesta of bodies. Cascades of banknotes scattered by some celebrant from the top of Mark Foy's building tumbled, flimsy portraits of a decapitated Buchanan stalling, flipping about, wavering, side-slipping and looping, his profile facing right, left, upside over, always always falling. Opportunists were found to have brought loud-hailers, which they put to use inflaming the crowd's wrath and jubilee, howling for their dead and their imprisoned, cursing years of penury, and announcing a new republic.

— I was in jail, Lavinia cried and held up hands still blood-caked from her escape through the lavatory window.

— Give her a go, they shouted. Shut up, they rejoiced. And give her a go! They lifted her bodily on to a car roof.

So just here, in this crowd, this odd nook of a great city, at this place she had known all her life but never thought of when locked away, this two-bit crossroads of obscure lives and uncommemorated passings between dingy buildings, Lavinia felt love swell her throat and sharp gratitude as tears. Elsewhere, the farrago of an unfettered city hooted and blasted on, but at this road junction the new Sydney began, framed in grubby walls, nondescript awnings, shabby advertisements. She had, as she knew by their sudden quiet, a responsibility to those around her: the responsibility of a woman still capable of tenderness.

— I have been through it all, she said, her voice errupting from the other end of the megaphone, disconcertingly grotesque. I was jailed without trial. And I am here to tell you.

What *was* she there to tell them, as if she had known they would call upon her, as if she had set out along that lane under the green umbrella rehearsing her lines, as if she had arrived here from the studio not like a fugitive but a leader?

— To tell you there is still time to do it right.

Suddenly everybody seemed to know everybody else, just waiting for the signal to switch on greetings and kisses, to hug, hugging quick and hard, or long and exploratively. They had been playing a game when they were young, the rules of which said you must pretend not to recognize a soul. But someone forgot to announce when the game finished, so the whole city, the whole country, had played on through the grey suspicions of quiet but attentive minds, through tunnels of despair and flat open vistas of treachery, till now. Now at this o'clock, common knowledge came by inspiration that the game had ended. So they kissed, they were old friends, brothers indeed and sisters, all the more passionate with relief for the long breath they had been holding.

— Lavinia! came an astounded and astoundingly heart-known cry. Fear and hope touched her.

She was in his arms. Yes, she was tumbling down from the top of that parked car with the driver still inside, down from her past of miseries, folded against the shape of a man she had once boasted would walk through fire for her.

Manciewicz could not speak. In his full vigour, he felt her yielding to him. Even as violent hands tugged at his coat collar, ripped one sleeve loose, and slit his shirt, he held her, impressing upon her the memory of how they had loved.

— Thank you, she whispered to her husband.

Then Lavinia smelt his jacket, belatedly she did, and she knew what this told her. She did not need words to explain why she suddenly buried her teeth in his neck at the tender part just below the ear, or reached blindly to claw his face while the mob ripped the Watchdog uniform off his back and booted his kidneys as he dropped like an unwanted foetus to the roadway, nor how she heard in his elderly sighs of a pneumoniac answering each kick that he had already been on the run when he first called to her.

Greta Grierson stepped into her sister's studio, caught up in the warm flow of a certain Captain Lonigan, one-time friend of Marcia Connor and hero of the arrest of a boy over the road, to find the place absolutely packed with a motley crowd flickering around her, strangely elusive, seen as an elbow here, flickering hints of nose and eye, a gesturing hand, the neck on which a head turned to see over its shoulder, a silhouette that was gone as soon as looked at, fingers tugging and tweaking at her. While Lonigan forced open the bathroom door and his swearing could be heard echoed in there, calling a couple of his men to witness what he had found and ordering them to the pursuit. While they clattered heedlessly past her as if she were burnt-out and no further use, she stared agape with outrage at a fancydress party: men in periwigs and pantaloons, women of all descriptions from fat whores to glacial Edinburgh ladies cavorted in an unseemly manner. They rushed round her, pulling her through the studio which she said she would never set foot in, turning her about to look at a bare patch on the wall where the Buchanan portrait had hung, at a stained washbasin, the grubby detritus of forgotten work; they prodded and pinched her and drove her to the window to look down as Lavinia's footprints and the green snailtrack of a fugitive umbrella, wobbling just above headheight, faded. They stuck her finger in the door crack and tried to entice Captain Lonigan to slam it, they pulled her hair and snagged her cardigan and made lewd gestures up her tartan skirt.

With absolute torment in her eyes, Greta caught the return look the captain gave her, a look coldly questioning her as to why she had become so agitated, a look which could be made to include cynical acknowledgement that she (this suspect so oddly known as Mama) had outwitted them by forewarning the Manciewicz woman.

111

A million new cereal packets went on the supermarket shelves carrying the final Part 10 of Series 50. Adorned with drawings of kangaroos, the flag, an Aborigine, and Captain Cook, the printing this time almost filled the whole back of the packet.

Of all the tales told in our set of 500, this is the last and the most remarkable. Because it is Australia's own story.

Early in the history of mankind there were people here who learned to live in this great harsh beautiful land without war or armies, without setting their gods against other people's gods, or dictating what is right and wrong beyond their own boundaries. Perhaps they had a wisdom no one else on earth could match, not even today. However narrow and restricted their life, this they did have.

36,000 years passed, and this order still reigned. The wheel was never invented here. Folk in other parts of the globe started building pyramids and temples. The recorded history of wars and bloody conquests had begun.

In Asia and Africa tribes massacred other tribes. Then in Europe too. For 2,000 years the massacres grew more terrible and more self-righteous. Wealth was invented. Empires rose and were crushed. New religions, Judaism and Buddhism among them, grew up all unknown to the elders in the Great South Land. Jesus lived and preached, and then Mahomet. And they were gone.

Exciting advances in science developed alongside appalling tortures. The Dark Ages plunged Europe into turmoil. Under noble dynasties in China and India magnificent civilizations flowered and perished. In South America and South-East Asia too. Countless millions of lives paid the price of religion, science and art. But the peoples of Australia lived on, untouched by any of this, untouched by the excitement and discovery, untouched by the beauty born of power and the abject misery as well.

Then the competing empires of China and Java, of Portugal and Holland, of England and France, sent sailors to see what was here: and they did not understand what they found because they came from societies built on slave labour. So slaves were imported when the invasion began (slaves called convicts), an invasion still not admitted for what it was: brutal, bloody and merciless.

We have all heard the story in one version or another, usually beginning with Captain Cook. And a romantic story of golden opportunity it is. But to the heroism of pioneers we should add the heroism of the Aborigines who resisted them.

The struggle for independence has never ceased, in one form or another. The 1992 referendum led to the 1993 republic and the first dictator since colonial days. Now he has fallen. It is time for Australians to take full responsibility, not just for the future, but for what has already been done in Australia. IT IS UP TO YOU!

(This handy compendium of knowledge in 500 parts has been brought to you by the Friends of Privilege.)

112

Sir William Penhallurick sat, a palpitating hunter, in the living-room of his villa. Downstairs, his wife could be heard bossing the cook. Outside, one after another, a dozen of his finest racehorses walked by, head to head with their strappers. Sweet sounds of life and success, far from the war-torn treachery of childhood, the smoking ruined buildings, the daily hunt for dogs or rats to eat, the bestial sexuality of occupation troops. No one here in this country, placid even in crisis, could possibly know what drove him.

Drizzle came drifting, ballooning against the big windows, floating his way from the city and possibly even bearing a trace of salt. Above the television set, the Kékszakállú coat-of-arms gleamed with reflected light.

This changed everything, this libel. From the first moment of her taking his hand on the yacht, he had recognized Dorina Buchanan as an enemy: she alone saw what there was to fear, and was not afraid. He must act. Not a minute to be lost. She caught him on the hop just at a time when he was sure of renewed success.

Yet he did not move from the chair. What kept him anchored there was the numbing weight of recognition that in IFID's view he might be every bit as finished as his protégé. Only the solid wealth of the empire he brought them could save him. Even so, he must hold off selling and play them on his line a little longer. Of course, to stay in the game, he would eventually sell because IFID could not afford him now, him personally, that is. It was a gamble.

Who else was capable of bringing about this courtroom catastrophe but Bernard's filly in her ivory tower of culture and morals?

Also, he realized that the excitement of choosing a new presidential candidate must already have happened without him. IFID kept at least one step ahead, including a military coup. Very much the CIA style of diplomacy. Admiral Todd, another of their men, called in only yesterday but mentioned nothing.

He had been left out.

Zoltán Kékszakállú, survivor of so many tedious and petulant wives, turned to find Alice approaching over the thick carpet, bearing a glass of his favourite sweet red wine on a tray, Alice, who had brought him respectability plus the priceless goodwill of a major newspaper, now stood over him, seeming almost youthful. Alice, flushed with envy at Dorina's public notoriety, perhaps, or love for him in his moment of need. He accepted the glass. Drizzle drifted in against the window. The clop of horse hooves, that sweet regular eccentric rhythm, dwindled. She toyed with her diamond rings, counting them as always, being a simple soul and the despair of her father and brothers who had left her the business for want of anyone less silly to bequeath it to.

Well, IFID may think they could treat him as finished, but he had more fight in him than they ever imagined. He had a plan.

— Drink up Bill dear, she invited firmly and hovered, a plump cod at the mouth of a cave, fanning ruminatively while her eyes remained unblinkingly alert.

And before he had time to think the unimaginable, he had taken two thirsty gulps. She stood looking down from under malnourished eyebrows, her reproach packed in under her gills and her body assembled to the lumpy shapes of disapproval, rings choking her soft fingers.

— You may finish it if you wish. That is up to you. It doesn't matter any longer. You have had enough. I could never forgive the drug thing you've been mixed up in, she explained, she who forgave him everything else for having brought her her title. She blew her nose. You know, she added (but was too stodgy to appreciate how funny her lines were). If you don't get into the Guinness Book of Records for anything else, you'll probably make it as the oldest suicide in history.

Lady Penhallurick brought the poison balanced on a saucer to show him what he'd taken and placed it beside the tray. He dropped his glass and picked up the tiny bottle, throwing it across the room.

— Thank you dear, she said with genuine gratitude. That provides us with all the proof we may need.

And she dared kiss him then.

113

Some years prior to this, work had begun on restoring the tugboat. Dorina Buchanan, true to her word and with Rory's encouragement, had consulted the maritime museum, hired a boatbuilder named Thommo Thomas and prepared for the satisfactions of getting something done. As a result, her peaceful mornings were disrupted by workmen sawing and hammering, accompanied by a radio belting out hooligan jingles at the top of its voice. She bore it just so long before she rang and offered the contractor an extra loading to have the radio switched off. To soften the blow she took a lesson from Bernard and sent down a case of beer, which she herself followed.

— I do apologize for being neurotic, she'd explained, making a long face to amuse them. I am rehearsing for a concert and it is impossible to practise with other music playing. She could not tell them that the hammers themselves were music to her, a remote impersonal Godly music, fierce cold and irrational, which she needed.

— We hear the piano hard at it, one admitted.

They thawed. She smiled. They liked her strangeness and they liked the way she seemed to take no interest in her husband's second election campaign (for that was how long ago she had commissioned the restoration). Dorina climbed back to the house feeling she had succeeded in striking up a friendship despite Rory's shame at her making fools, as he said, of the whole family. These were good men who cared about the job.

At night she had looked down on the harbour, seeking tranquillity as the black glittering water lapped round slipway rails. What appalled her was that the very experiences which ought really to have some cutting-edge accumulated in dull unfelt lumps: here she was, she and the boy and Buchanan, at a shaping-point of the future and she knew Buchanan's power seemed no more tangible or satisfying to him than it seemed to her. Naturally, he could say we shall close this coalmine or open that, but he could not experience the shock of young families suddenly facing poverty, shut out from the adventure of a country where everyone's right was to have a roughly equal chance at the lottery; and more alarming because less predictably, neither could she. She saw what was wrong, as well as what could be right, she debated the issues with herself and occasionally with him, but the grip of actuality had been taken from them by the very power Dorina wished to gauge. The world of making do and planning futures skittered delicately away over the skin of treacherous waters. The tugboat stood in a pool of floodlighting, already afloat on its own deep shadow. Cleared of vines, the deck appeared extraordinarily clean and crisply outlined, larger and more possible than it had when half-hidden by overgrowth. She looked out to the rind of sparkling suburbs round the harbour, lights reflected as dancing needles on the tide. Curious how she had always been rather afraid of sea travel but simultaneously fascinated, as if ships held a secret for her, a private magnetism she had not yet solved.

When, that same anaesthetized year, Dorina supposed they must launch the tugboat soon, Thommo Thomas agreed. He sanded his rough hands together with satisfaction and swore this was the kind of job he'd like to do till the day he might drop. Being Dorina, she considered the word drop an oddity. Yes, the traditional craftsmanship, as he explained, puts you in touch like, with a long line of the old fellows. Mr Thomas, she replied, I like you all the better for that. We shall invite the press. No, she corrected herself, we shall keep her in the family, your family and mine. We shall have the private satisfaction of watching her float out there, and then find somebody who wants to use her. Yes, to keep her in trim, he agreed, sanding his palms some more, she's not one of them useless females, just a pretty face and that (Dorina wondered if his feeling free to say this in front of her meant she was safe from such accusation), she's a worker the old *Felice*. Dorina expressed herself entirely in agreement with this view.

The job was finished at last. In its later months the final details dragged on interminably. The restoration had taken years, all told. And now she could not make up her mind to a launching. The wrench of allowing *Felice* to float out of reach, leaving the decayed slipway empty, suddenly shocked her. She had not really confronted this alteration to her view. But what I love, she explained, is looking down on her, the intimacy of knowing she will soon start a new life. Besides, Dorina's daily visit to the waterfront had become her sole regular outing. They delayed the launching to suit. She invented excuses which Mr Thomas accepted. Then she began resenting his casual enquiries as to whether she had yet made up her mind, and informed him somewhat abruptly that she would let him know in good time. Eventually she invited him to finalize his accounts. Once he'd been paid, she refused all further communication. Vines began to creep out from the enclosing walls, the new timbers weathered in sun and rain. The glitter died on *Felice*'s fittings. Dorina still went down daily, even more affectionately, took herself aboard and made a tour of inspection. A letter came twelve months later from the boatbuilder warning that the caulking would need redoing if the boat was not put in the water immediately to allow the timbers to swell. She wrote back that he must come and do what needed to be done (meaning the caulking), but affairs of state kept her from considering any other decision on a matter which was, in truth, no more than the satisfaction of a whim on her part. Perhaps he understood better than she anticipated; he paid an occasional visit to the yard and checked the boat without needing to be asked. She accepted this and, once, even waved to him briefly from the music room.

Now, years afterwards (having betrayed Buchanan and not even been allowed to see him, not even escaped her hateful shuttered life because, the new regime insisted, she would be more vulnerable than ever with so many people lusting for vengeance against the ex-president), the time had finally come. Mr Thommo Thomas was busy with his assistants, who had then been youths and were now men. They checked the rails and rollers. Meanwhile diffident security guards checked *them*. Till Dorina insisted, actually tearful with fury, that the guards return to their station on the bunker roof. Lagging impudently, they went, and the workmen were left to get on with the job in hand.

— I couldn't bear to have them intrude on something which is, by rights, ours and nobody else's business, she explained though there was no need, and smiled. This is what I have had to live with for years, all this prying. I thought I would at least be free now.

At sixty tons *Felice* presented few problems. The consultant from the maritime museum received an invitation. And no children please, she requested. It's your boat, Thommo concluded, unable to conceal his disappointment.

— She won't be quite the show job she was, he warned. But she'll do nice enough just the same. Sweet as a nut she is, and I'm glad to see her put in the water.

The men were most kind. They behaved as if they knew nothing of her disgrace.

Dorina had been permitted to telephone her husband in custody, but the so-called Caretaker Regime wouldn't let her see him. I still think of you, she told him, as my husband. The divorce seems quite unreal. I am the same and you are the same. No, he told her, you are not the same or you would never have taken me to court. She knew he was still alive, at least.

— I think, Dorina called where she stood, right on the caked mud in the shadow of the stern. I shall watch from down here, Mr Thomas. I am taking photographs to record each stage of the launching. We shall have them made into an album.

— She's your vessel, Mrs Buchanan, all said and done.

You sound sorry, she had told the phone. It's not that kind of thing, he replied. Well *I'm* sorry, she said. You were doing your duty, Dorina, as you saw it, he explained. I was doing my duty, she agreed desperately, aware that he had no idea what torment this cost her. He had begun to sound buoyant.

— Could I have a picture of the whole team together, please? A memento of everybody who worked on her.

Would *Felice* at last be launched and sail successfully? Wasn't success a name for surviving failure? The men began to sing as they clambered down for the photograph. They chaffed her shyly because she remained a celebrity still, even though the president cooled his heels behind bars until Admiral Todd got things ironed out. Also, being a character, she could afford to appear a bit weird. She took shots of the (then) apprentice being threatened with a mallet, of the carpenter kissing the tugboat's hull while Mr Thomas shook his head, and of all three, arms across shoulders. She caught the sly smile of the boy and the weariness of the old man. Gaiety and disillusion were to be in her photographs. Then the museum consultant insisted she join the group while he operated the camera. So she did, being taller than all of them, and more angular. In the viewfinder he saw her, reduced, with hectic colour in her eyes, hooking loose hairs over her ear and wind blowing them free again. With one hand she held on to a fender housing the chunky metal propeller, held it as if testing her grip. Behind the slipway the house towered as a concrete block completely blanking out any view of headland or cliff, while up on the flat roof stood two sentinels wearing the metal sheath of grey lounge suits, each with one hand concealed in his coat pocket.

The private ceremony went ahead as planned. The consultant, once more managing the museum's movie camera, positioned its tripod high on the bank above the north wall. Dorina waited, ready, near the water's edge to one side of the slipway. Workmen swung sledgehammers to a rhythmic stroke which in that confined space echoed sharp as detonations. As the first pair of chocks rang with orchestral brilliance before they fell away. Dorina also heard the deep chimes of her beloved *Cathédral engloutié*. She glanced fleetingly at the tide lapping just behind her and felt a twinge of worry that she might have left a kettle boiling in the kitchen and that the door to Rory's room might still be standing open where his kit, the syringe and blackened spoon, lay displayed for anybody to see. A guard on the roof yawned, politely covering his mouth. Above gaped the inscrutably blue sky. An inquisitive gull fluttered down to the rotting bollard and squirted tiny highlights of white paint for posterity's benefit.

— Stand clear please, Mr Thomas called in his simple voice, a bare voice, Dorina had already noted, devoid of the least self-importance, and she loved him for this with a terrible yearning love which could be called nothing less than childhood trust, momentarily restored as it ought to have been.

— Will she go? the ex-apprentice squawked, also surprised back into youth by the excitement.

Yes, with a strident rasping, *Felice* began to roll astern toward her old life, the calm harbour, the workaday world. A painful struggle against neglect shuddered through her timbers during the first centuries of yielding to the future. She grew ponderous, hull teetering, a bulbous whale shape, a hulk, a freight of cries and moans, a clatter of chains, and broke free from restraint with wild shrieks. She settled to the rails, wood rumbling against metal, to meet a destiny too long promised. The brackets heaved and held, mud quivered alive underfoot. The bay deepened to receive her. The gull balanced on one leg. The one-armed security men on duty up there planted their feet wide apart. Dorina, aiming the camera for an action shot, leapt into her own photograph. She clutched the raw metal fender, her face pressed in against the propeller blade still ringing from a knock it had received. A shoe fell off. Gongs were sounding. She was being carried, limbs twisted, like a person in a fit. The hull of her beloved *Felice* went grinding its massive splintery weight down the incline, pushing her before it and burying her lost shoe, to whisper into the oil-traced water of a peaceful corner of this great harbour with a music so subtle Dorina must strain to catch the drift as she felt her body driven under. Up rose the vessel, sides glittering violet, plated with a skin of steely cold. The bird flew off in shrill panic. Her hair swirled to the surface as she came within a breath of rescue. Then the vessel settled back and, breaking her grip, slid over her, forcing her deeper beneath its mammalian body.

Mr Thommo Thomas swore with the vehemence of hindsight, broad hands shaping the air to his distress. That's why she insisted he must not bring any children! The carpenter ran to where she had dropped her camera. The ex-apprentice dumped himself in the dirt and held his head in his hands, eyes black with shock as those of a removalist who, in the days of innocence, had looked down at a runaway piano gashing livid wounds in the world of respectable trade. He saw the water's surface as pocked with dead insects and miscellaneous bobbing particles of rubbish.

Belatedly, one guard looked at the other. They peered off the concrete parapet.

The tugboat floated to the limit of its tether, being held back from eternity's expanse, thrumming the rope so tight it threw up an arc of bright crystals, and then came gliding obediently home, perfectly shipshape, to nudge the landing stage. Sky wrinkled across the bay. The seagull flew simple circuits of greedy cries and alighted on the bollard as if for the first time. *Felice* had been launched.

In the clear pool welling astern, a corpse emerged and rolled over, it might be thought, joyfully. One fine hand slapped the water. Her mouth opened, hungry for those last moments; her eye reading, through the dazzle of new insights, Schopenhauer's assertion that it is the most pernicious of errors to claim that the world has no ethical but only a physical significance. Dorina's hair had pulled loose from its comb and snaked free along the current. She showed no sign of knowing she still had one shoe on. Her body drifted now without aim, just as Miss Gardiner had warned might happen to her in life if she did not show more enthusiasm for study while still a child and young enough to influence her destiny. She did not hear the musical chuckle of dying ripples. She did not lift her head to listen even when the infernal cruise boat arrived creaming round the point on a crescendo of *The Blue Danube* while passengers threw off their sloth and rushed to the rail, agog with rumours of mortality while the deck listed precariously. Guards, conducting an emergency drill by numbers, simultaneously drew revolvers from their pockets. At long last the boredom had broken. They meant business.

An alarm in the guardhouse began ringing madly.

POSTLUDE
A New Voice

114

Gruesome to think of it. Ha. Who would? Can't help it, though. Hooked. The predator padding round the old brain. Duty tied tight as a headache. A straight line right round from front to back. Done now. But not forgotten. If you had been in my situation, would you have behaved so differently?

Crass. Creepy really. They must know I hate him and what he has done to me all through my life. They only got a bit of it. Plus they were big enough to buck if they had the guts. Forget about the *others*. They despise the *others* as he despised them while he was still on top. One and the same.

O boredom. Still stirring the pot, the usual sludge. Let's be honest. We saw each other through a nightmare. Thank you Admiral Todd. Bring on the next. Nothing is ever any different in life. Out of purgatory: into hell. Wallowing around fighting for breath. Todd had me in his sights all along. Dear old Uncle Willy saying, let me introduce you and a career in the navy just the thing when you know the best people. Careful planner, Todd. Big career. Creepy. Us sat there to watch one another. Good as chaining us thigh to thigh, neck to neck. Two men in one room for months and nothing else to watch all day. Nothing to listen to all night but what if the snoring stopped? Wrecked father watches son through withdrawal. Race Special, read all about it. Wrecked son watches. Father craves what he has lost. Need, need. Are we supposed to have learnt something? No. Todd put us here because he knew that just being watched by the enemy would be the worst of all. No privacy allowed in hell. Judged and found animal. Him losing bags of fat. Lessons in forgetting he was someone special.

You can see us, can't you: each with his supply cut off? We just hoped our bad spells didn't coincide. That has been how much we've come together. I must get this down before too late. Because, who knows?

I can tell you what my tendons felt like when they came unstrung. They felt split. And that must have been the way I looked too. Him watching me collapsed in my corner, always a corner. Down to the bitter fact. I found I was looking at myself. Gooking. Caught with body huddled up, knees under chin, rock-a-bye blackness floating snorting and swollen inside. But me shrinking. You have no idea. The pain of standing up, the willpower. Head going out of range, up there choked in a cloud. On my feet; making out okay. But aching, suffocating in fear. I was to consider him and what he was going through.

One day, standing behind where he slumped. On our bench, he was. Big grey head in focus, with all the force I was pulling together at that moment. I had the advantage. But it slipped away. The true moment of murder was knowing I could live with myself afterwards. Shit man, I said, they've got you. You won't believe what small thing held me back. Distaste. That's it. Laughable. I couldn't bear taking hold of that sweaty neck. Not even for my mother's sake. Not even for killing if able. When I had a lust to satisfy. Pumping through the sluggish maze, blood getting lost. Forget me. The dregs. Who cares if this makes sense? You know the feeling: your tongue covered with. . . what?. . . lichen, something stale and furry and breakable. Ha bloody ha. It's all behind us now.

Two people shut away in one room eat each other, cry each other, shit each other, dreaming, fighting against claws in your throat, falling through sudden apertures into sunlit gardens where respectable people run away in the distance or zoom close and lunging daggers, smack and stink of blasts aimed to kill, how could you help knowing everything?

To give one example. For a whole day he tried to conceal the mice. Yes, funny as it was, I saw. Eventually I did. A mouse ran out of a hole in his belly, down from under the waistcoat which would have fitted round him twice. Skitter of claws on a hard floor. The race from corner to corner looking for cover. In that room! I could have told it a thing or two. Skitter, then silence. The mouse crouching. Darted back up his leg to safety. Warmth. You name it. The meal of a lifetime. The old man winced. He had been dozing and the mouse caught him out. He pretended a yawn, no worries. He spread his hands, examining the back of them. I examined them too. (Because now I was right behind him, my own hands feeling so terribly strong they trembled with it. I'm doing my best to tell you.) The tufts of hair between the knuckles and joints made me sick, especially his little fingers like a monkey's. You could watch the blood shoving out from his heart along the veins. Shove. Shove. Difficult blood, more sluggish to move than blood should be. The skin had rubbed shiny with age. Useless hands, ugly from uselessness. What else did he give them to do than scrawl his signature? The hands of a man who has forgotten how to fasten his own zips. Hands dead to the touch of a woman's face. Certainly the one woman who was so much too good for him. Or me. His fingers were. . . tumours of self-importance. There you have them, that's what they were like. As close as I can get it.

Lost deep in the empty building a door slammed. If I failed, you can blame that remote bang. Something snapped in me. Neither of us moved, just my hands ready and trembling. Just the faded head trembling the same way, only for a different reason. Even the mouse poked its frightened nose out and twitched its whiskers a moment.

Suppose he was dying. So was I.

This is the point I had to get through to him. In fact I said, keeping my voice calm (surprised that it came out shouting): What about me? Do you think I'm okay then? Remembering, through this hell, the old radiant insights, the old skill with feeling at home, making the body belong in a hutch, under some stairs, in the space between two bald armchairs, and the feeling I was in a reassuring rut, oh yes, doing the rounds of an actual beat, one home to another, poky nooks that the genius of heroin raised to dignity. Always comfort.

Do you think he gave me any peace? He turned his hands over. I saw them fill with daylight. Dawn had come; as a mystery. He splashed this daylight on his tired eyes. I heard him give an answer. Hands, cupped over his nose, kept things private. Like a person speaking from the bathroom with the door shut. You too, his nose said, you too! The hair faded. The tips of it shook so much he might have been laughing. I can see that now. The thought eats away at me.

When he spoke, he wasn't like a man who can afford to laugh, though. And he had a habit of losing the thread before coming to the point.

The day he called for pen and paper they were fetched straight away. Did I say that my own ratings were given the job of bringing us our food and performing ablutions-duty twice every twenty-four hours? They supplied him pronto. I thought: so they were waiting for this. Did old Toddler expect a confession? More fool him. I can show you precisely what the deposed president wrote because he gave it to me. I keep it folded in my pocket. Just a minute. This is the message, for what it's worth.

There are times when I wonder if I might not be truly damned, as you've wished on me in your vengeful moods.

The fact is that my body seems determined to survive.

I shall offer no excuses for my life of triumph. But one explanation, as a father, is perhaps owing.

Once we get caught in the system we can't get out, especially those at the top and trying to be all things to all people. The powerful man needs to be limited. I speak from experience. Another thing I learned while in the desert: just because you cannot see what your enemies see doesn't mean they see nothing. I made it a game. Fables, for those who can interpret them, may pick your world up by its heels, shake the money from its pockets, and bang its head against a rock for it.

Please do not imagine the coup d'état took me by surprise. The mob moved unbelievably slowly! Our one hope was young Taverner, who had the necessary imagination and style too.

Waiting for my ankles to grow strong I am given time to consider a more foolish young man, who lacks the manliness to kill when he knows he ought. What can he possibly amount to? I shall tell you because I am sure you will be attentive. He amounts to a warning: and here we are treading the boundary Dorina drew between physics and metaphysics. Within the animal we christened Rory is implied a community of such animals. There you have it. I have said enough. He belongs to a generation which inherits a big hole in the ground.

My specimen of a son stands here right now, snooping perhaps. Whether he is shaking with rage or nerves or just the shakes I can't tell. During these weeks I have met him for the first time. Of course he will look surprised to read this, because we do not converse. Even when he comes out of his fits, he never offers me the least attention unless in the line of duty to his new masters. A skinny twisted wreck, in my opinion, he behaves quite coolly and impersonally. This is the point. By a combination of his presence in my room, suffering every bit as much as I suffer, and yet able to put our relationship at a distance, he imposes himself upon me. I will explain this. I scarcely knew him when he was a boy, given to sulking and a craze for boats. Until now I did not know he had become an adult. I felt hampered by his weakness. All I wanted to do was shake him off.

If I am afraid of anybody, I am afraid of him. Because he is impervious to further injury.

Even now he looks on to make sure my pen is still going and that I have enough paper. Isn't that right? Though he doesn't know what I am putting down. So you see, I am a thing to this young fellow. When he comes to clean himself up, he will cope. I am to treat him as Sub-lieutenant Buchanan, officer in a navy liberated from my own service. Such a short while ago one word from me and admirals jumped. Now my comfort and my life are in the hands of an untried junior officer totally without commanding presence, let alone the charisma of a leader.

But I have seen Rory carry out his duty, however unpleasant. I have watched him behave with perfect rectitude (there, another echo of Dorina). Though I am the victim, it suddenly matters to me that he should succeed. The colder he is to me, the more I discover joy in my heart.

Is this intended for publication? I asked him in one of my good spells. No, he replied after long deliberation, I don't want to make out I knew it all.

I could not begin to speak to him. In the silence, a mouse scampered across the floor and that mouse had more confidence than I had: this place was his now, this warm air breathed over and over by ourselves, the stillness. The odour of belonging, I suppose, marked trails as fixed as highways.

So the time is coming. My father has been imprisoned here long enough to be able to walk unaided. He has lost an immense amount of weight. At first I thought he must be dying, he changed so dramatically. For the past several weeks we've practised a circuit of the room. I had to teach him every step, he was like a baby with no idea of balance. He could never have managed alone, needing me to take his arm, but even this was a far cry from the days of eight weightlifters carting him on a litter. Then last Monday he succeeded at performing his functions on the lavatory by himself. This, let me say, I welcomed as a deliverance. Though I still had to tie his shoes for him when I was well enough and help his legs into his trousers, he began to achieve everything else needed to dress himself fit for seeing (fit to kill, as he used to say when I was a boy). He still gets his coat collar twisted each time he puts it on, so it looks disreputable, but I don't point this out. He has to learn to do things for himself. You may imagine how loathsome I have found the whole process, watching him attacked by rodents, his flesh rotting and sagging and shrivelling away. But once he gave up raging over his fate and plotting vengeance his whole condition improved. The mice disappeared overnight.

This morning our good clothes were delivered, my dress uniform and a suit of his dating from the era when he first entered politics, the one he wore for the election, still with the badges pinned on. So it will happen today. Actually this is no surprise, I already guessed because after breakfast the building began echoing with peculiar sounds, deep booming cries and squeaks. This still goes on. Big things are being shifted around. The only time I remember hearing anything like it was once when I was a kid. We had a holiday on a yacht in Queensland. I think my mother was there too, but I can't be sure. When we went below we heard these faint muffled noises from underwater that they told us were whales, though it might have been anything, for all I know.

I hold the door open and show him out. There is small chance I'll be spared any part of the punishment. Television crews will be ready, I suppose, cameras rolling, to film every step he makes, and every stumble. He has one thing to say as we leave our room: Don't talk to me about hallucinations, I gave mine actual names!

His ankles will not let him down either, he cannot rely on them to save him. He must walk out into the street to discover he is somewhere very familiar in the heart of Sydney, right in the din of daily life. No good covering his ears. And he won't be able to shut out the stares either. That's the price he'll pay for being the most famous face in the country still. And for years to come. A life-sentence really.

He will learn to recognize the new banknotes without his portrait on them, and if any of the obsolete currency comes into his hands he, like anybody else, must surrender it at once in exchange for real money to the same nominal value.

All the doors are unlocked. We are prepared. Is it from nerves that I catch myself tugging my uniform straight when I know it is already immaculate? So I escort him to the lift and down to the foyer. We stand a moment just inside the portico, a few steps higher than the passing crowd. The street is amazingly packed with people jostling this way and that or simply standing, glancing at the clock up there, or fishing bunches of keys from their pockets and picking the coins from among them. Like the background buildings, they are aflutter with colour. Are they all here to see us? Who blames them? These clockwatchers key-sorters and jostlers have shed a shock which lasted years. Wearing new faces already. Yesterday their families would not have recognized them. Oh, I can just see how they were yesterday. For me, I find this intolerable. So filled with clear sight. Terrifying and beautiful beyond words to be free. Not ridden into the dirt. The days are going to be incredibly long now I can use them for so many things. A junkie is a primitive being: you spend nine-tenths of your time hassling. So here we are (not to avoid a cliché) on the steps of a new life. This is no laughing matter. Him making a stupendous effort to face what-ever is out there.

Now it hits him.

My father looks stunned. This is a completely unexpected blow. Memories, no doubt. Bunting billows from How to Vote booths along the balustrade by the footpath. Spruikers bark into microphones while shoals of suburbanites drift past. In all that milling, no one takes any notice. They are still happy. The issues mean nothing. Indifferent. As if suffering could never be recalled to mind. What he can't take his eyes off, the old man I mean, are the placards. They hypnotize him with serious simplified por-traits. In the foreground of the scene we're looking at is this: three booths, each one a picnic table with a sun umbrella stuck through the hole in the middle. At two of them, people sit on folding chairs or stand round passing out propaganda. I shall start from the lefthand booth where the campaign helpers wear dark blue, the men in suits and ties and the ladies decorously powdered. They drink tea from thermos cups, the flasks sitting snug in padded baskets. Here the portrait is the sober face of my old boss, Admiral Todd, touched up to remove the bags from under his eyes and those irritable folds at the sides of his mouth. The second table has no photograph. The ladies there, and they are all ladies, wear the red and white made famous as the protesters' colours outside Friends of Privilege camps, the colours of blood and milk as they used to tell us. There is no photo on this placard, only a message *The Port George Vote: Informal*, plus a slogan, *Don't vote for either one, you'll only encourage them*. The third table has a photograph okay, but no helpers. Under this flapping umbrella already buffeted askew, a brick weighs down the agitated pile of leaflets. A display board anchored to one table leg shudders. On the board is a grumpy picture of my father himself. Judging by the enormous neck, it was taken just before his fall from power. The mouth is set and the eyes empty. The caption reads *More of the Same*.

That's it, then.

The president of all those years says nothing. He just takes it in. We both know now. The day chosen for his release will be an occasion: the pantomime of his final defeat.

He looks at me with eyes very different from those in the portrait, eyes full of wildness and betrayal. I know he wants to ask why I did not forewarn him. I shan't confess I had no more idea than he had. This gives me a bit of power for a change. Let him think what he likes.

Through the thronged street, though it has been cordoned off to traffic, a solitary car comes gliding slowly among eddying heads and shoulders. We first saw it half a block away. Nearer it glides, nudging voters out of its path. And passes.

Now we are left, after the event, with a picture to interpret, a perfectly clear image. In the back seat by the window on our side sat Luigi Squarcia: his hand opening as a flower and being offered to his companion whose face I could not see. The Organizer (as I have always called him) was smiling. He did not look out. The car never hesitated. It went sleeking evenly along, unstoppable, while the crowds had to divide and make way. There it goes still, the roof a black mirror.

— Business and politics taught me the same thing, the old man says. You cannot have friends, only competitors. . . but not all lessons are worth learning.

He has reached the second step down and he is doing it by himself. His hands are finding uses: one brushes me aside while the other clutches the brass rail. Dear Father hobbles out to join the jostle of civilians. They sense a drama and turn to gloat. What else? He has nowhere to go:

— This one is just for me.

He means goodbye and his voice comes clear and young.

— I hope they give you hell, I answer, remembering the whole catastrophe.

Another step and he is out where raw sunshine slams at him. Wincing. The light is such a blinding torrent I can hardly look into it. He falters. I do not save myself falling victim again. This time to compassion. Unaccountable, I know. Yes, unless it is the compassion of a son for his disgraced parent. I follow. Is it merely to steady him? Or is it so he will not have to bear the first moments unsupported? People cluster round. His name is spoken with derision. A young blonde woman spits in his face.

He starts back at the impact: painless though humiliating. He wipes his cheek with a sleeve still smelling of mothballs. His open mouth convulses, then clamps shut. She looks baffled by her own anger.

My reason is clear. Because I have reached out to correct his twisted collar, I've claimed him as mine, I suppose.

But he moves away from me suddenly. Jerking out of reach. What now? Of course. I should have guessed. He has noticed the television cameras. We visit the information booths. He takes no account of his own, however. Instead, he shuffles up to the ladies at the booth next door.

— Here Ruth, look who's come to wish us good luck, calls a plump one wearing bunting for clothes.

— Get away! Ruth screeches in fury.

It is easy to see why. The camera crews must be delighted with the scene. Crass. What can I do? Am I ready to help him out of trouble? Apparently I have learnt very little. But the large lady copes okay. She must see the cameras trained her way too. She must know the danger to her cause.

— Roll up, roll up, she shouts. It's your right to do what you like with your vote. It's your vote like the nose on your face is your nose.

I see what this means: voting being compulsory, but no choice offered. Where are the famous thirteen political parties?

The woman referred to as Ruth is still screeching. It lays your ears back. But by now she is screeching with laughter. The other, weighed down by rosettes, acts cool and takes no notice:

— A hundred years to the day since Federation, she bellows, going red. And look what comes crawling from the woodwork, will you!

My father holds out his hand for their leaflet. The laughter rises harsh as a pain in my head; the old creature padding on the loose again, round and around. The brain just keeping up.

— What do I do? I hear him ask simply. We all hear him.

— You write this across your ballot slip: Remember Port George.

— There's nowhere like Australia, Ruth is laughing and yelling at the same time. (Freedom and torture, I know what she's going through.) Once, when we heard it was the CIA who kicked out our government back in 1975, we said oh yeah? She laughs. Oh yeah? Dear God. There's no. No anger in us.

An audience has gathered, crushing me closer. I don't like it. My father faces us and, among us, the cameras and the press.

He is used to them. He is lost without them. And now he is going to give them what they want, wouldn't you know? On his first day standing by himself, he leers like a movie star.

—This is the one, he trumpets in his irresistible hustings voice, wagging the Informal leaflet. This is the one! he shakes it, spoiling it, with his usual impatience.

Ruth laughs a flock of black stormbirds. There's no stopping her.

— We're only a nudge away from farce, she gasps. And always were.

There is a chance, I suppose, that the crazy idea could work. This must be the only place in the world it could. The vote is compulsory, so if enough of us opt out of the game, can any party claim a mandate? It doesn't look too promising, but might be a beginning. No more crazy than Captain Cook sticking a flag in the ground and saying, this is now a piece of Britain, this great unknown. And people *believing* it.

The lady's rosettes tremble. All weird. She does what I thought I would never see. She steps up and kisses Dorina's husband on the cheek. The loud wet kiss makes him actually blush.

— Lord love us, she declares. For the fools we are. And on a stinker like today. I'm fair melting under this finery. What dill thought of calling an election in January! Vote Informal, she yells at the top of her voice. For cooler elections. Get cracking Ruthie. Keep the good news coming. Here, love, do you want a thump on the back? The hiccups can kill you, they say. Women for a fair go. Now's your chance, sailor (to my mortification she waves at me and the television cameras swivel), you can have a kiss too if you like.

My father is becoming quite confidential, but she has no more time to listen, there's a job to be done.

—Free kisses for Informal voters! she cries at the top of her voice. That's an offer you can't well refuse.

Now I see it. Only now the penny drops. Their real message is simpler and more dangerous than I thought. The election is a farce. It has come to mean nothing. To keep our own country, we're going to be forced to fight for it.

This very moment, coincidentally, a shot is fired quite nearby. I reach for my father. So, did I already expect to see him assassinated? He is listening critically rather than smiling. Echoes ricochet along the street. The rabble falls silent. Flocks of pigeons clatter away, escaping above the Queen Victoria Building. I think the shot was probably a random enthusiasm.

On my ballot paper, I decide to write *Remember Dorina Buchanan*. She saw the truth but could not live with it. She saw there is no use pretending greedy people will play by the rules: they made them up, they know what the rules are worth. And we have to face the fact that the only lesson they'll understand at this late stage is violence.

Crowds begin swaying. From our slightly elevated position we see them breaking apart and running along George Street. Is the car roof among them? I can't make out clearly enough. Without warning they are swirling in that direction, flocking together like a religious meeting. Suddenly I think of the suburbs they come from and live in. The frenzy has grown terrific. Swarming as far as I can see down towards the station in one direction and the quay in the other. Like a simple creature, simpler than a single person is, an impenetrable pack with one brutal idea, thousands surging and sweeping round the spot where I last saw that car.

A wild outcry wells from the centre of action and what must already be history by now, startled, frightened, dangerous, massed voices yelling words in rhythms that are something deeply known but cut short, bursting out again, only to be swamped by pandemonium too soon for us to catch what they say. It has a bad taste like sweet and rotten fruit. Shadows of it arrive as a mighty gasping roar over our heads. Still no clearer, the same words are being bellowed at the faces of those about us, and by them. I catch one last glimpse of my father trying to take the rosettes lady by her arm, and her shaking him off angrily. The cameras are no longer interested. He is irrelevant. Look out! A vast push of excitement wells around us. The rule of the mob. Okay. You can smell this. He is utterly irrelevant and forgotten. Everywhere solid seething bodies block eddying backwaters, aimless people being shifted by clumps to one side or the other, closer or away. Most, like ourselves, only at the fringe. The real force is no longer visible, some emergency farther along the road, closer to the heart of what it means. I know this familiar feeling, this helpless deadlock, dark anger, thick dusty sunshine. I know this trip. Murderers get their sweaty fingers on you. Yet here we cling to crazy hopes of rescue. The flood of chaos lifts our hearts. You can't help it. People begin to understand. They smile all round me, showing their teeth as weapons. Ridiculous smiles, clean as the open sea.

Some smiles bold, some apprehensive. It's an epidemic of hope, all of us anonymous, recognizing our kind, necks swollen with the effort of shouting. Was that a second shot? A bit late. Again, the mass intake of expectation. Also frantic activity along there, where the car was last seen. Give me breathing space. Watch where you're going. This is wild. And now, who would imagine such an agreement of hands thrust up? An endless harvest of hands waving. Just look. Think of them finning. Think of a single undersea creature vast as a reef with a million fluttering gills. Thunder breaks over us in a wave of our own voices. Look out! It seems to me as if we are in the middle of